D0040948

An Absence of Light

ALSO BY DAVID L. LINDSEY

Body of Truth
Mercy
In the Lake of the Moon
Spiral
Heat from Another Sun
A Cold Mind
Black Gold, Red Death

An Absence of Light

DAVID L. LINDSEY

DOUBLEDAY
New York London Toronto Sydney Auckland

ROCKWOOD

PUBLISHED BY DOUBLEDAY
a division of Bantam Doubleday Dell Publishing Group, Inc.
1540 Broadway, New York, New York 10036

DOUBLEDAY and the portrayal of an anchor with a dolphin
are trademarks of Doubleday, a division of
Bantam Doubleday Dell Publishing Group, Inc.

All of the characters in this book are fictitious, and any resemblance to
actual persons, living or dead, is purely coincidental.

Book design by Gretchen Achilles

Library of Congress Cataloging-in-Publication Data

Lindsey, David L.
    An absence of light / David L. Lindsey. — 1st ed.
        p.   cm.
    1. Murder—Texas—Houston—Fiction.   2. Police—Texas—Houston—Fiction.
3. Houston (Tex.)—Fiction.   I. Title.
PS3562.I51193A27   1993
813′.54—dc20   93-35730
                                                                          CIP

ISBN 0-385-42311-X
Copyright © 1994 by David L. Lindsey
All Rights Reserved
Printed in the United States of America

May 1994
First Edition
10 9 8 7 6 5 4 3 2 1

For Joyce

as always,
as it should be.

". . . and he that increaseth knowledge increaseth sorrow."

—ECCLESIASTES 1:18

Sunday
THE FIRST DAY

HE WALKED BAREFOOT IN THE DARK ACROSS THE CLIPPED, DAMPISH lawn, the muggy breeze from the Gulf of Mexico fifty yards away gently tugging at the legs of his silk pajamas which he had rolled to mid calf. He was shirtless and though his torso carried its weight a little differently now than it had a couple of decades earlier, at fifty-eight his muscles were still firm. He was a handsome man and he knew it, and every day he lifted weights to maintain a thick chest and spent half an hour in the coastal sun to keep a nut brown patina to his olive complexion. Because his hair was beginning to thin a little, he now wore it slightly longer than he used to, his gray sideburns brushed back rakishly to blend with the gray hair at his temples.

Carrying a tall, thin glass of ice and rum in one hand, he walked toward the pier that jutted out into the murky Gulf where a seaplane was whipping the night waters as it taxied toward the docking slip, its red and white lights winking, the dying whine of its props dropping to lower and lower registers as it approached the two men on the pier who were waiting to secure the craft to the pilings.

Panos Kalatis could not see any of this very clearly, the men, the plane, the pier were all gray upon darker gray upon black, for the night was moonless and clear and the scattered lights on the long sweep of the shoreline cast their illumination straight to the stars where it was swallowed in the vast, empty, universal darkness. He scratched the salt-and-pepper hair on his chest and waited, listening to the peculiar hollow sound that things made when echoing off the surface of water, the doors of the plane clicking open, the metal pontoons thumping softly against the pilings, water lapping against shore and pier, the shuffle of men's feet on the wooden dock, and the furtive sound of their voices.

Kalatis ate a piece of ice from his glass and waited. He loved the

Gulf, its breath-warm nights filled with the salty odors of other worlds brought along on the swift, strong currents of the Gulf Stream. It reminded him of other salty waters, other gulfs, other shores, and intrigues.

At the moment, however, his overriding emotion was restlessness. He stepped a few feet away nearer the point where the pier joined the breakwater below. In the almost total darkness he could see the cusp of sand below the pier and make out the vague movements of the men on the dock. From among the scuffling sounds of feet on the dock he could make out a single set with a rhythm all its own. He concentrated on those as they separated from the others and grew louder as they approached along the pier. When they reached the stairs they turned short and choppy as the man mounted the series of steps that brought him up to the edge of the lawn.

"Panos."

"Over here." He spoke from the dark, not too loud, knowing his thick voice carried like a foghorn.

"Nice craft," the man said, a little out of breath, coming toward Kalatis across the lawn.

Before he got to him, Kalatis walked a few paces back toward the house so that Colin Faeber had to keep walking to overtake him. When Kalatis stopped he turned to face Faeber and ate another piece of ice. They looked at each other, each face barely discernible in the low light. Kalatis said nothing, and after a moment he turned and looked back toward the house which was on higher ground, palm trees scattered around it, a low-slung structure with deep verandas that made one think of British Colonial settings. Kalatis could see Jael on the veranda, moving back and forth, her long-limbed silhouette drifting in the dusky half light coming from the tall windows behind her. Even from this distance he clearly could see that she was naked. When he turned around he just caught the movement of Faeber's head looking away down the beach, as though there were something that way he wanted to see, out there in the dark.

Faeber was wearing a suit with a pocket handkerchief. He must have been somewhere, a party maybe, some kind of event. Kalatis could just make out the expression on his face in the wan light from the windows of the house, a light that died all the way across the broad sloping lawn to the beach until it was hardly anything at all by the time it got to them standing just a few yards above the water.

Faeber was feeling awkward because of Kalatis's silence. He looked down the beach the other way, and then he looked around to the plane on the water. There was nowhere else to direct his eyes except at Kalatis, or at Jael on the veranda where he already had looked and was afraid to look again.

Kalatis watched him and waited a moment more so that Faeber would be absolutely grateful to hear him speak. He drank some rum looking out toward the dark ghost of the plane on the water.

"I received a telephone call about an hour ago," he said. "It was not good news."

He could see Faeber stiffen, and he thought that if he were a dog he would have been able to smell the fear riding on the gusts coming off the water from behind him.

"What's the matter?" Faeber asked.

"Arthur Tisler has killed himself." He pronounced the name Tee-sler.

Pause. "God . . . !" The ejaculation from Faeber was an aspirant, a hiss.

Kalatis thought he saw Faeber's left leg move, maybe to steady himself on the slope of the lawn.

"Wh . . . when was this? Christ . . . that's incredible. Jesus Christ. When was this?"

"A few hours ago."

"Goddamn . . . Arthur Tisler."

"Yes."

"Was he alone? I mean, someone found him I guess. Who found him?"

"That's irrelevant."

Faeber was silent. Kalatis did not interrupt him. Years of experience had taught him that good people—and Faeber was a good man—responded to very little stimulus. If they were intelligent enough, venal enough, and if he had brought them along with enough skill and just the right tincture of anxiety, they would make the right decisions. They would be dependable—for his purposes, at least—even when they were caught off balance.

Faeber had turned to look down the beach, at the curving line of lights, as though he could do his best thinking if he were not looking directly in Kalatis's face. Kalatis studied his profile. He was a typical American businessman, a kind of perennial, overgrown boy who always would be impressed by—and who always would try to impress others with—his odd sense of masculinity, a concept that was comprised in large part of financial competitiveness. Kalatis had never met an American businessman who didn't eventually try to puzzle out your approximate financial worth by circuitous conversation during which they tried to elicit your occupation, where you lived, what you drove, what clubs you belonged to, whom you knew, where you went on vacation, and what kind of toys you employed for your leisure—boat, car, skis, guns, et cetera. It was a kind of penis comparison, a sophomoric measuring of oneself against the next man, using dollars instead of genitals.

Faeber turned to Kalatis. "You said you got a call. Is this going to be on the news?"

"No. I understand this can be handled very quietly. They've had some luck on that."

Faeber didn't pursue the question further or ask Kalatis to elaborate. He didn't need to. He loosened his tie.

"Then I guess the Seldon operation is dead in its tracks," he said. He paused and shook his head. "Suicide. Goddamn, can you believe that? What a butt stupid thing to do. Unbelievable. Okay, uh, there'll be a flurry of departmental investigations. Homicide and IAD. Graver will conduct an inquiry of his own to make sure nothing was compromised. If it's suicide . . ." He stopped and focused on Kalatis. "They're sure it's suicide . . ."

Kalatis nodded. "They are saying suicide."

"Then since it's suicide there's no problem with Homicide or IAD, only Graver's inquiry. But we should be covered there. Our people are good, very careful. I'll keep an eye on it, make sure nothing's unraveling."

Kalatis drank the remaining rum and tossed the ice out into the grass.

"I'm sure you will keep everything under control, Faeber," Kalatis said. "But two things bother me about what is happening here," he said. "Very serious concerns. It has been my experience that a suicide in this business always means trouble. I have seen it before. Mexico City. Brindisi. Montevideo. Marsala. Tel Aviv. Marseille." He named them slowly, hesitating a beat or two between each as though he first had to visualize the incident in each city before he could speak the name. "In each of these places I saw suicides, and in every instance they caused confusion, unexpected reversals. Other people died. Trouble."

He paused and rolled the cold glass across his bare chest, wiping the chilled sweat from the glass onto his skin. He wanted Faeber to listen to his words, to think about what he was saying.

"Men like this," he said, "do not kill themselves for ordinary reasons like money trouble or women or depression. They kill themselves, often, out of fear. Because they believe they cannot escape something. Or, perhaps, because they have done something they know will guarantee that they will have to be killed and, for some reason that I have never understood, they want to cheat the assassin."

"Maybe," Faeber said. "But this isn't the Third World, for Christ's sake. It's not the same here, Panos."

Kalatis nodded indulgently at the American chauvinism, an assumed superiority so deeply ingrained in this man that he wouldn't even have understood the sense of it if you had stopped him and explained it to him. A gust from the water tugged at the baggy legs of his pajamas.

"No, this is not the Third World, my friend," Kalatis assented. His voice was patient, his manner polite. "But what you don't understand yet is that you are no longer in the First World either. Or the Second. When you got involved in this work, Faeber, you got yourself into a different world altogether. I tried to tell you this, remember? This world is the same all over the globe. Believe me. You will not survive if you do not grasp that completely . . . and quickly."

Faeber looked at Kalatis and in the pale glow coming from across his shoulder from the house above them Kalatis could see the other man's eyes shift ever so slightly away from him as he looked at the woman on the veranda beyond. Kalatis smiled to himself. He had been waiting for that. Men, even intelligent men, perhaps especially intelligent men, were such predictable animals. There were very few who could have kept their eyes off that veranda. He had known men who, even when they knew they were about to die in the next few moments, would have had to look at that veranda.

With a blink Faeber quickly brought his eyes back to Kalatis, but the Greek had looked down toward the dock so that Faeber would not detect that he had been caught stealing a look at Jael.

"You said there were two things that bothered you," Faeber said. "Graver."

"Oh?"

"I have taken the time to study him in a little more depth than what was provided in the dossier you gave me," Kalatis said. "You know, he could be an easy man to underestimate. This is a serious thing, for him to conduct an inquiry. He will not be so easy to deceive."

"No," Faeber agreed. "I think you're right there, but we've got a bit of luck on our side—in the timing here. These are not good times for Graver. He's had distractions lately."

"You mean because of his wife."

"That's right. Your wife runs off with a society doctor it tends to break your concentration."

"That's not quite accurate."

"Okay, she had a long affair with the doctor, and now she's left Graver to marry the guy. The thing is, this doctor's a gadfly, this has been in the gossip columns for Christ's sake. Graver's a very private kind of man. It's got to be driving him nuts."

"Yes," Kalatis said. "I can imagine how he must feel."

Down on the docks a man laughed softly, and feet shifted on the planks. Kalatis had spent many nights listening to waiting men talk. They smoked; they talked softly about everything from sex to death; they waited for signals; they waited for something to make their adrenaline squirt and shock them to life. When Kalatis was young he was one of those men, but now he was the one they waited for. Men had waited in the darkness for him all over the world, and he had learned that the feel of night was different everywhere, different in Trieste than in Prague, different in Lima than in Lisbon, different in New Orleans than Milan. But the darkness, well, the darkness was always the same.

"Then is there something specific you think I should do?" Faeber asked.

"No." Kalatis dug his toes into the moist grass. "I only recommend that you second-guess yourself every time your heart beats. You know what must happen and what must not happen." There was a pause, but Faeber said nothing. "Okay," Kalatis said.

He whistled once sharply, and the murmuring voices stopped. Suddenly there was the sound of hurried footsteps on the pier, something bumped against the metal pontoons of the plane, and then the engine coughed and caught.

"They will take you back to Clear Lake and then drive you into the city."

Faeber seemed suddenly uncertain, hesitant to leave as though he thought he had missed something, some instruction, something more specific. Kalatis only looked at him in silence knowing that with the pale light coming from Kalatis's back Faeber could see little more of his features than his silhouette.

After an awkward moment, Faeber turned away and headed down the slope to the pier. Kalatis watched him and then when the darkness had covered him he listened to his choppy footsteps descending the stairs, his stride changing as he got to the dock and headed toward the plane.

Kalatis sucked his lungs full of the smell of the Gulf of Mexico and shrugged his shoulders forward to stretch his back muscles. He waited there on the sloping lawn while the moorings were untied from the plane and its engines slowly revved and whipped the water as it pulled away from the dock. Moving out into the Gulf, it picked up speed and then the pilot bore down on the throttle and the engines whined and beat the night air and in a moment it was airborne, climbing into the spangled black, its receding lights eventually becoming indistinguishable from the stars. He lost sight of it and even lost the sound of it as the surf reclaimed its rhythm on the night.

He turned around and looked toward the house. Jael was lying on her stomach in the hammock, and he could see it swinging, swinging. The cotton webbing of the hammock was white, and he imagined her dark skin against it and the way it protruded softly through the weave of the pattern in cocoa triangles.

2

FROM HIS CAR ON THE NEARLY DESERTED EXPRESSWAY, MARCUS
Graver watched the late June rain pass over the western margins of the
city as the fading evening stained to a deeper green the dense canopy of
water oaks and loblolly pines and magnolias that stretched to the horizon. A thin gleam of glaucous light, all that remained of the day,
appeared briefly between the drifting, bruised clouds and the darkening
trees, as if an unconscious eye had opened slightly, one last time.

Graver switched off the wipers and watched the eye close through
the last spatters of the departing storm that stippled the windshield.
Though he was agitated, impatient, only those who knew him well
would have been able to tell. He was driving fast on the glistening,
black ribbon that banked gently southward, the tires of his car sucking
up rain from the pavement and spewing it out behind in a white hissing
plume. The city's lights had begun to coruscate against the Sunday
dusk.

Graver would not have chosen Arthur Tisler if he had been asked
to imagine this. Of all the men and women who worked under him,
Tisler seemed the least remarkable, the least likely to have "things
happen" to him. Arthur Tisler was the quintessential invisible man,
and invisible men lived their lives without creating eddies of air around
themselves; they died without incident, and in no time at all people
found themselves saying, Arthur Tisler, my God, I haven't thought of
him in years.

Uninteresting was not a word inherently descriptive of low-key
personalities, but, as Graver thought about it, in Tisler's case this pale,
lighter-than-air adjective was singularly appropriate. In his middle thirties, Tisler was of middle height and middle weight. His hair, light
brown, straight, baby-fine, was prematurely thinning in a little fuzzy
swirl on the back of his head. He wore glasses, squarish metal frames

of pewter color with a dark brown plastic trim on the upper half. He hadn't much of a beard, tiny eyelashes, modest eyebrows that almost apologized for not making more of an impression, and a smallish nose that came rather to a point. He possessed, in fact, a forgettable face. Not too far in the future Graver would have to look at a picture of him to remember what he looked like.

Or, maybe not. Maybe after what had happened tonight, Graver would never be able to forget him.

He drifted to the right-hand lane, slowed, and took the Harwin exit down off the expressway. He lifted his chin, to stretch his neck a little underneath the knotted tie as he made a mental note to move over the collar button. It would be the second one he had done in a week, confirming in a practical way what the bathroom scales had been indicating quantitatively for several months now. Which was fine with him. He always had thought he was too thin anyway. He was the only middle-aged man he knew who never gave a damn about what he ate.

Harwin was a long street. It ran east and west from the Southwest Freeway into Sharpstown, through good and not-so-good parts of the city depending on how long you stayed with it. To Graver's right the streets grew sparse as he crossed over Brays Bayou, and vacant lots gave way to empty fields, black stretches of unlighted land. The tracks of the Southern Pacific Railroad angled in from the north as he approached the overpass of the Sam Houston Tollway, and then they turned parallel to Harwin as the lights of Andrau Airpark appeared in the near distance.

He turned right onto Willcrest, slowed immediately, crossed the railroad tracks, and then rolled down his window and began peering out into the darkness to his left, out across the tracts of urban emptiness toward the isolated end of the airstrip. The odors of wet grass and weeds washed into the car. He was surprised that he couldn't immediately see the lights of the patrol cars. The field appeared flat. He shifted his attention to the edge of the pavement. Pio Tordella had given him precise directions. The homicide detective told him he should begin looking for a little dirt road just after he crossed the railroad tracks. The road was unmarked, just ruts actually, going into the weeds and high grass.

Since his was the only car on the long stretch of street, he crossed over to the oncoming lane and drove beside the caliche shoulder so the headlights could more easily pick up any break in the smooth margin of grass. Immediately they did.

He turned off and quickly caught sight of the cherry and sapphire blips of a patrol car a hundred yards or so out into the emptiness, level with and almost obscured by the tops of the tall grass. Apparently it had not rained enough to make the ruts impassable. Leaning forward over the steering wheel, he followed them as well as he could, listening to the rasping of the high weeds as they bent and swept against the undercarriage of the car.

The ruts fell slightly into a shallow, saucer-like depression, and then silhouettes of three or four cars popped up against the backdrop of the city lights far beyond the airfield. As he neared the cars, his headlights picked up bits of debris, ragged strips of plastic bags or wrappers caught in the weeds, a rusting chunk of something resembling a car fender, a glint of glass in the ruts, a sun-bleached crate, a flap of tin wedged into the dirt and weeds. The depression apparently was used as an illicit dumping ground, a catchall for the detritus that urban dwellers sloughed off continually like dead parts of themselves.

Graver's car rocked gently in the ruts as he approached the scene and pulled up beside the nearest patrol car. There were only two of them in addition to the detectives' unmarked car, a police crime scene van, and the coroner's van. And of course there was the other car, which had to be Arthur Tisler's, a small-model Chevrolet several years old, the driver's side door standing open. The car was of an unidentifiable dark color, blue perhaps, or green, from which the sun had leached its richer pigment leaving a powdery, scaly finish. Though it was the center of attention, it was peculiarly inconspicuous, a black hole, swallowing light.

As he cut his headlights and got out of the car, two uniformed officers emerged from behind Tisler's car unspooling a yellow crime scene ribbon in a generous parameter. Pio Tordella, stocky and dark-haired, waded toward him through the tall, wet grass that was beginning to be tramped down around Tisler's car. He walked in front of the lights of one of the patrol cars and came over to Graver.

"Captain," Tordella said, approaching Graver's car as Graver closed the door.

They shook hands, and in that first moment Graver observed Tordella's soft eyes assessing him before they turned aside. Graver had spent six years in Homicide shortly after he came out of uniform, but for all of the fourteen years since then he had been in the Criminal Intelligence Division. Most of his career had been in intelligence work, chiefly as an analyst and, in the last four years, as the captain of the Division. He hadn't been to a crime scene in nearly five years.

But that wasn't what put the uneasy look in Tordella's expression. Rather, that had to do with Graver's work. Criminal Intelligence was a controversial division. It was sometimes disdained, sometimes resented, sometimes feared, but invariably it was regarded with a degree of deference. Graver had tried to develop a thick skin against these attitudes. He understood them and tolerated them. People who were known to collect secrets for a living could not expect to be treated with warm cordiality. Graver knew that the look of concern in the detective's face reflected his understanding of what fate had set in his path. The death of one of the secret keepers was a death of import, in fact, it was unprecedented, and Tordella did not know what to expect. It was not a case he would have chosen to be assigned to if he had had the opportunity to make a choice.

"It's a mess, Captain," Tordella warned him tentatively. His voice was soft and modulated, his pronunciation precise. He had a thick mustache that threatened to become unruly, and he had a habit of nibbling at one corner of it with his lower teeth.

Graver looked around at the collection of glistening cars, their shiny surfaces beaded from the passing rain. The metally smell of hot car engines mixed with the odor of damp weeds. The headlights of the patrol cars, the angle of the vehicles, including his own, reminded him of a study in visual perspectives, all the elements in the composition situated to draw the viewer's attention to the focal point of the canvas: the car with the open door, one of Tisler's legs protruding stiffly across the sill.

"He had his ID with him?" Graver asked.

"Yeah," Tordella said. "In his inside coat pocket." He reached into his own coat and pulled out a plastic bag, with Tisler's wallet and shield in it. The inside of the bag was smeared with blood.

Graver felt a momentary optimism. Then maybe it *was* suicide.

"By the way, you had some good luck," Tordella said.

Graver pulled his eyes away from the bag and looked at the stubby detective. "What."

"I wasn't first out," Tordella said. "Not ten minutes before this call came in there was a shoot-out at a convenience store out in Kashmere

Gardens. The clerk at the store shot a couple of guys who tried to rob him. Killed one on the spot. Wounded the other one who then killed the clerk and ran off, shooting every which way and wounding a woman outside. Right now he's holed up in a garage apartment about a block from the store—with a hostage. Caused a lot of radio action. *Every*body in the pressroom headed out there, and by now I imagine all their cruise cars are either there or headed there."

Somebody swore sharply with a hiss, and Graver and Tordella looked over to Tisler's car where a man in street clothes, maybe the coroner's investigator, was walking away from the opened car door, stamping his foot and wiping it on the grass. He swore again.

"Anyway," Tordella said, turning back to Graver, "Then this came in. The kid over there who called it in"—he looked in the direction of one of the young uniformed officers—"thought he was a detective and said over the radio that he had a 'suicide.' If anybody was listening, I imagine it was a pretty dull prospect compared to the Kashmere show. I don't think anybody in the media even knows we're out here."

"Yeah," Graver said, "that's a break, a good break." He looked toward Tisler's car again.

"He was an investigator, wasn't he?" Tordella asked.

"Yeah."

"Was he working tonight?"

"Jesus, I wish I knew," Graver said.

Tordella nodded. His large, dark eyes were heavy and, despite his anxiety, lent an air of calm to his demeanor. "What squad?"

"Organized Crime." Graver knew how that must have sounded, replete with implication.

Tordella nodded again, meditatively. "IAD guys are on their way out," he said.

Internal Affairs automatically made every officer-related shooting. This was going to give Jack Westrate a heart attack.

"And Captain Katz is on the way too," Tordella added. He was referring to Herb Katz, Graver's counterpart in Homicide. "Lieutenant had already gone out to Kashmere Gardens," Tordella explained.

That was irrelevant, Katz would have been called anyway. And Katz probably already had called Jack Westrate who, as assistant chief in charge of Investigative Services, was Graver's and Katz's superior. But Westrate wouldn't be appearing in the dark, weedy field. His domain of concern was the gassy, background realm of ramifications and politics, not events. He would be frantic about this, of course, he even would be in a state of panic, but for all the wrong reasons.

"What do you think?" Graver asked finally. He wanted a measure of Tordella's gut reaction. He wanted the experienced detective's feel for the scene.

"Well, I've been here only a little while myself," he said pointedly, shaking his head, "but not knowing anything else about it, just looking at it, I'd lean toward suicide."

Graver was relieved, but only momentarily. Still, at this point, even a temporary reprieve was welcome. They didn't say anything for a minute, watching the woman from the Crime Scene Unit as she video-taped the car and its contents, working it from every conceivable angle and perspective. When she was finished, Graver felt the detective looking at him. Taking his eyes off the car, he looked around. Tordella's sagging eyes were emotionless, his mouth slightly puckered on one side as he worked at the ends of his mustache.

"Okay, let's take a look," Graver said.

Tordella ducked his head, and they started toward Tisler's car. Though there hadn't been enough rain to create mud, it was damp enough to cause the soil to cake to Graver's shoes. Tordella stopped him behind the yellow ribbon that had been stretched on the ground in front of the open car door and was held in place by a couple of sticks jabbed into the dirt.

"We're still looking for something over there," he said, gesturing vaguely toward the other side of the ribbon.

In the headlight beams of the patrol unit, Graver could see Tisler's leg under the steering wheel, slanting awkwardly with his foot out the open door, his body slumped into the darkness toward the passenger seat. The beams backlighted the window of the open door on the driver's side, setting aglow the rusty splatter on the glass, the particu-late matter that had been part of the contents of Tisler's head.

Buttoning his suit coat so the tails wouldn't be in the way, Graver stepped over the yellow ribbon and walked up to the door, careful about the grass at his feet. He put his hands in his pockets, set his jaw, and looked inside.

Tisler had been sitting behind the steering wheel when the shot was fired, but his upper body was now laying over on the passenger side, his blasted head partially submerged in the black syrup that had pooled in the depression of the seat. His right leg was twisted awkwardly under the steering wheel column, his left one stretched full-length, sticking out the door. His right arm was flung out, hanging over the edge of the seat, and under it on the floor was a handgun, an automatic. There was a world of blood, and Graver could smell it, an oddly precise odor, a kind of musty sweetness, like something that had been stored in a dank cellar, something old. It was, he thought, an odor that probably had not changed in all the millennia of human history, that surely had smelled exactly like this ever since the day that Cain became the first man to breathe it.

Tordella pointed at the inside of the doorjamb, at the button that allowed the light to come on when the door was opened.

"He wedged a wooden match next to the button to keep it pushed in," he said. "I guess maybe he sat here a while before he did it and didn't want to attract attention." He gestured toward the dashboard. "Radio's on, but the volume's turned down. You wonder why he didn't just turn it off."

"And the door was open like this?"

"Yeah, just like this. And look." Tordella leaned across in front of Graver and pointed to the edge of the open door. "I think the damned bullet nicked the door frame. That's what we're looking for in the grass there, the slug."

"There's no note?"

"We haven't found one"—Tordella shrugged, nibbling at his mustache—"but we haven't gone through all of his clothes yet, or the car."

He shone his flashlight around inside the car. A pair of trousers on a coat hanger covered with clear plastic was hanging behind the passenger's side in the back; a pink laundry slip was stapled to the plastic. There was nothing else in the back seat, no litter, no clutter, no overlooked gum wrappers.

"Was he a neat person, like this?" Tordella nodded at the back seat.

"He was neat," Graver said.

"Somebody might've cleaned it up. Or I guess he might've. You know, the way they do sometimes."

There were a lot of myths about suicides, about how they often carefully planned their deaths, about their oddly scrupulous behavior before they died, about the strange logic of their dementia. But Graver never had been impressed by any of that. He did not find such generalities particularly convincing because he did not think of suicides as a single, peculiar species with specific, identifiable characteristics. Mentally disturbed people committed suicide. Intelligent, well-balanced people committed suicide. Cowards committed suicide and heroes too. Richard Cory killed himself, as did Judas. And Socrates. Graver saw very little in such a diversity that lent itself to generalization. He was invariably suspicious of simple, formulaic explanations to anything; axioms made him uneasy.

A small, twin-engine aircraft came whining down the tarmac toward them and lifted off so low over their heads that Graver could feel the props rumbling in his chest. Everyone turned and looked up at it, toward the sound of it, lifting up into the darkness.

"I guess we'll get started, then," Tordella said, pulling on a pair of latex gloves, popping the latex at his wrists. "I don't suppose you have any ideas about this."

Graver shook his head. "Not a clue. His squad supervisor is Ray Besom. Normally he would know if Tisler was working tonight, but he's on vacation, a fishing trip down near Port Isabel. And I imagine Dean Burtell might know."

"Burtell?"

"He's the analyst who works with Tisler most of the time."

Tordella nodded some more, studiously avoiding Graver's eyes as he interlaced the fingers of his hands and tamped the gloves tight.

"Okay. Well, look, stop us if you want to see something or have questions or anything," he said, flicking a glance at Graver. "Otherwise, considering who we got here, I'm going to work it up in detail."

Graver turned and walked back to his car, out of the white glare of the headlights. Pio Tordella was only the first in a long line of people who were going to be looking over Graver's shoulder on this one. The unexplained death of an intelligence officer had the effect of producing the maximum amount of suspicion with the least hope of having it resolved. There was no way to avoid the immediate assumption by others that something had gone terribly wrong in the Division where secrets were the stock in trade.

Leaning against the front fender, Graver watched them play out what had become a modern ritual of American urban culture. For a few hours the evening had been cooled by the passing showers, but now the stifling heat was already returning, and the night was growing steamy. It was difficult to tell whether the moisture enveloping his skin was from the incredible humidity or from seeping perspiration. The unusually wet spring and early onset of summer heat had spawned a richness of insects in the tall, weedy grass from which they now emerged in swarms that grew thicker by the minute, fogging to the bright beams of the squad car, flitting like sparks in the reflected light.

While Tordella's partner disappeared behind the dark side of Tisler's car, Tordella consulted with the coroner's investigator and the woman from the Crime Scene Unit. Standing in the glittering cloud of insects, he talked, gesturing with his pale latex hands, his figure casting jerky shadows across the gaping door of the car behind him.

Graver looked at Tisler again, at his skewed leg glimpsed in the fluttering darkness, and he could almost make himself believe that Tisler had moved, that the awkward sprawl of his torso was a posture of resistance, as if, in the unexpected terror of that God-abandoned last moment, he had changed his mind and was struggling desperately to keep from being swallowed headfirst into the black throat of eternity.

3

HERB KATZ LIGHTED A CIGARETTE. HE WAS WEARING A JOGGING suit, though Graver knew that Katz probably had not jogged fifty yards since he left the Police Academy more than twenty years ago.

"What did Westrate say when you called him?" Graver asked.

He and Katz were leaning back against the front of Graver's car watching Charlie Bricker and Hodge Petersen from the Internal Affairs Division pore over the car and its contents with Tordella and his partner. The lights on the patrol car had been replaced with portable floodlights from the CSU, and the two unit investigators were dusting the car and gathering samples.

" 'Son of a *bitch!'* " Katz said, imitating Westrate's strident voice. "Why didn't you call him?"

"I knew you would."

Graver was standing with his arms crossed, his legs crossed at the ankles. He and Katz were about the same age and first had met when they were in Homicide. Swarthy and good-looking, Katz had thick black hair and the kind of genes that would keep it black long after most people his age would be using special shampoo in the hope of keeping what was left of their gray hair. Graver had always thought there was something Slavic about his features. He had a wife, two daughters, and a son. Like Graver's own son and daughter, they were all in college now.

Katz also had a mistress. As long as Graver had known him he had always had a woman on the side, though Graver had never heard anyone refer to this. Katz was discreet. He was clever. There had been a few times in the past several years when Graver could tell that Katz was itching to know if Graver was aware of his dalliances, but Katz never made the mistake of trying a coy probe to find out. Graver saw that kind of thing a lot. When you had been in CID as long as he had, you saw it in everyone's behavior sooner or later. They wondered just how many of their skeletons you knew about. Those who tended to indulge in guilty consciences avoided you. The cynics assumed you knew just about everything and treated you with a rakish indifference. Katz was a cynic but, aside from that, he wasn't the kind of man who allowed himself to be haunted by guilt.

"He told me to get back to him as soon as I knew something," Katz said. "I could hear the panic in his voice. I think he was having a party. His wife answered, and when he came to the phone I could hear a lot of voices in the background."

Over at Tisler's car they were making efforts to move his body so that they could look under him. Everyone was trying to keep the blood off of them, but Tisler's limbs had stiffened at awkward angles, making the job impossible.

"If they make it a homicide," Graver said, "Jack's going to go head to head with Lukens."

Ward Lukens was the assistant chief responsible for Management Services and Westrate's principal rival in the power politics that constantly embroiled the ten assistant chiefs. Internal Affairs was his dog, and a homicide in the Intelligence Division would give him an opening to investigate Westrate's prized possession and the most protected division in the department. It meant an interdivisional imbroglio that could easily break out in the open.

"Okay, what about it, Marcus?" Katz tilted his head toward the bloody car in front of them. "Would suicide surprise you?"

"Suicide would surprise me," Graver assented. "Murder would surprise me even more—and scare the hell out of me."

"Then he wasn't working on anything that you think could have conceivably led to this?"

Graver shook his head. "Not really."

Katz turned and looked at Graver. "Creeping Jesus," he said. "What does that mean?"

"I wouldn't have thought so. Not him, not any of the investigators. His informants, maybe. You think of the informants, the sources, being at risk, not the investigators."

"Even if it's suicide you're going to have a hell of a time convincing some people that it wasn't related to spooking."

"Some people?"

"Just about everybody, I guess."

"Yeah, that's what I guess."

"Jesus, that's grisly," Katz said.

They were watching the morgue van attendants and the detectives wrestle Tisler's rigid torso out of the front seat. His stiff sprawl was causing his arms and legs to hang on the door frame and then a corner of the seat as they turned him and twisted him and maneuvered him out of the car.

When the deed was done, when the doors of the morgue van finally closed on Tisler's demise, the four detectives stood in the floodlights just inside the yellow ribbon and pulled off their latex gloves, tossing them into a paper sack. Charlie Bricker was the first to speak. He was tall and lanky, and he spoke to Tordella, looking down at the stocky detective. Whatever he said caused Tordella to nod and nod and then shake his head. Hodge Petersen put in a few words. Tordella shrugged. Tordella then seemed to make a point, turning partly toward the car behind him, gesturing over his shoulder. He asked his partner something, and the young man shook his head. Petersen took out his notebook and a ballpoint pen and made some notes. Tordella leaned forward and made a point of saying something to Petersen; Petersen nodded and kept writing. Bricker thrust his hands into his pockets, rocked back on his heels and said something as he wagged his head side to side as though he were reciting a set of rules. They all nodded in agreement.

"This ought to be interesting," Katz said.

At that point they broke from their loose huddle and came across the grass, through the dizzy fog of insects attracted to the floodlights.

"Well"—Tordella was the first to speak as the four of them approached—"we all pretty much agree that we just don't see anything indicating foul play here." He was addressing Katz this time, his boss, who was leaning his forearms on the fender of the car as he smoked, as if he were watching a game of pick-up basketball.

"It just looks like he shot himself is all," Tordella added. "I mean, that's what the physical evidence seems to point to. But there are still the fingerprints to think about, the autopsy, whatever the CSU might come up with, all that. IAD's going to need some stuff."

Charlie Bricker nodded. He was actually assigned to Narcotics but was pulling his eighteen-month stint in IAD, a requisite tour of duty that rotated among officers in all divisions. This was a universally dreaded duty, partly because the job involved investigating fellow officers, which no one liked to do, and partly because there was no overtime allowed in IAD, which adversely affected your monthly income. Internal Affairs detectives were often in a bad mood.

"I guess the best way to handle this," Bricker said, fixing his eyes on Graver, "is for us to get a synopsis of the investigations Tisler was involved in. And some kind of risk factor assessment for each one. We've got to have some way of making a judgment as to the job-related possibilities here."

"I'll see what I can do," Graver said.

"I'm going to put that in my report," Bricker said, making it clear to Graver that he wasn't going to be finessed, "that I'm requesting that kind of information from you before I can conclude my part of the investigation."

"I understand," Graver said. "Fair enough."

He couldn't blame Bricker for being a stickler about it. His captain was going to insist on that. And besides, Graver could afford to be amenable. Whether or not he ultimately gave Bricker what he was requesting would not be solely determined by him anyway. The CID file was the most sensitive repository of information in any law enforcement agency, and persons having access to the entire file could be counted on the fingers of one hand.

The intelligence unit of a police department stood apart from all the other divisions in one central aspect: it had no active interest in crimes already committed. Instead, the intelligence division's objective was preventive, to identify criminal trends, and to provide assessments of these trends to policy makers by collecting information about people and organizations who were either known to be, or who were suspected of being, involved in criminal acts, or who were threatening, planning, organizing, or financing criminal acts.

The key phrase in this mandate was "suspected of." It was the source of a world of trouble. Suspicion carried with it a responsibility as delicate as nitroglycerin. Because the law gave intelligence officers the authority to act on their suspicions, implicit within that authority was the assumption that they would act responsibly. They were given considerable latitude in determining who should become a target of their "collection efforts." (The term "spying" was considered a dysphemism, though many believed it to be a more honest description of domestic intelligence work.)

Intelligence investigators often collected information about persons who, at first glance, were not clearly seen to be involved in criminal activities. The intelligence file, therefore, invariably contained allegations, rumors, and hearsay that were in the process of being either corroborated or disproved. This information was known as "raw data."

For this reason, the file was highly sensitive. In reality, every Intelligence Division operated under a tentative condemnation. If the raw data they gathered eventually was validated and the resulting intelligence was used to avert criminal activity, then the intelligence process was a prima facie success. It was justified.

On the other hand, if the raw data eventually proved to be false, then the information was purged from the intelligence file. However, during the time in which these allegations were in the process of being evaluated, the intelligence unit was in fact maintaining a file of spurious information about persons or organizations who were entirely free of any criminal taint. In the eyes of many people this was clearly a violation of the individual's right to privacy, a violation that was hardly justified by the system's other successes.

For this very reason, then, the intelligence file was considered inviolable by the men and women who were responsible for keeping it. The file's raw data was considered unstable and susceptible to abuse, and only those persons who knew and understood the context in which the information was collected were allowed access. However, this narrowly restrictive guardianship of the CID file created an information elite, and like any privileged group the Criminal Intelligence Division was often resented. It was itself continuously under suspicion by those on the outside.

Marcus Graver had made a career of collecting other people's secrets. He had learned early on that most men were so complex a mixture of what was traditionally considered good and bad that to assign either value to any one individual was to commit a gross oversimplification. His personal philosophy about human nature had ranged all the way to the farthest margins of cynicism and back again, and now his own views were so bedeviled by disappointments and buoyed to hope by those rare, but inevitable, acts of selflessness, that he no longer had a coherent philosophy at all. No one theory or doctrine seemed to him to contain a suitable explanation for the astounding diversity of behavior of which a single individual was capable.

He also had learned that if you were in the business of collecting the kind of information about people that they ardently wished to keep hidden, for whatever innocent or evil reasons, you had better accept the fact that you never would be free of suspicion yourself. Knowing other people's secrets was, in itself, a kind of tainting knowledge.

They talked a few more minutes while the morgue van disappeared through the high weeds and the tow truck pulled up and hooked onto Tisler's car. Graver said he would take the responsibility for notifying Tisler's wife. The detectives finally left, and the Crime Scene Unit broke down its equipment and packed the van. Katz lighted one more cigarette.

"Well, congratulations, Marcus, this is a first," he said. "I don't believe a CID officer has ever died in circumstances that required an investigation."

"No," Graver said, "I don't think so."

It was completely dark now except for the jerking beams of flashlights as the two CSU investigators put in the last of the equipment and closed the doors. They had a brief conversation with the remaining uniformed officer who was waiting to be the last to leave the scene, and then they climbed into their van and plowed through the weeds to the ruts that led them back to the paved street.

The uniformed officer started toward them, his flashlight bouncing across the trampled grass.

"It's all right, go on in," Katz said to him across the darkness.

"Okay, sir. Just checking."

"Yeah, thanks," Katz said.

The flashlight beam bounced back to the patrol car, the door slammed, the headlights came on, and the car made a turn away from them and headed for the ruts that everyone else had followed.

For a moment the city seemed far away, having nothing to do with them. There were no more planes taking off from the airport. Katz's cigarette glowed brightly then faded, absorbed by the darkness that was close around them. Graver was waiting for him to make his observation. He knew Katz had something on his mind, or he would have been gone with the rest of them.

"I'm not telling you anything, I know," Katz said, clearing his throat and spitting a whorl of smoker's phlegm into the weeds. "God knows you've steered CID like a Kremlin gambler, but if I were you, I'd watch out for the cross fire on this one. I don't think Lukens is going to let Westrate off with a simple 'suicide.' The rumors about

Hertig retiring have got the AC's jumping from foot to foot like a bunch of little boys needing to pee."

Katz was a schmoozer and a lover of scuttlebutt. It came naturally to him. He would risk a trip to hell if he thought the devil could give him some juice on St. Peter. As it was, he was satisfied with regular happy hour visits at the right taverns and with belonging to the right health club where his sole exercise was lifting Bloody Marys—in one of his jogging suits—the tomato juice standing in as a health food.

"Westrate's like a rutting buck for that slot," he went on. "But I think Lukens's determination to keep him out of it could be just as nasty an ambition. I wouldn't expect you'd matter much if you got in the way of that fight."

Graver stood up from leaning against the fender. "No, I guess you're right about that."

He didn't want to have this conversation. He hated talking departmental politics. In his job he had to take it into consideration every time he stepped off the sidewalk, but he didn't like to talk about it. No matter what you said in a conversation on this subject, people like Katz inevitably would pass it on, usually with a spin on it. Graver didn't need that.

"Sorry you had to be dragged out here," he said.

Katz straightened up too, dropped his cigarette and stepped on it. He was used to Graver cutting conversations short. Graver was well known for it, for never kicking off his shoes, sitting back, and gossiping with the boys.

"What about Tisler," Katz asked, spitting between his feet, "was he a good investigator?"

"Yeah, actually, he was," Graver said. He paused. "I'm just hoping he wasn't better than I thought he was."

He guessed Katz wouldn't understand that.

4

AS GRAVER DROVE TOWARD THE WEST LOOP ON THE SOUTHWEST Freeway, he rolled down his windows despite the warm and dense humidity. He wouldn't have cared if it had been raining, he had to have some fresh air, and he wanted a lot of it.

Graver eventually would have to pay his respects to Peggy Tisler. As the captain of the Division, that was his responsibility. But he had met the woman only once or twice, three or four years ago, and he did not want to be the one to break the news to her of her husband's death. The messenger's role properly fell to Dean Burtell.

Dean Burtell probably knew Arthur Tisler better than anyone. In order to run a successful "collection operation," it was imperative that a symbiotic working relationship exist between the investigator and the analyst. As an analyst Burtell was on the receiving end of the operation's take and was responsible for applying critical thought to it, trying to ferret out the tortured patterns of criminal relationships and activities, and envisioning new possibilities not only for the way the targets might operate but also for the way law enforcement might act to preempt them to the greatest effect.

But in addition, he played a significant role in shaping the collection process itself. If he needed more information to confirm or disprove his suspicions about expanding linkages and connections, he consulted with the investigator. Working together, often for long periods of time, they designed a collection plan that each considered feasible and realistic.

In this way, step by step, they created a "folder" on their target, a process that might require years to develop. It was a long-term working relationship and was rarely successful if the investigator and analyst were unable to establish, at some level, a compatible association. Simultaneously, moreover, each investigator and analyst also worked in tandem with other investigators and analysts, sometimes carrying as many as six or seven targets. It just so happened that over time, Tisler and Burtell had worked a lot of targets together, and Burtell had come to know the reserved investigator very well.

Burtell was Tisler's physical opposite: strikingly good-looking, just over six feet tall, an enthusiastic handball player, a smart dresser, slightly wavy black hair which he wore full but well cut, a heavy beard that, even when closely shaved in the mornings, contributed a faint shading to his complexion. His personality, too, was in opposition to Tisler's. Dean Burtell had the at-ease manner of a man who never doubted himself. He was a fluid conversationalist, articulate and adept in social situations. Though he was gregarious by nature and enjoyed being around people, he was never so extroverted as to draw attention to himself. He was unusually polite, in an old-fashioned sort of way. In former times he would have been called a gentleman.

He had only two things in common with Tisler: he, also, was in his mid thirties; and he and his wife had no children.

Dean and Ginette Burtell lived in an upscale condominium complex just off Woodway in the vicinity of the Houston Country Club. This was more than a little out of the reach of an analyst's salary, but Ginette had a very good position with an international marketing firm headquartered in Houston, and her salary far surpassed her husband's. Ginette Burtell was a good match for her husband both in physical attractiveness and intelligence, though she was decidedly quieter.

Turning off of Woodway, Graver drove through the limestone pillars that marked the entrance to a complex of two-storied clusters of condos that the developers had given a distinctly Gallic flair, and which sat well back from the street behind a thick stand of loblolly pines that rose on stalky legs into the darkness.

He found the right cul-de-sac and parked at the curb in front of Burtell's home which, he was relieved to see, was lighted. Locking the car, he made his way along a meandering sidewalk through dampish odors of freshly mown grass, to a walled courtyard with an iron gate. As he opened the gate and went in, he immediately noticed the scent of roses which he barely could see on either side of the sidewalk in the soft light coming through the front windows. He pressed the doorbell and heard the muted response of distant chimes somewhere in the house.

The front light came on over his head, and while he was considering asking Burtell to join him outside rather than going in, the door opened and Ginette stood in the light wearing a pair of brief peach shorts which were very nearly hidden by the loose tail of a tank top.

"Marcus," she said with a smile of surprise. "Dean didn't tell me you were coming by." She stepped out and hugged him.

"Sorry, Ginette," Graver said. Her neck smelled vaguely of perfume. "He didn't know I was coming . . . I just need to see him a few minutes."

She looked at him with just a flicker of worry in her eyes and then pushed it aside. Even if the men and women who worked in intelligence told their husbands and wives more than they were supposed to about their work, the spouses were well trained to act dumb about it. In reality, they consistently behaved unnaturally incurious.

"Well, come on in," she said, stepping back into the entry. "We were sitting out in the patio. It was cool after the rain, but it's already warming up." She closed the door behind him. "We're having drinks . . . would you like something?"

Throughout the ordeal of Dore's well-publicized affair, Ginette Burtell had been exceptionally compassionate. He had learned that her late father had been through something similar years earlier, and she gave Graver all the understanding that she had gained in her own experience. In doing so, she had won Graver's lasting appreciation, and an unspoken bond grew between them that, despite a long friendship, had not been there before. She was a good bit shorter than Graver, with very white skin and short, jet hair. She was the kind of woman who woke up in the morning looking fresh and unruffled, showing none of the rigors of sleep.

"No, nothing," Graver said. "I'll only be a moment . . ."

They started walking through the living room toward an open, very modern bone-white kitchen.

"Dean was going to work in the yard," she said, "but the rain gave him an excuse to put it off."

"I doubt if he needed much of an excuse," Graver said.

She laughed and tucked a bit of hair behind one ear. "No, he wasn't looking forward to it."

Just then the back door in the kitchen opened and Burtell came in, barefoot in jeans and an old rugby shirt with the sleeves pushed up almost to his elbows. He had their drinks in his hands and was concentrating on maneuvering the door closed with his foot when he looked up and saw Graver.

"Marcus." His face ran through several emotions in the space of a moment—surprise, puzzlement, foreboding, recovery—before he collected himself and feigned a relaxed smile. He came toward them, handing one of the glasses to Ginette. "What's up?"

It was probably Graver's ill-disguised uneasiness that he reacted to so quickly, but whatever he sensed, he tried to remain nonchalant, though he surely expected the visit was not a social one.

"I'm sorry for not calling first," Graver said.

"It's all right, no problem," Burtell said. "Come on, let's sit in here." He gestured toward the living room with his drink. "It *was* cool outside, but it didn't last long. Oh, uh"—he held up the glass—"want something?"

"No, but thanks."

"Ginny"—Burtell turned to his wife—"would you mind making sure I got everything outside? I know I left some pretzels out there."

Ginette Burtell would make herself scarce.

They sat down, Graver in an armchair, Burtell on a large silk sofa. Graver sat back in the overstuffed chair, the tufted back feeling good against his spine, which had begun to ache. Burtell sat forward on the sofa, sipped from his glass, then rested his forearms on his knees, holding his drink casually in both hands, his eyes fixed on Graver.

"No easy way to get to this," Graver said. "Arthur Tisler's dead. It looks as if he killed himself."

Burtell dropped his glass.

There were only a few sips left, and it sloshed out on the creamy carpet with a couple of pieces of ice.

"Shit," he said, his eyes locked on Graver, his voice falling dead, the expletive in reference to Graver's announcement, not the spilled drink. He looked down at the spill—it was clear, gin or vodka—and then reached down and picked up the glass, fumbled with the few ice cubes, and finally captured them and put them in the glass. Taking a handkerchief out of his hip pocket, he laid it on the damp spot and pressed it, and then put the glass on a side table. He moved slowly, almost as if he were anticipating having to catch his balance. He looked at the handkerchief between his bare feet.

"Holy shit," he said. His face was drawn.

Neither of them said anything for a moment as Burtell stared down at the handkerchief.

"I went out there tonight—"

"Out there?" Burtell interrupted, his eyes still on the handkerchief. "He did this at home?"

"No. He'd parked in an empty field near the runways at Andrau Airpark. A patrolman just happened to see it and checked it out."

Burtell hadn't moved. "How?"

"He shot himself."

Silence.

"In the head?"

Graver nodded. He was watching Burtell closely. The two men were good friends. They didn't socialize all that often outside their professional relationship, but they were closer than most within that context. Graver almost felt like an older brother to Burtell who was a decade younger, and the feeling was reciprocated. They each knew how the other's mind worked, and both of them probably invested more of themselves in the intelligence game than was healthy for their marriages. They were kindred spirits and knew it.

"In the mouth?"

An odd thing to want to have clarified, but sometimes a person's curiosity about suicide, the precise activity of it, was as unexpected as the act itself.

"His right temple, Dean. He used his own gun."

Burtell's eyes were still fixed on the handkerchief. "Suicide," he said.

Graver heard the flatness in Burtell's voice and found his preoccupation with the handkerchief between his feet a curious behavior. Graver noted that Burtell was actually wan, seemingly nauseous.

"Well, that's what it looks like. That's not official yet. There was no note, not there with him, anyway." Graver spent a few minutes telling Burtell how the evening had unfolded, all of it just as it had happened. When he stopped, Burtell looked up.

"What about Peggy?"

"She doesn't know yet," Graver said. He hesitated. "I hate to ask you this, Dean, but I'd appreciate it if you'd break it to her."

"Jesus Christ," Burtell said. He reached down and picked up his handkerchief and tossed it on the table beside the glass. "Sure," he said, sinking back on the sofa. "Sure, it's fine. I don't mind. It ought to be me. I know that." He looked at Graver. "Is that all there is to it? That's all you know?"

"I'm afraid so."

Burtell frowned incredulously, but when Graver didn't elaborate Burtell's eyes drifted away. "What in the hell did he think he was doing?"

"I was really hoping you could give me some insight into that," Graver said.

Burtell's eyes jerked back to Graver. He seemed taken aback.

"You probably knew him better than anyone," Graver reminded him.

"Look, I don't . . . I just . . ." He paused, then, doing what he did best, he collected his thoughts, organized his thinking. "Okay," he said, raising his opened hands, palms out, a gesture of calming himself, starting over. "We weren't *that* close, for Christ's sake, Marcus . . ." He thought about it, staring past Graver, out to the blackness through the windows, shaking his head slowly.

"God, I don't know . . . uh, at home," he began. "I can't imagine anything going on at home, between him and Peggy anyway, that was eating at him . . . enough . . . you know, for this. Honest to God, I don't. Their marriage was . . . I don't know," he cleared his throat. "It would seem boring I guess to some people. Art wasn't . . . he didn't play around. He didn't hang out with a bunch of guys even. Peggy wasn't a sports widow, anything like that. He went to work; he went home. They pretty well did everything together.

"They didn't have any obvious troubles, serious ones anyway. Art was content with going to Peggy's cat shows, helping her with that kind of shit. That was actually their big 'outside activity,' her cat shows."

He paused, his thoughts straying for a moment before he caught himself and shook his head. "I just don't see anything there to kill yourself about. No lovers or crazy sex or frustrations." He caught himself. "I mean . . . I never saw any evidence of that kind of stuff. All I'm saying is, Art and Peggy . . . you just never saw anything like that. Nothing extreme about either of them, nothing that was in danger of getting out of control."

He laid his head back, twisted his neck in an effort to relieve the tension. He straightened up.

"What about their families," Graver asked. "Any complications there? What about money? Debts?"

"Family worries," Burtell said. "Art's dad is dead, five or six years ago. His mom lives in Dallas, in a retirement community near his only sister. He's never expressed any concern about any of them. I think Peggy's parents live in Corpus Christi. I don't really know anything about them.

"As for money problems, hell"—Burtell smiled thinly—"Art is 'fiscally conservative.' I doubt if he knew the definition of squander. He would have to be *taught* how to live beyond his means. One of the few people in the United States who operated on a cash basis. Really. I'd bet the only dime they owe is on their house . . ." He stopped. "In fact, Christ, I would have thought Tisler would be the last person in the world to kill himself, if for no other reason than it would cheat Peggy out of her insurance. He's paid premiums for years . . . money down the tubes . . . that's the way he'd see it. He would have thought it was a damned stupid thing to do. I mean, it would have been the first item crossed off his list of options. He just wouldn't have considered it . . . practical."

"You think he *didn't* kill himself?"

Burtell looked up. "No, that's not what I meant at all. I'm not implying anything . . ." He stopped and stared at Graver, who remained silent. "We've got to go into his investigations, is that it?"

"Regardless of what Homicide comes up with, we're going to have to audit them for our own internal satisfaction," Graver said. "We've got to make sure there's no connection, you know that."

Burtell swallowed and nodded. "Sure . . . I know."

"Was he holding something?" Graver asked.

It was a legitimate question, and Burtell knew it. Intelligence investigators were no different from other people when it came to occasional judgment calls that crossed over the line. Though a proper intelligence organization used a voluminous paper-trail system to account for—and justify—its activities, and to keep a firm rein on its investigators, there was no process that could anticipate acts of omission. For an infinite variety of reasons, there were occasions when investigators did not put everything they knew into the mountain of reports they were responsible for filing for each target they investigated. A good investigator had a side of him that was intensely private. He never told anyone everything he knew, not even his superiors who relied on his integrity. A good superior officer would know this, and he would know that there wasn't anything he could do about it. In this business secrets were the coin of the realm, and everyone had a few coins put away—just in case.

Ultimately, however, you had to believe the system would work because it *was* a system. You had to believe your investigators would not withhold information to the detriment of the operation or the Division, or to the detriment of the ideals inherent in the profession. In the end, as in all things, it came down to trust. It was an irony not lost on Graver. He knew from experience that the number of people any given intelligence officer would trust at any given time, inside or outside the business, would fall in the low single digits.

"Honest to God," Burtell said. "You knew him well enough to know he didn't have a loose tongue. If he was holding anything significant, he didn't give me a clue about it. The Seldon operation was definitely on his mind. It was getting tougher, but I just can't see how it would, even remotely, have a connection to something like this."

"Jesus, Dean. You don't think the combination of dumping toxic waste and drug trafficking held potential dangers?"

"Of course, but my point is that Art wasn't that far into it yet. He wasn't *near* anything. You've seen his contact reports. He was just beginning with this informant. The guy had potential, but Art was having to work his ass off to develop it. But he didn't know enough yet to get him killed."

"That you know about."

"Well, yeah," Burtell conceded, "that I know about."

"He wasn't working on anything else that had the potential of turning nasty?"

Burtell shook his head and stared away toward the night beyond the windows. "The three other targets he was working . . ." His voice trailed off and again he seemed to let his thoughts drift on to something else. For a moment neither of them said anything. Then Burtell continued, his gaze still directed outside, ". . . with me, they were pretty much on idle." He shifted his eyes back to Graver. "I don't know," he said. It was a statement of puzzlement, not ignorance.

Graver studied Burtell. He had expected him to be shocked, to be sobered, even stunned by the news of Tisler's death, but he had no idea that Burtell would be affected like this, that he would be so . . . disturbed.

"Okay," Graver said. He had heard enough. Maybe Burtell would have a new perspective on it in the morning. "Look, maybe I should go on over there and tell Peggy myself. Or I could go with you . . ."

"No, it's all right," Burtell said, shaking his head. "I really ought to. Ginny and I." He looked over at his glass as if he expected there might be something there to drink. He looked at Graver.

"Tomorrow was supposed to be the first day of my vacation," he said. "Guess I'll hold up on that."

Graver had forgotten. "Were you leaving town?"

"No, not the first week. Ginny couldn't get away just now. But we were going away the second week."

"Maybe we can clear this out in a couple of days."

"What about Besom? He can't be reached can he?"

"No, but I think he's supposed to be back in the city late tomorrow, though he's not scheduled to return to the office for another week."

"This is going to be a stunner for him."

"I'll try to get him as soon as he's back in town."

"Westrate, what about him?"

"I haven't talked to him," Graver said.

"He's going to shit."

"Probably."

Graver wasn't surprised by the question. Jack Westrate kept so much pressure on the Division that every time something happened out of the ordinary, every time there was an administrative or budgetary change or an investigation became "sensitive," everyone wondered how Jack Westrate was going to react. No one ever believed he would go to the wall for them. Westrate was consistent; he always put himself and his own concerns first. Every time there was a ripple in the water his first thought was how was it going to affect his own little boat. Arthur Tisler's self-centered act of despair would be an enormous annoyance for Westrate's own self-centered preoccupations.

Graver watched Burtell absently wind his watch. It was a dress watch, the classic kind that didn't have a battery. You had to wind it regularly. Graver guessed it wasn't even water-resistant, that kind of a dress watch. Burtell fidgeted with the band, a leather band with a gold buckle. You didn't see much death in the kind of work they did. You never really got much of an opportunity to see how people would react to it.

5.

AS HE WALKED OUTSIDE AND RETRACED HIS WAY ALONG THE
gently curving sidewalk to his car, Graver thought the night air seemed
even more oppressive than before. Feeling uneasy, he unlocked his car
and got in, started the engine, and looked toward Burtell's house as he
turned on the headlights. There wasn't much to see through the staggered, straight silhouettes of the pines, only glimpses of the lighted
windows in the chalky black haze.

He pulled away from the curb and drove out of the cul-de-sac.
Burtell, he thought, had reacted pretty much as Graver had expected.
And then again he hadn't. Though Burtell was indeed shocked at the
news of Tisler's death, shocked even that it had been suicide, his reaction seemed, somehow, to exceed the import of this grim news. It
wasn't that he had behaved inappropriately or ingenuously, or that his
reaction was emotive. Burtell was not given to melodrama. It was just
that his response was more inclusive, as though there were another
dimension to the news, and that he was understanding more than
Graver had told him. Graver didn't doubt anything he saw. He simply
had seen more than he was expecting.

But then the way Graver was looking at this might say more about
himself than about Burtell. Perhaps the fact that Graver thought
Burtell's reaction to the news of Tisler's suicide was more . . . reac-
tive . . . than Graver had expected was because Graver himself felt so
little. Or, at least, Dore would have said that. According to her, Graver
was an "emotional cripple." Someone else might have said that he was
too analytical or reserved or low-key. But Dore had said "emotional
cripple," and the description had stung. In fact, Graver remembered at
the time how much he had been hurt by that. Sometimes those words
ran through his mind when his eyes and thoughts stopped momentarily
on the cobblestone memento on his desk. Graver had spent a lot of

time second-guessing his feelings after that, and he regretted that Dore had saved those words as her parting shot, after she had already filed for divorce, and they had almost stopped speaking. He would like to have talked with her about that, before the emotions that once had tied them together had been severed and cauterized. But it was too late now, and he was left to puzzle over this unflattering description in solitude. Maybe that was the way Dore had intended it to be—to leave the barb in the flesh after the sting, a lasting, reminding hurt.

It could be, though, that Burtell's reaction was not really noteworthy. How was he supposed to have reacted? Could Graver have described a more appropriate response? What was an acceptable response when one is unexpectedly confronted with such things—outrageous acts that seemed to occur outside the realm of the probable? Tisler's suicide had gone against the grain of everything they had understood about him, and perhaps such a deviation from expected behavior had elicited an equally surprising response from Burtell.

There is, after all, a natural framework for everything, Graver thought, ambits of behavior that evolve from a given society and a person's place in it. There is an accretion of expectations that attach to our lives after a certain point. It is assumed that we will continue to behave as we always have behaved, that our personalities are set, an unavoidable amalgam of all the experiences we have had from birth to the present. If someone deviates from a behavior that we have come to expect from them, we are startled by it and remember it far more clearly than if they had acted predictably.

But it occurred to Graver that if by killing himself the benign and unremarkable Arthur Tisler had exceeded the parameters that others assumed of his personality, then perhaps he had done so with a clear, keen vision. Perhaps he had viewed his closing hour as an opening door, a way to liberation. Perhaps it was an act of rebellion against thirty-five years of docile predictability. By acting contrary to others' expectations of him, he may have entered for the first time in his existence into a limitless freedom, though he had had to end his life to do it.

The old Georgian home of red brick and white wood trim sat back from a wrought-iron fence with fleur-de-lys finials that long ago had rusted away all their original paint and had acquired a dark, mossy patina. The fence and the lawn and the house were shaded by the canopies of third-generation water oaks that hovered over the property like silent old aunts whose job it was to observe the comings and goings of the generations and, perhaps, to whisper about them among themselves when the Gulf breeze, prowling inland from the sea, moved through their vast, heavy limbs.

Graver had grown immensely and immediately fond of the old house which he had bought from an elderly doctor, a childless widower who, with the practical bravery of a reasonable man of science, had decided to sell the house he had lived in all his adult life and check himself into a nursing home while he could still understand what he was doing and why he was doing it.

The house always had seemed to be just the right size for them, even when the twins got to be teenagers and the place was filled with their migrations of friends, and the smell of Dore's cooking permeated the large rooms. For years he and the twins together had mowed the rambling lawn and cleaned the pool where the languorous summers were animated by swimming parties and barbecues. Dore had loved the place as much as he had, and most of their eighteen years there had been full of good times and good memories. Mostly. Then several years ago, after the twins had gone away to college, a worm had gotten into the apple. It was as if every minor incompatibility that he and Dore had managed to subordinate, in deference to the welfare of the family they had made, began to grow into insurmountable differences. In the end it all came to no good, and he was left with the house, a kind of consolation prize for having lost everything else. And now the twins were in graduate schools on separate coasts, each engaged to be married, and he was left pretty much to himself.

He parked in the gravel driveway, locked the car, and followed the sidewalk to the front porch. He had forgotten to leave on the front porch light, so he fumbled in the dark for the keyhole, finally found it, and let himself in, turning on the porch light behind him as he closed the door. He threw the dead bolt and took his suit coat off as he started up the stairs.

Throwing his coat on the unmade bed, he sat down and started taking off his shoes. He undressed, hanging his clothes in his closet across from Dore's, the door of which he kept closed. Walking into the bathroom, he took off his underwear and kicked them into the clothes basket. He took his swimsuit off the hook near the shower door and put it on, avoiding looking at himself in the mirrors. Grabbing a towel along with his goggles and lap watch, which he kept on a shelf near his washbasin, he walked out of the bathroom, removed his dress watch, tossed it on the bed, and started down the stairs. As he walked through the house, he turned on the lights and left them on behind him, through the main hallway, into the kitchen, and out into the back patio.

It was a simple pool, rectilinear, and long enough for lapping. Graver did not turn on the pool lights or the yard lights, though he could see the dial of the watch in the cast-off glow from the patio. The summer night air enveloped his bare skin like a warm breath as he walked to the edge of the pool, dropped his towel, and sat on the edge with his legs in the water as he pulled on his goggles. When they were in place, he slipped into the water which had a slightly cooler feel to it because of the passing rains. Normally, after soaking up the sun all day, it was as warm as a womb.

He swam forty minutes in the dark, the steady back and forth of his laps causing the waves in the water to rock the flappers in the skimmers, a gentle, hollow clapping that died out as it crossed the lawn to the hedges of honeysuckle and jasmine. He had done it so much he could tell within five minutes when he almost had swum his allotted time. Tonight he pushed himself a little more, added ten more minutes to the half hour and picked up the pace as well. When he finally finished, his lungs were sucking for air, and he had to hang on to the side of the pool a while before he could pull himself out.

Upstairs he changed into a pair of casual trousers and an old dress shirt, stepped into a pair of loafers, and went down to the kitchen. It was too late to cook anything, and nothing in the refrigerator looked good to him anyway. Bored with the prospect of eating, even though the laps always made him ravenous, he poured out a bowl of cereal, sliced thin slivers of a nectarine onto it, added milk, and sat down at the kitchen table to eat.

He didn't know what to do with his thoughts. Not wanting to think about Tisler for a while, he tried to make his mind blank. It was an exercise in futility. His *Weltanschauung* was thoroughly Westernized, and a blank mind was not an easy thing to come by. His meditations tended more toward the baroque.

Finishing his cereal, he stood wearily and took his empty bowl to the sink and rinsed it out, opened the dishwasher, and put the bowl and spoon into the washer. Taking a glass from the cabinet, he ran water from the faucet and stood at the sink as he drank it, looking out at the back yard. He could see the pool, and here and there a few yards from its margins the silhouettes of sago palms and palmettos; and in the near-dark he could make out the lower boughs of the oaks, too, with Spanish moss hanging from them in cheerless festoons that he found somber even in the best of times and which he now regarded with a painful sadness.

Then he heard the doorbell ring.

Instinctively he looked at his watch; it was nearly twelve o'clock. He set the glass on the counter, grabbed the hand towel that hung on the cabinet and dried his hands as he walked down the hallway to the front door. The light was off in the entry, but the front porch light was still on, and he could see the fractured figure of a man through the beveled glass of the door. He didn't readily recognize this Cubist silhouette. Tossing the hand towel over his shoulder, he threw the dead bolt and opened the door.

6.

JACK WESTRATE WAS STANDING IN FRONT OF HIM, HIS HANDS jammed into his pockets, his dark silk suit rumpled, shirt collar and tie undone. He was several inches shorter than Graver with a body frame that brought to mind words like bulwark and redoubt. He was decidedly stout, but it was the kind of heaviness that suggested a hard aggressiveness. There was nothing at all soft about Jack Westrate, in either his manner or his appearance.

"We'd better talk," he said and clamped his mouth shut, his long upper lip and dimpled lower lip clinched tightly in determination.

Westrate was like a bully cur; he always tried to set the rules of engagement in his favor with an immediate challenge in the first seconds of encounter. But it was too goddamned late to be "challenged," and Graver was in no mood to feel any sympathy for Westrate's predicament. So he didn't move or say anything, just hesitated long enough to make Westrate a little less confident, and then slowly backed away, pulling open the door. "Come on in," he said.

Westrate was immediately inside the front hall, bringing with him his familiar dense odors of cologne and cigar smoke. He wheeled to the right where he saw lamps turned on in the living room, and walked in.

"Sit down, anywhere," Graver said, gesturing vaguely around the room.

Westrate passed up the sofa and a wing chair and sat in a deep green leather armchair beside a table with a small Oriental lamp. Graver sat in his usual reading chair near his old mahogany desk, draping the hand towel on the brass handle of a magazine stand.

"I talked to Katz a little while ago," Westrate said immediately. "After you guys left the scene out there."

He sat forward in the chair, his forearms resting on his thick knees. His black hair was thinning, but he wore it military short anyway—

screw the balding. Sometimes you could tell he had tried to comb it, but most often it was just there with no particular direction except on the bit of a forelock that he swiped occasionally with a little black comb he carried in the inside pocket of his coat. Like Burtell, his beard was so thick it always shadowed the tight skin of his round face and hid like coal dust in the cleft of a belligerently square chin.

Graver said nothing. He crossed his legs and waited.

"Herb said they thought it was suicide."

"That's just . . ."

"Yeah, I know, preliminary. Still, it's not a by-God-for-sure homicide."

"No."

Westrate worked his thick, diminutive shoulders nervously, his suit coat bunching up in a roll behind his stubby neck. He always dressed in expensive custom-made suits, silk and linen blends, tropical wools appropriate to the steamy climate of the Gulf Coast, but he wore them without regard, seemingly unaware of their cost, wallowing in his thousand-dollar "pieces" as though he were wearing Katz's jogging uniforms. Graver rather liked that profligate flair about him, though he really couldn't say why. It was just about the only thing that he could tolerate about the man.

"Okay. So. I wouldn't have expected you to tell them, of course, if you had any reason to think differently. What about it?"

"I don't know anything, Jack. I don't disagree with what they've got to say because I don't have the slightest idea why the guy's dead."

"No shit." Westrate's face was immobile. He was trying to discern a feint in Graver's response, wondering if Graver was holding out on him. His suspicions were insatiable. Westrate had come out of the womb reading Machiavelli and suspecting his father of being a cuckold.

"No shit," Graver said. "And I talked to Dean Burtell a while ago. If this has anything to do with Tisler's work—suicide or homicide— Burtell doesn't have a clue about it either. Can't imagine."

"Oh, Jesus," Westrate seemed genuinely surprised. "That's good to know. A relief." He had expected the worst. He was the gamesman's equivalent of a hypochondriac. Ironically, however, Graver had the uneasy feeling that this time Westrate had a good reason to be worried, though he didn't say that.

"But beginning in the morning we're going to review his investigations—"

"Yeah, great, that's good," Westrate interrupted. "I wanted to cover that with you. Get a white paper to me, something I can pass on to Hertig, confirming there's no way the intelligence file has been compromised by this stunt."

Stunt? Jesus Christ.

"The thing is," Westrate said, his mouth tight with determination, "not to let this get out of hand. Get on it; stay on it; get it out of the way." He chopped the space between his beefy knees with a thick hand.

Graver didn't say anything to that. Westrate was so immersed in the profession of covering his ass that no form of reasoning that worked to any other end was capable of penetrating his myopic self-interest. He was a savvy player without question, but he lacked the ability to see the larger picture insofar as it extended beyond his own person. It was a modern failing, this inability to think in terms of anything that did not affect you personally, so, in this, Westrate was a product of his times. His own career was the largest concept in his intellectual inventory, and whatever affected that career was the most important thing in life. He was a hollow man. And he probably would realize all of his ambitions.

Graver looked away, toward the hallway floor just outside the double doors. A solitary lamp in the entrance hall was throwing a gleam across the polished hardwood floor like the trail of the moon on water. There was more than just an air of desperation in Westrate's manner and that made Graver cautious. Suspicious and cautious. He reached over to his desk and got a notepad off the top along with his old green fountain pen. He unscrewed the cap from the pen and made a few notes on the tablet, only doodles, but Westrate couldn't see that. He took his time, underlined a few things.

"Let's just talk worse case, here," Graver said, looking up. "How are you going to handle this if it's a homicide?"

Westrate's face changed from sober to grim at this question. He clearly had been thinking about this.

"Nobody gets into the file," he said. "Not without written *and* verbal approval from me."

Westrate was no clumsy buffoon despite his street-wise, bully-boy manner. The man could play power politics with as much sophistication as the best of them, which was precisely why he was sitting here now. Inside maneuvering was as second nature to him as his bluster. But even though Graver disliked him, he had to admit sympathy with

Westrate's situation. He was going to have to make some decisions for which there were no clear precedents, an agonizing position for a bureaucrat. Tisler's death was going to require a criminal inquiry and, naturally, the investigations he was involved in would be central to the inquiry. And therein lay the problem.

Westrate had to consider not only how best to protect the integrity of the CID files, but he had an additional concern. As assistant chief in charge of Investigative Services, he was responsible not only for CID, but also for Homicide, Narcotics, Auto Theft, and the Crime Lab. Tisler's death had put Westrate in the unenviable position of having his left hand (Homicide) investigate his right hand (CID), a situation which was made even worse by the fact that his right hand was the most secretive Division in the department and never opened its file to *anyone.*

So Graver asked the next sticky question. "What about IAD?"

Westrate shook his head slowly, emphatically. "I'm going to deal with that. I've already talked with Hertig, before I came over here."

No surprise there.

"Are you going to try to restrict them?"

"Damn right I am," Westrate snapped, his eyes boring in belligerently as if Graver himself had challenged him. "Nobody wants to relive that shit in the seventies. I'm not going to have anything like that on my watch."

"That was an altogether different situation, Jack. They were using the CID to compile dossiers on political enemies. It was stupid. They should have expected to have their files seized. They had nobody to blame but themselves."

"That may be," Westrate said. "But Lukens is going to have to climb over my dead goddamned body to get to that file."

Graver capped his fountain pen. "That may be wrongheaded thinking," he said.

Westrate looked at him. "What?"

Westrate was bowing his neck at this hint of anything less than total endorsement.

"Come on, Jack. An intelligence officer's death complicates the question of confidentiality," Graver said. "We can't very well refuse to turn over material evidence. I think we can argue for some editing of what they see, but I don't know how we can refuse to let them see anything."

"If Tordella determines this is a suicide, that's great, best case," Westrate said evasively. "No formal investigation. I'll handle the administrative wars . . . you *memorize* Arthur Tisler." He pointed the two index fingers of his clasped hands at Graver. "If somebody throws a question at you about that guy, I want you to be able to answer it with documentation, if there is any. I don't want anybody to know anything about Arthur Tisler that you don't already know about Arthur Tisler."

Westrate was still sitting forward, the soles of his shoes planted flat on the floor, his forearms anchored to his knees, the shoulders of his suit hunched and rumpled, a physical reflection of his emotional disconcertion—and determination. The lighting in the living room was not all that good, but Graver clearly could see the moisture glistening on Westrate's contentious upper lip. A lot was at stake, careers, and at least one man's entire psychology. It seemed that Westrate was convinced—or knew—that a scandal was about to break. He seemed to be developing a siege mentality, to be taking his concern way beyond a prudent anticipation of events.

"Why did you come to me like this?" Graver asked after a moment. "You could have told me all this in the morning."

"Okay," Westrate said. "Fair enough." He laced the fingers of both hands together and clenched them until the knuckles turned white. "We got a break with those turds shooting each other in Kashmere Gardens. That was an incredible piece of luck. I want to hold on to that." He raised a forefinger and wagged it slowly. "Insiders are going to know that we've got to be investigating this. SOP. But what I want to avoid is the suspicion that there's something more than routine shit going on here. I hope to hell—I pray—that you find out that Tisler was up to his nostrils in gambling debts, or that he was a closet queer, or that he was a pedophile and was diddling half the four-year-olds in Harris County. But the last thing I want to discover is that he was dicking around with the intelligence file. I want his sin to be *personal*, not professional."

Westrate was on the edge of the chair now, his stomach and pugnacious, tight-lipped face thrust forward, on the attack.

"The thing is," he said, "I don't want to give the impression that we're afraid that it might *be* professional. I don't want anybody to see me go into your office, and I don't want anybody to see you go into mine. From now on we communicate only by *secure* telephone. Or, we meet like this, face to face, somewhere we know we won't be seen. I don't want the staff, yours or mine, to see us putting our heads together. I don't want any scuttlebutt. I don't want any leaks. That's how the press gets on to something like this. Some little tight-butted secretary, some damn daydreaming file clerk, sees shit and reports it. I don't want the internal rumor mill to feed on this. And I've already made this clear to Katz, too."

Graver imagined that Westrate had been all over Katz, badgering him mercilessly to do this, to avoid that. He very definitely had worked up a lather over this. Graver couldn't make up his mind whether Westrate's paranoia was routine theatrics or whether he was hiding something that Graver should have been smart enough to pick up on. The truth was, if Westrate was trying to maneuver him because of one of his innumerable hidden agendas, there simply was no way Graver could see it coming. Not at this point, anyway.

Westrate stood. "I've got to go," he said. "Listen, Graver, I want you all over this. Any doubts, any questions, anything doesn't look right, doesn't add up, you get to me quick." He opened his eyes wide. "Understand?"

"I think I do," Graver said.

Westrate gave a snappy nod as if to say good, then we understand each other and that is that. He wheeled around and headed out of the living room like a wild boar, on to other business. In a few seconds he was at the front door, pulling it open. "Call me," he said without looking around and walked out.

Graver closed the door behind him and waited in the darkened entry hall, looking at the broken glow from the porch light as it came in through the refractions of the beveled glass on the door. He waited until the headlights of Westrate's car came on and then watched as they moved slowly and crookedly away from the curb and disappeared obliquely skyward down the street.

7

"I DON'T MUCH LIKE THE IDEA OF YOU WATCHING," SHE SAID, looking out the car window down the little lane of trees which still glistened from the passing rain. The lane, too, was glittery from the shower earlier in the evening and an occasional wisp of steam broke loose from the pavement and hovered momentarily under the glow of the lamps before it rose slowly and joined the darkness.

"I want to see this," Kalatis said. "Don't think about me. Just do what you do."

The woman was in her early forties with roan hair which she wore pulled back loosely and gathered behind her head. She was well built, having a figure that was not lean but which she kept much younger than its years by a lot of sweat and a grim determination to do battle without quarter against gravity and failing elasticity. Determination had marked her life. Her will was lapideous. Her ability to concentrate was singular. Her nerve was inflexible.

Panos Kalatis liked to use her because, over the years, she had learned to be afraid. The accumulating years had done that to her. That which constant threat had not been able to instill in her when she was younger, when he first had met her in Trieste, the creep of days passing one into the other, month into month, year into year, had accomplished with nothing more threatening than the moving hand of a clock. Diminishing time, the slow inevitable shrinking of it, had made her less rash. Life, which had been nothing to her in the past, acquired a looming significance. She still was deliberate, but the motivation now involved an equation of self-preservation. Kalatis liked to see her afraid. Thirty, even twenty years earlier, simply watching her walk across the street used to make the hair prickle on the back of his neck. Today her silent menopausal body had done what neither gun nor knife nor poison had done in her youth: it had taught her to fear, and her fear, though she kept it hidden, unacknowledged, had unmasked her mythology. She still was death, but now she was death of another sort.

He looked at her. She wore a bone-white silk blouse with long sleeves and a straight black dress. The flesh visible above the first button of her blouse was as white as the silk. He had not seen her breasts in fifteen years, and he wondered about them. So different from Jael's . . . in every way.

"I don't like it," she said again.

These few—two, maybe three jobs—would be her last for him. He thought she had just about outlived her usefulness.

"How much longer do you think you can do it this way?" Kalatis asked. It was a cruel question, but for Kalatis cruelty was an amusement, his own feelings long ago having been seared beyond such subtleties.

"What do you mean?" she said, opening her purse and looking around inside for something.

"Using your body. Maybe you ought to consider another angle. Something more . . . suitable . . ."

"Suitable," she said, looking into her purse. She took out a tube of lipstick and applied it without looking in a mirror. "Suitable . . ." She nodded, lightly pressing her lips together, staring out the windshield.

Kalatis guessed her insouciance was only feigned. He imagined she was furious. He thought that if the light in the car were brighter he would be able to see on the pale flesh across her cleavage the appearance of the blushed marbling that flared there when she grew impassioned. In the old days, in Trieste, he would watch for that delicate reddening whenever they went to bed together. She was always in such control he couldn't tell what she was feeling—her sexual engagement, like everything else she did, was done with a cool deliberation that did not give way to abandon until the very last moment. At first it was a puzzling thing for him because he never knew how he was doing, and sometimes the end caught him by surprise. Until he discovered the secret of her blushing bosom. She could control everything except that very specific behavior of her anatomy.

"What did he do to you?" she asked, closing her purse.

"This man?"

She nodded.

Panos put his hands on the steering wheel and stretched his legs and sighed. "He is very wealthy. He has two airplanes. One of these airplanes was seen where it should not have been. He knows it was there. He knows it should not have been there." Panos turned and looked at her. "I believe he has been unfaithful to me . . . in his way." He grinned.

The telephone between them rang before she could respond to that, and Panos answered it.

"Yes." He listened a moment. "Thank you." He put down the telephone. "He is with two other men, but he has just asked for his bill."

She opened the door of the Mercedes and got out. The private club was in an old, ivy-covered brick building and sat in the center of a thickly wooded grounds. The narrow lane that led to it was one-way, entering from one side of the grounds to a small parking lot and exiting on the other side. Kalatis was parked very near the entrance to the small lot, and she had to walk nearly fifty yards, passing through the dim wash of a streetlamp before she rounded the end of a hedge to the parked cars.

As he watched her walk, Kalatis had to admit she was far from losing her touch, or her shape, or, certainly, her sexual appeal. Though he would never let her know that. Whatever her fears of aging might have been, they were premature, but he liked seeing her afraid nonetheless.

There were only six or seven cars in the small lot that could not have held more than twice that number when it was full. The club was very exclusive indeed. She had met the man on two occasions only recently, while she was in the company of someone else, but it was enough for her to have made an impression on him, enough to give him a reason to think about her after she was gone. This would not have worked with ninety-five percent of the men Kalatis knew, but in his middle age Toland had become rash about sex. Irresponsible.

She waited in the darkness of a tree's canopy at the edge of the parking lot, and when the front door to the club opened she started walking. Kalatis watched with interest.

Having opened her purse again, she was looking in it as though searching for something, as she approached him in the dimly lighted car park. He saw her first, of course, and just as she looked up and closed her purse, he said something to her and she stopped. She turned, and oh, yes, recognized him.

Kalatis watched their body language and followed the gist of their conversation. Toland straightened up a little, tightened his stomach a bit. What in the world are you doing here?

She explained she was supposed to meet X here, but the arrangements had been made quite early in the evening and then she had got delayed and could not reach him by telephone, and a cab had just dropped her by on the off chance that he might still be here.

No, he wasn't here, Toland said. She tilted her head with good-natured disappointment. He asked a question, and she shook her head and explained something. He asked another question and gestured to his car only a few feet away. She tilted her head again, thinking a moment as she looked toward his car, and then nodded in appreciation.

She took him to the parking lot of a condominium not far from the club where her car was already parked anonymously among the others. She told him where to park, the precise spot. By now she was teasing him shamelessly, and he would have driven off the bank of the bayou into the water if she had allowed his hand another inch inside her panties. Instead of going up to her place, she suggested, why didn't they . . .

Kalatis had choreographed the event, but it would not have worked so well if his principal dancer had not been so talented. When Kalatis pulled into the parking lot behind them with his lights off, Toland was oblivious to everything but the increasingly revealing glimpses of the unfamiliar flesh in the seat next to him.

Parking among other cars a good distance away, Kalatis rolled down his windows, took out his binoculars, and balanced them on the steering wheel. He focused them on Toland's car, the interior of which was illuminated by the streetlamp behind it, presenting the two figures inside in sharp silhouettes. He gave them a few moments, until she had removed her blouse. He would have let her go further, but he was afraid she wouldn't remove her bra, that she would end it before he wanted. He still would have to pay her, but he wouldn't get the satisfaction he wanted. So, he adhered to the plan and picked up his telephone and dialed.

It rang four times before Kalatis saw her push Toland away. He could only imagine what was being said.

"Yeah . . ." Toland's voice was tense, irritable.

"Robert, this is Panos Kalatis."

Pause.

"Kalatis?" Pause. "What are you doing calling my car phone at this hour?"

"Somehow I knew you would be there to answer it."

"What do you want?"

"It's payback time, my friend."

"What?"

"I know what you've been doing, Toland." Kalatis kept his voice reasonable, relaxed. "You are not nearly good enough at this to try to steal from me. You're such a stupid pig, Robert."

Pause.

"I think there's a misunderstanding here . . ." Toland began. His voice had changed.

"I believe you're right," Kalatis said, "so let me explain it to you." He watched Toland's profile closely through the binoculars. "The woman sitting next to you . . . she's going to kill you for me. And I'm going to listen to it on this telephone and watch it through my binoculars. Robert, you are really so stupid . . ."

Kalatis didn't actually hear the two gunshots, not as gunshots, just as phuut! phuut! at the same time as part of the window behind Toland's head flew out into the parking lot sounding like crushed ice as it scattered across the pavement. The remaining parts of the window were glazed in rusty smears.

Kalatis counted to twelve before the passenger door opened, and she got out and closed it behind her. She walked through the few cars with business-like deliberation until she stopped at one, unlocked it, and got in. He counted to eight before the headlights came on, and she drove away.

Just for the hell of it Kalatis dialed Toland's number again. He felt better, much better. He listened to the busy signal with satisfaction.

8

GRAVER TURNED OFF THE PORCH LIGHT, THREW THE DEAD BOLT
on the door, and walked back into the living room. He went over to his
desk and sat down, picked up the notepad and looked at his doodles.
Jesus, what a situation. What a goddamned night.

He tossed the notepad aside. He was restless still, far too wired by
the events of the evening. He picked up the dish towel from the magazine stand and absently began folding it lengthwise, matching the corners, letting his thoughts drift. He thought about going for another
swim, to clear his head, but then, too quickly, even before he could
avoid it, he was remembering the weedy field and the fight that Tisler's
stiffening limbs had put up against the final confirmation of his death.
Tisler had managed to surprise everyone, had managed to set minds to
work on his death that had never given him a second thought when he
was alive. That was, of course, a sad inversion of the way life *should* be
played.

But Graver learned a lesson every day on the fallacy of the concept
that life "ought" to be a certain way. Everyone believed in that, of
course; perhaps it was the last vestige of a long-submerged Platonism—
the idea of the ideal, that somewhere there was rightness and perfection and if we could only adjust or fine-tune ourselves or society or our
environment, then life would be as it "ought" to be.

Maybe Tisler's suicide was his own comment on the "oughtness"
fallacy. Maybe he decided that was a screwed concept—or maybe he
decided that just a little more pressure on the trigger was the precise
amount of fine tuning needed to bring the idea of "oughtness" full
circle to perfection.

When the telephone rang on the corner of his desk, it startled him.
He cringed to think that there were still developments breaking in
Tisler's grim death. It was approaching one o'clock. It occurred to him

that he might not answer it, though there was never really any possibility that he wouldn't. But he did let it ring six times. Still holding the dish towel in one hand, he reluctantly picked up the receiver with his other.

"Hello."

"Marcus?"

It was a woman's voice, not Dore's, not instantly recognizable. His mind began reeling through an inventory of voices.

"Yes," he said, waiting for another audible clue. And then immediately he was cautious, even suspicious, afraid she might disconnect without speaking again.

The next voice was a man's. "Graver, this is Victor Last."

Graver recognized this voice immediately, even though he didn't think he had heard it in eight years. Last's voice was distinctive for its softness, even kindness, and its peculiar accent. Last was the son of British parents who owned a shipping business in Veracruz, Mexico, where Last was raised. His pronunciation was a wonderful amalgam of several languages.

"Well, this is a surprise, Victor," Graver said. He was wary.

"Yeah, well, I'm in the city now," Last said. "Thought I ought to check in with you."

Graver could hear the hollow, rushing-air sound of Last attempting to cover the mouthpiece while he spoke to someone with him, probably the woman who had been on the telephone when Graver answered it.

"Uh, look," Last said, coming back on the line, "I'd, uh, I'd like to talk to you. Could we get together for a drink?"

"Victor, you've caught me at a bad time. I've got a lot of fires to put out at—"

"It actually would be best tonight," Last interrupted. His voice was calm and natural, agreeable, as though Graver had called *him* to ask for a meeting at Last's convenience.

This polite disconnect with the reality of their situation put Graver on guard even more. Graver looked at the dish towel in his hand. Shit.

"Okay. Where are you? North? South?"

"The best place, I think, would be where we used to meet," Last said casually. Graver noted that he had avoided saying the name.

"Is it still there?"

"Sure."

"It's late. It'll be closed."

"I checked it out," Last said. "It'll be open."

"Fine," Graver said in resignation. "I'll be there in twenty minutes."

"Twenty minutes," Last said, and the line went dead.

9

THE SMALL LA CITA CAFE WAS ONLY A BLOCK FROM THE SHIP channel, near the neck of the turning basin in a barrio that never changed. Two languid Guadalupe palms still flanked the dirty, mandarin red front door, their huge, rough trunks rooted on the little spit of dirt and weeds between the buckled sidewalk and the rock building. A single strand of flamingo pink neon light still bordered the two horizontally rectangular front windows with their rounded corners, and the porthole in the front door still allowed a glimpse of the murky interior before you entered.

Graver parked across the street and waited a moment. He surveyed the neighborhood of small bungalows tucked back under old trees, their dim interiors glimpsed through the cinnamon vines that laded the dilapidated fences of thin wire and wood and the banana plants that lent a cool grace to the graceless, bare yards. He saw no cars parked along the street that seemed out of place.

He got out of the car, locked it, and walked across to the cafe. The neighborhood night smelled of the ship channel, a mixture of bayou and bay water, of diesel engines and foreign ports, of neighborhood kitchens and other-country foods. Graver inhaled deeply of the smells and let them carry him back eight years.

He pushed open the door and stepped inside. La Cita had never been much of a place, but it had been a good cafe. Now the once warmly lighted interior that had smelled of Greek and Mexican food was a gloomy twilight of neon beer signs, and the air was a bad breath of stale bodies, dead cigarettes, and rancid grease. Behind the bar a heavy Mexican woman was huddled under a small, goose-neck lamp reading a magazine. There were a few dark visages in the corners, but he walked past them to the back door and stepped out into the patio where strings of low-wattage, colored lights were draped back and forth above the stained concrete dance floor. Here everything was the same, the cinder-block walls that formed the sides and, across the back, a series of low-arched openings through which he could see the slow-drifting lights of ships moving through the channel. And the chunky wooden tables that randomly bordered the edges of the patio were still there too. But on this hot summer night only three or four of them were occupied by a few men and women who looked as though they had never had a chance at anything or, worse, had thrown it away and never had learned to forgive themselves.

Walking to an empty table toward the back corner, Graver sat so that he could see the door that opened onto the patio from the tavern. Behind him, through one of the arches, he could hear a tug grumbling softly past the wharves. He ordered a bottle of beer from a young man who had one side of his chest caved-in, causing a shoulder to sag and making him walk crab-like as though always having to correct a drift. He distinguished himself in this shabby setting, however, not by his deformity, but by having an immaculate haircut which he had combed to perfection. He also wore a dazzling white waiter's apron which, in this setting, undoubtedly was considered a foppish flair.

As Graver drank his beer, a wraith of a man in his early thirties got up from where he had been sitting alone and put some coins in the jukebox on the far side of the dance floor. He returned to his table, and in a moment the accordions and cornets of a *conjunto* began playing while the man lighted a cigarette. As if by request, two worn prostitutes wearing tight dresses that barely reached past their crotches and accented their obtruding stomachs, left their male companions at their table, stepped onto the dance floor, embraced, and began dancing. Seemingly oblivious to the sprightly rhythm of the *conjunto,* they moved mournfully about the floor, the calves of their thin legs knotted tightly as they crane-stepped on high heels that scratched across the gritty concrete floor, stomach to stomach, the arms of each draped over the other's shoulders, their foreheads together in unsmiling partnership.

Graver watched them, as did their companions and the wraith. Nearby a man and woman ignored them and shared a thick joint of marijuana in a sweet, mauve haze. When the music stopped the women returned to their companions, and Graver finished his beer.

Five minutes later Victor Last walked out the back door of the cafe, looked quickly around the courtyard, and started toward Graver, passing through the patches of colored lights in his casual, loose gait with which Graver was so familiar. He was wearing straw-colored, full-cut linen trousers with pleats, a blousy and wrinkled long-sleeved silk shirt, and a light tan, soft-shouldered sport coat with patch pockets. His dun hair was stylishly long, though barbered around the ears and neck, and combed back with a lock falling carelessly over his forehead.

He smiled modestly as he approached Graver who stood, and the two of them shook hands.

"Sit down," Graver said, motioning to the chair across from him.

Last nodded and sat down. Graver could see him better now and was surprised to see that Last must have had some hard years. Though he still was lean and had a good tan—the sun had streaked his dun hair with blond strands—his face was incredibly wrinkled, his eyes pinched with crow's feet and the corners of his mouth beginning to pucker. He looked like he had suffered a lot of sun and had given in to the rum and tequila of former days. Whatever he had been doing in the last eight years, he had done it with a vengeance.

Last grinned at him from across the table, slumped back rakishly in his chair with his legs crossed at the knees. Graver noticed his teeth were still white and even.

"You don't look any differently, Graver," Last said. "You must've made a bargain with the Deevil himself."

"You know I don't make bargains, Victor," Graver said. "The Devil will have to stand in line like everybody else."

"Shit." Last grinned broadly. That was all he ever did. He didn't laugh. There were only small grins or large ones. No laugh.

Graver noticed that Last's nose had suffered a severe break. It had not been flattened; it still had a strong narrow bridge, but it was seriously out of line. Graver guessed that as far as women were concerned, it hadn't hurt his looks at all.

"Well, I'm glad to see you," Last said.

And Graver believed him. Eight years earlier Last had been Graver's key informant in Graver's final and largest case as a CID investigator. They had worked closely together for nearly a year and had, indeed, become friends, though Graver thought that Last's definition of the term was probably much more fluid than his own. Graver noticed that Last's Masonic ring with its garnet stone, of which he was so proud, was missing from his ring finger.

"Can I buy you a beer?" Graver asked, motioning to the crooked waiter.

"Absolutely." Last reached into his coat pocket and took out a pack of cigarettes. He looked at Graver. "You still don't smoke?"

Graver shook his head.

Graver ordered himself another beer and one for Last, and Last watched the crooked waiter drift away toward the outside bar.

"Jesus," Last said, and sucked hard on his newly lighted cigarette. He turned back to Graver. *"El capitán,* huh?" Another grin, a small one.

"Yeah, about four years ago," Graver said. He was watching Last closely.

"I understand . . . I gather . . . you must've divorced."

Last's expression had changed to one of sympathy. Graver thought it odd that he would bring this up. Everyone was "gathering" that. The gossip columns had kept the masses appraised of Dore's imminent remarriage.

"He's 'socially prominent,' then? Must've been painful."

"I didn't much like it," Graver said. What was Last trying to do?

"Well, I'm sorry," Last said.

The crooked waiter brought the beers, and Last wiped the mouth of the bottle and held it up for a toast. Graver raised his bottle also, and they clinked them together.

"To the good old yesterdays," Last said, "and better tomorrows."

Last drank the cold beer like it was a glass of water, glubbing down throatfuls. When he lowered the bottle to the table it was more than half empty. He pursed his mouth, savoring the aftertaste, and looked around the dance floor.

"Place hasn't completely gone to piss." He dragged on the cigarette. He studied the women. "Whores used to be better ladies than these, though."

"Nothing's changed here, Victor. Maybe your taste is improving," Graver said.

Last smiled at this and turned to Graver again and smoked his cigarette. Victor Last was an unusual informant. In fact, he was an unusual man. He had a university background in the fine arts and when his criminal tendencies kicked in to gear they did so with a distinctly arty flair. His entire criminal history consisted of two years spent in a minimum security unit of the Texas Prison System for selling rare books and botanical prints and engravings that had been stolen from British libraries, museums, and private collections.

By the time Graver came across him, Last had served his sentence and had drifted back into the business, only now the danger of his game had gone up several notches. He had spent almost a decade as an "exporter" from Mexico with a sideline trade selling stolen pre-Columbian artifacts. And he was dabbling in forgeries of historical eighteenth-century colonial documents. Graver pegged him as raw material for a first-class informant, which he became. Graver looked the other way regarding some of Last's rumored involvements, and within a year an appreciative Last had put Graver onto a network of illegal arms dealers which developed into one of the largest gun-running operations on which the CID had ever tracked information.

As it turned out, Last liked the nature of the game. He liked the matching of wits involved in being a "spy," and he even liked the spurt of adrenaline that accompanied the edge of danger inherent in all high-dollar criminal schemes. Victor Last was indeed a gentleman adventurer, as at home in the jungles of Central America as in the mansions of Houston's wealthiest residents who collected the artifacts that he "acquired."

"Okay," Graver said, setting down his bottle, "what happened to you?"

Last nodded and slowly swallowed his mouthful of beer. He smiled almost apologetically.

"Dropped out of sight, didn't I?" He pulled on the cigarette again, looking across the concrete dance floor washed in patches of soft colors. "I overplayed my hand a little on that last one, Graver. It was time for a sabbatical. Went to Oaxaca first. Got back into the exporting business. But it wasn't what it used to be. I'd heard there was a new market opening up in Hispanic colonial documents. I checked into it; it was indeed a coming field. I moved to Madrid and spent a year combing the archives there. Fantastic archives. God, cavern-sized museums and extensive private collections. Some of the museums don't even know what they've got. Hell, some of those places don't even know how *much* they've got, let alone the value of it. Wonderful places."

He paused and polished off his beer. He held the bottle up and waved it at the crooked waiter across the patio. The waiter held up two fingers with a questioning look, but Graver shook his head.

Last ground out his cigarette in the tin ashtray on the table. The muggy night was stifling now in the early hours of the morning and beads of perspiration began to show up on Last's forehead and upper lip. He took a handkerchief from the breast pocket of his jacket and dabbed at his face, at his upper lip.

"Was in Spain, what, almost two years," Last continued, stuffing the handkerchief back into his pocket, deftly leaving a puff of it showing. "Made a bit of money, some good contacts. But all in all I preferred dear old Mexico. It's got a more 'entrepreneurial' quality about it." He smiled. "So back I came. Mexico City. I started working with private photographic archives. Surprisingly lots of them there. You know, all that European influence during the *Porfiriato,* before the Revolution. Some of the older families who have these big mansions in the grand parts of the city, they've got all kinds of things stuck away in those dowdy old places."

The crooked waiter brought Last's beer and took away their empty bottles. Last picked it up, the cold amber bottle already beaded with condensation, and held it to his forehead and temples. Then he took several big swigs.

"I got into some trouble in Mexico City," he continued. "They have finicky laws there about archives and things . . . historical artifacts . . . I don't particularly have anything against their legal system . . . you know, based on the Napoleonic Code . . . but you add to that all the corruption and it's hard to make a buck down there. Legitimately." He shrugged, looked at the people around the patio. "Even so, I kept at it for a couple of years."

He reached into the side pocket of his jacket again and took out another cigarette and lighted it. He tilted his head back and blew the smoke up into the still night.

"About six months ago," he said, "I went to Veracruz looking for some colonial maritime documents that were rumored to be in the possession of a family whose ancestors had been dockmasters in the port there during the Spanish viceroyalty. I was flush then, having just made a good deal on the sale of a collection of Mexican Revolution photographs, so I treated myself by staying at a very expensive little inn not far from the beach. I met a Houston couple, and during the next three or four days we became acquaintances. About a month after returning to Mexico City, I got an invitation to attend a party at their house in Houston."

Last took another drink of beer, and while he was savoring it, his pale eyes stayed on Graver. He was getting to the point of whatever it was.

"At the party, I met two other couples who interested me. One fellow owned an art gallery, and another was a businessman. Owned a huge business of a certain kind. I know nothing about this kind of business—it's an innocuous business—so I was just asking questions and this fellow grew very wary, suddenly evasive with his answers. Now this was curious to me because this was like asking questions of a grocer. I mean, it was an innocuous occupation."

Last smoked his cigarette.

"Now, before I go any further than this, let me ask you something."

Graver nodded.

"Have you had any inkling"—Last clenched his teeth and softly sucked air through them—"any inkling of police corruption?" He held up his hand with the cigarette. "On the detective level, I mean."

Graver felt his stomach tighten. "In what division?"

"I don't know."

"You know I wouldn't tell you something like that, Victor."

Last nodded understandingly. "Yeah, I know." He smoked his cigarette and tapped the amber bottle with one of his fingers. He made a face, one of indecision, not knowing what to do.

"Do you know something?" Graver asked.

"No," Last said quickly. "No, I don't. It's only a suspicion at something I overheard. I didn't understand what I was hearing and this was one of the possibilities. There are other possibilities."

"And where did you overhear this something?"

"Here in Houston. At a tony party about three months ago."

"Three months?"

"I had distractions," Last said, explaining his delay in bringing this to Graver. "But this kept . . . hanging back there." He tapped himself on the side of the head. "It was one of those things that I thought if I mentioned to you, you'd know right off if it meant anything or not."

"But you haven't told me anything."

"No, but I asked you about a subject, and it doesn't seem to ring a bell. I think I was wrong."

Last suddenly was uncharacteristically ill at ease. His aplomb was a distinguishing feature. It was what made him a good con artist and a good informant. He was one of those men who accepted dares with an easygoing smile and did outrageous things with a sophisticated fear-lessness that made good stories for other people to tell years afterward. But just now he was not feeling very sure of himself.

He began drinking his beer with the clear intent of getting it all down so he could leave. Graver guessed that Last was just now realizing he had miscalculated, that whatever he had stumbled into wasn't what he had thought it was.

Down on the wharves a gantry crane started up, whining like something hurt, moving cargo off the docks.

"Well, I apologize, Graver," Last said. "Getting you out and all. Really sorry . . . I, uh, must've"—he smiled unsteadily—"really been off course here."

"Look," Graver said, "how can I get in touch with you? Are you living in Houston now or still in Mexico?"

"Houston," Last said, putting his cigarette in his mouth as he reached inside his coat pocket for a pen and a small notepad. "More or less," he added cryptically. Squinting around the smoke of his ciga-rette, he jotted something on the paper and ripped it off the pad. He handed it to Graver. "You'll most likely get a woman. Her name is Camey." He spelled it. "She'll always know how to get in touch with me."

Graver didn't ask any questions about Camey. He nodded.

"Let me think about this," he said. "If you have any other thoughts, get in touch with me."

Last finished the beer and reached for his wallet inside his coat pocket.

"No," Graver said. "I'd rather you owe me."

"Ah." Last nodded once, his roguish smile returning. "Clever po-lice psychology." He put out his cigarette in the ashtray. "Well, Graver, despite the misfire it was good to see you. If ever you need me, call Camey."

He stood and reached over, and they shook hands.

"I'm glad you called, Victor," Graver said. "Take care of yourself."

"Good-bye, Graver." Last turned and walked back across the dance floor through the pastel patches of colored lights. In a moment he was opening the back door of the shabby little tavern and was gone.

Graver stood too and took out his wallet and got enough money for the drinks and a good tip for the crooked waiter and put it on the table under Last's empty beer bottle. Taking one final look around at the doleful patrons of La Cita, he walked across the dance floor, into the rancid tavern, and out the front door into the barrio night. The narrow little street was empty, just as it had been when he arrived. Victor Last was nowhere in sight.

Monday

THE SECOND DAY

WHEN THE RADIO ALARM WENT OFF, GRAVER OPENED HIS EYES
to a muted gray light. Without even moving, he could tell that the
muscles in his neck and shoulders were drawn into knots.

After getting home late, Graver had sat up in bed for another hour
trying to make notes for the next morning's meeting. Though he found
it hard to concentrate, he stayed with it until weariness and an aching
back forced him to put aside his pencil and pad and turn out the light.
Then he had lain awake until the early hours of the morning thinking
about Last. He replayed their conversation, picked at every word Last
had spoken, and wondered at his having appeared out of nowhere.
Graver cautioned himself. This was no time to start believing in seren-
dipity. Eventually he slipped into a restless sleep and the previous
twelve hours melted into dreams of absurdity.

When he rolled over to get up, he found the legal pad and pencil
among the rumpled sheets and threw them onto the floor at the foot of
the bed. Resisting the temptation to fall back onto the pillow, he
swung his legs over the side and sat there a moment, feeling heavy-
headed and stiff. Then he stood slowly and walked into the bathroom,
stepped into the shower, and turned on the cold water.

After bathing and shaving, he dressed and gathered up the dirty
clothes that he had piled on the settee near the windows. After
dropping off the clothes at the laundry, he stopped by a neighborhood bakery and bought a cinnamon roll, a small coffee, and a newspaper. The Kashmere Gardens shooting did make the headlines. The
gunman holding the hostage had been killed in a barrage of gunfire
after he shot his hostage on the small stoop of the garage apartment.

Graver quickly searched the rest of the paper, but there was no
mention of Arthur Tisler's death. Not a news item. He tossed the news-

paper into a trash can and finished the cinnamon roll and coffee on the way downtown.

The Criminal Intelligence Division was located on the top floor of a doleful, three-story building at the back of the police headquarters compound on the northwestern edge of downtown. Separated from the architectural splendors of Houston's building-boom years by the thundering concrete maze of ramps, piers, girders, and abutments of the Gulf Freeway, the homely, cement building had the peculiar distinction of having its single front door face outward from the back of the police compound rather than inward as did the other buildings. As a result, its ground floor had a marvelous view of the underbelly of the expressway where Buffalo Bayou screwed its way under the concrete superstructure, and the sticky weeds of summer grew out of control.

Graver parked in a small parking lot across the alley-like driveway that circled the building, and which was surrounded by a jungle of weeds that grew higher than his head and crowded right up to the lot's margins. He got out of the car, locked the door, and inhaled the musty odors that emanated from the oozing and fetid cocoa waters of the bayou fifty yards away on the other side of the weedy embankment.

Lara Casares was always the first person in the office every morning. Always. She had been Graver's secretary since the first day he stepped into the captain's position four years earlier when he had pulled her from the stenographer's pool where she had been a wasted talent. Nearly everything about Lara was a surprise, beginning with her appearance. She was an attractive thirty-three-year-old Latina with an astonishingly fine figure, which included a bust of admirable proportions and killer hips which she thrice weekly Jazzersized and pounded to a white-hot firmness. She wore her clothes the way musclemen wore tight shirts, self-aware and lustily pleased with the whole damn thing. Though she had only a high school education, Graver guessed that her IQ must have been off the charts. She was everything a first impression might have suggested she wasn't, dependable, discreet in a position where discretion was paramount, organized like a computer, always two jumps ahead of his every request, considerate, and sober as a nun when it came to her work, though she was something of a raucous lady on a personal level. Graver relied on her without reservation.

Beyond that, they shared a mutual attraction that had gone unacknowledged for longer than either of them ever would have predicted.

Despite her strong personality, Graver knew that Lara was too smart to be the first one to openly address their attraction, which they both knew was loaded with potential problems. This was one instance in which she would not take the lead. As for Graver himself, his shattered marriage had not had the same effect on him that it might have had on most men. He was not more prone to fall into an affair. Rather, for reasons he did not allow himself to examine too closely, he was determined to keep his feelings for Lara at arm's length, though now that the divorce was final he had to admit that there really was no longer any reason to do so. In fact, the truth was that at this time in his life he was probably closer to Lara than to anyone else.

When he walked into the office late, at half past eight, he said good morning to the receptionist and looked down the bare, narrow hallway to his left where the Division's offices opened off both sides of the corridor, a series of identical doors, their façades appearing increasingly narrow as they progressed to the opposite end of an exceedingly long hall.

Nowhere were the strapped finances of the city's budget more apparent than in these quarters. All of the offices, with the exception of his own, could not be described as anything more than cubicles. The offices on the right side of the hall were the more desirable ones because of the enormous advantage of being on the exterior wall of the building and therefore having small windows. On the other side of the hall the cubicles were like Cappadocian caves dug into the inside of the building. They were little more than coffins.

The door to the communications room was open and one of the printers was hammering away, dumping a roll of paper on the floor which was already littered with paper from reports that had come in over the weekend. The computers stayed alive around the clock to receive "contributions" from police officers—patrolmen and detectives —anywhere in the city.

Graver turned and walked past Lara's office and stuck his head in. She was on the telephone, and he pointed to his office and went on. By the time he had settled behind his desk and made a couple of notes, Lara came in the door with his Charlie Chan mug full of fresh coffee. She set the mug in front of him with a napkin, straightened up, and tugged once sharply on the hem of her red suit jacket.

"You left this on your desk over the weekend—with coffee in it. There was mold in it this morning," she said pointedly.

Every morning when Graver came into his office, he found his desk clear and neatly arranged, a condition in which he seldom left it. Lara was responsible. She dusted the amber glass shade on the lamp he had brought from home to offset the anemic fluorescent lighting in the ceiling. She made sure that the marbled fountain pen that Nathan had given him was in the narrow green glass tray on the front of his desk. She made sure the bone-white coffee mug with its silhouette of Charlie Chan on it that Natalie had given him was clean. And she made sure that his book-style calendar was held flat open with the black, smoothly worn cobblestone that a hundred years ago he and Dore, slightly inebriated and laughing, had dug out of a narrow lane near St. Paul's Cathedral.

That was another thing about Lara. She had an intuitive understanding of the lingering power of small things, of old gifts from a son and daughter, or of a mnemonic cobblestone that was not a reminder of the woman who was no longer his wife, but of the girl he once had married.

"Sorry," he said, motioning for her to close the door, which she did, coming back and standing in front of his desk.

"Some bad news," he said. "Arthur Tisler was found dead in his car last night. It looks like he killed himself."

Her mouth dropped open, and she sat down slowly in one of the chairs.

"My God," she said. "He *killed* himself?"

"That's what it . . . seems."

"Seems?"

"It's got to be investigated, Lara, that's all."

"I know, but . . . My God . . ." Her black eyes looked at him, and he could see her remembering Tisler.

"Of course Westrate's worrying about damage control, the way it's going to look."

"Nobody knows about this yet?"

"Burtell knows. He notified Peggy Tisler last night."

"Jesus, poor woman."

Graver would have liked to talk to her a while, just discuss it as he would have done with Dore years ago, but there wasn't time. Reluctantly he moved on.

"I guess you'd better call each of the squad supervisors and have them meet me in here at nine o'clock," he said. "I'll let them take care of telling their people. And you'd better hold all calls for me for the rest of the day except any from Jack Westrate or anyone in Homicide or IAD."

He briefly explained to her about the requisite inquiry and how it would have to take precedence over the normal routine of his responsibilities. Graver monitored the activities of his squads by the daily review of a steady stream of investigation summaries, intelligence reports, initial investigation summaries, operational requests, contributor management reports, and on and on, a seemingly endless flow of cumbersome but necessary forms, files, contracts, vouchers, records, summaries, lists, and logs. All of these—all but the most urgent of them—would now have to be set aside until Graver could complete a report that would give the CID's file a clean bill of health, free from any stain of Tisler's suicide. Lara was going to have to help him deal with more than he could handle.

At nine o'clock the three squad supervisors filed into his office. Ray Besom was the fourth, though absent on his fishing trip. Graver told them straight out what had happened. He told them as much as he had told Burtell the night before, but none of them was close to Tisler and kept their reactions to a soft curse or a wincing, jaw-clenching frown. He explained everything, the situation at the scene, who was on the investigation from Homicide and IAD.

"And I'm going to head our own inquiry myself," he said. "Review his investigations, make sure we're all right." They all knew what he meant. He looked at Matt Rostov, a thin, angular man in his early forties, who supervised the Research and Analysis Squad. "Matt, if it's all right with you, I'd like to pull Dean Burtell and Paula Sale to help me. Can you spare them for a week maybe?"

Rostov nodded and said sure.

"When you go back to your office would you let them know I'll be calling them a little later in the morning?"

Again Rostov nodded. Sure.

"I'm going to get Casey Neuman out of OC also."

"What about the people in OC," asked Lee Stanish, "they know yet?"

Stanish had been in Ray Besom's position as head of the Organized Crime Squad four years earlier. He was a superb supervisor, and Graver had moved him to the Anti-Terrorist Squad when the supervisor there had retired. He had had an excellent relationship with his investigators and never had thought that Besom had done a good-enough job with his old group.

"Not yet," Graver said. "I'm talking to them after this. I decided against making a general announcement. It's touchy, and there's a lot pending. I just thought it would be best if we kept it low-key."

Everyone nodded, everyone understood, and Graver dismissed them. Only Bob Penck, who supervised Technical Services had said nothing, which was normal for him. He might have said something if a bomb had gone off in the office . . . or maybe not.

After they left, Graver asked Lara to go ahead and call in all nine of the Organized Crime Squad's investigators. He got a fresh cup of coffee from across the hall and waited for them sitting at his desk. When they filed in, all of them expecting a bombshell since they never had been called in as a group before, they all stood around the walls, none of them wanting to take any of the three chairs in front of Graver's desk. So Graver stood too, and repeated the story of Arthur Tisler's death for the fourth time.

"WE'VE GOT A LOT TO DO AND VERY LITTLE TIME," GRAVER said, putting his hand on the stack of manila folders. He was leaning against the front of his desk, and the three people he had just called into his office wore grim expressions.

Dean Burtell was sitting in the chair nearest the windows, and despite a fresh shave and his predictably neat appearance, his normally bright personality was nowhere in sight. He was glum and the loss of sleep had changed the appearance of his face. Earlier Graver had spoken to him briefly about his visit with Peggy Tisler. She had been understandably distraught, and Dean and Ginny had stayed with her all night. They had called her family in Corpus Christi, and they had arrived in Houston near dawn just in time for Dean and Ginny to go home, shower, and go to work. Still, something more than the loss of sleep seemed to be at work in Burtell's demeanor.

Graver looked at him, and then looked out through the windows where the morning's smutty Gulf clouds were drifting rapidly inland, forming a muted backdrop for the downtown skyline. The southeastern exposure of Graver's corner office gave him a sweeping view of the city's western face. It was the only felicitous attribute this grim little building offered. The traffic on the expressway rumbled by in deep undertones that at times Graver actually could feel.

"I've already pulled all of Tisler's folders. You're going to work with the hard copies at this point because I want you to be able to see the original documents in case there's a handwritten marginal notation, a check mark in the text, anything that might catch your eye."

Next to Burtell, sitting a little farther back from Graver, was Paula Sale, the second person Graver had pulled from Rostov's R&A Squad. Thirty-six years old, she had a doctorate in sociology from Rice University and was one of four civilians Graver had managed to bring into the Division despite Westrate's objections. She had turned out to be a brilliant analyst. Right now she sat with one long leg crossed over the other, one hand holding a cup of coffee she rested on her knee. She was staring at him with critical, gray eyes as she tried to read between the lines. Paula wore her light chestnut hair with a blunt cut just above her shoulders. Straight, no permanent. She favored shirtwaist dresses which she wore with an unexpected panache. She liked bracelets. Divorced for three years, she could be abrasive to men who showed an interest in her. She most decidedly was not interested in men. Graver sometimes wondered if there wasn't more than a small degree of perversity in her rather forward sexuality and the way she bristled at men who reacted so predictably to it.

"Unfortunately we're not looking for anything specific," he continued. "Nothing that could narrow this down for us. There's just a single fact: Arthur's dead; and a single question: Is there anything in the files that speaks to that? I want you to come up with more questions, a lot of questions. Anything. Everything. I don't care how tenuous they are, if they make any connection at all in your mind, bring them forward for discussion."

Casey Neuman sat near the door. He was the youngest investigator in Besom's OC Squad. Innovative and a quick study, Neuman never had to be told anything twice and most of the time never had to be told anything at all. He was an anticipator, he could see things coming—an invaluable asset. With a shock of thick, light brown hair that he wore boyishly long, Casey favored plaid or tattersall shirts with button-down collars that he never buttoned and khaki suits or the odd sport coat with casual trousers. Though he was quiet, he was a born mimic and liked nothing more than having to change his appearance or take on a role to collect information. He was one of the few men the waspish Paula got along with without some kind of sparing tension. Maybe it was because he was young and boyish, or maybe it was because he never reacted to her acidic tongue with anything other than an openly amused smile. She never got a rise out of Casey.

"I'm going to give Paula the four investigations Tisler was working with you, Dean," Graver said, picking up the largest stack of manila folders and stepping over to Paula. She uncrossed her legs and lifted her coffee mug to let Graver set the stack on top of her legs.

This was standard, good management, and everyone there knew it, but everyone also knew that on a personal basis it was awkward.

Burtell had already told Graver that he couldn't think of anything in Tisler's investigations that might relate to his death, and now Paula was going to be second-guessing him. She was going to have to ask questions that could easily seem like caviling to Burtell. They each understood, and each of them wanted to be responsibly dispassionate.

Graver took the other stack from his desk and handed them to Burtell. "You take the other four, Dean. They're equally divided between Rankin and Derr. They're the only other analysts Tisler's worked with besides yourself. But I don't want you to talk to them about this."

Burtell accepted the folders and nodded. Graver's attention lingered hesitantly on him, and then he turned to Neuman. "Okay, Casey, I want you to work up Arthur just as you would any other new target. Start at the beginning. Run everything. Don't let anything slide, don't make any assumptions."

He paused. Casey and Paula were looking at him with fixed, sober expressions, still trying to absorb the news they had received less than an hour ago.

"This might seem a little distasteful," Graver acknowledged, "but we're going to do it. We've got to pick him apart."

"You don't *know* . . . anything, do you?" Paula interjected.

Though it might have sounded accusatory, it was asked with the kind of affrontive inquiry that was sterling Paula. She knew her place; she knew about hierarchy, but she also possessed an artless honesty and self-assurance that had a leveling effect on all of her relationships. She knew damn well that if he wasn't telling them something it was for a reason he would not share with them, and that he would have to lie to her and continue withholding it. But that was Paula. She wanted to see his face when he said it.

"No," he said. "I don't know anything." He picked up his Charlie Chan mug and sipped his coffee. It was his third cup of the morning, and many more would follow. "Last night they were leaning toward suicide, but that was just an on-the-spot hunch. Maybe later on this morning they'll have something to back that up. But right now there are no suspicions about anything, nothing to guide us in one direction or the other."

He stopped a moment and let his eyes drift to the clouds that were breaking a little now, the bright morning sun piercing through to the skyscrapers in brilliant shafts.

"Everyone clear about what we've got to do here?" he asked. They all nodded. "If there are any surprises waiting in those folders, or in Tisler's background, I want to see them coming. Okay?"

Everyone nodded again.

"You want our assessments on each target worked up in reports?" Paula asked.

"No, and that's a good point. If you think you've got something, come to me, let's talk it through first."

He started to dismiss them, then decided he had better underscore the seriousness of their situation. He crossed his arms and sat back on the desk again.

"Obviously if Tisler's been mishandling the file in some way, this is big trouble," he said. "Anything we discuss here dies here. I didn't choose you for this by tossing a coin, but because I thought you could do best what needs to be done." He hesitated only a second. "You report only to me. *Only* to me. If you want to talk and I'm not around then keep it to yourself until you find me. There aren't any other alternatives, no Plan B. Don't put anything in writing except your notes unless I ask you to. While this is going on I'm available around the clock; it's never too late, never too early. You've got my pager number. Use it. That clear?"

It was, and there were no questions.

12

GRAVER HAD SAVED TWO ASPECTS OF TISLER'S LIFE FOR HIM-self: his personnel file and his contributor documents. He went to the back of the personnel file and started at the beginning.

After graduating from the Academy, Tisler had spent three years in patrol and then began a steady tour through four of the departments in the investigations command, Robbery, Vice, Auto Theft, and a short stint in Narcotics. He twice had taken the exam for a sergeant's slot, but his scores had never been high enough to put him in a good position for a promotion. His security clearance check for his entry to CID was routine and seemed generally to reflect Burtell's assessment that Tisler was an orderly man. His credit report was immaculate. His indebtedness was small: a car, some household appliances, and a new house note that was only three years old. Job performance evaluations were remarkably lacking in distinction throughout his career, even during his first few years in CID.

But eighteen months earlier he seemed to have come into his own as an organized crime investigator and had developed two lengthy and complex operations which ultimately resulted in joint operations with federal authorities and which yielded a dozen or more major arrests. The ongoing Seldon investigation was still another operation that promised to net him some significant players. Burtell was the analyst on each of these three investigations.

Graver reached for the file box that contained the diskette copies of Tisler's folders. There were ten investigators in OC, and each of them was responsible for eight to ten targets. That was too many for Graver to keep in his head. Swiveling his chair around to the computer, he popped in the first diskette. For the next two and a half hours, ducking out only for cups of fresh coffee, he pored over Tisler's first big success.

At twelve-twenty, he ejected the first diskette and stepped outside to go to the bathroom. Lara and several of the stenographers were heading for lunch, and he asked her if she would pick up a hamburger for him when they came back. He gave her some money, walked down the hall to the bathroom, and was back at the computer in ten minutes. He popped the second diskette in the CPU. The second investigation was more complex than the first one. When Lara brought his hamburger, he ate it at the screen, creating a pile of wadded paper napkins and filling his office with the heavy odors of mustard and onions.

At a quarter to five Lara knocked on his door and came in with a sheaf of pink message slips in one hand and a cup of ice and a Dr Pepper in the other. She put the messages in front of him.

"You'd better see these messages before I go home," she said, pouring the Dr Pepper into the paper cup of ice. "And Chief Westrate called just now and said he was going to call you back in ten minutes." She set the iced drink in front of him and straightened up, holding the empty bottle in one hand, the other hand on her hip.

"Fan-tastic," Graver said, stretching his back which seemed to have calcified in the shape of the soft curve of his chair. He reached for the cold drink. "You must've been reading my mind."

"Uh-huh. A pepper-upper." She eyed his desk, still cluttered with the trash from his hamburger. "You've been cooped up in here too long," she said, and started gathering up the greasy paper sack and the dirty napkins and tossing them in the trash. She went over to the windows, opened one of them with the leveraged help of a quick twist of her hips, and flapped her long fingers with their fire-engine red nails in front of her face. "Those onions! My God."

She turned around and looked at him. He was sipping his Dr Pepper, watching her.

"So what's the gossip," he said.

"About what you'd expect, I guess," she said, hands on her hips again, palms vertical. "Art was so . . . un-extreme, if that's a word." She hesitated a second. "I went into his office to clean it out like you asked. Put his stuff in a box in my office to give to his wife. There weren't many personal things." She rocked one high-heeled foot sideways absently. "You been in his office much?"

Graver shook his head, taking in the small movement of her hips as she rocked her foot.

"On the inside of his door—you couldn't see it unless the door was closed—was a centerfold. A black girl. And it wasn't from *Playboy*.

This was from some magazine that went in for the gynecological poses. I mean, she was spreading herself." Pause. "I left it on the door. I don't suppose his wife would want a 'personal effect' like that."

Lara was not being cute about this. In fact her expression and voice portrayed an element of sadness that Graver couldn't quite interpret.

"Well, I appreciate you going through his things," he said. "Dean seems to be taking this a little harder than I would have expected. I just didn't think I should ask him to do it."

"I didn't mind it," she said. "What about you? How are you doing?"

"Fine," he said, sipping the cold drink.

She smiled, knowing he would say that, and nodded.

"That's good," she said. Pause. "Anything else I can do for you?"

Graver had to hand it to her. Lara had never once stepped over the line—albeit, for Lara, the line was a little further out there than it was for most people—during the past year, ever since Dore's affair had made its way into public view of the gossip columns. But she certainly had given him every opportunity to find solace with her whenever he might have desired it. And he had been sorely tempted. That he had not done so had nothing to do with professionalism or the fear that intimacy might ruin an enviable working relationship. He had never had any doubt that Lara could have managed to handle both. He wasn't so sure about himself.

He started to speak, but the telephone rang.

"That'll be Westrate," she said, her smile fading to good-natured resignation as she headed toward the door. "I'm gone. See you in the morning."

"Lara," he said.

She stopped and turned around with her hand on the doorknob.

"I do appreciate . . . everything."

She smiled again, this time with warmth and the intimacy of an unspoken understanding.

"Wash out that coffee mug before you go home. Okay?"

"It's done," he said, and picked up the telephone as she opened the door and walked out.

"Graver."

It was Westrate, though he didn't identify himself. "Katz called me just a few minutes ago," he said. "He'd just gotten a call from Tordella who was still at the morgue. Coroner's calling it a suicide too." Graver could hear the relief, the near joy in Westrate's voice. "Nobody sees any reason to suspect otherwise."

"Did they interview his wife?"

"Yeah, early this afternoon."

"Who conducted the interview?"

"Tordella and Petersen, I think."

"Nothing?"

"I guess not. I just know Katz said they were satisfied so far, and that they'd probably write it up as self-inflicted tomorrow. He just wanted me to know."

Graver slumped back in his chair. He felt more than relief; it was almost elation.

"But I still want a report from you people," Westrate said. "We've got to give the CID a clean bill of health. His wife's already screwed on her insurance, anyway. Might as well confirm it, at least make a report on the probabilities. Guy doesn't kill himself for nothing. Maybe there was a chippy or . . . I don't know, something."

"It'll be a while, Jack. Several days if we don't want it to look like we're sweeping it under the rug."

"Yeah, okay, take a week," Westrate said. "Let me know how it's going."

Westrate was off the telephone, and Graver turned his chair toward the glass wall. Early in the day the clouds had burned off and the hard blue sky stood empty and hot. No thunderstorms today. The expressway was jammed chrome to chrome, a creeping flow of glittering glass and metal wrapped around the girth of downtown.

He looked at his watch. It was five thirty-five, and the offices were empty. He thought about Westrate's call. Everybody was relieved. Nobody's ass was going to get singed over this after all. Everyone was pleased that Tisler seemed to have been so desperate as to have killed himself. The man had been driven to blast away his life for reasons none of them knew anything about, and so far no one, with the exception of Dean Burtell, seemed capable of working up anything more than a wince at his death.

13.

HE TURNED HIS ATTENTION AWAY FROM THE WINDOWS AND pulled Tisler's contributor files over in front of him. "Contributor" was an umbrella term for persons who supplied the CID with information about criminal activity. They were the bread and butter of intelligence work and fell into two categories. "Sources" were contributors with no criminal involvements. They included police officers, federal agents, witnesses, and private citizens, mostly people who felt a moral duty to share information or suspicions about criminal activities.

The other category was "informants," people with criminal backgrounds, prisoners, parolees, probationers, bailees, arrestees, or suspects. Informants were most frequently motivated to share information for quite different reasons than their counterparts. Often they were simply offering information for money. Sometimes they informed for revenge, or jealousy, or in an effort to have "competitors" eliminated, or as "pay back" for some past service on their behalf by law enforcement officials. The reasons were endless, often complex, and usually emotionally charged.

The personal identity of all contributors was closely held information, and their continued anonymity was a matter of enormous importance. Each contributor was assigned a control number which was used on all documents in place of the contributor's name. Graver had gone to the Central Index File, which could be accessed only through a stand-alone computer system, and pulled Tisler's name. Then he pulled up his contributor file which produced a column of four-digit control numbers. He then went into the confidential records safe and pulled the contributor folders bearing these control numbers.

He opened the first folder with the same feeling that Paula and Dean Burtell must have had when opening the folders Graver had handed them that morning: What in the hell should he be looking for?

"Graver."

He started, but wasn't surprised that the voice he recognized was Paula's.

"I thought I was the only one here," she said, leaning against the door frame, a manila folder dangling from her hand.

"Come in," he said, sitting back in his chair. He was glad to see her, glad to have someone to talk to. "Sit down."

Paula pulled herself away from the door frame and sat in one of the chairs in front of Graver's desk, crossing her long legs and looking out the windows. Across the bayou the reflection of the falling sun ignited the skyscrapers like molten pillars against the cobalt sky.

Paula frowned at the burning glass escarpments thinking, unhurried, absorbed in her thoughts which were, he imagined, so unlike everyone else's thoughts, so singularly faceted, that if he read them in an anthology of thoughts he would recognize their style immediately. Normally Paula's acerbic sense of humor was very much in evidence, and her attitude and conversation were sprinkled with wit heavily laced with sarcasm. Not a personality to everyone's choice. But Graver liked her; and he liked the woman she was hiding. At the moment, however, he sensed a distinct sobriety.

"What do you think about all this?" she asked, turning to him and raising the folders in her hand, her bracelets clacking on her wrist.

"There's something new on that," Graver said. He told her about the call from Westrate.

"No shit?" She was frowning.

"Surprised?"

"I don't know. I just . . ." She shrugged. "Then I guess that takes the pressure off."

"It does, but we've got to write an assessment report anyway." He rubbed his eyes, wiped his hand over his face, and leaned his elbows on the desk "What do I think? I scanned Tisler's investigations on the computer. Most of them were pretty much in overdrive it seemed to me. Except the Alan Seldon opening. Everything was taking a back seat to that."

Paula nodded, and though she said nothing, he could tell she had something on her mind.

"What about you?"

She leaned her head back and looked at the ceiling. Paula's spontaneity sometimes made her seem ten years younger than her age. He could see her eyes fixed on the acoustic tile above them. She swallowed, and her Adam's apple rose and fell the length of her long throat. Finally she raised her head and straightened up in the chair, turned a little more squarely to him.

"You know, five years ago when I first came here, Tisler was a mediocre investigator," she said bluntly, getting right down to business. "Actually, less than mediocre. His track record was lousy. But about eighteen months ago things changed. He had two long investigations in succession—Probst and Friel. Remember them?"

"Sure. They were good operations."

"Oh, yeah," Paula said. "They both netted big-time results when we turned them over to operations. Now, with this Seldon thing, it looks like he was onto another big one." She paused and looked squarely at Graver. "I know I was supposed to be reviewing only the five open investigations Tisler was working with Dean, but I happened to think of those other two cases and went to the archives and pulled them. As I read over those two operations—and the beginnings of the Seldon business—one question kept popping into my mind over and over: How in the hell did he get so good all of a sudden?"

Graver had settled back, resting his elbows on the arms of the chair.

"I don't know that he was suddenly all that good, was he?" he asked. "Probst and Friel were outstanding collection efforts, no doubt about it, but Tisler had eight or ten other targets whose progress was anything but exemplary."

"Okay, fine, but to my way of thinking that makes Probst, Friel, and Seldon all the more . . . curious," Paula persisted. "They're outstandingly atypical."

Graver watched her closely.

"All day I've been reading over the reports of these three investigations," Paula went on. "They share some interesting commonalities: an extraordinarily lean and orderly collection plan, big results, Dean as the analyst, and . . . all the contributors were sources."

"All of them?"

"All that mattered," she said. "There were a couple of informants thrown in, but they provided only incidental take. Think about it. We'd be lost in this business without informants, right? Even with all their detrimental baggage. But what we'd really like to have are sources. Sources have no criminal histories for defense attorneys to parade out to discredit the witness. Sources have no plea bargains to arrange in exchange for their testimony. Sources have no messy criminal personalities to baby-sit and fret over. They're just well-informed, conscientious citizens, clean and smelling of soap, eager and willing to help law enforcement with their little bits of invaluable information. Right?"

Graver nodded.

"Well, it seems that in these three investigations Tisler stumbled onto an embarrassment of riches. Suddenly he had nothing but sterling silver sources. These are the only three of his investigations in all his years in CID in which this has happened. The rest of the time he had to make do with a pretty shoddy line-up of informants."

She paused to let this soak in, and then her crossed leg began swinging. Something changed in her expression too, a slight adjustment in her mouth, a tightening at the corners of her eyes. She seemed to be hesitating before making her next point. But she went on.

"The initial leads in these things—all three of them—may have been Tisler's," Paula said, tapping the folders on her lap with an index finger. "But from then on he would have worked closely with Dean. It's a sure bet Dean guided the investigations and constructed the format for collecting the information. And Besom, of course, as Tisler's squad supervisor, would have followed every bit of this step-by-step."

Graver straightened up in his chair. He leaned forward with his forearms on his desk, picked up a pencil, and began bouncing the eraser end of it off the top of the old, iron-gray cobblestone. He was interested.

Paula turned her chair sideways and pulled another chair around to face her. She kicked off her shoes and propped her feet on the horizontal brace that supported the legs and used her inclined thighs as a lap desk. She flipped to the first page of her legal pad.

"First, just a quick overview of two cases where Tisler's sources did such an extraordinary job for him. Okay?"

Graver nodded, watching her. Paula was quite capable of becoming obsessive about an investigation. It was one of the characteristics that made her a superior analyst.

"The Probst investigation," she said, looking at her notes. "Ray Probst owned a temporary employee service that specialized in providing temps to banks and insurance companies. He used his temps as spies to acquire information on persons who had sizable personal incomes. Using their computers, the temps targeted the homes and even the items there that could be easily stolen, certain kinds of PC's, televisions, jewelry, art work, silver, everything. After the thefts, all the stuff was warehoused in small outlying airports and eventually flown to Mexico and points south for resale in the black market.

"Two sources and an informant. The take from the informant was insignificant. The two sources made the case, but they never had to testify because Tisler and Dean turned over so much corroborating information to operations that they were able to make the case without the sources' testimonies. In orchestrating the collection process Burtell seemed to intuit precisely the right information needed to open another facet of the case. Even more astonishing, Tisler's sources could always get it for him. Very clean. A model investigation."

Graver swung his chair around almost sideways to his desk. Leaning back, his elbow resting on the top of the desk, he started toying with the cobblestone, turning it clockwise, counterclockwise, clockwise.

Paula flipped another page of her notepad, her bracelets rattling.

"The Friel investigation. Lawrence Friel was in the business of transporting illegal drugs. He didn't buy, didn't sell, just got the stuff from one place to the next. He used his computer to plug into the computerized schedules of trucking companies originating out of Houston and going all over the country. His men would load the drugs into specially-made magnetic boxes which they would then piggyback somewhere on the truck's chassis. From that point on Friel's people never touched the stuff again. His men followed these vehicles in another car, and when the product reached its destination they contacted the receiving party and watched while they picked it up at a truck stop or warehouse or trucking yard. Then Friel's men picked up the pay.

"Again, the operation developed quickly, almost as if Dean and Tisler were using a blueprint of the operation. Two sources, no informants. Again, neither source had to testify because our boys came up with a bumper crop of corroborating information making it unnecessary."

She looked at Graver as she flipped another sheet of her legal pad. He could tell by her expression that she was wondering if he was getting the drift of where she was taking this. She needn't have worried. He was following it all too well.

"Now this brings us to Tisler's active Seldon case. So far, one source"—she reached out and tapped the two folders turned crossway to the others on the front of Graver's desk—"still developing. According to Tisler's source, Alan Seldon owns a chemical waste disposal business. Tisler's source says he has proof that Seldon is buying off EPA inspectors. Seldon is dumping the stuff on ranch land in Starr County in South Texas, way out in the boonies, on the border. According to the source the ranch is owned by a man fronting for a group of drug runners who put up the money for the ranch. The source is telling Tisler he can give him chapter and verse on how all this is happening, but has yet to put names to any of the parties involved, except Seldon's. But the guy's super touchy. Very careful."

"Jesus Christ . . ." Graver said.

"Wait a second," Paula interrupted him, tossing her legal pad on the desk. "There's more, but before you say anything I've got to pee, wash my face. I need a drink." She stood. "I'll be back in a second," she said, and walked out of his office.

14

GRAVER GOT UP AND STEPPED TO THE WINDOWS. THE SUN RE-
flecting on the skyscrapers had burned to a deeper and duller shade of
brassy fire and then, as he watched, with one last, laser-like dazzle, it
dropped behind the horizon, extinguishing the conflagration inside the
millions of square feet of tinted plate glass and transforming them into
palisades of lifeless gray.

He looked back at the scattered files on his desk. Paula was laying
out a scenario that was alive with implication. He guessed that she did
not have to go to the bathroom so much as she had to collect herself.
Graver was afraid she was going to be giving him some bad news, and
she wasn't altogether sure how he was going to take it. He wasn't sure
either and tried to ignore the warm, wandering nausea beginning to
move about in his abdomen.

"What do you think?" Paula asked. She was standing in the doorway, wiping her face and neck with a damp paper towel. She was
barefooted, having left her shoes by her chair.

Graver looked at her. "I'm ready to hear the rest of it," he said,
and walked back to his desk and sat down again.

Paula pinched the placket on the front of her dress and fanned it
lightly. "Fine," she said.

She tossed the wadded paper towel into the trash and sat down.
She had brushed out her hair, and he noticed a few damp wisps on
either side at her temples as she picked up the legal pad again.

"Okay, because all these contributors are sources, *new* sources,
this means there's a lot of information we don't have."

"No 'track record,' " Graver said. He already had seen it coming.
"No parole records or probation tracking data. Since they weren't
trading information for plea bargaining leverage, there's no prosecutor's contract. And they weren't selling their information so there's no

paperwork—or additional commitments—for that. It also means there is no history of reliability. We know only that their information was good in this one case."

"Exactly." Paula tapped her legal pad with the back of her hand and shook her head. "As a matter of fact," she said, crossing her arms on her lap, "we can't even be sure anyone has ever met these sources other than Tisler." She lifted her arms to look down at her notes again. "Aside from your review signature, the operational documents were all signed by Tisler, as the control officer, and witnessed by Besom."

Paula, typically, had surprised him. As a creative analyst she rivaled Burtell. Even though she was meticulously limning the framework of a nightmare, he could not help but admire her ability to intuit the invisible. She looked at him and, using her middle finger and thumb of one hand, combed along the center part of her hair to get the sides of it out of her face.

"Now"—she nodded at the folders on Graver's desk—"those contributor ID documents indicate they were updated five months ago, in January, as per operational directives. According to the updates, two of the five sources changed addresses this year, two last year. One in each of the Probst and Friel cases each year. Nice and neat. Balanced."

Paula shook her head, her eyes fixed on Graver. "Not so. This afternoon I made four telephone calls. On the first one, Bruce Sheck, I got an answering machine that told me I'd reached the number I'd dialed and to leave a message. At the number of the second source, Colleen Synar, a woman answered. She said that Synar had shared rent with her and another woman several years ago, but that she hadn't heard from her in over two years. At the other two numbers, I reached people who'd never heard of the person named in the file. They'd both had their present numbers for years."

They stared at each other. Graver was trying to swallow a growing anxiety.

"I didn't make any calls on the Seldon investigation," she said. "I didn't want to risk screwing it up."

"Who signed the audits?" Graver asked. "Besom?"

Paula nodded soberly. "You got it."

Graver's mind was still, the kind of breathless still you experienced in that first moment when you realized that the unbelievable was inevitable and was about to happen.

"My God," he said. Paula had done exactly what an analyst was supposed to do. She had stepped back a little way from the trees, and she had seen the forest. Slowly Arthur Tisler's death slipped out of the bright light of forensic surety and receded once again into the murky margins of doubt. Graver straightened up in his chair and leaned his forearms on the desk. "What else?"

She shrugged. "Nothing else." For the first time she looked drained.

"Son of a bitch," Graver said. He felt light-headed, maybe even slightly claustrophobic.

"They developed the cases too easily," Paula said, her voice portraying an awkward combination of caution and conviction. "Too slick. Those sources are tainted, Marcus. Somehow. Maybe they lied. Maybe they set up somebody." She shook her head. "It beats me."

"They didn't lie," Graver said. He was tired too, and shaken. "Everything the sources provided was good, the take was corroborated by second, sometimes third parties. There were *convictions,* for Christ's sake."

"But they're shielding the sources. Besom probably. But for sure Tisler . . . and Dean."

An EMS siren warbled on the expressway, its lights flashing in the dusk as it moved past them on one of the turns heading north. Graver stared out the wall of glass long after the ambulance had disappeared.

"Jesus, Paula," Graver said, "I . . ."

He couldn't believe it, and he had just come within a hairsbreadth of blurting his disbelief at Burtell's involvement. It was easy to entertain the idea of Tisler's corruption. He was dead, and Graver had no personal attachments to him anyway. And Besom was one of his least favorite people on earth, one of Westrate's buddies whom the assistant chief had foisted onto Graver. But to see this kind of incriminating evidence against Burtell was stunning.

He stared at the cobblestone. The implications of her analysis were undeniable. He stood and stepped to the windows. There wasn't enough air in the room; his heart labored with little effect.

Paula nervously toyed with her bracelets, clacking them back and forth on her wrist. Graver knew it was clear to her what he was going through. Christ. The world had not stopped, but it had slowed suddenly and dramatically.

"Okay," he said, staring out the window but seeing nothing beyond the glass. "Then what do we have? Let's say they're protecting sources. Why would they do that? I mean, to what purpose?"

"Maybe the sources aren't legitimate," Paula said. "Maybe they

. . . What if there's only *one* source and this thing is being run from the outside, not from here."

"That would be asking a lot," Graver said. "It's not like these three operations had much in common."

"They wouldn't have to. The common denominator would be the motive of whoever's outside. It's not likely we'd see a connection from this side of the picture."

Graver knew she was right. She obviously had given this a lot of thought before bringing it to him. He anticipated where her logic had taken her next.

"This has been going on a long time," he said, turning around and coming back to his desk. "And it's been working well. By now all the kinks have been worked out of it. We're not likely to find anything to connect these investigations in the documentation. No frayed ends."

Neither of them spoke for a moment.

"We can't confront Besom or Dean," Graver said finally, sitting down behind his desk again. "At the first hint that we suspect something, this entire thing will evaporate."

"When is Besom supposed to be back from his fishing trip?"

"Day after tomorrow . . . Wednesday." Graver was getting a headache. "But he's got another week of vacation. He's not due to be back in the office until a week from Wednesday."

"You think Dean can get in touch with him?"

Graver shrugged. He stared at the cobblestone, forcing himself to move on, to push Burtell's image out of his mind, to think in the abstract about the logistics of Paula's discoveries. The implications were mushrooming in his mind.

"I've got to cut Tisler's inquiry short," he said.

"What?"

"Wrap it up as quickly as possible," he said. "I won't take the week I told Westrate it would require. Casey's going to come up empty-handed on that background check. I'm sure of that now. Dean's not going to 'find' anything. I'll close it out, write a clearance paper and put it to bed. That's all Westrate wants anyway, a tidy ending. We'll give it to him."

"Then what?" Paula was frowning, uncertain where he was taking this.

"If Tisler wasn't murdered," Graver said, "then his suicide is likely to have caught them by surprise, just as much as it did us. They've got to be off balance, probably worried that he's left something behind that would blow this wide-open. It could be that whatever drove Tisler to kill himself is also bringing pressure to bear on the others. Maybe something's unraveling and Tisler couldn't face the consequences. His suicide can only have made things worse. I've got to avoid spooking them. It would be better if we made it look like we're buying the suicide and want to sweep it under the rug as quickly as possible."

"What about the Seldon investigation?"

Graver shook his head wearily. "I'll have to replace Tisler. It's got to go on . . . routinely, as if we have no suspicions."

"Christ. How will they handle that? You don't think they'll actually go ahead with a bogus 'source,' do you?"

"No." Graver shook his head emphatically. "They won't do that. I think . . . I think when I put it to Dean he'll say the source has dropped out of sight. Vanished. Tisler's suicide is definitely a good-enough reason for a 'source' to spook and disappear. He'd be wary, unsure of what was 'really' happening. That would be entirely logical under the circumstances."

Paula said nothing, waiting.

Graver reached up with one hand and pressed his fingers into the base of his neck where the muscle had been tensing tighter and tighter all evening.

"But I've got to get something more to substantiate our suspicions," he said. "They're going to rely on Dean to be their first line of defense, the one to know if anything's amiss. We've got to be careful with him." The words almost stuck in his throat. "Maybe this thing goes laterally and other investigators and analysts are involved. Maybe it's vertical, goes higher up . . ."

He stopped and shook his head slowly. This was goddamned unbelievable. And, on a personal level, it was excruciatingly painful.

15.

RAY BESOM HAD BEEN WALKING FIFTEEN OR TWENTY MINUTES when he saw the wooden hull of the old wreck emerge above the dune grass a hundred yards ahead of him. Unconsciously he quickened his step, his excitement almost making him forget about the weight of the tackle box and rods and bait bucket he had been lugging for the last three quarters of a mile from the point where the hired skiff had dropped him off. The guy would be back at nine o'clock, well after dark, to take him back to Port Isabel. Boca Chica was the end of the line. You couldn't get any farther south. If he walked another mile and a half he would come to the broad sand flats where the Rio Grande emptied into the Gulf of Mexico, and then on the other side of that nasty hemorrhage—maybe two hundred yards—was Mexico. That's why he came here. Except for an occasional wanderer, it was isolated.

Besom looked at his watch and then looked into the wind, out to the Gulf. The water was a dull, grayish brown with an occasional hint of pale turquoise and sometimes even a paler blue in the curls of the breakers. The Gulf of Mexico was not a pretty thing, not in the traditional sense that someone thinks of coastal waters as being pretty. But to him that characteristic, unlovely color of the warm Gulf Stream was beautiful, even exotic, and nothing at all in his experience compared to the tangy smell of these salt-laden breezes which, if you caught them at just the right time early in the morning or late in the evening, like now, carried with them the smoky aura of Mexico.

This was his sixth and last afternoon. His brother-in-law, who had driven down with him from Houston, had gotten sick on the second day and had flown back home. That was fine with him. The guy wasn't much of a fisherman, really, and he didn't like to hang around the bait shops and bars and icehouses when the dead tides made the fishing bad. But those were the places you learned things, those little dives where old farts with beer bellies, burned skin, and bad teeth laid up in the shadows in the heat of the day. These guys could tell you a thing or two about how to handle yourself if the tides were right and you wanted to get a hook into a redfish or speckled trout or flounder. This was the one week that he lived for during the other fifty-one.

He checked his watch again as he walked up to the old hull of the shrimp boat that had washed onto the beach seven years ago. He had checked the tide tables and in half an hour he wanted to be in the water. The sun was way behind him, going down somewhere in Mexico. He had a good two hours to fish before dark. But first, just to enjoy the moment, he dropped his equipment next to the hull and sat down in the sand. He pulled a cigarette out of the pack in his shirt pocket and lighted it, and then he reached for the waders he had been carrying, put his hand down into one of the legs and pulled out a single bottle of beer. He popped the cap on the sweaty, amber bottle and sat back against the bleached hull of the shrimper. Seagulls slid across the sky above him, squeaking, hovering, dipping down to look at him. If this could last forever you wouldn't hear any complaints from him.

When the cigarette gave out, Besom tossed it away and tucked the bottom of the beer bottle into the sand. He reached for his waders and began pulling them on, stopping a couple of times to work on the beer before it got warm. Standing, he finished buckling the waders and then reached down for the beer and finished it, tossing the bottle in the sand near the hull. He picked up the largest of the two rods—Go for it, he told himself—and checked the shimmering green Ambassador 5500 casting reel. Opening his tackle box he surveyed the trays of lures, having already decided against the shrimp tails in the bucket. He selected a Gold Spoon, rigged it, and walked across the beach to the water.

Wading into the water until it was just above his crotch and just below his waist, he spread his legs slightly for balance and began casting. It was a hell of a pleasure, a real pleasure like sex, to hear the reel whine in the casting, to let the lure settle a second and then begin bringing it in, feeling the tug and nuzzle on the line as the surf pulled and pushed at his pelvis.

He had been fishing a little over half an hour with only one bite, something that hit the spoon and screamed away with it and then spat it out, something playing with him, making his adrenaline squirt and his heart hammer as his imagination created a monster redfish way out past the sandbar, when he saw the girl.

She was coming toward him from up the beach, coming from civilization. He caught her out of the corner of his eye as he was casting, and when the lure hit the water and he started reeling in, he looked back at her. A dog was with her, of all things, a greyhound. When he was a kid living on Baffin Bay before the development of Riviera Beach, he used to have a greyhound, him and his best friend, a greyhound each. They would sneak into the King Ranch with them and chase coyotes and jackrabbits in the limitless, empty brush country that stretched all the way to Laguna Madre.

Besom couldn't see her face, but in the softening light of evening he could see that she had long black hair and that she was damn near naked. It was a bikini, of course, but from where he stood in the surf she was all thighs and bosom, moving along the beach toward him, eating something. Actually she was sauntering, that was the word for it, sauntering, walking leisurely, her long legs as long in proportion to her body as her greyhound's legs were to his, two graceful creatures coming along the beach as if this were not as deserted a stretch of sand as he could find.

By the time he had cast a couple more times, she was within shouting distance of him, and she had stopped at the edge of the water and was watching him, her head tilted a little, the dog loping around her, in and out of the sand and water like a racehorse. When he reeled in the next cast, he turned and looked at her. She was smiling at him. It was a red bikini . . . and more tight, tanned flesh than he could ever remember seeing.

"Any luck?" she shouted above the surf. The wind was blowing her black hair, and she shook her head, shook it out of her face.

"Not a hell of a lot, no," he shouted back. He hesitated, thought better of it, and turned back to the water. Casting again, as far as he could toss the spoon, he began reeling. He tried to be patient with it, tried to concentrate on the action of the lure far out in the gray water, but more than that, he wanted to turn around and look at the girl again. He could feel her still back there.

When the line was back to him, he turned. The girl was closer now and had waded a little way into the water to watch. He smiled at her.

"You like fishing?"

"I like watching," she said. "They're not biting, huh?"

"Not yet."

She had a slight accent. Not Mexican. Something else. Some kind of cute little accent.

She held up what she had in her hand. "Want a few slices of orange?"

Slices of orange? Oh, Mother Machree. Besom cut his eyes up the beach. Not a soul in sight. He hesitated. Shit. He shrugged "why not" to her, nodded, and turned slowly in the water and headed toward her. By the time he got to her she had backed up a little, and the edge of the surf was swirling around her ankles.

"How long you been out there?" she asked as he walked up to her.

He looked at his watch. "Forty minutes."

"What are you fishing for?" she asked, breaking off nearly half of what she had left of the orange and handing it to him.

She was a little older than a college girl, he saw, now that he was close. Her hair was thick with the humidity of the salt air, and she had that lusty weathered look about her that gave him the impression that she had been on the beach most of the afternoon. The girl had an incredible body, and he just couldn't help looking at her. She tossed her hair off her shoulders with the back of a bent wrist and when she did her breasts wobbled heavily behind the two small patches of her bikini top.

"Redfish," he heard himself say, and he broke off the first wedge of orange and tossed it into his mouth, his rod cradled in the crook of his left arm, as his eyes found the little pad of pudendum where the mile of thighs came together at her pelvis. The wild, fragrant buds of citrus burst and squirted in his mouth as he bit into the fruit.

"Redfish," she said.

He nodded. "What are you doing way down here?" he asked, managing to drag his eyes back to hers.

"Beth," she said, turning to her dog. "Sometimes we go all the way, right down to the Rio Grande and old Mexico. The walk's nothing to her, with those legs. And it keeps me in shape, too."

"No shit," he said, tossing a second wedge of orange into his mouth. He bit into it, a second burst of citrus, and she cocked her hip and smiled at him.

"You like that." She grinned.

He was looking at her breasts when the second wedge of orange turned to napalm in his throat, vaporized napalm, a spray of napalm instantly saturating his sinuses, ripping up into the hollows behind his eyes, actually coloring his vision. He saw scarlet everything, bikini, breasts, navel, smile, and as he staggered back into the red surf he knew he was dying. His trachea and lungs and heart were melted, already dissolved by the napalm, and even the murky Gulf water could not extinguish it.

The last thing he was aware of was the girl bent over him trying to open his mouth, but his jaws had locked down tight on his tongue, and she could only grab and pull at his lips and cheeks.

Frustrated, she gave up and stood for a minute watching him convulse, watching him suck in enough surf to drown even though he was past drowning. When he stopped jerking and flailing in the water, she bent down and worked at his mouth again, finally managing to pry it open. She took out the piece of his tongue he had bitten off and fished around in the sides of his mouth for the orange pulp, digging around the base of his gums, sloshing the frothing salty water into his mouth to make sure it was all washed out.

In a few moments she was finished, and she stood and stepped back away from him. She bent and washed her hands in the water, picked up some sand and rubbed her fingers with it and then washed them off again. Then she stepped back out of the water and watched him roll in the tide, watched him finally go face down, and pitch heavily with the slam of each wave in the rolling surf. After a minute or two, she looked up the beach where she came from, and then she called the greyhound and started walking back, her long, tan legs sauntering, her thick black hair blowing in the Gulf breeze.

Some of the seagulls stayed with him, reluctant to leave, sliding along the margins of the water, back and forth, dipping down, squeaking in the wind. Finally they, too, moved on and in a little while they were all gone, the girl, the dog, and the gulls.

16

THEY SAT IN THE CAR WITH THE WINDOWS ROLLED DOWN, ONE of only two cars in the small, otherwise empty lot, a niche carved out of the vast Memorial Park that surrounded them like a rain forest. The lot was at the terminus of a narrow lane that circled around and down behind a chic condominium tower that overlooked the verdant margins of Buffalo Bayou. In the failing light of dusk an arched footbridge with a wrought-iron gate was still visible fifty yards away where it led from the parking lot across a creek to the walking paths that followed the northern bank of the bayou. On the other side of the bayou, obscured by the dense wall of the park's semitropical vegetation, the emerald golf links of the River Oaks Country Club sloped up toward the city's most prestigious neighborhood.

Panos Kalatis let a gentle blue tendril of cigar smoke leave his mouth and drift out the car window into the boggy evening air. He was sitting behind the steering wheel, his seat pushed back so that he could turn a little to the passenger beside him and at the same time, with only the slightest movement of his head, be able to see the other man in the back seat.

"No one had any inkling of this, I suppose," Kalatis said, throwing a quizzical look at Burtell in the back seat. "No *intelligence* about the possibility." He had just pushed the buttons at his elbow and rolled down all the windows in the car.

"No, nothing," Burtell said. "You normally don't have intelligence about suicide," he added dryly. He wanted to say something else, but he held his tongue. There would be time to say what he wanted to say.

"Then you do think he killed himself?" Kalatis asked, still looking over the back of the seat.

"Yeah, I think he killed himself," Burtell said grudgingly. He was having a hard time swallowing his anger, his disgust at the two men in front of him.

Kalatis nodded, regarding Burtell with a meditative silence.

"You don't think they could've gotten it wrong?" Faeber asked.

"I doubt it," Burtell said tersely. Faeber was out of his element. The questions sounded stupid coming from him. He was merely mimicking Kalatis's role, hoping that by going along with his own needless interrogatories he was ingratiating himself with the Greek.

"But if he was murdered, they'd want to keep that quiet, wouldn't they?" Kalatis offered.

"You mean a cover-up? No way. Not a cop killing, not in CID."

"I've seen it done before," Kalatis said.

"Oh, Jesus, Panos. Come on." Burtell shook his head, impatient with the idea.

Kalatis nodded calmly and leaked more smoke into the failing light. Just then two women in bright nylon jogging shorts and sport bras jogged into sight on the other side of the footbridge and stopped, their run completed, in the clearing at the end of the path. They paced restlessly as they caught their breath and then after a few moments they started across the footbridge to the parking lot.

Kalatis followed them with his eyes as they made their way across the lot and started up the narrow lane toward the condo. "The question is," he said, still watching the women, "how is this going to affect us?"

"The question is, did he leave anything behind?" Faeber said.

Kalatis looked into the back seat, the dark circles around his eyes visible even in the twilight.

"If he left anything in that area it would have to be personal," Burtell said. "His own little record-keeping operation or something. There's nothing like that in CID. He didn't have any kind of setup like that at the office."

"How can you be sure of that?" Faeber asked.

"It's my goddamned business to be sure of it," Burtell said evenly. He hated having to answer Faeber. Faeber was important to Kalatis, no doubt about it. His data banks, his sleazy nature, his venality were all useful tools to Kalatis, but the man seemed to enjoy a closeness to the Greek that his talents did not warrant. Burtell was frustrated that he had not gotten beyond the business of these investigations. He had thought that by now he would have, but for some reason Kalatis had closed the door. Perhaps he had sensed a greater ambition in Burtell than he saw in either Besom or Tisler; perhaps he was wary of a more clever man.

No one said anything for a moment. Kalatis was turning the cigar in his mouth, keeping the butt of it damp, tasting the tobacco. With the women out of the picture there was nothing to distract their attention from the cicadas throbbing in the thickets of the park, the late June heat intense enough to keep them singing hours into the night.

"I wouldn't want to lose everything we've gained so far," Kalatis observed.

Burtell was attentive to every nuance in Kalatis's voice. His tone was not threatening, but it might have carried a thin imputation, or maybe it was simply an old-fashioned portent of imagined consequences, the kind of thing you perceived between the lines when the juices in your glands squirted into action and turned you cold even before you understood why. In this business, there was an entire language, an invisible lexicon that was only apprehensible in just that way, with your juices, elliptical communications conveyed solely in those absent spaces between the apparent. You understood because there was a portion of a primitive instinct left within you that you could not define or explain, except that it had to do with survival.

"All this preparation, this significant capital investment," Kalatis went on.

Burtell had to reassure him. "Look, Marcus Graver is writing a report that will close this down. Everybody wants this over, and everybody wants it clearly to *appear* to be over."

Kalatis had been staring through the windshield at the park where the surrounding trees were quickly turning from deep blue-greens to sooty black, their towering presence darker than the darkening sky. He turned and looked into the back seat again.

"What about Graver? He's good enough to get onto this, isn't he?"

"Yeah, he's good enough," Burtell said matter-of-factly. But he suspected Kalatis already knew that.

"Then we've got to worry about him."

"I don't think so."

"You don't think so."

"He's in a very awkward situation, Panos," Burtell said wearily. "I think he'll follow Homicide's lead. He'll almost have to. If he insists on pursuing suspicions of conspiracy, he's going to run into resistance from Westrate. Westrate's not going to want to hear any of that kind of talk. No matter how suspicious Graver may be—and I don't know that he is, this is just for the sake of your argument—regardless of any suspicions he may have, he's the kind of guy who's very good at making reality checks on himself. Homicide says suicide. IAD says suicide. He has no tangible evidence that Tisler was doing anything out of the ordinary. No matter what his suspicions, he's going to let it go. He's an empiricist."

Kalatis emitted a coil of cigar smoke, still looking over the back of the seat. "An 'empiricist,' uh-huh," he said with pointed boredom.

Burtell doubted the Greek knew what that meant. To hell with him, let him wonder.

"You have confidence that Tisler didn't have some kind of mental meltdown and leave something behind?" Faeber challenged again. "I mean, the man shot himself, for God's sake!"

"Colin, you son of a bitch," Burtell snapped. "The poor bastard told me what you did." Faeber quickly looked at Kalatis, who turned away, undoubtedly disgusted with Faeber's clumsy double take. "You wanted to 'guarantee' his loyalty? How goddamned bumbling can you be?"

"We had to do that," Kalatis interjected. He pulled at the knot of his tie, twisting his neck this way and that and unbuttoned his shirt collar, opening it wide. The heat seemed to have grown more oppressive with the fading light. Burtell had pulled off his suit coat a long time ago and laid it in the seat beside him. Faeber hadn't loosened anything or removed anything.

"You *thought* you had to do that," Burtell clarified. He wasn't going to let Kalatis weasel out of that so easily. Faeber cut his eyes at Kalatis to see how he was going to react to Burtell's challenge, but Burtell didn't give a damn. He went on. "Whatever reason you had to doubt him was a stupid reason. Somebody way overplayed this. Somebody didn't know what they were doing. You pushed him, and you lost him. Now you've got a dead man on your hands, and you want me to make sure it doesn't mean anything. Well, I can't do that."

"We're only suggesting," Kalatis said with calculated patience, "that you need to be sure about what you're telling us."

Faeber nodded in agreement.

Burtell didn't like this alliance he was seeing between the two men in front of him. He didn't like being on the defensive. Something was poisoning the well.

"There's . . . nothing . . . in . . . CID," Burtell emphasized. "If he's got something squirreled away outside, I can't be responsible for knowing anything about that. If he did that, it's because he was desperate, felt like he'd been pushed up against the wall." He let this hang in the sticky air for a moment. "It didn't have to be that way."

There was a long silence, Kalatis and Faeber half-turned in the front seat, Kalatis looking away now, out the windshield. He was big, and he often reminded Burtell of a minotaur. It was an apt image: Kalatis, his feet planted firmly in front of the doorway to darkness, guarding a subterranean maze of lies.

"What about Seldon, then?" Kalatis asked. He was holding his cigar, looking at its glowing tip. "What do we do now?"

"You forget about it," Burtell said. "It's gone, done."

Kalatis turned his head slowly toward Burtell. "Oh, I don't think so, my friend. I just said a moment ago that I didn't want to lose my situation here."

"You'll lose that and everything else if you try to force this," Burtell warned. "We can't screw around with Graver too much, Panos. We won't get by with it very long."

"What do you mean?" Kalatis asked softly, smiling. "We've been screwing him for two years."

"No, we've been lying to him for two years," Burtell clarified. "There's a difference. Tisler's death, that's screwing with him. Any idiot can tell lies, but you've got to be at the other end of the IQ scale if you want to deal successfully with Marcus Graver's suspicions."

"So it's over?" Faeber was incredulous.

"Seldon is, yes," Burtell said. "We put everything on hold for right now. Let everyone relax over there. Wait until Ray gets back from his vacation and then see if we can't restructure, pull this back together."

Kalatis had turned back to looking out the windshield. From where they sat they could see the tops of the downtown skyscrapers rising out of the darkness, just beginning to glitter in the twilight.

"Okay," Kalatis said suddenly with a huge sigh. He tossed his cigar out onto the asphalt of the parking lot. "We'll get with Besom when he gets back. When is that?"

"Tomorrow," Burtell said.

"Okay," Kalatis continued. "We'll get with him, get his opinion. Let's give this some thought. Work up the options. If we want to go on with the operation, how do we do it? Are the gains worth the risks? What do we do if Graver does come up with something?" He looked at Burtell and then at Faeber. "You know what we need." Again to the back seat. "I'll be in touch."

That was all there was to it.

Kalatis turned around to face the steering wheel and hit the buttons on his armrest that controlled the windows. As the windows were going up Burtell picked up his suit coat, feeling as though he ought to say something else, but not knowing just exactly what or just exactly why. Nothing more was said, so Burtell opened his door and got out. He closed the door just as the windows locked into place, and Kalatis started the car and flipped on the air conditioner.

Burtell hesitated a beat beside the dark windows of the Mercedes and then turned and walked across the small lot to his car, unlocked it, and threw in his coat. He looked back at the Mercedes which didn't move, just sat there with its motor running, its air conditioner humming along with the cicadas in the dark heat. He got into his own car and started the engine, feeling a little queasy as he adjusted the air conditioner vents to blow directly on him. The goddamned Greek was just too spooky. He was so goddamned byzantine he made intrigue look like a game of checkers.

Burtell put the car in gear and turned toward the narrow lane that led up past the condominium. The lights were coming on here and there in the condominium, and he wondered if the two women lived there or somewhere farther back in the neighborhoods. He drove past the Greek's car, which sat motionless and dark, seeming to have an intelligence about it, a mute and incomprehensible cunning like one of those crusty bayou cockroaches that lived in the layered armor of the palm trees. Jesus Christ.

"What do you think?" Kalatis asked as they watched the taillights of Burtell's car climb the lane and disappear.

Faeber was cautious. "He seemed sure of himself, that he had it under control."

"I think he was squirming," Kalatis said. "Maybe he hasn't got the guts to go through with this."

"Go through with it?"

"If we don't call it off. If we go through with it."

Faeber suddenly felt as if he had missed part of the conversation, that he hadn't picked up on something crucial. Confused now, his mind scrambled to sort it out. But he chose to say nothing else. He simply sat there wondering what in the hell was operating behind the black eyes of Panos Kalatis.

17.

DRIVING HOME, GRAVER WENT OVER AND OVER THE DISTURBING
evidence Paula had laid out during the past two hours. There was no
mistaking she had uncovered a breach in security that could have disas-
trous consequences. It was an intelligence director's worst fear, and the
bad news was compounded by the fact that an old, good friend seemed
to be involved, if not at the very heart of it.

In truth, this was something Graver still had not accepted, though
he had given Paula every indication that he had. It simply was unbelievable. He was going to have to think himself into it. Like a mathe-
matician, he possessed the problem and the theorem, but he had yet to
construct a formula of proof. And he would have to see that formula
played out, step by step, before he would be able to bring himself to see
Dean Burtell as a traitor.

The sticking point was motivation. Graver knew Burtell like a
brother, and the motives seen most often in circumstances of betrayal
simply did not figure into the equation. Greed? Dean liked to live well,
but his affinity for upper-middle-class comforts hardly added up to
avarice. Sexual obsession? Graver knew enough about human nature
to know that that sort of thing could be held in secret for decades, even
lifetimes, but often, if not always, there were indications, hints, of this
proclivity in other aspects of the personality. But not in Dean Burtell.
Revenge for imagined or actual wrongs? Burtell had never uttered a
word along these lines. That, too, commonly exhibited itself sooner or
later in someone who felt it strongly enough to seek it. Conflicting
ideology or philosophy? Not a factor.

But supposing Burtell had changed, and one of these elements had
become an obsession for him, obsession enough for him to betray everything and everyone for it. Would not Graver have noticed the
change? Even if Burtell had managed effectively to disguise the motive,

would Graver not have noticed something, even some other alteration in his behavior? How could he possibly have missed it? Had Burtell, like Tisler, suddenly acted contrary to character without anyone seeing even minor indications of something amiss—in either of them?

Graver had to admit that Paula's line of deduction was artful and well constructed, but it did not seem to track with the human factor, an understanding of which also required a kind of sixth sense. Surely there was something here that didn't add up. Surely, in this instance, appearances—the appearance of Burtell's involvement—were deceiving. But then that was the problem, wasn't it? Appearances *had* been deceiving. And now Graver, while accepting the axiom in the first instance, wanted to force it onto the second. It was the everlasting danger of counterintelligence, mirrors arranged to create the appearance of an infinity of the same image. Graver was on unstable ground, and it scared him.

He stopped at a seafood restaurant on Shepherd and the hostess took him to a small table for two by a window. Graver had not eaten at so many tables for two in his entire life as he had in the last six months. It was a constant and ironic reminder that dining, like sex, was an activity that, ideally, was expected to be done in pairs.

After ordering a dinner of fried shrimp and a bottle of Pacifico beer, he took out his pocket notebook and jotted down a few points that Paula had made that he wanted to rethink. Taking notes was an old habit that was hard to break, and he collected his thoughts much better in the company of old habits.

When his food arrived, he put away his notebook and ordered a second Pacifico. As he ate, he let his attention wander to the other diners, imagining the relationships of the people at each table. It was a favorite diversion, but one that he forced on himself now in a deliberate effort to take his mind off Burtell. It was not an entirely successful endeavor. When he finished eating, he did not order coffee, but quickly motioned to his waiter for the bill, paid it, and left.

As he was walking out to his car, he felt the pager on his belt vibrate. He looked down at the number, and then turned around and went back into the restaurant. There was only one pay telephone in the anteroom outside the rest rooms, and it was occupied by a young man in his twenties, a post-modern boulevardier with an attitude. He wore his black hair in a ponytail and was dressed in a fashionably baggy tan suit with a black shirt buttoned at the neck, no tie. When he saw that

Graver was waiting, he turned his back and kept talking. He was telling the person on the other end that he and a friend were going to a few clubs after dinner and why didn't she catch up with them at Tocino's at ten-thirty. Oh. Why? Well, tell him something. Tell him you've got a girlfriend who's sick, throwing up all over the place, and you have to go see about her. What? Well, tell him . . .

Graver took out his shield, opened it, reached over the man's shoulder, and dangled it in front of his face.

"Give me five minutes," he said. The young man flinched and turned around slowly, his eyes fixed in cautious surprise. "Tell her you'll call her back in five minutes. It'll give her time to think of something."

The young man did as he was told, then pressed down the hook with one hand, and gave the receiver to Graver. "Jesus," he said with mocking respect, his machismo requiring some kind of disparagement to cover his loss.

"Thanks," Graver said.

Neuman answered on the first ring.

"Everything all right?" Graver asked.

"Oh, sure . . . I just need to see you for a few minutes."

"Where are you?"

"I'm just finishing a hamburger at a diner called Sid's, off Montrose."

"I know where it is. I'm not far away. I'll be there in ten minutes."

When Graver got to the diner, Neuman was sitting in his car in front where he had parked to one side under an old mimosa. Graver pulled up beside him, and Neuman got out of his car.

"The place was too small to talk inside," Neuman explained through Graver's window.

Graver came around and each of them leaned against their cars. Though the night was clear, the air was damp, and heavy with the sweetness of the honeysuckle that grew in great clumps, frothy white with blossoms, against a board fence that disappeared around behind the diner.

"What's on your mind?" Graver asked.

Neuman was holding his car keys and jangled them gently as if to get himself started.

"Well, first of all I checked out Tisler," he said. "Thoroughly. Went after hidden income possibilities, real property—he's got a little rent house in Sharpstown. Had it a couple of years. Paid minimum down, fifteen-year mortgage, and he's plunking away monthly payments. I checked business involvements, savings accounts, all the banking possibilities. Nothing. Toys: vehicle and boat registrations. Nothing. I did all this in Peggy's name too. And in Art's middle name, Sydney. And in her maiden name, Mays. Nothing. If he had an extra income he wasn't stupid about taking care of it. I don't know how far you want me to go with this. Background checks next? Whatever."

Graver started to speak, but Neuman went on.

"But that's not why I wanted to talk to you."

Graver waited.

"I hope this isn't out of school . . . or . . . out of line." Neuman shifted his weight from one leg to the other. He had left his jacket and tie in the car and his shirt was wrinkled the way shirts get after long days squirming in chairs in front of computers, rummaging through files, sitting and standing, sitting and standing. "This, uh, I guess this falls into the 'it-seemed-odd-at-the-time-but . . .' category, for what it's worth."

Neuman's nervousness was uncomfortably reminiscent of Paula's behavior earlier. Graver sensed the chill of foreboding. Neuman jangled his keys and then plunged in.

"I think there may be something . . . irregular . . . about the way Art and Dean were working their investigations," he said.

Graver's stomach clinched. He couldn't even imagine what he was about to hear, but as of that moment he accepted as fact what had been only a premonition up until then: the surprise he was about to hear would be the rule, not the exception, regarding whatever the events that precipitated Tisler's death would come to be called. Whether it would be known in retrospect as a scandal, or an affair, or an ordeal, it was clear to Graver at this moment that he was involved in something that was going to cause an uproar. He was as sure of it as if he were looking back from five years in the future.

"I haven't read the Seldon documents," Neuman went on, "but I'd like to. Dean's been helping me develop the Darley investigation, that protection racket stuff. In the past month it's been moving fast, very fast, and Dean's been pushing me to move quicker, collect a wider variety of information, move, move, move . . . I've been chasing the damn ball from one side of the court to the other, just barely keeping up. But at the same time Art's Seldon operation has been really cooking too, and sometimes Art and I were in and out of Dean's office on a revolving-door basis. Documents flying back and forth, stuff breaking that couldn't wait. We got a little sloppy, I guess, leaving raw data notes, report drafts, stuff like that, on each other's desks instead of hand-to-hand delivery . . . not being too careful, or careful enough, anyway."

Neuman paused and swallowed, a shake of the keys.

"About a month, no, three weeks ago, I was working through the lunch hour to complete a report before I had to leave for a one-thirty meeting with an informant. Dean had my folder on that particular informant and was writing up notes for me, things he wanted me to watch for, things he wanted me to get if I could. I was actually meeting two informants that day, and Dean said he'd leave the contributor folders for both of them, along with his notes for me, on his desk. He was hurrying out to meet his wife for lunch.

"When I was finished, I ran across the hall to his office. His desk was a mess. I grabbed the two folders and took them back to my office. I flipped open the first one, read his notes, flipped open the second one. The documents were out of order. The most recent reports should have been at the front, Dean's notes on top. Instead, it was all scrambled. I leafed through the typed reports and found Dean's handwritten notes buried almost at the back. But when I started reading them, they didn't make sense. I didn't recognize anything. In fact these were not *pre*-interview notes at all, but a *post*-interview contributor contact report. It didn't take me but a second to realize that what I had was a Seldon case document."

"Then it was Art's handwriting, not Dean's."

"No. It was Dean's handwriting."

"What? You're sure?"

"Positive. I see it every day."

"Was the typed report in the folder with it?"

"No," Neuman said. "It wasn't." His voice was flat, and he actually had to clear his throat, a gesture that made Graver heartsick. "That's the deal. At the top right-hand corner of the first page Dean had written in the date, underlined it and circled it. This was on . . . a Thursday. The report was dated for Friday—of the *next* week."

"You're sure?" Graver asked again. He had to. It was hard to believe that Neuman wasn't making a mistake. His heart was pounding.

"Oh, yeah. I had a calendar right there, and I checked. I kept reading. There were references to events that 'had' occurred on the Tuesday and Wednesday of the coming week—I checked those dates too. The whole thing was written in the past tense, as if the events had already happened."

"Incredible," Graver said.

"Yeah." Neuman nodded, looking at him. "Pretty wild."

Graver looked away. An occasional car had passed by on the street while they were standing there, and as his eyes took notice of yet another one, he realized that it was at that moment accelerating. Had it been stopped across from them? Had it only slowed? Was it something he should have noticed? He turned back to Neuman.

"So what did you do?"

"I, uh, I quickly looked at the other documents in the folder. It was in my folder all right, my CI. This thing had just gotten in there by accident."

Neuman shook his keys. Graver could tell that he was pained by having to come out with this.

"I took the folder and ran back to Dean's office," Neuman continued, after taking a deep breath. "I picked through the pile of papers and folders there, trying not to disturb them. I played a hunch and went to the bottom, and sure enough I found another contributor contact folder. There was a two-digit difference in the contributor control number between this folder and mine. A transposition. It was a Seldon case folder. I found Dean's handwritten notes to me about my CI inside the folder, right on top where I'd expected to find it. I switched the handwritten pages to their proper folder, put the Seldon folder back on the bottom of the pile where I'd found it and got the hell out of there."

"Afterward," Graver asked, "did Dean ever indicate to you that he suspected something might have been disturbed?"

"No. It was just dumb luck that I realized what had happened and that I actually found the Seldon contributor folder at the bottom of the pile. But then, I guess that accounts for Dean's misplacement of his notes in the first place."

Graver stared past Neuman to the diner. It was a bare minimum eatery, mostly a counter with stools and a few tables next to the windows that faced the street. Inside, a waitress was wiping off the counter. She stopped to adjust a hairpin and then went back to wiping the counter. The only other person in the place was an old man with a bulbous nose sitting at a window table holding a newspaper in his hands. But he wasn't reading it. He was staring out the window, daydreaming, his eyes fixed on the night.

Graver shifted his eyes back to Neuman. "You've had plenty of time to think about this," he said. "What do you make of it?"

Neuman was quick to shake his head. "I don't know. I don't understand it. I don't know how Dean works his other cases, the tricks he uses to develop them. I've still got a lot to learn." He paused. "But . . . uh, I don't . . . I haven't been able to put together a scenario that could explain what he was doing. I don't know what he was doing."

"Yes," Graver said, "you do."

Neuman was embarrassed, a little flustered. The keys jangled again. Graver stared at him.

"Looks like he was fabricating a contact report," Neuman said.

"Yeah"—Graver nodded—"that's what it looks like."

Casey Neuman didn't say anything, and as they stood there at the edge of the light from the diner windows Graver realized that he wasn't going to say anything.

"Okay, Casey," Graver said. He knew exactly what he was going to do. "You're going to get your feet wet here, in a major way."

18

GRAVER SAT IN HIS CAR AND WATCHED NEUMAN'S TAILLIGHTS DIS-
appear into all the other lights of the city. These revelations indicting
Dean Burtell were hitting him hard. But he would have been a fool to
start looking for innocent explanations. He wasn't going to find them.

Instead of driving away, he got out of the car and went to the pay
telephone near the front door of the diner. Taking a slip of paper from
his wallet he dialed the number written there.

"Hello?"

It was the woman's voice he had heard the previous evening when
he had answered the telephone in his living room.

"I'd like to speak to Victor, please."

"Who?"

"Is this Camey?"

Pause.

"Yes."

"Victor told me you might be answering the telephone. This is
Graver. I need to talk to Victor."

"Oh. He's not here."

"Will you give him a message?"

"Okay."

"Tell him I need to talk to him as soon as I can. He has several
numbers. Tell him to call them until he gets me. I'll be at the home
number in half an hour."

"Okay."

For some reason he didn't feel as though she was getting the full
import of his message.

"Do you understand?" he asked.

"Yeah, sure, I understand."

"Thank you," he said.

He went back to the car again, got in, and closed the door. Turning an investigative eye on Burtell was going to be painful, not unlike what he had just been through with Dore. Jesus. His profession was built on the study of deception, he had seen it from every angle, examined it with a telescope and a microscope, dissected it, read about it, written about it, thought about it, watched it, listened to it, experienced it, done it himself, and still he seemed no less immune to it than in the beginning. Certainly Dore had proved that on a personal level. Now Burtell was making the professional point.

But then no one was really immune to it, ever. If you were going to have any peace of mind at all, if you didn't want to live your life alone and in a misanthropic rage, you had to trust people. You had to allow them the freedom to be Judas. And it didn't do you any good to indulge in philosophical indignation, because if you did—and if you were honest with yourself—eventually you would find yourself eating your philosophy along with your crow. Deception was too handy a human tool not to employ it sooner or later yourself.

The thing was, as with everything else deception had its dimensions. There were vast deceptions and small ones, there were trivial ones and mortal ones, there were those that hurt for a little while and those that devastated. Tonight, sitting alone in front of a nearly empty diner, Graver wasn't sure anymore if the distance between these dimensions actually was all that great. It seemed to him that when men and women determined to employ this oldest of Satan's skills, they implicitly agreed to sacrifice a little piece of themselves in the process. Perhaps it was only a bruise in the beginning, something easily sustained without great harm, hardly noticeable. But it never went away and every deception added to it and made it worse until it was large and rancid and began to eat at them from the inside. How much rot could a person tolerate, he wondered, before the rot began to be the thing that defined them?

He ran his fingers through his hair, started his car, and drove away from the diner.

19

HALF AN HOUR LATER GRAVER PULLED UP IN FRONT OF HIS HOUSE. Looking at it through the windshield he thought the place looked particularly dreary in the darkness. He never left a light on for himself, even when he knew he was going to be working late, and he never had gotten one of those little timers at the hardware store even though he had been meaning to for months. He just didn't think of it except at moments like this when he would like to have seen a light inside, even if it had to be one that he had turned on himself.

The headlights of his car panned across the lawn as he turned into the cinder drive that was two cars wide and extended all the way back to the garage and the brick courtyard at the rear of the house. The instant they squared on the garage's closed doors, they also picked up the glint from the chrome bumper of a car that had pulled around back into the courtyard.

Graver cut his headlights and stopped. Neuman or Paula would have parked in front. Slowly he eased the car along the cinder drive until he was even with side of the house. If anyone was inside and hadn't already seen him, they wouldn't see his car sitting in the drive if they looked out the front windows.

Cutting the motor, he opened the car door and stepped out onto the cinder drive and eased the door closed until the latch clicked softly. He took a deep breath of the darkness which was heavy with the combined fragrances of the blossoming mock oranges and the huisache that grew against the rock wall on the other side of the car. For some reason his mind recalled the image of the spent flowers, yellow and white, which would cover the drive in a few weeks as the last of the blossoms retreated in the face of the scorching July temperatures. He reached back for his Sig-Sauer in its holster at his waist. It was something he hadn't done in a dozen years except when he had to qualify at the firing range.

Holding the gun down at his side he eased along the cinder drive until he approached the back corner and the small Mercedes came into full view. He noted the license plate. He stood silently and scanned the night yard, hoping his eyes would quickly adjust to the varieties of darkness and shadows. The pool. The palmettos. The wrought-iron patio furniture. The bulky trunks of the oaks. He smelled cigarette smoke. Back to the pool.

Jesus.

His heart lurched at the realization that someone was sitting in one of the wrought-iron chairs on the patio at the near end of the pool. It was a man, staring straight across at him. Graver assumed the man had seen his car lights as he came into the drive, though he didn't know whether he could yet see Graver at the corner of the house.

"Graver. Is that you over there? I saw your headlights."

It was Victor Last. Graver was both relieved and furious. He always had kept his private life private, and especially from informants. It was bad business to let them know anything at all about your personal life. Maybe Graver had treated Last a little differently in this regard, but even so, showing up like this was clearly out of line. Or maybe Last himself saw it differently now that Graver was living alone.

He scanned the yard one more time, though feeling pessimistic about his chances of spotting anyone else who might have been there. He returned the Sig-Sauer to its holster and stepped out from around the corner and started across the courtyard to the pool.

"What the hell are you doing here, Last?" Graver asked, trying to control his voice.

"I heard from Camey within five minutes of your call," Last said. "She said you'd be home in half an hour and that you wanted to see me as soon as possible. I thought I could save some time."

Last said this in a most natural manner, as though he hadn't the slightest idea that Graver might have objected to his showing up at his home.

Graver sat down in one of the wrought-iron chairs across the table from Last. The night was not overcast so the city lights did not provide a reflective glow by which Graver could see Last's face. He did not like this. Last was much better at masking his voice than his facial changes. As far as Graver could tell, he was dressed much as the night before.

Graver put his forearms on the wrought-iron table. The water in the pool was still and silent, the surface occasionally catching a glint of light as though it were a tightly stretched sheet of clear cellophane.

"I want to hear more about what you alluded to the other night," Graver said.

"Oh?" Last's head was motionless, alert. "I see."

"Don't jump to any conclusions," Graver said. "Did you expect me to let that go?"

"I hoped not," Last said, a touch of a smirk in his voice.

"What is it you need, Victor?"

"I find myself a little short just now," he said, resting an elbow on the edge of the table, the cigarette in the air. "I'd like to reestablish our former relationship."

"Same as before?"

"Well . . . not quite. I'm *very* short, actually."

"How much?"

"Double."

Graver looked at Last's silhouette. His voice was very firm on this. He was sure of himself.

"Victor, I couldn't give you that if you had proof the mayor was a pedophile. It's not a matter of bargaining. It's a matter of empty purses up there. We just don't have it. At the time we were working together you were the highest-paid person we had. I can't do it."

"Come on, Graver," Last scoffed gently. "That was eight years ago. Doubling it is not really like *doubling* it, for Christ's sake. Inflation. Cost of living. The bloody economy, all that. Even if you paid me the same rate it would be more."

"I can't do it."

Silence. Last smoked his cigarette.

"I can give you twenty percent more," Graver said. "That would put you at the top again."

"I'm flattered," Last said dryly.

"That's all I can do. I'm sorry." Pause. "But I won't pay even that if your information's no good."

"Okay, fine. When can you pay me?"

"Let me hear your story."

Last was still again. The cigarette's ember moved from the table to his face and there was a brief, rosy glow as he sucked on it and fleetingly lighted his upper cheeks and eyes. Then he was back in the dark.

"You're a gentleman, Graver. I'll trust you on that."

Graver was relieved. He knew that Last trusted him, that wasn't it. It was the fact that Last didn't hold out for bigger money. If his information had been stunning, he would have. What Graver might have here was a good lead. It wasn't going to be something that was going to knock him out of his chair.

"Okay," Last said. He dropped his cigarette on the tile under the table and put his shoe on it. He dropped his arms to the arms of the chair, relaxed. When he began talking, his voice was mellow, soft, unhurried.

"I started to tell you last night about going to a party at this fellow's house here in Houston—"

"What was his name?" Graver interrupted.

"I'll get to that," Last said, unperturbed. "This man and his wife had a very strange house. Ugly, actually. Modern. One level, spare design, glass rooms around a series of atria. Kind of modular and rambly, if you can imagine. Odd. There were a lot of people, but it wasn't a raucous affair. It was a talking party. A little combo doing soft, white noise stuff and people standing around in clutches holding drinks. Yuppie sorts. New Age sorts. And the ever-present *business* sorts.

"At one point in the evening the lady who accompanied me to the party went to the loo. When she same back she was all atitter. Seems the loo was rather vulnerable visually, to an outside courtyard. The toilet was actually out in the open in the bedroom—so was the shower —and the only privacy was provided by the thick foliage surrounding the bedroom. No privacy in the room itself, so that you pissed away right there in front all the other ladies who might wander in to check their hair, or cosmetics, or whatever. She, of course, didn't trust the density of the foliage on the other side of the glass walls. She said there was another bedroom around the corner, and a woman she met in this first bedroom said the arrangement was similar. My lady friend asked this woman if she'd been here before, and she said, oh, yes. And my friend asked what about peepers. The lady laughed and said, no it wasn't at all what it seemed. No one could see in because of garden walls and all that. That was part of the intent in the architectural design. To make one feel that one was living *au naturel*.

"I decided to check it out. The place had a kind of honeycomb arrangement, rooms and atria interconnected. You could be in one glass room and look across one of the several atria to the next glass room. Glass and mirrored hallways connected these sort of modules.

"Anyway, after a while I slipped outside for a smoke. Everyone was inside, of course, addicted to the air-conditioning, not wanting to muss themselves with the humidity. I didn't know but what there might be someone outside, so I was very casual about it, lighting a cigarette right away so as to be able to explain myself if I needed to.

"Of course, it turned out that the visual security of this place was not at all what this woman had believed, not once you were inside the garden walls, which you achieved by simply coming inside the house and then going outside. Each of these eccentric bedrooms was indeed enclosed in its own small, high-walled courtyard, and stuffed with plants, palms and such. But, each courtyard also had outside the wall a small, unobtrusive ledge built along the footing of the wall. If you stepped onto the ledge you could look over the wall and see everything inside. There were also hose bibs there, and a watering hose, the ostensible purpose, I'm sure, for the ledge being there."

Last stopped and lighted another cigarette. He smoked a moment.

"The house was roughly the shape of a hexagon or octagon or something, you know, roundish but having straight walls. I stayed well out of the light in the irregular lawn interrupted by shrubbery. Came to the first bedroom. Stepped up on the ledge and looked over. Sure enough, laughably, a woman perched on the potty, her dress gathered up around her, looking rather defiantly, I thought, straight out the glass wall at me. I ducked reflexively and then came back up and saw her still there, still staring at me, her feet splayed, her hands resting in her lap and holding a bunch of tissue. She couldn't see me at all, even if I'd raised my hands and waved at her. I think the glass walls were coated somehow, to make the outside more opaque. I watched her finish, dry herself, and get up, and flush the toilet.

"I watched for a bit, two more ladies. This was rather fascinating, I found, the different little ways they tended to themselves. I finished my cigarette and decided to go around to the other bedroom. I passed the next atrium, another room of guests, and was just about to round the next shallow corner when I became aware of voices ahead of me, just around the corner. I stopped, held my breath, and listened. Yes, indeed. Two men's voices. I eased to the corner, next to which, luckily, a loquat tree was standing. Using this as a screen, I peeped around. Two men were standing on the ledge at the foot of the garden wall of the next bedroom. They were watching whatever women were in the bedroom, but they were doing so as though the action in there was rather sort of incidental entertainment. Their drink glasses were sitting atop the wall, as were their raised elbows, and they were smoking and in conversation."

Last paused to take another puff on his cigarette. He seemed to be thinking of how to proceed, maybe even, Graver thought, savoring the story.

"Now, this is weird, I know," he said, "but I *overheard* this one guy expressing disbelief, believingly expressing disbelief, if you know what I mean. The second man said, no, it was true. It had been some time getting arranged, but that they finally had done it. He said their 'access' to intelligence 'and its processes' was solid and had been tested several times. The first man wanted to know how long this had been going on. 'A while,' was all the second man said. They paused a bit, sipped their drinks, and watched someone in the loo. The second man stepped down off the ledge, lighted a cigarette, and stepped up again.

"Second man said he understood the first man was having trouble with a certain competitor. He asked what it would be worth to him to rid himself of this guy. First man said his volume would jump thirty percent. Second man asked would he be interested in eliminating him. First man asked was a pig's ass pork."

Last stopped at this and laughed. "American eloquence. I hadn't heard that one. Stunning." He smoked. "The second man said they needed to talk about that. First man said he didn't know of anything his competitor was doing that was illegal. Second man said that didn't matter, things could be worked out." Last paused. "They got interested in someone in the loo again and then the first man wanted to talk about it some more. Just think a bit about it, the second man said. They would get together again and explore the idea some more. They polished off their drinks, very quietly watched someone in the loo for a few minutes, and then the second man said they'd better get back or they'd be missed. That was it. I had to get out of there."

Last brought his hand to his mouth again, and the tip of the cigarette glowed and died.

"I didn't hear anything about the police in that," Graver said. "Everyone has intelligence capabilities now. Business, industry."

"But when the second fellow asked the first if he wanted to eliminate his competitor, the first said his competitor wasn't doing anything 'illegal.' Why would that figure into the picture at all if they weren't cops? Who moves against illegalities? Who could use an 'illegality' as a means to close down a business?"

Graver shook his head, not altogether convinced. This wasn't exactly the kind of thing he thought he was going to hear. It was too vague.

"Did you get a good look at these guys?"

"I think so. Their profiles, anyway."

"The owner of the house wasn't one of them?"

"No."

"Who owned the house?"

Last shifted in his chair. "How's that going to help you?"

"I don't know. It sure as hell won't help if I don't know."

"You want me to find out these two guys' names? I'll do that."

"What's the matter?"

"Look, this man collects 'native American' art. I'm trying to interest him in pre-Columbian stuff. It could be very good for me. Pre-Columbian is going to be very big. The free trade business is going to open up Mexican-interest marketing possibilities. I'm the newest thing in his life right now, Graver. Some of your clubfooted boys start mewling about asking questions, and this guy's going to ask why people are snooping around him all of a sudden. He's going to say to himself: Victor Last shows up and now people are asking questions." Last took one more hit off his cigarette and dropped it to the tile and stepped on it. "I don't have to explain this kind of thing to you, Graver."

"No, you don't. And I don't have to explain to you that what you've just told me is interesting. I think it's mildly amusing that men stand outside bathrooms and watch women urinate, but this definitely is not good take, Victor."

Graver could see enough to see Last grinning across the table.

"Well, I suppose it depends on what it is you're looking for, doesn't it," Last said. He shifted in his chair, crossed his legs the other way. "You want names."

"Of course I do. And let's see if we can't find out if 'the second man's' intelligence operation is in the police department or in the American Southwest Meat Packers Association."

Last clucked his tongue at Graver's sarcasm and stared across the table. "Come on, Graver," Last said softly, "tell me. Didn't I hit on something?"

Graver's response was immediate and a surprise even to himself.

"Okay, Victor. The truth is, no, you didn't hit on anything. If you've discovered a breach in CID security, it's news to me. But if you *have* discovered something, I sure as hell want to know more about it. I'm just not convinced you have, that's all."

Last nodded, slowly and for several moments. "Okay, Graver," he said finally, pushing his chair back and standing up. "I'll see what I can do."

Graver stood too.

"You still swim laps?" Last asked, his hands in his pocket as he looked down at the water.

"Yeah."

Last nodded his head. "Very disciplined. Admirable. Really."

He started toward his car and Graver followed him a few steps across the patio. When Last got to the Mercedes, he walked around to the driver's side, put his hand on the door handle and looked across the top of the car. "I'll be in touch," he said.

"That's fine," Graver said, and Last opened the Mercedes door. "But, Victor," Graver added, "don't ever come back here again."

Last grinned at Graver across the top of the car, got inside, and closed the door. Graver watched as Last backed down the cinder drive to the street and drove away.

Tuesday
THE THIRD DAY

20

TOO MUCH WAS HAPPENING; SLEEP HAD BECOME A RARE COMMOD-
ity, and Graver no longer had the peace of mind to acquire it. After
Last's departure there remained only a few hours for him to toss
among the sheets, trying to turn off his mind. When the alarm finally
sounded, he was both exhausted and grateful and rolled out of bed
with a headache. He showered and dressed and left the house without
even considering making his own breakfast. Instead, he stopped at a
coffee shop on the way downtown and sat at a window table while he
downed several cups of stout, black coffee with his bacon and eggs and
watched the city slowly awaken to a clear hot day.

Because he had got out of bed immediately and had not taken the
time to make his own breakfast, he beat Lara to the office by nearly an
hour. That was fine, he needed the time to get himself together. After
putting his briefcase on his desk, he went across the hall and started a
pot of coffee. While he waited for it to brew he stepped into Lara's
office and left a note on her desk to tell Paula, Neuman, and Burtell to
be ready for a nine o'clock meeting in his office. He also asked her not
to disturb him. Then he poured himself a cup of coffee and went into
his office and closed his door.

There was a lot to think about, and while he had eaten breakfast he
had made some decisions. The first was that he resolved to have Westrate's report ready by the end of the day.

He turned on his computer and tapped in the license plate number
he had seen on Last's Mercedes. The car belonged to a Camilla Reeder
who lived in a condominium in far west Houston. Ms. Reeder was
thirty-one years old and listed her employment as a cosmetics representative for Laurel Cosmetics. She had no criminal history. Last seemed
to have become acquainted with an unmarked woman—on the face of
it at least—which was an improvement for him.

Graver then turned his computer inquiries in another direction. He typed Last's name into NCIC to get a report on Last's most recent activities. He hadn't kept up with his career in nearly a decade, not in detail anyway. After that, he typed a brief inquiry document to be sent to the major intelligence agencies requesting MO and crime analysis subject category matches on Victor Last's career markers. It was time to see if Last had been back to his old ways.

After sending this out on the lines, Graver turned back to his desk and set about making notes on these as well as the essential elements of his conversations with Paula and Neuman.

At five minutes before nine o'clock, he opened his door and said good morning to Lara. Standing at her desk, he gave her a list of things he wanted done, briefly discussing each item on the list before he turned and went back into the office.

He went over his notes again and was making last-minute notations when he heard Paula's voice outside in the hallway followed by Lara's laughter. The door opened and they came in one after the other, Paula, Burtell, and Neuman, each of them carrying notebooks and folders and something to drink. Everyone said good morning as they shoved their chairs around to suit them and sat down.

Graver, trying to cover the self-consciousness he felt in Burtell's presence, moved brusquely into business. He knew Paula and Neuman would be watching to see how he was going to play it.

"First thing," he said. "Late yesterday afternoon Jack Westrate called and told me that Homicide and IAD had agreed to call Tisler's death a suicide. Nothing sinister to it."

Casey Neuman sipped from the canned soft drink he had brought in, and Paula stared straight at Graver without comment. Burtell turned away and looked out the windows. The file folders of the five Tisler investigations were on his lap, and he was holding a mug of coffee which rested on the folders. Graver couldn't really tell how he was taking this news. He did not want to dwell on it and was glad Burtell was going to let it pass without comment.

"That, of course, is a big break for us," he went on. "I don't know if you've come up with anything, but the momentum of presumption is in our favor with that ruling. But I've still got to produce a summary, a 'clean slate' document to put in the files. So let's get down to it. You guys finding anything in Tisler's folders that raise questions?" He went straight to Burtell. "Dean, what about it? You see anything noteworthy in the documents you reviewed?"

Burtell turned from the windows and shook his head. He looked down at the folders resting in his lap.

"No, I didn't see anything in here," he said. "Nothing even remotely curious. Art had routinely updated them as per regulations, but nothing significant had changed in any of them in over a year. Unremarkable in just about every way."

Graver waited a moment, looking at Burtell who had recovered considerably from the day before. He appeared to have got more sleep, got his emotions in order, though he was subdued as the occasion required. But Graver watched him for something else, perhaps an unnatural insouciance, a glimmer of an affectation in his manner, however slight.

"Okay," Graver said. He turned to Paula.

"No, nothing here, either," she said. "But for the record I want to state that I had only one day to look over these folders. I can't say that represents a thorough examination. It was just enough time for a . . . cursory review. But, no, in my cursory review I didn't find anything that would make me suspect anything untoward in the collection process."

Burtell kept his eyes on some vague spot on the front of Graver's desk and sipped his coffee.

"Do you think you need more time, is that it?" Graver asked. He had to. Paula had practically said she didn't have enough time.

"I don't know that that would be justified now, in light of the ruling from Homicide," Paula said. "I just don't want it recorded that I conducted a major audit here."

"Okay, noted," Graver said.

Paula, as usual, was playing her game with unyielding rigor. Even when deceiving Burtell, she didn't want him to think he could put something over on her. If there was something there to discover, she implied, she would bloody well find it if she were given the proper amount of time to examine the documents. Jesus. Graver could have shot her, but, in the end, her reaction was probably best. Burtell might have sensed something awry if all three of them had just rolled over. Paula, after all, was being Paula.

"Casey?"

Neuman repeated essentially what he had told Graver the night before about his search of Tisler's records, though he now went into more detail. As Paula had done, he said there was a lot more he could do, but a preliminary check of the records, with the view that Tisler might possibly have had financial difficulties, turned up no flags that would make him want to pursue the issue further.

Graver nodded and tapped the eraser of his pencil on the cobblestone. For a moment no one said anything. Neuman was studying the top of his soft drink can again, Paula was still looking straight at Graver, and Burtell had lifted his coffee mug and was straightening a document inside one of his folders.

"Okay. If no one has anything they want to add, then I'm going to go ahead and write a summary reflecting that we turned up nothing suspect in our audit, and as far as we're concerned their judgment that Tisler had died of a self-inflicted gunshot wound will go into his file. End of inquiry."

He looked at Burtell again. "Dean, will you continue to follow up with Peggy Tisler? Lara's going to get the details about when the family can claim the body. You can check with her on your way out. She's also going to see to it that the necessary paperwork is put together regarding the suicide ruling. Tisler's insurance company is going to want that. And there are a few other things . . . arrangements for a memorial service . . . whatever."

Burtell nodded. "Okay, sure, be glad to."

"Now, let's see, the next thing I want to get out of the way is deciding the best way to move ahead on the Seldon investigation."

There was a quick stirring behind Burtell's eyes.

"It looked to me like it was on track, a fast track," Graver said.

"Well, yeah"—Burtell straightened up in his chair, trying to move smoothly past his surprise—"it was. But Art . . . on this one his source was the linchpin to the investigation. In fact, the guy was all there was to it."

"Okay, all the more reason to get right back on it. Are you the alternate controlling officer?"

Burtell nodded, but it seemed tentative. Graver couldn't quite read it.

"Good," Graver said. "I'd like Casey to work with you on this. I know we don't normally do this, but under the circumstances I'd rather you didn't continue the case alone." Graver was too close to Burtell. He had no idea how he was carrying this off, if the incredible tension he was feeling was showing through his feint. "From the looks of it there's the potential that it could mushroom, and I think you ought to team up on it again. You think the guy will go for that?"

Burtell involuntarily shot a look at Neuman and then back to Graver. He shifted in his chair. "Jesus, I, uh, I don't know, Marcus. He's already paranoid, and Art was really having to massage him, coax him along. When he finds out Art's dead . . . I don't know. I just don't see how we can."

Graver looked at Burtell and hesitated as if he was trying to figure out just exactly what it was Burtell was getting at.

Burtell went on, putting the best face on it that he could muster.

"This guy . . . was having a hard time believing we could keep his identity confidential. I know that's a routine concern, but . . . he's not a routine source."

There was a moment's silence.

"What do you mean?" Graver asked, but he wasn't sure his tone of voice conveyed what he had intended.

Burtell looked around at each of them. Had Graver unintentionally betrayed something? Paula and Neuman both met Burtell's glance. Then everything turned, and it seemed to Graver that at that moment Burtell realized there was no way he was going to be able to finesse this. Graver could see it coming. As he had predicted, Burtell was about to pull the plug.

"We need to go into this, Marcus," Burtell said. Suddenly his tone was brittle, clinical. "Just the two of us."

Neuman and Paula didn't even have to be asked. They simply got up and walked out of the office.

21

WHEN THE DOOR CLOSED BEHIND THEM, BURTELL STOOD, PUTTING his files and his coffee mug down on the corner of Graver's desk. Though he tried to appear composed, something that normally came easily to him, his agitation was apparent, just beneath the surface. He stepped to the windows and looked out at the city which was hard and bright in the clear morning, collecting his thoughts. A handsome man, well dressed . . . and composed. Almost.

"The damn case wasn't that healthy," he began, leaning one shoulder against the glass wall, one hand in his pocket. "You saw yourself there aren't that many documents in the folder. Not that much corroborated information." He looked outside again, squinting into the eastern skyline. "Art had only three meetings with this guy."

Graver looked down at the opened folder on his desk. "Nieson."

Burtell nodded, not bothering to hide a look of disgust.

"Right, Parnell Nieson. At each meeting Nieson wore a wig, an expensive one. Art thought it was a hairpiece after the first meeting, but he couldn't be positive. Second meeting he was satisfied it was. Nieson . . . always had several days' growth of beard, though Art said it didn't hide the fact that he was obviously an executive type, expensive clothes, *manicured* nails, obligatory Rolex, all the stuff. He wore blue contact lenses. Art said he didn't try to pretend he wasn't disguised, though the alterations in his appearance were subtle enough, well done. Art never saw him drive anything. The guy always arrived at the meeting sites after Tisler, and he always left first."

"What?" Graver zeroed in on the irregular procedure. *"Every time?"*

"I know, I know." Burtell nodded, placating. "I jumped him about this. I told him he was crazy to let the guy dictate the terms of the meetings, that he was violating the basic rules of handling contributors. But Art smelled something big, and he argued that compromising on the meeting arrangements was insignificant compared to what he stood to get from the guy. He said he would humor him on that point. He didn't want to risk alienating him right from the beginning by insisting on something that, at this stage of the game, Art thought was trivial."

Burtell paused, stepped over to Graver's desk, and picked up his coffee mug. He sipped the coffee tentatively and returned to the window. Graver didn't take advantage of this hiatus to speak. He didn't want to relieve any of the pressure Burtell was feeling, or give him an extra moment to collect his thoughts. He let all the silence fall on Burtell's shoulders.

With his free hand still in his trousers pocket, Burtell bent his head in thought and continued.

"Nieson told Art from the beginning that he hated Seldon. He knew that much, that Art would be looking for a legitimate motive, and he gave him an 'honest' one. They were competitors in the same business and Seldon had burned him once, burned him big-time. Nieson wanted to see him hurt." He nodded to the folder opened before Graver. "You can see from the contact reports that he gave Art a lot of information relating to Seldon's business, detailed information that he knew Art could corroborate. He knew what he was talking about. But he never named names other than Seldon's, never gave away a piece of geography that Art could work from—the ranch for instance—never mentioned relationships we could draw inferences from, never . . . well, shit, never gave us anything we could work back on. If we went any further with this, he was going to have to take us there."

Graver turned a couple of pages in the folder before him.

"What about the information on the contributor's ID record? What did you find when you checked into that?"

Burtell nodded, knowing this question was coming, and he clearly wasn't looking forward to it.

"Yeah, I went into it." Pause. "None of it checked out."

"None of it?" Graver was genuinely surprised. The Seldon investigation was losing blood with every revelation.

"None."

"How long have you known this?" Graver flattened his tone. He wanted to sound cold, not worked up, as if he had gone past agitation to something more serious.

"After the first meeting we corroborated everything he'd told us about Seldon personally," Burtell said. "After the second meeting, we corroborated everything he told Art about Seldon's business. It was all checking out. This was looking good, both of us could see the potential of these relationships considering the enormous price tag on the chemical industry here in Houston. The drug business speaks for itself. It was checking out. It was solid. I have to admit, we were both getting worked up over this one."

Burtell was good, aligning himself with Tisler and hoping to avoid the appearance that he was foisting all the blame for the investigation onto a dead man who couldn't defend himself. He was putting just enough *mea culpa* into his explanation to keep Tisler from being a total scapegoat. He took a deep breath and exhaled. The deceit was painful for Graver to watch. Burtell did it so well, with just the right nuance of uncertainty to make it look like he was defending himself—or admitting to poor judgment.

"Third meeting," Burtell continued, "he gives us information about the actors on the drug end of the deal. We check it out through DEA, it's good. But he doesn't give us too much, not enough for us to initiate anything on our own. He still held the key to the relationships. He also finally gave Art his name and showed him an ID. That was two weeks ago. When Art came back and filled out the paperwork I got right on it. There is in fact a Parnell Nieson who is an executive with Rochin and Leeds Chemicals. But Tisler's source was not Parnell Nieson. I found a picture of Nieson in Rochin and Leeds's most recent annual report. Showed it to Tisler. Wasn't him."

"And Tisler confronted the source with this?"

"Yeah, four days later. Guy just laughed. He said we'd worked a lot faster than he'd thought we would."

"What happened then?"

"Art finally went out on a limb. He told the guy we wouldn't be able to work with him. Told him he wasn't reliable, that we couldn't deal with him because we had to have a dependable relationship in order to assemble a proper investigation. Art gambled and just walked away from it, which was pretty gutsy considering how much he wanted this to work. He was betting the guy wanted it as bad as we did."

"And when was that?"

Burtell calculated. "Ten days ago, I guess."

"That was a fourth meeting. Why wasn't that meeting recorded in the folder? There's no contact report on that."

The question was disingenuous. Graver knew exactly what was happening, or he would have known if any of this had actually taken place. Contrary to by-the-book regulations, the working relationship between analysts and investigators commonly involved a mutual agreement to relax the rules of the game. This was especially likely when a new investigation was being developed and an investigator, and/or the analyst, wanted to massage a reluctant contributor long past the time when a prudent superior would have advised them to walk away from it.

Such was the situation here. Tisler's source was proving to be reliable as far as the information he was providing was concerned, but his actual identity was crucial, and if he wasn't willing to provide it, working with him was going to be difficult to justify. Tisler and Burtell wanted more time to try to bring the man around. It was a cat-and-mouse game everyone was used to playing. To buy more time, they agreed to pretend the last meeting never happened.

At least, this was the scenario Burtell was offering. Despite a growing disgust at Burtell's egregious lying, Graver was fascinated. Burtell was incredible. If he was in fact fabricating all of this to cover for the nonexistent investigation—which Graver was sure he was doing—then he was even inventing a subtext for Graver to discover, knowing that as an old hand Graver would know how these things "really" worked. This was a deception within a deception within a manipulation. The full realization of the sophistication of Burtell's betrayal began to work its way to the surface of Graver's understanding, and for the first time he sensed something eerie creeping into the equation.

"We thought we could work it out," Burtell continued. "Art didn't want to file another daily report that would reflect that he'd come up empty-handed again. I agreed to go along with it." He looked at his coffee and decided not to drink any more of it. It was probably cold. "Art waited a week, and sure enough the guy called him. He was ready to do it. Everything. He swore. They were supposed to have met Saturday night."

"Do you know if they did?"

Burtell shook his head. "No, I don't know."

"Jesus Christ, Dean," Graver said, making his voice portray disappointment now, rather than impatience or anger. "And Tisler was the only one who knew what he looked like?" This was the central point of the entire game here; this was going to be Burtell's "explanation."

Burtell looked at him. "That's right."

Even in this, Burtell was playing his role perfectly. His eyes met Graver's as though he was admitting his fault like a man. He would courageously swallow the medicine, admit that he had let the investigation get away from him. Graver felt like he was in a theater group. His next question was calculated to see if Burtell could keep this up.

"Did Ray know you were pushing this?"

At this there was a slight bobble in Burtell's demeanor and in what had been, up to this point, a smoothly-played hand. Now Burtell had to ask himself some quick, tough questions. Should he drag Besom into the deception? Should he expand the cast of characters? Burtell's answer demonstrated how well he could balance on the wire.

"No, he didn't know. Art and I were skating this on our own."

Graver reached out and gave the cobblestone a few thoughtful turns.

"Did you ever get the impression from Art that there was anything . . . sinister about Nieson? Do you think there's even the slightest reason to suspect that he killed Art?"

"No, honestly I don't," Burtell said. "I've been over and over that too, Marcus, don't think I haven't. But . . . I just can't see it."

"Did he ever call Art here?"

"Yes."

Graver stared at the Seldon documents in front of him. That was it. Burtell had not hesitated to commit himself wholeheartedly to a course of action that was a clear abandonment of everything that Graver, at least, had thought he stood for. Burtell was embracing a deception that could not be explained away. If he ever had an inclination to get out of it he had to know that now was the moment to do so and that Graver was his best hope for effecting an extrication. He had to know this, and yet Burtell did not hesitate to step over the line that would separate them for a certainty. For Graver it was a truly painful display of hypocrisy. Graver felt as if Burtell had walked up to him and hit him in the stomach.

"Okay," Graver said, closing the manila folder. "I've got to think about this." He sat back in his chair and leveled his eyes at Burtell. "You shouldn't have let yourself get caught empty-handed—I mean *completely* empty-handed."

He wanted to say something entirely different, but that, at least, was expected of him. As he sat there staring at the man who was like a younger brother to him he came within a hairsbreadth of dropping all pretense, of stopping the charade. He wanted to take Burtell by the shoulders and shake him and ask him for God's sake what was he doing; how could he do what he was doing; what in the hell was happening to him.

Burtell was nodding at him, his eyes cast awkwardly to the side as he pretended to swallow the reprimand. "Yeah, I know," he said. "I screwed it up."

Graver was suddenly assaulted with a confusion of emotions. He was furious at Burtell's performance, standing in front of him dressed immaculately in lies, wearing them so well he was fluid and articulate and—if it had not been for Paula's and Neuman's discoveries—believable. He was furious that Burtell had played the altar boy for more than two years while at the same time he had operated some kind of shell game that Graver didn't even yet understand. He was disgusted with himself for having let it happen. He was frightened that the dimensions of this game were still unknown. He was baffled and maybe even a little rattled that he didn't yet know how to deal with it. And he was stung to the quick by the betrayal.

"I'll get back to you," he managed to say dismissively, hoping that his face was not giving away the turmoil he was feeling. Burtell nodded and for an instant Graver thought he hesitated. But he could no longer allow himself to trust anything he saw in Burtell's behavior. It was as if Dean Burtell had died right there in front of him.

Burtell bent down and picked up his files from his chair and headed for the door. But then he stopped and turned. He looked at Graver and then advanced a few steps to Graver's desk.

"Uh, Marcus. Did you . . . remember that I was scheduled for vacation?"

Graver looked at him blankly. "Sorry," he said. "I'd forgotten about it."

"Do you have any objections to me going ahead with it now? Under the circumstances . . . I . . . frankly, I could use it."

Graver shook his head. "No, of course not. I can't see any reason for you to hang around now." He pushed aside the paperwork on his desk and looked at the calendar. "That's two weeks. Starting tomorrow," he said.

Burtell nodded. "Thanks, I appreciate it." He seemed to hesitate again, then turned abruptly and walked out of the office.

Graver slumped back in his chair and stared at the closed door. "Jesus Christ," he said.

22.

GRAVER OPENED HIS DESK DRAWER AND GOT HIS CAR KEYS. He needed to talk to Paula and Neuman, but he also had to do something else, and he had to do it now. After locking his desk, the files, and the safe, he walked out of the office and told Lara that he had to leave for several hours, and it probably would be after lunch before he would be back.

She looked at him, and as their eyes met he could tell instantly by her expression that she saw something on his face that caught her attention. He turned and walked out of the office without telling her where he could be reached. It was something he never did. He felt her eyes on him until he was out the door.

Four or five blocks away from the office, he pulled into a self-service station to fill the car with gasoline. He set the nozzle on its slowest automatic setting and made a brief telephone call from a pay phone outside the station. After the call he gave the attendant fifteen dollars and got back to the nozzle just in time to catch the fifteen clocking around on the pump dials. He checked his watch.

It took him longer than he had thought it would to get to Arnette's. She lived in one of Houston's older neighborhoods where the ethnic diversity was reflected in almost exactly the same proportions as the city's demographic pie charts. It was a mixture that pleased Arnette Kepner just fine.

She lived in a World War II-vintage house that backed up to one of the city's bayous. When Arnette cashed in her twenty-five-year retirement from the federal government eight years ago, she looked for a long time before she found just the situation she wanted, a modest-to-low-income neighborhood, three houses in a row. It took every penny of her savings, but she bought all three of them and then proceeded to transform the yards of the three lots into something resembling a tropical nursery with the outside property lines of the two outside houses fortified with thick walls of rangy Asian bamboo. Although from the front each house appeared to have an entirely different owner, Arnette's three properties actually formed a compound with each adjacent house accessible to the other through a common back yard from which the interior fences had been removed creating one large, wooded lawn that was not visible from the street. Aside from this slightly overgrown appearance, nothing distinguished Arnette's houses from the others in the neighborhood since all of them tended toward a careless woodiness.

Within the perimeter of Arnette's bamboo wall was a well-hidden security system that encircled the three lots. It was a very thorough piece of technology. The mailbox of each house was set into a rock pillar by each of the front gates and was accessible from the back side; one was completely covered with fig ivy, one was moss green with a lichen patina, and the other was almost hidden in Paradise bamboo.

Graver parked in front of the middle house, which was Arnette's residence, and got out of the car. He knew the security lock on the front yard gate already would be opened for him, so he didn't hesitate to open it and step inside the yard. The winding street, which closely followed the curves of the bayou for a dozen or more blocks, was shaded by large pecans and oaks and cypresses which seemed to be populated with every kind of bird that could inhabit a coastal, subtropical region, and their screeching and whistling and burbling filled the still, late morning air. As Graver made his way along the short brick path through the elephant ears and plantains and palmettos, he thought how closely Arnette had come to making the place seem like "a little bit of 'Nam," as she had said she wanted to do.

He opened the screen door of the long, screened-in room that ran the length of the front of the house just as the door to the house itself opened.

"Baby!" Arnette said softly, smiling at him, and Graver stepped to the front door to hug a wiry, smallish woman with large brown eyes who was still a few years away from sixty. Arnette wore her thick, brindled hair pulled back—though it rebelled and strayed in a spray of salt and pepper filaments—and woven in a single braid which she habitually wore over her left shoulder in the rather coy manner of a much younger woman. She was trim and had the face of a gypsy, with a strong narrow nose and white teeth. As always when she was at home, she was dressed in a high-necked Vietnamese silk blouse and pants, today of bright saffron.

"I couldn't believe my ears," she said, holding Graver's arm in a kind of embrace as they entered the living room of the house. "It's been close to a year, mister. Where the hell have you been?"

"Wandering in the sloughs of bureaucracy," Graver said. "Lost in the Valley of Darkness."

She laughed knowingly as they stepped into a large room as eccentric in appearance as Arnette herself. Of the three houses in a row, only hers had been completely renovated, its dominating feature being its most immediate one, a sprawling and spacious living room with heavy teak pillars holding up the ceiling where walls once had been. Much of the lighting came from a continuous cornice that circled the room near the ceiling, which had been raised to include the higher spaces of the attic and which provided an unusual soft glow throughout, as though the room existed in a perpetual dawn. This lighting was supplemented by table lamps sprinkled among comfortable armchairs and sofas and small incidental tables stacked with books. The furniture and the walls were decorated with fabrics and artifacts that Arnette had picked up in Southeast Asia and Latin America during her years of work there. The effect was as if they were entering the enormous tent of a nomadic tribe or a large *marao,* the communal grass hut of the Montagnards of South Vietnam.

Arnette was still smiling as she gestured for Graver to sit down and then took her place on one of the sofas. Above her head on the wall behind her was a display of wicked-looking blades with wooden handles, a goose-necked *chuang* and smaller *siput* and a variety of hook-tipped *maks.* They were not weapons, however, but farming tools used by the rice-farming Jeh tribe of Montagnards who lived in the murky Dak Poko valley where Arnette had spent several lifetimes when she was younger, during the early years of the Vietnam War.

Surrounding them here and there as if in a museum were glass cases with pre-Columbian Mexican statuettes in the Remojadas style from Veracruz, life-sized stone masks in the Classic Teotihuacán style, and ceramics of every sort, including tripods decorated in the carved relief technique as well as Thin Orange ware. Weaving from the Guatemalan highlands hung on other walls, *huipiles* and *cortes* and *cintas* in the brilliant, exploding colors of the Indian imagination. There were black and white photographs in thin black frames, Arnette on a bridge in

Vienna, Arnette and Mona in a restaurant in Buenos Aires and at a cafe table in Montevideo, three people with no identification standing on the front porch of a cabin surrounded by aspens, a cur with three legs and a ribbon tied around his neck somewhere in Latin America.

Arnette tucked one of her legs up under her and sat back on the sofa, smiling at him.

"God, baby, it's really good to see you," she said. "I told Mona you were coming. She'll be over after a while, if that's all right with you."

"Sure, I'd love to see her," Graver said. Mona Isaza was Arnette's companion. They had met when Arnette had spent a year in Mexico City in the early 1970s and had been together ever since. She lived in one of the houses next door.

"How have things been with you, anyway?" Arnette asked, still smiling, seeming to relish his being there.

"Busy," he said and left it at that. Normally he would have brought her up to date on everyone, but he was sure she knew of his recent divorce, and he saw no reason to go into it. But if he mentioned the twins it would be uncomfortable to leave the subject of Dore just hanging there, so he chose not to say anything about any of them. "Just like everyone else."

"When are you going to get out of this work?" she asked. "If I calculate right, this is your twenty-third year with the department . . . fourteen in that wretched intelligence maze."

"Yeah, well, I'm going for twenty-five. Better benefits."

"That suits you, huh?"

Graver shrugged. "Mixed feelings."

"Oh, hell, that's the business, isn't it? Mixed feelings are the least of it. Everything else leaves a scab of some sort."

Graver nodded.

She looked at him a moment in silence, and her smile softened. She could tell he was in no mood for visiting.

"You've got something on your mind."

"I need some help."

"Good."

"Unofficially."

"Oh."

"Not for me, personally, it's for the department, but I'm the only one who's going to know about it."

"Uh-oh. You've got internal problems."

"I think it's bad."

"Jesus."

"I need you to do twenty-four hours on Dean Burtell and his wife."

Arnette thrust her head forward, her eyes wide open. "Burt-*tell?* Goddamn!"

Graver took the better part of an hour to tell her what had happened during the last two days. He told her everything. While he was talking she got up and lighted a joss stick and set it aside, the incense curling up into the twilight above them. Outside the birds were boisterous and shrill.

"The thing is," Graver said after a while, "I've decided that I don't want to turn this over to anyone just yet. I don't want to go to anyone in the department, not even IAD. And I don't want to go outside—DA's office or FBI—until I know more about what I've got here."

Arnette was sitting with one leg tucked up under her as before, the room now filled with the smoke of sandalwood. It was the waft of conspiracy, and Graver wondered if the fragrance put Arnette's mind in the way of contrivance and secrecy, the way a mantra called to mind a meditative discipline. He was afraid she was going to say something about Burtell, but she was more savvy than that and, to Graver's relief, stuck to the immediate business.

"Afraid they'll cut you out?"

"I think it's a distinct probability."

She thought a minute. "I'm sorry if I sound . . . mercenary, but if this is an 'unofficial' contract, how am I going to get paid? This is going to take a lot of people—five to seven for Dean, four or five for Ginette—at least. He hasn't been on the street in a long time, but I'll bet he knows a team tail when he sees it. We can't mess around here."

"I have a small discretionary fund," Graver said. "It can buy me several weeks if it needs to."

Graver had met Arnette Kepner more than a decade back when he was lecturing on network analysis at the Georgetown University's Consortium for the Study of Intelligence. After his lecture she was among the people who came up to the podium to ask more questions and talk for a few minutes. But she lingered until she was the last one and then asked to take him to dinner. It turned out to be a fascinating evening and was the beginning of a friendship.

He learned from her that she had spent nearly twenty-five years with the government, all of it in various intelligence branches, traveling to hot spots around the globe, first with army intelligence and then with "various other" agencies throughout her career. She said she was considering retiring and had thought that Houston would be a good place. They talked about the city in general terms, and she told him enough about her life for him to understand that she was a very unusual woman.

Eighteen months later he received a telephone call from her saying she was in town, that she had bought a home and why didn't he come by to see her. When he did, he discovered her three-house compound and learned that she had retired only from the federal government, not from the business. She already had been in Houston six months and had all the work she could manage, solely by word of mouth, freelancing special operations for practically every agency from whom she used to draw a salary.

The age of the personal computer had brought about a sea change in the private investigation and intelligence business. Now anyone who could afford a modem could enter the voyeuristic world of "databanking" where a subterranean network of information resellers, known as superbureaus, had assembled in a limitless number of categories every fact imaginable about most American citizens. Every time an individual filled out an information form, whether he was registering for a free prize at his local grocery or answering a "confidential" medical record form at his doctor's office, he was providing data that in all likelihood eventually would be purchased by an information reseller. Bank records, medical records, insurance records, personal data, credit records, everything was fair game in the information reselling business where practically nothing was protected by law. And virtually everyone who collected information—including doctors, bankers, and creditors—would eventually sell it. The fact was, in the United States today, the individual had no way of controlling information about himself. For a price, everyone's privacy was for sale.

This ongoing boom in information had been a boon to the burgeoning private investigation business, so much so that anybody and everybody was doing it. Now anybody could do a skip trace, search for a missing person, check the background of a job applicant, check criminal history records, track down an old girlfriend, check out a competitor's financial status and credit standing, locate anyone's address, telephone number, bank account, and medical records. The data was so easy to obtain that it was like picking it up off the sidewalk.

A surprising number of these agencies had even turned their investigation businesses into huge corporate entities like Kroll and Associates of New York (with branches all over the world), Investigations Group Inc., of Washington, and Business Risk International based in Nashville, whose annual gross incomes were in the tens of millions. These high profile agencies often specialized in money chasing for corporations and even for foreign governments. They provided credit assessments of corporate acquisition targets, conducted forensic accounting studies, collected environmental research, and investigated computer crimes, all logical criminal extensions of a modern, technological age.

Heraclitus, and a good number of wise and observant men after him, had remarked on the constancy and inevitability of change. It was now axiomatic, and anyone who ignored the importance of evolution did so at their own peril. But as the world entered the closing years of the twentieth century, few of those sages could have imagined the neck-snapping speed at which change would one day occur. Only human nature, with its abundant and ineluctable follies, continued to defy the philosopher's wisdom.

There was one other way in which all investigative and intelligence work had changed during the past several decades. Now that the Computer Age suddenly had given private investigation the means to be enormously profitable, the budgets of literally hundreds of agencies— and corporations who had their own competitor intelligence divisions —outstripped those of many budget-stressed law enforcement agencies. Because of this, the private sector could offer much larger salaries to experienced officers and agents, and as a result private investigative and intelligence agencies were aswarm with ex-police officers, ex-DEA agents, ex-FBI agents, ex-CIA officers, and personnel from practically every agency in the government's vast intelligence community.

Some private agencies had become so specialized in certain fields of data collection and analysis that law enforcement agencies at every level—all the way up to the CIA—were utilizing these specialized information resellers and private agencies whenever those entities had an edge on them in any given arena of activity. They didn't like having to do it, and they didn't publicize it. But they did it.

Now, more than at any other time in world history, "private" information was in danger of becoming only a nominal concept. The information business, legal and illegal, governmental and private, commercial and political, personal and public, legitimate and underground, was in an era of explosive growth. And, as in all boom-time businesses, abuse was rampant. Unfortunately, the American public didn't have a clue about what was happening to it.

But there were a few independent—private—intelligence operations like Arnette Kepner's whose work was nothing akin to the highly visible corporate swashbucklers like Kroll. Her experience was in the world of international intelligence, not merely investigation, and in her profession a high profile was the kiss of death and anonymity was the mark of a right-thinking operation. She did not work for businesses or governments, but for other intelligence agencies, and her computers, which occupied most of the rooms in one of her adjacent houses, were packed fat with rarified data about intelligence networks and thousands of individual agents, officers, and operatives which the traditional private and corporate investigative agencies knew nothing about.

Arnette stared at him through the thin haze created by the smoldering joss stick, her errant gray hair forming a lively aura around her face.

"Okay," she said. She leaned forward and took a cigarette from an ocher pack of a foreign brand sitting on the coffee table in front of her. She lit it and blew the smoke up into the midday dusk to mingle with the incense. Sitting back, she folded one arm across her waist and rested the wrist of the hand holding the cigarette on her knee. "What do you want?"

"A log of their movements and photographs of everyone they talk to. I want to be briefed daily."

"This kind of thing can be a long haul, Marcus. Two weeks is nothing."

Graver nodded. "Yeah, I know. But I don't have much of a choice here."

She looked at him seriously. "Okay, let's see what comes up. What's his address?"

Graver told her and gave her Ginette's office address as well. She nodded thoughtfully but didn't write down anything.

"Tomorrow Dean starts two weeks of vacation," Graver said. "I think his wife will have to work during the first week, but the second week they're off together."

"I'll put someone out there right now," she said, "something to hold it until I can get a team together later on in the evening. You have any reason to think he'll bolt?"

"No. I think it's too soon for that kind of panic. He'll try to sweat it out. He knows Westrate—everyone—wants to see this thing put to bed. He'll wait to see if it is."

"Okay, well, by tonight I'll have this together anyway." She pulled on her cigarette and then studied him, a sober expression on her face. "I know this is eating you alive," she said. "I'm so sorry it's happening."

To his surprise, Graver was suddenly relieved she had just come right out with it. He felt like he was wrapped in a straitjacket, and he alternately panicked and despaired at his condition.

He shook his head. "It'll soak in, I'm sure," he said. "But right now it doesn't seem very real . . . I just don't understand it . . . why in the hell he's in this situation. It's absolutely . . . senseless."

Arnette nodded. "It's going to take a lot of guts to do this, baby. It'll be hard on you. It's going to tear you apart. You've got to know that."

He didn't respond immediately. "I just want to know why he's doing it," he said.

"And you think you'll 'understand' it then? You don't really believe it'll be that simple, do you?"

Graver shrugged. He didn't even know if what he had just said was that simple. If he had thought about it for ten minutes he might have said something else. If he had this same conversation half an hour from now, he wasn't sure it would be anything like it was now. Maybe if there was one thing he did know it was that nothing that had happened to him in the last year was "that simple," least of all what was happening to him now.

"You know," Arnette said, a kind of smile softening her face, "I've been in this business so long . . . Most of the people in this work, when you get to know them well enough, have an element of the unchaste about them, at some level or other. Even the bureaucrats who don't actually get their hands dirty in the real blood and earth of the business." She narrowed her eyes in thought. "It has something to do with secrets, it seems, with *dealing* in secrets. You know, it's like trafficking in the power of the Holy Ghost. It's not something a person ought to do. But a person has proclivities . . . in that direction, I mean toward 'uncleanliness,' as the old Hebrews used to say. A person has proclivities, so he gravitates to a business that has the appearance of respectability, but which allows him all manner of vicarious indulgences . . . in the name of something higher, something cleaner. Very common men and women get into this work. It's almost a stereotype of the profession. The ordinary, workaday fellow, the 'invisible' plodder who years later, well into his retirement, is revealed to have been a longtime 'famous spy.' " She stopped. "But if you really dissect him, psychologically I mean, this banal old man, he is anything but benign. His perversity is only more cleverly dissembled. He's uncanny, disguising his moral petulance as a virtue."

She smoked a moment more and Graver waited, knowing all of this was prologue, watching her, suddenly and strangely aware of the extreme nature of this profession and how quickly logical steps could take you, one at a time, to such outrageous places.

"Except you, Marcus," she continued. "I've known you a good while now, longer than many. But I've never sensed any perversity in you at all. And I can tell you, dear, I look for it. Oh, I look for it in everyone I have anything to do with."

Her smile was very faint now, almost not there at all. Outside, the world seemed to be populated only by birds.

"It could be," he said, "that you've never met anyone who was so adept at guile."

It was a remark both cynical and self-condemning, one that Graver himself almost had come to believe. It was the kind of extreme thinking one came to when one began searching inside one's self for the reasons for other people's actions. Maybe it didn't make sense, but for some people it was instinctive, and it took an equally extreme act of will not to believe that the search was justified.

Arnette studied him, the smoke coiling from the cigarette beside her gypsy face, so exotic in saffron, in the twilight.

"Well, it could be," she drawled thoughtfully, her voice barely audible. Then stronger, her tone changing: "Anyway, this looks like a rough one, baby. I hope you're ready for it."

23

ON THE WAY BACK TO THE OFFICE GRAVER STOPPED AT A SMALL steak house that catered to businessmen, a place that had sat very still and very quiet while the last two decades had passed it by. It was a sunless retreat with heavy wood furnishings that smelled of liquor and cigarettes and cigars, and whose waitresses dressed in little Heidi uniforms with white ruffled scoop necks and push-up bras. The steaks sizzled in their own grease; there were only three kinds of salad dressings, none of them low cal; and the only kind of sweetener on the table was sugar. Everything was unhealthy and delicious.

He ate alone at a corner table and reviewed his conversation with Arnette. He remembered the look on her face when he told her he wanted her to put Dean and Ginette Burtell under surveillance. For just a flicker of an instant she had looked as if she doubted *his* loyalties, rather than Burtell's. What in the hell was he doing putting a tail on Burtell? That's the way it was with everyone, Dean Burtell was beyond reproach, his integrity was a given, so solid you just didn't bother to give it any thought. He was the kind of guy you would want standing beside you if one day the world suddenly turned nasty on you and all the rules changed and everything seemed stacked against you through no fault of your own. You'd want Dean there because you knew there would be no recriminations, an abundance of understanding, and an assurance that he would see you through to the end. Graver knew that was the way people felt about him. That was the way he felt about him too.

Graver's chopped steak arrived swimming in its own juices and with a side of fries that were long, thin, limp, and golden brown. As he ate, he tried to force his thoughts out in front of events. He really didn't have a lot of time to mull over his options. He knew that. And he also knew he didn't have much room to maneuver in a conventional sense. By the time he polished off the last bite of steak he had made some major decisions. There were certain points of reference he had to establish. There had to be one or two things he could rely on unequivocally.

It was nearly one-thirty when he got back to the office. He stopped at Lara's door and stuck his head in.

"Have you got a minute?"

"Sure," she said. Grabbing a steno pad and pencil, she followed him into his office. He closed the door behind them, and she went over and stood in front of his desk. He noticed she had freshened up after lunch, brushed through her hair, put on fresh lipstick, tucked and pulled at her suit until it looked as crisp and fresh as it had when she came in that morning.

"Sit down," he said, and he walked around her and sat in one of the other chairs opposite her in front of his desk. She held her steno pad and pencil in her scarlet-nailed fingers, resting on her lap. Her expression was anticipatory, though not anxious. She already had sensed this was not going to be a routine conversation.

"Lara, I need your help with something that's . . . out of the ordinary," Graver said.

Her expression did not change, but a slight vertical shadow, the beginning of a puzzled frown, appeared between her dark eyebrows.

He crossed his legs, trying to appear more relaxed than he actually felt, though he suspected that none of his consternation was escaping Lara. As always, there were things that passed between them about which neither of them ever spoke. It was one of the peculiar characteristics of their relationship that much of what they felt for each other, whether it was amorous or simply the affection of friendship, was never articulated. That, of course, was Graver's decision, or, as he thought of it more often lately, his fault.

"I'm going to be asking you for a favor, Lara, something that goes beyond your job description," he said. "It's something you'd ask of a friend, a close friend . . . someone you'd trust . . . no matter what happened."

The shadow in her expression lightened at these words, but the uncertainty remained.

"Is it personal or business?" she asked.

"Both," he said. "And that's the problem."

He saw her stiffen. "Does it involve a woman?" There was an unmistakable tension in the question.

"No," he said, "it's nothing like that."

As he looked at her, he realized how much he relied on her, how much he wanted to rely on her in order to weather the storm of the coming events. He felt like a doctor looking through a microscope at the cells of his own recently discovered disease. There was the danger of the loss of rationality. There was the tendency to see the vague, squirming shadows swimming in their own viscosity as something other than what they were, an inclination to see them as manifestations of Evil, Death, Divine Judgment. Graver wanted someone—Lara—to be there when his fears grew to mythological proportions, when his doubts grew more articulate and wiser than his convictions, and he was in danger of believing a lie.

She might have seen something of this fear in his eyes, in his manner, or sensed it in the tone of his voice. Whatever it was, her face softened as they stared at each other, and she nodded.

Jesus Christ. If he had any sense at all he would not let this woman out of his sight. Without any further explanation, Graver began at the beginning and told her everything. Everything. More than he was going to tell either Neuman or Paula. More than he was going to tell Arnette. As he talked his voice grew quieter, an unconscious habit when he was preoccupied beyond the moment about what he was saying. He talked to her as if she were the only other person in his life, allowing her to see the fear and the doubt, making no excuses for his confusion and the pain he felt for all the betrayal. He tried to give her the perspective from inside his own mind, to give her some semblance of the stress of his own emotions.

When he finally finished talking, she sat silently, looking at him. She hadn't moved a muscle. Then she dropped her eyes to her lap, to her hands.

"This is hard to believe," she said, her voice studied, thoughtful. "You must be . . ."

"In a state of shock," Graver said.

She looked up. "Yes, I would imagine so." Then hesitantly, "I'm sorry about Dean. Very sorry. I can see . . . I know how this is hurting you."

Graver shifted uncomfortably in his chair.

"You understand . . . the risks will be real," he said. "This is off the books. You'll be putting your job at risk. There aren't any guidelines, no operating procedures for this. I'm just going to do what I think has to be done. It's a judgment call; my judgment call. I don't want to mislead you about this."

"No, I understand that," she said. "It's just . . . so unexpected, a little breathtaking." She tried to smile, but it didn't happen. "It's just so . . . I don't know, strange, I guess, when you know these people."

One hand slid to the hem of her skirt, and she pulled at it to keep it from creeping any higher on her thighs.

"I apologize for putting you in this position, Lara. It's awkward for me too. I didn't do this lightly. And, honestly, I'll completely understand if you feel that you can't . . . see your way clear to do this."

This last sounded disingenuous to him, hackneyed, and contrived, which he regretted. But he was desperate enough to do it anyway.

Again she was silent. He was surprised at himself, that he could not discern what she might be feeling. He was sure that he would be able to read her reaction in her manner, in her face, but he was wrong. He saw nothing. He felt like a gambler waiting for the dice to stop spinning. But, deep down, he didn't believe she would refuse to help him.

"I'll do this," she said finally, looking up. "But you're right, this is as much a personal favor as a professional one. It's both, really . . . and then it isn't."

Her eyes burrowed into his eyes. In this brief moment, by her manner, by her tone of voice, by the expression on her face, she was letting him know that such a request from him, and her agreement to it, would not be without its consequences.

Graver waited.

"The reality is that you are now asking for something of Lara Casares, not of your secretary," she said. "And I will gladly do this, not as your secretary, but as Lara." She raised a dark eyebrow slightly, wanting to know if he understood.

Graver nodded.

"I trust you," she said. "Completely. But I'm not a fool. I understand enough of this business now to know that sometimes it's necessary for you to lie—to withhold the truth—whatever it is you find yourself having to call it." She paused, her black eyes still holding him across the short distance between them. "I have only one request: never lie to me. Lie to your secretary, if you must. I'm not so naïve as to think I can ask you not to do that. But never lie to me . . . to Lara." She paused again. "And if you don't understand the difference between the two, well, then, I guess it's time for me to know that about you."

She stopped and looked at him, almost sadly, he thought, and suddenly he realized there was a story here, behind this request, a story that had much to do with who she was and which had been entirely invisible to him for all these years until this moment. Either Lara was a master of secrets herself, or he had been shamefully obtuse, having been too self-absorbed to detect a vulnerability where he had thought none existed.

"This is important to me," she said. "Do you understand that? No lies . . . between you . . . and me."

Graver nodded. "I understand," he said. "Agreed."

"I believe that," she said. "I'll do whatever I can to help you."

Graver was tremendously relieved and, at the same time, chagrined. In a real sense he already had lied to her by his vague approach. Or, if he had not exactly lied to her, he had not been entirely honest either. She saw that, and that was precisely the kind of thing she was talking about. Even so, she had consented to work with him under decidedly bizarre circumstances. She had consented, but she also had put him on notice. Gently.

24

HE CALLED THEM INTO HIS OFFICE SEPARATELY. PAULA FIRST, because she did not yet know of his conversation the night before with Neuman. When Graver told her of Neuman's discovery, she was uncharacteristically quiet. Like many deskbound thinkers, Paula's understanding of life, while brilliantly analytical, was largely acquired through theories and paradigms rather than experience, and she was visibly disquieted by this harsh and untidy intrusion of flesh-and-blood reality. It was one thing to read and write about subterfuge and betrayal and quite another to find yourself wiping away the actual sweat of it.

She was sobered but not intimidated. She immediately agreed to work with Graver without any higher authority for what they were about to do. Graver was a little uncomfortable that she so readily assented to step into unchartered country with him. On the other hand, though, it was Paula's characteristic refusal to shrink in the face of the formidable that recommended her to the job they were about to take on.

After Paula, he called in Casey Neuman.

"At this point only the three of us know about this," Graver said. "Since I don't know where in the hell this thing goes, it's got to stay that way."

The two of them were sitting in Graver's office again, and it was late in the afternoon. Everyone had gone home. Neuman was turned almost sideways in the straight-back chair in front of Graver's desk, one leg crossed over the other at the knee, his left arm draped over the back of the chair. As Graver spoke, Neuman was looking down at a piece of paper he had been using as a bookmark and which he was now folding and unfolding as he listened.

"What you've got to consider now," Graver continued, "before you even agree to go along with this, is that something like this could go both ways. At some point down the road, next month, next year, if we deal with this thing successfully, we could be testifying for the prosecution. Fine. On the other hand, it could blow up in our faces. Let's say we've discovered the breach, but we've botched the inquiry, or we're hauled up on charges of running a rogue investigation that should have had authorization and direction from a higher level."

Neuman was still listening with his head down, and Graver was beginning to wonder if he was doing too good a job with this, maybe even talking him out of it. It didn't matter. He didn't want to get Neuman into something he hadn't thought through to the end. Which he probably had. Still, Graver wanted to *know* that he had.

"The thing is," Graver emphasized, "you've got to imagine having to defend yourself in front of a court, in the newspapers, on television. Just make the assumption now that someday it'll hit the media and your actions will be questioned . . . in public. You've got to think about that, and—if you decide to stay on—you've got to think about it tomorrow and the next day and every day until this is over. I'm telling you right now, if you can't live with yourself after you've done something I've asked you to do, then you'd better have the guts to tell me no."

Graver had been leaning on his desk, talking straight across it to Neuman, turning the cobblestone around and around on a stack of papers. Now he picked up the stone and tapped the wood of the desk with it. Neuman looked up.

"I don't own your soul, Casey," Graver said with a softly measured emphasis. "I'm not going to have to grow old with what you do, and I'm not going to have to answer to your conscience. I've got my own to deal with."

Neuman stared back at him, and Graver did not see any signs of trepidation, no uncertainty, no fear of the inexperienced. He didn't know if that was comforting or not.

"I understand the rules," Neuman said. "And I also understand that you think I can do this, or you would've cut me out and we wouldn't be having this conversation."

"That's right."

"Then I'm ready to work."

Graver looked at him and put down the cobblestone. Jesus.

"Okay." He picked up the telephone and punched in a number. "Paula," he said, "bring in the files."

As Graver had driven back from Arnette Kepner's he had wrestled with the logistics of what he was about to do. He wanted to keep the investigation as small and tight as possible. Since Burtell would be out of the office now for two weeks, it would be relatively easy for Graver to communicate with Neuman and Paula about their progress. He would tell the other analysts with whom Neuman was working on other investigations that he was pulling him for a couple of weeks. The routine compartmentalization of an Intelligence Division at least eased some of the covert maneuvering that would be necessary to do this. Intelligence officers at all levels were used to not being given explanations. It was part of the business and worked to their advantage more often than not. It was this claim to silence, justified by the necessity to maintain security, that so often rankled intelligence outsiders and struck them an unnecessary arrogance.

Graver had already talked with Matt Rostov about using Paula, and even though Graver would be handing in his report on Tisler the next morning, everyone would assume there would be loose ends to deal with. And Ray Besom was still out of town. These arrangements would allow Neuman and Paula to work in isolation from the others and enable him to see them regularly during the course of the day without raising any particular notice.

The first thing he would do would be to complete the report for Westrate. If there were others within CID involved along with Burtell and Besom and Tisler, they would be able to pass along the fact that the case indeed had been closed out.

Now, as they each sipped fresh cups of coffee that Neuman had stepped across the hall to make before they got started, he explained how he was going to handle Burtell.

"I've got someone from the outside for surveillance," he said bluntly. Both Paula and Neuman registered shock. "There was no way I could use anyone in law enforcement in this city. Burtell's been around too long, knows too many people. Besides, if I'm going to keep this unofficial . . . I couldn't risk a leak."

"These people," Paula said, "they're another agency?"

"No."

"A *private* investigator?"

"No," Graver said firmly. He wasn't going to explain, and he didn't want any questions about it. He went on immediately. "As soon as we have something from them, from surveillance, we'll follow up as quickly as possible. In the meantime, we've got plenty to do."

He opened a folder in which he had been filing away notes since Sunday night after Westrate's visit.

"First," he said, "we've *got* to determine the status of the sources listed in Tisler's contributor files for the Probst and Friel investigations. Did Tisler and/or Dean simply steal the names of real people, or do these people actually know Probst and Friel? Paula, you've already found out that most of these people can't be located. Bruce Sheck, we don't know. Colleen Synar, maybe. Let's get to the bottom of what's going on here. But be goddamned careful. We're working against our own people here. They know all the tricks; they can read all the signs. And they're expecting us."

"If we locate them, do you want us to go ahead and talk to them on the telephone?" Paula asked.

Graver hesitated. "No. Hold off on that. Just make sure we know where we can find them."

"What about the Seldon thing?" Neuman asked. Graver was expecting it. After all, neither of them knew what had happened that morning with Burtell after they had walked out of Graver's office. He told them Burtell's account of what had happened.

"Jesus Christ, Marcus." Paula was incredulous. "I don't believe that. Did he expect you to swallow that?"

"I don't know. Maybe. I hope so."

"Son of a bitch." Paula was shaking her head. "That's outrageous. That means the investigation is just vapor." Her eyes were wide as she gaped at Graver. "Besom. What about Besom? What are we going to do about him? We at least ought to go through his office. And Dean's too, for God's sake."

Neuman was shaking his head. "No, that'd be a mistake. They're not going to have any tangible evidence in their offices, Paula. And they'd know for sure if we went in there. We'd only be giving ourselves away."

"Look, when he left to go fishing he didn't know Tisler was going to kill himself," Paula said, turning to Graver. "Like you said, they've been doing this for so long they have their routine down pat. But maybe they've grown complacent, too, a little careless, maybe." She turned back to Neuman. "Look at Dean's screwup with your folders, Casey."

Graver stood and walked to the windows. Once again late afternoon was muting the colors of the city. He was beginning to hate this office. He had seen too much of it, and he was dreading how much more of it he was going to have to see before this was over.

"No, I've thought about going through their offices, too," he said, half-turned away from them, "but I think Casey's right. Besides, I can't believe they'd leave anything incriminating while they were away for any period of time."

"But Dean . . ."

"Yeah, I know that, Paula, but I think he must've been working on those drafts at the time he left. Yes, he left them there . . . even in the wrong folders, but he was only going to be gone for an hour. Yes, he was careless, maybe even complacent. But he's not going to do something like that and leave it overnight or for two weeks while he's on vacation. Especially now, after what's happened. I think Casey's right. It wouldn't be worth the risk."

He stepped back to his desk and, standing beside it, turned another page in his file.

"Casey, you said Tisler had rental property."

"Right. In Sharpstown."

"Did you check it out? Did you see if there were renters?"

"No."

Graver sat down at his desk and turned around to his computer. "What's the address?"

"Six twenty-three Leiter."

Graver pulled up the street index in the city directory.

"Lewis O. Feldberg, 555-2133."

He pulled up the name index. "Four Feldbergs," he said. "Lewis O. at 623 Leiter . . . is retired."

Graver tapped the keys a few more times and brought up the Water Department records. "The old man sure as hell doesn't use much utilities. Minimum billing. And, apparently, he moved into the place shortly after Tisler bought it. Feldberg started paying the utility bills just a few weeks later."

He kept tapping. "Mr. Feldberg's never had a traffic ticket."

"That's hard to believe," Paula said.

Graver tapped some more.

"Last time Mr. Feldberg registered to vote was in 1956," he said. *"That's* hard to believe," Paula repeated. "Go to vital stats."

Graver made a few more entries and then waited for the screen to quit flashing. When it stopped, he read the information: "Lewis O. Feldberg. Christ, he died in Fort Worth on August 3, 1958."

25

IT WAS NEARLY DUSK AND THE STREETLIGHTS ALREADY HAD COME
on by the time Graver found the address of Tisler's rent house in a
dying neighborhood off Beechnut inside the Southwest Freeway. The
area looked as if it had been developed in the late fifties and had
started its decline fifteen years later—several streets of small ranch-
style houses with low-pitched pebble and asphalt roofs and brick veneer wainscoting. He drove by the house once very slowly.

There was nothing about it that distinguished it, a fact that did not
surprise Graver. Tisler wouldn't have owned anything that distinguished itself. There was an old mulberry in the front yard growing
close enough to the straight, short sidewalk for the tree's roots to have
burrowed up under it, buckling the concrete until it broke. Graver was
glad to see that on either side of the front yard a dowdy ligustrum
hedge marked the property lines. The front door was introduced by a
little stoop with a wood railing the same height as the brick veneer. A
dull black mailbox was tacked to one of the wooden posts that held up
the stoop's roof.

Turning around at the end of the street, Graver came back by the
house just in time to see a light go on in one of the windows fronting
the street. Momentarily startled, he quickly guessed what had happened and turned into the driveway, pulling his car right up to the
garage door that faced the street.

Before he got out of his car, he bent down and picked up a crowbar
from the floor on the passenger side. He had bought it in the hardware
department of a discount mart just off the freeway only minutes before. Quickly closing the car door, he walked around the side of the
garage and saw with relief that the hedge continued to the back of the
property. At the rear of the garage he came to a gate in the chain-link
fence which enclosed the backyard. He lifted the gate's latch and

went in. Even in the dull light he could see that the yard was badly in need of mowing and that, since it grew in dark clumps and tufts with bare spots scattered here and there, it was probably mostly weeds.

He stepped onto an uncovered concrete slab "patio" attached to the back of the house and walked to the door. An aluminum storm door was on the outside with a solid wooden one behind it. Taking a small penlight out of his pocket, Graver shined it on the door frame. He didn't believe that Tisler would have gone to the expense of having an alarm system installed, but if he had, it would have been difficult to hide on a house like this. Satisfied that none was there, he put the penlight in his mouth and directed the small beam at the edge of the aluminum door where he inserted the thinnest end of the crowbar and popped it open. Holding it open with his back, he did the same with the wooden door, which should have been more difficult but wasn't, though it was noisier, which required him to work more carefully.

When he pushed open the door he found himself in a bare kitchen, and immediately noted the stale smell that a house acquired when it was long unoccupied. There were no tables or chairs, and there was nothing on the cabinets except a coffeemaker, its pot washed clean and sitting in its receptacle. A dish towel was folded beside it with a coffee mug turned upside down on the towel. The kitchen was separated from the adjoining dining room by a small bar and through the dining room Graver saw the soft glow from the light that he had seen come on earlier. He put down the crowbar on the kitchen counter and went through the dining room which was also bare except for a few cardboard boxes scattered in one corner. He continued into the living room. Here a few pieces of furniture were clustered together, an old sofa, a couple of armchairs, the lighted lamp on an end table beside one of the armchairs, and a coffee table with a few magazines neatly stacked in one pile in its center. Graver went over and picked up one of the magazines. They were all old issues of *Newsweek*. He put down the magazine and stepped around the coffee table to find the wall plug for the lamp. As he had guessed, he also found the electric timer that automatically turned on the lamp at irregular intervals.

The house was hot and stuffy, but Graver remembered seeing a window unit on the end of the house opposite the garage. He entered the hallway that opened off the living room and came immediately to a bathroom. Reaching around the corner in the dark, he found the light switch and turned it on. Again the room was empty except for a towel on the towel bar beside the sink, and on the rim of the sink, a bar of soap that was well used but cracking from the heat in the house. A packet of paper towels was torn open and sat next to the sink. There was a half-used roll of toilet tissue on the spool beside the toilet. Nothing in the medicine cabinet.

Leaving on the light, Graver continued to an open door on his right, a bedroom. Empty. There was one more door at the end of the hallway, on his left. It was closed. That would be the room where he had seen the air conditioner unit in the window. He went to the door, opened it, and flipped on the light.

In the center of the unfurnished room, with Venetian blinds pulled tightly closed over its windows, was a sizable computer setup. Graver stared at it with a mixture of dread and hope. This clinical-looking piece of hardware, the smell of its heat-warmed plastic filling the closed room with an odor distinct from the rest of the house, represented simultaneously a potential disaster and, perhaps, his best hope of dealing with it.

The work station itself was a flimsy-looking, L-shaped structure of thin metal and pressed wood, laden to overloading with what appeared to be a substantial computer system and laser printer. Graver walked over to it and surveyed the books on the single shelf above the monitor. They were only operating manuals for the hardware and the software. He looked at the system. Though not totally ignorant regarding computers, he was far from being proficient enough to be able to walk into a room, sit down at an unfamiliar system, and puzzle out its operation. He knew he would be lucky if he could even bring up the menu.

Still, just by looking at it, he could tell that this was a fairly large system—that much was given to him on the front of the CPU—and that it had a hard drive, two disk drives, and a port for a back-up tape. Graver pulled out the chair under the desk and sat down. He looked over the shelves and found the two tapes Tisler used for backup along with a small spiral pocket notebook where he recorded the alternating tapes and dates. Tisler's last backup had been the day before he died. Graver flipped on the computer and waited for it to clear. When it was ready, he began tapping at the keyboard. After fifteen minutes he had used everything obvious and still hadn't gained access. He began to have the uncomfortable feeling that he shouldn't be pressing his luck.

Hoping that Tisler had not toyed with the backup procedures, he pecked around for a few minutes, found the parameters, and copied them down, knowing he would need them to access the backup tapes on another system. He double-checked his notes, suddenly afraid he was going to transpose some of the characters in the paths. After he was satisfied, he took the older of the two tapes and used it to run another backup of the hard drive.

While he was waiting, he went through each book on the shelves and found nothing. By this time Graver thought he knew Tisler well enough to know that anything significant was going to be on the tape, and that it would be well protected by a labyrinthine cryptosystem. The loose ends—and there were always loose ends—all seemed to have been kept neatly swept into an unseen corner of what once had been Arthur Tisler's mind.

When the backup was completed, Graver retrieved the tape, put each of them in his pocket, and turned off the computer. The two tapes would give him everything that had been in the computer files the day before Tisler died, and everything that was on it now. If there were any discrepancies between the two, then Graver would know that someone other than Tisler had access to the computer. If there were no changes, he couldn't be sure. The question was, did he now erase the hard drive to prevent anyone else gaining access? He decided to wait until he knew the two tapes were good. He took one last look at the computer, not entirely sure he wasn't making a mistake by walking away from it, turned off the lights, and walked out of the room.

Leaving the house the same way he had come in, he made sure both back doors were firmly closed even though their locks were broken. As he was pulling out of the driveway another light went on in the house, this time in the empty bedroom across the hall from the computer. Arthur Tisler was very thorough.

He stopped at a convenience store and called Arnette from a pay phone.

"You're damned impatient," she said, hearing his voice.

"I'm not checking up," he said. "I've got something for you." He told her what it was.

"Did you get the parameters?"

"I did."

"This is going to take some crypt work," she cautioned, "and crypt work, baby, is not what it used to be. These days, sometimes its simply impossible to get where you want to go."

"I'm bringing them over."

"We'll be here," she said.

26

IT STRUCK BURTELL AS AN ODD PLACE TO MEET, BUT HE PAID his three dollars in the lobby, asked the location of the Modern Israeli Photography exhibit, and ascended the north foyer steps of the Museum of Fine Arts. Tuesday night was not the usual night for the museum's late hours, but the hours had been extended this week because of several special exhibits. Even so, the viewers were sparse as Burtell ascended another tier of stairs to a maze of exhibit panels set up in the largest exhibition hall.

He crossed his arms and began looking at the photographs. In less than five minutes he rounded a set of panels and met Panos Kalatis, a program rolled up in one hand, the other hand in his trousers pocket, leaning slightly forward to study a photograph among a series taken in a kibbutz. He was wearing gray dress slacks, a pink shirt opened at the neck, and a navy linen blazer with a gold crest on its breast pocket.

Kalatis continued to study the photograph as Burtell stood there.

"Sometimes parts of the Israeli coast remind me of Greece," he said, straightening up, but keeping his eyes on the photographs. "Harsh. Olive trees. Rocks. You can't really tell in these black and white photographs, but the light is the same too. Especially in the late summer."

He moved to the next photograph. A young couple in khaki walking shorts and sandals were moving just ahead of him, talking softly. He said nothing more until, after a few moments, the couple rounded the exhibit panels to the other side. Burtell came up beside him again.

"I thought we ought to talk, just the two of us," Kalatis said. "Without Faeber." He stepped close to another photograph, but then moved quickly to the next one. "You don't much like him, do you?"

"Not much," Burtell said.

"Why is that?"

"He's a little too ready to please."

"But that's what I pay people to do, to please me."

"Do you want them to lie to you?"

"Is Colin Faeber lying to me?" Kalatis asked, backing away from a photograph to see it better. He didn't seem to be too concerned about his question.

"He's the one who advised you to come down on Tisler, wasn't he?" Burtell said.

"Maybe," Kalatis said.

"He gave you bad advice."

"Well, bad advice is hardly lying, is it?"

Kalatis moved around the end of the panels to the next aisle. It was empty. They kept talking.

"I guess you know a lot about computers," Burtell said.

"Computers? Not a lot, no. That's why I hire people like Faeber. They know computers for me."

"Hiring someone to run your computer for you is like hiring a lawyer or an accountant. Before you turn your business over to them you'd better be damned sure you can trust them."

"I trust him," Kalatis said. "I trust everyone who works for me." He leaned a little sideways to look at a picture of an Israeli girl in a swimsuit. She was standing close to the photographer and with a slender index finger thrust under the piping of her suit at her groin, she was delicately tugging on the elastic to adjust the fit of the suit. She was smiling, wincing a little into the sunlight.

"Why?"

Kalatis turned away from the photograph and looked at Burtell. "Because," he said without a trace of a smile, his mellifluous voice modulated to accommodate the resonance of the granite and marble surroundings, "every one of them knows that if he screws me over I will have four big men hold him down while one of those blue-snouted baboons rips out his throat."

He turned and stepped to the next picture. A couple of men came around the corner and locked onto the pictures. One of them whispered something in Israeli to the other, and Kalatis turned and looked at them. For a moment he studied them, and then he moved efficiently to the end of the aisle and rounded the corner into the next branch of the maze. Burtell followed.

"I'm not sure Colin Faeber understands that," Burtell said.

"Oh, he understands it," Kalatis said. He had rolled his program into a tighter cylinder. He touched it quickly a couple of times to his trousers' leg as though he were going to give in to a nervous gesture and then caught himself. Burtell was glad to see that.

"Maybe he forgot," Burtell said.

"What the hell are you getting at?" Kalatis said in the same relaxed tone of voice that he might have used to make an observation about one of the photographs. He continued looking at the pictures, but there was a slight tension in his demeanor now, a tight pitch to his shoulders.

"I'm not at all sure I can tell you," Burtell said, more sure of himself after seeing the crack in Kalatis's porcelain cool. "A few days before he shot himself Art came to me and wanted to talk. He said he thought Faeber was having him watched. I asked him why he thought that, and he told me he had picked up surveillance. I asked him why he thought it was Faeber, and he got nervous and started hedging. He would only say that Faeber had it in for him, but he wouldn't explain why. I talked to him a long time about it, but he wouldn't go into it. Then he told me about receiving the envelope of photographs. He was distraught. He said Faeber had photographed him with the black woman for insurance." Burtell looked at Kalatis. "I couldn't get him to calm down. That was Friday afternoon. I didn't hear anything from him again until Graver came over Sunday night and told me he'd killed himself."

Kalatis stared at a photograph, but now Burtell could tell he wasn't seeing it. A woman laughed somewhere in the exhibit hall, and the laughter echoed off the hard surfaces of the museum and then suddenly died faraway in another gallery.

"You believe this?" Kalatis asked.

"Yes."

"Why would Faeber want 'insurance' from Tisler? Was Tisler trying to blackmail him with something? Another woman? Faeber screws his secretary. Everybody knows that. Christ. That's not anything to use against a man."

"I give Art more credit than that," Burtell said.

Kalatis snorted and turned and stepped to another photograph. Several people milled into their aisle, and Kalatis continued on to the end of the exhibit panels without saying anything further. Burtell guessed he was taking the time to collect his thoughts. Burtell went past him and turned another corner. The maze of panels seemed end-less and Burtell hadn't paid any attention to where they had started.

Kalatis came around the corner and looked at the first photograph. "I've seen these," he said and went to the next aisle. It was empty, and again Burtell joined him.

"Do you think you could find out what Tisler was talking about?" Kalatis asked.

"Regarding the insurance?"

"Yes, of course," Kalatis said with slight irritation.

"Maybe."

"Find out," Kalatis said. He stopped and looked down the curving wall of photographs. "I've seen enough," he said. "This is depressing."

The two men walked out of the main exhibition space, descending to the foyer, then to the lobby, and out the north entrance of the museum to Bissonnet Street. As soon as they were outside Kalatis stopped and lighted a cigarette. Without speaking they crossed Bissonnet and turned left along the sidewalk, passing scatterings of people strolling in the sweltering June night. They came to Montrose and Kalatis stopped. He looked to his left at the three lighted, circular fountains inside the traffic ellipse. South Main stretched straight off the ellipse, flanked by colonnades of massive water oaks, the underside of their canopies illumined softly by streetlamps that shrank to tiny, faint sparks as the lines of the boulevard converged in the distance. Kalatis looked at this scene a moment and then turned on his heels and walked in the opposite direction to the entrance of the Cullen Sculpture Garden.

They entered the walled garden which was laid out on the order of a small plaza with granite walkways, islands of emerald lawn, mani-cured shrubbery, and groomed trees. The sculpture sited variously within this environment was softly illuminated with special lighting that seemed to make some of the works hover in isolation out of the gray night.

Kalatis did not immediately stop to study these works. Still walk-ing, though not so briskly, he swung his hand holding the cigarette in a generalized arc.

"A lot of modern stuff," he said. "I've never liked the abstract. What the hell is abstract anyway? Represents modern man's confu-sion? His fragmented psyche? Shit. The disorientation of the twentieth century? Alienation of modern man? Jesus Christ. I don't know."

Burtell was patient. He reminded himself that it was Kalatis who had contacted him. After a few turns on the pathways Kalatis suddenly stopped in front of a single, isolated sculpture bathed in a haze of warm illumination.

" 'Flore Nue,' " he said, gesturing at the statue as though he were introducing Burtell. "Aristide Maillol." His French pronunciation was fluid, subtle, perfect. The bronze nude stood before them in uncontrived simplicity, her hands hanging straight down by her sides, one foot slightly advanced before the other, knee bent.

"This is real art," Kalatis said. "Look at her. The way of her shoulders. The shape of her breasts, her stomach. The simplicity of the way she presents herself to me."

To me? Burtell had been looking at the statues, but at these last two words he cut his eyes at Kalatis. The brute was almost salivating over the woman. He licked her with his eyes and smiled at her in a way that would have made a man who loved her want to kill him.

"Maillol knew how to shape a breast, and this little one . . . carries it very well."

Kalatis studied the sculpture for a few more moments and then abruptly turned away, flicked his cigarette away into the dark, and began walking very slowly, his head down.

"I am worried about something from yesterday's conversation, when we met with Faeber," he said, his voice low. "The idea of Graver keeps crawling right up into my forehead. When something squirms into my thoughts that much I have to pay attention to it. I'm not satisfied, my friend, that Graver is going to ignore this . . . business of Tisler."

He took a few steps.

"That's one thing. Another thing: I know very well that you would like to be more, let us say, involved a little more in my business."

Burtell's heart jolted. Did this monster know more about him than he thought? Had he given himself away somehow?

"I am an astute observer of human nature," Kalatis said. "For your information, I know that Faeber has . . . limitations, but what would the world do without such people? Think about it. His intelligence is very narrow, but it is very uncommonly concentrated. He serves a purpose, that's the most important thing. The second most important thing is recognizing when something does not serve a purpose . . . and getting rid of it. If something does not serve, don't keep it around you. This is a very clean way to live."

A few more steps, the rolled program still in his left hand, his right hand in his pocket.

"So," he said, as if everything had been explained, "I want to make sure Graver stays away from me. You want to have a little bite of my business so you can make a load of money. It's clear to me that we can serve each other well."

Kalatis stopped talking as they passed other night strollers, all talking softly as though viewing art from out of the darkness was an act of inherent holiness.

"What I propose is this," Kalatis resumed. "For the next five days I want to know immediately if Graver learns of my existence. After five days other arrangements will come into play, and it will not be so important. Now, if you do this . . . I will make it possible for you to retire . . . with a generous 'pension.' "

As they continued walking, Kalatis reached into the breast pocket of his jacket, took out a small paper booklet, and handed it to Burtell.

"This is a Belgium bank account in your name. It is empty now. At the end of five days, if you have done as you were asked, it will contain five hundred thousand American dollars. Only three people in the world will know about it. Me, the Belgium bank officer with whom I opened the account, and yourself. After I make the deposit, only one person in the world will be able to touch it—you."

Burtell was stunned. Unaware of the act of walking, he could only feel the weight of the little paper booklet in his hand, as heavy as thirty pieces of silver.

"I doubt that's likely to happen," he said.

"What?"

Burtell realized his mistake. "Graver—it's not likely he'll get that far in the investigation."

"Fine, but if he does I want to know about it."

Burtell was still wary. He thought he hadn't yet seen the whole picture. Kalatis wanted something more for his five hundred thousand dollars.

"This is a lot of money for such a small service. Just a telephone call," Burtell said.

They walked a little farther together before Kalatis said:

"Well, some men think betrayal is no small thing."

Burtell's face burned. It was like Kalatis to be so cruel as to refuse to use euphemisms. He could have let it pass, but he wanted Burtell to know, to be reminded just what it was he was doing for his money.

Burtell could live with it, but he hated Kalatis for being the kind of man who would go out of his way to corrupt another man, who would entice him with a fortune for only a moment's effort, and then when the man took the bait, ashamed and groveling, would pull his head back and shove a mirror in front of his face. There was something carious at the very core of Kalatis's dark life, something that brought out the worst in people who associated with him. Art Tisler had discovered that with tragic results.

27

THE DENSE FOLIAGE OF THE OVERARCHING TREES THAT COVERED
the serpentine street where Arnette lived reflected Graver's headlights
so that it seemed as if he was being drawn into a coiling green tunnel, a
meander that led to the Sibyl's cavern. If ever he needed a necromancer
it was now, someone like Arnette to summon Tisler's spirit for an
interview or, failing that, to summon the next best thing, his former
thoughts from whence he had locked them in a timeless silence, em-
balmed to perfection inside another kind of memory, not of man, but
of man's making, hundreds of thousands of words in a few minuscule
coffins of silicone.

This time Mona Isaza answered the door. Graver had missed her
earlier that day, so they embraced in the dark screened room as he had
embraced Arnette earlier, and Mona called him "bah-BEE" and kissed
him on the neck. She smelled, as always, of cooking, of something
oniony and of the cornmeal *masa* she used almost every meal to make
fresh tortillas. Mona was about the same height as Arnette, though
heavier, despite which she was in many ways the more feminine and
graceful of the two women. She was pure Zoque Indian from southern
Oaxaca, with the finely defined lips, heavy eyebrows, and black eyes
that were often seen in the sculptures and drawings of Francisco
Zúñiga's beloved Indian women. Whereas Arnette wore her hair in one
thick braid, Mona wore two long ones, each falling in front of her
shoulders over heavy bosoms. She customarily wore simple, cotton
dresses, thin from long use, as if she were a poor *campesino*.

"The Lady wants you next door," Mona said, smiling and perhaps
mocking just a little bit the imperious manner Arnette sometimes employed to control the cadre of eccentrics who worked for her. Closing the door behind them, she and Graver entered the twilight of
Arnette's living room. "It has been such a while since I have seen

you," she said softly, unhurriedly. "I was sorry to miss you yester-day."

Graver chatted with her and followed her through the twilight and out a back door into the dark again. Mona moved slowly and loved to talk, which she did with the same lack of urgency as she did everything else. Her speech was heavily accented, but markedly precise, each word a whole thing separated beautifully from its neighbor. Though she preferred the domestic role, Graver knew that Mona had a university education and was actually more widely read than Arnette. He always enjoyed her company and was fond of the sound of her voice, to which he now listened with pleasure as they entered an arbor covered with grapevines and walked the short distance to the next house. They entered another screened porch there and with a few words and another kiss, Mona left him to enter the back door to the house alone.

The large room that he stepped into presented a dramatic change. It was brightly lighted with half a dozen computer work stations sitting against the surrounding walls. Two of the stations were occupied by matronly women who appeared to be data input clerks. A third station, a more complex system with an oversized screen that was jumping with colors and what seemed to be a series of continuously changing graphs, was being operated by a young man with a ponytail and a General Custer mustache and goatee. He wore a black T-shirt with a brilliantly embroidered parrot on the back, khaki pants, and tennis shoes. His right leg was bouncing hectically as he slumped back in his chair and occasionally jabbed at the keyboard as he sipped coffee from a Styrofoam cup that, for some reason, had a bent paper clip laced through the side of it like an earring. In the center of the room Arnette sat at a long table with a blond girl who looked like a college student, too young to be doing this kind of thing, Graver thought.

"Hey, baby," Arnette said, looking up as he came in. She and the college girl, who was wearing a headset with a thin wire microphone that curved around in front of her mouth, were poring over the contents of a pile of ring binders. Every once in a while the college girl, who was wearing a bandanna-patterned halter top and, Graver presumed, a pair of shorts under the table, would turn her head aside and speak *sotto voce* into the microphone which was attached to a large transmitter that occupied one end of the table. With her left hand, she would touch this or that dial lightly, without looking at it, almost without thinking, as though it was an old habit, fine-tuning whatever it was going into her head. The room hummed with the white noise of electronic equipment.

"You have the tapes?" Arnette asked, putting a pencil behind her ear and reaching out her hand.

Graver retrieved them from his coat pocket and handed them to her along with the piece of paper with the parameters.

Arnette looked at the parameter notations and then handed everything to the girl.

"Get Corkie," she said. The girl hit a button on the receiver's control panel and muttered something into the thin mouthpiece. "There's nothing to tell you," Arnette said to Graver. "Apparently Ginette didn't go to her office. Her car was home when my people got there about four o'clock. We called her office. She had called in sick that morning. But Dean didn't show up there until half an hour ago."

Graver looked at his watch.

"What time did he leave the office?" Arnette asked.

"Must've been around three or three-thirty."

"Five hours out of pocket, more or less," Arnette calculated.

Graver felt the chest-constricting frustration of having lost the first move, though at the time he hadn't seen those few hours as especially critical. He had moved as quickly as he had thought prudent. But now prudence seemed less desirable than knowing where Burtell had been for those five hours.

A young Asian woman with a masculine haircut and wearing a man's undershirt and lace, spandex leggings came out of the next room and walked up behind the blonde, who handed the two tapes back over her head without looking around. The Asian took the tapes, looked at Graver, and walked away. She was wearing a single, red plastic earring about the size of Graver's thumb and in the shape of an erect penis, complete with dangling scrotum.

"Have any idea about these tapes?" Arnette asked.

"No. Could be his personal bookkeeping for all I know."

"But you think no one else knows about the computer."

"I don't know."

Arnette's eyes rested on him a moment, and then she turned her head slightly toward the blonde, but without taking her eyes off Graver, and said, "Tell Corkie to verify the integrity of those tapes."

The girl muttered again into the microphone.

"And if I were you, Marcus, I'd tap him. You'd better let us tap him. You don't have that much time."

It was understood, of course, that they didn't have authorization for a wiretap, but such formalities were never a consideration when you were operating in Kepner's world. She also had access to technology that was several cuts above what the CID could afford on its stressed municipal budget and which significantly reduced the risk of detection. Getting the Information was the name of the game. Not Getting Caught was the other name of the game. There was a lot of ingenuity in between.

Graver stood there and looked at her waiting for him to answer and could feel the sweat oozing to the surface of his skin. He knew that unless he explicitly instructed otherwise there would be no tapes of the Burtell wiretap, that it would be only a listening effort, a means by which he could hope to steal a march against the target, of gaining an edge in the contest. And he knew, too, that in this level of competition people didn't break into a sweat over what he had to decide. Still, he could feel the sweat.

The blonde at Arnette's elbow leaned to her and said a few words.

"Okay, you got a good copy on the tapes, Marcus," Arnette said. She stared at him. "What about it? You want the tap?"

He nodded. "Go ahead," he said.

28

GRAVER THOUGHT ABOUT IT ALL THE WAY BACK TO TISLER'S rent house. Did he really know enough to justify what he was doing now, going completely outside channels with his own investigation? Considering Westrate's outsized ambitions, considering who was involved and who *might be* involved, yes, he thought it did. What he had to keep in mind, however, was that in the end it was not Westrate to whom he ultimately would have to answer. The implications here were larger even than Westrate's ambitions. And if the conspiracy went no further than the three men he had identified so far, the fewer people involved in the investigation the greater the chance—though still a slim chance—that the police could keep it entirely under wraps.

So, until Graver had a more informed perspective, he was going to keep what he knew confined to the few people he trusted. One of his greatest fears was that his inquiry, if discovered by people at the command level, would be derailed for political reasons. He had seen it happen too often.

He found that going back into Tisler's rent house was far more eerie than entering it for the first time. The first time he had not been so much anxious as curious. Then he had expected to find some*thing,* though he had no idea what. Now, however, he was fearful of encountering some*one.*

But it was a groundless anxiety, and he easily entered through the back door again, went to the bedroom at the far end of the house where he quickly turned on the computer and erased the hard drive. He hoped to God that Arnette's people didn't screw up the only thing that was left of Tisler's curious cache.

Just as he was making his way through the kitchen to the back door, he felt his pager vibrate at his waist. He pushed the button to turn it off but didn't look at the calling number until he was back in his

car and headed away from Tisler's house. As he was driving, he held
the pager near the dash lights and saw Westrate's office number. He
pulled off the street at a car wash and called in.

Westrate answered on the first ring.

"Jesus Christ," he said, hearing Graver's voice. "Where the hell are
you?" Graver told him. "Better get down here to my office. Something's happened."

That was all Graver knew for twenty minutes, the length of time it
took him to come in on the Southwest Freeway, park in front of the
Administration Building, and get upstairs to the fourth floor where he
found the stout assistant chief alone in his office. Others had been
there, however. Two Styrofoam cups with the dregs of coffee sat on the
front edge of Westrate's desk, and there were cigarette butts in the
ashtray along with one of Westrate's half-smoked cigars.

Westrate was sitting behind his desk in an incredibly wrinkled
white shirt, tie undone, cuffs turned back, a thick hand nervously taking occasional swipes at the thinning bristles on his ball-like head. He
didn't get up as Graver walked in, and he didn't ask Graver to sit
down. The place reeked of smoke, and Westrate's desk was in disarray.

"Ray Besom is dead," Westrate said, scowling from under his
heavy eyebrows. He said it as if Graver had something to answer for,
and Westrate was by God expecting the answer right then.

Graver had the sudden, irrational thought that he had somehow
been at fault, that he had miscalculated something and, as a result,
Besom was dead. Burtell popped into his mind, Burtell and the five
missing hours.

"What happened?" He felt short of breath.

"Heart attack while he was fishing. They found him still in his
waders, washed up on the beach."

"Heart attack?"

"Yeah, goddamned heart attack!"

"He's in Brownsville?"

"Yeah."

"Who's 'they'?"

"Brownsville police," Westrate said heavily. He bent his round
head and held it in his two thick hands, elbows on the desk, the thinning spot in his short hair tilted at Graver. "Sit down."

Graver sat in one of the chairs in front of Westrate's desk. Westrate
dropped his hands and looked up at Graver and noticed the two Styro-

foam cups. "Shit, give me those." He stood and snatched the two cups with one hand, slopping some of the coffee as he dumped them into the trash can at the side of his desk. "Shit," he said again, opened a desk drawer, yanked out a wad of tissues and mashed them down on the splash of coffee. He rubbed it around as he leaned over, stretching his short arms across the desk. Graver could see a tuft of wiry black hair on his chest sticking up through his open collar. There was wiry black hair on his forearms and on the backs of his hands and on the tops of his fingers. Westrate flopped back down in his chair as he leaned over and with one hand dunked the wad of wet tissues into his trash can.

"Yesterday he was fishing at this spot, a place called Boca Chica near Port Isabel," Westrate began. "Goes there every year. Some old fart took him by boat. You can't get there in a car. This is about five yesterday afternoon. According to Besom's wife it was his last night down there. He was supposed to get up early this morning and drive home. Anyway, this old guy's supposed to come back later last night, nine o'clock, and pick him up. Nine o'clock comes, old fart is there, but no Besom. He waits an hour. Waits an hour and a half. Says he putters his boat in the direction Besom said he'd be walking, shining his spotlight on the beach. No Besom. He goes back to Port Isabel. Docks his boat and goes to a bar and drinks and worries about it. Tells some friends what's happened. They say, well, shit, if the guy wanted a ride he should've showed up."

Westrate let his head flop back against the high back of his chair.

"This is all coming from the Brownsville police," he said. "Old fart goes home and goes to *bed* for Christ's sake. But he's had a lot to drink and doesn't wake up until ten o'clock the next morning. That's this morning, today. But he can't get Besom off his feeble old mind. Gets in his boat and goes back out there, putters along the beach again, goes a mile or so and finally spots this bunch of fishing gear piled up beside an old beached shrimper. But no Besom. He goes back in, calls the Brownsville police because this place, Boca Chica, is in Brownsville's jurisdiction. They do a search party. It takes most of the afternoon, but they finally find Besom's body washed way down the beach, fully dressed, still in his waders. He was chewed up some. The fish had been at him a little. But not a lot. It hadn't been that long."

"He had his ID with him?"

"No, no ID, but the old man remembered that Besom said he was from Houston and was staying in a 'motel' in Brownsville. They start checking it out, calling the motels. In the meantime the Brownsville ME does an autopsy. Heart failure, drowning. They finally locate the motel, get in, find out from his things he's with HPD and call us."

Westrate was leaning back in his chair now, his arms up, his thick, hairy hands gripping the high back of the seat above his head. He was staring at Graver, his long upper lip taut and challenging.

"What do you know about the Brownsville ME?" Graver asked. "Is he reliable?"

"How the shit would I know?"

"Did Besom have a history of heart trouble?"

"God, I hope so."

"What about IAD?"

Westrate nodded. "I talked to Katz just a little while ago. Pio Tordella and his partner—and Bricker and Petersen—are driving down there tonight, right now."

"Who knows about it?"

"*Every*body. The Brownsville police didn't know what this was. Goddamned border town hicks. So when the local news says it wants to go along, they say sure, fine. They *filmed* the whole thing. Besom's wife already knows, but we got the news people to hold off on the ID anyway pending notification of the family. But it'll be on the news tomorrow night."

He was still staring at Graver, almost in an accusatory manner as if he was waiting for Graver to justify what was happening.

"He needs to be reautopsied back here," Graver said.

"Yeah, that's what Katz wants too." Westrate's face hadn't lost any of its tension in the telling of the story. He still looked as if he was going to explode. "You've already written the paper closing out Tisler?"

"I'll finish it tonight." From Westrate's expression Graver guessed someone had already suggested there was a smell of fish here. "The second autopsy is critical."

Westrate was still looking at him as he dropped his arms down and rested them on his desk. His forehead was oily. He looked like he'd been hot for a long time.

"Listen," he said grimly, "I don't care what the autopsy shows, this is too damned coincidental for me."

Graver agreed with him, but he didn't say so. He could hardly keep his thoughts on what Westrate was saying. He needed to get to Kepner.

When Dean Burtell heard about this he was going to do something. Whatever was happening here, it didn't look good for Burtell.

"You don't believe it was a heart attack," Graver said, trying to think in two directions at once.

Westrate's eyes widened slightly as he tilted his head downward until he was again glowering at Graver from under his woolly eyebrows.

"Heart attack." His voice was a mixture of anger and disdain. He was looking over his clasped hands, his two meaty fists gripping each other so tightly that Graver imagined them suddenly bursting and squirting all over the desk like tomatoes. "I don't care if we find a living, breathing witness to Tisler's suicide and the guy swears on a Bible that Tisler shot himself. I don't care if we find a witness who saw Ray Besom fishing, saw him suddenly grabbing his chest and gasping and falling down in the goddamn water. I don't care if we *KNOW* that's exactly how they both died . . . it *by God . . . looks . . . SUSPICIOUS!"*

Dramatically jerking his head from side to side for emphasis as he spoke these last words, Westrate literally spewed spittle as he hissed "suspicious." His face was as pink as a pistachio pod, and Graver could see even his scalp flushing through his thinning hair.

"*HO*-ly *JE*-sus!" Westrate exclaimed, falling back into his chair. Then suddenly he was up, jamming his hands into his pockets and stalking around his desk to the open door of his office where he stood looking out into the dark anteroom, jangling the change in his pockets.

Westrate's histrionics were wasted on Graver, who could only think of Burtell and of how critical it was to be close to him now. He wished to God he had asked for taps the first time he spoke to Kepner. At that time Ginette would have been at work and, as it turned out, Burtell wouldn't have been at home either. Kepner's people would have had plenty of time. Graver looked at his watch. He had to get out of Westrate's office.

"What do you want from me, Jack?" he asked.

Westrate didn't answer immediately, but when he turned around Graver was disconcerted to see that his wrath had physically altered his features. His eyes were puffy, and pasty swags of flesh were forming beneath them; his cheeks, normally taut with obesity, now appeared swollen with a scattering of unhealthy, livid blotches. He unhurriedly closed the door to his office and came over and gave a quick jerk to the other chair in front of his desk and sat down in it, facing Graver, his short, log-like legs spread out.

"What do you think about all this?" he asked. His voice was uncharacteristically quiet, and for the first time ever Graver saw an expression on his face that conveyed, however slightly, a vague vulnerability.

Graver braced himself. He could see that Westrate was at his wit's end, and he guessed the assistant chief was beginning to imagine, to see the foreshadowing of plots against him, against his career. What Westrate wanted was for Graver to say it first. He wanted to hear Graver say that something was wrong here.

"I think Tisler killed himself," Graver said. "And I doubt if we'll ever know why. And, until another autopsy proves otherwise, I'm going to assume Besom had a heart attack."

Westrate's face fell. "That's it?"

"That's what I think," Graver said.

"These two deaths are exactly what they appear to be?" His voice rose with incredulity.

"I've got to think so in the absence of any evidence that indicates otherwise."

"But just the fact that they died so close together . . . that doesn't make you suspicious?"

"As a matter of fact it does . . ." Graver said.

Westrate's eyebrows lifted in anticipation.

". . . but I think we've got to be careful, Jack. I think we've got to be suspicious of our suspicions. It would be too damn easy to read something into these events that the facts don't support." He paused and looked at Westrate. "You ever heard of 'Occam's razor'?"

Westrate stared at him.

"William of Occam was a fourteenth-century English philosopher who stated a kind of commonsense principle regarding lines of inquiry into the truth of a situation. It was stated in Latin, but translated it means: 'Plurality must not be posited without necessity.' A modern rendering might be, 'An explanation of the facts should be no more complicated than necessary,' or 'Among competing hypotheses, favor the simplest one.' Occam's razor advocated cutting away all the unnecessary considerations that can clutter up a line of inquiry and sticking to the simplest theory consistent with the facts."

Westrate's expression portrayed a disgruntled impatience.

"I've got a lot of data that tells me Tisler committed suicide," Graver elaborated. "The simplest explanation is that he did. I've got a lot of data that tells me Ray Besom had a heart attack. The simplest explanation, consistent with the facts, is that he did. So, unless we obtain other facts, facts that are *in*consistent with the explanation, then the weight of my suppositions will have to fall with the simplest explanation."

"Give me a break, Graver," Westrate snapped, his small nostrils flaring with agitation at Graver's professorial anecdote. "I've got four divisions to manage here."

That sounded like a non sequitur to Graver. He wasn't sure what Westrate meant, but it was clear he was sweating pearls over this. If he had suspicions that something was terribly wrong in CID, he sure as hell wasn't going to say so now. He was too sly for that. If he did express such a belief and it turned out that Besom did indeed have a heart attack, Westrate would end up sounding like a conspiracy theorist and an alarmist—one of my men kills himself, another one has a heart attack, ergo the CID is riddled by spies and cabalists. No, Westrate wasn't going to risk that with anyone, especially not with Graver. But he believed it.

Once again the pager on Graver's belt vibrated. Without looking down he turned it off.

"Is there something you want me to do?"

"No," Westrate said, getting up quickly.

"Does Hertig know this?"

"Goddamn right he knows it. I called him."

"What was his reaction?"

"What do you mean—he goddamned couldn't believe it. Wants some answers . . . just like the rest of us," he said pointedly. He waited a beat. "It's only a matter of hours before the media's going to catch on to this. CID's going to get some publicity. They're going to call you spies, secret police, all those kinds of liberal shit buzz words." He thrust his head forward. "Any suggestions?"

"Yeah," Graver fired back. "You handle it. Put whatever spin you want on it."

Westrate came to his feet and glared at Graver. Managing to get the best of his tongue, he stalked around behind his desk again. He fumbled in the debris there and found a cigar box, opened it, and took out a cigar. He jammed it in his mouth without lighting it and stood there, looking at Graver, mouthing the cigar, hands once again thrust deep into the pockets of his wrinkled trousers.

"Let's put it this way, Graver," he said, talking around the cigar. "You'd better get all over this situation like a sailor on a whore. If there's something to these 'coincidences,' if there is, and you don't snap to it until it's too goddamned late . . ." He took the cigar out of his mouth and said calmly, ". . . I'm gonna be so far up your ass you'll have to shit through your nose for the rest of your life."

Ray Besom's death was indeed a potential disaster for them, but Graver didn't think you should try to damage-control a disaster by letting your brain explode. Westrate was going to have to get a grip on himself if he was going to handle the media intelligently. But Graver couldn't do anything about that. He imagined Westrate and Chief Hertig's public relations crew would convene early in the morning. They would start putting together something that would be palatable and would effectively cover up the panic. Then they were going to turn to Graver.

"Anything else?" Graver asked, standing.

Westrate jabbed the cigar into his mouth again and sat down in his chair. "No," he said, and started pawing around in the mayhem of his desk.

Graver walked out into the semidarkness of the reception area and paused long enough beside a table lamp to look at his pager. The number was Paula's. She was still at the office.

He took the elevator downstairs to the lobby and went straight to the pay phones. He called Kepner, told her what had happened. She didn't have to be told anything else. After hanging up, he walked back through the lobby and out the back door and through a covered driveway that led in one direction to the motor pool, and in the other to the squat, smog-begrimed building where the CID occupied the southeast corner of the third floor.

29

GRAVER STARED AT THE DARKNESS JUST IN FRONT OF HIM AS HE followed the crumbling asphalt drive around to the back side of the compound. He had been shaken by the news of Ray Besom's death, though Westrate had not realized it, so preoccupied was he with his own over-the-top performance. It was hard to believe Besom had had a heart attack, especially in light of what Graver knew about Tisler and Besom's involvements. No, he didn't think it was a heart attack. But that was instinct. His judgment reminded him that if the Besom/Tisler/Burtell conspiracy—whatever it was—was indeed coming apart, it would be logical that the fear of the consequences would be exacting a severe toll on the participants. Weren't heart failure and stress undeniably linked? So what the hell was he supposed to think? The grim fact was, he still didn't know much of anything.

He stopped in the spartan lobby beneath the CID offices and called Paula on the pay phone. "I'm downstairs," he said. "Catch the security system for me, will you?"

She met him just as he approached the receptionist's glass booth and reactivated the security system after he came through.

"Were you on your way here when I called?" she asked.

"Kind of," he said, pushing past her and walking straight to his office.

She followed him and stood in the doorway and waited as he sat down behind his desk and quickly jotted down a couple of notes.

"What's the matter?" she asked.

He looked up at her and saw that she was barefooted, and her hair was pulled back in a bun, much of it working loose from the few pins she had holding it together. "You've been here all this time?"

"Yeah, me and Casey. We think we may have something."

"Good. Get him in here. Is there any coffee in there?"

"Yeah, we made a fresh pot about half an hour ago." She was staring at him with a puzzled frown, knowing something was wrong.

She stepped out into the hall and called Neuman from her office down at the other end as Graver went across to the coffee room and poured half a mug of the Division's stout generic coffee. When he came back, he took off his suit coat and hung it on the hat rack in the corner and then sat down behind his desk. As Paula and Neuman came in, he was taking his first sip of coffee. Paula sat down, but Neuman remained standing, his arms folded, a notebook sticking out from under his elbow as he twisted his waist and shoulders. He had already had enough sitting.

"You guys had anything to eat?" The air-conditioning seemed not to be working well, and Graver loosened his tie.

"We brought in sandwiches," Paula said.

Graver nodded. "Look, before we get started, there are two developments. First, when I got to Tisler's rent house I found a computer setup. Nobody lives there, apparently, but it looked like Tisler must have spent quite a bit of time there. It was a fairly good-sized computer. I wasn't able to get in, but I did manage to copy the hard drive."

"My God." Paula looked as if she had been given another clue to the location of the Holy Grail. "So where is it?" Neuman took a step forward.

"I've got someone working on it."

Paula was incredulous. She started to speak, but Graver quickly preempted her.

"And some worse news," he said. "Ray Besom has been found dead down near Port Isabel."

Paula gasped as if she had been punched in the stomach, and Neuman unfolded his arms and walked behind her to the windows.

"Holy shit." Neuman looked outside, then turned and walked back to where he had been standing.

"Heart attack," Graver explained quickly, "according to the autopsy. Apparently he died while he was surf fishing."

"Oh God, Marcus," Paula said, placing the flat of her hand on her forehead, her bracelets rattling, "I'm not going to believe that." She dropped her hand. She shook her head slowly. "I can't believe that."

Graver looked at her.

"We know too much . . . just too damn much to swallow that," she said. "What's going on here?"

"There's going to be another autopsy," Graver said. "Here."

Paula was still shaking her head. "It doesn't matter, even if the Harris County ME says it *was* a heart attack—"

"Wait a minute," Neuman interrupted. He was moving back and forth between the windows and the door again, his eyes darting back and forth between Paula and Graver. "The thing is, *if* Besom was killed somehow—in whatever way—it was meant to be disguised as a natural death, wasn't it? *If* we believe that, if that's true, then this is . . . this is definitely a high-octane situation. I mean . . . what kind of people do shit like that?"

Neuman, of course, had quickly closed on the central question. Each of them knew at this point that even they, with all their suspicions, had probably underestimated what they had stumbled upon. And Graver suspected all three of them were turning their suspicions in the same direction.

"What about Dean?" Paula asked quickly. "Maybe he's in danger."

"Or maybe he isn't"—Graver shook his head—"which is even scarier." Now he had confirmation that he hadn't overreacted by going to Arnette Kepner. He thought a moment and then he said, "I've got to call him."

"What?" Paula was lost. "What the hell for?"

"It's what I would do," Graver said. "If I didn't know about all this other I'd call him to let him know about Besom."

"I hope you've got good people on this," Paula said. "When Dean hears about this he's going to freak out, he's going to do something."

"Unless he already knows," Neuman said.

Graver was a little surprised at Neuman's remarks. He was quick to see a deeper, meaner undercurrent here, and Graver thought he was justified. Graver also guessed that each of them was feeling a sudden trepidation at the realization that the water was deeper and far more treacherous than they ever had expected.

Picking up a pencil from his desk, Graver tapped the cobblestone a couple of times.

"Whatever this is, it's coming apart," he said. "We may be getting here just in time to see its back going out the door."

"Marcus, maybe we ought to go ahead and confront Dean," Paula said.

Graver rubbed his face with his hands. "Our only *leverage* is that they don't know we're onto them. That's not much, but we sure as hell can't give it up."

"God," Neuman said, "can you imagine what must be at stake here for them to have risked killing Besom within twenty-four hours of Tisler? They've got to know, no matter what kind of evidence there is to support natural causes, that it's going to look suspicious to a lot of people."

"What are the odds Tisler was killed too?" Paula asked.

It was a moment before Graver looked up. "Good, I think now," he said. "Pretty damn good." He looked at her. "What did you call me about?"

"Oh," she said, looking down at the notepad in her lap, remembering. She moistened her lips. Everyone's thoughts had been derailed. "We've made some progress. Uh, in the Friel case, apparently the entire source documentation is bogus. *All* the contributors listed there are in the same category as Tisler's tenant Lewis Feldberg. They came off the vital statistics records. It's total bullshit."

"What about the Probst sources?"

"Real people . . . we think. Bruce Sheck—he's the guy who's supposed to have flown Probst's stolen goods to Mexico and Central America. Remember yesterday I only got an answering machine when I called his number. We started checking him out. Essentially everything in the Contributor Identification Records is accurate. His TDL photo matches the ID records photograph. As far as it goes. He's not on the computers, no aliases. He lives in Nassau Bay in a home that's in his name, no lien. He pays his utility bills with money orders, for Christ's sake, so there's no bank to follow up on. No traffic tickets. No military record. Not registered to vote. No marriage record in Harris County. Owns a 1993 Honda, no lien. We checked with the FAA. He has a pilot's license and owns a plane—no lien—which he hangars at Houston Gulf Airport, not far from his home. The guy lives a very unincumbered existence."

"What about Synar?"

"Absolutely nothing. Again, nowhere on the computers, everything the same as Sheck . . . no traffic violations, not registered to vote, all that," Paula said. "I called her old roommate again. She said Colleen wasn't from Houston, thought Los Angeles was her home. She remembered Colleen referring to a cousin in New York who was also a Synar. But there were no Synars with telephone numbers in either Los Angeles or New York."

"You know what," Neuman said, stepping over and picking up the contributor's ID record sheet from Paula's lap, "I've been thinking. That's a bullshit name." He held up the sheet and pointed to the small photograph of Colleen Synar in the lower right corner. "This is not Colleen Synar. No way. But I'll tell you what you do. You drive over to that address right now and talk to that woman who said she was her roommate . . . What was her name?"

"Valerie . . . Heath," Paula said, looking down at her notes.

"Yeah, you talk to Valerie Heath, and I'll bet you a hundred bucks you'll be talking to 'Colleen Synar.' I don't know where they came up with that name—Synar—but that woman took a flyer when she gave you her 'lead,' the two biggest cities in the country. That was right off the top of her head. She probably thought there ought to be Synars in those cities if there were going to be any anywhere, and by the time we ran them all down she would have bought some time."

Paula stared at him.

"In fact," Neuman said, "we ought to run a computer check on her right now. My hunch is her stats are going to look like Sheck's—bare bones."

"I think you'd better do it," Graver said to Paula. "If he's right, if they used that name only for this one reason, then it's a trip wire, and they're already on to us. If they're as finely tuned as we think, they'll know we've found a loose thread and are pulling on it. I don't know if we could have done it a better way, but it's too late now for us to go at this as if we were doing background checks on these two. We've got to go right to them. So run the computer check on Heath right now."

"Casey," he said, getting up and walking to the safe cabinet, "I want you to go down to the tech room and get three radios with secure frequencies." He opened the safe and got a key and tossed it to Neuman.

He looked at the two of them, Paula now standing and looking apprehensive, quite a different expression on her face than when she was so hungry to pin Burtell to the wall with her research findings. Neuman, on the other hand, looked like he had been born to the task; he was ready to hunt.

"After you've run the computer check, the two of you go out to Heath's place and talk to her."

Paula looked at her watch. "It's almost ten-thirty."

"It'll take you, what, thirty minutes to drive out there?"

Neuman nodded. "If we push it."

"Then push it," Graver said. "Keep in mind: unfortunately, except for Dean, she and Sheck are the only two people we know about who *might* give us access to the bigger picture here—if there is a bigger picture. Keep checking in with me. I don't want to have to wonder where you are or what you're doing."

They walked out of his office without saying a word, and Graver went back to his desk and sat down. He stared at the cobblestone. Jesus Christ. The single feeling that weighed most heavily on him now was one of urgency.

Graver was used to taking suspicions seriously, but everything that came to mind to explain what was, and had been, going on right under his nose seemed so radical that he doubted his own abilities to read the meager facts with any clarity.

Within a few minutes Neuman and Paula came by the office again and gave Graver one of the three handsets. Paula's first pass through the computers had yielded exactly what Neuman had predicted. Nothing. Valerie Heath seemed to live a life as tenuously attached to society as did Bruce Sheck.

They coordinated the radio frequencies, and Graver followed them to the outside door, reset the security system behind them, and then returned to his office. He sat down at his desk and turned to his own computer. With a few clicks on the keys he brought up his internal report regarding Tisler's death. Actually he was already through with it, but he wanted to read it over very carefully a few times before he turned it in for Westrate's approval in the morning. When he was satisfied, he printed out the final document, put it in a departmental envelope, stamped it Confidential, and put it in the locked distribution drawer so that it would be hand-delivered to Westrate's office first thing in the morning.

Returning to his desk, he picked up the telephone and dialed Burtell's number. Graver waited as the telephone rang two, three, four times, nervously hoping he would be able to discern something informative from Burtell's reaction to the news. On the fifth ring Ginette Burtell answered.

"Ginny, this is Graver," he said.

"Oh, hello," she said, and for some reason he was surprised at the animation in her voice. Before he could speak again she said, "Oh, if you're wanting to speak to Dean, I'm afraid you've just missed him."

"Yeah, I did need to talk to him."

"I'm sorry, but he left not four or five minutes ago."

"You don't happen to know how I could get in touch with him, do you?"

"No, actually, I don't even know where he was going."

Graver was surprised by this. How often did this happen? She must have sensed his surprise.

"Uh, he got a telephone call . . . and . . . he said he had to go out for a while."

Graver waited.

"I don't always, uh, ask him where he's going," she said hesitantly.

"You have any idea when he'll be back?"

"No, I really . . . Well, he said . . . 'a couple of hours,' I think."

He wanted to ask if she knew who had called, but if Burtell quizzed her, he didn't want her to say that he had asked.

On the other end she was hesitating. "Uhhhhh . . . can I take a message, have him call you or something?"

"Sure, if you don't mind asking him to call me when he gets in. Tell him it doesn't matter how late."

"Oh . . . okay, Marcus. Sure, I'll see that he gets the message."

"Listen, Ginny," Graver said, "I appreciate you and Dean going over to Peggy Tisler's. I know that wasn't easy. I owe you."

"It was something we would have wanted to do anyway," she said. "I felt so sorry for her."

They visited a few moments longer, and then Graver told her good night and hung up. For the fourth or fifth time that night, he hoped Arnette's people were in place and prepared. He resisted the temptation to call her. He knew the curious little control room he had been in earlier that evening would be buzzing now. Their target was on the move.

Wearily he started cleaning off his desk and discovered among the paperwork a packet of faxed reports stapled together with a note from Lara. "These came in one right after the other (note times circled) between 5:00 and 6:15." He must have shuffled the packet aside several times while he was putting together the Tisler report. Lara even had attached a red translucent plastic "Alert" tag to the staple.

He picked up the packet and sat back in his chair. The reports were responses to his inquiries that morning about Victor Last.

30

THEY PICKED HIM UP THE MOMENT HE LEFT THE HOUSE. FOUR cars, two with only drivers, two with drivers and a single passenger each. Three of the cars were Japanese models, and the fourth was American. Each car was light in color, none of them new, none older than five years. The cars were driven by Arnette Kepner's own heterogeneous mix of specialists who, for purposes of their radio communications, were identified only by their first names.

Connie was a woman forty-two years old, a former detective in sex crimes with the Chicago Police Department. Three years ago she had moved to Houston when her husband's employer, an engineering company, transferred him down to corporate headquarters. The mother of two high-schoolers, she had deep red hair, an Irish sense of humor, and a no-bullshit attitude about the jobs she worked for Arnette.

Murray was fifty-seven, retired four years from the army where he spent his entire career in numerous branches of the army's Intelligence Services. Stocky but still muscular and athletic, Murray favored tennis shoes and jeans and white T-shirts with the sleeves rolled into tight cuffs that revealed his weight-lifter's arms. He was balding, had striking blue-green eyes, and a clipped, graying mustache. He was the group leader once they were on the job.

Remberto was a thirty-two-year-old Bolivian who first came to the United States eight years earlier when he was part of a small, select contingent of Bolivian police officers who were brought to Virginia by the DEA for a special intelligence training course designed for drug agents. Remberto learned English quickly, spent three years undercover in La Paz and in the jungles of the Beni River valley radioing out information about the ever-shifting coca plantations that supplied the cartels in Colombia. He married a DEA agent's daughter, and was now in the University of Houston law school.

Li was a twenty-eight-year-old Amer-Asian whose mother Arnette knew during one of her Vietnam tours. Li's mother was killed in 1971, a fact Arnette did not know until 1978 when she tried to find them in the chaotic months after the U.S. pullout. When she finally found Li in a Catholic orphanage, she went through a year and a half of red tape to adopt her and then brought her to the United States. Li was educated mostly in Virginia public schools and was now working on a master's degree in Art History at Rice University.

The two women were accompanied by passengers, Boyd, a photographer with Li, and Cheryl, a sound specialist, with Connie. Murray had been briefed about the target, but the others knew nothing about him except that he was thoroughly familiar with surveillance techniques, a fact that let them know that they couldn't take anything for granted and a lack of watchfulness was likely to be detected.

Burtell left the condominium complex, passed through the entrance gates and turned east on Woodway, a curving, wooded street that eventually would go under the West Loop and merge with Memorial Drive just inside Memorial Park. Murray pulled out of a parking slot in front of another condominium, let a couple of cars get between him and Burtell, and then nosed into the traffic. The other three quickly entered the traffic stream from different streets a block away, Connie, Remberto, and Li. Murray was immediately on the radio.

MURRAY: "Okay, Connie, go ahead and get in front of him. If he goes for the Loop we'll stay with him. You double back when you can. If he goes all the way into downtown peel away the first chance you get after the merge with Memorial."

CONNIE: "Okay, here we go."

She pulled out and passed Murray and then Burtell, getting in front of him before the next light and adjusting her speed so that she didn't go through without him. When the light turned they went to the next one which they caught green and passed under the Loop, staying on Woodway as they entered the one-hundred-and-fifty-five-acre Memorial Park, its dense stand of loblolly pines turning the city-lighted night to a deeper darkness. Suddenly Burtell hit his brakes and turned off Woodway before it merged with Memorial Drive and entered the drive to the Houston Arboretum and Nature Center.

MURRAY: "Remberto. Li. Stay outta there. Don't go in. This is a bullshit stop. It's a dead end. He's not going to meet anybody in there, not this early in the game. He's trying to pull us off. Everybody watch for countersurveillance—they're gonna see who panics. Remberto, turn off on Picnic Lane ahead and look to pick him up if he goes on to merge with Memorial when he comes out of there. Connie, Li, the three of us are going to spread out and start circling Memorial, North Post Oak, and the access road. We'll pick him up if he comes out and heads west."

For a minute there was silence on the radio as they each did as they were told, Connie, being the farthest away already coming back and beginning the first leg of her circle as the others turned around. It was still early enough in the night for the traffic to provide a moderate flow of headlights.

Burtell did not come out for fifteen minutes. When he did, it was Li who picked him up.

LI: "I've got him, Murray. He's coming at me on Woodway."

MURRAY: "Keep going. I'll pick him up if he gets on the Loop. Remberto, come on in. Connie, turn off and wait for him. If he goes back west on Woodway one of you let me know who picks him up first."

Silence again as the disrupted surveillance team rearranged itself to accommodate Burtell's maneuver. Within seconds he had made another choice.

MURRAY: "Okay, he's mine. He's on the access road heading north. We're going up on the Loop."

Everyone followed, each at his own pace, from three different directions.

MURRAY: "We're heading into the interchange. Going east into . . . Son of a bitch! Heading west! Heading west! I lost him. I lost him . . . He's . . . Son of a bitch!"

REMBERTO: "It's okay, Murray. I've got him. No problem." The Bolivian's voice was calm, undisturbed. "We're on I-10 heading west. Somebody let me know when you're in line behind me in case he goes to the access roads again."

LI: "I'm five cars behind you, Rem."

CONNIE: "I'm three behind Li."

REMBERTO: "He's braking . . . No—no . . . He's going on. He's moving way over left. Oh, man, picking up speed."

CONNIE: "I'm in the left lane, Rem, but I'm too far back to identify him."

REMBERTO: "He's behind an RV, alternating red and orange lights . . . braking . . . braking."

CONNIE: "Okay . . . I see him."

REMBERTO: "Li stay right. I have a feeling he's going to whip across traffic and exit as soon . . . There he goes! . . . There he goes! Gessner! Gessner!"

LI: "I've got him. Gessner exit."

Remberto continued down the expressway past the exit.

MURRAY: Remberto, stay on the expressway. He could shoot back up. Connie, steady with traffic, I'm coming up on you. Li, what's he doing? Come on! Come on, kid, what's he doing?"

LI: "We're going through the Gessner light . . . not turning off . . . The light caught me . . . I'm stopped, I'm stop— There he goes . . . he's going back up . . . he's going back up on I-10 . . . Shit! He's flying, he's cooking."

CONNIE: "I've got him." Like Remberto her voice was laid back, conversational. "He's coming up on your tail, Remberto."

REMBERTO: "He's not leaving the right lane . . . Holy God . . . he's going to run right up my tailpipe!"

MURRAY: "Watch him! He's going to take the interchange . . . He's going . . ."

At the last possible moment, just before Burtell rammed into the back of Remberto's car, they came to the interchange exit and Burtell rocketed off to the right, careening into the climbing turn and, as he banked off the expressway onto the Sam Houston Tollway, headed south. It was too late for Connie to turn off, but Murray and Li both easily followed him in the flow of traffic. It was a good move, perfect timing to do what he did, an expert maneuver. Remberto and Connie would have to pass up the next exit to avoid having to brake quickly and possibly give themselves away to any countersurveillance. They would have to continue on to the next one, signaling, keeping cars between them, let a traffic light separate them, and then circle back on the access road to the interchange and join the tollway traffic behind the rest of them.

From here on Burtell played another kind of game. The tollway was wide, long, and straight, and Burtell tried to isolate himself. This was the tactic that Murray found the most difficult to deal with. The traffic here was more sparse, strung out on the newly completed tollway. Burtell slowed down and waited until a traffic cluster by-passed him, and he was fairly isolated on the long stretch of roadway. He drifted along and then suddenly pulled to the shoulder right before one of the exits that came at regular intervals. Anyone following him very closely would have to continue on the tollway and from his vantage point he could easily see the next two exits to identify any car that pulled off. He wouldn't forget the make of anything that did.

MURRAY: "He's pulled to the shoulder just past Richmond. He's getting out, raising the hood of his car. Li, we'll keep going. Remberto? Connie?"

CONNIE: "Exiting at Rodgerdale." That was the exit a mile before Burtell. He would never even see them pulling off.

REMBERTO: "I'm behind her, getting off at Briar Forest."

CONNIE: "On Rodgerdale, coming up on Richmond. I can see him up there, hood's up . . . He's looking down the tollway toward Li and Murray. Remberto. Get off in one of the neighborhood streets here. He's right at an exit. I'm pulling over to a gas station."

There was dead air for a while as Burtell continued to look down the tollway, watching the next two exits. Finally he closed the hood.

CONNIE: "Okay, he's satisfied, putting down the hood; he's moving. Remberto, he's pulling off right in front of me. He's ducking under the tollway, going back . . . Okay, he's turning under again . . . No, wait, no he was signaling but he's not turning . . . He's staying on Parkway . . . Parkway all the way."

Burtell was good at what he was doing, keeping all four of his tails off balance, though none of them had been able to determine if he had even picked them up. From all indications he did not know they were there. Even so, the game continued, across the south side of the city through neighborhoods and expressways, through one, two, three, four, five massive interchanges that took them west and then north, suddenly cutting right to the heart of downtown and careening back out again on another angle to take them once again on I-10 and, incredibly, once again onto the Sam Houston Tollway. Then to everyone's amazement he suddenly pulled aside on the same overpass as before and lifted the hood of his car again.

This time it was Connie and Li who shot past him and Murray and Remberto who caught the stall on the access road. When Burtell got back into the car the second time, he pulled off on the access road, doubled back under the tollway, and headed into town on Richmond.

MURRAY: "Well, kids, this is looking different. Something's up. Connie, Li, where are you guys?"

CONNIE: "We're off the tollway at Bellaire headed for Southwest Freeway. Keep us posted, and we'll intersect you as soon as we can."

The drive down Richmond was without any evasive maneuvering by Burtell. He was a model driver, going exactly the speed limit, never going through an amber traffic light. But this was deceivingly dangerous. Now they were down to only two vehicles, and they couldn't stay on him long. Remberto passed him.

MURRAY: "We're leading and following, Connie. Where are you?"

LI: "We're hauling ass on Southwest. What's your cross street?"

MURRAY: "Coming up on Ann Arbor. But he's just puttering along."

LI: "With luck we'll see you at Chimney Rock."

Which was exactly what happened. As soon as they came on Murray pulled off but Remberto remained in the lead. Nothing changed for another five minutes, Burtell the model driver staying with the flow of traffic which had gotten increasingly sparse. Then:

CONNIE: "He's turning left on Sage."

Connie, behind him, and Remberto, ahead of him, kept going. Li fell in behind him, but dropped way back because the street was almost deserted. In front of them only blocks away was the Galleria complex and slightly to their right the Transco Tower and its attendant fountain and park. Burtell turned right on Hidalgo and pulled to the side of the street across from the Transco Fountain. Li and Murray both continued by out of sight, and then Murray doubled back and entered Sage himself. He also turned on Hidalgo, but drove by and turned onto Post Oak and then into Bercher, where he parked.

MURRAY: "Be damned. He's going to the fountain." He looked at his watch. Burtell's evasive maneuvers had lasted a marathon hour and five minutes.

The Transco Tower was the tallest office building outside downtown, a perfectly symmetrical tower of sixty-four stories topped by a rotating beacon that was lighted every night from dusk to midnight and was powerful enough to be seen twenty miles away. On the south side of the tower was a long, mall-like park having a sunken lawn with grassy slopes. At the end of the lawn was the Transco Fountain, a granite wall several stories high and ten or twelve feet thick built in a half circle and facing the tower. Water gushed out of the top of the wall and fell down the sheer, grooved sides of the granite semicircle in thin roiling sheets to a stepped stone base and pool. Standing on the inside of the semicircle, as the water thundered and sprayed around you, produced the strange sensation of levitation.

A few feet away from the fountain another wall stood between the fountain and the lawn, a neoclassical façade with three Roman arches through which the lower portion of the lighted fountain could be viewed from the lawn. In the evenings the lighted fountain and sloping sides of the sunken lawn were a favorite site for strollers, Frisbee-throwers, and families who let their children play along the long, grassy slopes that were lighted obliquely from the rippling reflections off the fountain.

By the time Burtell got out of his car and started walking casually toward the fountain and the scores of milling people along the mall and around the fountain, Murray's drivers had parked at strategic places on opposite sides of the fountain complex, watching Burtell work his way slowly into the crowds.

MURRAY: "Everybody stay put. There are a lot of people out there, but not enough. We'd need a swarm of people to keep from getting nailed. Boyd, Cheryl. How you guys lined up?"

CHERYL: "If they don't go to the fountain I think I'll be able to pick them up okay."

BOYD: "I'm okay for now."

MURRAY: "Okay, go ahead and shoot."

Burtell strolled to the sidewalk that ran around the perimeter of the sunken lawn and began walking around it, beginning on the west side of the water curtain. As he walked he took something out of his suit coat pocket and began to eat.

MURRAY: "What the hell's that?"

BOYD: "Looks like peanuts."

MURRAY: "Peanuts?"

BOYD: "No, sunflower seeds."

MURRAY: "Well, shit, which is it?"

BOYD: "Sunflower seeds. He's cracking the hulls and spitting them out."

MURRAY: "Jesus, that's a good camera, hotshot."

BOYD: "Yeah."

Burtell walked around the entire lawn perimeter, stopping now and then to watch the kids rolling down the grassy slopes, looking up at the tower light, eating sunflower seeds, pausing, looking the length of the sunken lawn to the fountain. People milled all around him, a Frisbee sailed perilously close. He didn't speak to anyone. He was totally relaxed.

MURRAY: "Anybody see anything?"

No one responded. Burtell had almost made it back to the fountains approaching its east side, when a man in a suit joined him. Together they walked up the steps to the inner curve of the fountain curtain.

MURRAY: (excited) "Where the fuck he come from?"

CHERYL: "Goddamn it . . . I knew it, I knew they were going to do that."

MURRAY: "Boyd!"

BOYD: "I'm shooting . . . I'm shooting."

CHERYL: "I can shoot this, Murray, but the water's going to screw it up. I can't filter out the goddamned water . . . It's not going to work."

MURRAY: "You getting *any*thing?"

CHERYL: "Snatches . . . here and there . . . Oh, wait. They're behind the . . . you know, columns . . . I can only shoot the sound if they're in the open, under the arches. They're walking in and out of the arches."

MURRAY: "Boyd."

BOYD: "Same here. I'm shooting, but they're moving in and out of sight."

MURRAY: "What's he look like?"

BOYD: "He's an *old* guy."

MURRAY: "Old?"

BOYD: "God, he must be fifty, late fifties."

MURRAY: "Shit, kid."

Murray could hear them laughing.

Burtell and his companion walked back and forth the entire time they were at the fountain. By Murray's watch it was a thirty-two-minute meeting. They walked back and forth for thirty-two minutes inside the misty half circle of the water curtain, during which time Cheryl cursed intermittently and Boyd said, "Got 'em . . . got 'em . . . got 'em . . ." each time they stepped under one of the Roman arches.

Suddenly, without any body language that indicated they were finished talking, they parted, each exiting opposite sides of the fountain.

LI: "Murray. The guy's heading down the slope to a car fifty yards in front of me. Do I go with him?"

MURRAY: "Not part of the deal, kid. Tell you what, though. Pull out and go down to the parking lot of that dorky restaurant at Westheimer. Catch his license plate. Okay, people. Heads up, here we go."

Within three minutes they were coordinating their moves again.

LI: "Murray. Sorry, I don't know, I guess I missed him somehow."

MURRAY: "Figures."

31.

PAULA SAT IN THE PASSENGER SEAT AND USED A FLASHLIGHT TO locate Valerie Heath's address on the Key Map while Neuman drove, heading south out of the city on the Gulf Freeway toward Galveston. It seemed that Heath and Sheck both lived in the same area on Houston's extreme southeastern edge, a suburban sprawl of several incorporated cities that had grown up around NASA's Johnson Space Center and the shores of Clear Lake which was connected to Galveston Bay and the Gulf of Mexico by a narrow, crooked channel. In recent years Clear Lake had become a burgeoning sport and recreational playground for Houstonians who migrated from the city to the area's numerous yacht clubs, marinas, and restaurants.

Valerie Heath lived on a peninsular development across the lake from two of the larger yacht clubs, not far from the channel that led into Galveston Bay. The peninsula had been scored with canals along either side of which homes had been built with individual docks for each house. The streets in front of the houses ran straight into the mainland.

They found the street Heath lived on, and Neuman slowed to a crawl as they looked at the addresses perfectly stenciled on the curbs in front.

"Jesus," Neuman said as they eased past the spotless lawns, the magnolias and palms and sprays of oleanders. "This isn't the kind of neighborhood I'd expect a couple of hardworking secretaries to be able to afford on sharesies."

"Oh, really?" Paula said. "You would know?"

"Hey, not *this*," Neuman insisted.

"There it is," Paula said, leaning across to peer at a house on Neuman's side of the street. "Miami Vice," she said. It was a modern white stucco affair with a clay tile roof and a tile circular drive. There were palms scattered in front of it, and a sprinkler system was throwing up a mist that floated across the lawn in a shimmering drizzle punctuated by landscaping lights that shot up the trunks of the palms to burst into green sprays at the crowns. The windows were lighted in several rooms of the house.

Neuman went to the end of the block and turned around and came back, parking in front of the house next door.

"Look at that," Neuman said. "We must've had three inches of rain in the last ten days. They've got that damn sprinkler system on automatic, and they just forget about it." He cut the motor. "She drove a what?"

"A Dodge van."

"Well . . . that's not a Dodge van in the driveway," Neuman said. The black Corvette was glistening from the mist that floated out of the green light. "And there's no garage. If they're going to park at this house, they've got to park there."

"Maybe it's the roommate's."

Neuman leaned over and popped open the glove box and started digging around. "How about some light?"

Paula flicked on the flashlight. "What are you doing?"

"I keep some IDs and stuff in here," Neuman said, fumbling through a clutter of maps and envelopes, vitamin bottles and flashlight batteries until he found something in a single-fold leather holder. He put it in his pocket. He undid his tie and grabbed his sport jacket which lay between them. "Come on."

They got out and walked to Heath's driveway, following it up behind the Corvette to avoid the lawn sprinkler.

"This thing is spanking new," Neuman said. He bent down and looked at the small metal dealership logo on the lower left side of the trunk. "Bought it in El Paso."

They went around the car and into a courtyard to the front door. The night air was sticky, coming off Galveston Bay less than three hundred yards behind them. The mumbling of an inboard motor started up somewhere in the canal behind the house, and they could hear people calling to each other, friendly voices, a woman's laughter. The sound of the inboard grew deeper as it began moving along the canal. Neuman rang the doorbell and quickly checked the mailbox, which was empty.

"This is too damn late," Paula objected quickly.

The woman who came to the door looked to be in her early forties. She had dark hair chopped off short and kind of ragged at the neck and was wearing a pale blue terry cloth romper set. She was barefooted and holding a spatula in one hand.

"Valerie Heath?" Neuman asked.

"Yeah." The woman looked at Neuman expectantly and then took in Paula with a quick up-and-down of her eyes.

Neuman held up the ID he had gotten out of the glove box. "I'm Raymond Shiffler and this is my assistant Gail Aldridge. We're with American Universal Life Insurance Group—"

"You gotta be kidding," Heath interrupted him. "You people must be desperate."

She was closing the door, but Neuman's hand stopped it as he said:

"Ms. Aldridge is the woman who called you today about Colleen Synar."

The door stopped, the woman's face went slack, and her eyes returned to Paula. She opened her mouth, but said nothing.

Neuman didn't wait. "Ms. Heath, I'll quickly explain," he said, talking fast. "We are client locators for American Universal. Ms. Synar's father died five weeks ago. He had a thirty-thousand-dollar policy with us and had named Ms. Synar as the beneficiary. Now we've got to find her within the next forty days or so or she forfeits being able to collect. We are obligated by our charter to make every effort to find these beneficiaries, but, frankly, you're the closest we've been able to come to Ms. Synar."

The woman's mouth was hanging open slightly, and she seemed to be trying to decide what to do. The smell of frying food was coming out of the house.

"Do I smell something burning?" Neuman asked.

"Oh, shit." The woman turned, leaving the door open, and fast-walked back into the house.

Neuman looked at Paula. "She's sure as hell not the woman in the photograph on Synar's Contributor ID sheet." He turned back and shouted into the house.

"Can we come in, Ms. Heath? Thank you very much . . ." He looked at Paula again and tilted his head for her to follow. "I really appreciate this," he said, keeping his voice loud so that she would know he was coming in, though he counted on her being too busy to object. "This isn't going to take but just a minute of your time. We're out of the Baltimore office, Ms. Aldridge and I are, but we've been from one side of this country to the other looking for Ms. Synar—"

"Look, just wait a damn minute . . ." the woman was saying. She was standing at the stove frantically taking up whatever it was she was cooking. The stove was behind a bar that looked out into a family room at the end of a broad entrance hall through which they had just walked. Neuman and Paula were standing in the middle of the room looking at her across the bar. In the brighter light of the kitchen Neuman could see that Valerie Heath's hair was an unnatural pitch black and though he still guessed her to be in her early forties, he could see now that they must have been a hard forty years.

Neuman quickly assessed the contents of the house. The place didn't look as if it was occupied on a regular basis. There were only a couple of pictures on the walls, generic seascapes, and only the bare minimum of furniture. The bar behind which Valerie Heath was trying to rescue her food was bare, no personal items such as a few favorite seashells or goofy ceramic knickknacks or photographs of people or pets. The house looked like it was a time-share property and no one ever lived there long enough to really make it feel like a home.

Valerie Heath finally got the stove under control with a good deal of banging and flinging, and then she came around the counter where they were standing in the middle of the room. Smoke was filling the kitchen, and she marched over to a glass wall and pulled apart double sliding glass doors to open the family room to a stone patio and the canal. There were a lot of banana plants and potted palms and the glimmering lights of other houses across the narrow canal. A cabin cruiser was docked immediately across from them.

"Now listen to me," she said, turning away from the doors and planting herself in front of them, hands on her hips. The terry cloth romper had seen better days. It was stretched out of shape, and its elastic top, having been hoisted up many times too many over her pendulous, sun-speckled bosoms, was oozing down with each flounce of her body. "I don't know a goddamned thing about . . . Colleen Synar," she blurted, one hand flying up from her hip to poke around in her matte black hair before going back to her hip. "I've told her"—she nodded at Paula—"all I know about it . . . her . . . Synar."

"Ms. Heath"—Neuman twisted his head around, stretching his neck as if it was stiff—"if you could give us just five minutes . . ." He let his shoulders slump. "We've been working night and day on this; I mean, that's why we're here so late. We're under the gun on the dead-line on this thing. If we don't put an all-out effort into this it could look bad, you know, like American Universal didn't *try* to find the beneficiary so we wouldn't have to pay out the indemnity."

Valerie Heath stood in front of them and studied them. She was practically devoid of eyelashes, which made her common brown eyes smaller in a face otherwise dominated by generous features, a rather wide mouth—with a tender-looking fever blister in its right corner—heavy cheekbones, and a nose that was somehow masculine in its pro-portions. Her skin had forfeited a lot of its resiliency and whatever beauty it might have had to the unforgiving Texas coastal sun. She was angry and didn't try to hide it, but Neuman knew that she had to be curious too. Pissed and curious.

"Five minutes," she snapped.

"I appreciate this, Ms. Heath," Neuman said quickly as he guided Paula around a coffee table strewn with magazines and newspapers to a sofa against the wall facing the kitchen. "I really, really do." They sat down.

Valerie Heath reached down and snatched a pack of cigarettes off the coffee table and lighted the cigarette with a little sports car. When you mashed the trunk, the hood flew up to reveal the wick and flame.

She turned and got a chair from a chrome-and-glass table near the bar. The shorts of her jumpsuit were slightly soiled on the seat, old stains that would no longer wash out, and the limp legs of the mis-shapen shorts revealed too much of how she was put together in that region, more than she would have wanted anyone to see. But that was the furthest thing from her mind at the moment. As she sat down in the chair facing them across the coffee table, she was not only pissed and curious, she was nervous. She dragged on the cigarette and then held it aloft in her right hand, her elbow resting on her other forearm which lay across her stomach. Neuman noticed her fingernails were short, the dull red polish flaking off. She periodically puckered the side of her mouth that had the fever blister. The lady was tense.

"How long did Ms. Synar live with you?" Neuman asked quickly, getting right to it, making every effort to accommodate her obvious wish for him to get the hell out as soon as possible.

"Two years."

"Even?"

"What?" She glared at him.

"Two years even?"

"Yeah," she said acidly, daring him to challenge the fact. "Even."

"Ms. Aldridge checked Los Angeles and New York," Neuman said. "There aren't any Synars there."

Valerie Heath glanced at Paula and shrugged. Not her problem.

"Where did she work when she was living with you?" Neuman had his notebook out and was pretending to take notes, his arms on his knees as he sat forward and read from the notebook on the coffee table.

"You don't know where she was working?"

"On our policy forms," Neuman said, sighing hugely and pretending an impatient weariness at having to back up and bring her up to speed, "our policy holders are asked to list their beneficiaries' name, address, place of employment, date of birth, and Social Security number. Now, since this policy was taken out nearly eight years ago, and had not been updated—people never update them, they should, but they never do—everything on it was stale except her date of birth and Social Security number. Okay? So we had to start from scratch. In the past couple of weeks we've come this far, right here to you. And you say you haven't seen her in almost two years. If I knew where she was working at the time maybe there would be someone there who was close to her and would know more about where she might be or maybe they're even still in touch with her."

Valerie Heath studied him. She had crossed one leg over the other and was swinging it gingerly, the cellulite dimpling the lower sides of her weathered thighs. If Neuman had guessed right, she was one hell of a confused woman right now, and he didn't think she was having any luck puzzling through it.

"And you traced her to here," she said stiffly, slapping the cigarette in her mouth and sucking on it.

Neuman nodded his head slowly.

She glared at him, her eyes flat with anger.

"You told Ms. Aldridge that you had another woman living with the two of you at that time," Neuman said. "Is she still with you?"

"No."

"Where is she?"

"She's moved."

"Oh. Well, do you know where she moved to? Maybe she knew where Ms. Synar went after she left here."

"I don't know where she is."

Neuman nodded. "What was her name?"

This last question seemed to bring Valerie Heath to the boiling point.

"Look, goddamn it, I don't know you from Adam," she said. "You just walk in here . . ." She was shaking her head in frustration. "Let me see that ID again."

"Oh, sure," Neuman said, and he took it out of his pocket once more, stood, and leaned across the coffee table to hand it to her. This time she actually read the card which, of course, she hadn't done when Neuman first showed it to her. Moving it away from her until it came into focus at about arm's length, she concentrated on the words though her hand was shaking so badly Neuman couldn't imagine how she could read it. As she squinted at the ID, Neuman nudged Paula with his knee and tapped the mailing label on one of the magazines lying upside down on the coffee table.

After studying the card a moment, Valerie Heath gestured at Neuman with it though she didn't get up. Neuman stood again and took it back.

"I'm going to check you out, mister," Valerie Heath threatened, her lips quivering with emotion. "Tomorrow I'm calling . . . I'm checking you out, mister. I'm not going to answer any more questions."

"Ms. Heath," Neuman said slowly. "Please, I can assure you . . ."

Valerie Heath jumped to her feet, almost losing her romper top which she quickly retrieved, yanking up on the sides.

"Get the hell out of here," she said. She was trembling, her eyes blinking furiously, her anger tinged with something besides antagonism.

Neuman and Paula stood, and Neuman started to say something else, but Valerie Heath beat him to it.

"Get out of here!" She stretched a leathery arm toward the front door, a trail of cigarette ashes following the arc of her gesture.

"Look, I apologize if I offended you"—Neuman was keeping up the patter all the way to the door—"but I had to ask these questions. I mean, this is just part of the job. It's what we have to do if we're going to help . . ."

They were outside, and Valerie Heath slammed the door behind them.

"Jesus," Paula gasped as they walked out through the courtyard. "I thought she was going to start hitting you. I really thought she was going to."

"You were a lot of help in there, Paula," Neuman said, grinning at her.

"Next time, hotshot, why don't you let me in on the game plan and you might *get* some help. What did you expect me to do?"

They walked back along the drive through the drifting mist of the sprinkler system which was still hissing.

"What was your impression?" Neuman asked as they got into the car.

"Well, for starters, it was a total washout. She didn't give us one ounce of information we didn't already know."

"Yeah, but what was your impression about how she reacted to the whole thing about Colleen Synar?"

Paula thought a second. "Frightened. Yeah, she seemed scared, actually. And confused."

"Yeah, I thought so too," Neuman said, starting up the car. "And I noticed she didn't threaten to call the cops if we didn't get out." He turned on the headlights and drove past the house. When he got to the intersection where the street entered the mainland, he made a U-turn and started back.

"What's the deal?" Paula said. "You're not going to go back there . . ."

"Just wait a second," he said. He cut his headlights just before reaching the house again and glided past, doubling back at the end of the street. He pulled to the curb and parked behind one of several cars between him and Valerie Heath's. He cut the motor.

"I think we really rattled her cage," Neuman said. "You saw the name on the magazine subscription label?"

"Irene Whaley."

Neuman picked up the radio and called in the license plate on the Corvette. Paula rolled down her window and flapped the top of her dress for air. The night had grown sultry and with the dead air came an occasional waft of strong harbor odors. When the call came back on the car they both listened. It belonged to Frances Rupp, same address.

Paula looked at Neuman. "What the hell's going on?"

Neuman shook his head, watching the house. "I do not know." And then: "Okay, here we go."

Valerie Heath came out of the front courtyard gates in a hurry. She was still wearing her less than wonderful romper, still smoking furiously, and she was carrying a purse with a shoulder strap. They heard the chirrup of the security system on the car as she hit the disarm button on her key chain, and in a matter of moments she was in the car and was pulling out of the driveway.

"We're going to follow her?" Paula asked.

They watched her taillights grow smaller and smaller.

"You'd better move it, Casey. She's—"

"I'm not going to follow her," Neuman said, taking off his tie and jacket and tossing them in the back seat. He rolled up the sleeves of his shirt. "I'm going to go around to the back of her place and get her trash. Watch for me at the left front corner of the house. When you see me, pull up into the driveway."

32

THEY PULLED OFF THE GULF FREEWAY WHEN THEY WERE WELL OUT of the subdivisions around Clear Lake, and Houston was still just a glow on the night horizon. Neuman drove down the access road until he came to a dirt track that seemed to lead to nothing but darkness through miles of the flat coastal plain. He turned off and drove a hundred yards or so until the uneven ruts dropped slightly, and the tall clumps of plume and muhly grass hid them from the highway.

"Okay," Neuman said, cutting the motor. "If you'll hold the flashlight, I'll do the shit work."

"No argument from me, but why don't we just shine the headlights on it?"

"Because this is going to take a few minutes, and I don't want anybody seeing us and deciding to drive out here to see what it is we're doing."

They got out of the car and Neuman opened the trunk and took out two large plastic bags of garbage and set them beside the road. He took a pair of surgical gloves from a box of them that he kept in the trunk, pulled them on, and walked over to the plastic bags.

"If this doesn't pay off, I'm going to be pissed," he said. He bent down and tore open the first bag and began dumping everything out in one of the sandy ruts of the road, walking backward as he shook out the contents of the sack. The hot humid days had steamed everything in the sacks, and the odor was horrendous. Paula held her nose and quickly found the downwind side of the refuse. Taking a step or two into the tall grass, Neuman came back with a stick, straddled the string of garbage, bent down, and set to work.

There was a soft breeze coming across the grasses from the coast, but it was warm and gummy and there was not enough of it to carry away the stench of what Neuman was stirring around with his stick.

But more important it wasn't enough to blow away the host of mosquitoes that quickly found them. The spring rains had provided these insects with enough pools and puddles and mud holes to multiply themselves into numbers that approached plague proportions and within minutes they were swarming as thick as a fog. Paula swatted at them furiously and swore and fidgeted while Neuman inched his way along the rope of garbage. After ten minutes of this Neuman stopped and looked up.

"Paula, if you don't hold the damn light still I can't do this," he said, his voice rising slightly.

"We've just got to figure out something else. This is *not* going to work." She was writhing. "They are *eating* me!"

"You wearing a slip?" he asked.

"Yeah . . ."

"Squat down, pull the slip down over your legs, pull the dress up over your head, stick the flashlight out of a hole, and KEEP IT STILL!"

While Neuman waited, Paula did as she was told, taking a few minutes to arrange herself in the manner Neuman had described, squatting in the grassy median between the two sandy ruts and finally managing to get the flashlight through a hole near her face and guide the beam onto Valerie Heath's garbage.

"Beautiful," Neuman said, and returned to perusing his cache, flicking at pieces of paper with his stick. Now and then he would pick up something crumpled and unfold it or pry sticky things apart from one another or pull wadded pieces of paper from cans or waxed cartons. If it was something with printing on it, he picked it up and looked at it; if it was something he couldn't identify, he picked it up and looked at it. Not wanting to use his hands to swat at the insects, every few moments he would duck his head and wipe at the mosquitoes on his face with his shirtsleeves. Neither of them spoke. They just wanted to get it over with as quickly as possible.

As trucks whined by on the highway, Neuman gathered up a little pile of papers he had salvaged from the debris of the first bag and put them in the trunk of the car. Then he went to the second bag, ripped it open, and strung out its contents a little way from the first line of garbage.

"This is actually going pretty damn good," he said, picking up his stick and waiting for Paula to rearrange herself near the second line of garbage.

"Aren't the mosquitoes killing you?" she said from under her dress.
"Not that bad," he said. "Come on."

She focused the beam of the flashlight on the new row of refuse in the road, and Neuman started the process all over again.

It seemed like an hour, but it was only a little over twenty minutes from the time they got out of the car until Neuman said, "That's it." Paula stood quickly and pulled down her dress and held the flashlight while Neuman hurriedly collected his latest bits of salvage from the strewn garbage and took it to the opened trunk of the car where he put them with the others in a plastic evidence bag. He peeled off the surgical gloves and threw them down, grabbed another pair, slammed the trunk, and both of them ran around to opposite sides of the car, got in, and slammed the doors.

"This was a take," Neuman said enthusiastically. "I think we've got some stuff here, some good stuff."

"Jesus, I hope so." Paula was running her fingers through her hair which was disheveled from pulling her skirt over her head. "I don't *believe* those goddamn things out there," she snapped. She picked up the pair of latex gloves and pulled them on. "Let me see the bag," she said.

Neuman handed it to her as Paula opened the glove box, turned on the flashlight again, and laid it on the open glove box door. Neuman picked up his notebook and took a ballpoint out of his shirt pocket.

Paula carefully picked the first item out of the bag and leaned over and held it under the flashlight beam.

"Okay, we'll begin with the biggest pieces, the envelopes, three of them. One: from Gulfstream National Bank and Trust. Looks like maybe bank statements came in it. You know, a little window in it, so we don't know who's the addressee. Two: from Secure Maintenance Services, but this thing wasn't mailed. Uh, the name 'Doris W.' written in ballpoint on the front. Maybe she brought something home in it."

"Then shouldn't her name be on the envelope? You think she works there?"

"In the office, maybe. Casey," she said, dropping her hand in her lap and straightening up, "I'm melting. Since we can't roll down the window because of the damn mosquitoes, can we at least turn on the air conditioner?"

Neuman started the car, put the air conditioner on high and picked up his pen again.

Paula continued. "Three: from Excell Executive Secretarial Services, 'Olivia M.' written in pencil on the outside."

"Same handwriting?"

"Doesn't look like it."

Neuman nodded, writing.

"Okay," Paula continued. "Receipts." She slapped a mosquito on her arm. "Some of those little bastards are in this car." She scratched the bite vigorously. "One: from the Total Detailing, a car wash, one of those places that does everything that can be done to your car plus some more, over on Bay Area Boulevard."

"Gotta keep that 'Vette lookin' good," Neuman said.

"Yeah. Two: this one from—oh, you'll like this, Casey—Victoria's Secret in Baybrook Mall."

"Great. What'd she get?" Neuman asked, still writing.

"Four pairs of Chancery Lace bras and matching panties in champagne and toasted almond . . ."

"What?"

"Champagne and toasted almond, those are the colors."

"Whoa, no red and black?" He squashed a mosquito on his notepad.

"And some other stuff . . ." Paula said, setting it aside and going on to the next item. "This is a . . . lawn maintenance receipt. Next one is a . . ."

They went through the rest of the bits of paper which included receipts from a pharmacy, a laundry, a liquor store, and a grocery, and several sheets from a notepad with doodles on them including three different telephone numbers, and the name "Don C." which had been so decoratively embellished—perhaps during a telephone conversation—that it was difficult to decipher.

"And that's it," Paula said, putting the last scrap of paper into the plastic bag. She was scratching her arm. "Let's get the hell out of here."

"We'd better call Graver."

"I'll call him on the way in. Let's go."

"You want to run by Sheck's first?"

"What!" Paula looked at her watch with her flashlight. "Are you going to . . . ? It's after one o'clock, for God's sake. No way. I'm exhausted, really, really tired."

"Yeah, but I'd like to know if the lovely Ms. Heath went over there. It's just right there," he said, gesturing back toward the highway, "Nassau Bay . . ."

"I know where it is, Casey . . ."

"Okay, okay." Neuman slapped at a mosquito near his ear, put the car in reverse, and turned around with his right arm on the back of the seat.

"Wait, what about the garbage?" Paula asked.

Neuman looked at her, nonplussed. "I recycle at home—newspapers, green glass, clear glass, and cans. I don't buy plastic unless I have to. I go with a girl who takes her own canvas bag to the supermarket. My conscience is clean."

He turned around again, gunned the motor, and plowed back over Valerie Heath's trash and didn't slow down until he got all the way to the access road where he whipped the car around, threw it in drive, and roared onto the pavement.

"Roll down the windows," he said, cranking his handle as fast as he could. "We'll blow the little shits out of here."

Which they did, all the way back into the city.

"Well, we caught the meeting," Arnette said.

Graver had answered the telephone on the first ring. He had just spoken with Paula on the radio, had learned what they had done, and that they were on their way in. But they weren't coming back to the office. Neuman was going to drop Paula off at her car in the parking lot. They would have an early meeting in the morning.

"What happened?" he asked.

"He met one person, a man in his late fifties, early sixties. I'm relatively sure we got good photographs, but I'm afraid the audio is a very iffy prospect."

"Why? What's the matter?"

"They met at the Transco Tower park and walked straight to the fountain. Stood right in the cup of the waterfall and had a nice thirty-two-minute conversation."

"I'll be damned."

"Yeah. No dummies. Not only that, Burtell took my people on one hell of a road trip. The man's definitely got a technique."

"I guess that doesn't surprise me. Where is he now?"

"Looks like he's going back home. They're still on the streets, but that seems to be what he's doing."

"Were you able to get the taps in place?"

"Yes, but only after he left for his meeting. I've had to pull a lot of people in for this. The logistics haven't been easy."

"Okay, fine. I appreciate it."

"That's pretty weird about Besom," she said. "You sure they're going to do another autopsy?"

"That's what I was told."

"What do you think?"

"What the hell am I supposed to think? As a coincidence, the two deaths are pretty hard to buy, but every time I let my mind dwell on the alternatives . . . well, what I come up with is just as outrageous."

Arnette didn't speak for a moment and then she said:

"Marcus, listen to me. Trying to understand what the bad guys of this world are doing is like gazing at the stars. By the time you see their light it's all over, it's past tense, and they've long since gone on to something else. All you're left with is the evidence of what they were doing a million years ago. You can't wait for all the facts to come in to start figuring things out, baby. You've got to use your imagination if you want to get a jump on the physics of iniquity." She paused again. "Believe me, anything you can dream up, no matter how outrageous, is already happening. The thing is, most people won't figure that out for a long time to come. And that's exactly what the bastards are counting on."

Now it was Graver's turn to be silent, and when he finally spoke all he could think to say was, "When can I see the pictures?"

"You want to come over here early in the morning?"

"What time?"

"Seven-thirty."

"I'll be there."

33

"IT CAN'T BE VERY MUCH OF AN INSURANCE COMPANY," SHE said, throwing her fourth cigarette into the water. They were sitting on the dock of one of the marinas, their legs hanging over the side above the water, looking across the bay at one of the yacht basins, the strings of lights draped across the masts of the sailboats, the slightly different colored lights strung along the basin's docks. "I called 800 information, and it wasn't listed. Can't be *much* of a company."

She picked up the pack of cigarettes beside her and took out another one.

"Here, give me one of those damn things," he said. He hated seeing her like this. It only meant more trouble for him, every time.

"I think they were *cops*," she said, blowing smoke away into the soft breeze.

"Just because it was about Synar?"

" 'Just' because?" She turned and looked at him. He was only wearing jeans, no shirt, no shoes. She had called the service they used, and he had called her right back. She figured she had gotten him out of bed. She would rather have gotten him *into* bed. She guessed he just threw on his jeans and came like that. "I hardly remembered the god-damn name the first time she called. Then finally I did."

He smoked. "These are nasty little things," he said, holding the cigarette up and looking at it in the gloaming darkness. "This is one of those ladies' brands isn't it? Little thin things."

"Jesus!" She was exasperated. Don was always calm. He was so macho. Some guys acted macho, wore it like they wore their cologne, put it on just before going out and then washed it off in the shower afterward. But Don never acted anything. He *was* macho and never even seemed to notice it, which was like catnip to women like her. He was one of those guys who always knew just what to do in every situation. It had something to do with survival instincts, or something primitive like that, that had gotten bred out of most modern men, the suburban Happy Hour kind of guys. Don C. was always going to take care of himself; he knew exactly how to do it without even thinking. And he could take care of other people, too, if he wanted to.

"You sure you didn't tell them anything?" he asked.

"Not a damn thing."

He smoked the cigarette, slumped on the edge of the pier, swinging his feet a little. He could hear the basso moan of one of the big ships standing off in the bay. Jesus, he liked hearing those ships.

"If they were cops, I guess I don't understand what they were doing looking for Synar," he said. The Probst case was closed down over a year ago. What was happening here?

"What if there *is* a real Colleen Synar?"

"Naw," Don said. Faeber's people were supposed to have taken care of that. Now he wondered if they had. That greasy Greek was going to have to hear about this.

Don scratched the hair on his stomach with a thumb. She looked at him. Here he was, his wavy hair kind of wild from being in bed—she guessed he had just run his fingers through it—and even slumped as he was, unconcerned about how he looked, she could see the rows of muscles in his stomach, the lumpy divisions of the different muscles in his arms and shoulders, swinging his feet like a kid. It made her wet just sitting by him.

"Well," he said, "don't get too worked up about it. If they come back—and I don't think they will—but if they do, just stick with your story. There's nothing they can do about that, no way you can get in trouble, as long as you don't go making up any more than you've already told them. Hell, you can't be expected to know any more than that. Just stick to your story."

That was kind of smoothing it over, but there was no need in getting her worked up about all the what-if's in this situation.

Heath didn't know anything about the arrangements with the police department or anything about that whole operation, or that it even existed. All he had told her back then was that if anybody ever called looking for a Colleen Synar that she was supposed to tell them exactly what she apparently told them. On the other hand, it was decided that they would use *his* real name. The Greek told him they had it one hundred percent covered but, if for some unforeseen eventuality they had to have a real person to prove there was flesh and blood behind the information, then they wanted him to cover. He was good at that and could handle it. Of course, he got a bonus for allowing them to use his name for this "remote risk." A one-time chunk. Now it looked like that unforeseen eventuality had happened. He was going to have to think about this real hard. It was time to talk to that goddamn Greek. If he didn't know what was going on here, he'd better get his greasy ass in gear and find out. If he did know what was going on, then old Don C. wanted to know why he hadn't been warned.

"I'm not responsible for her not being a real person," Heath said.

"No, hell no," Don sympathized. "Just tell them to piss off." He dropped what was left of the shitty little cigarette between his bare feet into the water.

"Yeah, I don't even have to talk to them."

"Shit, no."

She was quiet for a while, and the water sloshed lazily against the pilings underneath them.

"I tell you what," she said, dropping her own cigarette into the water now, "for a long time I just took the money and didn't think about it. I mean, it's not like it's drugs we're dealing with here. I wasn't going to get busted. And the money's been so damn good, you know, unbelievable. But, I don't know, this now . . ."

"Why, what's the matter?"

He didn't like the sound of this too much. They had worked together a little over two years and everything had been fine. He had never allowed her to learn any more about him than his obviously bogus contact name. She didn't know where he lived or even what he drove. She had always been able to get everything he had requested. She was smart enough to follow the security procedures he had taught her and even smart enough to expand her own little network—the pyramid idea of acquisitions was something she snapped to pretty quick—but she wasn't that little bit smarter that she needed to be to give him any trouble, to be too curious. Or maybe it was just that she was too passive. She had told him one time that her former husband, the guy she had run away from just before he had met her, had knocked her around a lot, sent her to the hospital three times. Don guessed the guy must have beat all the spunk out of her. She was pretty easy to spook.

"Looking back," she said, "if I had it to do over and you asked me to cover for you on this Synar thing, I wouldn't do it."

Sometimes she sounded like a high school kid, he thought.

"I don't guess I can blame you," he said.

"Really?"

She seemed surprised by that, that he would understand. He was looking down at the water, at his white feet in the half light, the water moving under them, back and forth, back and forth around the pilings. He liked the smell of piers, of the way they smelled after years and years of standing in salt water, and people plopping fish up on them and cutting bait on them and spilling beer on them and the sun baking it all and drying it up and always the salt water. You didn't smell that kind of smell, that exact smell, anywhere else in the world except on piers. He had noticed that all the piers in all the countries he had been in smelled the same.

"I can't help but wonder what they do with it," she said.

"What?"

"That stuff we get for them."

He had meant, What did you say, because he had been day-dreaming, but he figured it out.

"Oh." He straightened from his slump and took a deep breath. "I'll tell you, I wouldn't ask myself that question if I was you."

She waited a second. "But I would like to know."

"Well, I don't want to know," he lied. "I just pass it on, take the money, and keep my mouth shut. I'll give you a little insight. The people I pass it on to, you don't want them to know you're asking yourself that question."

"I can guess there's big bucks in it," she said. "They're not going to give the 'little people' like us any percentage in an operation like this, so if I'm making what I'm making . . . and when you figure there's more like us . . ." She shook her head. "I mean . . . God."

He let her dwell on that a moment.

"What you've got to think about, Val, is where you'd be if this hadn't come along for you."

"Why, what do you mean?"

"I mean, that you've got to think about what the hell you'd do if this dried up on you."

"Why have I got to think about that?"

"Because you keep asking yourself questions about what they're doing with the information you give them," he said, his hands flat on the pier on either side of him as he looked down into the water, "and you could find yourself out of this deal quicker'n shit."

This was sobering for her, not only because of the prospect to which he alluded, which she had to admit, was indeed grim, but also because it was a none too thinly disguised threat. If she had learned anything over the two years she had been doing this, it was that someone had done a hell of a job in planning the structure of the "organization." She always paid her people in cash, and she was always paid in cash, even though the money was big. One of the first things Don taught her was how to deposit the stuff in banks without drawing attention, spread it out. She didn't know the real identity of anybody in the whole operation except the people below her whom she had recruited herself. But she had gathered from little snippets here and there in her conversations with Don over the two years that there were maybe half a dozen people like her that Don dealt with, and that maybe there were half a dozen people like Don that the guy above him dealt with. She couldn't even imagine how far it went.

"The thing is," Don said, interrupting her thoughts, "nobody's indispensable. They'll just get somebody else. We just do our business, make our deliveries, take the money, then we get to keep on taking the money. If we cause any trouble, hell, they just don't need trouble, everything dries up. No more Don C. That number you call? It disappears, and I won't exist anymore." Out of the corner of his eye he saw her looking at him again. "All they gotta do is say it, and it happens."

"Hey, Don, I was just wondering," she said defensively. "Hey, I don't care about anything but doing what I do. I don't care at all . . . about anything but just doing that. Just doing my job, that's all I want to do."

"Good," he said. "It's the best money you've ever made, and if this dries up you'll never make this good again, not even selling dope." He swung his legs bigger, sort of indicating a change of pace or subject matter. Not too far out in the bay some kind of craft, a big cabin cruiser, with red and green lights, plowed by and you could hear the frothy sound of the salt water spraying up from the bow and splashing back into itself. "How you like that new 'Vette?"

"How did you know I got a new car?"

"I saw you drive up in it, honey," he said, grinning.

"Oh, yeah," she said, somehow not entirely convinced. "It's great." She tried to brighten up, really wanted him to know she wasn't thinking about the other anymore. "It smells so damn new. I'd like to get a new car every time that smell wears off."

"Hell, you can buy that smell in a little spray can at the car wash," he said.

"Yeah, well I've tried that. It's nothing like the real thing."

"How's it handle?"

"You never driven a Corvette?"

"Nope." He was looking at her, grinning.

"Well, you've been missing something, Donny. It's better'n sex." Pause. "Well, as good as, anyway." Pause. "Nearly."

He laughed and ran his hand through his hair, and the muscles in his bare arm rippled when he did it, and she laughed too. She wished he would lean over and just pull down her top, just pull it down and put his mouth on her, and then she would lie back and he could have her right there on the damn dock. She didn't think there was a sexier man alive than Don C.

That's what she was thinking when he said:

"Okay, we'd better get out of here."

It took her a second to come down out of that imaginary thing that she would let him do.

"Yeah, I guess so," she said.

"You're supposed to have something for me in a couple of days, anyway, right?"

"That's right," she said, putting down one hand to steady herself as she got up. He got up too, and jammed his hands into the pockets of his tight jeans while she fished in her purse for the keys to the Corvette. She always left first. "I'll call you."

"Don't worry about anything," he reassured her. "I don't think they'll be back to see you. I'd even lay a little bet on it."

"You'd better keep your money," she said, finding the keys. She was pretty sobered by his abrupt interruption of her fantasy. "See you later."

She turned and started walking back along the long pier. There were a few people as she got nearer the land, a guy crabbing, a couple sitting on the pier looking out to the bay. When she got to the light where the pier connected to the land, she turned around to look back. He was still there, and though he was a little more obscured by the night she could tell he wasn't looking at her anymore. As a matter of fact, she thought she could see him pissing off the end of the pier.

34.

BY THE TIME PAULA AND NEUMAN HAD CALLED IN—THEIR CALL was closely followed by Arnette's—Graver had read several times through the intelligence reports on Victor Last as well as the crime analysis reports that detailed occurrences of MO's fitting the description of Last's known operations. The exercise was educational. He put a few things in his briefcase, grabbed his coat, reset the security system, turned out the lights, and pulled the door closed behind him.

Riding down in the moaning elevator, he thought of how Besom's death suddenly had galvanized the investigation. None of them, Neuman or Paula or himself, could imagine anything but the worst now. It still felt like he was living a bad dream when he thought of Burtell's role. Even when he spoke to Ginette on the telephone earlier, he felt as if the expression on his face was unnatural. He simply found the whole distorted situation too bizarre to know how to behave. The hardest part now was trying to decide whether Dean was in danger, or whether he *was* the danger. The thought of it ate at Graver like an ulcer.

His consternation was one of the main reasons he was keeping a detailed journal of the developments and of his reasons for his decisions and actions. He hoped that keeping a precise record somehow would help clarify the events. He felt like an alchemist performing rituals he didn't wholly understand in the hope that magic would happen and with the magic would come knowledge and the fine gold of the truth.

This journal remained in the computer in a password file while he kept a printed copy at home. His initial thought had been to keep the copy with him at all times, an impulse that was the emotional equivalent of the fetal position. Later a saner view prevailed, and he decided to keep the second copy at home. If the investigation became increasingly unstable, he would put a third copy in the safety deposit box at his bank. This was a flat-out effort to cover his ass, and even at that he had no idea how something like this would hold up in an inquiry, if it ultimately came to that.

Outside, the night was warm and moist, and the smell of sticky weeds and bayou mud was laced with the pungent odor of the oil-stained asphalt that, even at this late hour, was still radiating an uncomfortable fever. Pausing, he looked toward the city across the bayou, at the high urban sierras of scattered light. He recalled Arnette's observation that trying to anticipate the "bad guys of this world" was like gazing at the stars, by the time you saw the light it was all over. You had to use your imagination, she said, to get the jump on the physics of iniquity.

In her own inimitable way, of course, Arnette had been giving him good advice. Under the circumstances, he was dealing with this entirely too cautiously. In the normal course of events he was used to looking way out in front of the curve, having plenty of time to gather information methodically, to think it through. But this wasn't the normal course of things, and it clearly was looking like a Darwinian lesson: adapt to change or perish. He had better start thinking imaginatively, or this was going to be over before he even knew what it was that had happened.

The pager on his belt vibrated. He pushed back his coattail and looked down at the number. He didn't recognize it. But fewer than a dozen people had his new number, and he would want to talk to any of them. Without hesitating he turned around and walked back into the building to the pay telephone in the lobby. He set his briefcase on the floor, put a quarter in the slot, and dialed the number. It rang only once before someone answered.

"This is Graver."

"Graver, good." Victor Last sounded as controlled as ever, but there was an undercurrent of eagerness in his voice. "I've got something for you. I think you're going to like this. Can you meet me now, at La Cita?"

"Not there," Graver said. "Where are you?"

"I'm rather in the north part of the city," Last said vaguely.

"Okay. There's a little Italian restaurant called La Facezia just off Montrose. Do you know where Renard is?"

"Yeah."

"Okay, it's very near that intersection, on Cerano."

"I'll find it," Last said and hung up.

Graver pressed the lever on the pay phone, dropped another quarter in the slot, and dialed another number. When Lara answered on the third ring, her voice was husky with sleep.

"Lara, this is Graver."

Pause.

"Yes . . . hello . . ."

"I'm sorry to have to wake you, but I need your help for a little while."

"Now?"

"I'm afraid so, yes."

"Yeah, okay, sure." She was still a little fuzzy with sleep. "Uh . . . it'll take me a few minutes to get dressed," she said, sounding more awake now. "What do I wear?"

"Anything. I've got a meeting with someone at a small restaurant. I just want you to watch us from across the street."

"Oh."

"It's no big deal. I just need another pair of eyes."

There was a hesitation as if she were mulling over the questionable veracity of this claim. "Okay, where are you?"

"At the office."

"Okay, I'll be ready when you get here."

"Oh, Lara, bring a fairly good-sized shoulder bag."

He made good time since the traffic was sparse at this hour of night, and when he pulled up to her apartment fifteen minutes later, she was waiting for him at a small gate that led out of the courtyard that her apartment shared with three others. She was wearing a sleeveless summer shirtwaist dress of a dark color, maybe chocolate brown, and her thick hair was combed out, pulled back loosely, and clasped behind her head. She was carrying a shoulder bag which she held with one hand as she reached down to open the car door.

"You're quick," Graver said, as she got in and closed the door.

"Well, Jesus," she said, "once I finally woke up . . . I don't know why it took me so long to clear my head. Sorry."

A hint of fragrance—though not perfume, something softer, the way he imagined her body, her skin, must smell—wafted into the car with her, and as Graver pulled back onto the street she settled into her seat, putting her purse between them and turning slightly toward him, angling her legs.

"I hope this dress is all right," she said. "I thought, God, I shouldn't wear anything with a light color."

"No, that's just fine," Graver said. The dress, of course, fit her perfectly, buttoning up the front, the several topmost buttons left undone, the belted waist snug above her hips. Just having her there beside him relieved some of his exhaustion.

"You've been at the office all this time?" she asked. There was a note of concern in her voice, as if she sensed something important had taken place since she had seen him that afternoon.

"Most of it," Graver said.

"Okay," she said, "what's happened?"

He related chronologically the things that had happened since he had seen her late in the afternoon. He told her of the results of his meeting with Neuman and Paula, about the Feldberg house and its contents, about Paula and Neuman interviewing Valerie Heath, about Burtell being tailed and of Arnette's people getting photographs of his meeting with the unidentified man. The only thing he left out of sequence was Besom's death, and when he told her about it, her reaction was much like Paula's: a gasp of shock and instant suspicion.

She had been looking at him, but at this revelation she turned and looked out the windshield, watching the night go by and, for a few minutes, consulting her own thoughts. Graver would like to have been inside her head at that moment.

"This gets creepier by the hour," she said finally, still looking out the windshield. She had crossed her arms under her breasts. "Of course, you don't believe the heart attack business do you?"

"I don't believe the autopsy tells the whole story."

"God, I guess not. You still think the thing to do is to keep this closed? Just the four of us, and Arnette?"

"That's just about the only thing I am sure of now," Graver said. "I'm doing that right, if nothing else."

"I guess Westrate's all over you?"

"He's beside himself. He knows it's going to look bad, but I keep assuring him nothing's turning up. He smells something, and he's suspicious, but he doesn't know what to do about it except threaten me."

Graver changed lanes. He had been watching his rearview mirror, but he saw nothing to make him suspicious. And if there had been someone there he would have picked them up in the sparse traffic.

"So then you do think Besom was killed."

"I do," he said.

Lara turned to look out the windshield again. "This is scary," she said. "Really, really scary."

"The frightening part is not knowing what the hell lies behind it. Not knowing why. If I knew why, then I think some of the other stuff would fall into place. Motive at least would be an indicator of how they might be thinking."

" 'They'?"

"Whoever the hell 'they' are."

They passed under the Southwest Freeway. Graver was looking at everything, the side streets, the parking lots of restaurants, service stations, but trying not to let Lara see what he was doing. Suddenly he was seeing something suspicious in everything. Everything seemed to be a collusion between a car he had seen five blocks ago and the one he was approaching down the street, or the one parked on a side street with the one parked in the shadow of a service station.

"What is it you want me to do?" she asked, shifting in her seat. "You want me to sit in the car during this meeting, is that it?"

"No, not in the car," he said, pulling his mind back to the moment. "I've got to meet a man named Victor Last. Last was an informant for me years ago when I was still an investigator. He was a good source, productive, but I haven't seen him or heard from him in about eight years. Then late Sunday night, after the ordeal with Tisler was over, after Westrate had finally left the house, Last called me. Sometimes informants do that, years later. If you've had a good relationship with them, they crop up, get in touch with you. Since his call I've met with him twice. I met him at a tavern Sunday night, and then last night he showed up at my house."

"At your house? Christ. You didn't know he was going to be there?"

Graver shook his head. "No. And he's an intelligent man; he knew better than that. The fact that he did it anyway worries me. He never would have done it in the past. Last claims to have 'accidentally' come across some information about a security breach somewhere in the police department. Thinks it might have been in the CID. But he was vague about the details. Now, I think, he wants to give me a little more information."

"But you don't trust him so much now," Lara said.

"That's right. Though maybe I should. I just find it hard to believe he happens to be at the right place at the right time."

They were driving south on Montrose. There were only a few cars on the streets, and though there was no threat of rain, the humidity was high enough to make faint, hazy orbs around the streetlamps.

"So, what is it you want me to do?" Lara asked.

"I'm meeting this guy at a small restaurant called La Facezia?"

"In the museum district? Yeah, I know that place."

"All I want to know is whether there's someone watching us. Normally that would be a tricky thing to do. I mean, it's a countersurveillance job. But there's an odd intersection there that gives us an edge. Three streets come together, roughly in the shape of the letter "K," forming three corners. La Facezia sits on the bottom corner. There's another corner to the right, with a residence behind a high wall. Directly across from the restaurant, on the third corner, there's an old brick apartment building. Two floors. There's no security system. Front door's always open."

His right hand left the steering wheel, and he picked up a pair of binoculars that had been sitting beside him next to her purse. He handed them to her.

"I think they'll fit in your bag," he said. "They're night-vision binoculars. Everything will look greenish through them, but you'll get used to it."

She took the glasses and held them up to the window and looked outside.

"I'm going to drop you off about a block from the restaurant. I'll watch you from down the street, make sure you get to the building safely. I want you to go up the stairs. On the second floor, opposite the landing, there's a window that overlooks the intersection. You'll have a clear view of the entrance of the restaurant and the sidewalk tables. You should also be able to see all three streets for quite a ways."

"What do I look for?" she asked, putting the binoculars into her purse.

"Anybody hanging around, in cars maybe. Make a note—you have a steno pad?—of the kinds of cars you see, get license numbers if you can. Just be observant."

"And what if somebody comes out of one of the apartments, wants to know what I'm doing?"

"Just flash your CID photo identification. Give them some bullshit about 'security' and 'criminal intelligence.'"

She was quiet. He glanced at her as he slowed for the intersection of Main and the Mecom fountains.

"Are you okay with this?" he asked.

"Yeah, I'm up for it," she said, taking a deep breath and looking at him.

"But . . . ?"

"No 'buts' . . . It's just . . . Well," she said, raising her eyebrows in subdued surprise, "me doing this, this really is on the edge, isn't it? I mean, it's kind of like coming in on a wing and a prayer, isn't it?"

"That's right," Graver said, turning onto the heavily wooded Cerano Street. "That's exactly what it is."

35

GRAVER HAD BEEN GOING TO LA FACEZIA FOR YEARS, EVER SINCE the owner's daughter had provided him with information on a protection racket in the Oriental restaurant business where her boyfriend's parents owned several establishments. The restaurant was in an old stone building that sat on a neighborhood corner where three quiet, tree-shaded streets came to an intersection.

The restaurant had three faces which opened onto the intersection, and which accommodated an arbor-covered sidewalk with small bistro tables at which they served wine and coffee, but not meals, until one o'clock in the morning. Meals were served until ten-thirty, but only in the large interior dining room that was accessible through French doors that opened to each of the three faces of the arbored sidewalk. There were many other restaurants in this Left Bank-ish neighborhood of antique shops and bars near the museum district that was known as Houston's "art community," but only this one was so distinctive that when Graver sat down at one of its tables with a newspaper and a cup of coffee, he almost could forget he was in an American city. It was a family restaurant. There was no music, only the low murmur of conversations and the clinking of tableware and glasses. The chic and trendy crowd went elsewhere, places where there was more "atmosphere." Graver considered it a paradise, and since Dore had left he had gotten in the habit of eating here sometimes twice a week in the evenings when he didn't want to be alone. He would bring a book, get a table near one of the doors that opened onto the sidewalk, and settle in for a two-hour dinner.

Now, though, he took a table on the sidewalk next to one of the stone walls covered in a felt of fig vine. This would afford them some measure of privacy, though only a few other tables were occupied. He ordered a cup of coffee from one of the owner's several nieces who waited tables and settled back.

He didn't have to wait long. Ten minutes later Last came sauntering around the corner and stepped under the arbor and joined Graver at his table. He ran his fingers through his long hair and smiled.

"You're always surprising me, Graver," Last said, looking around, nodding approvingly. "This is a real find, a very nice place indeed." He looked at Graver. "I'll bet you this is your 'usual' place, isn't it?"

"I come here sometimes," Graver said. The girl came and took Last's order for wine. "What have you got for me, Victor?"

Last sat back in his chair and pulled out a pack of cigarettes. As he lit one, he looked casually around the sidewalk tables and then inside the nearby French doors at the empty dining room. He was wearing an expensive-looking linen sport coat with small brown and beige checks and a solid nut-brown silk shirt buttoned at the neck.

"Well, this did not turn out to be as, uh, easy to do as I'd thought," Last said, his voice softening. "But I have a name for you. Your 'mole,' as it were." He stopped as the girl brought his wine, thanked her, watched her go to another table, appreciating her hips, maybe even taking his time in order to whet Graver's curiosity. He turned to Graver. "Arthur Tisler." He lifted his wine, grinned, and took a long drink.

Graver could hardly contain himself. Goddamn it!

"Can you elaborate?"

"Not much," Last said, sucking on his cigarette. "I just heard he was selling information from your intelligence records."

Graver was almost beside himself. Victor Last was sitting across from him telling him that Arthur Tisler was selling information. For the past twenty-four hours he had agonized about this and, even with all the progress they had made, the breach in security was still a matter of conjecture. The only thing they knew for sure was that Tisler, Burtell, and Besom were creating bogus contributor interviews. The rest they had to guess. Now Last had laid it in his lap. And if Last could be believed, it was coming from a completely independent source.

But Last had delivered this astonishing information in a very relaxed manner, and Graver had the suspicion that Last did not understand the full impact of what he had just said. The information might have been parceled out to him. Graver did not believe that Last would have been so comfortable about giving this kind of volatile news to Graver if he had known what lay behind it.

"Arthur Tisler," Graver said.

Last nodded, appreciating what he must have thought was a shocking revelation to Graver.

"How did you get that name, Victor?"

There must have been something in Graver's voice. Last shot a look at him, his eyes regarding Graver with new interest, in a manner that sought an explanation for whatever it was he had heard that alerted him.

"What's the matter?" Last asked.

"Arthur Tisler's dead," Graver said.

"Wh-at?"

"You didn't know that?" Graver didn't even know why he asked that question. Sometimes when you were talking to a man like Last there was a point at which you might find yourself wondering exactly where you were in the game. The whole point of the exercise was to learn something you didn't already know, or to corroborate something you already had learned from someone else. Likewise, you later would take what you learned from this informant and try to corroborate it with another. You asked questions the answers to which you already knew, though you pretended you didn't. You asked questions pretending to believe the responses, though you probably didn't. You tried to discern the informant's hidden agenda, though he already had given you his reasons for what he was doing. You didn't give the informant new information. You didn't trade information. You fished and bobbed in deceptive currents, and you tried to discern the particles of truth suspended in the lies and half lies, and you tried not to overlook an actual truth when you stumbled upon it. You imagined a world of mistakes and tried to anticipate how you would explain why you did, or why you didn't, do something some other way. You imagined yourself coming. You imagined yourself going.

"Hell no, I didn't know." Last was frowning. He *didn't* know. "Dead when? A year ago or yesterday or what?"

Graver hesitated. It had been in the paper. It wouldn't matter.

"He killed himself Sunday night."

Last straightened his shoulders in surprise. He studied Graver, slowly bringing his glass to his mouth, sipping the wine to cover his uneasiness, keeping his eyes on Graver over the rim.

"Killed himself," he said, suspicious of that explanation.

"That's right."

"Was he dirty?"

"I didn't think so. But now you're telling me he was."

Graver could see Last thinking. He was going to hold on to it.

"Well, yeah, that's what I heard." He paused. "Maybe that's why he killed himself."

"Could be. What kind of information?"

"What?"

"What kind of information was he selling?"

Last was thinking again. He straightened up in his chair and leaned forward over the small table.

"You didn't know any of this?" he asked.

"You seem surprised." Graver was finding this a very slippery conversation. "Did you think you were telling me something I already knew? Did you think that was going to be helpful?"

"I thought I might be *corroborating.*" Last was indeed an old hand at this. He knew all the roles. And apparently he hadn't believed Graver the previous evening when Graver had said there was no breach in CID security. "I don't think I'm understanding what's going on here," he said.

He was decidedly uncomfortable. Which was fine with Graver. He was pretty damned uneasy himself.

"Is this it, then?" Graver asked. "Tisler was selling CID information, and that's it?"

Last didn't say anything. He sipped his wine and smoked his cigarette, once again slumped back in his chair. It was apparent he had been given good information, but maybe for the wrong reasons, which seemed to be Last's concern. Graver wanted desperately to know what Last had stumbled onto, and he was trying to decide how to get information without giving away any more than he had to. As Graver sat looking at his only direct link to an independent source who obviously knew invaluable information, he began to wonder if he was up to the opportunity. He began to wonder if there weren't extenuating circumstances.

Last straightened up in his chair, leaned his elbows on the table, and smiled uneasily.

"This is awkward, isn't it," he said. His voice was soft, soothing.

"Not for me," Graver lied.

"Well, I'm not at all sure . . . I mean, I thought you already knew this."

"You've said that, Victor."

"Yeah." Last looked away, his right hand on the stem of the wineglass as he turned the flat base of it on the surface of the table, the uncomfortable smile giving an enigmatic expression to his profile. "Okay, there's somebody else, too, in CID."

Graver waited. This was going to be telling.

Last looked back to Graver. "Guy named Besom."

Graver thought so. Three men involved, as far as Graver knew, and Last had named the only two who were dead. Last was giving him leads to nowhere. The question was, did he realize that? Last was looking at him closely, hoping to learn something himself from Graver's reaction.

Graver sipped his coffee, put down his cup, and leveled his eyes at Last.

"Before I react to that," Graver said, "I want you to tell me, right now, if you have any other names. Don't dribble them out to me, Victor. This is internal. I'm not inclined to joust with you over internal matters that affect the security of my Division."

A pause as Last stared into Graver's eyes and made quick mental calculations that Graver could only imagine.

"No. No other names," he said. He was almost squinting at Graver, puzzled, maybe a little apprehensive. Graver had the feeling Last didn't know what it was he had gotten into and was wondering if he had made a big mistake.

"Okay," Graver said. "The man you are referring to is Ray Besom. He's the supervisor of the Organized Crime Squad. He's been on vacation, fishing down on the border, near Port Isabel. About noon today he was found dead."

"Bloody hell . . ." Last swallowed; his face was rigid. It conveyed no self-assurance, no easy smile that connoted a smug knowledge that he was one step ahead of developing events. Graver guessed that not only was Last not ahead of developing events, but it was now beginning to dawn on him that maybe he was being used for reasons that had been hidden from him and which might have put him at great risk.

"Christ, and you people weren't suspicious?"

"I didn't say that. I only said we didn't know we had a breach in security." Graver paused and gave Last a moment to run over his options once again. He watched Last take another drink of wine and savor it, tasting it with the back of his tongue. "I don't have much room to maneuver, here, Victor."

Last looked at Graver as though he wanted to see if he could read in Graver's eyes what he thought he was reading in the inflection of his voice.

"I see," Last said, nodding a little. "Well, that's pretty clear, isn't it."

Graver said nothing.

Last looked around at the other tables under the arbor. It wasn't as if he was concerned about being overheard, rather it was more a gesture of restlessness. Again he picked up on the hips of the waitress and watched her bring coffee to a couple of girls who had just sat down at a table nearest the street. Watching the girl walk back into the deserted dining room, his prematurely old eyes followed her with the practiced imagination of a decadent. When she was out of sight, he looked into his glass. He swirled the wine.

"Fellow I met in Veracruz," Last said softly, speaking slowly and thoughtfully, "and at whose house I overheard the conversation, is Colin Faeber. He owns a computer company called DataPrint. I don't know much about the company, I mean, what it does, compiles data for businesses looking to buy other businesses or something like that. I checked it out a bit, though, you know, to see if the guy had a heavy purse. He does." He sipped his wine.

"But you don't know the names of the men you overheard talking?"

"No, I don't. And I don't know of any way to find out without raising immediate suspicion. I mean, I can't just ask Faeber outright, can I. And I didn't see them well enough to make some circumlocutious inquiry. Something tells me I'd be a damn fool to do that."

"What about the names? Where'd you get Tisler and Besom's names?"

Last nodded. He knew he was going to have to explain that now.

"Both were mentioned by the peeping Tom." He looked at Graver and saw the disgust on his face. "Well, shit, you can't really blame me for trying to string it out, can you?"

"Then he did mention the CID?"

"No. When he mentioned the names I made a point to remember them, but I only had a phonetic knowledge. Tisler. Besom. Those are not common names. But of course a conversation like that, I suspected the police department. So I called information at police headquarters and asked to speak to them—then your CID receptionist answered, and I hung up."

"And you overheard the names in that conversation?"

"Absolutely. But I'm telling you, I don't know who those two men were. That was a blind fluke, I'm telling you." He pushed his wineglass to the side and leaned in. "Frankly, Graver, this looks like this is very deep shit here. I mean, if these two deaths are not 'self-inflicted' and 'natural causes,' then I seriously believe I'm altogether in the wrong place. I don't want any part of this kind of thing. This is definitely not my kind of work, and you know it."

Graver sat quietly a moment, allowing Last to think he was just going to walk away from this or, rather, watching him try to convince Graver that that was just the thing he ought to do. Then he said:

"I've made a few inquiries, Victor. Someone's been shopping around forgeries of eighteenth-century Spanish land grant documents to private collectors in California. A curator at the Stanford Museum of Meso-American Artifacts reported being approached by a dealer who was offering what she believed to be stolen jade and clay sculptures. The curator at the Kimbell Museum reported being approached by a dealer offering what he believed were bogus stone masks." Graver stopped. "I have a list. And all the inquiries aren't in. There seems to have been a resurgence of this stuff in the last seven months. I called Alberto Hyder who heads the Art Thefts section of the National Police in Mexico City. They'd like very much to talk to you."

Last had sat back in his chair, crossed his legs, and put his hands in his pockets in a slouching posture as he regarded Graver with a sober diffidence. After Graver stopped talking, Last's pensive, pale eyes remained as still as opals in a setting of weathered wrinkles.

"What is it, exactly, that you want me to do?" Last asked.

"Nothing?" Graver was skeptical, looking in his rearview mirror as he pulled away from the curb where he had picked up Lara around the corner from the apartment house.

"Nothing suspicious, nothing like you described," she said, getting the binoculars out of her purse. "Incidentally, these things are incredible."

"What *did* you see?" Graver quizzed.

Lara settled into her seat, getting the long straps of the purse and binoculars out of her way, straightening her dress.

"First of all, I scanned the people at the tables along the sidewalk," she said. "There weren't that many. A couple of girls, a couple of guys. A man and a woman. One guy by himself. I was immediately suspicious of him, but he just sat there, wasn't doing much but staring out to the street, actually in my direction. Besides, he was the first to leave, and he just wandered off down the street under the trees until I couldn't see him anymore.

"After taking the inventory of people, I surveyed the cars parked along the street. I wrote down the numbers of as many license plates as I could see and made a note of where the cars were located." She pulled a steno pad out of her purse and opened it. "Made a little diagram of where they were. I didn't see anyone sitting in any of the cars. About halfway through your conversation, the two men got up and left. They walked out and got into one of the cars and drove away. The two girls left just before you and Last. They walked down the street and got into a car about a block away and drove off. None of the other cars moved; no new ones came and parked. And"—she shrugged, closed the pad, and tossed it onto the seat—"the man and the woman are still back there."

"Did you see people out walking?"

"I didn't see anyone else," she said. "I just didn't."

Graver pondered all this as he worked his way back toward Montrose. Lara reached into her purse again and took out several tissues.

"That old building," she said, blotting her face. "Window units in the apartments; in the hallway, nothing. The window I was looking out of was *open.*" She dabbed around her face with the tissues and then opened her blouse another button and dabbed at the tops of her breasts. She said, "What about the couple, the man and woman? They were there when you arrived, and they were there when you left. Could they have known enough ahead of time to get there before you?"

"Good question," Graver said. "From the time of the telephone call to the time we arrived was about forty minutes. Sure there was time."

"Did you get a good look at them?" Lara asked. She put her hand under her hair and raised it up off the back of her neck and held it there.

"I think I'd remember them if I saw them again," he said.

"Do you think they could have been countersurveillance?"

"They could've been."

"If they were, then that would mean . . . that Last tipped them off."

"Either that, or . . . let's say he's entirely uninvolved. Then for someone else to know about it they would have had to tap the phone." He thought a second. "But if that was the case, where had he been when he called? Whose telephone was he using that someone thought needed to be tapped?"

"God," Lara said. "I don't believe all this." She leaned forward, twisted a little, and let the cool air from the air-conditioning vent blow on the back of her neck, her face turned toward Graver. He looked at her bending forward in the darkness, the highlights of her dress and body enameled in a soft wash of sea-green light from the dash.

36.

"IT'S VERY SIMPLY AN ECONOMIC REALITY," PANOS KALATIS said, gesturing with his large Cuban cigar and speaking slowly, letting his deep voice resonate from his chest, his slight accent distinguishing his pronunciation. "The best shelters, triple A bonds, CD's, those things provide yields of only half what they did in the eighties. The stock market? You'd have to be crazy. It's a world market now. Who knows what's going to happen with the EC or in Eastern Europe or in the Middle East or Japan or with the next political party in power here? To play the market with any kind of consistency you have to work twice as hard as you did a decade ago, and it will still take you twice as long to recover the kinds of profits you did in half the time in the eighties."

The man sitting across from him knew what Kalatis was saying was true. That's why he was there. They were sitting on the veranda across the front of which bamboo blinds had been dropped so that the guest could not see anything but the interior of the long veranda and portions of the dimly lighted interior of the house. As was routine with all the others, the guest had been picked up earlier in the evening in Houston as prearranged, blindfolded, and taken up in Kalatis's plane. The pilot had flown for over an hour along the Gulf Coast and then had turned in several slow, wide banking maneuvers and returned an hour later to Houston. A two-and-a-half-hour diversionary flight. The guest was not told his destination, but had been led to believe he was somewhere on the coast of Mexico or Central America. Kalatis's men had been instructed to speak only Spanish or, when they had to communicate with the guest, English with a Spanish accent.

After the plane had landed, the guest had been led along the dock, up the beach stairs, and across the lawn to the house where his blindfold was removed only after he had been seated on the veranda. Then he was introduced to Kalatis who assumed the name of Borman for each of these meetings.

Though it was two o'clock in the morning, and they had been drinking Cuba Libres and talking since midnight, both men were wide awake. For the first hour Kalatis had talked about everything except the subject of their meeting. That was Kalatis's way. He had learned from his past mistakes—they were decades behind him now—that your quarry was more easily taken if he first was put at ease.

In the past hour, however, Kalatis finally had started way out at the margins of the subject and had been working his way in. Sometimes he had seen American businessmen grow impatient with this leisurely approach—they tended to think of themselves as ball-busters and wanted to get right to the business of "crunching numbers" and talking about "the bottom line."

But he insisted on doing everything his way from the very beginning, for two reasons. First of all because they would see in the long run that he had been right in everything he said. And secondly, having demonstrated this, he achieved an authoritative position at the outset. They tended to believe what he said after that, and every time he was right about something else he gained credibility. Everything was on his terms, or they didn't do business together. He was always polite; he was always gracious. But only by doing business on his terms could he gain even a semblance of control in what was essentially a very dicey enterprise. His guest was never allowed to suspect that Kalatis had only a semblance of control, however. The weight of that responsibility was Kalatis's alone. That was how he earned his living.

Even though the man had come to Kalatis on the recommendation of someone else, someone the man already trusted, Kalatis felt obligated to present very carefully as many facets of the arrangement as he thought wise, anticipating the questions his guest would want to have answered. Eventually, he would bring the presentation full circle, and the actual commitment to the deal would be as abrupt and as final as the thrust of a gaff through the gills of an exhausted marlin.

They were just about at that point now. Kalatis could smell it on the salty breeze coming across the lawn; he could taste it in the dark tobacco, hand-rolled by brown fingers in the steamy Vuelta Abajo. But still Kalatis spoke slowly, his voice mellow, his accent, usually kept in check, creeping more and more into his pronunciation. He was the picture of stability, assurance, right thinking.

"And, as I was telling you," he concluded, "it doesn't matter who is coming or who is going in Medellín or in Cali. It doesn't matter if the Escobars or Marquezes or Orejuelas are on top or if they have all fallen to the *sicarios* or the agents of the Dirección de Policía Judicial e Investigación. It just doesn't matter . . . the stuff is going to move *regardless*. The market environment is stable.

"Look at it this way. Last year was a bad year for the business in Colombia. Cocaine seizures reached record levels—fifty-five tons seized *inside* Colombia itself—and the three leading cartel bosses were arrested or killed in the last six months. Cocaine consumption in the U.S. is declining—though that is partly due to more people turning to heroin . . . and heroin sales are exploding. The extradition situation continues to be troubling, not much stability there. The DEA has once again wheedled its way into a stronger role, as has the U.S. Army, and of course the CIA. Sounds gloomy for the spice barons, huh?"

He shook his head slowly with a smile, drew on his Cohiba, and blew the aroma into the Gulf breeze.

"Not so. Last year nearly twelve hundred tons of cocaine was shipped out of Colombia. A very good year, a record year. Where is it going if the consumption rate is declining in the U.S.? Well, a lot of people don't believe it *is* declining. But even if it is, it's not declining much, and besides that in the past five years the cartels' expansion plans have paid off and their distribution routes have now established a solid footing in Europe and Japan. The rest of the world is going to become what the U.S. was in the sixties, seventies, and eighties. But don't think that leaves the U.S. in a backwater situation. Heroin is making a comeback . . . all over the world. Big time. The point is, the trade is not going away. If it's not cocaine in some form or heroin in some form, it's going to be the synthetics. A world of synthetics. It's only going to get bigger."

Kalatis paused to enjoy his cigar a moment. It was a testimony to his abilities as a raconteur that the guest did not take advantage of this hiatus. In the gloom of the veranda Kalatis's powerful figure was a dusky presence that presided ceremoniously over the occasion of this meeting. Presenting his strong profile to his guest, he looked toward the Gulf of Mexico and nurtured his Cohiba in silence while Jael appeared, barefoot and wearing something gauzy which afforded the guest a diaphanous profile of quite another sort, and replaced their drinks with fresh ones.

"Now, at this point I should mention the European opportunities," Kalatis said as he reached out and picked up his fresh Cuba Libre and sat back again, resting the cold drink on the broad arm of his wicker chair.

"There are wonderful investment opportunities there now, too, primarily in heroin and morphine base. The Europeans are acting as if they had just discovered candy, consuming three to four tons per month. Street value consumption is approaching two billion dollars a month there now, and we expect enormous growth as the borders between the countries are relaxed. The poppy crops are grown primarily in Afghanistan and Pakistan. As with the South American situation, the opportunities for us are in transhipping. The war in the Balkans has disrupted our usual overland routes, so now, for the most part, we are using ships. Ships also allow us to regularly move from one to three tons at a time. Typically our freighters leave the port of Karachi, Pakistan, and onload at sea very near the Iran-Pakistan border. The freighters cross the Arabian Sea, go up through the Red Sea, and into the Mediterranean."

A pause for a sip of rum, a tug on the Cohiba.

"At this point we listen very closely to what our counterintelligence people tell us. According to their recommendations we sometimes offload in Turkish ports, sometimes Greek ones. Other times it is best to go straight up the Adriatic to the Italian ports. Brindisi, Bari, Acona, Trieste. A good part of our investment goes to intelligence. This is a business. No one wants to lose money. We plan carefully, very carefully. As a result, our seizure rate is . . . zero.

"Of course, there are other European route investments too, but they involve relationships with the overlords of Istanbul's organized crime community, while others involve relationships with the Kurdish separatist rebels in Eastern Turkey. Right now our intelligence cautions us about these groups. The returns are greater—fewer parties involved —but the risks are higher because of the volatile political situations in which these people are currently involved."

Kalatis paused again. He knew his face was in the shadow so he took some time to regard his guest. The man was mesmerized. Kalatis knew he liked to hear about the security, the intelligence behind these operations. He didn't blame him. The drug business had long ago discovered the value of intelligence and counterintelligence, and they had developed it to a remarkably sophisticated degree. But Kalatis had taken his intelligence program well beyond the operational level. His intelligence capabilities were strategic. He was far ahead of the curve in that regard, and because of that his record was impeccable.

The guest waited for Kalatis to refresh himself with his tobacco and rum. If he had been anxious when he had arrived, the rum had settled him down. He felt no need to assert himself. And that was as it should be. He had come to listen to Kalatis.

"But for you, of course, the primary concern is Colombia," Kalatis said, his voice resonant and rich. "There is a kind of aristocracy of wealthy families there, old families of four and five generations, who have weathered every tumultuous surprise that that exotic society has produced. Wars. Rebellions. Terrorists. Foreign occupation. Coups. And finally democracy and capitalism. Everything. The men of these families are always there to wave good-bye to every passing event, always there to greet the coming of the next one. They are known as 'los hombres de siempre.' The men of always. These are the men who are responsible for Colombia being the only Latin American country that makes its debt payments promptly every single year. They are the reason its economic growth rate purrs along smoothly at four percent. They are the reason Colombia has a solid, educated, and growing middle class, the best universities in Latin America, and the oldest constitution in Latin America—which has just been revised, incidentally, and is a model of progressive politics."

Kalatis waved his cigar languidly. "The thing is, despite all that happens there, the place still works and it works well. There is a reason. 'Los hombres de siempre.'

"Now that the narcotics trade has proved its stability over several decades, now that it is easily into the tens of billions of dollars per annum without fluctuating or being appreciably affected by law enforcement or the vagaries of the world economy, these cautious men have gradually inserted themselves into the picture. Escobar, Ochoa, Gacha, men of that kind were the roughnecks, the pioneers, the cowboys. They were neither educated nor sophisticated. They were unpredictable. They had the mentality of street fighters even though they were dealing in billions. They were necessary, of course, every frontier must have its pioneers, but the 'drug culture' is no longer a new phenomenon, no longer a frontier. It is an established way of life now, all over the world, and as always happens when something new becomes an established part of society, the torch is passed from the pioneers to the settlers, to the men of commerce and politics. Change is inevitable, and the time for a more mature perspective in this business is long overdue . . . and now it's here."

He sipped the rum. He pulled a couple of times on the Cohiba. He let the fragrance and the taste of each meld together.

"I have been working with these people for four years. Never a single problem. They are businessmen, and they know that chaos costs money. Order and efficiency make money. And they know that publicity is for movie stars and fools, not businessmen. Before long—they are deliberate men, almost Oriental in their perspective on time—they will be all there is of the cartels. Anyone who wants the southern spice . . . will have to buy it from the men of always."

"Then it's agreed," Kalatis said softly. There were only the two of them on the veranda, and they had finished their last Cuba Libre. Each was leaning his elbows on the wicker table between them, and they were talking softly, casually, almost in a tone of indifference. "Five million."

"Cash."

"Oh, yes. Of course." He nodded meditatively. "You have this maturing from . . ."

"Everything, T-bills, triple A bonds, CD's . . . stock. That's flexible, the amount from the stocks, I mean."

"But you'll have five million? I'll need to know the exact amount."

"Yes. Five even."

"From four or five different banks at least. In several different states. That's important."

"It's been arranged."

"Two days from now."

The man nodded, and swallowed. Kalatis knew how he felt. He knew these guys. Men too much in a hurry, too much in love with the way it worked in the eighties to wait for the nineties to pay off. He was making a fortune off the impatience of men like this. Even so, even the real pirates among them got cottonmouth from giving away five million in cash. No collateral, no contracts, no handshakes. But Kalatis had never failed one of them, and that was why they kept coming, this one for the first time.

"And this is part of a 'mutual fund,'" the guest said, wanting Kalatis to reassure him one more time.

"Oh yes." Kalatis nodded readily. "This is one package—all Houston investors. Thirty-two million dollars. Your friend who recommended me to you is in for eight million. But you know that. There are two others. Yours is the smallest portion. All of the others have invested with me before. You understand I cannot provide their names. Many of our investors know each other because they have recommended one another. But some wish to remain unknown. You are the only newcomer in this particular program."

The guest nodded.

"Good. Okay," Kalatis said. "Now, for my part: I guarantee you a three hundred percent return. In sixty days you will receive a telephone message telling you where and when to meet my representative in Luxembourg. You will open an account there in your name for fifteen million American dollars. My representative will provide the documentation that will satisfy the bankers about the deposit. They want that now. Things have gotten a little more difficult in that regard, but it is only a matter of paperwork. Formalities."

Kalatis's cold cigar lay in the ashtray between them, and the ice cubes—all that was left of their Cuba Libres—had turned to less than half an inch of warm water in the bottom of each glass.

"Any questions?"

"You'll pick me up again?"

"One of my people, yes."

"At the same place?"

Kalatis nodded.

"Okay. I'm satisfied."

Kalatis stood. "So am I."

The other man stood too, and suddenly one of Kalatis's guards appeared at the edge of the veranda.

"He'll take you back to the States," Kalatis said. "It will be a pleasure doing business with you."

"Sir," the guard said, stepping up and touching the businessman's arm. The businessman started to shake Kalatis's hand, but the Greek turned away to light another Cohiba.

"Good-bye," Kalatis said through a haze of blue smoke, "and *bonne chance.*"

The businessman stood still while he was once again blindfolded. Then he was led down the steps and across the lawn to the seaplane moored at the dock below.

Wednesday

THE FOURTH DAY

37.

ANTICIPATING HE WOULD HAVE A DIFFICULT TIME GETTING TO sleep, Graver set his alarm late, allowing himself just enough time to shower and shave and drive to Arnette's. No time for breakfast. Within half an hour of waking, he was walking out the front door of the house. Avoiding the expressways, he negotiated the slower city streets and tried not to acknowledge his growling stomach. He would have given five dollars for a cup of coffee, but did not stop to get one. He already was cutting it close. When he pulled up in front of Arnette's house he was five minutes late.

He got out of the car, pushed the door closed softly and walked up to the front gate. The morning sun broke through the high overstory of water oaks and loblolly pines only intermittently, falling here and there on the leaves of the plantains and the palmetto fronds in brassy, molten splashes. Already the birds were clamoring high overhead.

Mona met Graver at the front door, smiling and barefoot and holding a mug of steaming coffee.

"Good God, Mona, I love you," Graver said, gratefully taking the mug from her and following her into the perpetual twilight of Arnette's living room.

"I love you too, bah-bee." Mona laughed. "The Lady is waiting for you next door," she said, and then hopefully, "Have you had something to eat?"

"Oh, I'm doing all right," he lied, wishing he had the time to sit down and indulge himself with one of Mona's incomparable breakfasts.

"Okay." She shrugged philosophically, as if it was Graver's loss.

He left her in the kitchen and continued out the side door to the grape arbor and over to the next house, entering through the screened patio.

The big room was empty except for a hard-looking woman with a mat of roan hair sitting at the big library table beside the radio. She was wearing the same headset the blond girl had worn the night before and was taking notes from one of the fat ring binders with which the table was still piled.

She looked up at him. "Graver?"

He nodded.

She pushed a button and returned to her writing, occasionally, like the blonde, reaching out to fine-tune the dials without looking at them.

Graver looked around. The computers were all quiet, each of them in a hectic limbo with different patterned screen savers, swimming and jigging and rippling in brilliantly colored silence. He stepped over to the doorway that he knew led to an adjacent room that housed Arnette's library. Looking in, he saw that she had significantly expanded her inventory with a larger section of publications that originated within the federal government's twenty-seven oversight intelligence services and their plethora of subordinate branches that comprised the United States intelligence community. Graver knew that most of these documents were classified. Apparently Arnette had lost none of her connections within the service. The country maps section also had been expanded, especially in those areas of the globe where the U.S. had its greatest vested interests.

"Good morning," Arnette said, coming into the main room from yet another doorway carrying a mug of coffee and a large packet which she took to the library table. The woman with the headset began clearing aside the ring binders. "Get some sleep?"

"Some," Graver said, coming back to the table.

Arnette pulled the photographs out of the large envelope and slapped them on the table.

"The photographer stayed up late last night," she said. "Let's see if it was worth it."

They both sat down and started turning through the photographs. There were forty-eight of them.

"The stippled effect on some of them is actually the spray coming from the fountain," Arnette said, picking up a photographer's loop and putting it on a photograph that was lying flat on the table. She put her eye right on the loop. "They must've been soaked by the time they finished talking."

Graver went through the four dozen photographs rather quickly, setting aside the ones in which the unknown man did not appear. The ones in which he did appear Graver then examined again more closely using the loop. The photographer had done a good job of getting the unknown man's face from several different angles as well as straight on. He appeared to be, as Arnette had said, in his late fifties. Shorter than Burtell, he was also heavier, though not obese. He was wearing a suit without a necktie, his shirt collar undone. His hair was thinning, but he kept it neatly parted and combed. Even though the photographs were in color, it was difficult to determine anything about his complexion or hair color because the lights of the fountain reflecting off the water and the beige granite gave an overall distorted cast to the photographs. He had a slightly bulbous nose and, in one photograph, a noticeable mole on the right side of his chin. He would have had trouble shaving around it.

Sometimes the man talked to Burtell while looking away, and the expression on his face did not change in any of the pictures. Once the photographer caught him looking back and up at the high curtain of water that almost surrounded them, and it was easy to see that his baldness was generalized over the top of his head.

"What do you think?" Arnette said after a while.

Graver shook his head. "Just a guy."

"He'd disappear in a room with half a dozen people," Arnette said. "He looks like a 'government' guy."

"I can't imagine that," Graver said, still looking at the photographs.

Arnette didn't say anything. She sipped her coffee, looked at a photograph.

"They didn't see him arrive?" Graver looked at her.

"No. He just came across the grass and was there. Left the same way. In fact, we tried to catch him leaving, but we just flat missed it. We would have had a better chance if we'd gotten out of the cars, but we decided against risking it."

Graver looked at the man in the picture with a degree of frustration that he found difficult to hide. This was nothing. What could he do with it? Where did it get him? No matter how much he looked at this man's face, it wasn't going to tell him any more than he could apprehend in the first few minutes. It was like having a fingerprint before the existence of the national fingerprint index. There was nothing to compare it with. There was no national index of faces.

"There's one thing," Arnette said. "We think we see some counter-surveillance there."

Graver looked at her.

"Yeah, no kidding," she said. She turned sideways and reached for the photographs Graver had set aside. She riffled through them, quickly arranging them in some specific order, and then held them up one by one so that she and Graver could look at them together. "The reason there are so many prints of the crowd is to check for this kind of thing." She picked up a pencil from the table to use as a pointer. "These shots were taken while Dean was strolling around the sunken lawn area. He made one full circle, eating sunflower seeds."

"Sunflower seeds?"

"Yep. See this couple here? They're walking together as Dean arrives."

At the mention of the word "couple," Graver felt his face flush as he leaned closer in to the photograph, bracing himself against the recognition of the man and woman from La Facezia. He focused on the woman whose face lay under the tip of Arnette's pencil. He stared at her. He did not recognize her. He focused on the man to her left. The face was not familiar.

"Dean starts walking along the grassy mall from the west end of the fountain," Arnette continued. "They meet him at this moment, but they're looking away at something. They pass by, Dean keeps going toward the north end of the lawn. The couple stops at the west side of the fountain to watch some kids throwing a Frisbee down on the sunken lawn. This gives them a view of the entire lawn area with Dean circling."

Arnette's pencil touched the faces on another photograph. Graver leaned in again, studying the man and woman from another angle. He simply does not recognize the faces. He is relieved, but puzzled. If he had been given the chance to bet that they would be the same couple from La Facezia, he would have done it.

"See, they're standing there facing the Frisbee players, but the woman is actually looking away toward Dean," Arnette went on. "Now she's looking back along the west side of the lawn. Here she's looking on the east side. Guy she's with is looking toward the fountain now. Dean circles the north end. Couple splits up. She walks to the north end; he stays at the fountain, and they mill around, watching the place from both vantage points. Here, the woman pretends to be watching some kids down in the sunken lawn. Now, Dean comes along the east side of the lawn, and when he gets to the fountain the Unknown joins him, and they step up to the fountain. Man at the fountain hangs around inside with them. He looks at the water falling. He looks at the arches, probably through them at the grassy mall beyond. Woman joins him after having come up the east side."

Arnette picked up several other photographs she had set aside. "Now, here, my photographer really goes close up." She put the point of the pencil on the man's left ear. "See this? I think this is an earpiece. There's disagreement here about this, but I think that's what it is. The couple stay a while in the spray of the fountain looking out through the arches, out to the sides. After a while they split up again and head to opposite sides of the grassy mall where they stay, just looking around as before, until Dean and the Unknown finish talking and split up."

Arnette put down the last picture and the pencil, took a sip of coffee and looked at Graver.

"In these photographs the couple do not appear to speak to each other even once. They don't lounge around on the grass, sit on the benches, go up to the waterfall, up close and look up and laugh about it—people always go up to the water and look up and laugh for some reason. The perspective gives you a weird feeling. But what's most important is that they do not look at what's in front of them. Ever. They're always looking somewhere else."

Graver was motionless, studying the pictures.

"We're seeing this all the time, now," she said, sitting back, cradling her coffee cup. "Everybody's a spy. The dope traffickers, the computer chip bandits, the stolen car rings, you name it. Business associates; business competitors. And middle-class America? Everybody's bugging everybody. Everybody's tapping into everybody else's modem, and eavesdropping on their portable telephone conversations. It's the technology. Radio Shack has turned America on to a new game . . . keeping up with the Bonds, the James Bonds." She smiled. "When the stakes get past who's cheating on whom, countersurveillance is a given. We automatically look for it."

Graver didn't say anything for a second.

"Do you think they picked you up?"

She shook her head. "No."

"What about the audio?"

"They worked on it late last night, but when they quit just after two o'clock, they hadn't recovered anything."

"Do you mean 'not much' or 'anything'?"

"I mean zip. Nothing."

"And Tisler's tapes?"

"Nothing. I told you those could be hard to crack. Again it's the technology. It's a two-way street. The computer chip has made it easier for us to maneuver through the mazes of cryptography, but at the same time it's made it easier for the other side to design ever more complex ciphers too. It's a constant struggle of one-upmanship. Sometimes they're ahead of us; sometimes we're ahead of them. It's a toss-up."

Graver sipped the last of his coffee. It was too cold to drink. He looked at the pictures scattered in front of him. He looked at Burtell, standing in profile facing the unknown man under one of the Roman arches with the waterfall shimmering behind him.

"He looks pretty calm, doesn't he," he said.

"Yeah, as a matter of fact I thought so too. They said last night he seemed completely relaxed. Do you think he knew about Besom when these were taken?"

"I hope not," Graver said. "I really hope not."

Arnette sipped her coffee too, waiting for him.

"Westrate was beside himself last night," Graver said, idly matching up the corners of several photographs. "He's thinking conspiracy; he's thinking corruption, but he doesn't want to be the first one to say it. I'm guessing that's the way they're all going to react, the administration. The emperor's new clothes will be greatly admired."

"What do you expect? Hell, take advantage of it. While they flap around in confusion, push ahead. It's got to be done, and by the time they get around to realizing that you'll be way out front. It's going to put you ahead in more ways than one."

Graver pushed away the photographs. "I don't see much here," he said. "Am I missing something?"

"No, I don't see much either. But the countersurveillance makes me think Dean's dealing with people who are bigger than local racket operators."

"Why?"

Arnette shook her head apologetically. "I'm sorry, Marcus, it's just a guess at this point. The appearance of the older man. Where he chose to meet. The way the countersurveillance went about its business. This is very slick stuff." She set aside her coffee and started gathering up the photographs. "Look, we've been on this less than eighteen hours. There's a lot to work with. Give us some breathing room."

Graver nodded, and got up. "Thanks, Arnette."

"What are you coming up with on your end?"

"We got some leads last night, some names. Today we'll start running them down."

"Look, when it begins to open up let us help," she said, putting the photographs back into the envelope. "We'll plug in the names on this end too." She stood. "It's too soon to get down about it, baby. You could be in for a long haul on this one. Get used to it."

38

WHEN GRAVER GOT BACK TO THE OFFICE IT WAS TWENTY MINUTES after nine. The receptionist was on the telephone as he passed her, and as he turned into the hallway to his office he caught Lara's eye just as she was concluding a telephone conversation as well. She raised her eyebrows and lifted her chin to stop him, and he stepped into her office as she was putting down the telephone.

"Nancy from Chief Hertig's office just called a couple of minutes ago," she said, writing something down as she spoke. "He wants to see you in his office as soon as you come in. She said to call before you started over."

"Jesus."

"And Paula wants to talk to you."

"Is that urgent?"

"She was standing here when Nancy called. She said she'd get back to you after that."

"Okay, fine. Call Nancy back and tell her I'm on my way." He turned around to walk out, paused, and turned back. "Listen, I appreciate last night," he said.

"My pleasure." She smiled. "Did you get any sleep?"

"Some. How about you?"

"Slept like a *rock,*" she said. "There just wasn't enough of the night left."

He grinned, nodded, and walked out, leaving the CID without even having gone into his office.

When Graver finally got over to the Administration Building and up to Hertig's office, he was not surprised to find that Hertig was not alone. Westrate was there looking as though he might have slept two hours the night before, and so was Ward Lukens. When Graver walked in Westrate and Lukens turned and looked at him from their chairs in front of Hertig's desk, but neither of them spoke or moved. It was clear they were both smoldering, and Graver guessed a considerable amount of heated conversation had preceded his arrival.

"Good morning, Marcus," Hertig said, smiling good-naturedly. He stood and came around from behind his desk extending his hand. The desk was a massive thing with an impressive telephone system taking up one side of it along with stacks of folders spilling papers, pictures of family, and a framed shield which Graver assumed was from his days as a detective. Behind him was a matching credenza so laden with awards and plaques and city seals and photographs of the chief with various people that it hardly was any use at all as a work space, though there was a stack of spiral-bound reports with colored covers, the sort of things that proliferated unstintingly in all kinds of government offices as proof and justification of employment.

They shook hands.

"Sit down," Hertig said, gesturing to a chair to the side of his desk, near Westrate. Hertig was one of those rare birds, a man of sixty-two who actually had a law degree when he joined the police force in the late 1950s. He even had left the force for a while, practiced law, and then came back and eventually became chief. He was tall and lanky, a good-looking man with graying ginger hair and pale blue eyes whose appearance seemed more to suggest perhaps an academician rather than a law enforcement officer. He had been around a long time and knew very well the kind of rivalries that drove men like the two sitting in front of him.

"We've been talking about Besom," he said, getting right to the point as he returned to his chair and sat down. "Actually about Tisler and Besom."

"Look, I haven't even had a chance yet to sit down at my desk this morning," Graver interrupted. "Does anybody in my office know about this yet?"

Hertig looked at Westrate.

Westrate shook his head.

"Late last night," Hertig resumed, "Besom's body was flown back to Houston, and at four-thirty this morning he was re-autopsied here as had been suggested."

"Who did the autopsy?" Graver interrupted again.

Hertig paused. "Stern."

Clay Stern was the Chief Medical Examiner. It would have been done right.

"He confirmed the results of the Brownsville coroner's findings,"

Hertig continued. "Essentially a heart attack. Apparently, according to Mrs. Besom and Besom's own medical records, he had no history of heart trouble. As it turns out, he had a condition physicians refer to as a 'widow maker.' Doesn't give any warning signs. No symptoms and therefore no suspicions." He snapped his fingers. "Then it gets you."

Hertig nodded at his own explanation, and for a moment his blue eyes lost their focus. He put his hands on the arms of his chair. He pursed his lips, his head tilted forward in thought. Then he reached out and picked up some papers.

"We've all read your report on Arthur Tisler, and what we've got here is a differing of opinions," Hertig said.

Graver looked at Westrate and Lukens. Both men had fixed their eyes on Hertig like spaniels. Graver suspected they were watching him for any indication of tilt, one way or the other, however subtle, however slight. Ward Lukens was a couple of years older than Westrate and about half as heavy. He had thick, wiry brown hair, wore unimaginative steel-rimmed glasses, and was so lacking in personality that Graver found him difficult to talk to. He was an honest man, however, and a stickler for rules, though these attributes were somewhat diminished by his maddening self-righteousness, and all of which made him the natural enemy of the conniving Westrate. Graver guessed that Hertig would have liked to strangle them both.

"About the report?" Graver asked.

"No. That seems clear enough. But about what to do now."

Hertig was enough of a lawyer to want to see where Graver would go with this given as little direction as necessary. But Graver wasn't going to venture anything without being presented with a specific question. He simply looked at Hertig and waited. Hertig waited. And then Graver thought he saw something like amusement come to the surface behind Hertig's pale eyes, and then it was gone.

"Ward has the feeling that two deaths, regardless of the seemingly innocent circumstances, are too much of a coincidence," Hertig said with a tilt of his head toward Lukens. "He thinks there ought to be a major audit of your OC unit." He paused, keeping his eyes on Graver. "How do you feel about that?"

"Obviously the deaths have startled us too," Graver said, looking at Westrate and back to Hertig. "And Jack has already grilled me about this." Graver chose the verb deliberately. It would be to his advantage if the other two men thought Westrate had treated the deaths with an appropriate skepticism, even though Graver knew that that skepticism had more to do with paranoia than a levelheaded consideration of the implications the deaths might have for the integrity of their intelligence system.

"I don't think an audit of the kind you're talking about is an advisable thing under these circumstances," Graver continued, "for several reasons. First of all, there's the matter of a lack of evidence—forensic or investigative—that would indicate anything is at play here other than coincidence." Graver went on to cover the same points he had covered the night before when he had spoken to Westrate and used the example of Occam's razor. If they decided to initiate an audit, it would be based solely on suspicion or hunch and not on fact or evidence or inexplicable inconsistencies or lacunae in the chain of procedure. Or, and Graver only implied this, it would be for some other reason . . . internecine squabbling, panic, butt-covering, or poor judgment.

"Two, if an audit is conducted it will have the inevitable effect of disrupting morale. It would be impossible to keep such an investigation quiet, and once it's known, there's no way we can avoid having it perceived as anything but a witch-hunt, no matter what we called it."

Hertig was still sitting with his forearms on the arms of his chair and his hands gripping the ends. His face had lost its equanimous and beatific expression of a mediator and had grown sober with concentration.

"Three, there's the inevitable question of parameters. If our internal audit of Tisler is to be redone it won't be such a problem. He was handling eight targets, most of them inactive except for semiannual updates. But Besom supervised ten investigators in OC. Some have as many as ten targets. That's well over a hundred targets. If you're concerned about Besom's role in regard to his investigators and their targets, you can't afford to let a single one of those go without a thorough audit. Otherwise there wouldn't be any use in doing it. This isn't the sort of thing that lends itself to random sampling."

Graver paused. He looked at each of them. "I'm not saying we shouldn't do it—though I personally don't believe it's justified—but I am saying we'd better be sure we've made our decision to do so based on sound reasoning."

That was it. Hertig's eyes were on Graver, and he was nodding, little shallow bobs as he thought. Without changing position in his chair he swiveled around slowly to the two men in front of him.

"Jack, I guess you go along with this."

"Yes, sir," Westrate said with alacrity, sensing the momentum turning in his favor.

Hertig looked at Lukens. "Ward, you have anything else to add?"

"I sure do," Lukens said, looking deliberately at Graver and then back at Hertig. "That all sounds wonderful and well thought out . . . and prepared. But it doesn't discount the circumstances, and I have to say that I just don't buy this coincidence scenario."

Lukens was tense, having to work hard to control his voice. He straightened himself in his chair. "Graver's little lecture sounds very neat, but all of you know damn well that if we always waited for substantial evidence to initiate an investigation in this business, we could cut our personnel by half. If something's going on in CID, the people involved aren't going to provide us with 'evidence.' "

He turned to Westrate. "You've got better people than that over there, don't you, Jack?"

Then back to Hertig. "That's an absurd prerequisite for suspicion, and an absurd prerequisite for initiating an investigation or inquiry." Lukens squared on Graver. "And I'm surprised to hear it coming from you, Graver. That was facile footwork, but I don't believe a word of it, and I don't even think you do."

Back to Hertig. "If something's gone wrong over there, Charlie, it's not going to hit us over the head. I think what we've got here is a break, and if we don't recognize that we're screwing ourselves. Jesus. Even if I'm wrong, we ought to audit the situation just to satisfy ourselves that I *am* wrong. Or let's just talk about PR, then. That's the worst possible reason for doing something, but it is another reason nonetheless. Tonight Besom's death is going to be on the news, and it's only a matter of time before you're going to find yourself having to explain these two deaths to those reporters who are always hoping to get a byline over another story of an HPD screw-up. Suicide? Heart attack? Trust us?" He paused. "At the very least we ought to be able to tell them a 'routine inquiry' is under way."

Graver was cringing inside, waiting for Westrate to explode, but much to his surprise it didn't happen. Westrate was a gamesman even more than he was a hothead, and he sensed that it was to his advantage right now not to do the obvious. But he had to say something, and though his face was livid, his tone was even.

"Routine inquiry, Ward? How do you do a routine inquiry into a heart attack? We've already got a report on Tisler. Why don't we tell them, 'Well, it's a hell of a deal, boys, but one killed himself and one died of a heart attack. Shit happens.' If there's no inquiry they've got a message right there that says there's just nothing to inquire about. Nothing to explain."

"That's your interpretation of what it would 'say,' Jack," Lukens rebutted. "To somebody else it might 'say': cover-up."

Everyone fell silent for a moment. Hertig was nodding, but he was looking at the calendar on his desk. Graver knew he did not want to have to tell the media that the Organized Crime Squad of the Criminal Intelligence Division was being audited following the deaths of two of its officers within the last forty-eight hours. That was like striking a match to gasoline. He practically would be writing the headlines himself. Lukens knew that too, but Graver guessed he figured his own angle was worth a try. He might get lucky. But he didn't.

Hertig leaned forward in his chair, rested his forearms on his desk, and looked at Lukens.

"Ward, I can't see committing all that manpower and time—which is money—to this," he said. "I think we've just got to call it hard luck, bad timing, a hell of a coincidence. I don't think we can justify it. I just don't."

That was the end of it. They were dismissed. Westrate had the good sense to simply walk out of the office without gloating, though Graver guessed he was cackling inside. He didn't even hang back to talk to Graver who was the last one out of the office. Each of them went back to their offices in silence.

It was hard to call which way the scales would go from one day to the other when it came to interdepartmental rivalries. Graver guessed that this time the well-known tug of war between Westrate and Lukens had worked to Lukens's disadvantage. Somehow his arguments for an inquiry seemed specious in light of his long-standing antagonism with Westrate. The next time it might go the other way. That was the kind of decision that men in Hertig's position had to make sometimes, and Graver wondered how comfortable Hertig actually was with his ruling. He wouldn't have been surprised to know that he had gotten no satisfaction out of it at all.

Certainly Graver himself felt decidedly frustrated. He had argued precisely in opposition to his own feelings, which were much closer to

Lukens's. It galled Graver that he had had to be so helpful to Westrate. But if he hadn't argued as he did, the decision might have gone the other way, and to have had his Division invaded by Internal Affairs investigators would have wreaked havoc on his own operation. Even so, Graver felt a little queasy about what he had just done.

39

THE MEETING WITH CHARLIE HERTIG HAD LASTED LESS THAN forty-five minutes and by ten-fifteen Graver was walking into his office. He tossed his briefcase onto his desk and was taking off his coat when Lara came in behind him with his Charlie Chan mug filled with coffee. She closed the door behind her and put the coffee on his desk with a paper napkin.

"Oh, God, fantastic," he said, sitting down behind his desk and pulling the coffee over in front of him. "Hertig wasn't in any mood to offer coffee this morning. I've been dying for a cup."

"How did it go?" she asked, sitting down in one of the chairs. She was wearing a straight skirt of off-white linen with a pearl-white blouse, her fingernails freshly painted, her long hair tucked up in a loose Gibson girl. He had no idea how she found the time it must take to look so perfect.

He told her about the meeting.

"That was awkward," she said.

Graver nodded, swallowing a sip of coffee. "Very. But for once, bureaucracy is in our favor." He looked at her. "Has the word seeped out about Besom?"

"All the way out. Some of our people found out about it this morning, while you were in the chief's office, when they received calls from newspaper reporters asking about it."

"Oh, shit."

"I've gotten together the forms and things for his family, and I've talked with personnel and put the paperwork into the mill over there. This is becoming depressingly familiar." She studied him. "You all right?"

"What's the matter, don't I look all right?"

"You look pretty tired."

"I *am* pretty tired." He sipped some coffee. "I'm not putting out any statements to the press, so if they call don't even bother with them. Refer everyone to Westrate's office. That's something I'm not even going to worry about."

They talked for a few minutes about the previous night, and he told her about seeing Arnette's surveillance photographs from Burtell's meeting at the fountain. He told her about the man and woman who were acting as countersurveillance and how he thought surely they would be the pair from La Facezia.

"Are you *sure* it wasn't the same couple?" She had leaned forward slightly in her chair, fascinated by his recounting of the surveillance operation against Burtell. "I mean, what about disguises?"

"I just don't think so. I don't think they were even the same 'type' of people. But then, maybe I didn't pay as much attention to them at La Facezia as I should have." He shook his head. "I don't know."

"This is just so incredible about Dean. I'm sorry, but I'm still finding it hard to . . . buy."

Graver looked at her. "Of course you do. That's the whole point of it."

"But you do too."

He nodded and could feel the weight of the whole ordeal pulling down on the flesh of his face. "That's the whole point of it," he repeated.

"Okay." She nodded, dropping her eyes. "I know."

"Now, why don't you have all the OC people come down here."

"All of them?"

"Yeah, I think so."

Within fifteen minutes the nine remaining investigators had crowded into Graver's office, sitting in the few chairs, leaning against the walls, a couple on the floor. Neuman was on the far side of the room. Graver went around behind his desk and proceeded to tell them what had happened. He was straightforward, told them everything he knew—at least what Westrate had told him—and said that, as with Tisler, they would be informed as soon as they knew anything about funeral arrangements.

He appointed Ted Leuci to be the acting squad supervisor—in Graver's opinion he should have had the job anyway, instead of Besom —and told them if they had any questions, problems, suggestions, requests . . . anything, to take it to Leuci first. He said he knew this was a weird set of circumstances, but sometimes life dealt these kinds of hands and all they could do was play them out as they came. It was an inane statement, but he felt he had to say something to acknowledge the eerie coincidence. He asked Leuci to stay back a moment and dismissed the rest of them.

He gave Leuci the security code to Besom's room and told him to go in there, gather Besom's personal things and put them in a storage box. He told him to go ahead and go through Besom's records, and start familiarizing himself with what he had to do to keep things rolling. If he had any questions, any at all about what he found among Besom's records, he should bring them to Graver.

After Leuci left he picked up the telephone and buzzed Paula. In a few minutes she and Neuman were walking through Graver's door.

"It's all over about Besom," Paula said, quickly sitting down in front of Graver's desk. Her hair was pulled back at the temples and fastened behind with a clasp. As always, one wrist was draped with a collection of bracelets that clacked as she gestured. Her slightly puffy eyes belied the late hours of the night before.

"Yeah, I know," Graver said. "What have you got?"

As Paula flipped open her ever-present legal pad, Neuman sat down in another chair and crossed his arms, ready to listen to Paula's summary. At least with one ear. He seemed preoccupied.

"We got fifteen separate pieces of paper from Valerie Heath's garbage," Paula began. "Three envelopes: one from Gulfstream National Bank and Trust with a window in it so we don't know who it was addressed to. One from The Secure Maintenance Services with the name 'Doris W.' written on the outside; one from Excell Executive Secretarial Services with 'Olivia M.' written on the outside. We found seven receipts from various places, grocery, car wash, pharmacy, that kind of thing. Of these seven, five were for cash, the other two we couldn't tell. We got three pieces of notepad paper with telephone numbers on them: one belongs to a male strippers' club called Phallacy; another is a beauty salon called La Riviera, and the third is a bar called Maggie's in Kemah, not too far from where she lives. We've also got a piece of notepaper with the name 'Don C.' doodled on it."

Paula looked up and nervously wagged a yellow pencil in her fingers. "Now. Valerie was driving a new Corvette, not the vehicle listed on the vehicle and tag listed on her Contributor ID sheet in the file. Computer tells us the Corvette is in the name of Frances Rupp at some other address. Neuman got the dealer's name off the trunk, and we talked to the guy who sold it to Rupp. The description fits Valerie Heath. While we were interviewing Heath, Neuman pointed out a magazine on the coffee table with a subscription label on it in the name of Irene Whaley. We ran a check on Whaley. No criminal history, but her Texas driver's license gives another address, not Heath's."

"Did the magazine have Heath's address on the label?"

"It did. We checked the bank. Valerie Heath does not have an account there. Neither does Irene Whaley or Frances Rupp.

"We checked with the Secure Maintenance Services and asked if anyone with a last name beginning with a W and having the first name Doris worked there. No. Did the same thing with Excell Executive Secretarial Services, asked about a last name beginning with an M, first name Olivia. No."

"What about Gulfstream bank?"

"We checked. No."

"Did you ask if Heath or Rupp or Whaley worked at either place?"

"We did. And we checked for Bruce Sheck too, and anybody with a last name that begins with a C, Don or Donald. They don't."

"I'm betting Heath has a bureau drawer full of false IDs," Neuman interjected. "Since the 'Doris' and 'Olivia' envelopes were found in her trash I'm assuming she was the recipient."

"Maybe someone living with her is using those names," Graver said.

"Could be," Neuman conceded, "but how likely is that considering we already have Heath assuming two other identities with false IDs? And since there were no last names on the envelopes, just initials, I'll bet these are the only names the addressers know her by. Heath is using the names as contact names."

"Spy stuff," Paula said.

"Yeah, something like that," Neuman said. "She has something to do with someone at those businesses who know her only by those names."

"Those envelopes could have been picked up entirely at random," Graver said.

Neuman nodded. "Could've been, but I'm guessing someone who works at those places, or who has access to stationery from those places, is giving something to Heath in those envelopes and writing her contact name on the outside." Neuman unfolded his arms and leaned forward in his chair. "Probably the envelopes were not hand-delivered from these persons to Heath. Really wouldn't be any need in writing the name on the envelopes if they were. They were dead-dropped."

"What about 'Don C'?" Paula asked.

"Let's don't forget how we got to this point," Graver said, holding up a cautionary hand. " 'Colleen Synar,' actually Heath, and Bruce Sheck were cited as sources in the Ray Probst investigation. Whoever placed them in that context—Tisler, Besom, Dean—put them on an equal footing. Let's do the same. Doris W., Olivia M.: Valerie Heath. Don C.: Bruce Sheck."

"Partners?" Paula frowned.

"Ohhh, I don't know." Neuman craned his head skeptically at Graver. "I can't imagine the woman Paula and I talked to being very high up in anybody's scheme. More likely they're just at the same level—low—of something bigger."

"Ray Probst ran a temporary employment service," Graver went on. "He was paying his people to steal information from the files of the banks and insurance companies where they worked. They would identify people who owned high-dollar consumer products that Probst knew he could quickly resell. And where were the envelopes from in Heath's trash? A maintenance service and a secretarial service."

"Then you think Probst was eliminated because he was competition?" Paula asked.

Graver didn't respond. He was staring at his own notes on the desk in front of him, one hand slowly turning the cobblestone. He began to shake his head.

"I just don't know . . . The thing is, I can't see that this kind of operation would turn over enough money, the kind of money it seems to me it would take to buy off three intelligence officers. If they were going to risk a career, jail, everything . . . wouldn't you think it would be for bigger money than this kind of operation would pull down? And if we're going to stick with our theory that Tisler and Besom were professional hits . . ."

"Yeah"—Paula nodded, glancing at Neuman—"we talked about that. That's why we think we've just scratched the surface of this thing. And, uh, this is where our imaginations got carried away, and after a while we were bouncing off the wall. We thought we'd better run some of this by you, see what you thought."

"Like I said," Neuman added, "we don't think Heath and Sheck are the heads behind all this. We see them as underlings, subordinates."

Graver looked at them as he turned the cobblestone. He thought

they were right on track. They didn't know that Burtell had been photographed meeting with an unknown man the night before and that the
meeting was overseen by a man and woman countersurveillance team,
a pair who most certainly were not Bruce Sheck and Valerie Heath.
And they didn't know about Arnette Kepner whose judgment in such
matters Graver trusted even more than his own. They didn't know that
she also suspected a larger, more important enterprise than the scam
Probst had been operating. Yet they were right on target.

"What we need to do," he said, "to give us a little more confirmation is to get a list of the companies each of those places have under
contract. Maybe what we find there will give us an idea of the direction
they're moving, even give us some sense of the dimensions, the size of
their objectives."

"Sooner or later," Neuman said cautiously—he didn't want to
seem too eager—"we're going to have to confront either Heath or
Sheck. I mean, in the interest of time. We don't have that much time,
do we?"

"What are you suggesting?" Graver knew Neuman was right about
the lack of time. It made their job seem nearly impossible.

Neuman was rolling back the cuffs on his plaid shirt. His tie,
though still knotted, was tucked into his shirt placket between the first
and second buttons to keep it out of his way.

"We could interview Sheck, just as we talked to Heath," he said.
"But odds are she's going to have talked to him already, and he'll
probably be expecting us. It'll be a tougher interview no matter what
he's like, unless he's completely spineless." He glanced at Paula.
"Heath though, she's vulnerable. I think we can panic her without too
much of a problem. We've got all this false ID stuff on her. I think we
can make her believe we know more than we do, put her in a corner,
press her, turn her around. I think it could pay off."

"But that really commits us, Casey," Paula hedged. "If we can't get
her to cooperate and she walks away, we've given ourselves away."

"I think we have anyway," Neuman admitted. "That insurance
business isn't going to hold up." He looked at his watch. "By now she
already knows there's no such company."

Graver stared at his notes, turned the cobblestone a few more
times. It was a close call. If he thought nothing was going to be forth-
coming from the tail and the tap on Burtell, if he thought the password
puzzle on Tisler's computer tape was not going to be broken within the

next twenty-four hours, if the audio tape of Burtell's meeting was not going to yield any information today, then he would be all for Neuman's plan. But Paula was right too. To try to turn Heath and to fail in the effort would scatter the pigeons without a doubt. The investigation would be out in the open.

"Here's what I want to do," Graver said finally. "As incredible as this may seem, I've got an informant who gave me something last night that may lead right into the middle of this." Without telling them anything about Last, Graver told them of the conversation Last had overheard at the party at Colin Faeber's house.

Paula's eyes widened in amazement as she turned to Neuman who simply shook his head at yet another weird twist. Graver entertained the idea of bringing them into the picture even more, telling them about Last, about Arnette, giving them all the pieces. But something warned him to hold back. As usual he was being cautious, and in doing so he knew he might be hampering their investigation by not having the benefit of their analysis of the entire scope of what they were dealing with. Still, he held back.

"Casey, I want you to do a work-up on Faeber," Graver said. "He may have nothing to do with the conversation these two guys had, I don't have any idea, but we need to try to find out. I'll keep after my informant. There's no way for me to corroborate this, obviously, but we can't be picky at this point."

Graver rubbed his face with his hands. His neck was getting stiff; he could feel the tendons drawing, growing taut and rigid. He shook his head.

"Jesus, we could use a dozen people on this. Paula, I want you to find out who's involved in Gulfstream National Bank and Trust. Officers, board members, that kind of thing. If it's owned by a holding company get the corporate charter from the Secretary of State's office, have them fax you everything they have. We've got to find out if there are any threads coming out of there that we can pull on."

He looked at his watch. "Check in with me. Maybe I'll have something from my end by the middle of the afternoon."

40

GRAVER CALLED LARA INTO HIS OFFICE AND FOR THE NEXT HOUR she helped him work through the stack of paperwork that had been piling up on his desk. It was important that his office didn't attract attention as a bottleneck to the paper flow. Whatever else happened, he didn't want it to appear as though Tisler and Besom's deaths were causing any disruption of routine.

At one thirty-five he realized that Lara had stopped writing and was sitting with her hands folded on a stack of files in her lap, staring at him. He looked up.

"I've got to have something to eat," she said. "Really."

He looked at his watch and slumped back in his chair. His head was splitting, and he was starving. "I'm sorry," he said. "I guess you're hungry, huh?"

"Oh, just a little," she said dryly, brushing the red-nailed fingers of one hand across her cleavage to pick up a wandering hair. "And you've got a headache, right?"

He nodded.

"Yeah, you've got that look. I'll bet you didn't have breakfast, either."

He nodded again.

"Right," she said, pushing her chair away from the desk. "What about it? What do you want to eat?"

He grinned at her. "Okay. If you'll go get it, I'll buy it. What about . . . Las Hermanas?"

"Perfect," she said, standing and giving a smart tug at the sides of her skirt to straighten it.

Graver reached back to the coatrack behind him and took his wallet out of his suit coat pocket. "I'll take a couple of beef enchiladas—ranchera—a taco, and a tamale."

"*A* tamale?"

"Just one," he said, dropping the twenty on the stack of folders beside her ballpoint pen.

"And beer," she said.

"Good try. How about an RC?"

She smiled and snatched up the bill. "Be back in twenty minutes."

Graver watched her walk out of the office and was still looking at her hips when the telephone rang. She looked back, he waved to her that he would get it, and she was gone. He picked up the telephone.

"This is Graver."

"This is your secure line, isn't it?" Arnette asked.

"Yeah, it is."

"We've salvaged a little of the audio from the conversation at the Transco Fountain," she said. "Not much on it in the way of context. But what has come through, twice, is a name. Marcus, you ever heard of a guy named Panos Kalatis?" She spelled the name.

Graver wrote it down, but he didn't have to think about it. "No."

"Okay. Well, I have. I think you'd better come over here, baby. We've got to talk."

Graver felt suddenly warm and queasy.

"I'm on the way," he said. He stood and grabbed his coat and headed out the door. Lara was already gone. As he slipped on his coat, he pushed through the door beside the receptionist's booth and told her to tell Lara that he would call in.

41

1:45 P.M.

HE PICKED UP A HAMBURGER AT A STALE-SMELLING LITTLE DRIVE-IN not far from the police station and ate it on the way to Arnette's. As he ate, he thought of the enchiladas from Las Hermanas and how furious Lara was going to be when she got back to the office.

Arnette met him at the front door. She was all business.

"This guy's name comes up twice, Marcus," she said, taking him through the twilight and out the back door into the shade of the arched arbor that led next door.

"Panos Kalatis. That's Greek."

"Yeah, the name's Greek," she said, yanking a grape leaf off the vines and starting to shred it as they walked. The cicadas were carrying on a rousing throb in the midday heat. "It's Dean's voice both times. Early on in their conversation he says something like he doesn't think Kalatis will do . . . something . . . and then later, toward the end, he ends a sentence with 'Kalatis.' That's it. They sure as hell knew what they were doing getting inside that fountain. Anyway, that's not much, just the name. But considering who he is, it's a huge break."

They came to the screened back porch of the other house, and Arnette pushed open the screen door without breaking stride and in a few steps they were entering the house and the computer room. The CRTs were busy again, and this time all of them were occupied. But Arnette didn't pause here at the table where the small blonde was once again at her station. Instead, she took Graver back to her library and closed the door. The library table was bare except for a computer monitor and keyboard at the far end, a glass ashtray and a single manila folder laying in the center. There was a green band code on the raised tab.

"I'm going to leave you here with this," Arnette said, lifting her chin at the solitary envelope. "After you've read it, step outside and have Quinn buzz me. Then we'll talk."

"Quinn's the blonde on the radio."

"Right."

Graver nodded and Arnette walked out of the library and closed the door behind her. Graver pulled out a chair and sat down. There was a code number along the left side of the file, a long string of digits and letters. He pulled the file over in front of him and opened it. It was a thick, single-spaced dossier on Yosef Raviv.

Raviv was born in 1936 to Jewish parents in Athens, Greece. His father was a locksmith in the Jewish district who in 1943 smuggled his family aboard a ship in Galatas and fled with them to British-partitioned Palestine. They settled in Ashdod on the Mediterranean coast, and the elder Raviv joined the prestate Lehi underground, a radical Jewish group that, along with another underground group known as the Irgunists, conducted terrorism against the British and Arabs in an effort to hasten the creation of a Jewish state. Three months before Jewish independence was announced in 1948, the elder Raviv was killed when a bomb he was assembling accidentally exploded. Yosef was twelve years old.

In 1953 at age seventeen Raviv enrolled in the Hebrew University in Jerusalem where he spent the next six years studying languages. When he left the university in 1959 at the age of twenty-three, he spoke French, English, Italian, and Spanish fluently and had a working knowledge of German, Arabic, and Russian.

After university, Raviv entered the Israeli Army for his mandatory three years service. At the end of that period, in 1962, he was immediately summoned by Tsomet, the Mossad's recruiting branch, at a time when a new era was beginning for Israel's foreign intelligence. Meir Amit, the Mossad's new director, was restructuring the agency and was emphasizing the recruitment of young men who had distinguished themselves in the military or university. He specifically sought men who exhibited "aggressiveness, cunning, initiative, eagerness for engagement with the enemy, and determination." After three years of instruction, Raviv graduated from the Institute in late 1965 as a Mossad *katsa,* or case officer.

Raviv was immediately sent to Marseille to replace a case officer whose Arabic language abilities were sorely needed in Israel at this time. All Israeli intelligence agencies, Mossad, Aman, and Shin Bet, strained to prepare for the war with the Arabs that everyone felt was inevitable. Raviv was still in Marseille in June of 1967 when the Six Day War rocked the Middle East.

Under the direction of Meir Amit, the Mossad policy known as the "peripheral concept" gained even greater favor and momentum. This philosophy was based on the belief that Israel needed to form alliances —sometimes secret ones—with the countries bordering the Arab world. In doing this, the Mossad also sought to form stronger ties with their counterpart agencies in the West. In the developing nations such as Africa and Latin America, they established diplomatic relations, proposed a variety of aid programs, and then opened embassies where Mossad agents went to work under diplomatic cover, offering their intelligence expertise to the host country's counterparts and thereby greatly expanding their own knowledge of that country's security operations. They also set up permanent Israeli military delegations in some countries. In Western Europe, the Mossad expanded its ties with their foreign security counterparts by joining a secret group called "Kilowatt" which was created to combat international terrorism. At every turn and available opportunity, Israel was increasing its knowledge of foreign intelligence and security operations all over the world.

In 1969 Raviv participated in a joint mission with Aman that was eventually to determine the shape of his career. After the Six Day War, the French clamped an embargo on munitions, aircraft, and boats that Israel already had bought and paid for, but which France had not yet delivered. The Israelis were in particular need of five missile boats that were part of the embargo, and they could not wait for the slow wheels of diplomacy to free them. Raviv received orders to travel to Normandy where the missile boats were kept in the shipyard at Cherbourg and to use agents to reconnoiter the weak points of the shipyard security so that the Israelis' naval operatives could plan a repossession.

On Christmas Eve, Israeli naval officers who had flown into France several weeks earlier and had been briefed by Raviv and his agents, entered the Cherbourg shipyards and sailed the five missile boats through Gibraltar and into the Mediterranean.

After this Raviv was asked not to return to Marseille, but to drop out of sight. He was instructed to go to London, get a job, and not contact the Mossad in any way. A year later, in December of 1970, he was contacted and told to go to Paris. There another three months passed before he was joined by a Mossad commander from Tel Aviv who spent a month with him. He had been chosen for a special kind of mission that was to become a trademark of his career.

It was a busy time for the Mossad in France. The 1970s would become the decade of terrorist revolutionary groups, the Baader-Meinhof gang in Germany, the Japanese Red Army, the Italian Red Brigade, the Basque ETA in Spain, the Action Directe in France, and five different Palestinian organizations. Sooner or later all of them found it necessary to pass through France and stay for various periods of time.

Raviv's languages expertise and his preference for working alone were considered indispensable under these circumstances. He had been made a "single," a rare *katsa* even by the standards of the innovative Mossad. He ran no agents and operated entirely alone, his existence unknown to other Mossad operatives anywhere. Even though the Mossad had three *kidon* units—small operational cells within the Metsada department that conducted assassinations and kidnappings everywhere in the world—there was a special need at this time for "veiled" hits, assassinations that appeared to be natural deaths. The targets were three men and a woman in the diplomatic corps of four different embassies who had significant clandestine connections to terrorist organizations. A traditional assassination—even if the Israelis were never linked to the deaths—would cause an uproar and create blowback that could only damage Israeli interests.

It took Raviv nineteen months to complete his assignment, a duration his superiors considered ideal. His hits were never detected.

In 1975 Yosef Raviv returned to Mossad headquarters in Tel Aviv. As one of Mossad's chief experts on terrorism, he spent the next year at the Institute teaching *katsas* in training and updating Mossad's training in operational techniques for their European stations. In late 1976 Raviv dropped out of sight.

In May of 1978 Raviv surfaced in Buenos Aires as Victor Soria, a wealthy Catalonian from Barcelona. Even though Argentina had a long and open history as Nazi sympathizers, both during and after the war, in the latter half of the 1970s the Mossad provided training to the Argentine military's secret police and shared intelligence with their counterinsurgency operations at various times during Argentina's "dirty war." They provided arms as well, and by the opening years of the 1980s Israeli arms sales represented seventeen percent of Argentina's total arms imports.

Israel's *Realpolitik,* however, had a face it never revealed, and it had a private memory as well as a public one. Although South America is well known as a haven for Nazi war criminals, when most people think of these men they think of prominent Germans like Adolf Eichmann, Klaus Barbie, and Dr. Josef Mengele. But there were others too, scores of nameless lower-ranked German officers as well as those men of the occupation who carried out the Nazi's atrocious directives, Croatian Ustashi, Romanian Legionnaires, Ukrainian nationalists. These men as well as the Nazis fled to South America to escape the retribution for their crimes, and more of them made new lives in Argentina than in any other country.

From 1978 through 1981 Victor Soria lived in Argentina and worked with the Argentine secret police. But this was not his sole mission. He lived alone among the eleven million people of Buenos Aires, but he also traveled extensively, sometimes renting a boat and heading up the Paraná, stopping at Rosario or Goya or Corrientes and traveling inland. He traveled to remote ranches in the central Pampas, south to the dusty and barren oil fields of Patagonia, and north into the swamps of the Gran Chaco. Sometimes he crossed the Pilcomayo into General Strossner's Paraguay, and at other times he crossed the Río de la Plata to Montevideo, Uruguay. No intelligence agency outside the Mossad has ever been able to obtain the statistics for Soria's work in Argentina, but by the time Raviv returned to Israel in 1981 he had become a legend in the intelligence world.

During the rest of 1981 he again taught at the Mossad Institute, but this time he taught methodologies in veiled assassinations to *kidon* operatives.

In 1982 Yosef Raviv spent a year at the Mossad station in Mexico City and then, once again, dropped out of sight.

In early 1984 Yosef Raviv returned to Tel Aviv and resigned from the Mossad. He was fifty years old and had been a Mossad operative for nineteen years.

Near the end of that year he bought a house in a smart district of Bogotá, Colombia, under the name of Panos Kalatis. The house was a large, Spanish-style residence that sat behind a high wall topped with barbed wire and equipped with an electronic security system. It was vastly more expensive than a pensioned-out Mossad officer would have been able to afford on his retirement.

For the next several years all of what is known about Kalatis is known by way of his associations. He entered a world that was largely a phenomenon of the 1980s, an era made possible by the postwar suspicion of governments who had for thirty years bred a generation of spies and operatives who, in the mid and late 1970s, faced retirement after a lifetime of deception and secrecy. It did not take them long to realize that their skills and contacts were marketable. Many of them became privateers, selling their services to the highest bidders, Third World juntas of the right wing, arms dealers, guerrilla movements, dictatorships, police states, drug cartels, and, even, their own governments who often found their "off the books" status a convenient means of deniability should their activities ever be discovered. The money was phenomenal, and the adrenaline-driving operations were just as good as the old days.

The difference with Kalatis was that he had never been a team player, and he never became one. Whatever he was doing seemed to be known only to him, and his movements could be charted only by his cohorts in the United States and Latin America, his chosen environments of retirement.

Between 1985 and 1989 Kalatis was seen with a wide variety of players, many of them having murky reputations in the world of intelligence and espionage: Mike Harari, a Mossad former who became Manuel Noriega's right-hand man in Panama, a dealer in information, arms (a participant in the Contra affair), drugs, and death; Pessach Ben-Or, a millionaire Israeli arms dealer headquartered in Guatemala who armed that country's right-wing army and death squads and who also helped arm the Contras; Rob Jarmon, an American rancher in Costa Rica who had close connections with the CIA who used the airfield on Jarmon's ranch to transport arms to the Contras; Rafael Cesar, a millionaire Mexican lawyer who had ties with the cartels in Colombia; Amiram Nir, Shimon Peres's adviser on counterterrorism from 1985 to 1988 and a key player in the Iran-Contra affair (after leaving the Peres government, Nir would die mysteriously in November of 1988 when his Cessna T210 crashed in Mexico where reportedly he had been to discuss the "marketing of avocados"); Brod Strasser, a South African industrialist who also owned a home in Bogotá and coffee plantations in Colombia's *Cordillera Oriental*; Lee Merriam, an American businessman who was reputed to be the key chemical supplier to the cartels' processing laboratories.

The list was long and curious, and it shed no direct light at all on

Kalatis himself or on what he was doing during these years. There are no records of business involvements with any of these people; he was known only to have been seen with them.

He has no visible means of income though he has bank accounts of undetermined amounts in Switzerland and Luxembourg.

Under the bold-face subtitle **Uncomfirmed:** "It is thought that somewhere around 1989 Kalatis may have bought a second residence in the Houston area. Since that time it has been rumored that he makes irregular trips back and forth between Bogotá and Houston in a private jet, a Desault Falcon which was at one time registered in the name of his pilot, a former Israeli Air Force instructor who is thought to have worked for Kalatis since the mid 1980s."

This seemingly trivial bit of information was the last entry. The last piece of paper was a single sheet with twenty-three lines of coded references. And then there was an 8 ½″ × 11″ glassine envelope. Graver opened it and took out three photographs. The first was a picture of Yosef Raviv during his last year in the Israeli Defense Forces. He was in uniform and wearing sunglasses. Broad-shouldered with a rakehell smile and a cigarette tucked in the corner of his mouth, he was holding an Uzi as he stood on a hilltop with a barren stretch of rugged desert valley behind him. It was 1962 and he was twenty-six. There was no one in the picture with him.

The next photograph was stamped simply: "Buenos Aires, 1980." Raviv was sitting at a sidewalk cafe. He was wearing a sport coat and shirt opened at the neck, and again he was wearing sunglasses. In eighteen years Raviv had acquired the solid frame of a man approaching middle age, though he was distinctly athletic. He looked hard and fit. The photographer had caught him in profile, one forearm resting on the small cafe tabletop, the hand of the other on the handle of a coffee cup which he had just put down or was about to pick up. He was alone and there was a folded newspaper at his elbow.

The third picture was in color, but it was very grainy. Stamped: "Mexico City, 1982." Raviv was walking along a residential street on a sidewalk next to a high wall. The second floor of a house with its red tile roof peeped up over the high wall. Raviv was wearing what appeared to be a light linen tropical suit, light shoes, and sunglasses. A bough of cerise bougainvillea was sagging over the top of the wall behind him. One hand—the one next to the whitewashed wall—was in his suit pocket while the other one, holding a cigarette, was in midair leaving his mouth where he had apparently just puffed on the cigarette. A foggy plume of smoke made a blurred spot in front of his face. He was alone and looking directly at the photographer, though Graver assumed the picture had been shot from a clandestine position. Raviv was looking straight into the lens with the considered suspicion of a wolf who had sensed something that his senses could not confirm.

Graver laid the three photographs side by side and looked at them again, each in turn, slowly. Then he picked them up, put them back into the glassine envelope, gathered together the pages, straightened them, placed everything back in the folder and closed it.

42

WHEN ARNETTE CAME BACK INTO THE LIBRARY, SHE WAS carrying two cups of fresh coffee. She was wearing common Vietnamese street clothing, a lemon, loose-fitting silk blouse with high collar and long sleeves and baggy white silk trousers. Without saying a word, she put one cup of coffee in front of Graver and went around to the other side of the table and sat down, placing her own cup on the table in front of her along with the ever present ocher pack of foreign cigarettes. She unhurriedly slipped a cigarette from the pack and lit it, looked at the thick dossier, and then at Graver as she exhaled the smoke.

"This is becoming a goddamned nightmare," Graver said, taking a drink of coffee. He needed the caffeine. He needed a jolt of something undeniably simple and immediately apprehensible.

"I'll have to say . . . this is extraordinary," Arnette said. "And it's big. There's no need in pretending it isn't."

Graver nodded at the dossier. "You think this guy's back with the Mossad?"

"There's no way of knowing about that," Arnette said, shaking her head. "There never is." She reached down to one end of the table and dragged the glass ashtray over in front of her. "We just have to go with the record in the file. Let's say he's not. In this case that actually seems to fit. With no system behind him he is even more dangerous. An organization—no matter how secret it might be—always has records, someone's personal diary, something tucked away in a vault for posterity, something to set the record straight someday. People can't help themselves it seems, most people anyway. But Kalatis isn't one of those people." She looked at the folder and shook her head again. "To a guy like that, other people—and organizations—are a liability. On his own he's not going to leave much of a trail. Most of the time he's not going to leave one at all."

They stared at each other for a moment.

"You think he killed Tisler and Besom."

"I think . . ." She pondered the question a moment. "Yeah"—she began to nod—"yeah, I think you ought to make that assumption."

"Christ." Graver looked away, let his eyes wander around the walls of books.

"They could have been doing anything, Marcus," she said. "Those investigations, Probst, Friel, the other one . . . Seldon . . . If Dean was fabricating the sources but had good information, then someone—Kalatis—was feeding them the information. Kalatis had inside knowledge, and it served his purposes, somehow, to have them go down. So he gave Dean the cases, and together with Besom and Tisler they made them look like they'd done the investigations."

"I don't see how Besom fit into it," Graver said and then, without waiting for her to respond, tacked in another direction. "They were doing it for money, a lot of money."

"Yeah," Arnette said, "I think you're right. Money is the whole story here." She gestured at Graver with the hand holding the cigarette. "I said you should assume Kalatis killed Tisler and Besom . . . or was responsible for it. You can also assume that you've probably stumbled onto the outer edges of a damned big operation. The people mentioned in that dossier, all of them are in business to turn hundreds of millions . . . per deal. They may have half a dozen deals going. Drugs. Arms. Information. Those are the big three. But to make those millions, and at the same time keep themselves in the background, they have to rely on a spider's web of small-timers. And they will mix as readily with these little guys as they will the money barons or Third World bosses or junta generals. They need them. Like all clever people, they know they can't be powerful unless they're surrounded by weakness."

She smoked. With her long braid, laced with silver strands and draped over one shoulder of her lemon silk blouse, with her gypsy complexion and straight, sharp-ridged nose, Arnette Kepner was a creature created by the dappled world of secrecy, every kind of secrecy, personal and professional, individual and governmental, official and unofficial. There was as much of her in the shadow as in the light, and that which was in the light never revealed so much as it implied. Arnette had been a long time in the deception game. It had affected her physiognomy, or the aura that surrounded it.

"The thing about Kalatis," she continued, "is that because he's a loner, there are fewer layers of small-timers between him and the dirty work. He's close. Just around the corner." She paused, and her voice assumed a note of calculation. "My advice: get your hands on one of the small-timers. Take them into a room and don't come out until you have the person above them. Get your hands on that person and do the same thing with them. Two, three 'interviews' like that and you'll be close enough to smell him."

Graver sipped the coffee and nodded, watching her. Jesus.

"What about Dean's contact at the fountain? What in the hell do you think he's doing?"

"Marcus, I told you I thought this guy looked like government, didn't I?" Arnette said, tapping an ash off her cigarette into the ashtray. "Well, we're checking into that. I'm trying to get wire photos of . . . relevant . . . CIA and FBI people." She was being uncharacteristically evasive. "Luckily, this part of the business is relatively small. I should get something pretty quick."

"This part?"

"The government doesn't know how to handle people like Kalatis. There's a lot of intelligence community overlapping. He's a former foreign intelligence officer—that's CIA. He's probably working drugs —that's DEA. Whatever he's doing, he's doing it Stateside—that's FBI. So who gets him? CIA? DEA? FBI? Usually, everybody feels free to pursue their separate courses of inquiry." She mashed out her cigarette in the ashtray. "And you know how well they cooperate with each other."

"Then you think Dean is working for a government agency?"

"Well, not exactly." Arnette lowered her eyes cautiously, and her thin fingers dropped to the ocher pack of cigarettes. She moved it a little, repositioned it, stood it on its side, stood it on its bottom. "The question is, does Dean know who he's dealing with? What they've been doing, Marcus, is pretty far out. It's dirty. Being co-opted by the bad guys is pretty . . . sleazy. I don't know who's fooling whom here. I just think the guy's got government written all over him . . . Dean has business with him . . . and they're talking about Panos Kalatis." She shrugged.

"Anyway," she went on, "with Kalatis getting into the picture, this becomes business to me, too. It turns out Dean's reference to Kalatis is the first action the intelligence networks have had on this guy in almost a year. This is a fantastic opportunity for me, for my business. I want to get all I can on him. Now that we've both got a stake in him, you won't have to bear the whole financial burden. And the guy at the fountain. I want to know who the hell he is, too. There are some things I can do that you won't have to pay for, and I'll simply pass along what I can."

Graver nodded.

She leveled her eyes on him. "And I'll expect you to do the same," she added.

Graver nodded again. "Sure, of course," he said. "I appreciate it." He straightened up in his chair, put his elbows on the table and held his head in his hands for a second and then dropped them.

"We could be making a big mistake here," he said, looking at Arnette. "Why should we believe that the information behind Tisler's bogus investigations has to be originating with Kalatis? What if they're coming from the people at the fountain? What if the unknown is providing the information, not Kalatis?"

"We're thinking Kalatis made the hits."

"Based on this, yes," Graver said, taping the dossier. "But what if we're wrong about that? Dean mentions Kalatis, but we don't know in what context. If we hadn't heard his name, if we didn't know he existed, wouldn't we be assuming the guy at the fountain was behind all this? We'd almost have to be. This dossier may have thrown us off track."

"Or put us on track," Arnette countered, slipping another cigarette out of her pack. "We could have been making the wrong assumption. But, okay, let's say we weren't. Dean is still talking to the guy at the fountain about Kalatis. Is he asking about Kalatis or reporting about him? Either way"—she waved the unlighted cigarette balanced between her thin fingers—"Kalatis is involved—somehow. Either way I can guarantee you're going to be dealing with him."

She lit the cigarette. The background noises from the computer room drifted into their silence, a telephone ringing, voices, the occasional shrill beep of a computer complaining of a wrong entry. Graver knew Arnette was waiting for him to tell her what he was going to do. She wanted to know, and both of them knew he ought to tell her. Though he had made a career in intelligence, what he was doing now had as much to do with operations as with intelligence. She was more experienced in these kinds of intrigues, and she had seen a hell of a lot more of the havoc caused by men who killed as unthinkingly as they took a piss. She had come from a world where the processes were the same, but the stakes were higher and the rules often didn't even fit in the picture at all. If he was about to do something that could have lethal results, he'd better understand that.

"Okay," he said. "Let me tell you what we've got." He told her of Neuman and Paula's interview with Valerie Heath and the subsequent take of names from her garbage. He told her how they were following up now. He did not mention Victor Last. Then he said:

"When I get back to the office, I'm going to have Neuman pick up Heath. He's been wanting to do that . . . and that's your advice too, assuming she's at the bottom of Kalatis's organization. We'll see if we can't get her to cough up some names. Time's running out."

"You know you can't let her out of your sight once you haul her in," Arnette said.

Graver could tell by her face that Arnette was eager to see this happen.

"Yeah, I know that," he said.

"That's a logistics problem. You can handle that?"

"Yeah." He didn't have any idea how, but he knew she would like to have the job, and he didn't want to give it to her.

She studied him a moment, trying to see what he was thinking, he guessed. Then she said, "Okay, I'm going to run these names through my networks."

Arnette always wanted more names. Intelligence files were encrusted with layers of aliases, an entire field of study in itself. They were invaluable connectors.

He nodded, and she continued to smoke. She was playing with the cellophane on her pack of cigarettes, and Graver imagined that if he could have been inside her brain the explosion of synapses would have resembled very much the static-like sound of that crinkling plastic. She was working on something.

Graver's pager vibrated at his waist.

"I've got to go," he said, pushing back his chair. "I guess you don't have anything on Tisler's computer."

Arnette mashed out her half-smoked cigarette. "No, nothing. But I've put a couple of other people on it. I'm more hopeful now that he was squirreling away a lot of information. It could be a gold mine."

"And Dean?" Graver stood.

"He's been at home all day, and he hasn't made any calls. And now that I know more about what's going on here, I doubt that he will.

He's way beyond that kind of thing." She picked up her pack of cigarettes. "But that just increases the probability he'll take another trip soon, maybe tonight. At the very least he'll have to go out to make telephone calls." She stood also. "What's your sense about Ginette? You think she knows? Is she involved?"

"I don't know. She seems . . . not to be as rattled as Dean, not as distracted maybe." He shook his head. "My first reaction is to think that she doesn't know. But . . . it's only a sense, a feeling."

"Okay, then," Arnette said. "Let's both keep plugging away. This can't go on much longer without something breaking open."

Arnette came around the end of the table and opened the door to the computer room where the work was still tilting along at full bore, the high-speed, light-speed, almost-silent chip labor of the twenty-first century enabling fewer than a dozen people to move a frighteningly vast amount of data in milliseconds. When Graver allowed himself to dwell on it very long, he almost despaired. It was marvelous what man had learned to do with nothing more than an electrical spark. But somehow, he felt as though man was also only the alchemist's apprentice. He knew a bit of God's technology, but he understood considerably less of the divine moral sense that would enable him always to use it wisely. As history had proved all too consistently over the millennia, man's head was still ahead of his heart.

43

WHEN GRAVER GOT BACK TO HIS CAR, HE LOOKED AT HIS PAGER. The call-back number was Paula's at the office. He made his way back through the neighborhoods to Holcombe and then headed north on Kirby Drive. By the time he got back to the CID offices it was just after four o'clock. He stopped in front of Lara's opened office door.

"I'm sorry about lunch," he said.

She stopped typing on her computer and looked at him. "No problem." She shook her head. "I ate as much of it as I could." She grinned. "Did you finally get something?"

"I ate a very bad hamburger on the way. Listen, would you check with me before you leave this afternoon?"

"Sure," she said, looking at him with dark-eyed curiosity, hoping he would elaborate.

"Thanks." He turned and walked away. But instead of going to his office, he started down the long corridor of doorways. Ahead of him people meandered in and out of their cubicles, and as he passed opened doors he heard snatches of conversations, telephones ringing, clicking of fingers on computer keyboards. The door to Besom's office was open and Ted Leuci was sitting in Besom's chair with a cardboard box on the floor between his feet. It was half-filled with a miscellany of knickknacks. Besom liked knickknacks, little stuffed animals with suction cup feet, a ceramic log-cabin with a pencil sharpener in the chimney, a little wooden outhouse that suddenly popped apart into half a dozen pieces when you pulled the tiny door handle, a jokey fisherman's yardstick with an exaggerated scale, a roadrunner made of nuts and bolts and wire welded together. The place was a junk shop.

"How's it going?" Graver asked.

Leuci sat back in his chair. He looked around the office. "Okay," he said, arching his spine. "I got rid of the paperwork first, to keep it moving." He looked down into the box. "Now this . . . stuff." He shook his head. "He had more crap . . ."

Graver nodded and moved on down the hall, past a few closed doors until he came to Paula's, which was open. He stopped. She was sitting with her back to the door, her swivel chair rocked back with her feet propped on the low windowsill. She was writing on the legal pad which was resting on her thighs.

"You have something?"

She swiveled around. "Yeah," she said, and motioned for him to come in, which he did, closing the door behind him.

Paula was definitely in her end-of-the-day mode. The belt of her shirtwaist dress was undone and hanging loose, and her hair was pulled back in a tacky little wad and held in place with a blue rubber band. Her lipstick was gone hours ago, and she wasn't wearing shoes. The expression on her face reflected some irritation. Graver leaned one shoulder against the door and put his hands in his pockets. The only other chair in the room was stacked with books and ring binders and catalogues and directories. It was too overloaded and had been that way too long for Paula to pretend anymore that the chair had been designed for sitting.

She rested a bare foot on the shield of one of the chair's ball casters and crossed her legs, again tilting back the chair.

"I went to the Red Book and checked into the bank," she said. "Gulfstream National Bank and Trust is owned by a holding company, Gulfway International Investments. I managed—after considerable hassle—to get a faxed copy of Gulfway's Annual Franchise Tax Filings. In addition to the bank's officers, there are five board members listed. Two live out of state, in California. I started checking into the local three. One is a petroleum engineering company executive. It turns out he's a huge donor to a Cistercian monastery operation out in the mountains of New Mexico—odd but true. I put him on the back burner.

"The second local is the founder of Hormann Plastics, a plastics manufacturing company, guy named Gilbert Hormann. Hormann's business raised a flag from the get-go because of the chemicals and drug combination of the Seldon deal.

"And the third local guy . . . Colin Faeber."

"Son of a bitch," Graver said, straightening up. "Have you talked to Neuman?"

"I've paged him. He's gone down to the courthouse."

"When did you page him?"

"Just now; just a minute ago."

Graver looked at his watch. "He can't be there much longer. The place closes in a few minutes." He looked at Paula. "What do you have on him—on Faeber?"

"Minimal: home address, business address. I didn't go any further because I knew Neuman was on it, and I didn't see any use in duplicating work. So I dug up this stuff on Hormann."

"Okay, fine. Look, if he calls tell him to come on back here and then the two of you come down to my office. We've got some planning to do."

44.

IT WAS ALMOST FIVE-TWENTY AND NEARLY EVERYONE HAD LEFT or was leaving. As he passed Lara's office she was straightening her desk, putting things away. They looked at each other, and she picked up a notepad and followed him into his office. She closed the door behind her.

"When I went out earlier I went to Arnette's," Graver said, taking off his coat and hanging it on the rack behind his desk. He rolled up his shirtsleeves as he walked back around his desk and looked out the windows. He reached back and put his hands on either side of the small of his back and pressed hard against the rigid muscles. He turned around. "She had some new information based on the conversation she had taped between Dean and the guy at the Transco fountain. Dean's in this very deep. Deeper than . . . I wanted to believe." He told her about Panos Kalatis.

By the time he had finished, he had paced back and forth the length of his office several times. He had massaged his back the entire time and had loosened his tie somewhere in the process. Finally he walked around and sat down behind his desk. When he finished he was sitting with his elbows on his desk, the fingers of both hands working the muscles at the back of his neck.

Lara said nothing for a moment. She was sitting with her back against the back of her chair, straight and correct, the way you were supposed to sit though no one ever did. Her posture conveyed a comfortable efficiency, a natural preciseness, and she studied him from a mind that rarely portrayed ambivalence, an attribute that appealed to Graver because it was so alien to him. He did not understand that kind of uncluttered mental process.

"I guess I'm missing something . . . significant," she said, the fingers of her right hand toying with the top button on her blouse, "but I don't necessarily see it that way."

"What, that he's mixed up in this?"

"I guess he's 'mixed up in it,' " she said. "I just don't think it's necessarily . . . a criminal involvement. I mean, what if this man at the fountain is a government person, like Arnette believes. Maybe Dean's working for him . . . undercover for a federal agency. If he is . . . he'd have to keep it from you, wouldn't he?"

"You're right," he said. "That's true, and that kind of thing happens. But it's rare. Rare enough for it not to be a serious consideration here. I'd like to believe it . . . but . . ."

"What do you believe, Marcus? What do you *really* think Dean is doing?" she asked suddenly. The use of his first name caught Graver by surprise and focused his attention. "Have you—Marcus Graver, not Captain Graver—honestly ruled out that . . . you might be misreading what's happening?"

Graver checked a quick response, something passionless and flavorless—and dishonest—right out of the knee-jerk guidebook. They stared at each other over the desk. She did not blink. Her expression did not convey that she had offered him a challenge. She simply had asked an honest question and was waiting for him to give her—and himself—an honest answer.

"No," he said finally, slumping back in his chair. "I haven't ruled it out. And that's . . . a very good reason why I probably should have turned this over to someone else." He paused, but she said nothing. "I haven't even admitted to myself what I'm doing. No, I'm not buying it yet. But if it's true," he said, his own eyes moving thoughtfully to the cobblestone, "if he's dirty . . . I want to be the one to deal with that. I guess that's part of the irrationality of . . . attachments, of a friendship. It feels like . . . as if it would be cowardly of me, maybe it seems it would even be cruel of me, to let someone else deal with this. If it turns out badly, I ought to be the one to handle it. I mean, entirely aside from my job, on a personal level, I ought to be the one to pull the switch."

His choice of words surprised him. Jesus. As Freudian slips go, that was a grim one.

She continued staring at him, her eyes almost losing their focus as she thought. She stopped toying with the button, and her hand dropped to her lap.

"I don't know if I could do it the way you're doing it," she said, "but I can see how you would want to."

"How *I* would want to?"

"After what you've been through . . . with your wife"—she looked him squarely in the eyes as if she were saying she was not going to dodge the hard issues anymore, the personal issues—"I'm not really surprised you'd want to see this resolved in a way that would allow you to have control over it."

"Why is that?" He could tell she was getting at something.

"If you turned it over to someone else, that would almost be like having another relationship dissolve without your having had anything to say about it. I can see why you'd want to be involved in this no matter how painful it was for you."

Graver was speechless at this observation. This wouldn't have occurred to him in a million years. Was this a valid line of speculation? Could something so deeply contained, so personal, as Dore's leaving him really affect the way he was handling this investigation? Jesus Christ. Unwittingly, Lara had raised once again the issue of his greatest fear. Whether it dealt with Dore and his failed marriage, or whether it dealt with his relationship with Dean Burtell and this case, or whether it even dealt with his relationship to her, the issue of self-deception nagged at Graver like an obsession, and he wondered if Lara had seen how thoroughly it had come to preoccupy him.

There was a knock on the door, and Paula pushed her way in with Neuman immediately behind her.

"Oh." She started, looking back and forth between the two of them. "Sorry, I thought everyone was gone."

Graver and Lara were looking around at her, obviously having been engaged in a conversation that was not entirely business.

"No, it's okay," Graver said, standing. "No problem, come on in."

Lara didn't get up, though Paula looked at her as if she expected her to.

"Lara's staying," Graver explained. "There's a lot to discuss."

"Oh," Paula said again, and Graver could see her brain working all over her face. She was cautious, suspicious, and clearly doubting the wisdom of what it seemed that Graver had apparently decided to do.

Neuman immediately read the situation and came in and sat down on the other side of Lara. From that moment on he accepted her as part of the team without reservation and wanted to be seen as having accepted her. He spoke freely in front of her and looked at her as well as the others when it came time for him to give his report.

Paula was less comfortable as she sat down on Lara's other side. Paula was always game, but she was not blindly game. She would have questions and inevitably would hold to the independence of her own opinions. She was going to reserve her judgment.

"Okay," Graver said to Neuman, standing behind his chair, "what have you got?"

Neuman loosened his tie, undid the collar button of his plaid shirt, and took a notebook out of his coat pocket.

"Colin Faeber's married to his second wife, no children. His first wife and a daughter live in Denver where he sends hefty alimony checks. Second wife is from a wealthy family in New Orleans where he went to college. Owns a new home—built four years ago—in the Tanglewood area. Nine hundred thousand plus mortgage . . . note at Southern Federal. His personal indebtedness, aside from the house, is about four hundred thou . . . a couple of cars, another residence on South Padre, some furniture. I went to the Uniform Commercial Code filings. His business, DataPrint, dates back seven years when he started it with an initial investment of two hundred thousand borrowed from a bank. That note was paid off after a couple of years. At first the company was a kind of processing operation. He had some pretty heavy duty hardware, and when a smaller firm needed data merged or sorted in a manner that was too complex for their own hardware, Faeber's company would do it for them. It seems to have been very successful.

"About three and a half years ago Faeber expanded suddenly and enormously. Bought new, more powerful computers with an enormous influx of capital. A new lien holder appeared on his UCC filings: Concordia International Investments . . . in Buenos Aires, of all places."

"Do you have anything on that?" Graver interrupted.

"Wait . . ." Neuman flipped back several pages. "I did take the time to check World Traders Data Reports, but the information was so sketchy I had to resort to tracking down an annual directory of firms in four Latin American countries, Argentina, Brazil, Mexico, and Venezuela . . . here. CII is owned by a holding company, Strasser Industries, which owns dozens of businesses worldwide."

"Strasser?" The word leaped out of Graver's mouth.

"Right."

"That's a surname?"

"Right. Brod Strasser. He's the CEO of Strasser Industries."

Graver kept his eyes on Neuman as he came around from behind his chair and sat down. They all looked at him as he motioned for Neuman to continue.

"Well, there's not a lot more. But from looking at the UCC filings it seems to me that CII owns more of DataPrint than Faeber does at this point. It looks like they just about bought him whole when they financed these huge systems for him."

"Has his business changed? Does he still do the same kind of work he did before?"

"On the books he does. I haven't had time to do any of my own legwork, so I don't know any more than that."

Graver nodded. "Well, I doubt if he does."

Paula, increasingly impatient, could not control her fidgeting, and Graver didn't blame her. It was probably clear to all of them now that he was holding a lot of information that he ought to be sharing with them if the investigation was to move forward with any speed at all.

"Okay," he said, "let me bring you up to speed from my end."

For the next hour he told them everything he knew except for identifying Arnette or Victor Last. As he spoke he watched their faces alternate through a series of changes from incredulity to grim by the time he had come to the end of Yosef Raviv's dossier and Brod Strasser's name.

Several times during his recitation, he saw Paula cut her eyes at Lara. She was still having a hard time believing Graver was including her in such a sensitive development. She would have been even more surprised if she had known how much more Lara knew about this than she did, as well as the Division's entire operations.

"So there's the connection to Kalatis/Raviv," he said. "Colin Faeber is well connected, and I doubt if Kalatis and Strasser are interested in the kind of business that DataPrint has described in the documents on file."

Neuman was slowly shaking his head.

"Then these . . . people . . . you've got tailing Burtell," Paula said. "They're . . . a pretty high-powered operation."

Graver nodded. Paula just looked at him. She was considerably sobered by what she had just heard, the way that people are sobered when they realize that they were mistaken about what it was, exactly, out there in the dark. She glanced once more at Lara as though Lara, too, now took on a significantly new dimension.

"What are you going to do, then?" Neuman asked. "What do we do now?"

"We keep moving," Graver said. "I'm convinced that Kalatis is the core of this. Dean obviously knows him, knows him well enough to discuss him with the man at the fountain. With Kalatis's Mossad background, we'd be fools not to go after him, not to make the assumption that he's the heart of this operation. I think Dean's involved with him" —Graver glanced fleetingly at Lara—"but I'm beginning to have my doubts about exactly *how* Dean might be involved. From here on I want everything we do to be directed toward one end: working our way to Kalatis."

Neuman's eagerness to take some of the weight of guilt off Burtell's shoulders was obvious.

"Then you think Dean's being—"

"I don't know *what's* happening," Graver cut him off impatiently. "But I do think you were right, Casey, about picking up Valerie Heath. We've got to do it; we've got to talk to her. Right now she's the only opening we have if we're going to try this without showing our hand, without confronting Dean."

"Then what?" Paula asked. "What are you going to do with her? We can't arrest her, and once we pick her up we can't let her go. There's too much risk."

"Lara's going to stay with her."

Paula gaped. "Where?"

"At my place."

"Oh, for God's sake, Graver."

"I don't see any other way," he said. "We've got to keep an eye on her, for her protection and ours."

"Fine, but what about a motel?"

"We don't have the budget for something like that or the means of providing any kind of protection without drawing attention. If we can get her to my place without anyone knowing it would be easier. Meals wouldn't be a problem there, and at night there'll be two of us to take turns."

"Do you think she'll actually be in danger?" Paula blurted.

"I have to think so."

"What about Lara, then?"

"What do you want me to do, Paula?" Graver was getting tired of her questions, and that she insisted on concentrating on the downside. "You come up with a better solution."

"When do you want to pick her up?" Neuman interjected a more practical question.

"Now," Graver said. "I'll go with you." He reached into his coat pocket and took his house key off the car key chain. He handed it across to Lara.

"Go home and get some clothes," he said. "Get something comfortable, something for several days. On your way to my place go by a grocery." He took out his wallet and handed her all the money he had. "I keep a pretty bare pantry. Get enough for several people for several days. Paula, you go with her. When you get there, pull your car into one of the two garages and close the door so it can't be seen from the street. When Casey and I get there with Heath, we'll talk about what to do next. A lot will depend on what we learn from her."

He stood up. "Keep your radio handy. If my surveillance people are right, Burtell will take another trip tonight. We need to be in touch with each other every minute. Okay?"

They all stood. Lara hadn't said a word.

45.

8:20 P.M.

BEFORE LEAVING THE CITY GRAVER GOT A SEARCH WARRANT FROM a judge he could trust to keep the issuance quiet, and Neuman maneuvered their unmarked car onto the Gulf Freeway into the sluggish flow of traffic that bled from downtown for several hours every evening.

Graver sat quietly on the passenger side watching the traffic, the congestion seeming to be an appropriate metaphor for the state of his mind at the moment. He kept going over and over the frayed ends of the developing investigation. It would have been difficult enough to conduct this kind of operation with the full knowledge of the administration and a full complement of investigators working with his own technical people. Difficult enough. But this covert effort with only two investigators and out-of-office technical support—regardless of how good they were—was an invitation to disaster. Having minimal control and keeping only a modicum of compartmentalization was very nearly counterproductive. He felt like he was hanging on by the tips of his fingers.

He brooded over this for half an hour in silence and then gave it up and turned his mind to the immediate task at hand. He took the Key Map out of the glove box and opened it to the harbor complex where Valerie Heath lived.

"You said she had a docking slip behind her place?" he asked Neuman.

"Yeah, one of those canals. It's a pretty narrow inlet. Two cabin-type boats could pass in there, but it would be close." Neuman reached over and pointed to the map. "I put a little dot where she lives. Ballpoint. A blue dot."

"Yeah, okay. Here it is." Graver studied the layout of streets and docks and slips and inlets. He knew the area. It was not inexpensive real estate. "The street in front of her place is a cul-de-sac."

"Yeah. She lives about four, five houses from the circle."

"So eight to ten houses have a good view of the front of her place," Graver asked.

"That's right."

"Describe the place to me, the inside."

As Neuman did this Graver listened, asked a few questions, verbally playing back the description to him as though he was looking in from the canal side. When he was satisfied, he fell silent again.

They took the 518 exit off the freeway and continued to Marina Bay Boulevard which they followed around toward the coast until they began seeing the entrances to the marinas and yacht clubs. Neuman slowed when he came to the long street that ran out onto the peninsula where Heath lived. It was late in the afternoon by now and the sun was low above Houston behind them, and the shadows were lengthening in front of them.

"Just go in far enough to see if her car is parked in front," Graver said. "If it is, turn around and come back out."

Neuman nodded and turned in to the street. They didn't have to go far before they saw the black Corvette.

"There it is," Neuman said.

"Okay," Graver. "This is perfect. We're lucky. I know someone near here who's got a boat."

Neuman looked at Graver but said nothing as Graver gave him directions. Within fifteen minutes they were pulling up in front of another house with boat slips in the rear. It was miles away from Heath's by land, but by water it was just a few minutes. The houses here were considerably more modest than those in Heath's neighborhood. There were more banana trees here than palms, and the oily smell of the shipyards nearby permeated the still air. An occasional camper or fishing skiff was parked here and there under the rows of shaggy oleanders that separated the houses, and the driveways here were made of crushed mussel shells from the bay instead of smooth paving stones.

Graver directed Neuman into a driveway and the crunching of the tires on the shell base made a comfortable sound in the late heat and softening light of the afternoon. The garage in front of the car had been converted into living quarters and the crushed shell ran dead into the wall. An enormous outboard motor lay across two weathered sawhorses in front of the car. Neuman cut the motor, and Graver got out and walked between the car and the outboard motor to the front door that was shaded by an old mimosa that bloomed as brilliantly as if it had graced a palace garden.

Graver knocked on the frame of the screen door and heard a parrot screech somewhere in the dark interior. He heard footsteps coming, heard them pause, then quicken as they approached the front door.

"God damn," a man said, and Graver stepped back and the screen door popped open as a stocky man in his mid sixties stuck out his suntanned arm to shake his hand.

"How are you, Ollie?" Graver said.

"Hell, I'm fine," the man said, stepping out of the house into the shade. "How are *you?*"

His gray hair was wispy, its thinness having allowed his scalp to become deeply tanned and speckled by the coastal sun. He wore khaki trousers rolled to mid calf over faded blue tennis shoes and a denim shirt that must have been washed a million times, its long sleeves rolled to the elbow. The shirttail was tucked into the waist of the pants which were hitched over a tight belly and held in place by a cracked leather belt that was much too large, its unused portion hanging down in front of his fly. He was grinning at Graver, looking up at the taller man with a cocky smile that revealed strong, even teeth.

"You want somethin', don't you." His grin broadened.

"Yeah, that's right," Graver said. "A little favor."

The stocky man looked at the car and at Neuman. "Business."

Graver nodded.

"Right now."

"I need a boat ride," Graver said. "Just a few minutes from here."

"Yeah."

"I need you to take us there, maybe wait a while. Twenty minutes. Something like that. We'll be bringing a woman back here, and then she'll leave with me."

"Yeah."

"And then I'll owe you . . . again." Graver smiled.

"No shit. That's the way I like it." He looked at Neuman in the car. "Well, come on," he said, jerking a thick arm at Neuman.

Ollie was always game for a game, having spent years in tactical operations before he retired out. If he trusted you, he didn't ask a lot of questions; he just followed instructions. He knew that whatever was happening here had already been thought through by Graver. Graver wouldn't be asking him in if it wasn't something that wouldn't pass Ollie's own muster . . . or could have been done without his help.

As Neuman got out of the car, the man eyed him and then he turned and started around the end of the house as Graver and Neuman followed. They passed under a tunnel of oleanders tangled in weedy vines to a back yard that was only thirty or forty feet deep and ended at a dock in the canal. Moored at the dock was an old inboard cabin launch, a small one, but well cared-for, if sparsely furnished.

Ollie stepped on board without hesitation and began flipping switches and pulling buttons as Graver and Neuman stepped off the dock and into the cabin.

"Where is it?" he asked as the ignition started grinding and the engine caught in a gruff cough that turned to a deep rumble. Graver told him. "Oh, yeah." He stepped out of the cabin, threw off the mooring ropes and got back to the wheel. Without any further questions he eased back on the throttle, and the launch pulled slowly away from the dock as the old man let it glide into a drifting turn and in a moment they were moving forward, headed out of the canal toward the bay.

No one said anything for a while as the old launch casually made its way along the shore, passing the entrances to other canals, the houses growing tonier as the dusk grew darker. Graver heard the engine ease up before he actually felt it. He had been watching the lights come on along the shore, watching their converging illumination flanking the narrow canals as they passed. The engine slowed yet again as they made another listless turn into yet another canal and glided past the docks of the houses.

"I figure it's the next one up," Ollie said in a husky voice.

"Casey," Graver said, pulling Neuman to the cabin doorway. "You recognize it?"

"Yeah, he's right. That's it."

Ollie grinned silently.

"Can you cut your lights, Ollie?"

The old man did.

"Can you dock at the very end? Not pull all the way up in back of the house?"

The old man nodded and did as Graver asked. It was almost completely dark, and his task was not all that easy. In a moment they felt the prow nudge the dock and the old man cut the engine. He quickly stepped out of the cabin and walked the gunwale to the prow and got out onto the dock.

"I want you to go around front," Graver said, turning to Neuman. "Just ring the doorbell. When she answers and recognizes you, identify yourself. Let her know immediately you're a police officer—but be sure to get in, at gunpoint if you have to. Don't let her lock you out. Then let me in from back here. I'll try to get in behind her if the door back here is unlocked."

No one said anything more as Graver and Neuman got onto the dock and stepped a few feet into the bushes at the back of the small lawn. There were lights on in the house, a dim one in the kitchen where Valerie had burned her food the night before and then lights on in what must have been the back bedroom. Everything else was dark, some of the soft light in the kitchen falling onto the stone patio just outside the sliding glass door.

Graver nodded when he was satisfied, and Neuman made his way around one side of the house and disappeared. Easing to the side of the back door, Graver peered into the kitchen and dining room for a moment and then backed up and put his ear next to the wall outside her bedroom where the light was. He could hear water running. Was she bathing? Would she hear the doorbell? He went to the patio door and tried it. He was startled to find it unlocked. Slowly he slid it open, praying there wasn't an alarm system, and stepped inside. He waited a moment, then moved across the family room to a short hallway that he guessed led to the lighted bedroom. He paused at the doorway. Now he could clearly hear the shower. Good. He hurried down the entrance hall to the front door and opened it to a surprised Neuman.

"She's bathing," Graver said.

"Is she alone?"

Graver shrugged and locked the door again after Neuman stepped inside. They made a quick check of the other rooms to make sure they were alone and then went into the family room where they could still hear the shower. Neuman looked at Graver.

"There's not going to be any easy way to do this," Graver whispered. "We've got to go in there, and we'd better do it before she gets out of the shower. She might be able to get to a gun if we give her the chance. She might scream. Get your shield out."

Graver went first. The bedroom was a mess. The bed was unmade, and the only light on was a lamp beside it. The bathroom door was open and the shower seemed to be running full blast. She sneezed, and then blew her nose. She coughed. The smell of soap and the dank of steam drifted out into the bedroom. A closet door was open and a tangle of clothes draped off crooked hangers above shoes and shoe boxes piled carelessly on the floor. There was a television under the windows that looked out to the canal and a large digital clock with red numbers sat on top of it. Her underwear was at the foot of the bed where she had shed it as well as a pair of shorts and a halter top. A bottle of suntan lotion lay on the floor in front of an armchair beside the bed. There was a copy of *Cosmopolitan* on the wadded sheets, its pages folded back to an article she had been reading.

"We'll let her get out of the bathroom," Graver whispered hoarsely. "Don't want her to lock herself in there. Stand back out of sight beside the door, and when she's out I'll identify myself. Don't let her get back in there."

Neuman nodded and started toward the wall and immediately the shower stopped. Neuman plastered himself against the wall adjacent to the bathroom door, and Graver moved back out of sight near the closet.

Both of them thought she would take some time to dry off, maybe brush her teeth, or blow-dry her hair, but to their surprise she came straight out of the shower and into the bedroom dripping water and without a towel. When she cleared the door Graver stepped away from the closet.

"Police," he said. "Freeze right there."

The minute he saw her he knew it wasn't going to work that way. She immediately bolted, not back into the bathroom, but toward the bedroom door.

"Police," they both yelled.

"Stop," Neuman blurted and then lunged at her before she got to the door, knocking her sideways onto the bed where she fell into the tangle of sheets and started screaming. Neuman was on top of her instantly, wrestling her into the sheets as he tried to get his hand over her mouth, get the sheets into her mouth, the two of them rolling over and over as she flailed her arms and legs and squealed, tossing Neuman first one way and then the other from the sheer strength of her panic. Graver jumped on the bed too and together they managed to pin her between them, Neuman beneath her on his back with his arms locked around her, pinning her upper arms to her sides, his fists gripping each other under her heavy breasts, her wet hair in his face.

She was facing Graver who was on top of her, pressing his knee into her sternum as he held a part of the sheet over her mouth with one hand and his shield in front of her face with the other. She stared at the shield wall-eyed. All three of them were heaving for breath.

"Goddamn it," Graver hissed. "We're police."

Pause.

Her eyes went back and forth between him and the shield.

"You got that?" he asked.

Pause.

"Police," he repeated.

She nodded frantically.

"I'm going to get off you," he said. "Let you get some clothes on." He shook his head. "Don't fight this, okay?"

She nodded, her wet hair flapping in Neuman's face.

He eased his hand off her mouth. "Say 'okay,' " he said.

"Okay," she panted.

Graver eased off her, pulling the sheet up over her as best as he could as he did so.

"He's going to let go of you," Graver told her. "Don't try to get away again. Okay?"

"Okay," she blubbered, snatching at the sheet from all over the bed as Neuman gladly scrambled out from under her and rolled off the foot of the bed.

The front of Neuman's sport coat and trousers were dark with the water he had soaked off of her backside. He wiped his face which was dripping from the water from her hair. "Great," he said, looking at his clothes as he slung the water off his hands.

Valerie Heath quickly got the sheets around her and sat up against the headboard of the bed, gaping at them.

"Do you understand that we're police?" Graver repeated, standing at the foot of the bed and holding his shield out in front of him.

"Yeah . . . yeah . . ." she stuttered. She looked at Neuman who was running his fingers through his rumbled hair.

"You remember me?" Neuman wheezed.

"Yeah . . ."

"Do you have any idea why we're here?" Graver asked, putting his shield back into his pocket.

She shook her head.

"I believe you do," Graver said. He stared at her. "Speak to me," he said, "so I'll know you're understanding me."

"I fuckin' understand you," she said, "you son of a bitch." Her black hair was plastered to her forehead, and without her makeup her face was as featureless as a sheet of paper.

"Good," Graver said. "Now listen to me. We're going to take you in for questioning." He would explain later that he wasn't exactly taking her in. "You've got yourself in a hell of a mess, Ms. Heath." He put his gun away, made a swipe at his own hair with his fingers and sat down at the foot of the bed.

"Listen," he said, trying to sound calm and sane to her, trying not to sound like a policeman, "I'll be honest with you. I don't believe you fully understand what it is you're involved in here." He paused. "The people you're working for have killed two police officers. Detectives." He looked at her in the dim light of the lamp. All he could see was belligerence. "As of this moment, your life isn't worth a dime either. I'll explain why when we have more time. If we decided we didn't want to talk to you after all, if we walked out of here right now and left you alone, you wouldn't make it through the night. Even if you got in that brand-new Corvette of yours and drove it like hell all night . . . you wouldn't see the sunrise." He held his eyes on her. "Believe me."

He didn't see anything in her face.

"We're getting ready to close down the whole operation, Valerie," he lied, "but we're going to try to save as many lives as we can. We don't want anybody else killed. We have reason to believe that they're going to start killing some of you. They know they're near the end of this, and they're trying to cut their losses. Unless we have your help, the people you work for, the people at the top, are going to get away with it. We don't want something for nothing. We want to deal. We can save your life, sure. But if you agree to cooperate with us we'll also do our best to keep you out of prison. After all, you've been used." He paused. "There's no need in you serving time for something you didn't really understand. Especially if they all skip out on you."

This time he saw something working in her eyes. As she calmed down she began to think, and Graver had the feeling that thinking was going to do her a lot of good. Maybe.

"Now listen," he said, "we need to get out of here as soon as we can. We've got a boat out in the canal. Why don't you get dressed. This is not a good place to be."

"Let me see that shield again," she said.

Graver took out his shield again and handed it to her. She took it and leaned over under the lamplight and looked at it very closely. She passed her fingers over the face of the shield. Then she handed it back to him. She looked at Neuman.

"I knew that goddamned insurance story was phony," she said.

"I need a little more practice," Neuman said.

"No shit." She relaxed a little.

"Why don't you get dressed," Graver said, standing.

"Oh, *yeah*," she said with exaggeration, looking at each of them.

"One of us is going to have to watch you," Graver said. "You know we can't turn our backs on you. Choose whichever you want."

"Oh, give me a *break*," she said, flinging aside the wet sheet as she crawled off the bed. "This jerk here has already had his hands all the hell over me. What am I gonna do, get modest all of a sudden?"

She walked naked to her dresser, opened the drawers, and started looking for panties and a bra. She didn't hurry, glancing at them a couple of times, letting them get a good look at her two-toned body as she seemed unable to immediately find what it was she was wanting.

"Get several changes and put them in a bag," Graver said, turning and walking out the bedroom door. He threw a look at Neuman who rolled his eyes and wiped his face one more time.

46.

BY THE TIME VALERIE HEATH HAD GOTTEN DRESSED—FOR SOME reason she selected a wraparound skirt with an orange and brown pattern of African motifs and a sleeveless white blouse—and had put some clothes in a weekender bag, she and Neuman were on pretty good terms. The same elements in his personality that enabled him to work easily with the ever thorny Paula seemed also to appeal to Valerie Heath.

While Neuman was charming her, Graver had picked up a small flight bag from another bedroom and had searched the house, gathering a considerable cache of false IDs and some paperwork and documents that he didn't take the time to read. He just swept everything into the bag.

Valerie was nervous at the idea of Neuman driving her Corvette into the city, but was finally convinced it was necessary. So as Neuman drove away from the front of her house, she and Graver stepped onto Ollie's boat, a craft that did not much impress her.

Graver avoided the issue of handcuffs until they got to Ollie's place, thinking any scene she might make there would attract less attention than on her own patio and dock. But he hadn't needed to worry. She accepted them, along with a waist chain, with a little obligatory grousing and willingly got into the passenger side of the front seat.

On the way into town Graver prepared her for her unorthodox "custody." He said that because of the deaths of the two police officers, a special undercover task force had been put together and that he was in charge of it. He said that there were two factions inside the police department. One faction wanted to throw the book at her because of her "role," while the other faction—himself, Neuman, and others—wanted to give her a break in exchange for what information she could provide them. What they would like to do when this was all over was simply cut her loose in exchange for her cooperation. She wouldn't need to call a lawyer because they weren't going to charge her with anything if she agreed to go along with them. Otherwise she was going to risk spending the rest of her life in prison.

Graver talked in a conversational way, explaining all of this to her as if she were being trained for a new job. He answered her questions, lying to her easily and readily, whatever it took to prep her to be ready to spill her guts once they started questioning her. He could tell by her questions what her fears were, and he played to those with the dexterity of a psychoanalyst. Valerie Heath was not a brilliant person, which was part of the reason she had found herself in her present situation.

By the time they got to the edge of the city and he told her he was going to have to blindfold her, she accepted the idea as aggravating but not necessarily unpolice-like. Graver radioed Neuman that he was going to pull over for the blindfold, and the two cars exited onto an access road. Once the blindfold was in place, Graver did not talk to her again. The first time she asked a question, Graver only said "Shhhh" very softly, and not another word was spoken until he slowed to pull to the curb in front of his house. He was glad to see the lights on in the house and the garage door closed as he had instructed.

He radioed Neuman behind him to go into the drive ahead of him and park the Corvette in whichever of the two garages Lara had not used for her car. Graver then immediately rolled down his window and turned his head to the outside as though he was talking to someone outside the car.

"Signal the guys at the back that we're coming around," he said, and quickly rolled up the window, waited a moment, then pulled down the driveway to the back of the house, parking the department car out of sight from the street as Last had done two nights before. He cut the motor.

"Okay, Valerie. Here we are," he said. "We're going to take you inside the house now."

Lara met them at the back door, stepping out of the way as she pulled it open. She had changed into a pair of jeans and a conversation-stopping tank top. Paula was standing in the entrance to the kitchen behind her.

Just as they all got into the kitchen Graver's pager vibrated at his waist. He looked down and recognized Arnette's number.

"Wait right here," he said, and walked out of the room leaving them standing there in silence. He went into the living room and called Arnette.

"Okay, baby, your man's on the move again," she said. Graver looked at his watch: it was 10:30. He could hear voices coming over radios in the background.

"You don't know anything about where he's going?"

"Nothing. No calls came in or out of his place. He just got up and left. But it looks like he's going through the same maneuvers as last time. The guy's relentless."

"I've just picked up Heath," Graver said.

"She's going to talk?"

"I think so."

"Good. Milk her. Let me know if we can use any of it. I'll call you with news from this end."

Graver hung up the telephone and stood at his desk a moment. A weighty disappointment settled on him again at Burtell's betrayal. It had never been completely obliterated by the fast pace of the developing events, but sometimes it confronted him anew, and it struck him hard again as it had when he had first realized it. He turned and walked back out into the hallway and down to the kitchen where everyone was standing just where he had left them.

"Okay," he said, taking Valerie Heath's arm again, "we're going upstairs."

He took her up, guiding her carefully, taking her around the landing to Natalie's bedroom. Once inside, he turned on the light and let Neuman untie her blindfold. He didn't remove her handcuffs. She blinked a few times and looked around.

"You know Paula," he said. Heath nodded, looking her over quickly with a sarcastic what-else-is-new expression. "And this is Lara," he said. Heath nodded again, giving her the same eye-flicking appraisal.

"What about the cuffs?" she asked, holding out her hands.

"Not yet," Graver said. He was curt, and didn't offer any explanations. "Are you hungry?"

She shook her head and sat down on the end of the bed. "Can I have a cigarette?"

"Not in here," Graver said.

"Coffee? Can I get a cup of *coffee* then?"

"Sure," he said. "Paula, will you give me a hand?"

Downstairs Graver went straight to the kitchen and started a pot of coffee while Paula dumped the overnight bag out on the kitchen table and began going through the documents. When the coffee was going, Graver sat down across from her. Paula had laid out six false Texas driver's licenses, all with Heath's picture on them—in a few she wore blond wigs—but with different names, birth dates, and identifiers, including licenses for Irene Whaley, who subscribed to magazines at Heath's house, and Frances Rupp, who had bought the Corvette. There were bank account cards for each of the licenses, all at different banks, all of them containing money. All of the accounts together totaled nearly three hundred thousand dollars.

"In-credible," Paula said.

47

"I MET DON C. ABOUT THREE YEARS AGO," SHE SAID, CRA-
dling the coffee in her cuffed hands as she sat at the foot of the bed
with her legs crossed yoga-style. Her white blouse was unbuttoned low
enough to reveal the long cleavage of her weighted breasts. "Met him
in a bar. I was coming off a bad marriage, a *bad* marriage, and I was
depressed and broke. Don struck up a conversation with me, heard my
story, and said he could use a kind of gofer girl to help him do his
little stuff. That's what he called it, his 'little stuff.' It didn't take any
convincing, that's for damn sure. Shit, I jumped at it."

She shook her head, remembering. "Truth is, I would've worked
for that guy for nothing." She looked at Lara who was sitting in a
chair across from her as if she thought Lara would understand.
"Guy's"—she nodded and lifted an eyebrow wryly—"a *stud*. A real
one. Not some Happy Hour Yuppie, but a guy who's got muscles and
never went to a gym an hour in his life." She shook her head. "Anyway," she said, glancing around at Graver who was sitting at the head
of the bed with a tape recorder, "all I did was, I went to parking
garages and malls and places like that and took manila envelopes from
people—it was usually women but sometimes guys—and gave them
envelopes of cash in return. I knew it was cash. Don told me. And I
knew it wasn't drugs . . . I mean, flat manila envelopes? Besides, I
opened the ones that weren't sealed good and looked. Sometimes it
was microfiche or computer printouts or just photocopies of documents."

"What kind of documents?" Neuman asked. He was sitting on the
floor leaning back against the wall, his legs straight out on the
carpeted floor. He was taking notes on a steno pad.

"Lots of time they were bank records. Sometimes it was corporate information, uh, market research, product development research, sales figures, financial reports, billing records. Anything, everything."

"Did you always give the money to individuals?"

"Oh, no. Most of the time not. At first I did because Don wanted me to get familiar with them, but not later. Don would give me a key and the money. If the key was to a car trunk in a parking garage, he'd give me the license plate number too. I'd find the car, open the trunk, leave the money, and take the envelope that would be there. Sometimes the key was to a locker at an airport or a mailbox at the post office. A few times even a safety deposit box. The drops could be anywhere. Whatever you could think of."

"How much money were you paying out?" Paula asked. She was sitting in a chair too, near Lara, her crossed leg swinging nervously.

"Sometimes hundreds sometimes thousands . . . per person. As much as thirty thousand, as little as a couple of hundred. But I was picking up from the same group of people all this time, same five or six people, so they were turning some serious cash.

"This was kind of my training. I did this for maybe six months before Don got around to talking to me about it, telling me what he was doing and how he was doing it. He said he had a client who gave him a shopping list of information he wanted. It was this guy who furnished the money to buy the stuff. Don found the people who could get the information, and then he started running them.

"Anyway, eventually Don turned these people over to me, and I'm still doing it. He passes me information lists, and I pass them on to the right people, make all the buys. It's so damn easy. The amount of money I get out of it goes up and down sometimes because I get a percentage of what my sources get and what they get depends on the kind of information Don is asking them to come up with. I can't always count on a certain amount every month, but it's always cash, for me, for them, all around, and there is so damn much of it it doesn't matter. I never had so much money."

"Do you put it all in one account?"

"Oh, hell no. Don taught me how to set up bank accounts all around, spread the money, never deposit more than eight thousand at a time in any one place. That's his personal, rule-of-thumb cutoff, eight thousand. The thing is, he didn't want to get the banks suspicious, thinking we were selling drugs, and report us to the cops."

"He got you the forged driver's licenses?" Graver asked.

"Yeah. His client can give us any kind of thing we want like that."

"But you don't have any idea who the client is."

Valerie Heath shook her head. "Naw. Nobody knows anybody. I don't even know Don, for Christ's sake. I always meet him wherever he says to meet, and he's always there ahead of me and makes me leave first so I can't see what kind of car he drives."

"You've never tried to hide and catch him leaving after you?" Paula asked.

Heath waited a beat or two before answering. "Yeah"—she nodded—"once. He caught me. That's when I found out he knew exactly what I drove. He knows a lot about me. He said if he ever caught me doing that again it was over." She paused and sipped her coffee. "I was already pulling down almost ninety thousand a year. Cash. I figured knowing more about him wasn't worth losing that. Hell, if he wants to be the mystery man, let him. I'll take the cash."

"What about the people you're buying from? Do they know you?"

"No way. I do just like Don. I use a different first name and last initial with each of them. Debbie E. Linda M. Whatever. Every one of them knows me as somebody different."

"Do you know any of them?"

"Nope. If one of them drops out for some reason—and I never know why they do, it doesn't happen very often—Don gives me a new one. First name only. New contact routines. I don't know them. They don't know me. I don't know Don."

"But he knows you."

"Yeah." She nodded. She put her coffee cup between her thighs and raised her hands to fluff her hair. "He does."

"What kind of business are your people working in?" Neuman asked.

"I got people in two banks, a few law offices, a maintenance service, and an executive secretarial service. The maintenance service guy is the biggest moneymaker."

"Why's that?"

"Because this guy isn't really a janitor. He's a computer freak, a hacker. The business he works for has the janitorial contract for one of the biggest buildings downtown. There are oil company offices in there, law offices, stockbrokers, real estate people, international businesses. This guy has access to all these offices all night, every night. Don has more laundry lists for this guy than anyone."

"Do all of your people have the same expertise?" Neuman was making notes frantically, not even looking up to ask the question. "I mean, are they all employed in the same kind of job?"

"No. That's the thing about this," Heath said, looking at Lara again. "All of them are fairly low-level. Secretaries, data input clerks. Desk types. That's why it works. Everybody's in low-paying jobs and always need the money, but they have access to records. Computers. They can get whatever it is you want on those damn computers. They have all this access, but they aren't getting paid shit. Everybody like that's strapped for money. It's easy to buy them. Cash. That's the thing. I mean, they don't have any loyalty to those companies. They know damn well if things get tight they're going to be the first ones to go. They're not kidding themselves. Big shots—they always think, you know, the average person is dim-witted. Those big companies. It's like the government. Average person gets a chance, they're going to screw them 'cause they know the company would do the same to them if their profits started suffering. That's what this shitty economy has taught a lot of people, if nothing else. Cover your ass."

Valerie polished off her coffee and looked around, waiting for the next question.

Graver asked, "Have you ever heard of a company called DataPrint?"

Valerie Heath pursed her mouth a second and then shook her head. "No."

"Have you ever heard of a guy named Bruce Sheck?"

Again she gave it a little thought and shook her head. "No."

"What was the deal with Colleen Synar?" Graver asked.

"That, Jesus. It wasn't anything. One day Don tells me, Look, if anyone calls you and asks for a Colleen Synar, tell them she moved away a long time ago. I said, What? He said, somebody might call you about her, just tell them she moved away and that's all you know. That pissed me a little. I didn't say he could do that, give my number to somebody. He didn't explain any more than that. I was pissed, but I didn't say anything else. I was afraid of losing my situation. At that time the money was already coming in big-time. I'd never had anything like that before. I didn't want to lose it. I worried about it a long time, was scared every time the phone rang. But when nobody ever called I forgot about it . . . until she called," she said, nodding at Paula.

"When you want to get in touch with Don, how do you do it?" Graver was leaning back against the headboard of the bed. His tie was undone.

"Telephone number. I call it, leave a message, he calls me back. The number changes every four or five weeks."

"What's the number?" Neuman asked.

"Forget it," she said. "I called him yesterday and the thing's dead. And I haven't heard from him."

"Do you think Don has other people like you, buying information from several sources?"

"Oh, sure he does. He told me. In so many words, anyway."

"How many other people do you think there are?"

"No idea. He just said this was a big operation. And he had this system down pretty good. Rules. Sometimes when we meet he says something like, well, he'd better get going and run his 'other' traps. Gives me the impression I'm not the only one he's feeding money to and collecting information from." She thought a moment. "To tell you the truth, sometimes I think there might be other people like Don, too. You know, working for this 'client.' "

"Have you ever heard of the name Panos Kalatis?" Graver asked.

She shook her head. "No, I think I'd remember that one."

"Have you ever heard Don speak of a Greek guy?"

"Greek?" She frowned then shook her head again. "No Greek."

They talked to Valerie Heath for more than an hour. Twice Lara went downstairs to get her more coffee and once Heath had to stop to go to the bathroom. Though Lara said nothing during all this, Paula, Neuman, and Graver went over and over the information, approaching it from different angles, rephrasing her answers into new questions that put a slightly different perspective on the subject. Heath's responses never wavered, and she responded as candidly as she had thrown off the sheets in front of Neuman and Graver. It seemed that having once decided to give it all up, she did so without reservation. At times it even seemed to Graver that she was oddly relieved to do it. And he noticed, too, that she was responding to the very human emotion of being flattered to be the center of attention.

"If we needed to talk to Don," Graver said, "how would we get in touch with him?" As he asked this, he took Bruce Sheck's contributor ID record out of a manila folder and held his picture up in front of her.

"Damned if I know," she said. "Just that phone number." Her eyes went to the photograph. She stared at it. Slowly her expression changed. "Well, I'll be damned." She started nodding slowly, a smile almost forming on her mouth. "That's him. That's ol' Don C. himself."

48

GRAVER WAS WALKING AROUND THE KITCHEN WITH HIS SHIRT-sleeves rolled to the elbows pulling sandwich meat and cheese out of the refrigerator, pickles and olives and onions out of the pantry, bread from the bread box, handing a knife to Neuman and indicating to him to start slicing. He was talking to Paula who was sitting at the table taking notes.

"I want you to drain every little detail out of her," he was saying. "What companies these people were in; what were their exact positions; what kind of data they were providing; what kinds of businesses Don wanted information from; what kinds of information; the names of the firms this computer hacker pulled information from; who was his shift supervisor—the supervisor was probably being paid off since he had to know the hacker wasn't cleaning offices. Everything you can think of that could help us later when we start piecing this together."

He took another knife out of the holder on the cabinet and started slicing the onion.

"All in all it wasn't a bad call," Graver said. "She did put Sheck in place for us, and there's a load of detail to be mined from those sources in each of those five companies."

"Sheck's going to be harder to get our hands on than Valerie was," Neuman said, stacking the bread slices on a plate. "It seems to me he's a pretty savvy operator, an old hand at this sort of thing."

"I think you're right." Graver finished the onion and started slicing tomatoes. "He has all the earmarks of a professional. Heath even used the term 'running' for Sheck's handling of his sources. She got that from him. The guy's got an intelligence background. And that brings us to Kalatis. This guy belongs to Kalatis."

"With Mossad? He sounds American to me."

"I don't think it makes any difference anymore," Graver said. He was frustrated and angry. "Boundaries are disappearing everywhere. For people like this, loyalties don't have anything to do with where you're born or where you live or with family or homeland. Their loyalties don't operate under flags. They put their lives on the line for international monetary units: the dollar, the deutsche mark, the pound, the yen."

He put the slices of onions and tomatoes on a large platter with pickles and olives, but left the cold cuts in the brown butcher's paper the way Lara had brought them from the grocery.

"The problem is," he said, "we haven't made a hell of a lot of progress on the big picture here." He opened a sack of potato chips and a sack of corn chips and then went to the refrigerator again and took out a bottle each of mayonnaise and mustard. "You guys want regular mustard or that other, the spicy kind?"

"Regular," Neuman said.

"Spicy," Paula said.

Graver put them both on the cabinet.

"There's beer and soft drinks in the refrigerator," he said and started putting together a sandwich while Paula began clearing the table of its collection of notepads and Heath's assortment of forged identities. When Graver finished the sandwich, he cut it in half diagonally, put it on a plate with both kinds of chips and some olives, and got a beer from the refrigerator. He opened it, put the plate and the beer on a tray with a napkin and walked out of the kitchen.

They were sitting on the floor at the foot of the bed like a couple of schoolgirls, the cards between them.

"Jesus Christ!" Valerie said, walling her eyes from beneath her shock of parched, black hair. "Look at the butler, will ya. You make that yourself?"

"Yeah," Graver said, putting the tray down on the floor beside Lara.

"Thanks," Lara said.

"You don't have a wife?" Heath asked. "You divorced or what?"

"You sure you don't want something?" he asked her.

"Well . . . not a sandwich." She grinned, running her eyes over him.

Graver walked out of the room and looked at his watch. Arnette had called well over an hour ago. Something should have happened by now. As he passed his bedroom he glanced in the open door and stopped. He stepped inside. His bed had been made and Lara's off-white linen suit was spread out on it. An open suitcase was on the other side of the bed. He walked over and looked in the suitcase. There were slips, a couple of silk blouses. Lingerie. The cups of the bras tucked into each other, the panties folded once. There was the familiar fragrance of fading perfume that lingered in women's suitcases, even when they were empty. He walked to Dore's closet and opened the door. There were three dresses hanging there, isolated in the empty space that echoed even in the silence. He closed the door and walked back into the bedroom, pausing once again at the opened suitcase. He stared at the lingerie and resisted an impulse to reach down and touch the lace on the upper parts of the bras, the slippery silk. He turned away and quickly walked out of the room.

Downstairs Paula and Neuman were sitting at the kitchen table eating and talking, a steno pad and ballpoint pen lying beside Neuman's plate. Graver went to the cabinet and started making a sandwich for himself.

"Okay, let me run this by you," Neuman said, wiping his mouth with a napkin and picking up the pen as he leaned over his notes. "Sheck is somewhere higher up in the chain for whoever's buying the information. It's a pretty good bet Sheck knows Dean, or at least Dean knows him since Sheck's name is in the Probst file. Kalatis is in the picture only because Dean mentioned his name when he met with the Unknown at the Transco Fountain."

"That's right," Graver said, slicing his sandwich. "And, incidentally, that telephone call earlier was from our surveillance people. Dean's been on the move for about an hour."

"Jesus," Paula said. She threw a look of incredulity at both of them. "Jesus, this is just wild."

"And there's Faeber. We connect him with Kalatis through Brod Strasser who bought controlling interest in DataPrint and who was mentioned as a Kalatis associate in the Raviv file."

"Just for the record," Graver put in, "I don't think it was a coincidence that it was at Faeber's house that my informant overheard the conversation where Tisler and Besom's names came up."

Paula nodded slowly, thoughtfully. "And I don't think it's too much of a leap in logic to assume that Faeber's company, or at least someone inside his company, is buying the take from Bruce Sheck's little data acquisition operation."

Graver opened a beer for himself, leaned back against the kitchen counter with his legs crossed at the ankles, and began eating his sandwich, looking across the kitchen at them.

"Which speaks also to Sheck's 'expertise,' " Neuman said. He ate a potato chip and drank a couple of sips of his soft drink. He looked at Graver as he wiped his mouth again. "And which makes me wonder about your informant. Do you . . . are you fairly sure . . ."

"You mean, am I sure he's not a plant?" He shook his head. "No. His timing—coming out of nowhere just now—is suspicious and his 'good luck' at Faeber's party strains credulity." Graver shook his head. "No, I'm not comfortable with it at all. But the one thing that doesn't jibe with his being a plant is his deliberately bringing Faeber's name into it. Why would they volunteer *anybody's* name? Especially the name of a key player."

"You said he seemed surprised to hear of their deaths," Paula said. "Maybe he wasn't told everything. Maybe he was just supposed to try to find out how much you knew, if you knew anything, and when he learned of the deaths that caught him off guard, he panicked, and gave up Faeber's name."

"No." Neuman was shaking his head. "People like Kalatis, this Strasser, they never would have let someone at an informant's level get close enough to them and run the risk of him doing something like that. They just wouldn't do it."

"Yeah, I guess I agree with that," Graver said, "and that's precisely the point that makes me want to believe him. His story is just too . . . clumsy. I can't see them deliberately setting up something like that. I just can't imagine what they would have thought they could gain by having him do what he's done."

"Let's say he's telling the truth," Paula said. "Who did he overhear? Sheck? You think Bruce Sheck is the kind of guy who would be at a tony party like Faeber's?"

None of them, of course, believed a "stud" who frequented the kinds of bars where he could have picked up the likes of Valerie Heath would also have been at a party in the polite company of a Tanglewood crowd like the one Last had described. They fell silent. Graver ate his sandwich as Neuman studied his notes again, and Paula stared at the kitchen floor. Graver didn't know what they were thinking, but he was increasingly aware that this thing was all over the place. What in the hell did he expect to accomplish? It would take an enormous task force and a lot of time to investigate this properly. He didn't have either the task force or the time. And even as he was thinking this, Paula was ahead of him.

"Graver," she said, interrupting his thoughts. She had turned around in her chair and was facing him, her bare feet slightly apart on the floor, her hands together in her lap pushing the skirt of her dress down between her thighs. It was a college kid's posture. "Do you really think anyone in the police department other than Dean is involved in this? Is that what you're trying to discover before you get someone else in on this?"

He put an olive in his mouth and bit into it, tasting the pimiento and the salty oil. He chewed it and then washed it down with a swallow of beer.

"Why?" he asked.

"Because you know as well as I do this is . . . impossible." She cut her eyes at Neuman, then back to Graver. "We're not doing this justice. There ought to be people all over this Heath and Sheck operation. It's enormous. There could be five or six Shecks and thirty Heaths and more than a hundred, maybe hundreds of people stealing information to sell to them. It's incredible when you think about it. I'm probably not even imagining on a big-enough scale. It gave me the creeps listening to that woman upstairs. These people . . . the information they have is spooky. And even spookier is imagining what they might be doing with it. It's just that . . . this is so big, for Christ's sake."

Graver nodded, chewing the last bite of his sandwich. He wasn't sure how he was going to answer her, but he was sure of how he felt about it.

"Look," he said, taking a sip of beer and wiping his hands on a paper towel he was using for a napkin. He pushed the nearly empty beer bottle back on the tile countertop and walked over, pulled out a chair, and sat down.

"You're right. It is big. You're right, we absolutely cannot handle it. Not in the long run. But we're actually only in the discovery stages of this thing right now. Do I think someone else from the police department is involved in this? I don't know, but I have growing doubts that men like Kalatis and Strasser and even Faeber, for that matter, would be involved if it was the kind of operation that didn't go any higher up than Dean Burtell. An analyst is nothing to these men. They may *need* an analyst, they may *use* him, but I'm guessing that what they're trying to get into requires a higher level of cooperation. Dean, for all his intellect and ability, is only a stepping-stone here. I've got to believe they're aiming higher than what he can provide. He's simply being used."

He looked at Neuman and then back at Paula.

"So what do I do? I make the assumption that a lot of money is involved here because the big players don't come to small games. There's a big game somewhere right under our noses. Now who among the HPD's top people am I going to trust with this? It's not that there aren't any good men and women here who can be trusted. Of course there are. It's just that there may be *some* here who *can't* be trusted, but I don't know who the hell they are. So how do I know who to bring into it? Who do I involve? Should I risk this whole operation that you've just talked about, this enormous something, on a bet that it stops with Dean? Or on a bet that I'll be able to pick the right people to reveal it to?" He paused. "I don't think so."

"What about the FBI? If it's so big, they ought to be the ones going into this. They've got the resources."

Graver looked at her. "All right, Paula, here's an honest answer to that. You're right, in a well-ordered world that would be the way to go."

Then he explained to her what Arnette had pointed out to him about the conflicting jurisdictions of the CIA, DEA, and FBI regarding Kalatis.

"If I go to them at this point," he said, "I might run the risk of having this melt right in front of my eyes. I shouldn't have to explain to you about jurisdictional squabbles. Well, at this point—maybe not tomorrow, maybe not the next day—but at this point, I want to be able to call the shots on the leads *we* develop. I don't want anything taken away from me. I don't want to be co-opted or condescended to. I don't want to be pushed into the background." He paused. "I guess when it comes right down to it I'm not any better than the rest of them about wanting to protect my jurisdiction. But Tisler and Besom were *my* people. Dean is *my* responsibility. I don't want to turn them over to anyone else."

He paused again. "Besides, from what I see happening I think we have as good a shot at Kalatis as any of the agencies. And I don't want to share this bastard with anybody. If we get our hands on him, I don't want to see him bargained away from us for some other agenda set by people in Washington or Langley or Quantico."

Neuman was looking down at his steno pad, doodling on it with his pen. Paula was staring at him, but she wasn't saying anything. She simply looked at him, lost in thought. He guessed that she was trying to work it out. He guessed she didn't know what she thought, and until she did she wasn't going to push it.

"But," Graver continued, "I don't think we're going to have much time to worry about it anyway. A lot of possibilities are about to come into play here. If Kalatis is moving on some kind of big project, those other agencies are going to be onto him anyway. I don't think for a minute we're in this thing by ourselves. If Kalatis suspects he's about to be compromised—and he probably knows more than we'd like to think—then he's going to speed up the program. Our window of opportunity here is very small and shrinking."

"How small?" Neuman looked up.

Graver shrugged and shook his head. "I'm guessing . . . a couple of days maybe. Tisler and Besom's deaths will hit the newspapers in the morning. If those news stories take the form of something speculative, if they hint at something dark behind the deaths, Kalatis is going to want to disappear. And then Sheck is going to miss Heath. I just don't think we have that much time before this turns into something a hell of a lot different than we have now."

12:18 A.M.

"ANY ROOM FACING THE HARBOR," THE MAN SAID. HE SAID IT quickly, having put his bag down in front of the registration desk without taking his other arm from around the young woman he was holding close to him. The desk clerk noticed the guy's thumb was rubbing the side of the woman's bra under her blouse. Or it would have been rubbing her bra. He didn't think she was wearing one.

"High up," the woman said, looking at the man and then at the desk clerk, smiling at him with a smile that the clerk would have described as mischievous if he had been familiar with the word. "I want to see the boats, the lights on the boats."

"High up," the man said, winking at the desk clerk. "Got to see those boats."

"High up," the desk clerk said, checking his computer. The man was some kind of Latin, not Mexican, maybe Colombian, a real macho hunk, good-looking, well-built, early thirties. The woman was in her mid twenties, the clerk guessed. A red-blooded American thing with caramel-colored hair streaked blond by the sun and a very fine set of hooters that this Latin character was getting his thumb all over and, now, even the rest of his hand. The clerk lost track of what he was hitting on the keyboard and had to mess around with the keys again to find his place.

"What about it, huh? Have you got something?" the Macho asked. "What have you got? We're kind of in a hurry." He said hurry with a kind of back-of-the-throat skitter across the r's.

No shit. The clerk cut his eyes at the girl. She was beaming at him. Jees-us.

"Yeah, sure do. Got one right here. A good view of the marina. A pretty view. It's not at the top, but it's two floors from it."

"Fantastic," the Macho said, finally taking his arm from around the woman and reaching into his suit jacket for his wallet. As the Macho filled out the forms, the clerk sneaked another look at the woman's breasts but he forgot to look at her face first and when he finally did she caught him. But she just beamed at him again and pulled back her shoulders perkily, or he thought that was what she did, and his eyes hit on her chest again on their way down to the registration form. The clerk envied the Latin Macho. The clerk's imagination did a little number on the woman as he looked at her one last time.

When the paperwork was done the clerk started to ring for a bellman, but the Macho stopped him.

"We don't need any help," he said. "We've just got these couple of bags," and sure enough there was another bag the clerk hadn't noticed that the woman was carrying, one of those fancy aluminum cases. "Many thanks," the Macho said, and they turned and walked across the lobby to the elevators.

Once inside the elevators Remberto pulled a radio from his waistband under his coat and spoke into it.

"Room 1202. She wants you to bring the other aluminum suitcase. Don't go in the main lobby door. There is another entrance at the marina end of the lobby with elevators out of sight of the front desk."

Within seven minutes Cheryl was standing at the floor-to-ceiling windows in their room looking down at the sailboats in the marina below. The lights were off in the room, and they moved around in the pale glow thrown up from the strings of lights draped up and down the docks and boat slips.

"Isn't this too far?" Remberto asked.

"Nope. Perfect," Cheryl said as she bent down and opened her aluminum suitcase and took out a tripod and began assembling it. Remberto took binoculars out of his suitcase and began scanning the rows of docked boats. Just as Cheryl was putting the tripod in place someone knocked at the door, and she went to the eyehole and looked out. "Good," she said and opened the door.

Murray came in carrying Cheryl's larger aluminum suitcase, and behind him was Boyd with his bags of photographic equipment and carrying his own tripod.

They worked quickly, Murray and Remberto standing on either side of the large window with binoculars while Boyd and Cheryl set up their equipment in the middle. In twelve minutes everything was in place. Cheryl sat behind her parabolic microphone mounted on its tripod, her headset in place, the receiver on her lap.

"Okay, guys. Any suggestions?"

"Yeah," Remberto said. His binoculars hadn't left his eyes since he got there. "See the first dock from the left? Boat slips on either side. Go out to the second dock light, from there . . . one, two, three . . . third boat. It's a small cabin cruiser, blue trim. There are people inside, more than two, talking."

Cheryl leaned forward over the scope of the microphone, found the boat, and began toying with the receiver dials. Everyone waited. Two minutes, three.

"I just don't think so," she said. "They're talking, uh, office politics. Lou got a lot bigger raise than this guy, and this guy's pissed because he did most of Lou's work on the 'Fleming deal' and Lou never gave him credit for what he'd done except in private . . ."

"Okay," Remberto said. "Fourth dock over. Between the main walkway and the dock, first boat before the first light."

The trial-and-error process was frustrating, but everyone was used to it and remained calm and focused. They found their targets on the fourth boat.

"Got 'em," Cheryl said, clapping one hand to her headphones. With her other hand she flipped on the recorder.

50

"I'VE WORKED FOR THAT SON OF A BITCH A LONG TIME," THE man said, "and I'm telling you, something's going wrong here. I mean, really wrong, not just some glitch."

"You have how many numbers?" Burtell's voice was immediately recognizable.

"Three. *Three* contact numbers. Always the same system. First one's routine. Second one's secure from everyone. Third one's the 'get the hell out of Dodge' number, when it's time to clear out, drop everything, save your ass. I can't get him on any of them, and he sure as hell hasn't called me on any of mine. That's damned unusual."

"Maybe he's cut you out, doesn't trust you anymore."

"The hell he doesn't! We started using this method in Buenos Aires, that far back. I've always worked the street-level stuff for him, and he depends on me to tell him when the people he's got me working with are starting to stink. That's what that second number's for. Just him and me."

They were sitting inside, the cabin table between them, two bottles of beer on the table along with a nearly consumed fifth of Wild Turkey. The cabin door was thrown open to the still, humid night. Outside, the lazy sound of an idling inboard motor carried across the water.

Burtell looked at Sheck. He was nearing forty, and he had lived in a moral wasteland most of his adult life. He made his living by doing casually and without hesitation deeds that were punishable by death or life imprisonment in every society in the world. His life was a rejection of every concept that comprised the glue that held together the societies that the mass of men called civilized. He was incapable of compunction. He was entirely self-serving. And right now, he resembled more than anything an alerted hyena, his hackles raised, his jaws slightly open and rigid, ready to maul as he snuffled the wind for verification of his suspicions.

"You know about Tisler," Burtell said.

"Yeah, sure, I heard that."

"Do you know about Besom?"

"What about him?"

"He's dead too."

Bruce Sheck stopped swallowing in the middle of swigging his beer. He lowered the bottle, putting it down on the table without a sound.

"Dead."

"Had a heart attack while he was surf fishing." Burtell watched him closely.

"Heart attack." Sheck's face was static, but at the same time reflected a thought process way ahead of the words that had been spoken. "When was this?"

"He died sometime Monday afternoon or night. They found him yesterday, brought his body to Houston last night."

"When did you talk to Kalatis last?"

"Same night Besom died, though none of us knew it at the time," Burtell lied. Sheck, especially a drunk Sheck, didn't need to know about the previous night's meeting at the art museum. "Faeber was there too. They wanted to know if Tisler's death had initiated an investigation, a witch-hunt inside the Department. They wanted to know if they should be afraid that Art had left behind something incriminating."

"Should they?"

"I don't know," Burtell said. "But I do know they shouldn't have blackmailed him. They miscalculated."

"Well, the guy sure had a sweet tooth for black ass, I'll say that. I saw those damn photographs."

Burtell flagged this remark. Kalatis's children ate each other, every one of them a scorpion. Sheck obviously had known about the spying efforts against Tisler, may even have been a part of it. Burtell wondered what kind of paranoia these people lived with. Were they ever free of the suspicion that they themselves might be the next ones to be fed upon? It took only a word from Kalatis to change them from victor to victim. In the long run, that had to weigh heavily on the nerves.

"He shot himself twenty-four hours after they showed him the pictures," Burtell said pointedly.

Sheck shrugged, smiled a little, and shook his head. The gesture infuriated Burtell, and he took a drink of the beer to help him hold his tongue.

"What did you call me for?" Burtell asked.

Sheck had sat back on the padded cushion of the cabin banquette, his back against a porthole, one leg drawn up so that he was resting one arm on his bent knee, a bare foot on the cushion. He was holding his beer bottle by its neck between the first two fingers of the hand resting on his knee, studying Burtell with a cocked head as though he was trying to see a flaw in Burtell's character. He seemed to be wanting to say something but not yet altogether sure it was the right thing to do.

"I don't know what your whole story is, Burtell," Sheck said. He wasn't smiling now. He seemed to be working up to some kind of confrontation with the leisurely swagger of a bully.

Burtell's heart raced and a hot, moist sensation bathed him in an instant. He deliberately did not take a drink of beer at this moment. Sheck knew to watch for that little trick. Burtell simply looked at him. He did not swallow even though he felt the saliva gathering rapidly at the back of his throat. He did not speak. He wasn't going to let Sheck draw him out. If Sheck had something on his mind, he was going to have to come out with it. Burtell had no intention of making anything easier for Bruce Sheck.

"Are you satisfied with the money you're getting out of this operation?" Sheck asked.

"Why do you ask?"

"Are you?"

"Why do you ask?"

Sheck grinned, but it was not a completely natural grin. Tension and risk lay behind it, a quivering at the corner of his upper lip that he could not control. The man was showing some stress, which instantly caused Burtell more concern than anything that had happened up to that moment.

Sheck's grin faded, and he dropped his foot to the deck, placed his forearms on the table, and leaned slightly toward Burtell. The grin disappeared completely, replaced with a grim, downward pull of the sides of his mouth.

"I think something's about to happen with this operation," he said. "I think my ass is in danger, and I think yours is too." He paused to see how Burtell was going to react to such a revelation. "The only reason I'm having this conversation is because I think Kalatis is getting ready for a big change in the way he operates, and I think he's getting ready to cut me loose. And not just me. He's getting ready to wipe out a hell of a lot of his past, start a new era."

Sheck stared at Burtell and Burtell could smell the mixture of beer and Wild Turkey with which Sheck apparently had been fortifying his nerves all night, long before Burtell's arrival.

"The way this is set up, Burtell, is ingenious," Sheck began. "It's a system in which knowledge flows only one way from a thousand origins through a nervous system that grows increasingly less complex as it reaches the top. Less complex, that's the brilliant part of it. If Valerie Heath and all the others like her were cut off, the people who bring her information would not know what to do. The woman who has a first name and an initial, who gives them money for photocopies, would simply never call them again. They wouldn't know how to get in touch with her. The money would dry up. The whole thing would be over for them. One day they have a contact, one day they don't. It's over, gone forever."

Sheck raised one hand and imitated a bubble bursting.

"And then there's me. If something happened to me then the Valerie Heaths are left without a thought in their stupid little heads. It's over. They don't even know enough to ask a question. Who are they gonna ask? One day they have a contact, one day they don't. If nobody calls them again, shit, that part of their life is over. Forever."

Sheck stopped, picked up the Wild Turkey bottle and took a nip from it. Burtell forced himself to be patient. Sheck was being frustratingly repetitious. Burtell reminded himself that he owed a lot to Sheck's tenacious curiosity. It was Sheck who had discovered Kalatis's scheme to end all schemes, an elaborate plan to reduce a multiplicity of intrigues to one simple equation and, ultimately, to one man. One wealthy man. Burtell owed him, even to the point of indulging his endless reliving of Kalatis's betrayal, a betrayal that Sheck could do nothing about.

Wiping his mouth, Sheck resumed speaking, his voice a husky, raspy sound that died in the dead air of the cabin almost as soon as it left his throat.

"The point is, all Kalatis has to do is eliminate four or five people —I don't know exactly how many, but just a few—and that whole, big, complex system that involves several hundred people is shut down"—he snapped his fingers—"just like that. Gone. And you couldn't piece it together again for love or money. Very clean. You sure as hell couldn't trace it to Kalatis.

"This system here in Houston has been running nearly four years now. Kalatis and Faeber have more shit in their computers about key people in this city, in this state, than the goddamn FBI and CIA combined. They know where all the money is. They know where all the scandal is. They know where the future is. They've gotten to this point by milking this big nervous system of theirs."

Though Sheck paused, letting his sometimes slightly unfocused eyes rest lazily on Burtell, Burtell said nothing. Sheck had called the meeting, and the whiskey and beer were lubricating a normally reticent personality. The best thing Burtell could do was to let the chemistry take its course.

"I'll tell you what I've learned, Burtell," Sheck continued, as though he had made a difficult thought transition through the vapor of alcohol. "I've learned that an operation has a certain life span. Kalatis knows this . . . like God. The son of a bitch sees the beginning and the end, and he controls both of them. But if you're a guy like me, just a peon in this deal, if you keep your eyes and ears open, learn to read the signs, you start to notice certain little shifts and changes, signals that some kind of shit's about to happen. You get to where you can predict the rhythm of the seasons, so to speak. Get to know when there's going to be rain, or frost, or when the sap is rising in the trees."

Sheck finished his beer and very carefully set the empty bottle to one side of the table, out of his way. He leaned closer to Burtell, resting his forearms on the table, and his raspy voice grew softer still.

"Well, let me tell you, Dean Burtell, the sap is rising. Things are going to heat up. This season has just about run its course."

He stopped. Outside a lanyard slapped with a hollow ping against an aluminum mast on one of the sailboats, and a dock creaked as the bay waters shifted on the tides in the marina.

"Give me something I can believe, Sheck," Burtell said after a pause. "I can't make any judgments about your feelings."

Sheck kept his eyes on Burtell and nodded slowly.

"I don't fly for Kalatis as much now as I used to," he said, easing back from Burtell, "but it's still pretty damn regular. So I know his two other pilots pretty well. Kalatis, he loves compartmentalization. Believes it's the vitamin C of intelligence work . . . keeps away infections, system screwups. So we're not supposed to talk to each other. But I've been with that greasy Greek longer than anybody, and when these guys came on board they discovered that working for him was so goddamned weird they'd sneak around and feel me out about things. This is happening, that's happening, they'd say. What do I think that means? I'd shoot straight with them. Give them some pointers about working close with the guy because they were right there at 'headquarters.' Flying was all they did. I was still in operations, not so close to the Greek on a daily basis. I couldn't see who was coming and going. But that's all they could see, who was coming and going, but they didn't know anything about what was happening in the background, in operations. So between us pilots—there's a comradery with pilots, people don't understand that—we can pretty well follow the fortunes of Kalatis's business. I mean, in a 'big picture' sort of way."

Sheck stopped, paused as he straightened his back, drew his neck in, and belched, not a croaking belch from his gut, but a loud, wind-rushing belch of hops and malt that hissed up through his throat. He shook his head like he was clearing it from a hard blow.

"Okay," he said, ready to go on. "For over two years now, two and a half years, Kalatis has had an export operation in Colombia called Hermes Exports—totally separate operationwise from what I've been doing . . . another compartment altogether—shipping flowers and coffee into the U.S. Colombia's the second biggest flower importer to the U.S. after Holland. And coffee, you know about coffee. But it's the flower business that's the heart of the Hermes story. It's a first-class operation, and the flower importers here love their products because they're all packed in a Styrofoam-like insulation. The shipments arrive in pristine condition. This insulation is made in a Strasser-owned chemical plant in Bogotá. The chemicals for the plant are shipped to Colombia from another Strasser-owned company called Hormann Plastics here in Houston. Now, to manufacture plastics in any volume—and Hormann's operation is huge—you gotta have access to big quantities of sulfuric acid and acetic anhydride. Both are used to make cellulose acetate, stuff you got to have if you're gonna make plastics and foam insulation.

"But"—Sheck raised a muscular forearm and held up his index finger—"as you well know . . . sulfuric acid is also used in processing cocaine . . . and acetic anhydride is used in processing heroin."

He grinned and shook his head admiringly. Even as upset as he was, even as fearful of his own life as he claimed to be, he had to appreciate the genius of what he was about to describe.

"Not only are Kalatis and his buddy Strasser shipping themselves the chemicals to process cocaine and heroin—and these chemicals are on the DEA's and Customs' hot list, so they gotta be paying off some pretty big boys because the feds watch that shit with a microscope. Not only are they doing that, but they have—or their chemists have—developed a shit-sure method of 'reconstituting' cocaine. Those damn flowers are packed in form-pressed cocaine 'insulation' which has been douched in some kind of hydrofluorocarbon or some such shit to cover the smell so the drug dogs can't pick it up. They've been shipping flowers packed in cocaine for nearly three years and no damn Customs hound has ever blinked. Not once. No, shit no."

Sheck suppressed another belch, and a sour expression crossed his face. "That ballsy Greek has used this very successful system, which has produced a hell of a cash flow, to entice Houston and Texas investors to their even bigger—their global—drug business. They make their pitch to legitimate businessmen who are so shit-faced greedy they can't stand seeing their money get less than a pirate's ransom in interest. These men have been giving their money—their cash—to Kalatis who has promptly turned around and tripled it for them. It's like a come-along thing, a Ponzi scheme . . . they win every time . . . they start trusting him . . . they start putting in bigger and bigger amounts. The money's so big now that they're able to buy commodity volumes of cocaine and heroin . . . all over the world. They're moving merchant ship loads of stuff . . . out of Afghanistan, out of the Golden Triangle, out of Peru . . . everywhere."

The combination of whiskey and beer was taking its toll on Sheck, but even in his increasing stupor he had just filled in a gap in Burtell's puzzle. Burtell knew the huge sums of money had built to the point that Kalatis had thought it was time to effect his final plan, the grand finale, but he just wasn't sure that the cash flow was all coming from information buyers. Now he knew it wasn't, and though he had suspected drugs all along, he had never been able to prove it or to draw it out of Sheck until now. Sheck had given him the beginning and the end—and now the middle, the part that was the driving force behind Kalatis's one-man stratagem for achieving financial Nirvana.

Sheck started to reach for the Wild Turkey again. But his hand had just gotten on the neck of the bottle when he froze. He cut his eyes at

Burtell. He sniffed a little. Then he sniffed again, deeply, loudly. His face blanched.

"What is that shit . . . ?"

Remberto and Murray both were looking through their powerful binoculars into the lighted cabin windows when the explosion turned the air into a liquid mist of fire that incinerated the oxygen and everything else within a one-hundred-foot globe, the epicenter of which was the boat they had been watching.

Everyone in the hotel room yelled reflexively. Remberto and Murray recovered instantly, alternately lowering and raising their binoculars, unable to see all they wanted to see with or without them.

Boyd's tripod camera began ratcheting frames as he quickly pulled out another kind of camera and went to work.

Cheryl flung off her headphones and stared out of the darkened hotel room at the billowing plume of orange light illuminating the silence and the astonishment on her face.

She still could hear him sniffing. What is that shit . . . she heard him say.

51

GRAVER SAT AT HIS DESK HOLDING THE TELEPHONE IN STUNNED silence as Arnette explained what had happened. Paula and Neuman watched him from the sofa and one of the armchairs. They had cleaned up in the kitchen and had moved to the living room where they were continuing their discussion of what course they should follow next. When the telephone rang Graver had expected it to be Arnette, but he hadn't expected to hear what she had to say.

"Yeah, okay," he said, and then he had to clear his throat. "I'll get there as soon as I can." He put down the receiver. "God . . . damn . . ."

Paula and Neuman exchanged glances.

"That was . . . the surveillance. They followed Dean out to Clear Lake, to the marina at South Shore Harbor. He went down to the boats. The team got a room in the hotel there . . . the audio specialist, photographer . . . The audio operator finally located him in the cabin of one of the sailboats in the marina. He was talking to Bruce Sheck."

"I'll be damned," Neuman said.

Graver could feel Paula's eyes fixed on him. She knew instinctively this was not the shock to which Graver was reacting.

Graver looked at his watch. "A little less than fifteen minutes ago . . . the boat blew up."

Silence.

"The surveillance team said . . . it was a hell of an explosion. Blew up, maybe, half a dozen other boats . . . set fire to that many more. They said . . . they'd be surprised if there's enough left to make an ID on either one of them."

Both Paula and Neuman were dumbfounded and said nothing. Graver almost could feel their racing pulses, the constriction in their chests. The room was thick with the paralyzing concussion of shock. Graver thought of Ginette Burtell. She would stay up all night waiting for Dean to come home, and by morning she would be in a state of panic. The odds were good that she would call Graver. Or maybe Dean had told her something that would turn her first efforts else-where. Dean had not, after all, ever returned Graver's call. Maybe she knew more than Graver suspected. There was no way to know, but he could at least make the assumption that she would not have expected this.

"This is sickening," Paula said shakily. "This is out of control . . . way out of control."

"What about the surveillance team?" Neuman asked. They were talking softly, almost whispering. "Did they get anything on tape, any of their conversation?"

Graver nodded. He didn't want to talk to them. He wanted to be somewhere else.

"Apparently so," he managed to say. "I didn't . . . I don't know what. Just that there was something to listen to. My contact was still on the line to the surveillance team in the hotel room. They were frantically packing their stuff, trying to get out of there." He shook his head. "Jesus . . . Christ."

"How did they know it was Sheck?" Neuman asked.

"Dean used his name."

"Oh, this is horrible." Paula was sitting on the sofa with her feet on the floor, her legs together, her arms together, hands clasped and resting atop her thighs as she leaned forward. She looked up at Graver. "We didn't have any idea that Sheck had a boat, did we? A plane. A car. But not a boat."

Graver shook his head.

"Maybe it was Dean's," Neuman said.

"We never checked on that, I guess," Paula said. She looked up at Graver. "What are you going to do about Ginette?"

"Nothing," he said. It was possibly the hardest single word he had ever had to say.

Paula frowned at him. It was almost a flinch, a reproach.

"We don't know anything," Graver insisted. "We have to re-member that. Dean's death will come to us—if it comes to us—from forensics. It'll be up to Ginette to report him missing. We'll deal with it then." He shook his head. "We're just damned lucky the surveillance team caught them in time, and that Dean wasn't as good at this business as they were. We're lucky we've got the recording."

Paula stared at Graver in dismay. "How twisted can this get?"

It was a rhetorical question, but Graver had been asking himself the same thing. He stood stiffly, deferring a little to his tired back, and put his hands in his pockets. He walked toward the entrance hall doorway and looked at the soft sheen of muted light on the burnished hardwood floor. It was impossible to stop thinking about the explosion, the actual chemistry of it . . . the impact, the heat, the instant tornadic destruction of it. He had seen explosions on film before, assassinations. The target never reacts at all because the firestorm happens faster than human reflexes are capable of responding. For a millisecond the target can be seen simply sitting immobile in the conflagration, burning alive like the Buddhist monks who set themselves afire in the sixties to protest the Vietnam War. An upright human torch, knowing in that instant they were aflame in hell but being too stunned to react. Then the impact of the explosion, and in the next instant they vanished in a shuddering mist. The rest of it was a mystery, whatever it was like to die.

Graver was too numb even to sob, though he felt it in his throat, a soft, choking lump of grief and anger and dismay. He was light-headed, but he stood very still drawing deep breaths, struggling for control, resolving not to give in . . . to anything. Not a damned bloody thing.

He turned around.

"Okay," he said, taking his hands out of his pockets and wiping his face with both hands. He waited a moment. "Here's what we've got to do." He swallowed. "This will in no way affect the CID, not for a few days, not . . . until the Bomb Squad's forensic team has had a chance to do their work. And maybe not even then." He walked a few steps into the living room. "First, Ginette will report him missing. When that happens, the CID will be brought back into it. I don't think even Jack Westrate will be able to scoff away the disappearance of another CID officer." He crossed his arms, took a few more steps, his head down, thinking. "All hell will break loose. If the newspapers were going to run something on Tisler and Besom, it will be bumped off the front page by this explosion. There's no way to anticipate if the reporters on the other stories will make any connections here. Again, they won't know who was on the boat. It'll probably take them a day even to determine which slip was the center of the explosion. So . . . we've got a little time."

He looked at his watch. He felt the flesh of his face sagging with exhaustion. It seemed to require every gland in his body to produce enough juice to keep him standing.

"As far as I'm concerned . . . there's only one reason for any of this now . . . to focus everything . . . on Panos Kalatis."

Graver actually was having to make an effort to control a nearly hysterical frustration at being so completely at a disadvantage. He could hardly contain his grief for Burtell's death or his rage at Kalatis's silent, anonymous audacity. He was forcing himself, at considerable expense to his nervous system, to be controlled and methodical and logical.

"Paula," he went on, "I want you to debrief Valerie Heath just as we discussed. Tonight, as soon as we get through here. Before you do, tell her what happened. Tell her Sheck was just killed by a bomb with another CID agent . . . no, just another man. When you're through, blindfold her again—I sure as hell don't want her to know where she's been—and you and Lara take her car and another one and drive her somewhere—a parking garage—and release her. Give her her keys and tell her to get the hell out of the state. Then both of you come back here and wait."

He walked a few paces into the room and addressed Neuman.

"Sheck lives in Nassau Bay?" he asked.

Neuman nodded. "Yeah, just across the lake from South Shore Harbor."

"You need to get over there, Casey, and pick the place apart. Take a garbage sack and fill it up with anything remotely informative." He hesitated. "There's going to be a lot of action over there. Spectators standing around in their back yards watching the excitement across the water. That's good for you. But be careful. Kalatis's people are going to want to make sure he didn't leave anything behind. They may have already been there. Or they may get there ahead of you and still be there. If not, they might walk in on you. Just watch your ass. Okay? But take the place apart. Unscrew air-conditioning grates, wall plugs. Shit like that. And call in every half hour . . . on the secure handsets. And wear latex gloves."

Neuman nodded eagerly. He was wired, ready to do it.

"I'm going to meet the surveillance people and listen to what they picked up. When I'm through, I'll get right back here. We'll go from there." He looked at each of them. "Don't use my telephone and don't answer it. I'll leave the answering machine on. It's important," he said, "that we keep in touch. But use the handsets."

52.

VICTOR LAST LAY ON HIS BACK STARING UP AT THE CEILING, HIS right arm hanging off the side of the bed holding a champagne glass. He was naked. The sheets were a pale tea rose silk. His left hand held one of Rayner Faeber's very generous, very jiggly breasts. She lay with her blond head tucked up under his arm, and when he looked down he could see her other breast with its peachy aureole, her so very white and nearly plumpish body, and her splayed legs—she liked to splay her legs—with her dusty pubis at their apex. She smelled of a kind of bath oil that she said she could buy only at this one small shop in the Rue du Bourg-Tibourg. It smelled like . . . heather. He loved the stuff, which he told her once and so she always put a dash of it in her bathwater when she knew they were going to be together.

He looked to his left, out through one of the bedroom's glass walls and through an atrium, through another glass wall and into the living room. Beyond that was another glass wall, another atrium . . . all of it washed in the wan light of a city night as though he were in Atlantis, looking through houses of water, the light refracting in undulations of aqua so pale and anemic as to be almost colorless. It was, he had to admit, the perfect environment for Rayner. She was almost translucent herself. So much so, that sometimes when he had sex with her in this watery glass world, he half-expected to see her inner parts working, expected, even, to see his own erect self in her in flashes of clarity that illuminated them like flashes of lightning.

She took a deep breath to sigh and her breast rose and filled out under his hand. He liked that. He really did like it when she did that. Rayner was sybaritic, as true to the concept as any woman he had ever met, and she had the money to indulge her nature. The first night they had been together in Veracruz—Colin, as usual, having left her alone to take a "business trip" to Mexico City—they had had sex on the beach. At one point during that extraordinary event, he had had the astonishing sensation that she had disappeared from beneath him, so alike had her flesh appeared to the water and the moon.

She raised one of her hands, which also held a champagne glass, and raised her head to meet it, the effort tightening the breast he held, and drank what was left of her champagne. Or almost all of it. She held the glass above her and let the remainder dribble onto her. He could see the snail trail of its rivulet reflected in the sourceless light. She lowered her hand, and he heard the whisper of the glass falling on the carpet. In the next moment her champagne-cooled hand found its way between his legs. His stomach tightened reflexively.

"Victor," she said, and she turned a little to him, her breast pulling out of his hand, and ran her tongue up the side of his rib cage. Again his gaze went to the partitions of glass walls, through light and water and light and water.

She suddenly sat up, her face right in the center of his line of sight. She wore no makeup—they had been at this a while, in and out of the pool, and at it again—so her face was only an apparition, though he could make out her wonderful mouth and her eyes that tilted upward on the outer edges.

"If you could have anything in the world," she said, "what would it be?"

"All of Colin's money," he said without hesitation.

Rayner's lips rose at the edges in a smile, and she was close enough for him to feel the little burst of breath as she gave a single voiceless laugh. Her hand toyed between his legs.

"All of his money," she said, leaning over him, the weight of her pendulous breasts resting on his chest. "And to that end, how are you progressing?"

"I'm not quite sure," he said, and he wasn't quite sure what in the hell she meant by the question, either. He turned his head, drank the rest of his own champagne and set the glass on the jade green marble of the small table beside the bed. He reached down to her breasts and kissed her forehead. "Not sure about the money," he repeated, "but I'm having a dee-vil of a time with his wife."

There were a few minutes of aggressive fondling and kissing which almost led to more heated action, but Last was able to avoid that without letting her know that he thought it was time to move on to precisely the issue he had just raised.

"Bloody champagne," he said, giving one last tongue-flick to a peachy aureole before rolling over and sitting up on the side of the bed. "I've got to get some coffee or something. I won't even be able to steer the bloody car."

"Why don't you spend the night?" she suggested, leaning on one elbow, facing his back.

"No, can't do that," he said, shaking his head and running his fingers through his hair. "We'll get shot in bed one of these nights. A very bad end to a very good thing."

She didn't say anything for a moment, and he waited with his head in his hands, his eyes cut to the side, as if he were a hunter listening with held breath for the single thwick of a broken twig to betray the approaching prey.

"I want to go ahead and divorce him," she said. "This is driving me nuts."

"That'd be crazy, love," Last said. "It's not time yet. He'd know. He'd have me shot."

"He doesn't know anything. Doesn't even suspect anything." She put a hand on his back, two fingers straddling the ripple of his spine, kneading and massaging it. "It's been years since he's noticed anything about me except whether or not I'm absent or present."

"The man's in the information business, Rayner. He knows. As a matter of fact, I've been half-thinking we've already pushed our luck too far. Something hasn't seemed right in the last couple of weeks."

Her hand stopped on his back. "What do you mean?"

"I don't know . . . exactly," he said, choosing his words carefully. "Something's going on with him. I can feel it."

Her hand dropped, and she sat up in bed. "Turn around," she said. "Let's talk."

Last turned around and sat with his back resting against the headboard. Rayner arranged herself beside him and facing him, her legs crossed yoga style, her hands straight down on either side of her for support as she leaned back slightly. This provided him a wonderful view of her bosom, which he loved to look at and which she loved to have him to look at. Her strawberry blond hair was tousled.

"You know once you asked me why I never seemed hurt or sad or bitter because of the way Colin treats me?"

"Yes."

"I gave you some fluffy answer."

He nodded.

"The truth is that by the time you and I met in Veracruz, I had already been through that 'hurt' stage of our so-called marriage. It was past, well past. I should have listened to his first wife. She actually came to see me once, before I married him. A nice woman. I liked her, which should have been warning enough." She paused and looked at Last. "That makes sense," she said, "but I'm not sure you'd understand it. Anyway, when everything she had warned me about began proving true, I saw the handwriting on the wall."

She paused and raked the fingers of one hand through her hair. "I'm not a total bitch," she said, "but I'm not a patsy, either. We'd been married a couple of years, this house was new, and his business had just undergone a giant growth leap. Boom. Suddenly the business was huge. That was because Brod Strasser and another guy had bought into it."

"Who was the other guy?"

"A Greek—a weird man if you ask me—named Panos Kalatis."

"Colin told you all this?"

"God, no." But she didn't say how she knew. "Actually, these men own controlling interest now, or Strasser does, through one of his holding companies. Poor Colin's just an employee for all practical purposes. A highly paid errand boy, no longer his own man. The man's smart, Colin is. I'm not saying he's not smart. It's just that . . . I didn't have much respect for the choice he made.

"Once he'd sold out, figuratively and literally, I thought to myself: okay, where am I, exactly? I'm married to a man who's indifferent to me, treats me like an outdated appliance. I could live with that, I guess, for a while, if the benefits were good. I mean extraordinarily good."

"But they weren't."

"No, not in the long term, I didn't think. Colin makes this fabulous salary, but he doesn't have a piece of the action. Fabulous salaries are great as long as you're employed. But people get fired. I mean, the 1980s are littered with surprised executives. They thought it would never end too. But it always does. People like Strasser and Kalatis *own* the action. They don't get fired. And when Colin's no longer any use to them they'll throw him away like something they've wiped their behinds on. He's only a breath away from losing everything . . . whenever it suits them. And then where would that leave me?"

She reached out and took one of the tea rose pillows and held it in her lap, her arms wrapped around it. She looked at him a moment before she continued.

"So I made up my mind to get something out of this . . . relationship. I thought, well, if they can buy information I can too. I hired a first-rate private investigator. He documented on film and tape Colin's affair with his secretary. In flagrante, as they say. It was rather erotic footage, if you could forget who they were. When I had had enough of it, when my sick curiosity had been indulged ad nauseam, I told the guy thanks and paid him off. Then I contacted the secretary and had her come over here one afternoon when Colin was out of town.

"We sat in the living room over there," she said, looking through the walls of glass, "and I showed the videos to her. She was stunned and frightened. Ashamed. I kept playing them until she simply ducked her head and wouldn't watch them anymore. It was cruel of me and, frankly, I surprised myself. By this time I didn't think I had any emotional investment left in the man, but I found that I was getting some kind of unseemly satisfaction out of this perverse humiliation of her. But finally I stopped.

"I really didn't blame her, after all. The woman's intelligent, a superb executive secretary. She knew sleeping with the boss was going nowhere but, on the other hand, it wasn't hurting her at all at bonus time, and he was continually giving her all these gifts. I know what executive secretaries do. I used to be one. I know what it's like. A good one practically runs the company, but she never gets any credit for it and compared to some of the men executive officers—who do a hell of a lot less than she does—her salary's paltry. She thinks, what the hell, she deserves the perks she gets from sleeping with the bastard. She knows all about the boss's personal life—this woman knew Colin and I hadn't had sex in two years. She knows all about the business. Where it's strong, where it's weak. Where all the corporate skeletons are buried. Who's got clout, who hasn't. But most important: she has access."

Rayner stopped and looked at her hands. She was doing something with her fingers, more precisely her fingernails, looking at them as though she could see what she was doing, though Last doubted she could in the pale, watery light. Then she looked up and went on.

"She was sobbing, distraught. I could tell that in her mind she had lost everything. I started talking to her. I said, look, relax, relax. Truth is, the marriage was over, and you were just the next in line. That's okay, really. I admitted that I was angry but not because I loved the man. I was just angry at being used by him. And I said that, frankly, she should be angry about being used too. I said I wasn't going to do anything with the videos. I said I didn't think either of us would get what we deserved out of a nasty divorce battle. I calmed her down, got her to thinking. And then I said that we'd both be better off putting our heads together and try to come up with a way to earn ourselves a little security out of all this. I told her that neither one of us had any protection, any security for the future. We could both end up on the sidewalk tomorrow with nothing. Nothing. And it could happen so easy." She paused. "I presented her with a proposition."

As Rayner talked, Last sat with his back against the wall and slowly felt the hair rise on the back of his neck. Surrounded by the aqueous light of Rayner's peculiar world, he listened to a woman he had been cultivating for eight months, waiting for just the right opportunity to use her and their affair as a stepping-stone to his own fortune, only to have it slowly revealed to him that he had been thrusting in the moonlight with Morgan le Fay. As she talked his heart alternately hammered and started as he thought that at any moment she was going to blast him to hell for his many months of calculated intercourse. He felt as though this woman had been reading him like a newspaper, and she was about to deliver the coup de grâce.

But it didn't happen. Instead, he listened to the story of how two women, invisible in plain sight, had gathered enough information—about DataPrint . . . and related businesses called Concordia Investments and Hormann Plastics and Hermes Exports and Strasser Industries—to have the two of themselves killed on the spot. When she finally came to a stopping point, they sat in silence among the silk and glass and fragrance of heather and for the first time in his life Last didn't know whether to scream in jubilation or horror. He had discovered either the mother lode of all his adventuring, or he had just listened to his own death warrant. He honestly could not place a bet on which it might be. The odds were skewed by the magnitude.

"Jesus . . . Mary . . . and Joseph," he said.

She was looking at him as though she were awaiting his assessment. She wanted to know what he thought.

"Rayner," he swallowed, "listen to me." His mouth was cottony.

"This could get you killed . . . I mean, I cannot believe you've gone this far. Do you have any idea how . . . exposed, how vulnerable you are? Both of you."

"Only in the last few months," she said. "When we began to piece together the drugs part of it. That scared the shit out of us."

Last looked at her. He thought he could sense the fear in her now, but at the same time he didn't know why he hadn't sensed it before. Who, exactly, had he been deceiving all these months? Her or himself?

"How long have you been doing this?" he asked.

"Nine months. We had to take it slow," she said with unintended understatement. "We didn't want to screw it up. You know, little by little, checking and double-checking, take a step and listen. Take another step and listen."

He waited a moment, not wanting to seem too eager.

"You have documentation?"

"Of course. That's what it's all about, isn't it?"

"But . . ." And then it dawned on him. "She—the secretary—continued her affair with Colin?"

Rayner nodded. "She had to. I don't think this would have worked otherwise. Every time he took her, she took him." She smiled. "Talk about poetic justice . . ."

"And she's still sleeping with him?"

"I hope so."

She was looking at him, her face only a few feet away from his, through the clear water. In the instant before she spoke he anticipated her.

"We've gone about as far as we can go," she said, "without some help." He could almost see her holding her breath, hoping she hadn't made a mistake about him. "Do you want in on this?"

53

NEUMAN COULD SEE THE GLOW FROM THE FIRE IN THE SOUTH Shore Harbor Marina even before he turned off NASA Road 1 into the Swan Lagoon development of Nassau Bay. Cars were slowing along the highway to puzzle over the orange light reflecting off the bottom of the Gulf clouds that were drifting inland, and when he turned into the neighborhood street that would take him to Sheck's house, people were standing on their front lawns looking toward the fire.

Sheck's house was a modern one-story bungalow on a winding street lined with palms and green lawns and in a price range not unlike Valerie Heath's. Neuman parked in the front drive, hiding the car as best as he could behind a screen of oleanders, and got out, hardly noticed by the scattered clusters of people standing in their front lawns across the street looking in his direction. The back of Sheck's house was right on the water and almost directly across the lagoon from the marina.

He didn't go to the front door but casually walked around to the side of the house, found a wooden privacy fence with a gate and went into the back yard. From here the fire in the marina looked like a conflagration as it reflected from both the clouds and the surface of the bay water, the fire itself the brightest point between the two illuminations. The entire marina seemed to be burning.

Throwing a glance at the back of the house to make sure he didn't miss the obvious—a light, someone standing at a window or door—he moved along the thick hedges that lined both sides of the back yard for privacy from the neighbors and stood near a pier at the edge of the water and looked across. He could hear sirens and bullhorns and the wailing of emergency vehicles, the cacophony hanging in the moist, still air as though the entire confusion were taking place in an amphitheater. As he stood there with his feet in the damp grass, it was hard for him to believe that Burtell was over there, burned up in a fire that no one understood yet. For a moment he wondered what it had been like for Burtell to be blasted into the next life.

He looked at the fire, which was close enough for him actually to see the flames, fed by the gasoline and oil from the boats. It was the first time he had ever had a friend die violently, and he was surprised at the disconnectedness of such an event. Somehow it seemed at once unreal and at the same time so real as to be nauseating.

The voices of people on the other side of the hedges brought him back to the moment. They were talking about the fire, speculating. Someone had a scanner and the crackle and scratch of transmissions came through the hedges more clearly than their voices.

He turned and walked back to the house, easing along in the darkness of the hedges. At the back of the house there were several doors. The first one seemed to open into the garage. There were sliding glass doors that opened onto the broad patio and lakefront, common to most of the homes that opened onto the view of the water. Then, beyond that, there was a kind of courtyard enclosed on three sides by another set of dense hedges and another door. It looked as if it might be an outside entrance to a separate apartment or room.

Neuman took the latex gloves out of his coat pocket and tugged them on and used his lock picks to open the door that he assumed gave access to the garage. He was right. Closing and locking the door behind him, he took a penlight from his pocket and shone it around the garage which was empty except for a motorcycle. He went over and felt the engine which was cold. Seeing nothing else of immediate interest, he went to a small workbench against one of the walls and selected several types of screwdrivers and put them in his coat pocket. Another door near the one through which he had entered opened into a laundry and utility room where he paused to look through the cabinets for plastic garbage bags. He found them, took one out of the box, and then went through another door into the kitchen.

Bruce Sheck's house was a bit more lived in than Valerie Heath's, though it reflected both the carelessness and selective habits of a bachelor's life. The living room at the front of the house facing the street was practically ignored with a modicum of furnishings. There were three bedrooms. Two of them were like the living room, furnished with the bare necessities but otherwise entirely untouched. But the combination family room and kitchen was where he seemed to have spent all his time. The television was there and scattered around were a few nudie magazines, a pair of sweat clothes in the middle of the floor as if he had just stepped out of them, some fishing poles stacked in a corner near the patio doors along with a pair of old tennis shoes and a small ice chest. There were some aviation maps lying on the kitchen table, the first thing Neuman had seen that he thought ought to go into the plastic bag.

The kitchen was better furnished than Neuman had anticipated. Sheck had not been a gourmet. There was an abundance of TV dinners in the refrigerator along with a good stock of beer, half a watermelon, orange juice, milk, and the miscellaneous makings for sandwiches. The pantry and cabinets held the expected staples and there were two old pizza boxes in the trash next to the electric range.

Neuman moved into Sheck's bedroom. The clothes in his closet ran to jeans and casual shirts, a few sport coats, and only three pairs of dress trousers. In the corner of the closet he found an expensive Weatherby deer rifle and shells, two extraordinarily expensive Italian-made shotguns and four or five boxes of shotgun shells along with two well-used bird sacks and an old set of deer horns tied together at the base with a short piece of cord lying on top of a pair of hunting boots. He checked the closet closely for hidden doors or compartments in the walls or under the carpet.

He found no place anywhere in the house where it appeared that Sheck might have kept "paperwork," and there was no evidence at all that indicated that anyone had been there before him.

Walking back into the family room, he unlocked the patio doors and stepped outside and around to the door inside the small courtyard. Again he used his lock picks to open the door. The room looked as if at one time it might have been a makeshift office, but now it seemed largely unused. There was an old metal office desk like those in CID, a small sofa, and a couple of chairs. A coffee table in front of the sofa was scattered with an assortment of old issues of magazines, *Texas Monthly, Commando, Aviator,* and *Sports Illustrated.*

Even though it seemed infrequently used, the room seemed to Neuman the most likely one in which Sheck might have been inclined to hide any code sheets or cipher paraphernalia. So, taking the screwdrivers out of his pocket, he set to work dismantling anything that could be taken apart. He went into the small bath first, covering one wall at a time, and then worked his way into the larger room doing the same methodical one-wall-at-a-time approach. Air-conditioning vents, electrical plates around plugs and switches. Lamp bases. The legs on the sofa and coffee table. Zippers on the sofa cushions; the upholstery curtain covering the entire bottom carriage. The desk was a project all unto itself. At the end of half an hour he had nothing, and was facing the daunting task of having to do the same thing to the larger house.

Leaving the room disheveled, he locked the door behind him and went back into the house through the patio door. Standing in the family room just off the kitchen, he decided to try to eliminate some of the more attractive sites that he might normally search. If he had wanted to hide something of irreplaceable value, something that his life might some day depend on, he would want to make sure that the object would not fall victim to the vagaries of chance, the most obvious of which was common theft. He would not use anything that could possibly be stolen. Stereo, television, appliances, the motorcycle, tools, furniture. He would begin by confining his search to the house structure itself. And he would begin in the room that normally would be considered the most personal. He started in Sheck's bedroom. Everything came apart, just as it had in the room outside off the patio, but nothing surfaced.

This was disappointing, but not altogether unexpected. If Sheck had been the kind of professional that they expected him to be, he was not going to leave anything significant lying around the house. Neuman guessed that Sheck was a survivalist and was proud to be a man who lived—who stayed alive—by his own wits.

He went to the other two bedrooms and did the same kind of search, even taking apart the thermostat in the hallway. Nothing.

As he was walking out of the second bedroom, he stopped. The showers. He hadn't looked in any of the showers. The showerheads. Not in Sheck's bedroom, because it was used regularly, but the other two were never used, or seldom used it seemed. He went back into the bedroom he had just come out of and went into the shower stall. The showerhead was a big fat one, large enough for a canister of 35mm film or something of similar size. He unscrewed it. Nothing. He went into the second bedroom. Same kind of showerhead. Nothing. He stood with the showerhead in his hand. Jesus. The shower was never used. He looked down at his feet . . . at the drain. He laid down the showerhead, took the Phillips screwdriver out of his pocket and undid the two screws from the chrome-plated grill over the drain. Nothing. He left them there and went back to the second bedroom, stepped into the shower, and looked at the drain. He got down on his knees and looked at the chrome grate that covered it. There appeared to be a piece of lint stuck to the lip of one of the little round holes. He looked closer, putting the penlight and his face nearer to the drain. It wasn't a piece of lint.

His blood pressure shot up instantly as he fumbled with the screwdriver and undid the two Phillips screws. Carefully he removed the grate from its seat and felt the tug, like a gentle nudge of a bite on a fishing line. He lifted the grate and saw the string, which actually was not a string but a length of clear monofilament fishing line, tied through one of the holes on the grate. The knot of the colorless line was almost invisible. He put the penlight in his mouth, carefully raised the grate with one hand, and grasped the line with the other. The monofilament was only three inches long and was tied through the eyelet of a threaded cap screwed onto a plastic, waterproof canister about five inches long, the kind of ribbed container in which an out-doorsman might keep matches to protect them from moisture.

Neuman's heart was racing. He couldn't believe his luck. He couldn't believe he had *thought* of this, of the goddamned drain. Gripping the canister in one hand, he stepped out of the shower and leaned against the vanity counter. Holding the canister up to his face he looked at it in the beam of his penlight. It was army green with a thick rubber seal between the screw cap and the case. It looked like the kind of heavy-duty equipment he would have expected of Sheck. He shook it gently and heard nothing. He wanted to open it in the worst way, but was afraid it might contain film that needed to be opened in a darkroom, and his fear of ruining such hard-won evidence canceled all thought of satisfying his burning curiosity.

Putting the canister in his coat pocket—still attached to the mono-filament and drain grate—he walked out of the bedroom, down the hallway to the kitchen and into the family room. Through the sliding glass doors that looked out onto the lawn, he had a perfect view of the burning marina across the lake. He was aware of an acidy, hollow feeling in his stomach as he thought that the night before Sheck might well have been standing where he was standing now, looking across at the bright display of lights that shone every night from the marina, lights strung on poles along the docks, lights running up and across the masts of the sailboats and around the cabins of the cruisers. Lights two times themselves, reflected upon the surface of the water.

54.

GRAVER SAT AT ARNETTE'S LIBRARY TABLE WITH CHERYL AND Arnette as Cheryl rewound the tape for the third time.

"You want to hear it again?" Arnette asked.

Graver shook his head. He was not likely to forget anything he had heard in Dean Burtell's last conversation. It was an eerie recording with its wavering beginnings as Cheryl zeroed in on the range and the frequency followed by a remarkably clear reception. Bruce Sheck's voice was whiskey raw and surly, and it was easy to imagine him after what Valerie Heath had already said about him. Good-looking, athletic, more savvy for sure than Valerie Heath could have imagined, an element of meanness sulking just beneath the surface.

But listening to Burtell was like listening to a brother. Graver didn't have a brother, but he imagined that Burtell could have been one and to know that with each word he spoke he was another syllable closer to imminent, violent death was a painful thing to experience. They were so unsuspecting. True, Sheck did say he thought they were in danger, but clearly it was a danger he had every intention of being able to deal with, and neither of them thought they were in danger then, at that moment. And then too, the entire conversation was almost a monologue by Sheck. It seemed that he had been drinking for some time, which had made him loquacious. Burtell spoke very little on the tape and when he did speak it was brief, an indication, it seemed to Graver, that he was either tense or angry or maybe even cautiously uneasy. But, the fact was, the few words he did speak were all the more painful to listen to because they were so few. Graver found himself leaning toward the tape recorder on the table, hoping to hear Burtell say something, anything, at length.

Graver looked at Cheryl. "Thank you," he said. He saw a flicker of surprise in her eyes, but that was all right. He didn't mind that his gratitude must have sounded a little odd to her. He was grateful for this last audible witness.

Arnette made a little gesture with her hand, and Cheryl snapped off the recorder, stood up, and left the room.

"That was a hell of a thing to have to listen to," Arnette said, reaching for her cigarettes that lay on the table in front of her. "I'm sorry you had to do it. I'm sorry it happened, baby."

Graver's stomach was a knot of queasiness and anger. He could hardly believe . . . any of it. It was outrageous, even grotesque. The events of the last two days seemed to be evidence of the unraveling of all that was sane and reasonable.

"That was pretty damn crude of Kalatis," she said. "I think it signals a major change in the game.

"You're convinced it was Kalatis."

Arnette flicked her lighter and looked at Graver over the flame, lit the cigarette and laid the lighter on the table.

"Think about it, baby," she said. "Or do you know something you haven't told me?"

Graver shook his head. "No, I know so damn little if I knew something it wouldn't be much."

"Christ, Sheck practically narrated his own death. He was pointing his finger at Kalatis when he blew up."

"What about the man at the fountain?"

Arnette looked as though she dreaded giving him any more bad news.

"The pictures have been rolling in here over the computers ever since I told you I was going to look. But he's not in there," she said. "I don't know who the hell he is. But that doesn't mean he's not government. It just means my source may not be as good as it used to be, or he'll be in the next batch that comes through."

"Or that he's *not* government."

"Okay," she conceded, her elbow resting on the table, the cigarette up in the air.

"I just don't understand why Kalatis would use a bomb, for God's sake," Graver said. "After he'd gone to all the trouble of making veiled hits on Tisler and Besom." He tilted his head at the recorder. "Dean obviously thought Tisler killed himself because of the photographs."

"Dean was mistaken," Arnette said coldly. "I don't have any doubt about that. Tisler's death may have caught you people by surprise, but I can assure you it wasn't a surprise to Panos Kalatis. What we're seeing here is a methodical burning of bridges, an elimination of liabilities. Kalatis is distancing himself from the little guys who've been doing his dirty work in this operation. I think Sheck was right about that."

"And do you also think he was right about Kalatis bringing something to culmination here?"

Arnette tapped her cigarette on the edge of the glass ashtray.

"It looks like it," she said. She read his thoughts and shook her head. "Forget it. What are you going to do? Go to the feds with what you've got? You don't even have enough . . . I mean actual documentation . . . to get them to stop him from leaving the country. And if you did find some goof who would authorize it for you, Kalatis's lawyers would shred it, and in twenty-four hours he'd be gone for good."

She stood up and crossed her arms, her cigarette lofted in the air next to her face as she paced to one end of the room and then back, stopping across the desk from him, leveling her eyes at him.

"You know what's happened here, baby?" she asked. "Misfortune. You got in on the tail end of a god-awful operation. You may never know what happened. Ever. You lost two dirty cops, and you gotta face it, maybe three. If there's more, odds are you'll never know. The bad guys were organized so far over your head that all you got was a glimpse of hell before they slammed the gates closed. Consider yourself lucky."

She smoked her cigarette and looked at him through the acrid haze. It was a brutal assessment and probably accurate, and Graver guessed there was a good reason why she had delivered it with so little finesse.

"But your instincts were right about one thing," she said. "Somebody else hasn't stepped out of the shadows yet. I'm guessing, too, that Tisler, Besom, and Dean could have ID'd that somebody else, and he, whoever he is, has benefited from their deaths as much as Kalatis has. Maybe he's safe now. Unless you come up with something."

She gestured at him with her cigarette.

"You can do two things. Bury it as long as you can while you keep hammering away at it on your own. Or write a goddamned elaborate, thesis-sized document about everything that's happened in the last three days since Arthur Tisler turned up dead." She stopped. "You did keep a personal log."

Graver nodded.

"Okay, good. Write it just exactly the way it happened, detailing what you did and why—leaving me out, of course—giving them every-thing in chronological order. Bypass Westrate and give it to Hertig. Let him decide for you. That's his goddamned job."

She stared at him, a small, wiry woman of dusky complexion and murky past, who at too young an age had had to learn to make hard choices, not the least of which was to remain in a profession that demanded hard choices of her as a matter of course. Having done so, she had discovered too late that living with such decisions was alto-gether another proposition from making them. It was the former that had aged her. But for a long time now she no longer flinched at having to make gut-wrenching decisions. She made them and then did battle with her conscience afterward and in private. These were the true ugly confrontations, she once admitted to him, facing yourself, being your own judge and jury—and, someday, if it became necessary, hang-man.

"We did some checking into Gulfstream Bank," she said, interrupt-ing Graver's silence. "Did you know the bank is only six years old? I'd guess that maybe seven years ago Kalatis conducted a kind of market survey of Southern cities. I don't know what his criteria might have been, but Houston seems to have fit the bill for whatever it was he wanted to do. Now that's long-term planning. When you think about it, this 'project' has consumed the greater part of a decade of Kalatis's life. That gives you some indication of the volume of money at stake here. It's got to be colossal."

She shook her head, staring at Graver, studying him though her thoughts were wandering.

"You know, more and more this business scares the shit out of me. Guys like Kalatis and Strasser, there are no limits, just no damn limits. They're like a rogue government that commands a fortune but has no physical territory, has no constituency except its victims, no raison d'être except greed." She paused. "Makes you wonder if this is the future . . . bigger and bigger appetites, rapacious avarice." She smiled cynically. "But I'm forgetting my history, aren't I. All the way back to King Menes the Fighter."

"Hermes Exports," Graver said, as if he hadn't been listening to her.

"Yeah, we're running them down, too. It looks like they sell to a hell of a lot of importers. They're probably scattering cocaine all over the nation."

"You think they're 'reconstituting' it all here, then shipping it out?"

"Why would they? If the stuff ships safely, why not let it go on?"

"Then the process can't be that difficult."

"I imagine Strasser's chemists have trained people . . . all over the place. Besides, the drug business, working with that shit, doesn't take a big brain. You could almost train an orangutan to do it. Sanitation and preciseness are not exactly the hallmarks of a good drug processor."

Graver let his eyes fall to the steno pad. He wanted to ask her to run a computer check on Victor Last to see if her data banks had anything he couldn't get from his own source agencies, but something made him hold off.

"You're cut off, aren't you," Arnette said, studying him. "Sheck would have been your next step. Failing that you could have hauled in Dean. That would have been a wild swing, but it would have been the only shot you had left if you wanted to stay hot." She smoked, studying him. "Now all you have is the prospect of a long, difficult investigation. No more sizzling fuse to follow to its source. You're going to have to piece it together a fragment at a time, in the tried and true manner of intelligence work."

He looked at her. She bent over the library table and mashed out her cigarette in the ashtray. Her fingernails were immaculate, no polish, precisely and smoothly filed to oval ends with narrow, bone-white outer margins. He chose his words carefully.

"I know it's out of my territory," he said, "and even out of my league, for that matter, but Kalatis is the only thing I can think about right now. For the present, he's the only thing I care about, and a 'long, difficult investigation' is not going to get him."

He saw a look of sober fear set in behind Arnette's eyes.

"What the hell do you mean by that?" she asked.

"I simply mean that this time patience and the long view have no appeal to me whatsoever. I'm not going crazy here. I know what the odds are that Kalatis will get away with this. I live with those odds every day, just like you do. Only this time I can't be philosophical about it. Sorry. The larger investigation is secondary." He paused, and they stared at each other. "Arnette, I want that son of a bitch so bad that it's become the *only* thing I want."

She didn't even blink. She was standing behind her chair, her thin fingers gripping the back of it.

"You'd better keep your head screwed on," she said evenly. Her face had hardened, and she was looking at him with an expression he couldn't quite decipher. If he hadn't been so wired, so nearly out of control inside his mind, the look on her face would have had a dark and restraining effect on him. He tapped the table thoughtfully with the side of his thumb.

"But I'm not cut off, Arnette. There's a direct route to Kalatis . . . through Colin Faeber."

"If you pick him up, the time you have to find Kalatis will be reduced to hours, not days," she warned. "The minute he's picked up . . ." She snapped her fingers once.

"If it looks like I'm going to lose Kalatis, I won't hesitate to do it."

"That's risky."

"That's desperate."

After a pause she asked, "How much time do you think you've got?"

Graver looked at the steno pad and pushed it back and forth on the table a few times.

"I've probably already had a telephone call at home from Westrate," he said. "Or from Ben Olmstead, my sergeant in our Houston Terrorist Task Force. I've got three men besides Olmstead in a joint effort with the FBI. They work out of the Federal Building, not even in our offices. I'll be getting immediate briefs from them, so I'll know what they're coming up with out there at South Shore Harbor as soon as it happens. At some point I expect Ginette to report Dean missing. They'll eventually guess Dean might have been one of the bodies, but won't be able to prove it. But because of his disappearance and the deaths of Tisler and Besom, somebody—probably Ward Lukens—will push for an inquiry. And they'll get it. That's when I'm going to have to cough up what I know."

"So . . . we've got . . ."

"I'd guess . . . a few days . . . maybe. I think it'll depend on how quickly Ginette panics."

The handset that had been sitting on the table at Graver's elbow rang for the first time. He picked it up and answered it.

"It's Neuman. I'm on the Gulf Freeway, coming in. I've got something from Sheck's."

"What is it?" Graver sat up in his chair, and Arnette froze, her eyes fixed on him. Graver flicked the conference switch on the handset so Arnette could hear.

"I'm not sure," Neuman said. "I've got some aviation navigating maps, but I also found a canister, a waterproof, military-style container a little over five inches long. I found it tied to a piece of fishing line hanging down inside the floor drain of one of the bedroom showers."

"Jesus, yes," Arnette hissed, suddenly leaning forward and placing both hands flat on the table.

The muscles in Graver's neck began a steady tightening.

"I didn't open it," Neuman said. "Afraid it might be undeveloped film."

"Have him bring it *here*," Arnette said, repeatedly jabbing a forefinger downward in front of her.

Graver looked at her.

"If you say it's okay . . . then it's okay," she said.

Graver nodded.

"Give him the address," she said.

"Neuman . . ."

"Yeah?"

"Listen, I'm going to give you an address. I want you to bring the canister to 4645 Rauer."

Neuman repeated the address.

"That's right. It's a residence. Someone will be waiting for you at the front yard gate."

"Give me twenty minutes."

Graver clicked off the radio.

"In a *shower drain*." Arnette grinned with admiration. "Your boy's pretty good."

Graver suddenly was hopeful again. His adrenaline had been so taxed in the last few days that he was surprised his glands could still produce anything.

"Everybody has some rainy-day security," he said, thinking of Sheck.

"That's the kind of business we're in, baby," Arnette said with satisfaction. "Spooks are as predictable as everybody else. They just think differently. Once you know *how* they think, the odds are good you can make some guesses about *what* they think." She walked back to the other end of the table, tapped a knuckle on the wood surface, and returned to stand in front of Graver. "Kalatis may have cause to regret that marina bombing," she said.

"I'm going to do everything I can to make sure that he does," Graver said.

The fact that they were addressing two entirely different matters was clear to both of them.

55

HE HAD FOUR PLANES IN THE AIR AT ONCE. TWO WERE FLYING back and forth along the Gulf Coast, each with a blindfolded client who thought he was en route to either Mexico or one of the many islands in the West Indies. All of the clients, the four he had flown in during the last two days and the four he would fly in during the next two days, thought they were going somewhere different. All of them, however, believed they had left the United States. Right now one client was being flown "back to the States" and another was due to arrive at any moment. A third plane had taken off from a point twenty miles out in the Gulf where twenty-two million dollars in cash had been loaded onto it from a cabin cruiser. This plane was headed for Grand Cayman. A fourth plane also had been loaded offshore, though at a different point than the third plane. It was carrying twenty-eight-million dollars and was headed for Panama City. This money was in the hands of capable accountants—as well as a generously paid security force—and would be scattered all over the Western Hemisphere in safe, legitimate accounts within fifteen days.

Kalatis was standing on the veranda of his house above the beach. He was smoking a fresh Cohiba and was wearing dark trousers and a loose-fitting pastel salmon shirt of lightweight silk. He heard the distant soprano drone of the next plane, and looked at his watch. Right on time. He thought of Jael. She would be wrapping up her business soon, too. By three or four o'clock both of them would be through with their night's work, and then they would crawl into a bed of fresh white Egyptian cotton sheets and stay there until noon. In the meantime, there were men he was paying to keep regular hours, and Kalatis's biggest operation ever would continue rolling toward its finale with the inexorable and accelerating pace of a boulder tumbling down a mountainside.

He watched as the plane dropped out of the night sky, its winking lights falling toward the Gulf waters until it banked sharply to make its approach, the sound coming straight at him though only the lights were visible, skimming over the top of the water, nothing but the lights until suddenly two tracks of white spray shot up out of the darkness as the pontoons touched and cut the water, and the engines pulled down to a grumble as the plane taxied toward the dock below.

Throwing an appraising glance at the setting of the table on the veranda, Kalatis sucked in his stomach and jammed his flattened hand around his waistband to double-check his shirttail. This client was much more entertaining than the usual. A fitting way to conclude his evening. He turned back to the dock and waited for the telltale sounds as the plane cut its engines and drifted the last few yards to the dock, the sounds of mooring, the guards giving instructions to each other— people of this caliber often traveled with a companion or two of their own—and finally the footsteps on the dock as his men brought the blindfolded client up and across the lawn to the steps of the veranda where they removed the mask.

"Greetings, Ms. Donata," Kalatis said in his most pleasing accent. "I am delighted to see you once again."

Ms. Patricia Donata was thirty-six years old. She had a law degree from Stanford; she was a certified public accountant. Her occupation seemed to be . . . consultant. She had small bosoms, but very long legs of which she allowed you to see an abundance. She also had cold water in her veins. Kalatis found her to be an astute and more than capable representative of her clients.

They sat on the veranda, and as usual the representative was seated so that she saw rather more of the interior of the large spaces of the house than of the coastline. Kalatis took no chances. They had drinks. Kalatis put away his cigar. There was a quarter of an hour of small talk, no business, as Kalatis reacquainted himself with the pleasure of watching Ms. Donata. She had a lovely face with something of a hint of Asia about it, full lips with mandarin red lipstick. Her black hair was shoulder-length. She was a little nervous, he thought, but was handling herself very well in spite of it. He thought her very sexy and did not try to hurry their meeting.

Finally he said, "Well, I know you have been in Houston for several days. I apologize for causing you inconvenience, but since this transaction is considerably larger than those we have arranged before, it required some extra accommodation on everyone's part. I have had to talk to many people such as yourself, and it has had to be done all in a short space of time." He smiled at her. "Has everything been handled to your satisfaction?"

She set her drink on the table in front of her and clasped her hands in her lap.

"I have to say," she said in her unadorned and familiar California manner, "you did it up right, Panos. The logistics were handled beautifully. It relieved the nervousness of a couple of my clients when you sent people out there to work with their own security groups. I don't normally travel with thirty-two million in cash. Everybody liked the way your people in Houston handled it."

"I am delighted to hear it," he said. "And I was also pleased that you were able to allay the fears of some members of your consortium."

"When you're working with eight different personalities, businessmen with strong egos, it takes patience and savvy—and you have to put up with a lot of shit—to get them to agree on anything," she said, providing herself with a nice, oblique compliment.

Yes, Kalatis thought, but they finally agreed to cough up the cash, didn't they. Ultimately greed, not Ms. Donata's patience and savvy, got the best of them. The magnetism of the sexual appetite, Kalatis knew, was not even in the same league as the pull of greed. Offer a man a three hundred percent return on his investment, and he will follow you panting into hell for it. If the percentage points are high enough, nothing is sacred, nothing is forbidden.

Kalatis looked at her with an expression of commiserate understanding.

"This kind of investment makes everyone . . . cautious," he said. "But you must remind your clients that this time we are buying in commodity volume. Metric tons. That is why their waiting time is shorter. They can check their accounts in sixty days." He smiled. "I think they will be satisfied."

"Have all of your consortia come through as you anticipated?" she asked.

It was a bit of a pushy question, but Kalatis wrote it off to her personality. She was, in short, a bitch.

"Exactly as anticipated, I am glad to say." He held up one hand and counted them off by fingers, beginning with his thumb. "Chicago, Atlanta, Seattle, Miami, Washington, D.C., and"—he held up the index finger of the other hand—"New York. Everything as planned. No surprises. It took the better part of a year to arrange this so that everyone who wished to participate could do so with as much assurance as possible."

"Does all the product come from the same region in Afghanistan?"

Ms. Donata was a curious woman, but he also thought she must find her role gratifying and rather found some adventure in using words like "product." Well, she should be gratified. She had put together a collection of businessmen who twice before had trusted him with their millions. And now for the third time. She had been a very clever woman, the arrangements for this venture had been complex— by Kalatis's design—but she had handled the negotiations astutely and creatively. Really an admirable achievement for such a young woman.

But in sixty days, Ms. Donata's life would become a living hell. Everything she saw now, all that she had schemed for and accomplished through the shadow ways of Panos Kalatis, would vanish overnight, and she would be ruined.

So he did not mind indulging her sense of amusement at this time. It was like playing backgammon with a woman who, expecting to marry a prince in the morning, was unknowingly whiling away the last hours before her execution. There was a peculiar kind of stimulation that came from entertaining a woman whose imminent ruin was certain, but unknown to her. It gave her an air of fragility that he very much enjoyed. Yes, Ms. Donata had been a clever woman indeed, but she should have been a little cleverer still.

He told her glib lies of the mujahideen and poppies, of pack trains out of the mountains of the Badakhshan and Hazarajat, of Deh Khavak and Kamdesh and Asmar. He told her enough for her to believe that she could believe what she heard. He often saw this sort of worldly naïveté in Americans who grew up in the United States and never left it, middle-class people who lived middle-class lives, and for whom an adventure was to move to a middle-class neighborhood in a different city. Having seen nothing of the world except the evening news, they were gullible and easily deceived. They might be well educated, as Ms. Donata surely was, but it was an education gotten among the homogeneity of people just like themselves. It was like being a well-educated sheep.

After a while the conversation turned to more benign topics, as a maid—Kalatis had thought that under the circumstances a woman was wanted for this job—brought out some small finger sandwiches and replenished their drinks. They talked of places they had traveled. They were killing time. Below them on the dock—there was the audible shuffling of feet and an occasional dull, hollow thunk as someone bumped a hull or pontoon—as the last twelve million dollars of her thirty-two million dollars in cash was being loaded from the plane to the cruiser. The previous twenty million dollars had been transferred in smaller increments during the course of the last few days.

Kalatis was suppressing a premature euphoria. He was very near to concluding a nine-year project. True, he had not planned *this* particular venture until just the last twenty months—when he saw how incredibly eager American businessmen were to abandon legitimacy—but it had issued from the larger picture, an exercise that he was already looking back on as his American years. The money. My God, the money these men were willing to part with in a calculated gamble to triple what they already had astonished and delighted him. But cogs and wheels were still turning elsewhere, everything was synchronized to terminate simultaneously, and while so many diverse events were still pending he did not let his mind dwell too long on the sweet potential of his rewards.

His thoughts returned to the task at hand as Ms. Donata was beginning an anecdote about Vail. And down below on the docks millions of dollars from the West Coast were about to depart from the South Coast, to points far removed and unknown . . . except to Kalatis.

56

GILBERT HORMANN PUSHED PANOS KALATIS OUT OF HIS MIND. IT was growing increasingly easy to do with every passing moment.

He had been working late at the office, a regular occurrence especially when there was a shipment to Colombia in the offing. The door was open to his adjoining private apartment where he had been to pour himself a drink half an hour before. His personal line in his apartment rang, and he walked in and picked it up expecting to hear his wife ask how much later he was going to be.

It was Kalatis. The Greek said he was rushed. He said he had just gotten the documents required for the Colombian shipment—these were counterfeited bills of lading and other forms that had to be filed with governmental agencies in order to be able to export significant quantities of sulfuric acid and acetic anhydride. Kalatis wanted Gilbert to have the documents tonight, and he was going to send over someone with them, just to drop them off. Gilbert knew there was no use arguing that he was just about to leave.

He hung up the telephone and looked at his watch. Kalatis had said the documents would be there in half an hour. Great. Gilbert had been only minutes away from quitting for the night anyway, and the telephone call had broken his concentration. He turned off the light in his office and walked into his apartment. There was a small kitchen there, a well-furnished bar, a sitting area with a couple of sofas and several armchairs for entertaining. There were plants scattered about, an enormous television, and a view of the entire Galleria area below and, just slightly to the right, the shimmering skyline of downtown. Around the corner was a large bedroom with a generous bath and a Jacuzzi with the same view as in the living room.

Gilbert made himself another drink, kicked off his shoes—he had taken off his tie long ago—and settled down in front of the television, flicking the remote control until he came to the Playboy channel. Forty minutes passed quickly, lubricated by several more drinks, and when the security phone rang he quickly punched in the numbers to let Kalatis's messenger into the elevator. Deliveries from Kalatis were not rare, and his emissaries had the routine well rehearsed.

In five minutes the buzzer to the main office reception area sounded, and Gilbert got up and walked out through his office carrying his drink and without bothering to put on his shoes. When he entered the reception area he almost dropped his glass. Standing on the outside of the glass wall was Kalatis's emissary, Jael.

Gilbert actually stopped. She was wearing a simple, deep-burgundy cocktail dress which hung off her shoulders like a sheet of water. Gilbert was stunned. She held up a manila envelope against the glass, a gesture that seemed to jar him into action. He walked to the receptionist's desk and buzzed open the glass panel door.

"I'm so sorry," she said, smiling and reaching out the envelope. "Panos called you about this?"

Gilbert nodded stupidly. He could see her goddamn *nipples.*

"I'm so sorry it is so late. You know Panos," she said with a rueful wrinkle of her brows and a little shrug. Gilbert would have given fifty dollars to see her shrug that away again. "Everything is so . . . hectic . . . so busy there. He was leaving for a business trip . . . everyone was busy. No one but me to come."

No one but her to come. Gilbert loved her choice of words . . . and her accent. He didn't know what the hell kind of an accent it was, and he didn't care. He always had thought she was one of the hottest-looking women he had ever laid eyes on. Panos's woman, some kind of Middle Eastern blood was what he guessed, but that didn't matter either. She was just an incredible thing. Lean and young and buxom and dark, eyes like a goddamn cat's. He may have been staring at her, he didn't know. He already had drunk enough to make such fine distinctions indistinguishable.

She looked at his glass and smiled. He reached out for the envelope, and he *thought* she kind of held on to it when he took it.

"What have you drinking there?" she asked.

"Oh, uh, scotch. Whiskey."

She nodded, still smiling like she had caught him doing something . . . naughty.

"Uh"—he gestured vaguely—"you . . . want"—he gestured more vaguely, maybe toward her with the glass—"something?"

She raised her eyebrows. "To drink . . . with you?"

And it was at that moment that Panos Kalatis slid out of Gilbert's mind for good. The spice of the present instant was overwhelming. He reached for the door which he suddenly realized she had been holding open with her . . . hip.

"I don't have to hurry to go back," she said, brushing past him. "It is so busy there, and anyway, they will everyone be gone away when I am back there."

"You came by yourself?" he asked with appropriate concern in his voice as they made their way through his office and into his apartment.

"Oh yes," she said, looking around, locking on the view of the city from the sitting room windows.

"What would you like to drink?" he asked, tossing the envelope into a chair and going straight to the bar.

"Cuba Libre," she said, standing at the windows.

Cuba Libre. She goddamned looked like Cuba Libre. He managed to make it, as well as another scotch for himself, though he was in a bit of a fog, and he wasn't sure he made it as good as he could have. He spilled some of each on his hands as he made his way over to her, and then was momentarily disconcerted to find her sitting primly on the sofa in front of the television, back straight, hands in her lap, breasts dripping burgundy, watching a man humping a woman on what appeared to be a motorcycle in a rainstorm.

"What is that?" he said stupidly, standing flat-footed with the wet glasses in his hands.

"They having some love," she said equanimously. She pronounced it "lowve."

She might have said it was going to be clear to partly cloudy, but then she smiled at him in such a way that entirely obliterated this alternate possibility.

Not once during the next half hour did Gilbert Hormann ask another question. Not of her. Not of himself. Not of Fate or of Good Fortune. Not of God. He never asked why it was that he should be naked on the sofa with this incomparable hetaera, Jael. He never asked why he should have her breast in his mouth or feel what he was feeling between her legs. He never asked himself why it should be his good, dumb luck to be in the Jacuzzi with her, swilling scotch and sliding all over her while the city lights went round and round in the vast, black firmament. He never asked any questions at all until he was aware of holding his mouth open because she had asked him to, and looking

past her glistening breasts above him to see her holding an eyedropper
. . . an eyedropper . . . over his opened mouth.

But then it was too late.

His heart stopped. While he was exhaling, something invisible
squeezed out what little air was left and held his chest and lungs in an
excruciatingly painful vacuum. He was agog with pain, specific pain.
He could feel his face turning scarlet, empurpling, and could sense the
arteries in his heart growing thin, attenuated, dissolving, flooding the
muscle in a hemorrhage of uncontained blood. He watched helplessly
as Jael pulled her hand away, the dropper still poised, hesitant, with a
clear drop on the very end of it. He could see it, right on the very end
of the glass ampule, and her breasts inviting even now at this very
terrifying moment when he was thinking, God he had screwed up, her
breasts inviting him to have one more mouthful.

She got out of the Jacuzzi very carefully and stepped onto a towel
she had laid out ahead of time. He hadn't noticed. She knelt beside the
Jacuzzi, turned off the circulating pump, and released the water. As the
basin emptied, she patted herself dry, watching the water disappear,
leaving the pinkish Gilbert Hormann lying in the bottom like a great
hairless bear.

Carefully folding the damp towel in a very precise square, she put it
on the step to the Jacuzzi and knelt on it as she took the sprayer hose
from its seat on the side of the basin and began washing down the
body and the inside of the tub. She got back in the tub with him and
turned him over, washing him thoroughly, washing the sides of the tub
to make sure none of her head hair or pubic hair remained. She opened
his mouth and sprayed it out and then took shampoo from the shelf of
the tub and washed his hair, and hosed him down again very thoroughly, having to turn him over once more.

When she was satisfied, she refilled the Jacuzzi and restarted the
circulating pump. The body floated awkwardly in the swirling water,
moving oddly as the currents pushed it about. She wiped down the
steps to the Jacuzzi with the towel on which she had been kneeling, and
then put it in a plastic trash bag she found in the kitchen.

Before dressing she went into the living room and got her glass,
washed it, and returned it to the liquor cabinet. Then she took a hand
towel from the kitchen and wiped down all the table surfaces around
the sofa so that there would not be too many damp rings for one glass.
She took Hormann's clothes that were scattered about and draped

them with reasonable carelessness on a chair in the bathroom, put his shoes near the chair, as though he had just kicked them off there, and put his socks on top of them.

When everything was to her satisfaction, she went back into the living room and picked up her dress from the floor and slipped it on over her head. She picked up one of the magazines from a coffee table —a *Newsweek*—and returned to the bath where she tossed it into the Jacuzzi. She also turned over the glass from which Hormann had been drinking and left it rolling around in a circle on the side of the tub.

All of this was probably unnecessary. Panos had thoroughly researched the man's medical records. Chronic high blood pressure. They had used precisely the right chemistry. Still, she liked to do everything every time. It was a good habit.

She picked up the manila folder she had brought, picked up her plastic bag containing her towel and walked out of the apartment leaving the lights on. Turning out the lights in his office, she walked out through the reception area, buzzed herself out, and disappeared down the hall to the elevators.

57.

THEY CROWDED INTO THE DARKROOM, GRAVER, ARNETTE, NEUMAN, who was still trying to absorb what had been revealed to him in the three common little houses on Rauer Street, and Boyd, who was handling the canister. In the room's cool redness everyone looked pale and conspiratorial, intent on the object in Boyd's hands.

"You don't think this is some kind of bomb, a booby trap, do you?" Boyd mused, only half in jest as he put the first twist on the cap. No one said anything.

"I just want to know if it's film," Graver said. "Then I'll get out of your way."

It was a long-threaded cap, as was customary with such water-proofed containers, and when it finally came free Boyd laid it on the worktable. Holding it over his opened hand, he turned it over in the palm of his hand, and a tightly coiled, shiny black scroll fell into his hand.

"It's film," he said. "Already developed." He stretched out the roll between his hands, one high in the air, the other down below his waist. "Microfilm."

"Okay, that's good enough for me," Graver said. "How long will it take you to get something."

"I can get you the first frame—microfiche—in about twenty minutes."

They stepped out of the darkroom leaving Boyd to his magic and walked around the corner to the main computer room. Every work station was being used and the room was chattering with keystrokes. Quinn was at her radio, writing in a notebook, and speaking with professional ennui into her pencil-sized microphone. Neuman took it in quickly, trying not to gawk, but naturally wanting to see as much as possible. Arnette smiled and stopped.

"This is Quinn," she said to Neuman, but not interrupting the girl for an introduction. "Right now she's fielding reports from the South Shore Harbor. We've got stringers, much like a newspaper does. When something big like that happens they bring us up to speed. Every call is computer-recorded and the reports are tallied and the information is assigned a value, very much like a value code is given to an informant or a source. We keep track of both the quality and the volume of information from each stringer. Sometimes that pays off in ways you wouldn't expect."

She walked around the room slowly, clockwise.

"These two women are working on Tisler's computer data. This is still a very long shot," she said, looking at Graver, "but they've gotten through some doors, made some progress. Over here, this guy's working on trying to ID the guy who met Burtell at the Transco Fountain. We haven't found him, but we're getting updates on these people so it's actually a useful exercise for us. It's been a while since I updated my photo file, and it's expensive, so you don't want to do it without a good reason.

"Dani," she said, pointing to the girl at the next station, "is running leads on Brod Strasser. You guys stumbled onto some of the most reclusive boys in the business. Take Kalatis. We *think* he bought a place in the Houston area around 1989. We *think* he's been spending about half his time here since then, but we can't verify it. Our real estate stringers say they don't think so, that there are no shell residential purchases they can't open up. They're wrong, but we can't prove it. He owns a private plane, a Desault Falcon. We know that it's in the name of his pilot, a former Israeli Air Force instructor. We know when he leaves Colombia in that thing . . . and that's all we know. Once, in 1989, we nailed it at Hobby. It stayed there three days. Now, I *know* the guy's been back here in it, but we can't prove it. We think he's paying off an air traffic controller in Honduras—Tegucigalpa. He enters the country at that little narrow Gulf of Fonseca, crosses Honduras, and comes out over the Bay Islands as somebody else. Then to be safe, he's using a private strip somewhere around Houston instead of one of the airports. But we can't prove it."

She stopped without explaining anything about the last three or four work stations.

"And it goes on and on," she said. "We're always chasing down something."

She headed toward the library and Graver and Neuman followed. As they walked in, Graver's handset that he had left on the library table was buzzing. He picked it up. It was Paula.

"Graver, everything went okay with Heath. She's gone. But as soon as we got back to your place Ginette Burtell drove up right behind us. She's hysterical. She thought you'd be home. She says she thinks that Dean is dead. She's really unglued. Lara's with her."

Graver's heart sank.

"Why does she think he's dead?"

"That explosion. Local stations broke into network programming with it. She says Dean kept a boat in a slip at South Shore Harbor."

"Christ."

"I think you'd better get over here. She says she has something to tell you. Apparently Dean had been afraid the last few days. She says he had given her a message to give to you in the event of his death. I think she's frightened, too. I don't know . . . there seems to be more to this. I think you'd better get over here."

"Did she wonder why you and Lara were at my place?"

"Yeah, but I just told her we were in the middle of something. You'd better come on."

"Okay, I'm coming right now."

"You heard from Neuman?" There was an edge of concern in Paula's voice.

"He's with me. He got something from Sheck's. I'll fill you in when I get there."

58

BY THE TIME GRAVER GOT HOME, GINETTE BURTELL WAS SITTING quietly with Lara on the sofa in the living room, each turned slightly to the other, their knees just touching as they talked. Lara, who had a softer touch than Paula and with whom Ginette was more familiar because she saw her every time she came into the office to see Dean, had a natural ability to communicate on a visceral level and a manner that was immediately discernible as genuine and without calculation. It was the kind of candid compassion that Ginette needed at that moment, and Lara apparently had been able to calm her.

When Graver walked into the room Ginette stood up immediately.

"Marcus," she said. "Thank God." She wore no makeup to hide the fact that her eyes were red and swollen, and her fashionable skirt and blouse were wrinkled as if she had been wearing them too long and had no interest in their condition.

"We've got to talk," she said quickly, her voice cracking on the last word. Her face wrinkled as Graver came over to her and took her hands, which were twisting a tissue.

"Okay, Ginny, it's okay," he said, getting her to sit down again with him as Lara stood and started to leave the room. "Ginny," Graver said, "you don't mind if Lara stays, do you?"

She shook her head and buried her face in the tissue, grabbing others from the box on the sofa. Graver glanced at Lara.

"Ginny, I know you've got something to say that you feel is important," Graver said. "I don't want to miss anything. This is all very complicated. I'm going to ask Paula to come back in too. We need all the help we can get on this, and of course Paula . . . works with Dean"—he almost said "worked"—"and needs to hear this."

She nodded again and Graver again looked at Lara, who left to get Paula from the kitchen where Graver had found her a few moments earlier nursing a cup of coffee and looking thoroughly uncomfortable. Graver had paused only a moment to speak to her when he came in the back door. She quickly had told him of his messages and handed a piece of paper with the calls on it: Westrate and Olmstead as Graver had guessed, each a couple of times—Graver deliberately had turned off his pager when he had left the house earlier—and Victor Last.

"Do you want anything to drink?" Graver asked. He was turned toward her on the sofa.

"No, I . . . no," she said, wiping her nose and putting all of her energy into an effort to gain control of herself. "I'm sorry."

"No need to be," Graver said. "If you'll just try to think of every-thing . . . every detail, it'll help us get to the bottom of this."

As Lara and Paula came back into the room and found chairs, Graver told Ginette to start from the beginning, to take her time, and not to be disconcerted if he had to interrupt her a number of times to ask questions.

"God, I don't know how to start," she said. "I saw the news bulle-tin . . . South Shore Harbor. We keep a sailboat out there and I think . . . I think that's where Dean was going when he left the house to-night."

"Why do you think that?"

"Because he had a meeting . . . with someone. When he had meetings he used the boat sometimes."

"How do you know?"

"He let it slip one time, a reference. Something hadn't been cleaned up when we went out there to go sailing, and he said oh he'd forgotten to take care of it after the last meeting. I saw him cringe, you know, kind of. I guessed it had something to do with work, so I didn't say anything further. I tried not to quiz him. That's always hard, trying to ignore all the . . . inexplicable things."

"But there are a lot of boats out there, Ginny," Graver said. "Why do you think Dean was on the boat that blew up?"

"Was he?" She looked at him, visibly bracing herself. It was a brave question, and one that revealed that she believed Graver already knew the truth.

"I don't know anything about what's happened out there," Graver lied. "The Department's gotten a ton of calls about it, but I doubt if I'll know much of anything until tomorrow. I understand it's chaos out there."

"The boat was in slip forty-nine," she said, stiffening.

"Ginny, we don't know that kind of detail yet. I'm pretty eager to know myself, and when I do find out something I'll let you know immediately."

He paused, and she continued to stare at him. He thought she might be seeing right through him, but he plunged on.

"Dean was officially on vacation, Ginny," he said. "He wouldn't be going to meet someone now, would he?"

She sat staring at the tissue she was kneading. "I, uh, I said to, Paula, that . . . Jesus"—she looked up and away toward the windows, her eyes batting back the tears—"Dean's . . . Dean's had something else going on . . . besides work . . . I mean CID work . . . something else . . ."

She stopped, finding it difficult to broach the subject.

"Did he tell you this?"

She shook her head.

"No, of course not," she said. "He wouldn't have done that." She took a deep breath. "Uh, about a year ago . . . or a little less . . . he began going out at night again. I got used to that when he was an investigator, but that was years ago. As an analyst it was pretty rare that he would do that. But it got to be he'd go out at least one night almost every week. I finally asked him about it, I said what's the deal with this going out? You don't have to do that." She dropped her eyes. "I thought . . . I thought he was seeing another woman. I blew up. He sat me down and said there was a special investigation under way and that everyone was having to put in extra time. It was a big project, a long one, and that this would have to go on for a while. After that he was very . . . sensitive about it, never tried to hide it or make it mysterious. But he reminded me that if I ever spoke to any of you, you know, when I came to see him at the office, that I must never mention that he'd been working late, that it wouldn't look good if it seemed that he'd been talking about his work at home."

Ginette reached a hand up and wiped it across her brow, brushing aside a wisp of her short, jet hair. She sighed heavily, exhausted from the tension that was eating every bit of her strength.

"About four or five months ago Dean began to change. He seemed . . . stressed. He grew kind of broody, irritable. I'd seen this before when he was an investigator, if something he was working on wasn't going right. And in those days he'd talk about it after a while, if I insisted. But this time"—she shook her head—"this time he just got angry when I tried to draw him out. He made it clear, in no uncertain terms, that it wasn't something we could talk about.

"Then he began going out more often at night. Sometimes I think he was going to meet Art. Sometimes Art would come by here, or he'd call and come over, and they'd stand outside in the drive and talk. So I knew it was business, not another woman. But it was eating him up. He couldn't sleep. I'd wake up in the night, and he wouldn't be in bed. I'd find him sitting out in the courtyard, or in the living room. Or I'd wake up suddenly, and he'd just be lying there, staring at the ceiling . . . or . . . or just be staring at me."

She stopped and swallowed and, though she didn't sob, tears rolled out of her eyes so that she had to stop and use more tissue. Graver glanced at Lara, whose large, dark eyes were fixed on him with sober concern. Again Ginette got herself under control and went on.

"Sunday night when you came over and told him about Art—God, it seems like a month ago—it was terrible. After you left Dean came in and told me. He told me we had to get over to Peggy's and break the bad news to her. Then he went into the bathroom and closed the door. In a few minutes I heard him vomiting. He stayed in there a long time. I went ahead and changed clothes, and he was still in there. He, uh, he was sick until there was nothing left . . . uh, I, uh, could hear him in there just, you know, coughing and coughing."

She started crying again, covering her face in the wad of tissues. Lara quickly got up and came over to the sofa and sat down on the other side of her, putting her arm around her. She took the wet tissues out of Ginette's hands and gave her dry ones and hugged her and said something to her.

Graver sat there helplessly, the image of Burtell vomiting playing over and over in his mind. Paula was sitting near Graver's desk with a pen and notepad, staring at Ginette with a drawn face. Graver saw that she hadn't written down a word.

It was a few minutes before Ginette was able to continue, and when she did her voice was thin and without strength. This time Lara stayed at her side.

"We went over and stayed Sunday night with Peggy," she went on. "We got a sedative for her and finally, about three in the morning, she went to sleep. Neither Dean nor I slept a minute. When Peggy's folks came in from Corpus Christi about five-thirty the next morning, we went home. We both bathed, cleaned up and went to work. But Monday night was miserable. Dean wasn't able to sleep at all. Tuesday morning the loss of sleep was killing me, and I called in sick. Dean got up and went to work as usual. I slept through the day and got up late in the afternoon. Dean had left a note on the kitchen table saying that he had left the office early, that, you know, you had let him start his vacation, and that he would be home again later.

"When he came in around nine o'clock that evening he looked terrible. He was carrying a computer backup tape which he said he'd tell me about later. We ate dinner and then about ten-fifteen he said he had to go to a meeting and would be back in a few hours. As soon as he left, you called. I was so glad to hear from you . . . I . . . almost told you I was seriously worried about him, but I rationalized. I thought, no he's had this big investigation, then Art's suicide. It's just that it's a terrible time for him. I didn't want to be an alarmist. Dean wouldn't have wanted me to run whining to you about how much stress he was under. So I didn't say anything to you about it. He came in late that night . . . God, that was last night . . . and went straight to bed with a sick headache.

"This morning I went to work and let him sleep. He told me later that he had slept all day. When I got home this afternoon we had a few drinks, and he started talking."

Ginette stopped and swallowed. "I'm sorry," she said. "I could use a glass of water after all."

Paula got up, went into the kitchen, and brought one back to her. Ginette took several drinks and then held it in her lap as she went on.

"He started talking," she said. "He said that he had been involved in an investigation that . . . you . . . didn't know anything about. He said that six or eight months ago he began to suspect someone was selling CID intelligence. He said after a month or so of looking into it he was sure it was happening, and he brought Art in because he trusted him and needed some help. But he said he hadn't involved you because . . . he said, you know, he didn't know how high up it went . . ."

"He wasn't sure if I was involved or not," Graver said.

She nodded uncertainly and shrugged. "I guess."

"He was right to do that, Ginny," Graver said. "He did the right thing. Then he believed people above him were involved?"

"He said he had proof that Ray Besom was selling intelligence."

"Proof?"

"Yes. He said he and Art had set up a separate computer system in a rent house that Art owns, and they had been putting everything they knew on that. He said that yesterday he had gone over to Art's rent house after he left the office and transferred everything on the computer to the backup tape he'd brought home. He said he then scrambled what was on the computer using special software for that purpose. He said he could use the same software to unscramble it later if he needed to, but the way it was now it was reduced to nonsense."

"Why didn't he just erase it after he'd copied it?" Graver asked.

She shook her head. "I don't know. He didn't say."

"Okay," Graver said. "Go on."

She took another sip of water.

"He said that in a little while he was going to have to go out to another meeting. He said that he was reasonably sure now that you weren't involved in this thing, and that if anything should happen to him that I should give you the backup tapes."

She stopped and drank some more water, using this to fight back the welling urge to break down again. It was killing Graver to see her going through this and to have to keep her at it until she had told him all she could. He felt cruel and, for some inexplicable reason, hypocritical.

"I just couldn't believe he had said that. I went crazy. He promised me . . . *promised* me that there was nothing to be worried about. He said the only reason he said that was . . . it was just the same as having life insurance. Nobody expects to be killed in a car wreck, but you make arrangements just the same. I didn't buy that," she said, shaking her head. "We went on talking for quite a while. But eventually he had to go. He said he wouldn't be late. That was around ten-thirty."

She started breathing heavily, fighting the tears. "And then I was watching television . . . and they broke in . . ."

"Ginette," Graver said, wanting to stop her before she began crying again. "Ginette, do you have the tape?"

But she was already sobbing. Still, she managed to point to her purse which was sitting under the coffee table in front of them. Graver reached down and picked it up, reached inside, felt around, found the tape, and held it up.

"Is this it, Ginny?"

She nodded, sobbing.

Graver patted her on the leg and got up and walked over to the telephone on his desk. He dialed Arnette's number. When she answered, he quickly explained what he had. She was incredulous.

"You *have* the tape?" she asked.

"I'm holding it."

"Can you get it over here now?"

"I can't come. I've got an answering machine full of messages that can't wait any longer. If it's okay with you I'm going to send Paula."

"Get her over here."

"What about the microfiche?"

"We've got the first few pages. So far it's a detailed record of how Faeber's collection system is set up. It's big, baby. They're buying information you wouldn't believe. We've got names, dates, places, codes. This is Kalatis's work. It's highly organized into cells. Compartmentalized. Backstops everywhere. From the looks of this Colin Faeber's computers are full of some heavy stuff. And there's CID information in there too. It's a massive operation."

"I'm sending her over," Graver said.

59

GRAVER SPENT A FEW MORE MINUTES TALKING TO GINETTE
Burtell, reassuring her, trying to say something to her that would ease
her mind enough to allow the sedatives that Lara finally had convinced
her to take to achieve their effect. He assured her again that he would
do all that he could to find Dean, and that she shouldn't automatically
assume the worst. He repeated his promise to her to let her know as
soon as he knew something definite. After a while Lara took her upstairs to Natalie's bedroom.

Feeling lousy about having had to lie to Ginette, Graver sat down
at his desk and called Ben Olmstead. He tried several numbers, his
pager, and handset, before finally getting him at South Shore Marina.
According to Olmstead, the impact of the initial explosion had destroyed nearly a dozen boats and as many more were set afire. Unfortunately the area of impact was on one of the docks that held a refueling
slip, and a couple of gasoline storage tanks had been ignited. One of
the tanks was full, so it was only burning. But the other one had been
nearly empty and had blown immediately, increasing the force of the
original explosion.

"Can they tell anything about the point of impact, where it originated?" Graver asked.

"No, but we're getting a slip rental list from the marina management now and ought to be able to get close, within a dozen or so
names here pretty soon."

"What about telephone calls?" Graver could hear the confusion in
the background, sirens, men yelling, the roar of water-pumping engines.

"Oh, yeah. They're coming in. Maybe five so far, but none of the
groups we're seriously concerned about."

"Is everybody out there?"

"You bet. Bomb Squad. Houston Fire Department Arson Squad. ATF. DEA. If you can believe it, the DEA had a stakeout going on over on the other side of the marina. When this blew over here they freaked out. They're confused as hell now, thinking their informant set them up. Oh, and we've also got a list of all the people registered in the hotel here. Going over that now. We're also having the hotel security pull all their surveillance films from their lobby cameras for the last twenty-four hours." He paused. "Westrate call you?"

"Yeah, I've got to call him back," Graver said, "but I wanted to talk to you first. You don't even know yet if the explosion was a bomb, do you? Whether it was accidental? A gas leak, a butane leak in one of the cabins?"

"No, we don't know. And the Bomb Squad can't make very good guesses since the punch of this one was obscured by the gasoline tank going almost simultaneously. Some witnesses say there were two explosions close together, some say one. And this is a hell of a fire, so we're not going to get to the source for another twelve or fifteen hours I'd guess."

"Okay, Ben. Thanks, I appreciate it. Keep in touch."

"Will do."

Graver immediately called Arnette and told her that investigators were pulling lobby tapes and hotel registrations for the last twenty-four hours. If her people think they got caught on camera she might want to do something about it.

Then he called Westrate.

"Where the hell have you been?" Westrate bellowed.

"I've just talked with Olmstead," Graver said, ignoring the question. "They've got it nailed down out there as well as can be expected."

"What does that mean?"

"They've done just about all they can do until the fire's out and they can get in there and study it."

"Do they think it was terrorists? Some kind of drug thing?"

"They don't have any idea." Graver told him about the DEA operation on the other side of the marina.

"This could have been theirs," Westrate said. "The sons of bitches wouldn't have let us in on that, though, would they. We'll have to spend good time and money to duplicate what they know and then they'll say, 'Oh, we could have let you have that information.' "

Graver didn't want to listen to this kind of thing, Westrate's favorite pastime.

"I've got to go, Jack."

"Look, keep me posted. But, shit, it's late. Just wait and get back with me in the morning . . . unless something spectacular happens."

"Okay, Jack."

Graver hung up and slumped back in his chair. He was limp with exhaustion. The day had begun around seven o'clock when he went to Arnette's even before going to the office and viewed the surveillance photographs Boyd had taken of Burtell meeting with the Unknown at the Transco Fountain the night before . . . just a little over twenty-four hours from right now. Then around two o'clock in the afternoon he was back at Arnette's reading the Yosef Raviv dossier after Arnette had picked up Kalatis's name on the fountain interview recording. By four o'clock he was back at the office and Paula had turned up Colin Faeber's name on the board of Gulfstream Bank and an hour later Neuman returned to the office with the news that Faeber's DataPrint was owned by Concordia International Investments, a subsidiary of Strasser Industries. Around eight-thirty in the evening Graver and Neuman had picked up Valerie Heath and around twelve-thirty Burtell was blown to bits in South Shore Harbor. And now the latest developments of the last few hours.

This had been one of the fastest-breaking investigations he had ever experienced, especially one of such complexity, all of which was complicated by the fact that he was trying to keep it off the books. He needed very badly to sit down and bring his journal up to date, but the thought of doing that now seemed an impossibility to him.

What he really wanted was a glass of wine, a rich, fruity Merlot that would almost be a meal in itself, but he knew if he did that his energy level would plummet right to the bottom.

The telephone rang. Startled, he snatched it off the receiver almost before it stopped ringing.

"This is Graver."

"It's Victor. Listen to me." His voice hushed and quick. "I've only a moment. We've got to meet in the morning, late morning. You're not going to believe what I've got for you, my friend."

"Give me a clue, Victor," Graver said.

"I'm going to deliver Faeber's ass."

In the euphoria about Neuman's discovery and then the immediate strain of confronting Ginette Burtell, Graver had forgotten about Colin Faeber, the only living direct link to Kalatis. Now here was Victor Last offering to "deliver Faeber's ass."

"What do you mean by that, Victor? Are you speaking physically or judicially?"

"Both, for Christ's sake! What does it matter?"

"When do you want to meet?"

"Ten o'clock. I can't get there before then."

"Get where?"

"Oh, that Italian place of yours. Good coffee."

The line went dead.

Shit! Graver buried his face in his hands, his elbows on the top of his desk. He seriously needed time to think. It was moving too fast, all of it, and he didn't like the feeling of . . . hurtling.

"Graver."

He turned around and saw Lara standing in the door.

"She's sleeping. Why don't you take time for a glass of wine?"

60

THEY SAT SIDE BY SIDE ON THE SOFA, THEIR HEADS RESTING ON the cushioned back, their shoes off, their feet propped on the ottoman with its tapestry picture of a Tuscan hillside.

"I needed this," he said. "I appreciate your thinking of it."

"To tell you the truth," she said, "I probably did this as much for me as for you. I'm drained. This has been hard, the whole ordeal, but these last few hours with Ginny have been . . . so painful. It's . . . You just naturally put yourself in her place. I feel so terrible for her, but there's nothing, really, that I can do." Lara sipped from her glass. "This is really torment for her."

"You were good with her," Graver said. "I'm grateful to you for how you've handled it. She needed the attention, the consolation."

"Well, anyway, how are you holding up?" she asked.

"I'm doing okay," he said evasively. "Much better right this minute than . . . in a long time."

She moved a bare foot over to his crossed feet and rubbed the top of it against the arch of his socked foot. The gesture was the kind of small thing that can mean so much at just the right moment. Neither of them said anything for a while. Graver could have kissed her just for these few moments, even if they proved not to last very long. He was thankful for this brief shared tranquility, for the companionship in silence, for the shared Merlot, and, even if their thoughts were miles apart, for her willingness to sit quietly with him and not feel that she had to keep up a conversation. He liked seeing her out of her dress clothes, jean-clad legs and shoeless feet beside his on the ottoman. He felt the uniquely human comfort of being with another person who cared whether or not you were tired or worried or simply wanted some company.

"What do you think about all this?" he asked, turning to look at her.

She did not answer immediately, and he watched her profile framed in her abundance of chestnut hair casually pulled back, her eyes fixed on something across the room as she thought.

"I think . . . that this is a pretty cruel business," she said. She looked at him. "I think it's complicated, and it's addictive, and it's cruel."

"Addictive?"

"Yes," she said. "I didn't really realize it myself until all this happened. There's this race to uncover layers and layers of secrets. You don't know where it's taking you, but you like the ride. It's challenging. There's risk. Like gambling. You have to put up something, a stake, to be able to play the game. And it's voyeuristic. You get to look at people from the back of a mirror. Or through cracks in the walls."

"You don't like that part of it. The spying."

"Well, that's refreshing," she said.

"What?"

"Calling it what it is instead of 'a collection effort' or 'strategic intelligence' or any of those other doublespeak terms."

She took a sip of her Merlot, and he watched her, concentrating on the shape of her lips on the rim of the glass, the way the dark wine entered her mouth.

"There's something . . . maybe there's something a little hypocritical about it. Or something like that. I don't quite know how to talk about it," she said.

She seemed suddenly embarrassed. The first time Graver had ever seen that in her face. She looked down at her glass.

"It's not a simple business," he said, not wanting her to feel awkward. That hadn't been his intention in asking her.

"I didn't like it that you lied to Ginny Burtell," she said suddenly. "That was . . . I don't know . . . very hard to watch."

"It was hard to do," he said.

She turned and looked at him. "Was it?"

He felt himself flush.

"I just didn't like seeing it," she went on. "I didn't like . . . seeing how easily it came to you."

For a moment he couldn't swallow. What she had just said, softly, almost kindly, was an indictment, and he was all the more embarrassed because, perhaps, it *had* come easily—or at least maybe it hadn't been as difficult as it should have been.

"Aren't you going to tell her at all?" she asked.

"Lara, I can't."

She took a deep breath and looked into her wine again.

"God, it's a terrible thing to see this at work," she said. "I guess . . . it's always been just paperwork to me before. I should have known better, that this kind of . . . messiness lay behind it all. It was stupid of me not to have thought about it."

He didn't know what it was that he felt, but he did know that she had seen something that he himself had not seen before. It was not that she had seen him deliberately lie. Surely she knew, too, that there was a larger purpose to his lying, maybe even that there were lives to be saved by it. It was, rather, that she had seen that it had come to him so easily. It was an appalling idea, and one that cut even deeper than having to admit—as he did more often lately—that all the reasons he gave himself for doing what he did were actually sounding more and more like rationalizations.

He could feel her sitting beside him in anticipation, waiting for him to say something, waiting for him to explain things he didn't understand himself.

The awkward silence was interrupted by the telephone ringing again. Graver got up and walked to his desk and answered it.

"Graver, I've got a suggestion." It was Arnette. "Paula's just come in here. We're going to put this thing on the computers and see what we come up with, but whatever it is we're not going to want to waste any more time than is necessary once the information starts pouring out here. I just got through talking to Mona, and your people have agreed, so we're going to put them up over here tonight. I've got people working in shifts here, but your two are going around the clock, and they're going to need some sleep or they're going to conk out on me. So, we'll work as late as we can, get three or four hours sleep, and then hit the ground running early in the morning. Okay?"

"That's your call, Arnette. I appreciate it. I'll cover for them at the office in the morning. I'm going to have to go in, probably early, so let me know what you can as soon as you can. And tell Mona I owe her."

"Good night, baby."

Graver put down the telephone and rubbed his temples with the thumb and middle finger of one hand. He sipped the wine, thinking.

"Okay," he said. "Paula and Neuman are staying at Arnette's tonight, and they won't be going in to the office in the morning. I'd like you to be here when Ginette wakes up because we've got a bit of a problem with her. I'll have to talk to her and get her to understand we've got to keep this quiet. I don't know anything about her family. We'll need to find out who's closest and get someone here to be with her when they confirm that Dean's boat was the site of the explosion."

He walked back to the sofa and sat down on the edge of it, turned a little to Lara.

"I'll be able to cover for Paula and Neuman," he added, "but I guess you'd better call in sick in the morning."

Lara nodded. Graver sat back on the sofa again. There was a little bit of wine left in her glass. His thoughts immediately turned to Last. For a while Lara had made him forget the brief but tantalizing exchange of a few minutes before. Could Last really have come up with something significant? Last was going to "deliver Faeber's ass"? How could Graver possibly believe that?

"God knows how this is going to end," he said, shaking his head. "I don't know how much longer we can keep up this ad hoc task force situation."

"Do you think someone higher up *is* involved in this?"

"There's not any way I can guess at that." He drank some of the Merlot. "Sometimes I think there has to be. Sometimes I think this whole thing was a rogue deal, a blip on the screen, an aberration." He looked at his hand holding the wine, the wine almost as thick and dark as blood. "And other times I know damn well that's not true. These people haven't died because of a blip on the screen. They died because someone set a process into motion, a complex process, that required them to die."

"And . . . where are we in this 'process'? How many more people are going to have to die?"

"Damned if I know. But I think Arnette was right when she said we're just seeing the tail end of it. Whatever is happening is happening fast, and we're going to be lucky just to get a whiff of what it was all about. If it continues to accelerate at the rate it's been going, it'll be over suddenly and soon. Too soon."

"What does that mean?"

"If something doesn't open up immediately I'm going to lose Kalatis. God knows how close—or far away—we are to him. He's making things happen all around us. If I can't get my hands on Faeber . . . then I really don't have much hope I'll ever even see Kalatis's face."

They sat a while longer, finishing their wine, going over the incredible events that had taken Ray Besom, Arthur Tisler, and Dean Burtell all in four days. Lara found it difficult to grasp the enormity of it, and though Graver pretended to deal with it as philosophically and professionally as possible, the truth was he, too, found it mind-boggling. Paula was right, this kind of thing happens to you only once.

As to the ramifications of this chaotic episode, Graver thought it would not end well for anyone. It was very likely he would be called on the boards for the way he had handled it, for keeping it to himself. The second-guessers would be all over him. It would be as clear as day that he should have done it another way. There was no avoiding that. Having to replay the game came with the job of calling the shots. But for right now, he had to wait once again. The waiting was unavoidable too, and it was easily the hardest part of the job.

Lara emptied her glass.

"That was good," she said. "Look, I realize I've got my stuff all over your bed," she said, starting to get up. "I'll go up and clear it off so you can get some sleep."

"No, don't worry about it," he said. "You go ahead and sleep in there. I'll use Nathan's room down the hall . . ."

They looked at each other a moment.

"I suppose this has reached the point of the ridiculous, hasn't it," he said.

She smiled, a gentle smile that reminded him of what a fool he had been, and of how lucky he was that what they were about to do was even still a possibility.

He took refuge with her through what was left of the night. He did not suppose that she ever would have imagined that word was appropriate, but that was what she was to him in those too few hours, an asylum from the strain of the silent calamity that he was feeling. All that he could touch and smell and taste of her was comfort to him. And when the passion subsided and silence and stillness returned unhurriedly to them, when they lay together for the first time as if theirs was an old familiar intimacy regained, he lay awake, hopeful, in the company of her comfort.

Thursday
THE FIFTH DAY

61

GRAVER HAD ONLY JUST GONE TO SLEEP WHEN HE WAS GENTLY shaken awake.

"It's six-fifteen," Lara said.

He was on his side, his back to her, and for a moment he thought he couldn't move. Exhaustion lay on him like a blanket of lead. He felt her shake him again.

"Marcus, it's six-fifteen."

Her use of his first name and the motion of the bed as she got up brought him to the surface, and with a tremendous effort he rolled over. Her back was turned to him, and he saw her untie her dressing gown, slip it off and hang it over the closet door where she had hung her clothes. She glanced back at him over a bare shoulder, her thick, tumbled hair falling down her naked back.

"I'm going to shower," she said. "Are you awake?"

"Yeah," he said. "Thanks."

He watched her hips and long legs disappear into the bath through the louvered doors. It was a sight he hadn't seen in a long time, and it almost seemed as if it was happening to someone else.

Getting out of bed, he pulled on his trousers and went downstairs shirtless and barefooted to make coffee. When he got to the kitchen door he could smell it. Lara had put it on before she woke him, and it was just finishing perking.

He poured a cup for each of them and then took them back upstairs. She was still in the shower, a large corner one which was nearer the vanity where she had laid out her things. He stepped over and put her coffee next to her basin, pausing to look at her through the glass door, her arms raised, her eyes closed, her hands buried in her hair piled with a lather of shampoo. She was leaning back to keep her head out of the shower's spray. He noticed she had laid out only one towel on the little bench near the shower door, and he stepped over to the cabinets and got out another. Dore had always used two, one to wrap her hair in, one to dry with. He put the additional towel on the bench, and then went to his own basin, turned on the water, and began shaving.

They maneuvered through the next half hour of bathing and dressing with a collaborative naturalness that seemed more like a resumption of old ways than a first-time experience. For Graver it was very much a healing activity, like something had been set right in his life that had been wrong for a long time.

She was wearing only a bra and panties and was bent over drying her hair when he finished dressing and, catching her eye in the mirror, motioned to her that he was going downstairs. Unlocking the front door, he stepped outside and got the paper off the front lawn. The coastal clouds were already clearing, and the day promised to be clear and blistering. The hottest days of the year had arrived with their unrelenting swelter and humidity. Unfolding the paper as he walked back into the house, he saw that the explosion at the marina had commanded a banner headline.

Tossing the paper onto the kitchen table, he set about making breakfast. He took out the toaster and bread and quickly made a couple of pieces of toast, took some strawberry jam out of the refrigerator, and sat down at the table with a fresh cup of coffee to read the coverage. There wasn't much to it, interviews with people who worked at the hotel and marina, with a couple of people who owned boats that were destroyed, with the fire chief who didn't want to speculate whether it was a bomb or a gas leak, with several people who were staying in the hotel and had a bird's-eye view of the scene. A lot of photographs. A boxed story on the background of the marina's development, whom it catered to, NASA people, well-to-do people who had summer homes in the area. A story about the estimated dollar figure on the damage.

The telephone rang on the near end of the kitchen counter, and he got up and grabbed it.

"This is Olmstead, Captain. I've got some interesting information for you." He paused.

"Okay, go ahead."

"First of all, they finally got the fire out about an hour ago. That gave us a chance to get a little closer and start estimating the slip positions. Close to ground zero, or pretty damn close to it, is a boat slip rented by a guy named Max Tiborman. On the rental papers he gives his address as Lake Charles, Louisiana. But the telephone company in Lake Charles has no listing for Tiborman. We got the police down there to go by and check the address on the papers. Turns out it's a U-Haul rental company. So we check out the boat registration number. That turns out to be in the name of Mrs. Ginette Sommer."

Olmstead paused. Graver said nothing. Olmstead continued.

"On a boat registration you have to give your home address, but on this form there was only a post office box number. I don't know how that happened." Another pause. "Now, Captain, I don't know, this could be an absolute fluke, but I happen to know that Dean Burtell's wife's name is Ginette, and I know her maiden name is Sommer. I know because I had a good friend with the same last name and that came up at a Division Christmas party one time and we talked about it . . ."

He stopped, his point made.

"Goddamn," Graver said. "What's the slip number?"

"Forty-nine."

"Shit. Anybody else know about this?" Graver meant anyone else on the HTTF, anyone in the FBI. Olmstead knew what he meant.

"Well, no. I mean, this is a little unusual, and I just kept my mouth shut when the registration fax came through. I didn't know . . . I thought maybe you guys had something working, an investigation cover set up or something. Thought I'd better run it by you."

Graver's mind was racing. He couldn't let Burtell's involvement surface so soon. It had to be staunched at this moment, at this point.

"Ben, we do have something out there," Graver said. "It's touchy, very touchy. Hell of a coincidence. Let me get with the people involved and see if we can agree on a way to handle this, who to bring into it, at what level. Dean's on vacation so it might take me a while to get to him, but I'll get right on it. You handled it right, Ben. Exposure now would have cost us the operation, a lot of time and work and money. It's been a long time in the making. Hold on to this, and I'll get back to you on it."

"Yeah, okay."

"Was anyone hurt out there?"

"God, we don't know. The fire's only been out about an hour, like I said, and everything's hot as hell. The Arson Squad and Bomb Squad people are just now beginning to pick their way into all the debris. You know, moving around in boats. The smoke's still hanging over the water. The docks are all unstable. It'll be slow going."

"Okay, Ben. Thanks. I'll be going into the office in another half hour. Let me know if anything else comes up."

"Will do. See you later."

Graver put down the telephone and looked up. Lara was standing just inside the kitchen watching him. She probably had heard the whole thing, his pretense at assuming that Burtell was still alive.

"They've already found out who owns the boat," Graver said, going over to the table to get his coffee cup for a refill.

Lara came over to the cabinet too and refilled her own cup.

"Thanks for the coffee," she said.

"Sure."

They both leaned back against the cabinet.

"They . . . haven't found anything?" she asked.

"You mean bodies, or what's left of them? No."

"What happens now?"

"I hate to ask you to do this, Lara, but Ginette's going to have to be looked after somehow until this mess comes together." He hesitated. "I mean, we've got to make sure she doesn't contact anyone else with the police department. She thinks everyone's going to be devoting a lot of energy to finding out whether or not Dean's alive, and no one there even knows that he's 'missing.' "

"What about her family?"

"When I get to the office, I'll look in Dean's personal file and get her family information. I'll call them, get somebody here as soon as I can."

Lara sipped her coffee, and Graver waited for her to say something.

"Do you want us to stay here?"

"Why, what do you mean?"

"Practicalities. She doesn't have any clothes. She's going to need some."

"Christ." His first thought was of their safety. Would Kalatis consider Ginette Burtell a risk? But Graver had had no similar fear for Besom's wife or Peggy Tisler. He couldn't allow himself to lose perspective. "Okay. Just don't stay there long, Lara. I'd feel better if she were here."

The telephone rang again, and Graver reached around and picked it up. It was Neuman calling from Arnette's computer room.

"I thought I'd try to catch you before you went to the office and bring you up to date," he said. "We're getting tons of stuff from Sheck's microfiche. It's going to be a lot of fun just deciding the best way to use it. Sheck's outlined this operation from the grass roots to the top. Goes into a lot of detail. We may want to keep some of these people running, see if we can't turn some of them. Sheck's infiltrated so many businesses and institutions it seems to me there ought to be a way to use his system. We need to talk about that. Anyway—we've got enough on Faeber to close him down."

"Is there anything there on any of our people?"

"Yeah. It looks like it started with Besom, a couple of years ago. He was selling investigation information to Faeber. Faeber wanted more. Besom couldn't do it by himself and brought Tisler into it. The money was just too good. Besom made a couple of hundred thousand his first year. Tisler over a hundred. Right now I'm reading about the kind of CID information Faeber was asking for. So far Dean hasn't come into the picture yet."

"And what about Dean's tapes?"

"Paula's back there working on that now. Dean had done some cipher work to protect it, even on this copy, but it was just elementary stuff and Arnette's people broke into it sometime early this morning. So Paula's only been working inside the files for about an hour."

"What about Kalatis?"

"Nothing on him yet."

They talked another few minutes and then Graver hung up. While he had been talking Lara had put a piece of toast in the toaster and was now eating it, sitting sideways at the table with her coffee, listening to Graver's end of the conversation as she watched him.

"They're making some progress," he said. "I don't know . . . are you going to be all right here?"

"Don't worry about us," she said. "I won't even bother about the clothes if she doesn't mention them. I just wanted to know what to do. We'll be okay."

Graver took one last sip of his coffee, and they looked at each other. A smile slowly softened Lara's face acknowledging what the night had meant to her and to a mutual intimacy long held in abeyance. At that moment Graver realized what Lara had known all along, that in some things, she understood him a hell of a lot better than he understood himself.

62

AT THE OFFICE, GRAVER KEPT ONE EYE ON THE CLOCK AS HE set about trying to put some order into a day that had begun with an assurance of disorder. It was a bad time for Lara to be out of pocket. The first thing he did was to pull one of the women from the data input clerks to take Lara's place. She was lost, of course, but at least she could take messages and keep track of the flood of calls.

Next he started checking with his squad supervisors to make sure they were already moving. Organized Crime investigators and analysts were double-checking with informants who might have any remote knowledge of explosives use, as well as reviewing their most active investigations involving competing crime families and organizations, especially those headed by and comprised of Canadian, Asian, and Greek members, as well as the Black and Latin gang organizations that were increasingly becoming an interstate problem. Research and Analysis was already on the computers pulling up names of individuals and groups known to have used explosives or had contacts with those who had used explosives or who were involved in any kind of marine activity or having marine connections. The Anti-Terrorist Squad was running down their possibles in extremist groups of both wings, those having connections with illegal ordnance and explosives, pro-life and pro-choice activists, racist groups, radical religious groups, and persons in the public disorder files.

Graver had a hard time keeping his mind on what he was doing. He knew the odds of any of this hectic activity actually producing a genuine lead was remote. It felt odd to be overseeing a storm of activity that he knew was absolutely futile, to be authorizing the expenditure of manpower and funds on inquiries that could not possibly produce any yield whatsoever.

After his review with his last supervisor, Graver punched an outside line and called his FBI intelligence counterpart in the Federal Building across the bayou to check with their progress. Luckily, the FBI was fielding most of the telephone calls from other intelligence and law enforcement agencies who knew automatically that the FBI would bear the brunt of the investigation. The Bureau's agents were scattered all over the Gulf Coast shaking down their informants in dissident and terrorist groups whom they considered the most likely candidates to use explosives. So far nothing had turned up, and his assessment of the situation at the South Shore Marina was very much as Olmstead had described it.

Westrate was next. Graver called him and brought him up to date on the morning's events and the wheels that had been set in motion. He told Westrate that he would keep him informed and that as of yet they still didn't even know if it was some kind of accident or a bomb. Westrate, ever mindful of his professional image, was getting nervous at being the man in the background of a headline story. Everyone knew that CID *ought* to have a bead on the possible perpetrators and that sooner or later—most likely sooner—the media would be coming to him with questions in that direction. The story had been on all three network morning news programs, Westrate informed him, and speculation was running high.

For Graver's part, he was more concerned about the timing of finding human remains at the scene. If Burtell was identified, it was all over. The information about Ginette Burtell owning the boat would hold for a while. Graver had the leverage of being Olmstead's superior, and he could use that leverage to stall for some time. So, unless Olmstead for some reason jumped procedural rules, Graver's ad hoc task force was safe for a while longer.

At nine-thirty Graver went to Burtell's personal file and found Ginette's record. She was from Seattle, and she had listed her sister as the person she would like to have called in case of an emergency. He got the sister on the telephone, explained who he was, and told her that Dean had been in an accident and there was a good chance he had been killed. He told her that Ginette did not know this yet, nor did she know he was calling, but he thought she might need someone within the next twenty-four hours. She assured him she would catch the next available flight.

Having just about run out of time, Graver was getting ready to walk out of his office on his way to meet Victor Last when his handset rang. He picked it up from the edge of his desk.

"Graver, it's Paula. We've been trying to get to you on your secure line, but it's been constantly busy. Can you call us back on it? Arnette and I want to speak to you at the same time."

Graver called Arnette's number.

"Okay, here's a quick recap of what we've pulled off of Dean's tape so far," Paula said. "It looks like Besom and Tisler were selling CID records to Faeber's DataPrint for six months before Dean ever began to suspect anything was going on. Just about the time he was figuring this out, he was contacted by a guy named Geis. No first name. Geis is CIA."

"Bullshit," Graver said instantly. "This is what Dean's got in those tapes? Is this his answer to the man at the Transco Fountain?"

Paula hesitated, surprised at his flash of anger. "Yeah, but wait a minute. Let me go on here."

Graver was silent, conscious of strong and confused feelings about Burtell. What in the hell had he done? Had he gone back and rewritten his own record to cover himself? Graver was embarrassed for him. This smacked of self-serving damage control, and to see Burtell trying to sweep his own culpability under the rug by rewriting the record of his own dishonesty was doubly disappointing. Graver could understand why Dean had lied to Ginette, being too ashamed to want her to know what he'd done, but at least he should have given the rest of them the credit for knowing a scam when they saw it.

"Burtell was contacted by this guy who told him what Besom and Tisler were doing, told him about the Faeber/Kalatis connection. He then gave Dean essentially the same data on Raviv/Kalatis that Arnette has here. He has in his record almost the identical information. So maybe Geis *is* CIA."

"Why would you believe that?" Graver interrupted heatedly. "Arnette, are on the line?"

"Yep."

"Why would you believe that, Arnette? If you have the information, why couldn't someone else outside the agency have the information too? Don't you think you should be a little skeptical about this?"

"Why don't you let her go on, Marcus?" Arnette said. She was cool, her voice even and steady.

"Shit." He was furious. "Go ahead." He felt like he was being led around by the nose, and he was getting tired of it. He was impatient and almost too angry to sit still.

"According to Dean," Paula began again, "Geis tells him that he thinks Kalatis is setting up some kind of enormous sting operation through his drug smuggling business with Brod Strasser. He outlines the same drug operation that we picked up on the tape from Sheck. Same bogus companies, same operational methods. Everything."

"His detail here is exact, Marcus," Arnette interjected. "Your point is well taken about other private intelligence companies having what I have, but you know as well as I do—and I'll write off your slight to frustration—that I'm a little different from 'most' private intelligence operations. I don't know of anyone else . . . *anyone* . . . with my access. That's why I was so excited to get onto Kalatis." She hesitated for emphasis. "Nobody but the majors have him, baby. We've got to take this Geis seriously."

Graver said nothing. All along Arnette had insisted the man at the Transco Fountain was "government." Now Dean's records were confirming her assertions. He couldn't blame her for wanting to believe him. Paula went on.

"Geis wanted Dean to work his way inside and help them find out what Kalatis was up to. Geis was pretty damned uncomfortable not knowing what Kalatis was doing besides the drug business. So he gives Dean what he needs to know. Dean 'discovers' Besom's and Tisler's information-selling operation and demands a piece of it, or he'll blow it. Soon, with Geis's background help and guidance, he's well into the operation."

"And getting paid off just like they were," Graver added cynically.

"Apparently so," Paula said. "He doesn't hide that. It's all right here. They were making a lot of money. Kalatis was paying generously."

"And the Seldon investigation?"

"Just what we thought, another cooked operation. Kalatis wanted Seldon out of the way. Dean never really spells out why, just that Seldon was the next target."

"Is that it? What did Dean find out for Geis?"

"Not a lot. It was months before Dean ever met Kalatis, but when he did it seems that Kalatis found him a little more to his liking than either Besom or Tisler. Before long Dean was handling most of the communication between the CID guys and Kalatis/Faeber. Kalatis came up with the idea of the bogus investigations as a means of eliminating competitors and put Dean in charge of the operation. Probst is the first target. It comes off beautifully. Kalatis is pleased. Friel is next. Then Seldon.

"But Kalatis was careful. Besom and Tisler never knew about anything except their own little areas of operation. They never knew about Sheck's network, for instance, or about his back-door connection to Kalatis. They never had a sense of the size of the organization.

"Dean was reasonably aggressive, though," she added. "He let Kalatis know that he was ambitious and wanted to be more active, more involved. He presented ideas. Proposed operations that could expand their data collection into other intelligence agencies. Geis was feeding Dean information to help build his credibility with Kalatis, helping him present some enticing projects, hoping Kalatis would come to rely on him and eventually pull Dean deeper into the organization."

"What Dean didn't know, however," Arnette put in again, "was that Kalatis wasn't taking on any new ideas. Whatever Geis suspected Kalatis of doing, whatever his sting was, it was on its last passage. If Dean had come along a year earlier, two years earlier, Kalatis would have found a place for him. But he wasn't about to bring in any more clever people this late in his game. He was already shutting down. Dean didn't have a chance."

"But," Paula said, "Kalatis did put him in touch with Sheck. That's how Sheck got into the Probst operation."

"That's most of it, the heart of the story," Arnette said. "Dean includes an encyclopedia of details about these operations, some of which are going to be useful in other ways. He was thoroughly familiar with Sheck's network of information buyers and adds another perspective to Sheck's own account of what he was doing."

"Let's go back to the sting," Graver said. "What's the story on that?"

"It's intriguing, but not very informative," Arnette continued. "Sheck, keeping his fingers in the works via his pilot buddies, thinks Kalatis and Strasser are getting ready to offer one last giant buy to their investors. They'll all be asked to come up with more money than ever before while being promised, of course, equally greater profits. But Sheck predicts Kalatis and Strasser are going to walk away with it— just vanish with the millions."

"Then he agrees with Geis."

"Apparently so. He also points out that by the time this happens, Kalatis and Strasser will have dismantled enough of their operation here that they'll be untraceable. And I'll have to say, as old intelligence hands they know how to cover a trail. They can probably pull it off."

"And Dean reported all this to Geis?"

"He did."

"Okay, then. What about Geis?"

"That's the big disappointment," Paula said. "Dean gives details of how he contacts Geis and where they met, how Geis contacts him. All of it is standard operations procedure. We have telephone numbers. We have dead drop locations. We have serial contact outlines. Dean was giving us everything. But, unfortunately, Geis also met Dean at the marina a number of times. We have the contact procedures that they followed when they wanted that to happen. It would have been a perfect opportunity to set the guy up. Would have been, but not now."

"Geis's hair must have stood on end when he saw the news of the explosion," Arnette put in. "None of the contact information Dean gave us is any good now. In fact, I doubt if we'll ever hear of Mr. Geis again. For all practical purposes, when Kalatis killed Dean, he killed Geis too."

Graver was silent a moment. He had to admit it did sound good. If he was condemning Burtell he might be condemning the wrong man. Still, he was angry. How could Burtell have so readily assigned his loyalty to Geis, a man he had never met, while at the same time withholding his faith in Graver with whom he had been close for so many years? It didn't make much sense to Graver, and he could not deny that it hurt more than a little to discover Dean's distrust. It would almost be easier to believe that Burtell had been dirty than to admit that when so much had been at stake—even, ultimately, his life—Burtell had not trusted Graver enough to overcome his suspicion. If that was, in fact, what it was that had caused Dean to keep his "undercover assignment" to himself.

But in all honesty, Graver couldn't blame Dean. Hadn't Graver himself done the same thing? When he first realized that the CID had a leak, and suspicion turned in Burtell's direction, hadn't Graver investigated him with a cold disregard for their close personal relationship? Graver had trained him, and both men had been more loyal to their training—and to the system that had taught them—than to each other. Graver always had believed that his quiet, invisible work was his personal contribution to a reasonable society's struggle to maintain its balance against the innumerable and ever-present tyrannies of social chaos. He didn't have a missionary zeal about it, but he never doubted he was doing what was right and necessary.

Now, he felt as if he had tricked himself. He remembered a quote from Aeschylus which had appeared at the beginning of a chapter on totalitarianism in a book he had used years before in a series of courses he had taken at Georgetown University. "For somehow, this is tyranny's disease, to trust no friend."

At the time, the quote had lodged in his mind as a reminder of the consequences of the evils he had sworn to engage. It was an acrid and disconcerting irony, then, to find that "tyranny's disease" was alive and well among the men who had dedicated themselves to opposing tyranny itself. The disease had invaded the physician, despite his skills and good intentions, despite his best efforts.

"This is too neat," he heard himself say. He swallowed hard to dislodge the lump in his throat. "I don't understand," he said, trying to sound terse and focused, "why Dean is giving all this up to us. Why, suddenly, at the last minute, is he spilling everything he knows—about Kalatis and Faeber, and especially about Geis? Why wouldn't he 'keep the faith' with the CIA?"

For the first time Arnette had no response.

"All the loose ends are falling into place," Graver went on, "but it's all happening a little too late, isn't it. We've uncovered a wealth of information in record time, but Geis has evaporated, and we're not a single step closer to Kalatis."

"That's right," Arnette snapped back. "Look, Marcus, I don't know how to answer your questions about Dean, but I do know he's put us onto some very serious operations here. Yes, all the big players are disappearing into the woodwork. That's what they're trained to do. That's their business. If they didn't sew up loose ends, they wouldn't *be* in business. But the fact is, Dean's given us a hell of a lot more than we would have had without him. I'm not going to agonize about his ethics this late in the game. We're not through here; we still need a lot of answers. I'm not going to blame Dean because he didn't clear up *everything* for me. As for his role in this, you may never figure it out. Or if you do, you might not like it. But does that really make a goddamned bit of difference as to what we do now?"

For a few moments the line was dead, no one spoke. Then Graver said:

"Okay, Arnette. You're right." He paused again. "But for right now I've still got just one objective . . . and just one more chance at achieving it. Paula, can you glean anything else from the files?"

"Oh, sure," Paula said. "There are a million details, stuff we can follow up on for months. As far as connections go, this is a bonanza."

"Arnette," Graver said, "you have no interest in the operational end here, I know. But if I get a shot at Kalatis can I get some backup from your people? Before you answer, you'd better know this: there's not a dime in it."

"I told you, I'm already making money off this, baby," Arnette said. "You can have my people anytime. I'm way ahead of the game here."

"Okay," Graver said. "We may have a long shot. I'll get back to you within a couple of hours."

63

BY THE TIME GRAVER GOT TO LA FACEZIA, HE WAS NEARLY twenty minutes late. He parked a half block away, locked the car, and walked back on the sidewalk under the shade of the catalpa trees, a welcome shelter from the mid-morning sun. The temperature already had climbed into the upper eighties and surely would not stop until it reached the mid nineties.

The tables under the arbor on the sidewalk were popular this morning, and the patio doors were thrown open so that the dining room was open to the shady cool. As Graver suspected, Last was not among the sidewalk coffee drinkers. He went through one of the iron gates, under the arbor, and into the dining room which retained a cavernous coolness, its three sets of French doors allowing a wash of arbor-muted morning brightness into the big room.

As Graver walked through one of the French doors that opened obliquely into the dining room, he paused a moment to let his eyes adjust from the glare of the street. There were a few diners, and he could hear a murmur of conversation and the clinking of tableware. One of the waitresses whisked by him with a tray of coffee and crois-sants on her way to the sidewalk tables. "Please, anywhere you wish," she said in passing, and following that he heard Last's relaxed, mellow English.

"Right here, Marcus."

Graver turned to his right and made out Last's shadow ghost sitting at one of the more choice tables, next to a window with a thick stone sill. An iron grille covered the window and a lacework of ivy covered the iron, forming a delicate panel of privacy separating them from the tables outside like the screen in a confessional. Graver walked to the table and sat down.

"This is untypical," Last observed. "So late."

"I couldn't help it," Graver said. "You've seen the papers?"

"Oh yes. I gathered as much."

One of the waitresses came and took Graver's order for coffee.

"Okay," Graver said. "Let's hear it." He was in no mood for pleasantries, and he wanted Last to know that. Last nodded.

"Of all the stuff I'd told you before," Last said, "I left out something . . . rather central."

"Really?" Graver couldn't resist a note of sarcasm.

"What I didn't tell you was, I've been boffing Mrs. Faeber almost from the beginning."

Graver looked at him. "Okay."

"This is a lonely woman, Marcus. I knew it from the moment I met her." Last paused to sip his own coffee when the girl brought Graver's. "I saw opportunity there . . . one way or the other. They had money; I had . . . artifacts. Surely we could work out something, I thought. But Rayner—Mrs. Faeber—was, is, a sexually aggressive woman and 'Colin,' apparently, has the sexual curiosity of a sheet of paper. By the time they left Mexico that first time we met, Rayner and I had . . . connected, so to speak." He paused to light a cigarette. "This woman, Graver, I tell you she's insatiable. I've never seen anything like it. Do you know that—?"

"Victor, I don't want to hear it. You know what I do want to hear."

Last paused and looked at Graver across the table. Graver's eyes had adjusted to the low light now, and he saw Last's handsome face with its glory of wrinkles, battle scars from his encounters with the bottle and from sleepless nights in bordellos, from the anxiety of a life of fleecing and deception, from the punishing pleasures and constant disquiet of silk-sheet adulteries, from never being sure of anything except the assurance that nothing was sure. He was smiling slightly, a smile that was at once boyish and wizened. He looked like a man who, on the brink of finally having to admit to himself that he had pissed away the better part of a lifetime with nothing to show for it, had spotted one more long shot—a good one this time—and was about to put everything he had left into the wager.

"Marcus, I was with Rayner last night. She told me an incredible story. I think it has enormous potential."

"You said you could 'deliver Faeber's ass.' "

"Better than that. I think . . . if we give it some thought . . . we can put our hands on Kalatis."

64

PANOS KALATIS LEANED AGAINST THE DOOR OF HIS BEDROOM and looked out across the veranda through the white heat of the sunlight to the murky waters of the Gulf of Mexico. Wearing only his white pajama trousers, he was barefoot and shirtless, his well-tanned barrel chest thrust out in general defiance. He was smoking his first cigar of the day, and he was worried.

Behind him, Jael lay across their bed, nut brown and naked, stretching her long limbs in the warm, late morning breeze that blew in through the veranda doors from the Gulf. Occasionally the squeal of a seagull broke the silence that was otherwise only interrupted by the wash of the water on the beach below and the rustling of the palm fronds moved by the breeze.

Kalatis was worried because his chief security officer had caused him to be awakened at eleven o'clock, thinking it unwise to allow him to go another hour without knowing of the explosion at the South Shore Marina. Though he had cut off all communication with Sheck and Burtell, his men had tried to renew them since news of the explosion this morning and had had no success. Kalatis had something to think about.

"Panos," Jael said from behind him, her voice throaty from sleep. "Panos."

He turned a little and looked over his shoulder. She was an absolute marvel. He knew of nothing more heightening to a sexual experience than sleeping with a woman who knew how to kill you in five different languages. A woman like this one. He could not get enough of this woman; he was capable of watching her for long periods of time in much the same way that an animal trainer might watch a prized cat, just for the pure pleasure of enjoying the incomparable marriage of sinew and movement. Her beauty was so unaffected and powerful that it nullified the dimension of danger she occupied, or rather transformed it, so that the violence of which she was capable was no longer a thing to be feared, but to be appreciated, if not altogether desired.

And he liked the way she said "Panos."

Nevertheless, he turned his back to her and squinted at the eye-watering brightness of the Gulf. Colin Faeber had been trying to get in touch with him. No doubt he had heard of the explosion too and was in a state of panic. Kalatis decided his best course of action with Faeber was simply never to see or speak to him again. Though Faeber had been one of the few people who had been to Kalatis's beach house without having been presented with the pretense that he was being taken out of the country, he always had been brought there at night and still was deceived as to its true location. But he knew Kalatis was not in Mexico; he knew Kalatis lived as close as an hour's flight. No, Kalatis did not want to see Faeber again—ever.

The explosion in the harbor had disturbed a very tightly scheduled series of events and possibly had ruined the rest of Kalatis's program. Possibly. Now he had to decide whether he thought he could salvage all of it, or whether he thought he should cut his losses. That would mean passing up nearly forty million dollars, and that kind of money was worth considerable risk.

But, there *was* considerable risk. Not the least of which was continuing his plan without knowing who was responsible for the explosion. Was this an accident? Burtell and Sheck were almost surely killed in that fire, since it was their habit to meet on Burtell's boat. If they were, what kind of a coincidence was that? None, he was sure. Kalatis had planned and escaped too many intrigues to believe in coincidence. Coincidence was a thing that occurred so rarely that he considered it almost an apocryphal concept. Like the unicorn, it was an idea of fools and romantics. As an explanation for anything as concrete as an explosion, it was a delusion.

He had so little time left—he was beginning his last day of collections—that it was hardly worth the effort of putting into operation any kind of serious investigation. His best course of action was to try and speed up the collection process which was, as always, to take place late at night and in the early morning hours. Now he had his people getting in touch with the three remaining clients, trying to arrange their appointments for earlier in the evening or, even better, late in the afternoon. This change would be catching his clients by surprise, and they would surely have procedural adjustments to bring about before they could comply with his request. All of this was to be negotiated during the next three or four hours. By daylight the next morning, Panos Kalatis would have disappeared off the face of the earth.

Of course, there was the possibility that Sheck, or even Burtell, had enemies Kalatis knew nothing about. The explosion did not necessarily have to do with him or with their relationship to him. There was no way of knowing who Sheck might have angered and for what reasons. It could be that this had nothing to do with Kalatis at all.

But Kalatis had not remained alive all these years by keeping faith with "possibilities" and "could be's." He had remained alive because at the slightest hint of the inconsistent or the inexplicable, he vanished. He did not wait for explanations. They would come eventually, but when they did Kalatis would be somewhere safe to hear them out. A man without a sixth sense was a dead man.

Thus his thoughts turned to Graver. Kalatis was well aware of Graver's friendship with Dean Burtell, but he had seen big money come between friendships before—it was almost the rule—and he had fully intended to cause such a breach—to his benefit—when he had offered Burtell the five-hundred-thousand-dollar retirement fund. That had been Tuesday night. Now it was Thursday morning, and he had heard not a word from Burtell. He had been willing to bet that the intervening silence was good news. Burtell, it seemed to him, was no less venal than all the other people whose loyalties he paid for every day of the week. He believed he had made a sound investment.

But with Burtell's death, all bets were off. He knew Graver well enough to know what to expect. If Graver didn't already know Kalatis was involved with one of his men, he would know soon enough. It was time to stop calculating and start moving.

Standing in the doorway thinking of these things, he flinched only a little when the two bare arms reached around his chest, and he felt Jael's breasts against the middle of his back, felt her pelvis tuck into his buttocks.

"What are your thought?" she asked in her accented and ungrammatical English.

Kalatis did not respond immediately. He was always polite to her, even kind, even indulgent, but he was never tender. He really did think of her as a cat. You kept it well fed and well groomed. You could scratch it and rub it, give it small pleasures, but you must never become its friend. You must never display a regard that hinted you would make any sacrifice, however small or insignificant, on its behalf. It was not a relationship that accommodated friendship.

So he ignored her because he did not want to be bothered at that moment. He smoked and shrugged her off irritably. She backed away, and in the silence behind him he heard the soft crunching of the mattress as she returned to the bed and the cool Egyptian cotton sheets. He had to think, not of her, but of himself. He had to make sure he was doing the right thing, dispensing with the right people, setting into motion the right timing.

In reviewing his plans there was nothing he regretted. Well, perhaps walking away from the house in Bogotá. And leaving forever the dusky loins of Colombia's remarkable women. That he truly would regret. But as for the rest of it, he gave nothing else a second thought. He had done it often enough for it to be almost familiar. In fact, all those Spartan vanishments over the years—those times when he had built a full life and then one day, because of a telephone call or a three-word note slipped under his door or a notice in the personals column of the newspaper, he closed the door behind him and walked away into another life leaving the alarm clock still set for the next morning—all of those Spartan disappearances when he left a life with only the clothes on his back to accompany him were like dress rehearsals for this final one in which he was taking as much of the world with him as he could possibly manage. His new life would be his last life. He did not intend to disappear ever again, nor did he intend to start all over with nothing, as he had every time before. This final time he would have millions, scattered over the globe in a dozen caches protected by codes and ciphers and shielded accounts. The plan was elaborate, extensive, with dozens of people needed to bring it to its conclusion, but in the end, after a lengthy unfolding, there would be only himself, walking through a doorway alone, to a new life. For the last time.

65

COLIN FAEBER PUT DOWN THE TELEPHONE IN HIS OFFICE AND WAS immediately aware of a clammy dampness around his mouth. He knew that a condensation of perspiration was forming on his upper lip. The woman had said that Gilbert Hormann had died of a heart attack in the suite adjacent to his office sometime during the night. His personal secretary had found his body herself, when she came into the office that morning. She was sorry, she said, but she couldn't talk anymore. There was so much confusion there now. They had just taken away the body. Everyone was very upset. It was tragic, so tragic.

Faeber sat immobile in his chair and counted them off: Tisler, suicide. Besom, heart attack. Burtell, probably in the explosion. He couldn't find Sheck. Possibly in the explosion with Burtell, since that was their primary meeting location. Hormann, heart attack.

And now he could not raise Kalatis on their code line. Had something happened to him as well? What the hell was happening? He put his hands on the edge of the desk in front of him as if he were steadying himself against the gunnel of a boat, as if he were fighting the nausea of too many hours at sea. Was there something going on here that he should see, something obvious that in retrospect he would see all too clearly and wonder why he hadn't detected it in the first place? His stomach tumbled at the thought of it. But since he couldn't "see" it, what should he do? Should he take the extreme step of contacting Strasser? He had been told never to do that. Strasser was "out of the picture" except financially. He was completely removed, and it was clearly his intention to remain that way. The idea was only fleeting, for if Faeber was intimidated by Kalatis, he was petrified by Brod Strasser whom he had met on only four occasions during the three and a half years since he had bought controlling interest in DataPrint.

He looked around his office which was modern in style as befitted his profession, chrome and glass and copolymer furniture, decorated in primary colors with touches here and there of Italian *moderne* furnishings, the coffee server, the cocktail pitchers in the liquor cabinets. He stood up from his desk. He didn't know why. He wasn't going anywhere. He didn't know what to do. But he couldn't sit still, either. There was no contingency plan for this kind of thing, everyone dying, nobody to contact. What the hell was going on? Was this thing coming to an end? Was he in danger? Christ! What would make him think he *wasn't?* Why *wouldn't* he be?

He started toward the door of his office, hesitated, turned back and stood at the window behind his desk. From the western edge of downtown he looked westward, over a sweep of the green canopies of trees toward the satellite commercial centers whose office towers punched up out of the carpet of thick woods like futuristic cities on a jungle-covered planet. Though he had stood at these windows and daydreamed over this view countless times, just now it seemed alien, as though he had awakened in an unfamiliar world. He felt only an unmistakable anxiety.

Turning away from the window again he walked to the door and opened it.

"Connie," he said. That was all he had to say. She was typing at her computer screen and stopped immediately, though without hurrying, and in one or two moments she was in his office. "Close the door," he said.

She looked at him as he turned around midway to his desk.

"What's the matter?" she asked.

Colin Faeber, like many businessmen the world over, had fallen, if not in love, then at least into serious glandular obsession with his secretary. Connie, like secretaries the world over, had allowed him to indulge his obsession. It was an easy thing to do. Convenient. Though the sex was usually mundane to forgettable, the perks were often superb. But Faeber's record with wives and other women was a poor one. His understanding of women in general was obtuse. It was something he never bothered to analyze, and therefore he never acquired more than an adolescent's comprehension about the opposite sex. It was, for the most part, simply a libidinal conversance, and even that was only rudimentary.

But it was just this lack of understanding of women that made Faeber vulnerable. With Connie he had found a more indulgent patience than had been his luck before. He had never stopped to ask why this was, but he had recognized it, and as a result he had begun to unburden himself to her. She had listened, commiserated, seemed concerned, and interested. In fact, she seemed interested not only in him, but also in the astute ways he handled his business.

During the last three or four months Connie had learned more about Faeber's business than just about anyone involved other than his senior officers. But even their knowledge was concentrated in their own areas of expertise and did not extend to the business overall. Connie's did.

As a matter of fact, the more he talked about his business with her the more she seemed to care for him. It was almost as though she found his work to be an aphrodisiac. Sometimes it seemed even to him that he droned on endlessly, but Connie was always willing, even eager to listen. She asked questions, which it flattered him to be able to answer.

And it wasn't too long before, as a special demonstration of his cleverness, he revealed to her what he called the "real" purpose of the business: the selling of "certain" information to persons undisclosed. He told her of the "intel" section, which employed only half a dozen data input clerks, a single coordinator, and a secretary. The operation of this section was buried in the accounting, and the billing for its services was off the books—and was quadruple the volume of the legitimate billing of the business. All cash.

He told her of intrigues, of the cells of paid informants scattered in businesses and buildings throughout the city, of low-level employees who were more than eager to tap into their employer's computers and withdraw vital information. Money was all it took. Cash. Nobody ever had enough of it. It could buy you anything in the world, and for the right amount of it everyone could be persuaded to do something.

She said she didn't believe him, about the "intel section." So one night after a fog of vodka tonics, after she had stripteased him to a pitch of silliness, they left his office in their underwear and, carrying the bottle of gin with them—and her purse, she laughingly insisted she would need it for "after"—wove their way through ghostly pools of isolated fluorescent lights until they came to a door where she watched him punch his code into the security panel above the doorknob. And he took her in. She was amazed. And gratified, so she let him have what he wanted. During this unseemly business, she repeated the security code over and over to herself so she wouldn't forget it. Afterward, he passed out on the scratchy, synthetic fiber carpet, amid the white noise of the humming microprocessors and the smell of heated plastic.

Quickly she wrote down the security code for the door and then set to work with the micro camera she had brought in her purse along with numerous rolls of film. Nearly an hour and a half later she snapped closed the camera, put it back in her purse, and began the back-breaking work of waking him and helping him back to his office.

After that night Colin Faeber had no more secrets, though he didn't know it.

So now, as he began to explain his fears to her, she had to remember to make him stop from time to time and explain himself, to clarify a point or two here and there. When he finally finished, though still pacing back and forth across his office, Connie, who thought she had known so much, had heard more than she had bargained for. She had known nothing, of course, of the "coincidental" deaths, and now Faeber, having rashly regurgitated everything in an effort to help her appreciate his fears, had caused her to wonder if she really wanted to go any further with this. She already had done things she had never dreamed she would do, or could do, emboldened by the prospect of enormous sums of money that Rayner said they would be able to extort with the information she was getting. But now, if she understood him rightly, Faeber was worried about being *killed*. This was clearly another kind of game altogether.

"I just don't know what to do," he said.

"You don't have *any* idea of what's going on here?" she asked.

"No. Kalatis, I don't know, that guy could be capable of anything."

"I thought you were afraid he'd been . . . killed." She couldn't believe she was having this conversation.

"I don't know, maybe, or maybe he's just . . . not answering."

"Which would mean . . . ?" She wished to God he would stop pacing. He was a goddamned caricature, a comic book character being "nervous," taking long strides with little U-turn marks behind his heels.

"I don't . . . *know*."

Connie wanted to scream. He had said "I don't know" four times in the last three minutes. She looked at him. The man was falling apart. He actually was pale, and perspiring on his upper lip. That was something she particularly disliked, but upon seeing it now it was not dislike she felt. It was fear. His fear was infectious, and she felt its warm hand creeping up her throat and contaminating her own imagination. But even in the midst of her growing anxiety, she had the clear, rational realization that she could use his panic as an opportunity to gain an advantage. Despite her alarm, she resolved to appear calm, to *be* calm. She resolved to present a composed and rational demeanor. She would become a point of stability that he could cling to. It was an opportunity she could hardly afford to pass up.

"Look," she said, not knowing what she would say next, "nobody knows where I live, do they? I mean, any of those people?"

He stared at her from across the room. He shook his head.

"Okay, go to my place, then, and stay there. I'll try to get some idea of what's going on."

"How are you going to do that?"

"Give me your contact numbers."

He stared at her, but she could see him thinking. What was his alternative? He clearly thought things had fallen apart. But was he misreading the situation? If he was, it would be a mistake to betray such numbers. Kalatis would have him strangled. But if he wasn't, if his suspicions were right and he was being hung out to dry . . . or if he was going to be killed . . . then he had nothing to loose, and might even save his life. But what could she possibly find out . . . ?

"What are you going to do with them?" he asked.

"You said you couldn't get an answer from Burtell or Sheck. You said you thought they were in the explosion at the marina. What if you're wrong? What if they're hiding too, or not yet aware that something's gone wrong?"

Faeber stood still and tried to moisten his lips with his tongue. It didn't work. His mouth was like sand.

"Then I ought to call them myself," he said.

"You're not thinking straight," she said. "You need to drop out of sight. Keep quiet. Wait." She couldn't believe she was saying these things. It didn't seem very real, helping an emotionally debilitated Colin Faeber elude an assassin.

Faeber's dry tongue came out of his mouth again, just a little, and retreated. He walked over to the coat closet, opened the door and took out his suit coat that was hanging there. Retrieving his wallet from the inside pocket, he took out a small plastic card and handed it to her.

"The instructions are on there," he said. "It's a series of digits, and you calculate them differently depending on the date and who you're trying to call. It's all explained. It's kind of like one of those perpetual calendars. It says on there."

She took the card from him.

"Just stay at my place," she said. "Just let me look into this a little."

He nodded, but he seemed preoccupied. All the failure that Rayner had predicted would come to him—because of his scheming with Kalatis—had arrived. They were through with him. He had served his purpose, and he wasn't even sure what it had been. Still holding his coat, he walked out of the office.

Connie watched him leave. Through the open door of his office, she saw him walk through her office and into the reception room. She heard the receptionist speak to him, but he didn't answer. She heard the soft ping of the door as he pushed it open and walked out into the hallway.

She stepped over to his desk, picked up the telephone, and called Rayner Faeber.

66

THEY AGREED TO MEET THE TWO WOMEN IN THE PARKING GARAGE of the Stouffer Hotel in Greenway Plaza. That was Rayner's idea. Graver didn't care where they met and considered himself lucky that she had hit Last's pager when she had because the two men were just about to leave La Facezia's and go their separate ways.

As they approached the top of the ramp on the level where they had agreed to meet, Last spotted their car.

"There they are," he said. "The BMW."

A large, midnight blue BMW sedan with deeply tinted windows was waiting in one of the parking spaces facing the outside of the garage, its nose up against the low barrier wall so that the occupants had a good view looking out of the shaded shelter to the northwest, toward the Galleria and the Transco Tower. The noon sun was baking the city, sending undulating heat waves out over the treetops and glinting here and there off glass and chrome.

Graver pulled up to the same wall, but parked several spaces away. As the two of them got out of the car and closed their doors, Last looked at him over the top of the car.

"Oh yeah. I said your name was Gray."

"Gray?"

"Yeah. G-r-a-y."

"Forget that. Don't use a name at all," Graver said, and they walked over to the BMW. Last motioned for him to get into the back seat behind the passenger while he walked around behind the car to the driver's side. Graver waited until Last opened his door first and then followed his lead.

When they closed their doors, Graver found himself very close to two attractive women who were turned half around in their seats, looking at him intently with professionally cosmeticized faces. The

BMW was purring softly, its air conditioner whispering a gentle current of chill air. These were women who did not believe that just because you were conspiring to extort millions of dollars you had to subject yourself to the tortures of sweating through your dress in a Houston parking garage. The air conditioner, therefore, was a necessity. Graver was grateful for it. The heavily padded interior was a cool, quiet world that smelled of secrets, of questionable intent, and of expensive perfume.

"Rayner," Last said, indicating the strawberry blonde in front of him. "And Connie," he said, indicating the woman in front of Graver. "This is the man I was telling you about," he said to the women.

They both nodded and said hello. Rayner looked at Graver as though she might have thought he was a professional killer, an assessment which she seemed to find pretty damn interesting. She was probably in her early forties, full-bodied, and wearing a dress that accommodated the white, liquidy cleavage Last had so precisely described. She was indeed a pretty woman, and Graver could see why Last had had no trouble seeing things from her point of view. She wore a collection of diamonds on one hand and an emerald cabochon on the other. She kept wanting to smile, but never quite managed to do it.

Connie was considerably more professional. In her early thirties, she was stylishly thin with frosted shoulder-length hair. She wore a double-breasted, black and white business suit, and her hazel eyes drilled into Graver as though she fully intended to see the bullshit in him before he even opened his mouth and revealed it himself.

"You said you had gotten some telephone numbers from Faeber," Last said, looking at Connie.

She hesitated, her eyes still on Graver.

"Wait a minute," Graver said. "I think I should set a few things straight first, so that we understand our situation more clearly." He looked back and forth between the two women. "Victor has told me that you might have a certain amount of access to a man named Panos Kalatis through Colin Faeber. I have business with Kalatis. For various reasons I've lost contact with him. I don't know anything about your intended business, and all you know about mine is that I want access to Kalatis—and that's all you need to know. But given that, I'm here to see if there's some way we might be able to help each other."

When he finished that brief statement, both women were looking at him with wide-eyed absorption. They were silent.

"I told him about the telephone numbers," Last said.

"Do you know about the deaths?" Connie asked abruptly. Her eyes had never moved from Graver.

"Which ones?"

He thought she winced.

"A guy named Tisler." She waited, but Graver didn't react. "A guy named Burtell." She waited. Graver didn't say anything. "And Besom and Sheck and Gilbert Hormann."

On this last one her voice cracked, and it was Graver's turn to wince. Jesus Christ.

"Yes," he said. "I know about them. How do you know about them?"

"Colin told me about them this morning," she said shakily. "I didn't know anything about any of that." She cut her eyes at Last and Rayner. "Nobody told me anything about any of that."

"Where is Faeber?"

"I thought you were only interested in Kalatis?" she said.

"I thought the idea was that we'd do what we could to help each other," Graver responded. "Faeber could help me get to Kalatis."

"Not anymore," Connie said. For the next few minutes she explained what had happened that morning, leaving out the part about sending Faeber to her condo.

Graver watched Rayner and from the look on her face she was hearing this for the first time too. Connie had played her cards very close to the vest. Several times during her explanation Rayner and Last exchanged glances. Graver kept his eyes on Connie. She was nervous, almost testy.

"When Faeber called those numbers," Graver said, after she had finished, "what was the procedure?"

"He called the number and left a message. They would call him back."

"Then it's almost certain we can't trace the numbers," he said. "I'd guess they're using a digital clearing box. It'll be in a rented apartment somewhere. Since there are different numbers for different dates, there are probably several locations, several boxes. The return calls will also go through the clearing boxes, scrambling the signals so that a trace will stop at the box. All we'll find at the end of the trace is an unfurnished apartment with a little black box sitting on the floor. They've probably got several apartments so if one is tracked down they'll be able to clear calls out of the others." He stopped. "Who do the numbers put him in contact with?"

She looked down at the card which she had been holding in her lap behind the seat and read the names. "Panos. Dean. Rick. Bruce. Ray. Eddie."

"Rick and Eddie? Do you know anything about them?"

She shook her head. "I just know they're pilots."

"You *know* they're pilots?"

"Yeah. They're a couple of the guys who pick up Colin and take him to Kalatis's place. He told me."

"Okay. Wait a minute." Graver got out of the BMW and walked to his car. He sat down in the front seat, picked up his handset, and called Arnette. Then he went back to the BMW carrying the handset with him.

"What was that?" Connie said as soon as he closed the door. She seemed to be the only one talking.

"You said Faeber would be flown to Kalatis's?" Graver asked, ignoring her question.

"That's what Colin says. Kalatis flies him there when he wants to talk to him."

"Do you recall Faeber ever saying how long the flight was?"

She glanced at Rayner as if to see if there were any objections to her going on with this. She got no reaction. She looked back at Graver.

"Yeah, as a matter of fact, I do," she said. "One time he was telling me about how they always make sure he can't see where they're going, even though he doesn't know anything about flying, and the flight's always at night. If he was in one of the smaller planes they'd put him facing backward into the cabin so he couldn't see, and then they'd put headphones on him and make him listen to Muzak or something so he couldn't hear the pilot giving his navigating coordinates to the towers. He said the flights were about an hour."

"Did he ever say what kind of plane he flew in?"

"No, he doesn't know planes." She hesitated, thought a second. "But he did say they always landed on water, so I guess it was one of those pontoon planes. They taxied up to a pier and then walked up to the house."

"What kind of a house?"

"He said it was . . . just this big white house. Palms in front. A porch . . . a, uh, veranda he called it."

"And Kalatis was there?"

"Yeah, on the veranda. Colin said he'd never even been on the inside."

"Was anyone else there?"

"He said there would be men waiting at the pier to tie up the plane. The pilots would stand around and talk to these guys while Colin went up to the house."

"You said, 'up to the house.' Was it hilly? A rocky cliff?"

"No, actually, I don't think so. He described it like . . . you know, up from the beach to the house."

"That's all? No one else there?"

"Well, yeah. There was someone else. Colin said that about half the time this woman would be there. He said she was maybe in her late twenties, a foreign woman, he thought maybe Middle Eastern. He said that on several occasions she would be in the house . . . naked or with very little on . . . and as they sat on the veranda he could clearly see her through the windows. He said he thought Kalatis liked that, for Colin to be able to see her naked through the window behind Kalatis's back. Sometimes she brought them drinks out on the veranda."

"He didn't know her name?"

"Kalatis never spoke to her. Just motioned to her to do what he wanted. Bring drinks. Take away drinks. Whatever."

There was another pause as Graver tried to push his brain in the right directions, tried to probe possibilities, the opportunities that would give him the most advantage with the least expenditure of time.

"Look, uh," Rayner said, speaking for the first time, glancing at Last with a look of impatience, "what is it, exactly, that you can do for us?"

Graver leveled his eyes on her. "What is it you want me to do?"

Rayner stared at him. She clearly was uncertain whether or how she should describe her plan to him. She seemed to be trying to figure out how to get to the subject without getting to the point. She said:

"We want to use the information we've obtained to convince Faeber and Kalatis that we need some retirement security."

"We?"

"Me and Connie," she said, tilting her head at the other woman. "There aren't any golden parachutes for wives and secretaries. It would be . . . only fair for us to have some financial assurance."

"You mean extortion."

"I mean," she said, glancing at Last, "that Victor led me to believe that you knew something about these matters and could help us . . . inform us how to protect ourselves from . . . legal complications as we go about doing this. That's what I mean."

She was a little testy.

"Well, what you seem to be suggesting might be a little hard to do now," Graver said.

Rayner frowned at him. Last squirmed in his seat.

"What do you mean, 'now'?" Rayner asked.

"From the way Connie described this morning's meeting with your husband," Graver said, "it sounds to me like he thinks his house of cards is collapsing. And he thinks he's been left behind to be buried in the rubble. It looks like Kalatis and Strasser are closing down the operation. They're burning their bridges—Tisler, Besom, Burtell, Hormann, Sheck. And if Kalatis doesn't kill your husband first, he'll probably spend the rest of his life in jail. As soon as the police put together all these deaths, it won't take them long to shut down DataPrint and its 'intel project.' " He paused, his attention still fixed on Rayner. "I'm afraid your idea is just a little late in coming," he concluded.

"Jesus Christ." Connie sank back against the door.

"That damn stupid pud," Rayner said, shaking her head, half-pissed at Faeber, half-pitying him. "He might as well have just waded out into the damn Gulf of Mexico, just kept going until he fell off the damn continental shelf. Wasn't even smart enough to get himself black-mailed."

Nobody moved or spoke in the cool, perfumed compartment. Graver watched Connie. Something had hit her harder than the other two. She was worried, staring out into the midday glare. Rayner's mind was churning, though, and it didn't take her long to come up with the obvious. But Last was there ahead of her, and tried to stop her before she opened her mouth.

"That's it then," Last said. "We'd better let this man get on with his business."

"Wait just a damn minute," Rayner said to Last. "There's a plan B here, and I think he"—she nodded at Graver—"might be able to help us out on it."

"I don't think we ought to worry him about any plan B's right now," Last said, trying to cut her off. "He agreed to help us if he could, but it's clear that he can't. He's not obligated to anything else."

"Plan B," Rayner said forcefully, ignoring Last and speaking directly to Graver, "is that we go after the biggest clients in the 'intel' file. These are big people, corporate people, who paid cash for personal intelligence on competitors, political enemies, people they wanted to ruin or outbid or outmaneuver or blackmail. There are politicians on that list, CEO's, bankers. If it became known what they had done it could ruin careers, bring down corporations, ruin marriages, destroy reputations . . ." She stopped. "But there's a small 'window of opportunity' here. We've got to move in a hurry. Once the police get onto this, once they have the 'intel' tapes, we won't be able to touch these people. It'll all be over."

She looked at Last triumphantly. "Hell, that could be the ticket right there. We could tell them up front: Look, the police will be onto this thing in ten days. We have access to the computers. In exchange for a little financial consideration, we can erase your name from the files, and when the investigation breaks your name won't even exist . . ."

She stopped and looked at Graver, then back at Last who was slumped against his door, staring at her like he could have strangled her.

"What's the matter?" she said.

Graver turned to Last. "I'll let you deal with this," he said. Then he looked at Connie. "You want to tell me where he is? I could probably get some more information from him that might be useful. That would take the responsibility off you. You wouldn't have it on your conscience . . . if something happened to him."

"What?" Rayner was looking around at everyone, confused that everyone was acting as if she hadn't said anything at all, that she didn't exist.

"He's at my place," Connie said, and she gave him the address.

"Colin?" Rayner snapped her head around to the secretary.

"Does Kalatis know where you live?" Graver asked.

Connie shook her head. "That's why I sent him there." She looked sick.

"Don't go back there," Graver said to her. "Not today, not tonight." Her eyes widened. "I'll call you when it's all right," he said. "Stay at a hotel tonight, at a friend's. Go on to work tomorrow as usual, and when it's okay I'll leave a message at your office. It won't be explicit, but you'll understand."

She nodded. Graver knew she would do whatever he said. She had crossed the line from out of control to under control.

"Hello? Hello? Am I missing something here?" Rayner sputtered. "Did anyone hear anything I said?" She had turned around now and was crouching on her knees, facing the back seat, her cleavage well presented.

"Bloody hell," Last said to her. "Give it a rest, love."

"What!" Rayner was incredulous.

"Don't get lost," Graver said to Last. "I'm going to want to reach you."

Last nodded miserably. Graver opened the door of the BMW and got out. He walked to his car, got in, started the motor, and backed out of the parking slot. Punching in Arnette's number on the handset, he started down the ramp, and looked in his rearview mirror. The midnight blue BMW hadn't moved. He could only imagine the conversation inside.

67

"NO, I DON'T WANT TO PICK HIM UP," GRAVER SAID. HE was headed back to the police department and had just given Faeber's location to Arnette. "I already know his lines of communications to Kalatis are closed so he wouldn't be any good to me in that regard."

"But . . ."

"But I suspect they'll try to hit him. And I don't know anyone who could have a more direct contact to Kalatis than a hit man. Kalatis would want to order something like that personally. And he's been doing a lot of it."

"Then you think they know where Faeber is?"

"If they don't they'll figure it out soon enough."

"And you want us to pick up the hit man when he comes for him."

"If you can. If you have people who can do that."

There was a pause on Arnette's end of the line.

"Yeah," she said finally. "I've got people who can do that."

Graver said nothing else. This was a big decision for Arnette. Though some of her people had had plenty of experience in operations, she always had stayed away from it, which was professionally prudent and legally imperative. Now she was stepping across the line too. This entire operation had been a study in crossing the line.

"I'll get them on the way as soon as we hang up," Arnette said.

Graver was relieved but said nothing about it. Instead he asked, "Any luck on those first names of those pilots?"

"Neuman is running them on Sheck's data, which we were finally able to scan onto a diskette," Arnette said. "And Paula's doing the same for Burtell's document. We ought to have something—or nothing—in a few minutes."

"If you get a last name and an address, have Neuman call me," Graver said. "I want him to be the one to pick them up, but I want to talk to him first."

"Will do. What's going on 'officially'?"

"I haven't heard anything. I don't think Hormann's death will cause even a ripple. He's not a subject in any file so his 'heart attack' will go unnoticed. Kalatis really has something there with his veiled hits. I still think this whole thing will stay under until they identify Dean's body. The amazing thing is that no matter how much the FBI and the DEA swarm around this bombing, they're not ever going to come up with Kalatis. It's hard for me to believe the guy's completely off the screen. It makes you wonder who else is out there we haven't got a line on."

"I wouldn't dwell on that if I were you," Arnette said. "Incidentally, I like your people. *Very* good. My compliments."

"Look, I've got to get off of this thing," he said. "I'm going to be waiting to hear from you."

When he got back to the office he had been gone almost three hours, so he checked once again with his squad supervisors. Nothing had come up, and it was still too soon for anything to have developed at the marina. There were check-in calls from both Westrate and Hertig, both of which Graver decided not to return since there was nothing to add to what he had already told them. He went through his messages, all of which could wait, and just as he was about to call in his temporary secretary to check on the paperwork his handset rang. He answered it immediately and was surprised to hear Lara's voice.

"Marcus, Ginette and I have just walked into her condo to get some clothes . . . the place has been wrecked."

"Jesus—are you sure there's nobody still there?"

"Yes, I checked. Ginette's really upset . . ."

"Lara, grab some of her clothes and then get the hell out of there. Listen, I've called her sister from Seattle. She's on her way. Okay?"

"Yeah, fine. She's getting her clothes now. After we made sure nobody was here I got her busy getting her things together. But what about someone following us? Should I worry about that? I mean, I wouldn't know what to do about that."

"Just get straight back to the house," Graver said. "I'll have a squad car get right over there to Ginette's and follow you back to my place. I'll have them go inside the house with you, make sure everything's okay. If you have the slightest concern about anything, call me."

"Okay," she said.

"Are you all right?"

"Yeah, I'm fine. This is just a little creepy, that's all."

"I know it is. I'm sorry to have to put you in this position."

"No, I didn't mean that."

"Lara, I'm going to call the shift lieutenant in patrol right now. You want to hang on?"

"No, go ahead. Really, we're all right. I'll check in with you later."

He hung up and called the patrol lieutenant. He explained briefly what he wanted without going into any background information. One of the advantages of commanding the CID was that if you didn't always explain yourself there was the assumption that you couldn't because of the nature of your responsibilities. Everyone accepted that, though sometimes grudgingly.

As soon as he put down the telephone, his handset rang again.

"Captain, this is Casey. I think we may have the two pilots. Found them in Sheck's document. He refers to a couple of pilots by last name only, Ledet and Redden. We went to the FAA records and found a Richard D. Ledet and an Edward E. Redden. Ledet lives in Atlanta, hangars a plane at a small airport there. Redden lives in Seabrook, a couple of miles from Sheck. He hangars a small Beechcraft at the Gulf Airport where Sheck kept his.

"Now, we checked utility records, and Redden is currently paying the bills at the Seabrook address. The place is definitely occupied. Telephone unlisted. We called Gulf Airport, and his plane is in the hangar. Arnette has a woman in Seabrook who's checking right now to see if she can tell if he appears to be home. Car in the driveway, newspapers in the yard, whatever.

"And it turns out that Arnette has both Ledet and Redden in her files. They were contract pilots for Army Intelligence *and* the CIA during the 1980s in Central America, most of the time stationed out of Tegucigalpa in Honduras, but doing regular junkets as far down as Colombia. They don't have a military background, just a couple of good ol' boys who got the flying bug in college, got their pilot's licenses, dropped out to fly and have been doing it ever since, for any-body, everybody, anytime, anywhere—for good money. Much of the time they fly together. They're single, late thirties."

"Has she got photographs?"

"Yeah, sure does."

"Okay, Casey, let's get out there. Ask Arnette if we can have a printout of their files, if not, read them before you leave, remember as much as you can. I'll leave from here in ten minutes and meet you at . . . Are you coming out the South Loop?"

"Yeah, that's closest."

"Okay, listen. Right after you go through the interchange coming onto the Gulf Freeway, look for the Broadway exit. Take Broadway south. A block or so off the freeway there's a branch post office. I'll be waiting in the parking lot for you."

Graver grabbed his coat, told his temporary secretary he would be gone for a couple of hours, and avoided looking down the long corridor as he went out through the reception area. He didn't want to get caught by anybody.

He guessed Arnette would not give Neuman a printout, so Neuman would be stuck there for ten or fifteen minutes reading the files, which would give Graver time to grab a sandwich on the way. He stopped at a barbecue place just east of downtown, bought a sliced beef sandwich with extra onions, a spear of dill pickle, and an RC in a bottle. Then he got on an up ramp to the Gulf Freeway and headed south.

Driving with one hand and eating the sandwich with the other, laying it down every so often on the greasy paper sack on the car seat beside him, he squinted into the high noon glare and thought about the best way to interview the pilot. So much depended on his immediate impression and on what Neuman had to tell him from Arnette's file. He wished he had been able to read them himself, but he knew he had used up a lot of luck just finding the guy. He imagined what a man named Redden would look like, his mind entertaining several types, none of which seemed right to him. Still, by the time he passed the interchange at the South Loop and slowed for the Broadway exit, he had settled on a fair-complexioned, Irish-looking Southern farmer's son. The South was full of them.

Graver waited at the post office parking lot for nearly fifteen min-utes—plenty of time to choke down the rest of the barbecue and gulp the RC to the bottom—before he saw Neuman coming along Broadway. Graver got out of his car, locked it, and was taking off his tie as Neuman pulled up.

"You get the file?" Graver asked, closing the door.

"Nope, no file." Neuman grinned, realizing that Graver knew all along that he wasn't likely to get it. He pulled out of the parking lot, got on the access road, and floated up on the freeway to join the traffic.

"Redden's from Sweetwater, Texas," Neuman began. "Father was a high school principal there. Went to college at Texas Tech, majoring in mechanical engineering, dropped out when he learned to fly. He was a crop duster for a while, a few years, then he got a job with a charter service flying people over the Grand Canyon. A few years at that, and he joined the National Forest Service in California flying firefighters into the summer fires. A few years at that. Next he turns up in the Rio Grande Valley, Mission, Pharr, that area. No visible employment, but visible money, so the DEA begins keeping tabs on him. They catch him one night in Ojinaga across from Presidio with a load of Mexican Brown. The State Department had the word out that they needed some pilots, and Redden was persuaded to go to Honduras and Nicaragua for some covert action. That's what he was doing when he landed a load of arms on a little private strip outside Villavicencio, Colombia. After that he seemed to have disconnected from CIA to 'independent' work, probably with Kalatis. His bio peters out very quickly after that. Just sightings throughout Central America."

"But there's no warrant out for him?"

"Nope."

"Christ. Kalatis. I don't believe that guy's reach."

"I don't believe a lot that I've seen in the last twenty-four hours," Neuman said. "I don't believe Arnette. That place is like a government installation . . ."

"What about Ledet?"

"I didn't spend much time on Ledet since he's in Atlanta."

"Remember anything about him?"

"He's from Louisiana, Baton Rouge. Went to LSU. Apparently met Redden when they both were flying drugs on the border. I don't think he was picked up by the DEA, he just showed up in Tegucigalpa shortly after Redden. Probably because of Redden. Their history generally parallels after that. I think they're pretty good buds."

Graver looked across the coastal flats as they left the city. The sun was fierce.

"Ledet from Red Stick," he said. He could feel the sun's heat radiating off the window beside him as it came through the glass like a laser and fell across his shoulder. The air conditioner in the car was cranked up as high as it would go as he stared out the window to the coastal flats.

68.

EDDIE REDDEN LIVED ON A PIECE OF EXPENSIVE PROPERTY. HE had a beachfront house that was protected from the street by a thick screen of pink and scarlet oleanders and clumps of cerise bougainvillea. Turning into the drive you could see a large, low-slung bungalow with a shallow-sloped roof, and Jamaican-style jalousies of bleached cypress. A deep veranda, flanked by palms, ran around to the back of the house where Galveston Bay glittered on the other side of a thick, emerald lawn that someone else mowed and fertilized and watered. Beyond that a dock ran out into the flats and a small blue skiff was tied to the pilings, bobbing in the southerly breeze.

There was a circle drive that exited on the other side of the lot, and where the front sidewalk met the drive a freestanding porte cochere of trellises covered with grapevines sheltered a black Alfa Romeo convertible. Neuman pulled up behind the Alfa and cut the motor. The two of them got out of the car and walked up to the porch and into the shade to the front door. The house was open to the breeze and you could see through to the porch in back. The daylight from the bright bay reflected dully off the burnished wooden floor in a long, luminous smear. Graver smelled gardenias on the breeze.

Neuman rang the doorbell. Nothing happened at first, no sound in the house. He rang it again, and a woman's voice from somewhere inside said, "I'm coming," politeness tinged with impatience. They didn't hear her walking on the floor because, as they immediately observed, she was barefooted. She was suddenly standing on the other side of the screen door, adjusting the drape of a white cotton shift she had just put on. The smear of light from the wooden floor behind her went right through the thin material to reveal to them the space between her legs all the way to her crotch. The cotton shift was all she was wearing. She tucked some dull brown hair behind an ear, and cocked her head up at Neuman, squinting a little at him.

"Yeah?"

"Hi," Neuman said. "Is Eddie in?"

"Who wants to know?"

"Joe . . . Dearden."

"*Jay Deer-den . . . ?*" She said it to herself like it was the most ridiculous name she'd ever heard.

"Yeah, Jay," Neuman said.

"Well . . ." she said, dropping her eyes, seemingly truly puzzled as to how to answer his question. Not a particularly intelligent-looking woman, she had sharp features and a weathered face with an abundance of sun-induced freckles. It was a common feature along the Gulf Coast. She did, however, possess a shapely figure.

"He was expecting me," Neuman said.

"He *was?*" she squinted up at him again. She turned and looked into the darkness of the house. Neuman reached out and quickly but softly tried the screen door. It was open. She turned back to him. "Well, shit, he's not here," she said.

"Who is it?" a man said from inside, his voice approaching.

"It's for Eddie . . . *Jay Deer-den?*" she said, emphasizing again the apparent peculiarity of the name to her.

Like her, the man was suddenly in front of them, frowning into the light of the porch, standing partially behind the girl and wearing only a pair of jogging shorts with the word "Athletic" on the front of the right leg.

Neuman immediately recognized him.

This was the best they could hope for.

"Hey, Rick," Neuman said in a long-time-no-see tone of voice, using his name so Graver would know they were talking to Richard Ledet. Then he jerked open the screen door.

Ledet hit the girl in the small of her back with both open hands, popping her head back and shoving her into Neuman who just as violently flung her aside as he lunged at Ledet. But the pilot's bare feet had better traction on the wood floor, and he was three steps ahead of Neuman on a straight course through the kitchen toward the back porch to the bay. Luckily the screen door that led out of the kitchen to the porch was latched, and when Ledet hit it with his arms outstretched to shove it open ahead of him, his arms went through the screen. The cross brace of wood midway down the door caught him in the stomach, and the momentum of his weight took him crashing through it, but slowed him enough for Neuman to tackle him. The two men hit the floor of the porch with a whump and loud grunts.

Graver was on top of Ledet almost as soon as he hit the floor, jamming the muzzle of his Sig-Sauer against Ledet's temple so that the pain of it alone would keep him there even without the threat of what it could do to him if Graver pulled the trigger.

Ledet froze.

Neuman was up instantly, running back into the main room where he found the girl just getting up off the floor. She started to scream, and he clamped his hand over her mouth.

Suddenly everything stopped.

"Anybody else here?" Graver snapped at Ledet.

The pilot hesitated and then said, "No."

Graver shoved the muzzle of the Sig-Sauer tighter against Ledet's temple.

"Swear to God," Ledet said.

"Put your hands behind your back." Graver kept his knee in the small of Ledet's bare back and cuffed his hands. Then he got up. "Okay, get up," he said, but he didn't help the pilot who took a moment to get to his knees, an awkward maneuver with his hands bound behind his back. When he was up, they walked back into the main room.

"If you scream when I take my hand down, I'll knock you out," Neuman told the girl. She nodded, and he cuffed her hands behind her as well and sat her on the sofa.

"He says there's no one else here," Graver said.

There was a sturdy rattan table and matching chairs to one side of the main room. A deck of cards was sitting on the table with a couple of empty beer bottles. Graver pulled out one of the chairs, turned it around, and told Ledet to sit down. Using another pair of handcuffs, Graver fastened one of Ledet's ankles to the leg of the rattan table. It would at least keep him from bolting.

"Watch them," he said, and walked through the house, three bedrooms, three baths, kitchen, dining room, wide hallways, all the windows opened to the bay breeze. When he got back to the main room everyone was in the same position as he had left them.

Graver pulled out another chair from the table where Ledet was sitting and sat down a few feet from him. The pilot was about Graver's height, well built, no fat, and good muscle definition. He had black hair, a couple of days' growth of beard, a straight narrow nose, and a suntan over an already swarthy complexion. He wore a very neat but full mustache. Graver studied him a minute. Ledet looked at him un-flinchingly, but without belligerence. He was trying to figure it out.

"Where's Eddie?" Graver asked.

"What's the deal here?" Ledet ventured. "Who are you guys?"

"The deal is we want to talk to Eddie," Graver said. He crossed his legs and crossed his forearms in his lap as he leaned forward slightly, the Sig-Sauer still in his hand.

"He's on a trip."

"Where?"

"Mexico, a charter job."

"What's he flying?"

"His little twin Beech."

"You know that for sure."

"Yeah, I do."

"Well, we drove by the hangar," Graver said. "The Beechcraft's still there."

Ledet swallowed. "Well, that's what he told me he was taking."

"Did he tell you where he was going?"

"You mean where in Mexico? No, just a charter he said."

"When will he get back?"

Ledet swallowed again. "He was supposed to be back today."

"Supposed to be?"

"Yeah. I haven't heard from him."

"We checked with the Gulf Airport office. The Beechcraft hasn't been flown in three days."

Ledet shrugged quizzically.

Graver looked at the girl. "Is this his girl you were in bed with?"

Ledet frowned. "Eddie's? Hell no."

"Who is she?" Graver asked, as if the girl weren't there.

"What, you mean her name?"

"That would be good to know, yeah."

"Alice."

"Just Alice?"

Ledet cut his eyes at her. "Uh . . . Alice . . ."

"Gifford," the girl said.

"Oh, yeah," Ledet said, remembering. "We just met last night . . . I didn't remember . . ."

Graver nodded. He thought a moment. "When did you leave Atlanta?"

Ledet's face flickered with a newfound suspicion as he realized that this man knew where he lived.

"Yesterday," Ledet said, studying Graver warily.

Graver had seen that look before, and it was not the expression he had hoped to see.

"This is actually very simple and straightforward," Graver said, hoping to turn Ledet's suspicions in another direction. "My code lines to Panos Kalatis are dead. I don't know why they're dead, but they are. I'm trying to get in touch with him. It's a matter of extreme importance to me. To both of us. I want to use your code line to contact him."

Ledet's mouth went slack, and he swallowed again as his demeanor changed to that of a man sitting in the hot seat. That was more in keeping with the reaction Graver had hoped for. But Ledet didn't respond. He seemed at a loss for words, suddenly seeing himself surrounded by a minefield. Considering the work Ledet had been doing for the last decade, Graver assumed that he understood some of the unspoken rules of the game. In the last few moments it would have occurred to him that these two men had barged in without any regard for hiding their faces. That had professional implications. They might be police—the suspicion of which Graver wanted to dispel for the moment—or if they were at the other end of the spectrum it could be that they didn't care if Ledet and Alice saw their faces because when they left they would not leave behind any witnesses. This latter possibility was the one clearly on Ledet's mind at the moment.

But he was having a hard time formulating a response. Normally he would have done his "Kalatis who" routine, but if this guy had a telephone code . . . or even *knew* that the telephone codes existed, then that ploy was not likely to work. He would have to resort to something else.

"Then you're out of luck," Ledet said, "Way out of luck."

"Oh?"

Ledet nodded. "Eddie's the only one who has it. That's always been the way we've done it. Just Eddie."

"What about when you're home?"

Ledet shook his head. "If there's work, Eddie calls me. I never talk to the guy. Kalatis, I mean. It's Eddie."

"He calls you, Eddie does?"

"That's right."

"If he calls you, then you come and you do the job?"

"That's right. That's how it works."

"Then you must be expecting some work," Graver said, motioning to Ledet with the Sig-Sauer. "Here you are."

Ledet stared at Graver and reluctantly nodded.

"And what is it this time?"

Ledet shook his head. "I don't know. Eddie calls me, says, Rick, we got work, and I fly over here. I don't know what the work is until I get here and he tells me."

"But you don't know now."

"No, I don't, because I haven't seen Eddie."

"He wasn't here when you got in yesterday."

"Right, he wasn't."

This Graver did not believe. "But you do know that he's on a charter to Mexico."

"Yeah, right."

"But you were wrong about him using the Beechcraft."

"Well, yeah, I guess so. I mean, I only know what Eddie tells me. If he tells me the Beechcraft, then I think the Beechcraft. What can I say? I can't do anything about it if he changes his mind or . . . the plans change."

Graver nodded, thinking. He unfolded his arms and his legs and stood, still nodding a little. Turning away he walked along the smear of light, through the doors into the kitchen, and out the shattered screen door to the veranda. He looked out across the bay, out to where the horizon grew hazy, and the water and the sky did not meet in a clean, sharp demarcation but formed a gray seamless distance. From the porch here, he could hear the seagulls. Here, the breeze coming off the water was much warmer, even hot, not yet having the advantage of coming through the shady coils of the house. And here, too, instead of the fragrance of gardenias there was the murky smell of Gulf brine. He turned around and went back through the kitchen into the main room.

He stopped beside the chair where he had been sitting and looked at Ledet and then at Neuman and Alice. Alice was petrified.

"Put something in her mouth," Graver instructed, and Neuman reached down and picked up the hem of Alice's shift and stuffed it into her mouth. This bared her legs and her lap, which was punctuated by the darker hair of the upper part of her pubic triangle.

Graver turned back to Ledet.

"We've all got choices here . . . except her," Graver said. "We're going to use her. Whatever happens to her is up to you and me." He waited a moment. Silence. This was all spur-of-the-moment ad-lib, and he suddenly had the feeling he had just made a terrible tactical error. "I know you've flown Colin Faeber to Kalatis's place a number of times. I need to go there."

Ledet stared up at Graver. He was scared, Graver could tell that, but Graver knew, too, that men who were afraid could also be very gutsy. Ledet was the kind of man who would call a bluff like this. After all, Graver had just handed him a nothing-to-lose deal. If Ledet was wrong it was the girl who would lose her life, not him. He could always talk, after he saw how serious they were.

"I need to know how to get to Kalatis's place," Graver said.

Ledet didn't say anything. He just sat there. At that moment Graver knew he had screwed up. If he hadn't been willing to pistol-whip one of them or both of them, then he should never have pretended he wasn't a cop. If he had been from Ledet's world, he would have already started with Ledet, and Ledet was now realizing that. He knew the girl was not going to get shot. Graver was furious at himself. He had pulled a rookie's stunt, and it had cost him the small advantage that he had had.

Ledet was almost grinning at him now. He knew he was dealing with a law enforcement officer of some kind. Graver knew some men who wouldn't have hesitated to beat that smirk off Ledet's face, to pound a little doubt into him, but Graver had never operated that way. It just wasn't in him.

The girl was crying, her body shaking with sobs, her mouth stuffed with her own dress, her eyebrows contorted, anguished, tears streaming down her face. Graver felt like a heel. The girl was the only one who had suffered here, and he hated himself for standing her up in front of a bogus firing squad. It had been an unnecessary cruelty, and he should have known better than to have subjected her to it.

Ledet looked over at her, and then looked back to Graver. He definitely knew that Graver was a cop. But Alice didn't. Between sobs she was trying to talk, yelling at the level of a high hum, a strident, muffled pleading.

Graver looked at her, and nodded for Neuman to remove the gag.

"I know, I know," she blurted, coughing, mucous mixed with tears stringing from her nose. "Don't kill me, God, no, I know, I know. I . . ." she gasped for breath and coughed.

Graver nodded for Neuman to remove her handcuffs, and then he looked at Ledet who was now watching Alice with a concerned frown.

Going into the nearest bedroom, Graver returned with a box of tissues which he gave to Alice who grabbed at them like a drowning woman. She blew her nose and wiped her face, blew her nose again, trying to get the best of her hysteria so she could prove that she was useful and didn't deserve to be killed.

"What is it?" Graver asked. "You know what?"

Alice wiped tear-logged strands of hair out of her face and coughed some more.

"I know about flying," she said, finally finding her voice. "I used to date a pilot . . ." she stopped in mid idea and looked at Ledet who was eagerly waiting to see what she was up to. "You *prick,*" she shrieked and spat at him, a mouthful that hit him squarely in the middle of his throat and slobbered down onto his bare chest.

"Hold it," Neuman said from behind her, reaching out and grabbing her shoulders as he forced her back down on the sofa.

Alice was glaring at Ledet so fiercely Graver believed she would have shot him if she could have gotten her hands on his gun. As far as she was concerned she had just watched Ledet demonstrate that he was willing to give her up to be shot rather than tell this man what he wanted to know. Maybe this was going to work to Graver's advantage after all.

"What is it?" Graver asked. "You'd better tell me what you know."

"Alice! You stupid bitch," Ledet croaked.

"I know where his goddamned navigational maps are, by God," she announced triumphantly. "You want to know where the son of a bitch flies, look on his maps. I found them this morning while he was sleeping." She looked at Ledet. "I've been around the block a few times, mister." She was furious. "When you went to get that coke last night I followed you into that other guy's room. You was so whiskey-whipped you didn't know shit from Shinola. I just stood in the door naked as a jaybird and watched you. Took you forever. Saw you take out the coke, a couple of guns"—she cut her eyes at Graver then—"I saw it all. Ammo"—eyes back to Ledet—"porno tapes."

"These guys are goddamn *cops,*" Ledet yelled. "Nobody was going to shoot you, dammit! Stupid bitch! Dammit!"

She frowned at Graver, then at Ledet, then back at Graver. "That right?"

"Sort of," Graver said. He came over and stood squarely in front of her. "Let me tell you something. If what you say is true, this guy is going to prison, and he won't be coming out again until he's old enough to collect his social security—if ever. If you take sides with him, you'll go down with him."

"What do you mean, go down with him? All I did was snort some of this asshole's coke and screw him. What do you mean 'go down with him'?"

"If you know about ongoing criminal activities and conceal it, you're an accessory," Graver said, not putting too fine a point on it.

She looked at Ledet. "I knew you were an asshole the second you walked into that bar, mister. I couldn't of had a better day in my life than the one I'd of had if I'd just walked out of that bar right then."

Wiping her nose one more time, she got up from the sofa, gave a tug to the hem of her shift and walked past Ledet, throwing a look at him that told him she was going to burn his ass.

The maps, the cocaine, and the guns were all in a window seat in what must have been Redden's bedroom. But the compartment was architecturally disguised to look as though it was part of a cantilevered bay window rather than what it was, a compartment large enough for two men to crawl into.

There was about half a kilo of recreational cocaine stored in a clear plastic container, three Uzi's, a Sig-Sauer like Graver's, a couple of Smith & Wesson M13's, and a Colt Delta. Ordnance for each was stacked neatly in separate wooden crates with the tops off. There was a stack of hard-core porn films as Alice had said—and there was a satchel.

Graver picked up the satchel and opened the leather straps. Folded in neat, nine-by-twelve squares were flight maps. There was a red, rubber-stamped rectangle on the front with a place for a date. The date, written in ballpoint pen, was the next day.

69

CONNIE'S CONDOMINIUM WAS ON A SHORT, QUIET STREET NOT far from Greenway Plaza, one of the city's eight "business centers," clusters of glass and steel architecture that punched up out of the heavily forested landscape that comprised the seven thousand five hundred square miles of metropolitan Houston.

It was not a large complex, only five units arranged around a regular pentagonal courtyard enclosed by high, rusty brick walls covered in Virginia creeper and English ivy, a barrier from the noise of the streets. There was only a single entrance from the apex of the pentagon, through a single-lane drive that circled a central garden plot of decorative plantings at the hub of which bloomed an enormous mimosa with shimmering pink blossoms. Each residence had a garage that was entered off the circular drive, though each garage was situated so that its entrance was not visible from the circular drive itself.

In many ways it was a good location to stake out. One entrance from the front. None from the back. But on the other hand it was a hell of a challenge because the architect had gone to a lot of trouble to guard the entrance of each building from its neighbors, privacy being a highly touted "amenity" of this particular complex. Access from the garage to the front door was from inside the garage so that once you entered and lowered the garage door behind you by remote control you were secure. The public entrance to the front door was through a walled courtyard with a wrought-iron gate that had an electronic lock that could be unlocked only with the resident's key or from inside the residence.

The problem was positioning. There could be no surveillance from a car. They needed access to one of the other condos, preferably an adjacent one. Using Arnette's computerized crisscross directory, Dani, with Arnette looking over her shoulder, called each of the adjacent units. The first one answered and Dani asked for a fictitious name and then apologized for the wrong number. The second one had a recording saying they couldn't come to the telephone right now, leave a message. Dani tapped into the computer for the resident's occupation. Lawrence Micheson, sales representative for Tectronics Aluminum Fabrications. She called the employer and asked to speak to Mr. Micheson. She was transferred to his secretary who said he was in Phoenix on business and wouldn't be back until Saturday, could she take a message. No, thank you. Dani tapped into one of the credit bureaus and learned that Mr. Micheson was not married. Odds were: the place was empty.

It was decided that Remberto would go in. Murray would stay outside the complex on a side street that had a clear view of the entrance and let him know when someone was approaching the entrance gates.

The afternoon was still and sweltering, and by the time Remberto walked inside the complex his shirt was beginning to stick to him. That was the thing about Houston, moving here was like having never left Bolivia. The heat and humidity was just like working the Beni River jungles. But of course there had never been air conditioners in the valley of the Beni River. Remberto loved refrigerated air. It made him smile.

While Remberto and Murray were crossing the city, Dani had gone ahead and called the other two condos in the complex. The residents were not home at either of them. So of the five residences, the only ones that were occupied were Connie's, where Faeber was waiting, and the one on the other side, the one immediately to the right as you entered the compound. Knowing this, Remberto did not have to worry about someone seeing him from behind or across the way. There had not been enough time to determine if there was an alarm system, and even if they had known that there was one, there had not been enough time to bring the electronic equipment to manipulate it or to contact their stringer at whichever security company had installed the system.

So, it was back to the jungle. Remberto was going to have to find a place outside in Micheson's courtyard where he could watch Connie's front door without Faeber being able to see him from inside the condo. It was just going to be a matter of scouting it out to see what vantage point best served the purpose.

Locating the right vantage point turned out to be easier than he had expected, though using it was going to be a tedious proposition. The brick wall separating Connie's front courtyard from Micheson's was ten inches wide. The design for the brick of which it was made called for a random placement of bricks to stick out several inches from the face of the wall creating a relatively accessible means of ascent. The garages of the two condos backed up to each other having a common wall while the wall of the garages facing the entrances formed the front wall of the courtyard. Just inside Connie's entrance court, in the corner created by the garage wall and the wall dividing the two properties, grew a healthy and shaggy Mexican fan palm, its large and verdant fronds just high enough to reach over the top of the wall.

Remberto used the jutting bricks to climb the wall and found a place to sit atop the wall leaning his back against the garage wall and under its eave. The fronds of the fan palm completely obscured him from the courtyard and from the windows on the front of Connie's condo. He called Murray.

"Okay," he said. "I'm in place, on top of the wall in her front courtyard."

"No shit?"

"Yeah, really. Listen, it's quiet here. If someone's coming just buzz me twice."

"Will do."

Remberto settled in to wait. He was fully aware that he might be there for hours, in fact, he expected to be. He also expected to be uncomfortable. And he was. Both courtyards were lush with vegetation which meant the humidity there was at the top end of the scale; and he felt every percentage point. The sun was just a little past meridian which meant the eave of the garage provided a ribbon of shade for the back of his head, but the ribbon was shrinking by the minute. Pretty soon he would be in full sun for an hour or so until the fan palm began to block it. The steam rose out of the courtyards, and colonies of gnats moved in small congregations like clouds from palms to oleanders to azaleas to plumerias and eventually to Remberto whose sweat-drenched clothes attracted them like bees to nectar. That was okay. Remberto had lived with gnats before. Sweat poured from his hairline and ran down the back of his neck, behind his ears, down his forehead and into his eyes. That was okay. He had lived with sweat before.

But the brick wall was something else. Remberto's butt was wider than ten inches, and after an hour he thought his spine was going to lock up on him. After an hour and a half he was beginning to get worried about what he was going to do. This was not something he thought he could endure for five or six hours. Instead of keeping his legs and feet together, pulled up in front of him, he shifted and dropped one on either side of the wall. That was a great relief—for about eight minutes—then the ridges of the bricks began to cut into his inner thighs, and he felt like his tailbone had no flesh at all between it and the bricks.

Then the handset buzzed twice.

Remberto froze and listened carefully. The signal meant only that a car was entering the compound. It could go to any residence, and he strained to try to determine which. Within a minute he heard the soft wheezing of an idling car pull into the concrete drive in front of Micheson's garage to his left. It idled for a moment and then stopped.

There was a brief wait before he heard the car door open. Girlfriend? Cleaning woman? Micheson sneaking back into town early without telling his employer? He knew Murray had been watching the car since it entered and would be observing where it finally stopped, and that he already would have called in the license plate for verification.

Remberto was not so well hidden from Micheson's side of the courtyard. In fact he was practically in plain view. His heart raced as his mind rushed past his few options, and then suddenly he heard the car door close . . . softly . . . the *single* click of a door gently pushed to, just enough to keep it from swinging open, though not fully shut. He froze. That was not the proper sound.

He heard footsteps leaving the concrete drive, but they faded away rather than growing louder as they should have if the person was approaching Micheson's gate. Then he heard them getting louder again—but they were at Connie's gate. Just as they stopped he realized they were a woman's footsteps, a woman wearing heels.

She had a key to the gate and opened it. Connie? Rayner Faeber deciding to try to reason with her husband? But Graver had told Arnette that the two women had been warned to stay away. Had one of them simply ignored his instructions?

Remberto's change of position had been a mistake. He could feel the nerves in his groins tingling which meant his inner thigh muscles were being pinched by the ridges in the bricks. But he couldn't move. Not now.

The woman came into view: early forties, roan hair, a little chunky, but stylishly dressed in a business suit. Attractive. She reminded Remberto of a realtor who might deal in the tonier parts of the city. There was something business-like and practical about her—maybe the way she handled her shoulder bag, sure of herself—expeditious in her manner.

She walked straight to the front door without looking to the left or the right and again used a key to let herself into the condo. And though she did this without hesitation, she also did it carefully, making no noise. As soon as she closed the door Remberto pressed the handset.

"Murray! Murray, what's the deal here? Who is this?"

When Murray spoke Remberto flinched because the voice came from back to his left side, through Micheson's wrought-iron gate.

"Berto!" Murray was panting heavily, his muscled arms bared by the short sleeves of his T-shirt holding onto the gate as he pressed his forehead to the bars in an effort to see around the corner of the garage to Remberto. "The plates are *stolen!*"

Remberto swung his left leg over the wall. There wasn't enough room to jump down behind the palm—he had to remain hidden until he got to the ground—so he turned around facing the wall and lowered himself by his arms onto the ground in the tiny space between the trunk of the palm and the walls of the corner. Then he moved quickly, if stiffly, along the wall and came out at the gate.

Murray was already there having run back around the garage, and handed his Colt through the gate to Remberto as he reached up, grabbed the top of the front wall and pulled himself up and over, dropping into the courtyard with Remberto.

"What's going on? What's the story here?" Remberto asked, moving his weight from leg to leg to massage out the tingling.

"Shit, we don't know. Computers say the plates are stolen, that's all we know."

Remberto was already moving to the front door, acting more on instinct now than a progression of reason. As he guessed, she had left the door unlocked, a bad sign, and he pushed it open as he pulled his own gun from his waistband.

Immediately inside there was a small foyer and a living room to their right and straight ahead stairs ascending to the second floor, turning halfway up and wrapping around over the entrance to the living room. They stood a moment and listened. Voices, distant and almost inaudible, came from upstairs. Luckily the stairs were carpeted, and they started up, Remberto first.

At the head of the stairs the landing went in both directions, so they had to stop and listen again. The voices were louder, from the left. Together they advanced down the narrow hall, past an open doorway to a darkened bedroom on the left, an open door to a darkened bathroom to the right, the voices coming from another room straight ahead. The woman's voice grew louder as she stepped to the door of the room, almost in the doorway, her muted shadow from the oblique light of the sunlit room falling on the opened door. She must have been inches from being visible to them. Remberto ducked into the bedroom; Murray disappeared into the bath on the opposite side of the hall.

"The sooner the better," she said. "I'll do it if you want. It's what I came for."

"Jesus," the man sobbed. "No . . . no. Just . . . just step outside . . . just . . . downstairs."

"Okay," she said. "I'm going." She stepped into the doorway and out of the room into the hall. Her left hand rested on a shoulder bag hanging from her left shoulder, and her right hand hung straight down at her side, holding a handgun with a silencer. She took several steps but then stopped, turned, stepped back to the door and raised her gun straight out level with her shoulder.

In that instant both Remberto and Murray burst out into the hall and yelled at her in the same instant that the explosion of a single gunshot reverberated from inside the room. Wheeling around smoothly, her arm never dropping from its leveled position, her silencer coughed one, two, three times, ripping into the door facings on either side of the hall as Remberto and Murray fell back into the rooms. They looked across the hall at each other and waited—the advantage was theirs.

Silence.

Murray turned on the bathroom light and found a hand mirror on the vanity. He turned off the light, and in a moment the mirror moved out from the door frame. She was standing squared at them, her feet planted firmly, slightly apart, her legs flexed in competition shooting form, both arms out in front of her now supporting the gun. The silencer coughed again, and Murray's mirror disintegrated.

Silence.

"What are you going to do?" Murray yelled. "Jump out the window?"

Silence.

"Who are you?" she asked, her voice calm, almost conversational.

"We're not police," Murray said. "And we're not a follow-up from Kalatis."

Silence.

"You didn't shoot him," he said. "We know that."

"Does that make any difference?"

"It does to me," Murray said cryptically.

Silence.

"I don't want this to have a bad ending," Murray said. "Why don't you—"

The silencer coughed again—once—followed by the sound of a falling body. Murray grabbed a shard of the broken mirror and held it out against the door frame. He could see her lying on the floor.

"Shit," he said, and darted his head out, then back. "I think she did it," he said, looking across at Remberto.

Remberto looked around and saw the dark spreading on the carpet under her head, her body lying almost inside the bedroom door she had just stepped through. The gun was out of her hand, partially concealed under the hem of her skirt.

"Yeah," he said, "she did."

They came out of their doorways and approached her carefully, nonetheless, but she was clearly dead. Remberto stepped over her into the bedroom which actually had been turned into a study with a desk and bookcases, a sofa, and chairs. Faeber was sprawled on the floor, his legs over the legs of an overturned chair in which he had been sitting, facing the windows. The blow from the large handgun he had used had knocked him over backward.

Remberto stepped back into the hall.

"Faeber shot himself too," he said.

Murray was down on his knees pulling off one of the surgical gloves that the woman had been wearing.

"I want to see just who the hell this gal is," Murray said. "Look in her shoulder bag. I need some paper."

Remberto opened the purse; it was completely empty.

"Shit," Murray said.

Remberto stepped into the study and found an envelope which he brought back. Murray took it, lifted the woman's bare hand, bent her arm back, and dipped the ends of her fingers in her blood. He carefully made two complete sets of prints and then dropped her hand and stood, waving the envelope to dry the prints.

The two men looked at each other.

"I don't know," Murray said finally, shaking his head. "What a goddamned creep show. Let's get the hell out of here."

70

EVEN IF GRAVER COULD UNDERSTAND THE MAPS, HE KNEW IT was going to be to his immediate advantage to have as much leverage as possible against Ledet.

The first thing he did was to bring everyone into the bedroom. He put Ledet on the floor, cuffed now at his ankles as well as his wrists, and had Alice sit on the edge of the bed. He laid out all the firearms on the bed and called out the serial numbers on each of them to Neuman who jotted them in his notebook. Then Graver called a friend at ATF and gave him the information, Redden's telephone number, and hung up.

Then he turned on the television that was standing on a bureau across the room from the foot of the bed, punched on the VCR, and slipped in the first tape. The first several were standard, low-budget, professionally-produced porno films, and Graver fast-forwarded through them, suspecting these weren't going to have what he was looking for. Cassette number four was home-produced right there in the bedroom where they were sitting. It "featured" Eddie Redden—Neuman identified him—and a couple of girls, a thin, black-haired girl with prune-sized breasts and bruises on her buttocks, and a narrow-hipped blonde with black pubic hair and bosoms as large and distended as overfull udders.

"Goood Lorrrd!" Alice blurted, leaning forward on her hands on the bed and gaping at the television. "My Gahhhd! That's Katie May-hew and . . . and that old girl that hangs out at Remo's Inn in Kemah! What's her name . . . Deena . . . or Reena or something like that? Look at thaaaat! Look at what . . ."

Graver hit the fast forward again and went to the end with Alice gasping and squealing at the skittering acrobatics of her fellow tavern habitués. The next tape was more of the same, this time including Ledet and two women whom Alice, with visible disappointment, did not seem to know. The last tape was what Graver had thought he might find. This one included Ledet, and Redden again—and two more girls. But this time they were little girls, clearly underage, just on the borderline of puberty.

Alice gasped again, but then clapped her hands over her opened mouth in a gesture of shock and, after a few minutes, with loathing on her face, she turned away. Graver turned off the tape.

As if on cue, the telephone rang. It was the report from the ATF. All the guns were from a shipment stolen from a South Florida gun shop nearly two years earlier.

Graver hung up the telephone and walked around the bed and sat down on the edge of it facing Ledet on the floor. He stared at him a moment.

"If it was up to me," he said, "I'd take you out back on the beach and shoot you in the head. I've never shot a man, but I don't think—in this instance—it would bother me. Not more than a few minutes, anyway." He paused. "But the truth of the matter is what ultimately happens to you isn't going to be up to me. There will be a prosecutor, a judge, and a defense lawyer. You'll get a lawyer who will do everything in his power to mitigate the circumstances here, the coke, the stolen guns, the little girls, but he won't be able to do you any good if this is all he's got to work with."

Graver looked over at the stack of guns, at the pile of tapes, taking his time to think about it.

"I wish I didn't need your help," Graver went on, "but I do. And if you help us, you'll also be helping yourself, though I regret this. Your lawyer will take what you do for us and milk it for all it's worth. I personally don't think you ought to benefit a scintilla—you know what a scintilla is, it's about as little as your mind can imagine—I don't think you should benefit even that much for helping us. I think you ought to be forced to do it by law. I think you ought to get the needle if you don't help us, maybe life if you do. But your lawyer will do a lot better than that . . . unfortunately."

Alice was listening to this with her mouth dropped open slightly, as if she couldn't believe this pretty sober thing she had gotten herself into when she agreed to this one-night stand.

Graver stood up from the bed and walked around and got the maps and came back and stood in front of Ledet.

"You want to try to make it a little easier on your lawyer?"

• • •

According to Rick Ledet, Eddie Redden was one of three principal pilots for Panos Kalatis. Redden kept a pager with him at all times and was on call twenty-four hours a day. His instructions from Kalatis were delivered to him in a variety of ways, sometimes by telephone, sometimes by personal messenger, sometimes at the conclusion of one of his flights. Ledet himself went along as copilot or flunky assistant, whatever was needed.

"What are the reasons for the flights?" Graver asked. They were sitting in the large main room again, at the rattan table, the flight maps spread out in front of them. Neuman was taking notes and Alice was in the back bedroom. Graver decided she had heard just about all she needed to hear of what was happening, so he asked her to stay in the bedroom while they finished talking. Now that she knew they were police, she was compliant and—after they removed the telephone and told her she could watch television—relatively content to wait it out and see what happened next. After all, this little ordeal was going to make good tavern talk when it was all over.

"Just about everything and anything," Ledet said. He was smoking, raising both cuffed hands every time he wanted a puff on his cigarette. "But about eighteen months ago Kalatis kind of reorganized the pilots and put me and Eddie exclusively on runs with people and money. That's our main cargo. We take out a lot of cash. A lot of cash."

"From his drug operation?"

"That's what Eddie says some of it is. And some of it's from other kinds of business. Kalatis and Faeber sold information of some sort."

"How much money, how often?"

"I do a money haul with them about once a month. How much? Shit, Eddie said millions, and I guess it must be. They load these reinforced cardboard storage boxes into the plane, you know, the kind with handles cut into the ends, and a top that fits down over it. I saw inside one of them one time, one of the guards let me look, and the bills were stacked in there nice and neat, banded and labeled. It'd already been counted, and they knew just exactly how much was in each box. Millions, like Eddie said. We have thirty or forty of these things stacked in the cabin. A box of cash is heavy, quite a load."

"So they take money out of the country about once a month . . ."

"No, I said *I* do money hauls about once a month," Ledet corrected Graver, mashing out a cigarette into an ashtray sitting on the table in front of him. "Eddie does it all the time. I only go when they're going to Panama or the Caymans or Colombia. They want a copilot who can speak pretty good Spanish on those jumps in case something happened to the pilot. They don't want to risk losing a load."

"Then where does Eddie take it when he's by himself?"

"Offshore. He runs loads to cruisers sitting out in the Gulf, past U.S. jurisdictional waters. Once every week he does that, a regular milk run." He looked down and tapped the maps. "That's what these are. The cruisers never wait at the same place. Keep shifting around. The coordinates change every week, every run."

"How do you get around filing flight plans?"

Ledet gave Graver a you've-got-to-be-kidding look. "Come on, man, flight plans?" He snorted. "Look, flying is one of the last great freedoms in this life. They've got all these rules, sure, but, shit, do you have any concept of how goddamn *big* 'airspace' is? The *volume?*" He gestured with a tilted bob of his head toward the hazy heat out the back door of the house. "The sky out there is full of planes that nobody knows shit about, not the DEA, not the Border Patrol, not any of the branches of the military, not NSA . . . 'Airspace,' man, it's just too damn big to know what's going on up there all the time. They can monitor *some* corridors *some* of the time, but that's about it. That leaves about ninety-nine percent of the airspace unaccounted for. It's a smuggler's paradise. Like the high seas two hundred years ago. You read in the paper where the DEA says they figure they interdict only about five percent, seven percent of the shit coming through? They're not lying about that. Poor bastards are just pissing into the wind, and they know it. And pound for pound there's probably more cash going out than dope coming in." He grinned and gave his head a little shake. "It's a 'free-flowing stream,' just like the old church song says."

When you heard a man like this talk you understood why so many law enforcement officers were getting out of the business. After a few years the futility of it was a persuasive deterrent to a career. Or, on the other hand, the temptation to skim a little off for yourself became too great. When there was so much cash that you had to talk about it in terms of its weight rather than its unit value, it began to lose its meaning.

"Then you think Redden is making a money haul now?"

Ledet looked a little uneasy at the question, though he had shown no uneasiness earlier when he gave up the information. He reached for a cigarette and lit it with a throwaway plastic lighter.

"I guess," he said.

"He's not on a charter to Mexico."

Ledet shook his head.

"Spell it out for me," Graver said impatiently.

"When Eddie called me he said something big was up with Kalatis. He, Eddie, needed me for a long-distance run."

"As copilot."

"Right. But I copiloted on other kinds of things, too, not just cash runs. Kalatis has people brought to his place, people he does business with. He always wants copilots on those."

"What people?"

"Eddie said they're 'clients,' people the Greek needs to talk to. I'm not sure about what kind of dealings. But I do know they're more cash customers of some sort, having to do with either the information business or the dope business."

"Then you think you're here for taxiing services, to take people to Kalatis for meetings?"

"Yeah. My understanding is tonight's going to be hectic. I think all the pilots are on duty tonight."

This was what Graver wanted to hear. He wanted to hear something about Kalatis. He wanted to hear the details of a plan of which Kalatis was an integral, necessary participant.

"Each pilot has a copilot as well?" he asked.

"Right. There're six of us."

"Three aircraft."

"Right. We've done something like this before, when he was closing deals, a big program with everything coming together in one tight time frame. All three planes, carrying people, money, dope. That's kind of Kalatis's strong suit. Organization. These big operations, men and schedules coordinated real close, planes and boats on the move, everything clicking like clockwork. And that's the way it happens too"—he snapped his fingers in a quick, measured cadence, snap, snap, snap, snap—"just like that."

"All of you taking people and money down to Mexico, to Kalatis's place."

"To Kalatis's place, yeah," Ledet confirmed, but his eyes slid away from Graver as he said it.

Graver and Neuman exchanged looks.

"You realize," Graver reminded Ledet, "that the point of all this is still the first thing I said to you. I want to know how to get to Kalatis."

Ledet nodded and dragged on his cigarette. His hands were resting on the rattan next to the ashtray. The one holding the cigarette was trembling. He seemed to be coming to some crucial decision, a personal Rubicon.

"I want to be in one of those special wings of a maximum security prison," Ledet said abruptly. "Where they put you if they think your life's in danger in there. I'm not saying anything about where Kalatis lives without that. I'll tell you that right now. I don't care how much you threaten me with this lifer shit."

Ledet was looking at Graver now, straight at him, his face pinched with the seriousness of his situation.

"This guy's not just any bad-ass out there," Ledet said. "He's quiet and methodical and never forgets anything anybody ever did to him. If you wrong him, he'll get you." He smoked his cigarette. "The man's got incredible reach. You could be half a world away from him and then wake up some night and realize he's got you by the balls . . . squeezing. I'd never tell you if I thought he'd outlive my prison sentence."

"Okay," Graver said. "It's a deal. The special section of maximum security."

He had no authority to say that. He wasn't even the right person to be discussing it. Nor did Ledet's almost pitiful, animal fear move him in the least. He just wanted Kalatis and would have agreed to any absurdity, would have promised this man any lie, to get him.

Ledet studied him a moment as if the readiness with which Graver had agreed had made him suspicious. He seemed to suspect that promised easy time was going to be a lot like promised easy money—it never was. But the weight around his eyes also betrayed his realization that he really didn't have much of a choice anyway.

"Kalatis doesn't live in Mexico," Ledet said. "Every time we take somebody to him we do a two-hour decoy flight. Tell them we're headed to Mexico when in fact we're actually riding around out in the Gulf or cruising down the coast to Florida. Kalatis's place is in Galveston."

"Galveston?" Graver was incredulous.

Ledet nodded. "Yeah. About thirty miles as the crow flies"— he tapped the top of the table with his middle finger—"from right here."

71

2:40 P.M.

GRAVER LEANED AGAINST A PILLAR OF THE PORCH AND STARED OUT across the bay, watching two freighters moving dead into Pelican Spit. Soon they would tack sharply to the southeast and steam between the peninsula of Port Bolivar and the eastern tip of Galveston Island and head out into the open Gulf. The hazy heat of late June made it seem as though he was seeing them through a mirage or a daydream, ghost ships, sea-bound for ports unknown.

The diversion lasted less than a minute, and then Neuman was coming out the battered screen door that Ledet had bashed through.

Graver turned. "He can't go anywhere?"

Neuman shook his head. "No." He squinted out to the bright haze over the bay. "Now what?"

Graver looked at his watch. He stepped away from the edge of the porch and sat down in a rattan armchair. Both he and Neuman had shed their coats and rolled up their sleeves, and Graver's gun, hugging his waist, had rubbed a raw spot on his side that was beginning to itch because of the sweat. He wasn't used to wearing the Sig-Sauer that much. It was too big to be comfortable.

"We've got enough evidence," he said, watching the two ships. They were like the hour and minute hands of a clock, you could see that they were moving, but you couldn't see them doing it. "But I don't think we've got enough time."

Before Neuman could say anything, Graver went on. He spoke quickly, thinking out loud, his mind almost tripping over itself as he tried to work out the best course of action.

"Enough evidence to justify a tactical intervention, to go out to Kalatis's and sweep up everything and everybody, and let it all get sorted out in the days and weeks to follow. I don't have any doubt that what we have in the computers from Tisler and Burtell will justify it. That and all the other crap, what we know, what we can substantiate, even keeping Arnette out of it . . . we have more than enough, enough even to spin this off into a dozen other directions and investigations.

"But," he said, wiping his sweaty forehead on the shoulder of his shirt, "there's not enough time to present all of this in the way it needs to be presented to convince the people who have to be convinced in order to get the raid authorized. And then there's the matter of the tactical preparation. If this thing isn't planned right . . ."

"If Kalatis is moving that kind of money," Neuman said, "he's going to have a lot of firepower. He doesn't strike me as the kind of guy to move around underprotected."

"No, you're right," Graver agreed. "And it's going to take time to prepare a tactical action against something like that. It's probably even irresponsible of me to ask our tactical people to try an operation on this scale on only four or five hours notice. To do it right, it ought to involve boats, helicopters, cars"—he shook his head—"who knows how many men."

"And we don't have any idea of the layout at Kalatis's place, do we?"

"No, we don't," Graver said. "It would be a nightmare. Frankly, I doubt if the tactical commanders would even consider it under the circumstances."

He stood impatiently and shifted the gun at his waist. "Shit," he said, and leaned again on the porch post. The freighters were at another angle now, headed into the strait.

The telephone in the house rang, and Graver whirled around and burst past the broken screen door, through the kitchen and into the main room where Ledet sat bound on the floor, looking at the telephone on the rattan table as though it were a cobra.

"If this is Redden . . . be careful," Graver said, putting his hand on the telephone. "If you screw this up, by God, I promise you I'll make sure you die of old age in a cage."

Ledet looked as if he were being confronted by Satan. The telephone kept ringing. Ledet nodded, and Neuman was on his knees unlocking Ledet's handcuffs. Then Neuman stood and rushed back to the bedroom as Graver took the telephone off the rattan table and put it on the floor with Ledet.

"Okay!" Neuman yelled.

Ledet picked up the telephone on the sixth ring.

"Hello." He tried to make his voice sound normal, whatever the hell that was. The past two hours had caused him to completely lose sight of it.

"Hey, Rick."

"Eddie, what's happenin'?"

"When did you get in?"

"About five-thirty yesterday. What happened to you?"

"Well, there's a lot of shit going down with our friend here. When I called you we had a routine job. We still have a job, but now there's nothing routine about it."

"Something wrong?"

"No, not wrong, just . . . serious."

"We going to clock some hours, then?"

"Yeah, a lot. Look, I need you to come out to Las Copas, okay?"

"When?"

"Right about dusk. Eight-thirty would be good."

"Can't do it." Ledet looked at Graver.

"What do you mean?"

"I came in with oil line problems, Eddie. I haven't fixed it yet."

"Why the hell not? You had time yesterday, didn't you? You've had all day." He hesitated. "You picked something up, didn't you."

"Well, yeah, I did . . ."

"Shit . . . is she still there?"

"Yeah," Ledet said tentatively, as though he expected to be reprimanded for it.

"Christ," Redden said. "Well, get the hell rid of her, Rick. Jesus, man, that was stupid."

"How was I to know this was going to be something special," Ledet said, looking at Graver. "Okay, I'll get her out of here. What about Las Copas? Why don't you just swing by and pick me up on the way?"

"I don't know," Redden said, sounding worried.

"What?" He raised his eyebrows to Graver, surprised. "What do you mean you don't know? What's the deal?"

"I told you this is serious, Rick. I've got a schedule, and it doesn't include stopping by to pick you up, know what I mean?"

Graver grabbed his notepad, jotted something, and shoved it in front of Ledet.

"Where are you now? Can't you just come get me now?"

"Forget it," Redden said. "Look, Rick, can't you patch up the oil problem? How bad could it be, for Christ's sake? Rick, listen to me, trust me, just by-God get there. We're going to pull in some big money on this one. Something's going on here. I'll tell you about it when you get there. Just believe me when I tell you you can't miss this, okay? Besides that, I can't go flying in there without a copilot. I don't know what he'd do."

Graver got on the floor and jotted another note on the pad holding it so Ledet could read it as he wrote.

"Okay, okay. Uh, I'll, shit, I'll try and patch it up somehow. But what about Las Copas, I mean is that where they're staging this, whatever it is? I mean, what if I come in there slinging oil? I'm not going to want to do that if all those—"

"Wait a minute, Rick . . . uh, Rick, stand by." Silence. "I'll call you right back."

The line went dead and Ledet sat on the floor looking astonished.

"Jesus. He just hung up, just like that," Ledet said, looking up at Graver, still holding the receiver. "You think he smelled something? You think he knew something was wrong here?"

"Put down the damn receiver," Graver snapped.

Ledet hung up. Neuman came into the room.

"I don't think he suspected anything," he said. "It sounded to me like he was interrupted from that end. I think we're okay."

"What's Las Copas?" Graver asked.

"It's a little strip Kalatis had cut in the boonies," Ledet said. "Inland from Kalatis's beach house, across Chocolate Bay in Brazoria County. It's a secret strip, no roads in, just air traffic. A dirt top, bayous and low-water ponds all around. The pilots use it as a rendezvous point, and sometimes to transfer goods from planes to boats. There's a navigable bayou within seventy-five yards of it, but it's a swampy place."

"It's near Kalatis's house?"

"Yeah. Ten, twelve air miles. He owns a shit-load of beachfront property across the West Bay from there, on the Gulf side of the island."

The telephone rang again.

"See what he says before you repeat the part about patching the oil line," Graver said as Neuman went back into the bedroom. "We want him *here*."

Ledet nodded. "Hello?"

"It's me," Redden said. "Okay, look, I'm coming to pick you up. That was Wade. The whole thing's been changed—again. New schedule. No problem about picking you up now. You're a lucky son of a bitch, Ledet. This is better anyway. I can refuel at Bayfield and we'll have time to get something to eat before we have to be in the air again."

"Bayfield? I thought you were at Gulf."

"No, man, change of plans. I didn't take the Beechcraft. We got *cargo*. I'm in the PC, needed the extra muscle."

"Oh," Ledet said, looking at Graver for vindication. "Okay. Glad we got that straight. Then when you going to be there?" Ledet asked.

"Uh, well, there's plenty of time now so, let's see, it's almost three now. Why don't you pick me up out there at . . . five. We'll run over to Kemah for some crab before we start this little circus the Greek's got planned. Gonna be a long night, Ricky. Hope you're rested up."

"Okay, five o'clock," Ledet said, and hung up. He looked at Graver for approval.

"What's a PC?" Graver asked.

"It's a Pilatus PC-12 turboprop, a Swiss aircraft. A very fine piece of equipment."

"What did he mean 'extra muscle'?"

"The PC's a power plane. It's new, a corporate class aircraft, but a workhorse. It's got a range of 1700 nautical miles, airspeed of 270 knots, and can carry up to a ton in payload—people, cargo, whatever, depending on whether you put in seats or decking."

"Put your hands out," Graver said, and when Ledet did Graver snapped the cuffs again and sat down in one of the rattan chairs, looking at Ledet on the floor.

"That's good," Neuman said, coming back into the room.

Graver nodded, but his eyes had shifted to the white heat outside, beyond the sunless rooms and the shady porch. No one said anything as Graver stared outside. The afternoon was hot enough now that you could smell it, the vegetation and soil and bay water heated to the point that they exuded odors all their own, odors that never occurred at any other time than on the most sweltering days of summer. It was hot even in the house now, the temperature outside outstripping the natural coolness inherent to the marriage of shadow and breeze. Now the hot breath off the bay intruded to the point of rudeness, leaving them no recourse but to sweat and wish it was later in the afternoon.

"Look, how much longer am I supposed to stay back there?" Alice asked, standing in the doorway to the main room. She was holding onto the door frame with one hand, standing on one foot, the other foot pulled up and pressed against the inside of her knee.

"Not much longer," Neuman said.

"It's three o'clock," she said. "Right at it, anyway."

"Maybe an hour," Neuman said, not having any idea.

"An *hour?* God dog!" She wheeled around in exasperation and returned to the bedroom.

Graver looked at Neuman, nodded his head sideways toward the porch and then got up and walked back through the kitchen again carrying his handset, with Neuman following. When he got outside he dialed Arnette.

"I've got some news for you," Arnette said, and she told him what had happened at Connie's condominium. "They just walked out, Marcus," she said. "There really wasn't anything else they could do."

"Goddamn." The deaths made Graver furious. He didn't feel exactly responsible for them, but he did feel connected to them somehow. They were deaths for which he felt a sense of guilt. Kalatis was at the root of two more acts of despair. The man was the angel of despair.

"What's happened to Kalatis's 'veiled' hits?" he asked. "A bomb, now this. What's going on here?"

"I'm wondering if it's him," Arnette said.

"Who, then? Geis?"

"Maybe. What puzzles me is the erratic pattern of the hits. They don't ring true. Bombing at the marina. Veiled hit on Hormann. Obvious assassination of Faeber. Either Kalatis is losing his grip . . . or someone with a heavier hand has stepped in."

"You're sticking with your 'government man' theory, then?"

"I don't know," Arnette admitted. "If there's a second hitter involved . . . if it's Geis . . . the government's coming unhinged."

"Before now I thought you were wrong," Graver said. "Now I think you're right, but I'm hoping you're wrong."

"I just don't know why—if I'm right about a second hitter—why is he playing into Kalatis's game? I mean, ideally Kalatis would have wanted Burtell and Sheck and Faeber dead anyway, as a part of his plan to burn his bridges. Why is someone stepping in and helping him out . . . so crudely?"

"I don't know," Graver said. "I don't know about any of that, but I do know I made a mistake by not pulling in Faeber. Honestly, I didn't anticipate that. I should have, I just didn't."

"What about Faeber—and the woman? Do you want us to put in an anonymous call to Homicide?"

"No," Graver said quickly. "That'll only bring everything down on me even faster."

"Jesus, baby, that's going to be a mess for that girl to find."

"I can't help that," Graver said.

There was a pause and then Arnette asked, "So what did you find out from your pilot then?"

He told her about their interview with Ledet and the options he and Neuman had been discussing.

"Well, you're probably right there," Arnette said. "This is going to be over by tomorrow morning. And I think you're right in assuming Kalatis is getting ready to disappear. I can't believe it. This has been one hell of an incredible run. Paula's still plowing through Burtell's account. He was thorough, Marcus. Everything's there. It's going to cause a sensation when you finally come out with it."

"It'll have to wait."

"What are you going to do?"

"I'm going after Kalatis. I'm going to try to turn Eddie Redden," Graver said. "What about Murray and Remberto?"

"What do you mean? You want to *use* them?"

"I want to know if they'd help me out."

"Do what?"

"I don't know. I just want to know if they'd be interested."

"Are you sure . . . you know what your doing, Marcus? No offense, but—"

"No offense taken," Graver interrupted. "If you don't feel good about it tell them so. I don't know any more than I'm telling you. I just want to know if I have anyone I can rely on if it looks like there's something I can do when the time comes. Guns blazing is hardly my style, Arnette, so don't worry about it. On the other hand, after what they went through at Connie's they know what kind of stuff they might expect. I just need some competent people who've at least been to a firing range in the last six months."

Arnette didn't say anything for a moment.

"Maybe they'll help you out," she said finally. "But probably not for the good of mankind. They've worked for the government before. It doesn't pay what it ought to for what you have to do. They may respect you, baby, but they've already given at the office."

"I can't pay them anything," Graver said, "but if I'm right about what we're going to be getting into here, we'll be picking up a lot of hot cash. Maybe millions. I could use some help keeping up with it."

Arnette was silent again. He knew she understood what he was saying. "Okay," she said. "I'll ask them."

"If they're interested, I'll have to have them here as soon as possible, but no later than four-thirty." He gave Arnette the address. "If they're coming, have them call me."

He disconnected and dialed Rayner Faeber's number. She answered, and he asked for Last. When Last came on, Graver said:

"This is for your ears only, Victor."

Last paused only a second. "Yeah, okay."

"I need your help. There's money in it." That was a bit of an exaggeration, Graver thought, but since Last was in the exaggeration business he ought to understand that. "If you want in you'll have to leave right now. I'll give you an address."

"I understand," Last said. "Give it to me."

Graver gave the address of a service station a couple of miles from where they were. He didn't trust the extension phones in Faeber's house.

"You need to be there at four o'clock," Graver said. "Okay?"

"I'll be there."

Graver hung up and looked at Neuman. "You okay with what's going on here?"

"So far," Neuman said.

It was the kind of response Graver appreciated. He could trust Neuman to tell him if it didn't smell right to him. With the exception of Last, who Graver thought would be the wild card in the operation, he knew he could expect the same from Murray and Remberto, if they decided to come in. They had seen a hell of a lot more of this sort of thing than he had.

"Okay, good," Graver said. The handset rang, and he answered immediately.

"Is this Marcus Graver?"

"Yes, I'm Graver."

"This is Remberto. We're on our way right now."

Disconnect.

Graver looked at his watch. It was ten minutes after three o'clock. An hour and fifty minutes before Eddie Redden was supposed to touch down at the small strip at Bayfield.

72

GRAVER SAT ON THE BACK PORCH WITH REMBERTO AND MURRAY. He had explained everything to them, trying to give them as much perspective as he could in a short time. All three men were sweating, all three men were drinking ice water, none of them wanting anything stronger which might cause even a momentary flicker in their judgment. Since Neuman had gone to pick up Last at the service station, Graver told them about Last, too. These were two men he could trust without reservation, and inasmuch as he could influence their opinion, he wanted them to have that kind of trust in him as well. The best way to get that, aside from having Arnette's endorsement, was to give them a clean view of the players and the circumstances, though the latter might change dramatically within the hour.

"What about the girl in there?" Murray asked. He sat up straight in his chair without leaning back, holding his glass in thick hands, the muscles in his arms and shoulders looking like they belonged to a man twenty years his junior. He had a ballpoint pen stuck in the neck of his plain white T-shirt, and an old Colt-Browning .45 service automatic stuck in the waist of his jeans. His face was so closely shaven it was slick, and his burr haircut, even though his widow's peak was thinning considerably, added to the air of no-nonsense professionalism that he exuded. Graver had no doubts about either the competence or the reliability of Murray.

"I thought I'd leave Last with her while we go to pick up Redden. I haven't thought about it beyond that. But I can't very well let her go."

"Good."

"And this Redden, he will be armed?" Remberto asked.

"Ledet says he will be."

Remberto was tall for a Latin, a little taller than Graver, rangy but with broad shoulders. A good-looking young man with thick black hair that was neatly barbered and combed, he wore slacks, a pale blue shirt, and a sport coat, all of which looked very much stressed after his hour-long sauna in Connie's courtyard. He wore a shoulder holster under his jacket with a Sig-Sauer like Graver's jammed into it and sat in his chair with a very relaxed and self-assured manner. But the stillness in his dark eyes belied a concentrated tension that he had acquired during his few, but densely experienced, years in undercover work and which now occupied the core of his personality.

Both men had kept their eyes on him since the moment they had walked out on the porch. For them there was no tendency to let their attention wander to the bay, the predictable reaction of anyone who sat on a porch with a beach view. But Remberto and Murray—Graver still didn't know their last names—had no curiosity about the water or the ship or the Gulf. They were only interested in Graver and what Graver had to say to them about the impending events.

"I've been behind a desk for a long time," Graver said, "and you two know more about the tactical end, but I've got a couple of suggestions about when it might be best to take him. Tell me what you think.

"The first good opportunity, it seems to me, is while he's refueling. Ledet says that at Bayfield the planes refill from a small tanker truck that pulls up to the hangars. Always two servicemen in the truck. I thought two of us could take their place. If that's not feasible maybe pose as other pilots, whatever, milling around the parking lot, the terminal office. Whatever it takes. The second opportunity would be at the restaurant where they eat. I've done that before, and I like it. It's easy to be on either side of him and have two guns on him before he suspects anything. Have Ledet sit at a table that would accommodate an easy approach.

"What I *don't* like about the second option," Graver added, "is that taking him at a restaurant would mean that he and Ledet would have to drive there alone in order to avoid raising any suspicion. Too great a chance for Ledet to think he could win a car chase . . . too much time for a lot of things to happen."

"No, I favor the airport too," Murray said.

"So do I," Remberto added, "but, if something goes wrong, if there is shooting, we will be risking fire with that fuel."

"Yeah, I thought of that," Graver said.

"What is his personality?" Remberto asked.

"I don't know, but judging from his telephone conversation, he's the one in control. Ledet seems to be going along, less concentrated. And, too, Redden's the one that Kalatis trusts, which says a lot. Kalatis seems to insist on personal contact with his three lead pilots."

"And we're just going to question the guy, is that it?" Murray asked.

Graver explained his situation regarding the bureaucracy he would have to negotiate in order to move officially against Kalatis.

"And while they're trying to work out the politics of such a move, Kalatis would vanish," he said. "And he wouldn't be the first big target to slip out the back door while the bureaucrats are trying to make up their minds. So, my intention in questioning Redden is to see if there's some way to salvage something out of this fiasco other than a long, drawn-out investigation that will wind down eighteen months from now with nothing to show for it but a few oversentenced small-timers."

He looked at them. "I'll be honest with you," he said. "I told Arnette they'd be moving money tonight, and they will be. But my sole concern here is Panos Kalatis. I want the money because Kalatis wants the money and my guess is wherever it is he's not far away. To me the money is nothing more than bait. I'm not going to be looking at that; I'm going to keep my eyes on the shadows."

He wasn't going to spell it out. He didn't think he had to.

"You're sure the cargo's not drugs," Murray said.

"Ledet says it's cash or people or both. Not drugs. According to him, these pilots never move drugs. That's another cell, another group."

"Goddamn," Murray said. "Organization."

"Yeah, and I don't think it's unusual for Kalatis to reorganize periodically or to change plans at the last minute. He expects everyone to keep up with this, not to be put off balance by last-minute shifts in time and place. I think Redden and his two counterparts are very good operationally. And since they know just about as much as anybody about Kalatis, I put them right up at the top. I really want these guys. They would be invaluable from an intelligence point of view."

Both men nodded, and it seemed as though they thought his proposition a reasonable one, if somewhat unorthodox. But then Graver guessed that neither of them was too fond of orthodoxy anyway, or they wouldn't be doing what they were doing.

Just then Graver's handset buzzed, and Neuman told them he was pulling up in front of the house.

The Pilatus PC-12 was indeed a beautiful aircraft, a long, sleek fuselage with wings mounted from its belly, the tips of the wings turned up like fins, the T-tail gaining extra support by a straight, sharp rib extending forward to the roof just behind the last of the eight port windows. Coming in from the Gulf and approaching the northwest-by-southeast runway, it looked like a sliver of ice falling into the lowering sun.

Graver sat in the car in the shade of one of several hangars flanking the runway where Redden had just touched down. Bayfield, he observed, was one of those airstrips that looked like it had been built during the 1940s to serve what had then been a remote naval station or some other wartime installation and then had been quickly superseded after the war by better installations that grew up nearer the expanding city of Houston. But somehow Bayfield did not die. One by one the four Quonset huts were replaced by corrugated tin hangars that quickly looked as old as the huts they replaced. A variety of men hangared a variety of planes there off and on over the years, and a pilot manqué who wore glasses with Coke bottle lenses ran the "tower," a two-room, cinder-block building with a radio and a picture window facing the strip. There were always a couple of guys hanging around working on old engines and to drive the fuel truck if someone dropped in and wanted to top off. Bayfield was almost deserted, but at the same time it was not unusual to see fancy planes parked there from time to time. They came and went. Nobody paid much attention.

Graver watched Ledet fifty yards away ease the Alfa Romeo along the skirt of the tarmac and stop at the opened doors of the hangar where Redden kept the Pilatus. Inside the hangar, Neuman was backed against the wall, watching Ledet only seventy-five feet away. A hundred and thirty yards away, inside the main hangar where Graver had already presented his credentials and impressed upon the four employees there the importance of cooperation and silence, Remberto and Murray were slipping into the bright orange overalls of the two airport mechanics who normally drove the small tanker truck. Remberto kept his eyes on another employee who was on the other side of a glass wall wearing headphones. The man gave Remberto a thumbs-up.

"There it is," Remberto said, zipping up the coveralls. "He just radioed for the fuel truck."

Using his handset, Murray relayed this to Graver as Neuman listened in, and then the two men climbed into the high-seated fuel truck, Murray behind the wheel, and pulled out of the shade of the hangar. Behind them, well back from the door, a clutch of men—the two tanker drivers, a mechanic, and the dispatcher—watched the unfolding scenario as though it was a spectator event with more than a hint of serious danger about it.

The sun glinted off the Pilatus as Redden turned at the end of the runway and began taxiing back toward the hangar, halfway up the tarmac.

Wearing sunglasses, Ledet got out of the Alfa and leaned back against its front fender and watched as Redden approached at a ninety-degree angle from the hangar and then twitched the flaps to swing the plane around so that it was headed straight into the open doors. He taxied the Pilatus almost to the door, the whine of the turboprop growing louder inside the hangar as it drew near, the powerful engine reverberating against the corrugated sheet metal walls. Then he cut the engine, and the turbo began its long whining wind-down.

Peering through a crack in the seams of the sheet metal, Neuman watched as Redden, his face unemotional behind dark aviator sunglasses, began gathering together miscellany from the cockpit, getting ready to open the door. Neuman shifted his eyes to Ledet who stood up from the car but didn't move away from it, while on the other side of him, behind the plane, the tanker truck advanced on the plane.

Neuman could see Redden crawling out of his cockpit seat into the center aisle, and then the full door behind the cockpit levered out and slid back against the body of the plane.

"Hey, Rick," Redden shouted, and jerked his head for Ledet to come over. Ledet hesitated. The fuel tanker was approaching the wing of the plane, and he didn't want to be anywhere around Redden when the guns came out. Inexplicably, he just pointed to the fuel truck.

Murray was pulling to a stop, and when he saw Ledet pointing at him he grabbed a clipboard off the dash of the truck and raised it and pointed to it. Redden looked toward the truck and saw the driver waving the clipboard. He laid something in one of the passenger seats, lowered the steps, and stepped down out of the plane. He was sandy-haired with a light, sun-flushed complexion. Though he was not a heavy man, he had a well-developed beer gut which was hardly camouflaged by his loose-fitting guayabera, a common garment for convenient handgun concealment. He wore cowboy boots and faded blue jeans, one leg of which was caught on the top of his boot revealing the boot's red leather top which served as the background for a hand-tooled Mexican eagle, its wings spread out on either side of the boot.

Murray and Remberto got down out of the truck, slammed their doors, and came around the end of the wing as Murray again raised the clipboard.

"They said you had paperwork to clear up before you could take on fuel," Murray said.

Redden looked around at Ledet. "What's this shit?"

Ledet shrugged.

Redden and Murray approached each other as Murray held out the clipboard, turning slightly as he did so to allow Remberto to approach Redden a few steps later than Murray and on Redden's blind side.

"I'm paid up. What the hell's the matter?" Redden said, grabbing the clipboard.

As soon as he jerked it out of Murray's hand, Remberto's arm went inside his bright orange overalls and came out with the Sig-Sauer, the muzzle of which went instantly into the fleshy reserve covering Redden's left kidney. Redden flinched, and as he did so the muzzle of Murray's .45 screwed into his stomach while at the same instant Remberto's left hand gripped his left arm just above the elbow.

"A forty-five and a nine-millimeter," Murray said, his face right up in Redden's. "And a Mac-10 right over there in the hangar."

As Redden rolled his eyes cautiously to look at Ledet, Neuman came out of the hangar with his gun leveled at Ledet who simply raised his hands in the air.

"Son of a bitch," Redden said. "Jeee-sus, I'm not believing this."

"Believe it," Murray said and his thick hand went around behind Redden and relieved him of the gun he had jammed into the back of his waistband. "Nine-millimeter . . . Beretta," Murray said before he had even brought it out in the open.

The instant Remberto's hand had gone into his overalls, Graver started the car and drove quickly across the tarmac, pulling up between Ledet's Alfa and the plane. He got out and came around the front of the car to where Redden was still trying to absorb the past twenty seconds. Graver handed a pair of handcuffs to Murray who stepped around behind Redden and cuffed him.

"Who the hell are *you?*" Redden demanded, leveling his dark lenses at Graver. His nose was hawk-beaked and raw from the sun. Graver guessed it didn't take much sun to be too much sun for Redden.

Graver reached out and took off Redden's sunglasses to reveal pale blue eyes and an extraordinarily woolly pair of ginger eyebrows. Redden immediately grimaced in the bright light.

"Shit," he said.

73

ON THE SPUR OF THE MOMENT GRAVER DECIDED NOT TO TAKE
Eddie Redden back to his house in Seabrook for questioning. Instead
he sat him down in the center of the empty hangar, his hands handcuffed behind his back, his legs crossed yoga fashion. He placed him so
that he faced the hangar's sliding doors that were pulled wide open so
that he had a good view of his precious Pilatus PC-12 fifty feet away.
Graver stood just to the side of the plane so that Redden just about had
to look at both of them when he spoke to Graver. The sheet metal
hangar was at its maximum heat level, having soaked up the coastal
sun all day long. Even though the huge doors were wide open, the
occasional breeze that slipped in was only a different way of feeling the
heat, and caused the hangar to function very much like a convection
oven.

Everyone removed their coats and hung them wherever they could
find a place, on a nail or over the handle of an hydraulic jack, or on the
hasp of a door latch. The empty hangar magnified their voices so that
no one really had to talk above a conversational tone to be heard.
Outside, the droning of cicadas and grasshoppers was interrupted occasionally by an airplane approaching or taking off. And occasionally,
too, when there was a pause in the talk, you could hear the sheet metal
walls of the hangar crackling and popping as they expanded in the
heat.

Eddie Redden was harder to deal with than Richard Ledet. For one
thing, he was not the sort of man who let his imagination play tricks
on him. He was long on common sense. You didn't convince him of
anything by trying to work on his anxieties—he didn't have any. He
seemed to face life with an unadorned philosophy of acceptance, a kind
of West Texas stoicism that had no use for breast-beating and wailing.
Sometimes life pissed on you, and sometimes it didn't. When it did,

you were unlucky. When it didn't, you were lucky. There wasn't anything you could do about it one way or the other. That could have been his credo. And in light of that, he had become adept at making the best of a bad situation. Life might piss on Eddie Redden, but he didn't moan about it. What he did was, he took a long soapy shower during which he gave some serious thought to how to stay the hell out of the way next time.

And that's what he was doing now, sitting cross-legged like an Indian—probably the first time he had done that since he was fifteen—trying to figure out how not to get pissed on any more than he already had.

Graver had laid it all out as methodically and dispassionately as he could, guessing that Redden would appreciate a right-to-the-bone explanation of his situation. Graver stated the facts like an accountant. The porno film with the little girls, the cocaine, the stolen ordnance, his employment by Kalatis, the weekly money jumps to the cruisers in the Gulf—Graver had the maps for documentation—the monthly money jumps to points south . . . for starters . . . enough right there to assure Redden that when he had taxied up to the hangar a few minutes ago he probably had piloted an airplane for the last time in his life.

Now Redden was thinking it over, breathing heavily—it wasn't easy to sit on a hot concrete floor with your legs crossed and your arms cuffed behind you while the too-tight waist of your blue jeans cut into your beer-induced and doughy overhang. He was sweating profusely, so much so that dribbles of it rolled down his forehead and clung to his ginger eyebrows like drops of salty rain. He had sweated through his guayabera which clung to his back and stomach, and the strain of his position was giving him something like a charley horse in his side, causing him to tilt slightly to try to ease it.

Redden was grunting softly with each breath. He looked up at his Pilatus PC-12. He shook his head. He grinned a little.

"Hey, Ricky," he said, speaking to Ledet who was sitting directly behind him in the same position, but out of his sight. "You cut a deal with these boys, didja?"

Neuman shook his head at Ledet.

When he didn't answer Redden grinned and said, "Shee-it."

Since they had walked into the hangar no one had said a word except Graver and Redden.

"Well," Redden said, shifting on his buttocks, trying to relieve the catch in his side. Sweat dripped off the end of his nose onto the concrete floor where it soaked up immediately. "The thing about cutting a deal is . . . the thing about this quid pro crow is . . . that I got to watch my back for the rest of my life."

"That's right," Graver said, wiping his face with his handkerchief. "But if you don't want to bother with that you can just spend the rest of your life in a cage."

Redden snorted. "Well, shit, we know where this is going, don't we? If I can help it I'm not about to spend the rest of my life in a cage." He grunted. "You sure it's really necessary to keep me cuffed up like this? Goddamn."

Graver stepped over in front of him and squatted down. He looked at him. "You smoke?"

Redden frowned. "Yeah, I smoke."

"Want a cigarette?"

"Yeah, I want a cigarette."

Graver looked at Neuman who went over to Ledet and took his cigarettes out of his shirt pocket, along with the disposable lighter.

"Take off one cuff," Graver said to Neuman who got the key from Murray and unlocked one cuff. As he did, Remberto loudly cocked the slide on his Sig-Sauer.

Redden flinched and then slowly turned his head toward the sound as he took the cigarette from Neuman and lit it. He looked at Remberto.

"You guys sure don't act like the law," he said. He didn't try to get up, but stretched his waist and shoulders, twisting this way and that.

"Okay," Graver said, still squatting in front of Redden, "tell me what's supposed to be happening tonight."

Redden was not given to dramatics, but his long pause before responding to Graver's question clearly reflected the pressure he was feeling from what he was about to do. It seemed that no one talked about Kalatis without behaving as though they were about to open the doors of hell. You just didn't do it unless you had no other choice.

"Kalatis has been working on some kind of a big business deal," Redden began. "I don't know anything about what the negotiations are over—drugs or information or arms, I just don't know—but the thing's going to be wrapped up tonight." He pulled on his cigarette. "Now, when something like this happens, these people he's dealing with are brought in to see Kalatis for the deal-maker meet. They bring their last cash payment with them. And usually, and this is just a peculiarity with the Greek, usually all this happens after midnight, early hours of the morning. That's just the way he likes to do it.

"The way it works is, these people, if they're from out of town, are put up in a hotel in Houston, and Kalatis's people pick them up and take them to whatever airstrip we're using."

"Do you always use the same ones?"

"Yeah"—Redden nodded—"all of them. On a kind of rotating basis, nothing regular. He keeps it random. But we'll use most of them sooner or later, West, Southwest, Clover Field, here, Gulf, Andrau, Hull, Ellington, Hobby, Intercontinental, Hooks, Midwest, Weiser— all of them.

"Anyway, these people and their cash are transported by Kalatis's security people from their hotel to the airport. They get in, the money's loaded, and we take off. Now, all these people think we're going to Mexico, somewhere down in there. But what we do is we take a two-hour diversionary. We keep them occupied in the cabin so they don't hear transmissions or see anything, even though it's at night, then we land at Kalatis's place if we're in a 'tooner—"

"A 'tooner?"

"Plane with pontoons—or we land at a little transfer strip, transfer to a 'tooner, and take it in."

"But you always go to Kalatis's in a plane with pontoons."

Redden gave a single nod. "Got to. He won't let that kind of stuff come in by car. Besides, it's part of the scam, them thinking they're in Mexico."

"Is there just one transfer strip or several?"

"One, just one. A place called Las Copas."

"But tonight is different?" Graver asked.

"Yeah, tonight is different," Redden said, nodding hugely, taking one last drag off the cigarette which he had smoked down to the filter. He mashed it out on the concrete beside him. He used the thumb of his right hand to squeegee the sweat off his forehead, the one loose handcuff making a jangling sound like Paula's bracelets.

"When there's several in one night like this, they all take off from the same airport. That way Kalatis's security people have to check out only one hangar. The timing is worked out so that the clients arrive one hour apart so there's plenty of time in between connections. None of the clients even know that Kalatis has met with anyone else that night. That's the way he does it."

Redden rocked on his buttocks again. "This is a hell of a place to sit down," he said. He shot a look of disgust at Remberto. "Shit. Okay." He used his thumb on his sweating forehead again. "Tonight all three are coming in at different airstrips."

"Which ones?"

Wade from Andrau. Maricio from Clover. I'm leaving from Hobby."

"And this will be after midnight?"

"Nope, not this time," Redden corrected. "That's another thing that's changed. First client will be here at ten-fifteen. Second one at eleven thirty-five. Third one, twelve fifty-five."

"That's"—Graver paused to calculate—"an hour and twenty minutes between each client arriving here."

"That's right."

"Why the change?"

Redden stared at the concrete in front of him for a moment, and then looked up at Graver.

"Well, actually, to tell you the truth," he said, "we were just a little worried about that point ourselves."

"We?"

"Me and Wade and Maricio . . . the three pilots. We've, uh, been watching all this, and it looks to us like Kalatis may be going to drop out of sight after tonight."

"Why do you think that?"

"There's a guy name of Sheck who used to fly with us," Redden said. "He's been with Kalatis a lot longer than the rest of us, and we kind of get together with him pretty regular and talk about Kalatis. Ol' Sheck's got some pretty good insights into the guy. He still works for Kalatis on some kind of secret shit they got going. Sheck seems to think he's winding down a lot of his operations here and that he's getting ready to do some kind of super scam and then just disappear. After these changes that have been developing today—first one thing, then another—me and the boys are getting a little skittish. I've been trying to get in touch with Sheck for the last four or five hours to run these last developments by him, but I can't find him."

"Did you read the paper this morning?"

Redden looked at Graver. "Yeah."

"Bruce Sheck blew up in one of those boats in South Shore Marina."

Redden blanched and his facial muscles went slack. "Blew up?"

"You know Colin Faeber?"

"Yeah."

"He was hit this afternoon."

" 'Hit'? Killed?"

"Gilbert Hormann?"

Redden nodded, already seeing it coming.

"He was hit last night."

Redden swallowed. His eyes looked like they would never blink again. He swallowed again.

"And three of my intelligence officers who were working on the case," Graver added without explanation.

Redden's stare dropped to the tarmac outside the doors of the hangar. "Sheck was goddamned right . . . the Greek's cutting himself loose. He's going to run."

"And where do you think his pilots fall into this scheme of things, Eddie? You think he's just going to let you go—with all you know about him?"

"Son . . . of . . . a . . . bitch." Redden seemed almost catatonic.

"This might have been your last day of flying anyway," Graver said.

Redden said nothing. He just stared at the tarmac that was dancing in the heat waves beyond his plane.

74

"TONIGHT," GRAVER SAID, BRINGING REDDEN BACK TO THE conversation at hand, "if you're going to be picking up the clients here, taking them on a two-hour 'diversionary' and then going into Las Copas, they'll be boarding pontoon planes there to hop over Chocolate Bay, right?"

Redden nodded. His rate and volume of perspiration seemed to have accelerated.

"How does that work? Does the pontoon plane pull up in the bayou there? There's a bayou nearby, isn't there?"

Redden nodded. "About seventy-five yards from the strip."

Neuman had rolled a car tire over and was sitting on the edge of it behind Redden. Murray and Remberto had pulled over a sawhorse and were sharing opposite ends of it. All of them sweating, all of them riveted to the conversation as they listened to Graver methodically extract every logistical detail.

"Anything different about the routine at this point?"

Redden nodded again, as if something was just now dawning on him, as if another piece of the Kalatis puzzle was falling into place.

"Yeah." He swallowed once more. "Yeah, normally the cash and the client are loaded onto the 'tooner and jumped over Chocolate Bay. When we get to Kalatis's pier, the client goes up to the house for his meet with Kalatis, and the cash is off-loaded onto a cruiser."

"Then what?"

"Cruiser takes the cash out to the Gulf rendezvous instead of the 'tooner. The 'tooner and pilot have to wait to jump the client back over the bay."

"You said 'when we get to Kalatis's pier.' You fly the pontoon plane too? There weren't other pilots for the pontoon plane?"

"No, we fly it. There's only one 'tooner. First pilot drops down on Las Copas, everything's loaded onto 'tooner, jump over Chocolate, jump back over Chocolate when client is through, pick up the regular plane and leave the 'tooner in the bayou for the next pilot and client. He does the same thing. The copilot on the last plane takes the 'tooner away. It's kept in a small Gulf-side hangar in Kemah."

"I assume someone stays with whatever plane is paused at Las Copas?"

"Oh, yeah, three of Kalatis's guards go to Las Copas by boat ahead of time. They take an electric generator and string lights along the strip. It's quite a job. The lights just come on momentarily during the landing, and then they're shut down again. The guards—they call them security—stay during the whole operation, just that one night, and help off-load the cash from one plane to the other and then 'secure' the plane that's not being used."

"Three guards, you said. Are there always three?"

"That's right. That's where Kalatis is different from your average, run-of-the-mill smuggler or bad guy. There'll be six armed guards, not fifteen or twenty. Just six. Three at Las Copas, three at his own dock. They're low-key kind of guys. In fact, every weapon they'll be carrying will be fitted with a silencer. The Uzi's, the Mac-10s, whatever they're carrying. Silencers. It's only common sense when you think about it. All those other cowboys like the sound of the blasting. Shit, with silencers you can do a lotta death before anybody even knows you're there. So they don't mind using them. I don't mean they're trigger-happy; I've never seen that. But they're not afraid of using them either."

Redden thought about that for a second and then he looked at Graver again. "Look, can I have another cigarette?"

Again Neuman took a cigarette from Ledet. When Redden had lit it, Graver went on.

"Okay, now, you said this time was going to be different."

"Yeah. This afternoon we had a meeting with Kalatis. The normal routine was suspended. Each one of us is going to have a slightly different schedule. Wade's first up. No diversionary—straight to Las Copas. Same routine at Las Copas, transfer client and cash to the 'tooner. But when he gets to Kalatis's, he drops off the money and the client and flies back to Las Copas without the client."

"Did Kalatis explain that?"

"He said the client's going into Galveston by cruiser, and then back to Houston by car."

"But what about the hoax of making them believe they were in Mexico?"

"Yeah, I asked about that. Kalatis said he'd hired me to fly planes, not to run his business." Redden grinned, the way a man grinned about a death threat instead of allowing himself to panic. "Anyway, so Maricio's next. Same thing, straight to Las Copas—"

"How long is that flight?" Graver interrupted.

"Half an hour. Maricio's 'tooner trip is the same as Wade's, drop off the cash and the client and back to Las Copas. I'm doing anchor. Same routine as the others."

A small plane that had landed on an opposite runway came wheezing by the hangar. It was the first one that had come close since they had been there, and they all turned and looked at it. Graver turned back to Redden. The pilot was staring at the nose gear of his plane. Graver guessed he was reworking what he had just told them about the night's schedule. He imagined that in light of what he had learned from Graver about the other deaths, Redden was having second thoughts about the implications of the new schedule.

"Let's get back to the guards," Graver said. "When the client comes to the airport and gets on the plane with his money, does he have guards who go along to guarantee the delivery?"

"No, huh-uh. That's not part of the deal. Kalatis hates high profile, hates all those guys strutting around carrying automatic shit. Deal is, when you bring your money on board Kalatis's planes Kalatis is responsible from there on. If you don't trust him by this time, don't give him your money."

"But what about traveling to the airport?"

"Kalatis allows the client to have two guards travel to the airport from the hotel. One of Kalatis's men is with them. The plane is inside the hangar. We open the door, the car drives in. All the loading is done in here out of sight. The client's heavies have to leave before we'll take off."

"Then there is one guard who makes the actual trip with the money."

"Right."

"Then Kalatis actually will have four guards at Las Copas."

"Yeah, I guess that'd be right. Three on the ground, one in the plane. But that one guard always stays with 'his' load. He goes on to Kalatis's pier. That poor bastard's life is tied to each box of money. If he loses one, he loses the other—sooner or later."

"You don't think there will be changes in the guards' routines too, like there were in yours?"

"I can't say about that. I just know it wasn't mentioned when we were going over the plans."

"What about the amount of time you've got to make the pontoon flight from Las Copas to Kalatis's beach house and back to Las Copas? Is that enough time?"

"Shit, barely. It'll be damn close. The jump across Chocolate and West Bay's not the problem. It's the time on Las Copas going in, off-loading the client and cash, going the seventy-five yards to the 'tooner and on-loading the client and cash. They're giving us twenty minutes on that, then there's the fifteen-minute jump to Kalatis's dock, ten off-loading at the dock, fifteen-minute jump back to Las Copas, ten to dock the 'tooner, get back to our planes, and get outta there. Then they've given us a ten-minute cushion from the time one plane leaves to go home and the other lands on Las Copas."

"And that's not enough."

Redden dragged on the cigarette and then shook his head as he pulled down the corners of his mouth. "Nope, not enough. Doesn't leave time for screw-ups . . . There's always screw-ups, especially when you're running out of a little ol' dirt strip like Las Copas. You've got to be careful with radio contact in there. It's crazy. And those damned generator lights. It's gonna be touchy."

Graver nodded and studied Redden a moment.

"Okay," he said. "What about a contingency plan? What happens if something goes wrong somewhere along the line?"

"Yeah, always a backup plan. Actually there are two." He used the toe of his boot to tap an ash off the cigarette. "If something goes wrong before the money's delivered, we call a coded number and tell Kalatis what happened. He makes a decision. If he's going to change airports, he's got to coordinate the money delivery, and he's got to make sure the guard who's going to be baby-sitting that load knows the score. Then he calls us back and tells us the alternate pickup site.

"If something happens *after* the pickup, there's a prearranged des-tination. It's prearranged because after we're airborne everybody's got to be thinking the same thing. Personnel will be spread thin because the guys at the original drop site—Las Copas—will be out of pocket. Kalatis's troops will be spread thin. That's another reason the in-flight alternate destination will be the same for all three pilots. Kalatis wouldn't have enough people on the ground to spread them out to cover three alternate delivery sites."

Graver looked at him. "You mean everyone meets at one airport."

"That's right. But the timing stays the same."

"Which airport?"

Redden raised his hand dangling the handcuffs and pointed an index finger down to the concrete in front of him.

"I'm sittin' on it," he said.

Graver stared at Redden. "Have you ever had to use a contingency plan?"

"Once."

"How did it go?"

"Clockwork." He shrugged. "Everybody's a professional. They can handle contingencies."

Graver nodded. The tin walls of the hangar crackled in the heat.

"Did you tell Kalatis you had your doubts about the schedule of the timing at Las Copas?"

Redden nodded stoically. "Yep."

"What did he say?"

Redden's expression was grim. He took a last pull on the cigarette and mashed it out next to the other butt on the concrete.

"He doubled our fee," he said. "Hell, we were already getting paid like damn CEOs, now we're getting paid like *two* damn CEOs." He looked around at Remberto and then back at Graver. "Just goes to show you, don't it. You pay a guy enough money, and he'll risk hell and high water to do the job. The bigger the money gets, the more he tells himself he can beat the odds . . . even if the odds get bigger too. All he can think about is coming out on the other end—smelling like brimstone and steam—with all that tax-free cash."

75

7:50 P.M.

THE FIVE OF THEM SAT ON THE VERANDA FACING THE BAY. PIZZA boxes and hamburger carry-out sacks were scattered around on the small rattan tables along with cans of soft drinks. Graver leaned back in his chair and looked through the kitchen into the main room of the oversized bungalow where Redden and Ledet were sitting in the middle of the floor, their ankles and wrists cuffed together, looking like hostages in the fading light. Alice was handcuffed too, but she was in the bedroom watching television. She had been told she was a material witness, and it was necessary to hold her for a while longer. Not being too bright, Alice accepted this without demanding to see a lawyer or screaming about her rights. And it helped that she had the television. It turned out she liked television a lot.

When they first arrived at the beach house and secured the three people inside, everyone had gone to the veranda and handed out the pizza and hamburgers. Graver had explained to Victor Last, who had remained with Alice, what had happened, and Last had listened without asking too many questions. Graver could tell that Last had sensed that questions were not the proper thing at this point in the proceedings, though it was not clear to Last just exactly what the proceedings were. Which was fine.

Then they had eaten their food, which was quickly growing cold, and talked about how Redden and Ledet's stories had jibed and what they thought about Kalatis's security, what they thought about his elaborate planning, what size plane the others might fly, and what the airspeed of the planes might be. In short, they talked about everything except the most important thing on their minds—what they were going to do—a matter that was totally absorbing Graver's thoughts as he ate in silence, staring out to the dying light in the bay, while the others talked.

After finishing his hamburger, Graver sat back in his chair and opened his notebook. He started jotting down an outline of the schedule of flights, when each pilot left Bayfield, landed at Las Copas, off-loaded and on-loaded cash and clients to the pontoon plane, departed Las Copas and arrived at Kalatis's pier, off-loaded cash and clients, and returned to Las Copas. At each juncture he noted the timing as related by Redden, keeping in mind that it was a schedule to which Redden doubted they could adhere. The plan was tight and efficient. But something about it was terribly wrong.

"Okay," he said finally, leaning forward in his chair and holding his notes in his hands in front of him, his forearms resting on his knees. Everyone stopped talking, wadded last bits of paper, put away boxes and sacks from in front of them.

Graver began reading the flight plans, stopping once in a while to listen to someone's different recollection of what Redden had said was going to happen at a particular point. In this way everyone reviewed a plan that was confirmed by consensus, no points remaining so unclear that anyone thought it was necessary to go back to Redden for clarification. When Graver was through he sat back in his chair again.

"Any observations?"

There was a momentary pause, and then Murray spoke up.

"Yeah, one." He was careful to keep his voice down. He wiped his mouth one last time with a paper napkin, wadded the napkin, and tossed it into a paper sack between his feet. "I personally think that seventy-five percent of this plan is total bullshit."

Graver almost smiled with relief. "So do I," he said. "Let's hear it."

"First of all," Murray said, passing a thick hand over his short haircut, "Kalatis has got this thing on a schedule that looks too tight. We know how Redden feels about this." He pulled his chair a couple of feet closer to Graver so he wouldn't have to worry so much about being overheard by the two men inside the bungalow.

"Second, Kalatis has decided to give up his gimmick about living somewhere in Mexico. Now this is a game he's gone to a lot of trouble to keep up for months, maybe a year or more. And now, at the last minute before bringing in the last of the big money, he's going to let all these people know where he really lives?" Murray shook his head. "No way. I don't buy that. Even if he is skipping out, I don't buy that.

"Third, he's changing—*at the last minute*—a schedule that has worked like clockwork for all this time. Why, right before his biggest haul, would he risk running an all-new schedule which is so complex that it is almost guaranteed to break down somewhere?

"Fourth, if I were in Kalatis's shoes, I'd be simplifying my last deal, just to make sure I didn't screw it up, instead of making it more complex. Or, I'd just leave it alone.

"Fifth, judging from Redden's account, Las Copas is as remote as hell." Murray was leaning forward toward Graver, and he turned and looked at Remberto. "What I think," he said, "is that the first stop at Las Copas is the last stop . . . for everybody."

Graver looked at Remberto who gave a very small nod of agreement, and then at Neuman who was stunned, and then at Last who was looking like he wanted to break out in a sweat.

"That's what I think too," Graver said.

"They're going to kill *all* of them at Las Copas?" Neuman was incredulous. "The clients . . . and the pilots . . . and the copilots?"

Graver nodded. "Yeah. I think the reason Kalatis wasn't concerned about how the tight schedule was going to work was because it didn't matter. The clients, the pilots, and the money—all stop for the last time at Las Copas."

"Goddamn . . ." Neuman was shaken.

"Yeah, and I think that was dawning on Redden too," Murray said. "That guy's no dimwit."

"What about the planes? They'd have four planes there," Neuman said.

"Probably only three," Graver said. "The pontoon plane might not even be needed. And they'll just have other pilots to take them away. But Redden, Maricio, Wade and their copilots know too much about this particular operation. The new pilots, they'll just be hired to pick up some planes at an old dirt strip. That's all they'll know. And they're not going to ask a lot of questions. The money's too good, like Redden said."

"And when it is all over," Remberto added, looking at Neuman, "there will be only three witnesses: the security guards who will do all the shooting. You can bet they will be paying those boys a percentage of the money brought in on the three planes. You have to pay people like that very well. You never let your tigers get too hungry."

"The question is, what's the best way to break this up," Graver said. "There're only five of us." He hesitated. "I see two chances. One: We leave now, immediately, for Las Copas. Ambush the guards when they come in early to string the lights, and then intercept each of the planes as it comes in. We'll have to get the 'all clear' signaling arrangements from one of the guards.

"But there are some immediate risks and problems with this idea. There can be only four of us at Las Copas. One of us would have to stay with Redden who would have to fly the other four in, drop them off, and get back to Bayfield. Also, we'd have to leave immediately to get to Las Copas as early as possible if we hope to beat Kalatis's guards there. Actually, it may be too late for that already. I'd guess Kalatis's three men would want to be at Las Copas plenty early to set up." He looked at his watch. "It'll be getting dark in less than an hour.

"Or two: to intercept them at each of the airports, right after the client's guards have left after unloading the client and the money. There would be only one guard to deal with in this scenario." He looked down at his notes. "The problem with this second course of action is that we'd get to intercept only one load of money and one client, because when that first plane—Wade's—doesn't reach Las Copas on schedule, Kalatis will be notified, and he'll send someone to see what went wrong. We'd have to forget about being able to intercept the other two loads of cash.

"And," he added, "it doesn't achieve my objective. I'm betting Kalatis will be attracted to that cash like a shark to blood. He's going to show up where there's the most of it."

Everyone thought about this for a while, running through the course of action, imagining each phase.

"What if we rode into Las Copas on the first plane?" Murray suggested. "We'd have only the one guard to deal with at Andrau, and when we got to Las Copas and overpowered the guards there we could radio to Kalatis that everything was on schedule. We could intercept Maricio. Redden wouldn't even have to take off. We'd have all three loads in one place."

"That's good only if we are right about what is supposed to happen at Las Copas," Remberto interjected. "If we are wrong, Kalatis will know something is wrong by eleven thirty-five when the first plane fails to arrive at his pier."

Graver drummed a finger on his notebook. "And I'm afraid we'll find more than three guards at Las Copas," he said. "If we do, we'll be trapped in that plane, maybe in a cross fire. And if we're right about them taking out everybody after landing, we don't know just how they're going to do that. They could have everyone get off and kill them right there on the dirt strip without even coming out of the brush. Then what?"

The haze of the dying evening extended in both time and space until it seemed to have swallowed the horizon in its progress toward the smoky sheen of dusk. It was as if the world ended just there, a little ways out in the bay, and the thick hoar of the Gulf summer evening spilled over an imperceptible edge into the cosmos. Seagulls screaked, invisible in the limitless, timeless gray.

"I don't see how we can do it," Graver said, finally. He dropped his notebook on the floor at his feet and rubbed his face with his hands. "I just don't think we can risk it. Too many unknowns, too little time. It could end in a disaster."

For a moment the only sounds that could be heard on the veranda were the shrills of the seagulls and the uncertain gasping of the surf.

"Well," Remberto said, his voice low, just above the surf, but clear and steady, "if you want all the cash at one place because you think it will bring in Kalatis, then I think there's another way we can do this."

76

10:40 P.M.

RICK LEDET BANKED THE CESSNA 185, AND NEUMAN LOOKED across the cockpit past him, out the window, and down at the black space that Ledet assured him was Chocolate Bay.

"I see the strip," Ledet said, pulling the Cessna back up to parallel with the horizon. They were headed back toward Houston and Neuman could tell by the glow from the city lights that they were upright again. "I'm going to bank again and head back toward the Gulf. Then I'll throttle down and do some turns, and every time I say so, you fire one off. We'll light 'em up like a damn firefight."

"Okay," Neuman said. It was all he could say. It was amazing how quickly up and down disappeared at night. He was gripping the box of military parachute flares between his knees in the cockpit seat, and the gun was cocked open. He jammed a flare into the breach.

"I thought if I made a couple of passes they might give us a flash," Ledet said. "Assholes. I should've known better. Disciplined bastards. It doesn't matter. I've made that strip enough times . . . hell, I can even see the bayou. Okay, hang on."

The Cessna banked and dropped at the same time, but it didn't drop far before Ledet leveled it out, and Neuman could see ahead of them the half moon on the Gulf. Jesus, it was a beautiful sight. The beauty of it surprised him.

"You ready?" Ledet yelled. "This first one's going to be for spotting."

Neuman pulled back the window flap, slapped closed the flare gun, braced it in the window, and cocked it. He felt the engine of the Cessna trim down and then Ledet yelled, "Fire one."

Neuman pulled the trigger. The whump filled the cockpit with its concussion.

"Holy shit!" Ledet laughed. "Whoooooeeeee! Look at that!"

The flare exploded in the night sky outside the plane with surprising brilliance. Phosphorous white. The parachute made the light bobble in the black, and then it settled to a gentle swinging back and forth like a lantern as it descended.

"God I'd love to be down there right now. Don't you know those assholes are *shitting!*"

Neuman was reloading.

"Okay, yeah!" Ledet yelled, confirming their positioning by the flare's illumination of the bayous below them. "Awww riiight! We're right on! Fire two!"

Neuman fired. Whump! The sky burned angel white. Neuman reloaded.

"Fire three!"

The Cessna was banking again and Neuman could feel the structure shuddering against the torque of the turn. He tried to ignore it as he reloaded and fired again . . . and again . . . and again. The maneuver was a blur in time. He had no idea how long it lasted, but as he felt gravity sling him first one way and then another, as he fired every time he heard the word fire and reloaded every time he finished, he watched the trails of the propellants followed by the explosion of the flares, and then the giant sphere of white light hanging in darkness, a darkness which, in contrast to the intruding flares, was no longer murky darkness but solid pitch.

He felt the plane bank one more time. The box of flares was empty. He looked out the window and saw half a dozen floating fires drifting laterally away from him through the darkness. It looked as if they had set fire to a corner of the night, and the fire was so dazzlingly bright that he almost expected to see it ignite the rest of the sky, all the way to daylight.

10:50 P.M.

Wade Pace had scanned the instrument panel of his Malibu Mirage for the tenth time and, satisfied with what he saw, took the time to look out the side window of his cockpit at the Houston skyline slipping away to his left. His copilot was doing the same. Wade turned and looked over his right shoulder at the passengers behind him. The client sat uneasily in the first pair of seats, also looking out his window at the skyline, and behind him in the next pair of seats was Kalatis's human Doberman, looking straight back at him. The Doberman wasn't interested in the view. Wade turned back to his panel of dials.

"Shit," he said to his copilot and shivered. The copilot nodded slowly and widened his eyes.

"Malibu. Malibu. This is Com One."

Wade instinctively put one hand up to his headphones and frowned in puzzlement at his copilot. They both recognized Kalatis's voice.

"Malibu, this is Com One. Do you read me?"

"Yeah, Com One, this is Malibu. Go ahead."

"There is an intrusion at your destination." Kalatis's voice was slow and deliberate. "Proceed to alternate field."

Wade shot his copilot a look of astonishment.

"Malibu, do you read me?"

"This is Malibu, I read you. I am now proceeding to alternate destination." He paused. "You need to confirm this with on-board security. Stand by."

Wade turned and looked back over his right shoulder again and met the gaze of the Doberman. He tapped his headphones and motioned for the Doberman to come up. The man unhurriedly unbuckled his seat belt and stood, crouching as he started forward. His face was expressionless—it was always expressionless. When he stopped behind Wade's seat his bulk filled the entire aisle space.

"You'd better listen to this," Wade said as the copilot took off his headset and handed it to the Doberman who was now leaning inside the cockpit. "It's Com One. Identify yourself first," Wade said, as the man put on the headset and adjusted the microphone.

"This is Malibu security."

Wade remained half-turned in his seat and watched him as he listened to Kalatis relate the exact same words he had just told Wade. The Doberman had no reaction. He simply said:

"Malibu security confirms a Com One directive to proceed to alternate destination."

That was it. He jerked off the headset and gave it to the copilot and turned around and went back to his seat. Wade rolled his eyes at his copilot. Kalatis had a collection of these kinds of guys. It was like having a collection of ugly beetles. They all talked in this quasi-military jargon, and they all took themselves very seriously. Well, shit, they were carrying a lot of money.

The copilot gave Wade the new coordinates, and he put the Malibu into a long, gentle bank. The pile of glitter that was downtown Houston slowly changed its orientation outside Wade's window. Now it was more forward, and it would stay that way until he banked one more time and headed into the runway. Then the city lights would be directly in his line of sight, just above the instrument panel. Now, with the change of plans, the new ETA put them thirty-five minutes out.

Panos Kalatis sat shirtless in his radio room, staring at the panel of dials in front of him, and calculating the odds of the success of several alternative moves. Suddenly he was perspiring, but he was as calm as a philosopher. The report of the flares over Las Copas had been entirely unexpected and had initiated a flurry of activity at the beach house. Jael was now hurrying back and forth between the house to the twin-engine pontoon plane waiting at the dock, loading last-minute cargo which included everything from their next change of clothes to the codebooks of Kalatis's foreign bank accounts. The final hours had arrived, a little ahead of time, to be sure, but not unplanned for.

He always had overplanned his operations, and they always had proceeded with a smoothness in which he took a great deal of pride. Tonight had been no different. Instead of three security guards at Las Copas, he had six. They were his most trusted employees and had been with him longer than anyone, even longer than he and Strasser had been together. All six of them were pilots and any of them could have flown the Malibu or the Mooney MSE or the Pilatus. Which, of course, was all part of the plan. All of them would have taken part in the executions.

But now, none of them would, and what was worse, they had gone into Las Copas by boat. For all practical purposes, they were out of the picture for good. Even if the flares were not a raid, even if they were some kind of diversion and nothing else happened—which Kalatis doubted—his six most reliable men would never be able to make it back in time to help him. Kalatis was about to accelerate the evening's events. He would now have to rely heavily on the three men he had been planning to have killed on Las Copas, the three guards who were responsible for getting the money and the clients from the hotels to the airports. But that did not bother Kalatis. They did not know he had been planning to kill them, so there was no harm done.

Nor did Kalatis allow himself to agonize over who was responsible for the "raid" at Las Copas. He assumed it was Graver. He wondered if Burtell had been alive if he would have given him a call. He wondered how deeply five hundred thousand dollars had burned into Burtell's sorry soul. Well, it didn't matter. What did matter was that he had a security leak, and the prospect of losing the nearly forty million dollars that soon would be in the air on the way to Bayfield began to nag at him. He already had sent two times that much out in the last week, but two thirds was never as good as one hundred percent, and Kalatis would take some risks for one hundred percent.

Picking up the white telephone, he first called a number in La Porte and left a code number. Momentarily his blue telephone rang. The return call was from a man, a Texan, Kalatis had known briefly in Buenos Aires in 1981. In 1985 the man had opened a trucking business in La Porte. In 1990, the man received a telephone call from Kalatis. Since then, Kalatis had not spoken to the man more than four or five times, but when he did the man "rented" one of his trucks to Kalatis for an exorbitant amount of money. Cash.

Kalatis picked up the white telephone again and called Maricio Landrone's code number. Within moments the blue telephone rang.

"This is Landrone."

"Maricio, are you at the hangar?"

"Yes, I'm here."

"There's been a foul-up at the original destination. We are going to use the alternate plan." Kalatis spoke slowly, almost casually. He had learned a lifetime ago, in the Mossad, that the very first step in controlling your men was in controlling your voice. For most men—and women—fear and panic were infectious. If they detected the virus of fear or uncertainty or futility, it was likely they also would contract the disease. It was the first responsibility of a group leader never to expose your people to the virus, even if you yourself were dying of it.

"The alternate destination remains the same," Kalatis said, "but the timetable is suspended. I want you to leave right now. The cargo will be ready at its hangar when you get there. Load and leave as soon as you can."

"Okay," Maricio said. "I've got it."

Maricio had flown cocaine for Kalatis for two years before he took over one of the money runs a year earlier. He was very good at last-minute changes.

Kalatis picked up the white telephone again and called Eddie Redden. Almost immediately the blue telephone rang and Kalatis gave the same information to his third pilot. When he hung up, he looked at his watch. The first load should be arriving at Bayfield in Wade Pace's Malibu Mirage in just over twenty minutes. With luck, the last one would breeze in on Eddie Redden's Pilatus somewhere around twelve-fifteen. Maricio Landrone's flight would be the questionable one. There was not much difference in the distance Landrone and Redden had to fly. It was possible they could come in on top of each other at Bayfield. Kalatis had no idea how they might handle that. And he wasn't going to worry about it. As of this moment he had done all he could do. From here on, whether or not he got his money was going to depend on other people.

He heard the twin engines on the pontoon plane sitting at the dock revving to a pitch that sounded to him like the sweet whine of escape. He could almost smell the burnt fuel thrown off the heated engines, a smell that reminded him of other nighttime assignments, years of adrenaline-driven timetables and rendezvous where trusting other people to hold up their end of the bargain was the only hope he had of getting out alive.

"Panos."

Kalatis turned and saw Jael standing in the doorway through the bedroom. She was wearing a man's white shirt tucked into a pair of jeans, her black hair pulled back into a single thick braid that dropped down the center of her back.

"We must go," she said. "The pilot say we must go if we want to see."

"Okay," Kalatis said. "Have you got everything?"

"Everything, yes," she said.

"Then go on down to the plane. I'll be right behind you."

"Everything" actually translated to very little. They were literally walking out of the door and away from a fully furnished house, closets filled with clothes, televisions, stereos—everything that made up a person's life. He felt marvelous, like a snake shedding its skin. It was an exhilarating experience, to walk away from everything.

He bent down under the desk on top of which were stacked tens of thousands of dollars of electronic equipment, radio and telephone equipment that had allowed him to communicate secretly with his people for nearly four years, and turned a timer dial on a metal canister about the size of a shoe box. It was actually a cake of enhanced C-4, a solid block of it. Wires leading from it led to two other cakes elsewhere in the house. He carefully felt the subtle clicks on the dial and set it on twelve minutes. By the time the dial reached "0" again they would be miles out into the Gulf, and the explosion would be a thing of beauty, viewed from afar.

77

THERE WAS VERY LITTLE WITH WHICH MARCUS GRAVER COULD salve his conscience about what he was doing. No matter what he told himself, he could not shake the anxiety of circumventing the system— he couldn't say circumventing the rule of law since that so often was obscured even within the system. And even more disconcerting to him was his knowledge that he had allowed himself to take matters this far because of a personal obsession with Panos Kalatis. If he had been professionally dispassionate he would not be taking these risks. A more reasoned plan would have recognized the imbalance of risk and objective. They already had a wealth of information that would enhance the intelligence holdings of several agencies. It would have been more prudent to wait for another time when he, not Kalatis, would define the closing gambit.

But Graver did not wait.

According to Redden, whenever the alternate plan kicked into play, the situation at Bayfield was not entirely known to the pilots. Their instructions were to taxi to hangar No. 2 and unload the money into a truck that would be waiting there. The client and the guard would stay with the money. The pilots could leave. And that was the end of the affair as far as they were concerned.

The hangar, luckily, had a back room, which was the rear end of the hangar partitioned off and having a flat ceiling which formed a loft under the high-pitched roof of the hangar itself.

Inside this back-room "office" Graver, Murray, and Last waited. There was a door in the partitioned wall and a sash window covered with a glaze of dirt and two walnut-sized clods of dirt dauber's nests. The place smelled of undisturbed dust and oil as they stood among stacks of used tires and misshapen cardboard boxes filled with disassembled parts of old airplanes. Just outside the partitioned office,

Remberto hid in the corner formed by the walls of the office and the hangar, wedged between another stack of old tires and an aluminum flat-bottomed boat which was leaning against the front wall of the office. The tin walls of the hangar were still crackling but now it was because the tin was cooling down from the day's heat.

They had not been in their places more than ten minutes, having hurriedly hidden the two cars in adjacent hangars, when a truck approached along the caliche road that led from the highway three miles away. From the sound of its revving engine, the driver was in a hurry, the sound growing louder until the truck roared up to the closed doors of the hangar and stopped. While the engine idled, a door opened, and someone quickly approached the hangar doors and started fiddling with the latch. Then suddenly the doors slid apart and a man stood between the headlights of a panel truck, its high beams illuminating the glaze of dirt on the office window. Graver and the others pulled back in the shadows.

For a moment Graver thought the man was going to search the hangar, but then he turned, got back into the truck and drove it into the hangar and cut the lights and the engine. Again the man got out of the truck and went back to the hangar doors and pulled them closed, or nearly closed, leaving a space of about a foot between them. He stood in the opening looking out and nervously took out a cigarette and lit it, blowing the smoke out the opening into the darkness.

Then, immediately, there was the distant sound of an airplane. The driver heard it too and threw down his cigarette, shoved the doors a little farther apart and stepped out. The sound of the plane grew louder as it approached until it changed tone slightly and suddenly burst low over the hangar and continued out over the Gulf.

The man hurried back inside the hangar, went to an electrical box installed on the wall to the right of the doors, and threw a switch. Through the larger separation of the doors, Graver could make out a string of weak lights spaced far apart along either side of the runway. It appeared to be a makeshift lighting system. The landing strip itself was very obviously only a daytime landing field. The man returned to the door, stepped outside, and looked either way.

Almost immediately the sound of the plane returned, but this time it was coming from the direction of the Gulf. Graver listened to it, imagining the aircraft coming in low over the water and leveling off. He heard it trimming its speed, the tone of the engine deepening, and then it cut way down, and the plane was on the tarmac. Graver saw the lights flick past the crack in the door as the plane wheezed to taxiing speed, revved slightly as it turned, and headed toward the hangar.

As the sound of the taxiing engine approached, the driver of the van began pushing aside the two hangar doors until they were wide open, and the plane taxied up to the opening until its nose was almost inside the hangar. Then the pilot cut the engine, and the prop feathered to a standstill.

The driver slapped open the latches on the back doors of the van, and flung them open. At the same time the door to the airplane, which was situated almost midway in the fuselage and contained the second window back from the cockpit, opened from its middle, the top half hinged at the top swinging up and out of the way while the bottom half folded down to make steps.

Graver watched with one eye peering through the dirty window as a large man wearing a sport coat without a tie and carrying an Uzi equipped with a silencer was the first to disembark.

"Everything okay here?" he asked, standing at the bottom of the steps and looking at the back of the truck where an interior light was throwing a splash of illumination on the concrete floor of the darkened hangar.

"I'm ready to load up," the driver said from inside the back of the truck, but not exactly responding to the guard's question.

The guard nodded unenthusiastically, and looked around as the pilot—Wade Pace, Graver reminded himself—came down the steps followed by a man who must have been the copilot, followed by a man in a business suit who was unsteady and unsure about coming down the narrow steps of the plane.

Pace came up to the back of the truck and looked in.

"I've got eight boxes," he said.

"Okay, fine. Bring 'em out, and I'll stack 'em in the back here."

Pace looked at the guard who was standing near the door of the plane now. The guard looked back at him.

"Go ahead," the guard said, jerking his head toward the steps of the plane.

"We could use a little help," Pace said.

The guard gave a jerk of his head that said tough luck and checked the silencer on the Uzi as if to make sure it was secure.

Pace hesitated, still looking at the guard, then turned and started to the steps of the plane.

"I want to call Kalatis about this," the client said, standing awkwardly near the hangar door. He was visibly jittery, one hand on his hip, the other one wiping his face. "This sort of thing's never happened before. This is a hell of a long way from Mexico."

"We can't risk radio contact from here," the guard said. "Security is Mr. Kalatis's special expertise. He knows what he's doing."

The client clearly knew he was in no position to demand anything. If his money was being stolen right now, there was nothing he could do about it, and he would be lucky not to be shot. If it wasn't being stolen, if this was a legitimate security maneuver, then he ought to keep his mouth shut and not alienate the people who were trying to protect his money.

Pace swore and climbed into the plane. In a moment he began handing out banker's boxes to the copilot. The client watched them. It apparently didn't occur to him that he might help, or if it did he had decided that it wasn't his job either. No one said anything else until Pace handed down the last box to the copilot who lugged it to the back of the van and plopped it down on the carpeted floor at the rear door.

"That's it," Pace said, coming down the steps. "We're outta here."

"You remember what to do?" the guard asked.

"I think I can manage," Pace said, pissed at the guard's surly haughtiness.

"You've got the coordinates . . . fifteen miles out, and then you can do whatever the hell you want."

"Let's go," Pace said to his copilot, and the two of them slowly pushed the plane back away from the hangar doorway into the darkness at the edge of the tarmac.

In the dim light coming from the back of the van, Graver could barely make them out climbing back into the plane and pulling the steps up behind them. In a minute the plane engine kicked alive, and Pace revved it to a whine, held it a minute and then maneuvered his flaps to turn the plane toward the tarmac where it taxied toward the end of the runway. He squared for the takeoff, revved his engine, and then the plane was barreling down the runway and lifting off over the water toward the Gulf the way it had come in.

The guard, the van driver, and the client stood just at the edge of the splash of light and watched the plane's lights disappear into the stars, and then the guard turned, lifted his Uzi, and shot the other two men.

The two muted bursts were startling, the rapid thupping sounds incongruously matched to their effect, which was to cause blood to spray from the two men's backs while simultaneously knocking them cleanly off their feet.

Graver felt Murray and Last flinch on either side of him, and as it happened his mind rapidly registered a decision to do nothing: It would do no good to shoot the guard now. They could not prevent the two deaths they had just witnessed. If they could have anticipated that and prevented it then shooting him would have been justified. But now, the guard was more use to them alive. Graver was grateful for Remberto's training. Another man might have shot the guard instantly.

So they watched as the guard slung the Uzi over his shoulder by its strap, came into the hangar, and cut off the runway lights. Then he went back outside, grabbed the feet of the client, and dragged him out of the light and around the corner of the hangar. After a while he returned and grabbed the feet of the van driver and dragged him away also. When he returned, he stepped to the side of the hangar doors, picked up a garden hose that was coiled there, turned on the hydrant to which the hose was attached, and started washing away the considerable amount of blood from in front of the doorway and into the darkness.

THE SIXTY-FIVE-FOOT *SPHINX* ROCKED GENTLY IN THE WARM waters of the Gulf Stream. The pontoon plane had gone, and Kalatis and Jael sat on the deck with binoculars, their feet on the railing gazing at a specific coordinate to the northwest. The area they were watching was fifteen miles off the coast and might as well have been fifteen hundred miles off the coast. It was the middle of nowhere and didn't exist at all until someone drew the navigational coordinates on a map to define it. For three hundred and sixty degrees there was nothing but emptiness and darkness and one direction could have been any direction; it was all empty, without boundary or meaning or relationship.

Kalatis checked his watch and then looked again in that one single direction that the navigational maps had told him was the right direction. He lifted his binoculars. The space around them was silent except for the whispered swash of the Gulf Stream nibbling at the hull of the *Sphinx*.

Suddenly there was a bright flash directly in line with Kalatis's gaze.

"Christ!" he said. "There it is. Close. Shit, closer than I was expecting. I didn't even hear the plane."

He took down his binoculars and watched the fireball the size of an orange against the star-speckled darkness.

"How much far away is that?" Jael asked, lifting her binoculars to see it more clearly.

"I don't know," Kalatis said, raising his binoculars again. "A mile. Maybe a mile."

The fireball died out quickly, leaving its afterimage in the stars.

"That's Pace," Kalatis said. "The first thirteen million is in the van."

THE GUARD CAME BACK INTO THE HANGAR AND STOOD AT THE rear of the van. He was out of Graver's line of sight for a few moments, but whatever he was doing didn't last long, and he soon closed both doors and slammed down the latch. But he did not close the hangar doors. Rather, he stood outside the opening, just about where he had shot the two men a few moments earlier, and worked with his Uzi. It sounded like he was fieldstripping the gun, a fact which gave Graver pause. As soon as the next plane landed Graver would be confronted with two armed men. Now was the perfect moment to cut that risk in half. But if he did, there would be no way of knowing whether or not this man had a role—a signal, some kind of all-clear communication— to play in the landing of the next shipment. And Graver wanted that next shipment right there in the van in front of him, just like the first one. So he waited.

The heat inside the back room of the hangar was exacerbated by the dead weight of the motionless air. There was no circulation, and everything Graver touched stuck to him. Like Remberto, he had shed his coat and rolled his sleeves to his elbows, and every time he put his arm down on the edge of the barrel or on a box or a board, a layer of dust stuck to the sweat on his forearm. Perspiration rolled down his ribs, staining his shirt in long, dark smears. In the faint light he looked at Murray who had pulled off his white T-shirt because of its visibility. His thick chest and arms made him look like a gladiator as he held his reliable old .45 in his right hand, his arms slightly out from his sides.

Graver then looked at Last who wiped his forehead on the arm of his expensive linen jacket and rolled his eyes. Last had done well. Graver had had secret reservations about giving him a gun and a role of responsibility, but by doing so without expressing doubts to Murray and Remberto, he was tacitly vouching for his trustworthiness in a squeeze. He had no idea, of course, if Last was indeed trustworthy in a squeeze, but Graver already had his neck out as far as it would go, and he needed another body—and another gun—on his side of this equation.

The guard reassembled his Uzi and then lit a cigarette which he left dangling in his lips while he stepped over to the side of the hangar, unzipped his pants, and urinated into the dried grass at the edge of the tarmac.

Just as Graver was beginning to wonder if something had gone wrong, the drone of Maricio Landrone's Mooney became audible in the distance. Hearing it, the guard finished his business, zipped his trousers and walked farther out onto the tarmac and looked up at the sky. As Pace had done, Landrone buzzed the hangar and headed out into the Gulf. The guard quick-walked back into the hangar, went to the electrical box inside the door, flipped on the runway lights, and then returned to the skirt of the tarmac to watch the landing.

While the guard was concentrating on the sight and increasing sound of the incoming aircraft, Graver nodded at Murray who slipped out of the door of the back room and signaled to Remberto. The two men went to opposite sides of the hangar, Remberto on the left side of the van as viewed from the office and Murray on the right. Each hid behind a piece of equipment that they already had picked out and which would provide only momentary cover, Remberto behind a four-cylinder caddy for an acetylene welding rig, and Murray behind a generator for an arc welder. If anyone decided to take a look around, even a cursory one, everything would happen fast. If all went as planned, it would anyway.

Graver's eyes were straining to see in the dull light of the hangar. From the moment Murray stepped out of the office door everything was out of Graver's hands. Arnette's men were perfectly willing to be led by Graver as to operational strategy, but when it came to tactical decisions they were on their own. They had had a long talk and an agreement about that. Graver was responsible for the decisions that set everything into motion, but the action itself was a second-by-second unfolding over which he had no control.

Landrone taxied his Mooney up to the door of the hangar as Pace had done his Malibu and the guard stood just inside the hangar, ten feet from the prop. Again the pilot cut the engine. The Mooney was a smaller aircraft than the Malibu, and the doors swung open from either side of the cockpit. Landrone and his copilot were the first out.

"Has Pace come in already?" Landrone asked, walking toward the guard, removing his baseball cap by its bill and wiping his forehead in the crook of his arm.

"Come and gone," the pilot said, turning to the van, unlatching the doors, and flinging them back. "Eight boxes."

"Okay. We've got eight too."

The other guard and client were climbing out of the plane now, both stooping to come under the wings of the plane and into the light.

"Everything's set," the first guard said.

The second one nodded. "Okay, let's unload this shit then."

At that point both guards had their backs turned to Remberto and Murray, one on each side of the plane, both just inside the hangar and dimly illuminated by the light coming out of the back of the van. Pace's guard was on Remberto's side, Landrone's guard was on Murray's.

What happened next had been discussed in advance, the probabilities analyzed, the practical matters posited and agreed to.

"Police—freeze!" Remberto and Murray yelled simultaneously, charging out from behind their concealments straight at their respective guards with their firearms extended. Graver and Last also burst out of the office yelling, "Police! Police!" to make the place sound like it was filled with law enforcement officers.

But the guards did not freeze.

As naturally as their hearts beat, their hands clapped onto their Uzi's which hung across their shoulders on straps, and they began spinning and dropping to a crouch. Neither Remberto nor Murray waited for them to get more than halfway around before they fired three times each as fast as they could from a distance of little more than twenty feet, their volleys knocking both guards off their feet and killing them instantly. Only Murray's guard managed to fire his Uzi, though he had not managed to raise the muzzle, and the sputtering burst from the barrel chewed off his left foot and splattered concrete splinters and blood all over Landrone and his copilot and the stunned man in the business suit.

Within seconds the two pilots and the client were on the ground being handcuffed as Graver and Last relieved the two dead guards of their Uzi's.

Graver quickly flicked off the runway lights and stepped over to the pilot.

"I want this plane out of sight," he said. "We've got our cars in that hangar right over there." He motioned to their right. "Are either of the other two hangars empty?"

"Both," Landrone said.

And then they heard the hum of Redden's Pilatus.

"Goddamn," Murray swore, breathing heavily. They were all breathing heavily from working fast and from the adrenaline. Killing always drove the adrenaline.

Murray's expression was one of surprise. The fate of Eddie Redden had been a hotly debated question during the planning stages several hours earlier. They all wanted the last load of money, but Murray had contended they should take it at Hobby airport where it was supposed to be delivered to Redden and loaded into his plane. But to do that, one of them would have had to go with Redden and take the responsibility of commandeering the load without help. Murray contended that could be done by one person having the advantage of total surprise. Graver wasn't so sure, and besides, he didn't want to spare the man here at Bayfield in the event that they ran into a much different situation than they were anticipating. The plan already had forfeited Neuman to Ledet's flare raid over Las Copas.

Graver contended they should send Redden alone. After a long private conversation with the pilot in which Graver assured him that if he disappeared—with or without the money—that he, Graver, would hunt him down even if he had to go to hell to get him and, conversely, assured him if Redden helped them he, Graver, would do his utmost to see that he got every break possible when it was over, Graver felt that Redden was worth the risk. Murray swore they would never see his crab-red face again if they let him fly off in the Pilatus.

Suddenly the Pilatus screamed low over them and shot out into the Gulf.

"I don't believe it," Murray barked.

"There's no time to get this thing across the tarmac to the other hangar," Graver yelled, frantically helping Last and Remberto stand the three men up and cuff their hands together behind their backs. "Cuff them back to back, and get them into the storeroom," he snapped to Last, and then ran back into the hangar and flipped on the runway lights he had just turned off.

Remberto was already pulling one of the dead guards around the corner into the darkness and Murray was grabbing the other, both bodies leaving a snail's slag of blood and dirt. Graver ran to the rear of the plane and lifted the tail as Remberto came back, followed closely by Murray, each man getting on the leading edge of either wing and pushing the plane out onto the tarmac. When the plane was out far enough for the wings to clear the turn, Graver swung the tail around, and they all began pushing from the trailing edge of the wings, rolling the light craft out into the darkness, into the weeds between the two hangars, past the four bodies, all the way down the length of the hangar and around to the back.

Running to the front doors again, Graver grabbed the garden hose and began washing down the blood. A wet cement skirt in front of the hangar would not raise the immediate questions that a bloody one would.

Graver felt like he was in a dream. Jesus Christ. He could not believe he had just let two men be killed so that he could have a slim chance at catching the man they worked for. Now, washing down the blood, he belched a mouthful of bile and bent over and spat it on the concrete, fighting to hold back the rest of it as he hosed it away from his feet. His face was hot, and he fought a persistent, destabilizing nausea.

He heard the Pilatus approaching from the water, just as Remberto and Murray returned from between the hangars.

"Murray," Graver yelled, "the guard with Redden will probably know the other two guards." He handed one of the Uzi's to Remberto and slung the other over his shoulder. "We can't let them see but two of us, and only from a distance."

"I'll get in the dark just around the corner," Murray said. "It's a toss-up which side of the plane the guard will get out of, but I want to get to him as soon as his feet hit the ground. We can't give him too much time to think about what he's seeing here."

Everyone agreed, but as Murray disappeared around the corner they didn't have time to discuss how to handle it.

"Do we leave the door of the van open?" Remberto panted.

"Maybe, only one," Graver said, checking his clip. "The guard's going to be looking through the cockpit window. If he gets a good look at the whole inside he'll know both shipments aren't in there, not enough boxes. But maybe we ought to let him see *some* boxes, and the Uzi's. He'll be looking for those."

Remberto closed one door, leaving open the one that controlled the interior light.

The turbo-powered Pilatus, sounding sure and powerful, its lights brighter than had been the lights of the other two aircraft, came off the water in a precision approach that allowed no seam of sound or sight to tell them when it had hit the tarmac. One moment it was airborne, and the next it was taxiing as though there were no tactile difference in the two activities. It went slightly farther down the runway than the others had done, and when it turned to come across to the hangar it did so without hesitation or uncertainty, almost as if it were being flown by a computer.

Graver's heart was working hard, still crazy from the shooting. It didn't help any that he now began to worry that the guard on the Pilatus was going to see something he didn't like and cause a standoff that might get one of them killed.

"Let's move across in front of the light," Graver said, "let them see us, but not too well." His legs were rubbery, and he hoped to God they didn't give way unexpectedly.

Redden, perhaps sensing the situation in front of him, cut the plane lights when he squared on the hangar door, and now the only light that could illumine their faces was the dim one coming from inside the van, which Graver and Remberto were careful to keep behind them.

The Pilatus stopped as had the others, about a dozen feet from the hangar doorway, and then Redden cut the engine and the turboprop whooshed to a standstill.

For just a moment nothing happened. Every one of Graver's pores was weeping perspiration. The Pilatus was large enough to have both a passenger door just behind the cockpit as well as a much wider cargo door behind that. But there was only one cockpit door, on the opposite side of the plane from Murray.

The passenger door opened first, the steps were lowered, and the client stepped into the doorway and started down. Almost to the tarmac, the passenger suddenly turned and looked back to the plane, and at that instant Graver heard shouting from inside and suddenly four explosions—bam! bam! bam! bam!—and a man's body flew backward out of the door, landing on his back almost on top of the client, half on and half off the stairway.

The guy in the business suit screamed and lurched back and was instantly grabbed by Graver who dragged him into the darkness a few feet beyond the body.

"Hold it! Hold everything!" Redden yelled from inside the plane. "I shot him, Graver! Had to, okay? Hear me?"

"Okay, Redden," Graver yelled. "Toss out the gun and come down with your arms straight out to the sides, shoulder high."

"Okay! Okay."

An autopistol flew out the door and bounced and skidded on the tarmac. That didn't mean a damn thing, of course. He still could be armed. But Redden appeared in the doorway, his arms straight out as instructed as Murray came under the belly of the nose behind the prop and stood at the steps.

"Son of a bitch smelled a rat," Redden explained, standing on the top step. "He got spooky from the very start when I showed up without a copilot. Watch his goddamn Uzi"—Redden nodded at the body at the foot of the steps—"it's cocked and off safety."

"Come on down," Murray said, his .45 trained on the considerable target of Redden's chest.

At the bottom of the steps Redden had to be careful not to loose his balance when stepping over the guard's body, and the moment his feet hit the tarmac Remberto was cuffing his hands behind his back.

"No one else in the plane?" Graver asked.

"No, that's it. But the money's in there, ten boxes of it."

Graver felt like a man who had just survived an explosion unscathed; he was doing the psychological equivalent of feeling his body, almost disbelieving the fact that he had been through something so incredible without having one of his limbs blown off. All three loads of money were on the ground. None of his people had been hurt or even fired on. He had two of the three clients. Each of them could be tremendously enlightening about Kalatis's operations from their own perspectives.

But even so, standing there in the silence of the aftermath, his relief at having escaped all the tragedies that could have befallen them, he was somberly resentful that Kalatis had escaped. Whatever means Kalatis had arranged to take possession of his money had died with the guards and the van driver. The clients would know nothing about what was to happen to the money after the delivery. And now everyone who did know was dead. Graver was, in effect, cut off from Kalatis by a very neat sectioning away of the middlemen. He hadn't even laid eyes on him, except for photographs. But like a greedy man, though realizing that fate had been good to him, Graver still was not satisfied. The very thing he had wanted most had eluded him, and that single deprivation turned all the rest of his good fortune to sour disappointment.

Then suddenly the darkness began to throb and thicken, and

Graver's nausea instantly leapt to the back of his throat with the chest-pounding, wind-beating, and almost deafening appearance of a sleek, black helicopter that slid over the tops of the trees across the runway. A glistening, pitch airship, it was nearly invisible as it hung in the night air, its lights winking against the stars, its dimly lit windows goggling at them like a giant locust's eyes from across a hundred feet of tarmac. Its mammoth rotors whipped up an invisible cloud of grit and sand that pelted them as though the chopping blades were hacking the black night into cinders.

REMBERTO AND MURRAY QUICKLY EDGED INTO THE HANGAR with Redden, moving back into the darkness behind the front of the van where Last was holding Landrone and the client who had flown with him.

Graver uncocked his Sig-Sauer, jammed it into its holster, and waited at the wing of the Pilatus. If this was Kalatis, Graver had no intention of allowing a shoot-out between the two groups of men. There were already too many bodies; he didn't want to be the cause of any more. Kalatis could have his money—but Graver wanted to talk to him first.

The huge Bell LongRanger rocked slightly as it descended from the darkness and then settled to the ground, its jet-driven rotors changing pitch of tone as the deceleration relieved them of the weight of their torque and they began a whining, whistling, slowdown.

Nothing happened in the helicopter for a few moments until the rotors were circling slowly enough for the eye to follow them, gliding, and finally whooshing to a standstill. Graver waited where he was. The doors opened. Graver would not have been surprised to have seen the hairy, black body of Satan emerge, hoofed and horned and goatish and smelling of the stench of his own corruption and of the death over which he reigned always, even this night, lying all about them.

Instead, the steps unfolded and a middle-aged, middle-sized man stepped out of the helicopter alone. He wore a beige-colored suit without a tie and started walking toward Graver. As the man approached, Graver noted that he was balding, that his suit was wrinkled and carelessly worn and, as Graver moved away from the wing of the Pilatus and started out to meet him, he realized that the face was familiar. When they were thirty feet from each other Graver recognized him and stopped.

"Geis," Graver said.

The man stopped also. He looked at Graver with an unconcerned but serious face.

"Very good," he said. "That's commendable."

The photographs from the fountain flipped through Graver's memory. The man at the fountain. Geis. As Arnette had pointed out, this Geis in front of him was unremarkable in appearance. The slightly rounded nose was indeed familiar. The man exuded . . . nothing. He was so common in appearance as to have been all but invisible had he been encountered on the street or in a mall or sitting in the car next to you in traffic. He was uninteresting in every way.

"What are you doing here?" Graver asked.

"Vested interests, Graver. Vested interests." He nodded at his own words. He said it wearily, as though he had had a long day but wasn't going to complain about it. "What, uh . . . Is all the money here?"

Graver hesitated, he didn't know why. More than likely Geis knew damn well where the money was.

"It's all here," Graver said.

"What about Panos Kalatis?"

"I don't know anything about Kalatis."

Geis sighed and nodded. "Did you know his house blew up about an hour ago?"

"I didn't know that."

"Big-time. Blew to shit."

Geis nodded at his own description of the severity of the explosion and then leaned sideways a little to look around Graver at the entrance of the hangar. His cheap, loose-fitting suit emphasized his rounded shoulders and dumpy stature. Graver noticed that the sleeves of his coat were a little too long, coming down onto his hands.

"You have people back in there with guns, I guess," Geis observed blandly. He might have been asking Graver if he had a ride home.

Graver said nothing.

"Well, look," Geis said, straightening up and putting his pudgy hands into the pockets of his baggy trousers, "I'm, uh, I'm going to have to take the money."

"Where?"

"Well, with me."

"I don't think so," Graver said.

Pause.

"Is it all in the hangar there, in the van?"

Graver said nothing.

"I don't think it's all in the van," Geis said, almost to himself. "You haven't had time to unload the Pilatus yet."

Pause.

Graver turned partway to the hangar and called back over his shoulder. "Use the handset and call Westrate," he said. "Get a tac squad out here. Tell them who's here."

"Don't do that," Geis said quickly, but without urgency. "I mean, we'll be out of here before anybody can get here, but if we leave without the money it will be very, very bad. Just have them hold off on that call. I'll show you what I mean."

There was something about Geis's sang-froid in the presence of so much death that made Graver take his words seriously. He raised his hand and turned and looked toward the hangar.

"Hold it," he yelled. He turned to Geis. "If you're CIA you'd better produce some proof. I'm not letting you take that money without some very convincing authorization." He hesitated a couple of counts. "I mean it."

Geis waved at the helicopter without turning around. "I'll show you," he repeated.

The door to the helicopter opened again and a man stepped out carrying a telephone and jogged over to them. He gave the telephone to Geis and then stepped back a few steps and waited. Geis pushed a button on the black instrument, listened a moment, and then said, "Put him on." Then he handed the phone to Graver.

Graver took it and put it to his ear. "Hello," he said.

"Captain, this is Neuman."

"Casey? Where are you?"

"I'm not sure."

"What do you mean? What's going on?"

"Well, they're holding us somewhere?"

"You and Ledet?"

"Yeah." Pause. "And Lara and Ginette Burtell."

Graver almost dropped the telephone. His muscles went limp, as if he had been swimming for hours, as if there was nothing left in him or in them, no strength at all, just quivering muscle.

"I want to speak to Lara," Graver said.

"I'll see . . ."

Pause.

"Hello?" Lara sounded scared. That was immediately apparent. It took only two syllables.

"Lara, are you okay?" Graver asked, fixing his eyes on Geis.

"Yes. Yes, we're okay. They broke into the house . . ." She started crying, stopped, recovered her voice. "I'm sorry . . . God . . ."

They broke into the house? Graver's throat tightened. Neuman was back on the line.

"We're all right," Neuman assured him.

"No one's hurt . . . ?"

"No, no, everything's fine, nothing like that."

"Okay," Graver said. "Don't worry. It'll be all right. We're working it out. Understand?"

"Yeah. Captain . . . 'Geis' is Strasser . . ." The line went dead.

Strasser.

The dumpy man reached out for the telephone, took it from Graver, and handed it back to the man who had brought it to them from the helicopter.

"You're Brod Strasser?" Graver felt like a fool. He had seen no further into this nightmare than if he had been a kid. The surprise was debilitating. Not only that, he knew that Strasser would kill everyone he was holding if he thought he had to.

"There's just a lot going on here that you don't understand, Graver," Strasser said.

"I have no doubt of that." Graver was almost ashamed of his stupidity. He had risked everyone's life. Somewhere along the way he had allowed himself to get sucked into a maelstrom of self-deception. Standing here, facing this powerful, disheveled little man, Graver suddenly realized how terribly wrong he had gone. Now this banal, dangerous creature was threatening four more deaths. Graver was appalled at what he had done.

"Do you know what Kalatis was doing?" Strasser asked. His voice brought Graver back to the moment.

"I assumed the two of you were robbing one more grave."

"Well, there you have it. That's precisely why we're standing here. *We* weren't doing anything. Panos was taking all of this for himself. I've most certainly seen the last of Panos Kalatis. There's a total of forty million dollars here. A little over. This was the last 'collection' of a series of collections that Panos has been making behind my back.

He's already gotten away with over"—Strasser paused and leaned forward toward Graver for emphasis, the hands of his short arms still jammed into his pockets—"one hundred million . . . in this deal. 'Our' money, as it were."

Strasser straightened up. "But he would have had one hundred and *forty* million if I hadn't stopped the hemorrhage. I've got men running my interests all over the world, Graver. Sometimes they manage to steal from me for a long time before I catch them. Panos was better at it than most. Silly bastard."

"Was he burning his bridges? Is that why everyone died?"

"Well, not everyone. Tisler, Besom, yes, of course. Faeber, Gilbert Hormann, yes. But Burtell was working for me, and he was catching on that . . . he was being used."

"That you weren't CIA."

Strasser gave a quick shrug.

"What about Sheck?"

"Oh, Sheck just happened . . . you know, to be in the wrong place, wrong time. That happens to people like Sheck. If it hadn't been there last night, it would have been somewhere else another night."

"Jesus Christ." Graver couldn't believe his ears.

"Kalatis," Strasser said, shaking his head. "Things began to unravel. It's too bad. There's this concept, a bourgeois concept you find even in the most un-bourgeois-like people—Kalatis for example—this bourgeois concept, that a person oughtn't to have to work all his life. That's just a bizarre concept when you think about it. I mean, where does that *come* from? That's what got Kalatis into trouble. He wanted this bundle to 'retire.' He just wanted to kick back and screw young girls the rest of his life."

"Strasser. Strasser." It was Victor Last, coming up behind Graver from the hangar where he was supposed to be holding the pilots and the two remaining clients. At the sound of his voice calling Strasser's name, Graver felt as if he were enveloped in an insulting cold breath. He knew instantly. Betrayal was everywhere a popular sin.

"Two thirds of the money is still in the planes," Last wheezed, jogging up beside them, glancing once awkwardly at Graver.

Strasser smiled benignly, the first time his face had shown any expression at all.

"Well, Vic, let's just get it all out then," he said. He looked at Graver. "I guess this is a surprise," he said, tilting his head at Last.

"Yes, this is a surprise." Graver turned to Last. "How long have you been working for him, Victor? From the beginning?"

Last didn't know exactly how to behave, at least he had enough scruples remaining in his soul to be ashamed. He mumbled something lame about it being "just business."

"We wouldn't have known where you were tonight if it hadn't been for Vic," Strasser explained. "He's been carrying a couple of special frequency beepers. He kept one turned on all the time so we knew where you were. Then, when he was sure where the money was going to be, he turned on the second one. We just homed in."

Strasser then turned and waved at the plane again and another man jumped out. Strasser turned back to Last. "Where's the other plane?"

"Around behind the hangar. They pushed it around there." Last was ingratiatingly eager to help. He didn't look at Graver again. Like a lamprey, he was firmly attached to Strasser's soft, hosting underbelly. Last was going to make enough from his usefulness in this affair to pull off his own bourgeois retirement.

"Take these guys around there," Strasser said to Last, as the second man jogged up to join the man with the radio.

Graver turned and waved for Remberto and Murray to come over to him. He looked at Strasser.

"I've got to tell them what's happening here."

Strasser nodded, understanding.

When Remberto and Murray approached it was clear they recognized "Geis" too.

"This is Brod Strasser," Graver said. Remberto and Murray shifted their eyes from Graver to Strasser who just stood there with his hands in his pockets as though he was waiting for an elevator to arrive. "Kalatis was 'stealing' this money from him. He's apparently already squirreled away over one hundred million. There's forty million over there," he said, nodding his head toward the hangar. "Strasser's people have Neuman, Ledet, my assistant from my office, and Ginette Burtell. He wants the money."

"Ho-ly shit," Murray swore.

Remberto looked at Strasser as if he had seen it all before. This was the drug business.

"Mr. Strasser," one of Last's helpers yelled, "it's going to be easier to push the plane over there. It's a small Mooney. We could use the spot from the chopper."

Strasser turned and walked back to the helicopter and told the pilot to turn on the spotlight.

"Did you talk to Neuman?" Remberto asked quickly as Strasser stepped away.

"Yeah, I did. And to my assistant. She was keeping Ginette Burtell at my house."

"Then Strasser's people *are* actually holding them?" Murray said.

Graver nodded. "I'm afraid so."

As Strasser started back toward them they all turned and looked at the path of the spotlight shooting down between the two hangars and saw the three men turn the Mooney and then begin pushing it toward them between the two buildings.

"I see some bodies over there," Strasser observed incidentally. "The guards?"

"Yeah," Graver said. "One of them killed—"

The explosion was a double impact: the bomb and then the Mooney's fuel tank, both combining into a mini-mushroom that lifted up between the two hangars, incinerating the plane, Strasser's two men, and Last in a fluorescing orange flash. The blast also blew the thirteen million dollars high into the night sky so that when the mushroom burned itself out in midair in a matter of one or two seconds, the only fire in the sky was another cloud, a floating, drifting, fluttering cloud of burning money, individual bills flittering crookedly like falling leaves, leaves afire, an autumn of burning millions.

Everyone gaped in stupefaction at the incinerating fortune that hung in a slow descent like a star-burst of fireworks.

And then Strasser screamed:

"God Almighty! God *damn* his soul to bloody hell! The son of a bitch . . ."

Everyone had the same thought at the same instant: Kalatis's guards had probably left bombs on all the planes. All of the pilots had been doomed the moment they unloaded their planes and flew away. Kalatis had come close to making a clean sweep.

"The Pilatus," Strasser croaked. When the Pilatus blew, it would take the van with it. Forty million up in flames.

Remberto and Murray and Graver ran for Redden's plane, lifting its tail and dragging it away from the door of the hangar. Since Last and Strasser's men had just begun to push the Mooney it was still near the rear of the hangar when it blew and the fiery concussion blasted the rear wall of the hangar all the way into the office. Redden, Landrone, Landrone's copilot, and the two clients could not have survived the blast.

Remberto was scrambling inside the van before anyone else could get to it. Throwing it into reverse, he roared out of the hangar and kept going all the way out to the helicopter which was already starting its rotors again. As Murray and Graver were running away from the Pilatus two more men bailed out of Strasser's helicopter and started running toward the Pilatus while Strasser shouted instructions to them. They ran past Graver and Murray who spun around in disbelief and watched in horror as the two men climbed into the still-open cockpit as Strasser had ordered them to do. Strasser himself watched without any visible emotion as the two men confronted almost certain death on his behalf. He might have been standing at a gaming table where life and death played no part in the wager. But he wasn't. And it did.

The prop on the Pilatus kicked on and almost simultaneously one of the men clambered out of the cockpit door with a briefcase with which he disappeared into the dark as the Pilatus revved and pulled away from the burning hangar, taxiing out onto the tarmac near the helicopter and the van.

In a moment the man came running out of the dark without the briefcase, running as hard as he could, and was well onto the tarmac when the bomb went off. Another red mushroom lighted the airstrip, and though they could feel the heat from its explosion, it was well away from the hangars and did no damage, the fireball dissipating quickly as the darkness rushed back into the space from which it had been driven.

It was only at that moment that Graver realized that both hangars had been on fire since the initial explosion, and their cars were burning inside the second one.

81

GRAVER AND REMBERTO AND MURRAY STOOD ON THE TARMAC AND watched Strasser's men unload the Pilatus and the van and stack the boxes of cash into the sleek body of the Bell 206L. Strasser walked over to Graver when it was all done.

"That's twenty-two million," Strasser said. "You know how much went up? *Eighteen* million. The biggest load was in the smallest plane." He snorted. "I don't know how Panos figured that."

"How do I know my people are all right?" Graver asked.

"They're all right," Strasser said. He lifted the telephone he was carrying and punched a button again. He listened a moment. "It's me. Give me fifteen minutes and then walk away from them. When you leave, tell them to call this number."

He punched a couple of numbers on the handset, tried to dial out, listened, punched another button and handed it the telephone to Graver.

"Here," he said. "Your people will call you in fifteen minutes. But you can't call out on that now. I just turned it into a receiver." He looked at the still-burning hangar. "I imagine somebody's on the way out here now anyway," he said. He studied Graver. "This has been a hell of a deal for you, huh?"

"Yeah," Graver said.

"What did you do, go around the bureaucracy?"

"What do you mean?"

"This whole thing started for you five days ago when Arthur Tisler turned up dead. Now you're standing here talking to me. To tell you the truth, this surprises me very much. I'm not a pretentious man, Graver. I don't see much use in crowing about anything, but I do know how I run things. I do know I'm good at what I do. Under normal circumstances you couldn't have gotten this close to me in five years, let alone five days."

"Well," Graver said, wiping his forehead on the arm of his shirt which was now gritty with soot and dirt and sweat, "these haven't been normal circumstances."

"No, that's true," Strasser conceded, "that's true. But still, bureaucracies don't move as fast as you've moved these last five days." He looked at Remberto and Murray. "And I don't think these two guys are cops."

"Tell me something," Graver said, "have I still got somebody dirty in the police department?"

"Hell, you know, I don't even know." Strasser shrugged casually. "All that was Panos's business. I never had anything to do with any of this except for buying out Faeber and Hormann through front companies. My people arranged that. I basically backed Kalatis's ventures. All the details were his. I'm just here because, you know, when you've got people like Panos for business partners, you've got to have somebody watching them all the time. Some of my people inside his works, people he didn't know were my people, told me they thought he was working on some kind of rip-off. Panos is about as good as they get. You know anything about him?"

"Yeah, I know he's Yosef Raviv. I know his background with the Mossad, all that."

"The hell you say." Strasser nodded, looking at Graver with admiration. "Well, okay, then you know how good he is. Compartmentalized everything. So this 'rip-off'—nobody knew much about it because he didn't tell anybody about it. That's why I moved on Burtell. He was already suspecting Tisler and Besom so I just gave him everything, told him I was CIA—which kept him from bringing you into it, you know, a higher calling—and he almost got to the core of it too. But he was too damn smart for his own good. He figured me out about the same time he figured out what Kalatis was doing.

"Anyway, Panos was my biggest success and my worst mistake all rolled into one. Like all high-yield propositions, he was also high-risk."

"Then he's disappeared . . . along with one hundred million."

Strasser crossed his stubby arms and looked around at the helicopter. The pilot had kicked on the turbos and the rotors were beginning to whine.

"Well, recovering the money's a moot point," he said. "I'll see if I

an't recover that. That's a maybe." He turned and brought his eyes
back to Graver. "But Panos . . . Panos is not a maybe. Panos is a sure
thing."

The rotors on the Bell picked up speed surprisingly quickly and
were hammering the night air.

"Sir," a man shouted above the swelling whine of the jet rotors,
"we're going to have to go."

Strasser waved a stubby arm without looking around.

"How many people burned up in there?" he asked.

"Two pilots, one copilot, and two businessmen who accompanied
their money for the delivery. I don't even know who they were."

Strasser nodded, looking at the two burning hangars.

"Could've been worse," he said, and turned and walked away
toward the helicopter, the rotors of which were whipping the air now,
working up to the familiar whumpwhumpwhump sound before it
lifted off.

Strasser climbed into the helicopter and the door closed. He sat
with his back to the cockpit, and Graver could see him buckling his
seat belt, and then he could see Strasser's face looking out the window
at them as they stood on the tarmac. Then the big Bell's rotors revved
up to a fierce speed, and the craft grew light on its skids and lifted up
into the darkness. Graver was looking at its belly as it started drifting
sideways, sliding toward the Gulf at the end of the runway, blending
with the night, black going into black as the darkness swallowed it.

August

82

IN LATE AUGUST THE BREEZES THAT USUALLY GRACE ITALY'S Amalfi coast succumb to the late summer heat and grow weak and listless in the long afternoons. There is a villa there, the color of a fawn, wedged into the rocky coast above the Golfo di Salerno with a view that skirts the island of Capri and looks across the fifteen miles of the Tyrrhenian Sea to Sardinia. It is a jewel of a villa, with a terrace that hangs on the edge of the cliffs and from which the view of the blue, lively western Mediterranean stretches unmarred to the horizon.

Panos Kalatis lay naked on a deck lounge. He lay on his stomach, his arms folded under his head. He was marvelously tanned, his rakish graying hair combed straight back from his forehead. Twenty feet away the pool where he and Jael had been swimming sparkled in the sun that was halfway past meridian in the west.

Jael, also naked, was on her knees, straddling Kalatis. Deeply tanned, her long, wet hair was put up on the back of her head and held loosely in place with a hairpin. She had filled a cupped hand with oil and was rubbing it into his back with her long fingers. The smell of herbal oils heated by the sun against his back filled Kalatis's nostrils with a fragrance as ancient as the Amalfi coast itself. As Jael massaged him and the sun warmed the muscles in his back, Kalatis felt the double lobes of her buttocks rocking back and touching his own as she moved up and down his spine with her oily hands.

Kalatis grew languid, allowing himself that lightweighted feeling of drifting, a slight sense of arousal at the touch of Jael's soft inner thighs against his sides.

Watching her own shadow on the tile terrace, Jael paused and reached up and took the thick hairpin out of her long hair. She shook it loose until it hung straight and untangled, almost to the middle of her back.

Taking the thick pin in her left hand, she lightly touched the point of it at a precise spot between the second and third vertebrae of Kalatis's spine at the base of his skull. She angled the pin upward slightly and then, with the palm of her right hand, she smacked the wide haft of the pin, driving the stainless steel shaft straight into his spinal cord. She sat back on his buttocks until his legs had ceased quivering, and he was still.

83.

GRAVER ROUNDED THE FAR END OF THE POOL AND STARTED THE
last half of his final lap. He was up to forty minutes, and by the time
his right arm had completed its stroke and his left hand touched the
edge of the pool, his heart was banging against the walls of his chest
like a diesel-driven piston.

He jerked his goggles off his head and hung on to the edge of the
pool, wheezing for air. Even though he couldn't have gone another lap
the workout felt good. As he rested, the late August sun warmed the
top of his wet head and burned its way into the muscles of his shoulders like a heat lamp. He waited for his heart and lungs to regain their
equilibrium as he felt his body being moved gently by the water that
was slowly settling from the disturbance of his laps.

As he sucked in the heavy afternoon air, he stared across the hot
green lawn broken by scattered sago palms and let his thoughts return
for the thousandth time to the recent events and their aftermath.

The mandatory suspension imposed for the duration of the investigation should have been a blessing, an opportunity to relax, to recoup
his sapped energies, and to think. But it didn't work out that way.
Though the media had been sluggish in connecting all the dots at the
beginning, they made up for lost time after the calamity at Bayfield.
The investigative reporters in every branch of the media suddenly came
alive, and within a week "new leads" were breaking every day and
continued to break through the blistering months of July and August.

The withering media assault effectively shut down the Criminal
Intelligence Division, and the complexities of what had happened during those five hot days in June promised an extended investigation.

Graver's report to the special investigating commission had been
lengthy and detailed, exceptionally detailed. During the entire period
he had been able to account for almost every hour of his time. He had

outlined the labyrinth of relationships among the players, pulling no punches for those under his command—or for himself—for not having detected anything amiss despite his having designed a new counter-intelligence program two years earlier that had been intended to prevent just such breaches. He had provided names, linkages, information to enable the commission to subpoena entire computer programs from DataPrint and Hormann Plastics and Gulfstream National Bank and Trust, and provided complete copies of Dean Burtell and Bruce Sheck's computer and microfilm accounts of their involvement. The detail—and amount of detail—had required nearly two weeks of assisted accumulation before the administration could even reach the point that they could suspend him and the commission's work could begin. Then he walked out of the office and went home.

The only thing that presented a problem was the involvement of Arnette Kepner and her people. Graver had refused to disclose her as a source and, much to his surprise and gratification, so had Casey Neuman and Paula Sale. Though they also had been suspended for the duration of the investigation, their silence was an extraordinary vote of confidence. There would be a way, of course, to resolve the problem. There always was with bureaucracies, especially bureaucracies that relied on secrets to assure their own survival.

That was almost two months ago. He swam twice every day. He drank more wine than he should have, but not too much. He gained weight, but not more than he needed to. His supporters within the Department kept him apprised of the rumors and, when they could, the actual facts. Apparently Westrate had rolled over immediately and had offered up Graver's career to mollify the fury of the bureaucrats for the shame the Department was suffering under the cloud of scandal. In all likelihood, Graver's career was gone. The fate of Neuman and Paula was less clear; their futures were still in the balance.

He never heard a word from Arnette. That was expected; that was as it should be. It was a tough business and certain things were understood. By helping him as she had, she had gone way beyond the understood rules of the game. Her silence now was nothing more than self-preservation. She would have expected the same from Graver.

But Graver was a realist and already had accepted the inevitable; he didn't need to wait for a sitting special commission verdict to know that eventually he would be relieved of his position. He would be lucky if he was allowed part of his pension. He spent most of his time, however, brooding over the events of those few days. The days passed one into the other without distinction as he replayed the mistakes, the disappointments, the bad luck.

All the dying had haunted him.

It would have been easy to blame it on others, on Panos Kalatis and Brod Strasser and their unconscionable commerce in the chemistry of sour dreams, their traffic in a merchandise that commanded unspeakable fortunes. It would have been easy to blame it on the businessmen like Faeber and Hormann and the nameless "clients" whose greed was so vast and dark it blotted out the light of common decency.

But in all honesty, he couldn't shift the blame so easily. He could have avoided much of the killing if he had kept strictly to his business of gathering intelligence. That's what he told himself on some days. On other days he told himself something quite different. On those days when he counted the deaths over and over again, it seemed to him that everyone who had died would have died anyway, regardless of what he had done. Their fate had been cast in a game of chance that had been designed and put into play by Kalatis and Strasser, a game that already had run a long course and was just coming to a conclusion as Graver stumbled upon it in its closing hours. Despite what he might think he could have done, it had been out of his control all along. No matter what he could have done Kalatis still would have disappeared with a hundred million dollars. Strasser still would have flown away with twenty-two million in crumbs. Neither man would miss a beat marketing drugs. They simply would move to new venues. They would surround themselves with a different cast of bit players, and in no time at all the river of sour dreams would resume its flow, swollen to its banks with wrecked hopes and the human flotsam of their trade.

As for those two nebulous personalities, little was said in the news reports. Their names appeared only twice and both times only in passing and in the context of rumors. Graver heard that a couple of men from the State Department had been in town for a few days, and after that Kalatis and Strasser were pushed out of the picture altogether by stories of Art Tisler having been selling CID intelligence for sex. Kinky sex and crooked cops were a jazzier story and pushed simple greed completely out of the headlines.

"Fed Ex," Lara said, coming out the back door of the house. She was wearing her swimsuit, carrying her towel and a large envelope.

Graver pulled himself out of the pool, shook off the water, and walked over to the wrought-iron table and chairs and picked up his towel. He dried off, watching Lara walk toward him across the grass. She handed the envelope to him by slapping it against his stomach. He took it as she tossed her towel on one of the chairs, walked to the edge of the pool, and dove in.

Graver looked at the sender's address. It had originated in Houston. He opened one end of the envelope and slipped out three eight-by-ten colored photographs and a handwritten note on a single sheet of paper.

> *Jael stayed with him until she had been able to obtain every one of the foreign account numbers. Within forty-eight hours of getting the last one, I had all the money, and she had finished her job. She was a good and faithful servant.*
> *I thought you would like to know.*
>
> *"Geis"*

Graver looked at the first photograph. It had been taken while the photographer was standing over Kalatis's nude body. He was lying on his stomach on a poolside lounge, his head turned to the side with his arms under his head as though he were asleep. A shiny piece of silver metal, about two inches long, was resting horizontally on the back of his neck.

The second photograph was a picture of the metal pin pulled halfway out of Kalatis's neck. Proof that it had been driven home.

The third photograph was a clinical close-up of the entry wound, the pin still in place.

Graver put the photographs back into the envelope, and thought of the innocuous figure of Strasser standing on the tarmac, looking like an overworked traveling salesman.

"What was that?" Lara asked. She was in the water at the end of the pool where he had been, her arms resting on the side of the pool as she pushed her wet hair away from her face.

"Just more stuff about the investigation," Graver said. "People still trying to tie up loose ends."

He looked at the note. "She *was* a good and faithful servant." The past tense of the verb was significant.

Perhaps Satan had in fact stepped out of that black helicopter that night at Bayfield. Graver's mistake had been that he never had been able to think in dark enough terms to have had any real understanding of what it was he had been dealing with. Arnette had hinted as much. Instead of thinking in terms of data or kilos or dollars, instead of thinking in terms of bits of information or accumulative intelligence, he should have been thinking in less tangible terms. He should have viewed his work, at bottom, as a struggle of abstractions.

His career had been devoted to shedding light on a subject of mystery, to illuminating the darkness through knowledge, albeit secret knowledge. He thought now that he had had the right objective all those years, but he had employed the wrong technique in trying to achieve it. And maybe, even, he had been looking in the wrong places for the answers. Perhaps it was not the business of shedding light on people's deeds that he should have been concerned with, because, after all, when light arrived the essence of darkness was changed; it was no longer darkness. It seemed to him that he was arriving too late in the sequence of events. Perhaps he should have been trying to understand, instead, the character of darkness itself, and what it was that happened when men's desires were shaped and formed in an absence of light.